JIM CONKEY

To order additional copies of this book, contact:
Xlibris Corporation
1-888-795-4274
www.Xlibris.com
Orders@Xlibris.com
45313

For Nancy
. . . these precious days I spend with you - Insha' Allah

Acknowledgments

This novel came about because of Vikki Ford, communications director at the University of Nevada Extension. Vikki was the author of my oral history. When the project was finished, she insisted that I write a novel based on some of my experiences, as a U.S. Navy officer, in special operations during the cold war. I resisted the invitation until my wife, Nancy, in collaboration with Vikki, shamed me into taking on the project. Vikki became teacher and editor for the first four years of research and writing and gave me invaluable help along the way. Nancy, in turn, has been the steady compass that kept me on track through the project.

It was my good fortune to have served with Commander Joe Plassmeyer, USN (Retired), and Lieutenant Commander Jim Bladh, USN (Retired), when Joe Plassmeyer, then a Lieutenant, Junior Grade, was officer in charge of Special Weapons/Explosive Ordnance Disposal Team II and Chief Jim Bladh was the senior enlisted man on my Special Weapons/Explosive Ordnance Disposal Team I. We were stationed at the U.S. naval ordnance facility at Port Lyautey, Morocco, from 1957 to 59. Their review of the manuscript and suggestions made on the technical aspects of the story were of great value. Their encouragement along the way was priceless. We have remained close shipmates through the years.

I want to thank my daughters Mary Murphy and Jayna Conkey for their valued contribution to this project. I asked Mary to take on the first-reader task because she would have little or no interest in buying a book of this sort. Her suggestions may have helped me tell an important story that many felt needed to be told to a wider audience. Jayna's computer graphics magic and suggestions made the story come alive.

Finally, Zahkia. Always there, always supportive.

Preface

The U.S. Freedom of Information Act provided public access to documents held by various branches of the U. S. government. The documents are a rich source of highly controversial, previously classified information, which may now appear in writings of historical significance or provide grist for historical fiction.

During the cold war (1945-1991), our response to the continuing threat of communist expansion beyond the borders of the Soviet Union was to encircle the Soviet Union with American military bases located in foreign countries and to deploy U.S Navy aircraft carrier forces to the eastern Mediterranean and western Pacific regions.

The strategy included placing U.S. Air Force Strategic Air Command (SAC) bombers, medium-range Jupiter and Thor ballistic missiles, and U.S. Navy aircraft carriers within striking distance of targets in the Soviet Union. All of these missiles and aircraft were nuclear or thermonuclear weapons capable. Supply and communication facilities, all strategically located in foreign countries, supported air force and navy fleet operations.

A number of American bases were located in the French Protectorates of Morocco, Algeria, and Tunisia at the time a bloody war for independence was being fought and won by Arabs in those states. With the impending defeat of the French military and the removal of the French colonial governments, the United States negotiated a treaty with the new Arab governments. The treaty included advantageous trade agreements for the host countries, provisions for leasing land for U.S. Air Force and U.S. Navy bases, and employment for native workers on the bases.

Guerilla units such as the FLN (Front de Libération Nationale) and a number of Islamic fundamentalist clerics turned their attention from the French to the American military presence, considering it to be a neo-colonial threat, a new invasion of infidels taking the place of the old.

The Soviets were concerned, not only about the American military presence in North Africa as a part of the American doctrine of encirclement, but also about what they perceived as the coming threat of American hegemony in that part of the world. They would do whatever possible to disrupt the mission of these forward bases and, at the same time, try to increase their own influence in these Arab countries. Although the cold war is over, the United States continues to have over six-hundred military bases in one-hundred and thirty countries as of this writing.

This is a story about one naval officer and a series of U.S. Navy special operations associated with Arab, French, and Russian interests in the end of the wars of nationalism that ended French colonial rule in North Africa.

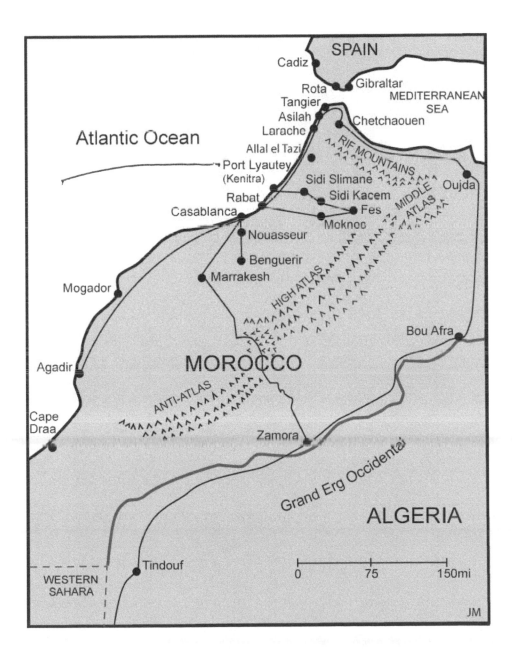

"THE EVACUATION OF FOREIGN TROOPS IS THE TASK OF THE HOUR."

"The central committee underlines that the experience and events have shown that the keeping of French and Spanish armies on Moroccan soil constitutes for us an immediate danger. Especially, now that the imperialists have thrown their masks and shown their intentions for reestablishing their domination on Northern Africa.
On another side the stocking of atomic and hydrogen arms on the American bases in Morocco shows the great danger that exists, not only in the case of war but also in time of peace like we see in the Sidi Slimane incident.
The Moroccan population must then gather their efforts towards the battle for the organization of troops and for the liquidation of American bases."

Translated from the Bulletin of the Moroccan Communist Party *Espour*
New Series, No. 27, dated 25 February 1958.

They are rioting in Africa.
They are starving in Spain.
There are hurricanes in Florida
and Texas needs rain.
The whole world is festering
with unhappy souls.
The French hate the Germans
The Germans hate the Poles.
Italians hate the Yugoslavs
South Africans hate the Dutch
And I don't like anybody very much.

But we can be tranquil and thankful and proud
For man is endowed with a mushroom shaped cloud,
And we know for certain that some lovely day
someone will set the spark off and we will all be blown away.
They are rioting in Africa
there is strife in Iran.
What nature doesn't do to us will be
done by our fellow man.

The Kingston Trio,
"The Merry Minuet (They Are Rioting in Africa)"
circa 1958

Chapter 1

2003

On a late Monday afternoon, the fall sun was disappearing behind the ridges of the Sierra Nevada at Lake Tahoe. As the light faded, it became more difficult for Dr. Burt Turner to see the shadowy details of a small square of x-ray film tucked in the lower right corner of his office window. It was an x-ray of his right knee taken by one of his former students as part of his annual physical six weeks ago. The joint showed somewhat less wear than expected for a man his age, and no abnormality to be concerned about. So much for his complaint. Still, it was another reminder of time passing and the possibility of retirement from the college where he taught.

Lake Tahoe College was a small 760-student liberal arts college near the town of Truckee, Calfornia. The faculty was dedicated to teaching at the expense of research, although some faculty members had small financial grants from a variety of granting institutions and did small research projects. The college offered coursework leading to baccalaureate degrees in liberal arts, graphic arts, information technology, nursing, X-ray technology, and teaching.

Ten years ago, Turner accepted a faculty position in the biology department after feeling assured the stress would be far less than what he had experienced during the last twenty years as a tenured faculty member and research scientist at the University of California at San Francisco (UCSF) Medical School. He was to find problems at the college far less in number and complexity but, like anywhere else, able to be ramped up in intensity by a few individuals hardwired to do these things.

Four years ago, he was asked to serve as chairman of the biology department. He accepted the position with misgivings, but things turned out rather well as he found he was quite good at budget management, curriculum improvement, and putting out "brush fires" so common in academia. In his long career, he really hadn't formed any close relationships with his coworkers. He was not antisocial, but he didn't have the need to be part of any group.

He was a physically attractive man. His hair was white, well trimmed and smart. The wrinkles on his face were deepening now, made worse by too much of the Moroccan Sahara sun of his midtwenties. His once-six-foot-one frame was now slightly less than six feet, and he presented a paunch reflective of a 15-pound weight gain over the 172-pound navy weight of forty years ago. When he was feeling sorry for himself, he would tell his daughter, "When you know the details of the aging process, experiencing it personally is like going through a geriatrics textbook, chapter by chapter."

She would answer with, "You look distinguished and maybe even worldly, Dad."

He stayed active by walking the three miles to the college and back, followed by weight lifting and stretching at home. The plan was designed for him by one of his students, a part-time personal trainer at a nearby health club. He hiked in the Sierras; sea-kayaked when he could, and cross-country-skied in winter. He was in very good shape, but didn't think so. His physician and friend, Dr. Fredric Haven (FACS, etc.), reassured him, "You are aging nicely and will live a long time."

He met his wife, Laura, in 1960, when he was a navy lieutenant junior grade, officer in charge of a special weapons/explosive ordnance disposal (SW/EOD) team assigned to the Naval Air Station, Port Lyautey, Morocco. She was a North Africa-Middle East analyst assigned to the Central Intelligence Agency (CIA) station in Paris. They were total opposites. Laura was sophisticated, thoughtful, and very bright. He was unsophisticated, spontaneous, and less bright. When something was to be put together or fixed, she would read the directions and go forward with success, while he would immerse himself in the problem at hand and deal with it intuitively. Their academic backgrounds were vastly different. Laura: bachelor of arts, international studies, minor in Arabic and Farsi languages, Harvard University, 1956; masters in Arab studies, American University, Cairo Egypt, 1957. Turner: bachelor of science, marine biology, minor in history, University of Southern California, 1956. After their marriage, Turner received his PhD in comparative physiology, from George Washington University in 1965. They became inseparable. Four years ago, she died of ovarian cancer. It was a terrible loss for him, and he never developed a relationship with another woman; there were opportunities untaken.

Two years after Laura's passing, it seemed like a good idea for his daughter Helen to move in with him. She was thirty-two, divorced, and without children. She taught fourth grade at Donner Elementary School, and though she and her father taught different age groups, they had enough in common to make after-work conversation interesting. The arrangement worked quite well. They didn't get in each other's way and were comfortable with each other intellectually. They simply liked each other.

He glanced at his old Rolex Submariner, got up from his chair, stretched for a moment, and then his phone rang. He hesitated, but then picked it up.

"Burt Turner speaking."

His secretary, Majorie, answered, "Dr. Turner, there is a Stephen Brannen calling from Albuquerque. Do you want to take the call?"

He thought a moment and asked, "Did he say what he wanted?"

"No, he didn't."

Out of curiosity, he replied, "I'll talk with him."

She put the caller through.

"Dr. Turner?"

"This is he."

"My name is Steven Brannen. I'm calling from Albuquerque, New Mexico."

The voice at the other end sounded like a telemarketer's; Turner almost hung up the phone.

The caller went on, "I'll be attending a conference at Lake Tahoe this week, and since you are at North Shore, I thought perhaps we could chat about an interesting historical occurrence we both know something about."

"I'm not sure I know who you are, Mr. Brannen."

"Well, we have never met, Dr. Turner. Let me give you a riddle: the subject is associated with Apple Tree, Poplar Tree, and Watermelon."

Turner could hear a suppressed laugh. There was a pause, then Brannen said, "I will be at the Hyatt Regency, Incline Village, room 406 from Thursday until Saturday noon. Perhaps you could think about Apple Tree, Poplar Tree, and Watermelon for a bit."

Before Turner could answer, Brannen hung up.

What the hell was that all about—Stephen Brannen, Apple Tree, Poplar Tree, and Watermelon?

He put the phone handset back on the cradle, thought for a minute, and decided to take his briefcase home. There were tests to be graded. The briefcase was loose of hinge, scuffed, bruised, and battered, but serviceable.

When he took this briefcase to class, it was his custom to put it on the table next to the podium before taking out his lecture notes. At the beginning of the semester, there would always be a student in the front row who would point at the briefcase and set in motion a series of questions: "How old is that?" (About thirty-eight years old.) "Where did you get it?" (His wife bought it at Woodward and Lothrop in Washinton DC when he first started teaching.) "Why doesn't she buy you a new one ?" (She couldn't. She passed away a few years ago.) And that would settle the conversation about the briefcase, although on an uncomfortable note. His answer on the last would have unwittingly touched some of the young women in class, perhaps.

Turner and his daughter lived in a small frame house built by the Central Pacific Railroad in the late 1800s. He and his wife bought the house at an estate sale after he accepted the position at the college. Over time, they rebuilt the house, being careful to retain its rustic character along the way. The house turned out to be quite comfortable and, most importantly, well able to handle the extremely cold winters for which the town of Truckee was noted.

On his way home, he stopped at the bakery and bought a loaf of sourdough and a baguette, spent a moment talking about the weather with the baker (it was unusually cold), and left for home. Approaching the house, he saw Helen's '98 Saturn parked in the garage at a strange angle next to his small truck. *Bad day at school for Helen*, he thought. He stopped at the mailbox near the curb, took out a few circulars, a radio guide from National Public Radio in Reno, an announcement from the Reno Philharmonic, and the culinary magazine *Bon Appetit*. He walked up the sidewalk, and as he went up the porch stairs, he made a mental note, a second time, to deal with three loose nails in the top stair. He crossed the porch, readjusted one of the fall decorations near the front door—Helen's work, and went inside.

As he walked through the front room and hallway leading to the kitchen-dining area, he could smell fried pork chops and onions; he thought there would be potatoes and gravy too. After hanging up his jacket in the hall closet, he kicked off his shoes, strapped on a pair of sandals, and went into the kitchen. His daughter was at the stove. He went over to her and, putting his hand on her shoulder, teased, "I thought you wanted me to lose ten pounds."

"Look, Dad, I had a lousy day, you don't seem to care about your weight, and I don't really care about your weight or mine right now."

He turned away and started setting the table for dinner. He took two wineglasses out of the cupboard and asked, "Why was school lousy today?"

"I had an after-school meeting with the same two women I met with two weeks ago. The same problem, both of their boys not doing their homework, and I continued to give them an Incomplete for their weekly grades. They both said that they didn't understand why I gave their kids an Incomplete, while they always got good grades from other teachers. Then it got worse. They said they were taking their boys out of our school and sending them to the charter school at Crystal Bay—where they have dedicated and student-oriented teachers! Then they left."

"Did you talk with the principal?"

"Mrs. Thompson was really great. She told me not to worry and that Frank Peters, the charter school principal, was going to have his hands full."

As she dished up their plates, her father filled the glasses with inexpensive but very good Australian wine (a grenache-shiraz), and they sat down to eat. Small talk continued, and Turner finally brought up the phone call from Stephen Brannen.

"You should call the Hyatt and ask what conferences are being held during that period of time, Dad. The answer may give you an idea of who Mr. Stephen Brannen is."

"I'll do that in the morning." Then he carefully asked, "Are you going to ask Pete Thomas over for dinner next Sunday?"

She rolled her eyes and said, "We'll see, Dad."

Pete owned and operated Pete's Garage in Truckee. He was Helen's age, had never been married, and the relationship between him and Helen had gone from casual to serious recently. Turner and Pete liked each other a lot, one reason being that both of them had served in the navy. Although Turner's four-year career was over before Pete was born, they still had much in common. They both enjoyed talking about world history; Pete was currently interested in British general Charles "Chinese" Gordon, of Khartoum fame, a favorite of Turner's during his college days.

The next morning, when Turner arrived in his office, he noticed the night custodian had put an apple on his desk and, next to it, a short carefully printed note. He sat down and read,

> Dr. Turner, I found *la manzana* on your computer table; did
> it fall from *el manzano*? I don't think you want me to tell your
> daughter that you are not eating your *frutas*.

Turner smiled. From time to time, he would practice his waterfront Spanish with the custodian. After a quick look at his lecture notes, he left his office and was making his way through the crowded hallway: Manzano *is "apple tree" in English*. A moment later . . . *"Poplar tree" in Spanish could be* alamos, *"watermelon" is* sandia. *I think I know what this is!* He was ill at ease with Stephen Brannen's joke.

After class, he looked up the number of the Hyatt Regency at Incline Village, a few miles from North Shore, and dialed. The front desk receptionist looked up conference scheduling and said there were two scheduled for the coming Thursday through Saturday, a Reunion of Retired Telephone Workers and a Hazardous Material Transport Safety Officers Conference. It was now Tuesday.

"Could you tell me if a Mr. Stephen Brannen has checked in?"

After a pause, the receptionist replied, "Sir, Mr. Stephen Brannen is not expected until late Wednesday afternoon. Would you like to leave a message for him?"

"Let Mr. Brannen know that Dr. Turner called and will call again about five, Wednesday."

Turner swung his chair around and caught a glimpse of a Steller's jay just taking off from a branch of one of the nearby Jeffrey pine trees. *Stephen Brannen calling from Albuquerque, the Hazardous Material Transport Safety Officers Conference, Alamos was Los Alamos National Laboratory, Sandia was Sandia National Laboratories in Albuquerque, and Manzano was Manzano Base. It's about the incident in North Africa . . . over forty years ago. What does Stephen Brannen want?*

He reminded himself that Laura was one of the players at the time.

Laura Brae graduated from high school in Alexandria, Virginia, with honors. She was a student gifted in the languages; she applied for admission to the international studies program at Harvard University and was accepted. She was granted a partial scholarship, and to defer additional costs, she worked for her dad (Brae's Pharmacy, Cameron Valley) during summers and holidays.

While majoring in international studies, she decided to minor in Arabic and Farsi languages. In her junior year, she had her first serious romantic involvement. He was a music major and played trumpet in the Yale University marching band. The involvement lasted seven months and ended badly.

When Laura was a senior, she attended a job fair at Harvard and was interviewed by a number of U.S. government agencies and other business and industry recruiters. Because of her academic background, she was heavily recruited, and being physically attractive didn't hurt. One agency in particular offered to send her to graduate school at the American University in Cairo, Egypt, if she promised to stay with the agency for six years after she received her master's degree. She accepted. The recruiter was from the Central Intelligence Agency (CIA).

Laura's master's dissertation was titled "Al Magreb: An Exploration of the Possibility of an Arab Nation from the Atlantic Coast to the Persian Gulf." When she graduated from the American University in Cairo, she had four weeks at home. After two years at CIA headquarters in Langley, Virginia, she was assigned to the CIA station in Paris, France, as an analyst in the section concerned with North African and Middle Eastern affairs. It was 1959.

———————

After dinner that evening, they were sitting at the table when Helen asked, "Did you see the article in the *San Francisco Chronicle* this morning about the old plane that went down off Newfoundland?"

"No, what about it?"

"I'll get the paper."

She went to the front room, came back with the front section of the newspaper, sat down, and read, "A U.S. Navy transport aircraft, missing since 1960, was found ten miles south of Lamaline, Berin Peninsula, Newfoundland, in 320 feet of water. The captain of the Canadian fishing boat *Easy Catch* reported to the coast guard that he snagged and hauled up a section of wing with *U.S. Navy* on the underside. The Canadian government has given the U.S. government permission to recover the aircraft or parts of the aircraft. A spokesperson representing the U.S. Navy said the aircraft was a navy R-6D four-engine transport that had taken off in bad weather for a flight from the Naval Air Station at Norfolk, Virginia, to the Naval Air Station at Port Lyautey, Morocco. Off the coast of Massachusetts, the aircraft flew into a hurricane that had been forecast to have been farther south of the aircraft's Great Circle route and, being unable to turn around, flew on with the intent to try to make an emergency landing at Newfoundland. Radio and radar contact was lost while the aircraft was approaching the coast of Newfoundland. After two hours without contact, the aircraft was presumed lost. When the weather finally cleared, there was an extensive search, but after five days, the search was abandoned. The aircraft had gone down at sea without a trace. There was no evidence of survivors.

"What do you think of that, Dad?"

"It sounds like a bad place to go down. The water there is really cold."

She became absorbed in a story about preventing suicide on the Golden Gate Bridge.

Slowly turning his wineglass with his thumb and forefinger at the stem, he thought about a night, long ago, when he was assigned courier duty at the U.S. Naval Air Station at Port Lyautey, Morocco, to receive and take custody of classified cargo being flown in from the United States. The classified cargo was plutonium capsules and explosive detonators for nuclear weapons, to be temporarily stored at the Naval Ordnance Facility at the Naval Air Station before being sent to the Sixth Fleet in the Mediterranean. During transport, each capsule was housed in a central canister within a carrying frame called a birdcage. The explosive detonators were transported separately in aluminum "suitcases." He and Chief Gunner's Mate Manuel Gallegos, the senior enlisted man in his special weapons/explosive ordnance disposal team, waited in a rainstorm for four hours beyond the estimated time of arrival of the aircraft.

Finally, with the flight long overdue, the duty officer at Naval Air Station Operations told Turner and Gallegos it was assumed to have gone down. The aircraft was an R-6D carrying four birdcages and three suitcases. The loss became one of the many unresolved incidents involving U.S. nuclear weapons or nuclear materials being transported by air. At long last, the mystery had been solved.

Turner abruptly got up, carrying his half-empty glass of wine, and left the kitchen. An hour later, Helen knocked on his study door, opened it, and found her father reading and taking notes from papers spread across his worktable. She saw a closed file folder; on it were written in bold black letters

U.S. Navy
Officer Service Record

She asked, "What are you doing, Dad?"

"I'm getting prepared for a meeting with Brannen. I think I know what he wants."

––––––––––––

The next morning, he arrived at his office earlier than usual. He checked his phone messages; there were none.

That afternoon, after class, he called the Hyatt Regency. When the front desk receptionist answered, Turner asked for room 406. On the third ring, the phone was answered with a smoker's cough, then, "Brannen speaking."

Turner introduced himself. Stephen Brannen cleared his throat and said, "I am glad you called. I guess my simple riddle stimulated your curiosity, huh?" Brannen laughed as he said this.

"Well, you certainly did stimulate my curiosity. You are taking me back in time quite a bit, Mr. Brannen."

"I would like to, and please call me Stephen."

"Well, Stephen, what is this all about?"

"Perhaps we could meet tomorrow, if you are available."

"I have a 9:30 a.m. class, and I'm tied up the rest of the day."

"Perhaps we might go to breakfast at 8:00 a.m. Is that possible for you?"

"Yes, I could do that. Where would you like to meet?"

"Would it be convenient for you to meet me at Gar Woods restaurant at North Shore?"

"I'll see you there at 8:00 a.m., Stephen." Turner hung up the phone.

He was just going out the door of his office when the phone rang again. He hesitated, returned to his desk, and picked it up. It was Helen.

"Hi, Dad, did your day go well? Did you make the call?"

"The day went well, and I'm meeting Brannen at eight tomorrow morning."

"That sounds interesting." She added, "I'm going to dinner with Pete tonight. Don't expect me 'til late. There're burritos and salad all made up in the refrigerator."

"Thanks. Why don't you ask Pete to dinner on Sunday?"

"I will, Dad, I will."

At seven forty-five on Thursday morning, Turner drove into the parking lot at Gar Woods. The restaurant was on the water's edge at Lake Tahoe, and this morning, the view of the lake and mountains, dusted with early fall snow, was unusually spectacular. He left his truck, and when he was about halfway across the parking lot, he looked up at the restaurant's wooden balcony and saw a large older man in a full-length brown coat, with a briefcase under his arm, looking down at him.

The man waved and shouted, "Hello, Dr. Turner."

Turner went up the wooden staircase to the balcony, walked over, and asked, "Stephen Brannen?"

The older man took a cigarette out of his mouth with his left hand and, putting out his other hand, said, "Yes, I'm Stephen Brannen."

They shook hands.

Turner asked, "How did you know it was me, Stephen?"

"Actually, I have a recent picture of you." Brannen grinned as he said this.

He discarded the stub of his cigarette, and they went into the restaurant. A waitress on the other side of the room recognized Turner and walked over.

"Good morning, Professor Turner. Here for breakfast?"

"Good morning, Tamara. Yes, we are."

Tamara was a former student of his.

"Where would you like to sit?" she asked.

Brannen said, "We have some business to discuss. Could we be over there, away from the others?"

"Of course. Follow me."

They followed her to a small table next to a window overlooking the balcony and sat down.

She asked, "What are you two having for breakfast?"

Brannen said, "I'll have a short stack, bacon, and coffee, caffeinated."

Turner said, "I'll have a bear claw and coffee, decaffeinated."

When the waitress left, Turner asked, "How did you get a picture of me?"

"Well, your college had a small informational display on a table in the hotel lobby. Part of the display was a stack of catalogues, and as I leafed through one, there were pictures of the faculty . . . and there you were, looking back at me."

"Stephen, what is this all about?"

Brannen lifted his briefcase to the table, opened it, and removed an envelope. Passing the envelope to Turner, he said, "Have a look."

Turner removed an eight-by-ten-inch glossy black-and-white picture and looked at it carefully.

"Do you know what this is?" Brannen asked.

"It's a burned-out hulk of a B-47," he replied and handed the picture and envelope back to Brannen.

"It belonged to the U.S. Air Force Strategic Air Command. I would like to talk to you about it, Burt. But first, the Los Alamos National Laboratory has had a number of inquires from two other U.S. government agencies concerning the incident involving this airplane—"

Turner interrupted, "Stephen, I don't really know who you are, or if this conversation should continue."

Brannen reached into the inside pocket of his coat, took out a wallet, and removed a white-and-blue laminated card. He passed the card to Turner. It identified Stephen W. Brannen as a consultant on hazardous material transport for Los Alamos National Laboratory, U.S. Department of Energy. It included a recent picture of Brannen. Turner returned the card.

"The data in the library archives at Los Alamos concerning this incident was collected from a number of different sources. In many cases, the sources provided classified information that was intended, it seems, to protect the interests of important military and political officials at the time. It is supposed that all these officials are dead now, and if there are a few alive, no one knows where they might be."

Leaning forward, he continued, "Historical evidence that has been collected recently pertains to inconclusive records found at Sandia Base and Manzano Base in Albuquerque, and at the Nevada Test site. The people at archives would like to update and make clear what really happened and file it all away for posterity. It will only be available to those having a certified 'Need to Know' and cleared for Top Secret/Restricted Data. You are the only one that can help us, Burt, in what was a most noble experiment."

"I have heard that one before."

At this point, the waitress brought them their breakfasts. Over breakfast, Brannen and Turner spoke about general things—the weather and personal opinions about geopolitics and, in particular, the problem of dealing with the war on terrorism and the difficulties in dealing with radical Islamic fundamentalism in the Middle East and North Africa.

"Burt, didn't you have some experience with terrorists when you were in North Africa?"

Turner lied, "Not where I was."

In time, Turner grew comfortable talking with Brannen, especially when the conversation came around to comparing notes about their time in military service. It developed that they were both serving at the same time as junior officers—Brannen was in the air force. After thirty years' service, he retired from the air force as a lieutenant colonel and had worked at Los Alamos National Laboratory for the last twelve years. His early background was in biochemical warfare, and later, he was one of the first members of the Nuclear Emergency Support Team (NEST). The NEST teams were under the Department of Energy and were responsible for dealing with nuclear accidents and their possible biological implications.

Brannen asked Turner if he still liked teaching and if he thought about retiring. Turner told him that teaching was not like it used to be and that, yes, he was thinking about retiring. Brannen told him he was ready and was going to retire soon with a comfortable air force retirement package.

The waitress saw they had finished their breakfasts and were chatting quietly. She walked over and asked, "Would you like anything else?"

"I'm fine, Tamara. How about you, Stephen?"

"No, thanks."

The waitress presented the check, and Brannen said, "I'll take care of this, Burt—or rather, our government, in its generosity, will take care of it."

Brannen paid the bill, added a generous tip, and they left the restaurant. In the parking lot, Brannen lit a cigarette and said, "Burt, tomorrow afternoon I give my show-and-tell at the conference. My part should be over at four thirty. I would really like to continue our conversation. Could we meet again about 5:00 p.m.?"

"I'll be finished a little after five. Why don't you come over to the house about five thirty and have dinner with my daughter and me?"

"I haven't had a home-cooked meal in quite a while. I would really enjoy that."

"Would you like steak or fish or anything in particular?"

"Anything but pizza or hamburgers."

After Turner gave directions to his house in Truckee, they shook hands. Brannen went to his rental car, Turner went to his truck, and they left the parking lot.

By the time Turner arrived at his office, he thought he had the situation pretty well worked out. Stephen Brannen seemed to be a decent guy and was straight up about what he wanted. He wasn't some young superpatriot out on a mission; he was a seasoned professional, and nonthreatening in his approach. Turner thought when they met again he would try to find out how much Brannen really knew about his tour of duty in North Africa; it could help him decide how cooperative he wanted to be with the other man.

He finished class at noon and was eating a peanut butter and jelly sandwich when the phone rang.

"Burt Turner speaking."

"Hi, Dad. Well, what happened?"

"What do you mean what happened?"

"Come on, you know what I mean."

"Stephen Brannen seems to be a very interesting man. I invited him to dinner tomorrow night."

There was a pause, then, "Oh, that's nice. I have to go. See you tonight!"

At dinner that night, Helen asked, "Come on, Dad, tell me about your meeting."

"Mr. Brannen is very easy to talk with. He's a retired air force officer and is employed at Los Alamos National Laboratory. He's a consultant in hazardous material transport there, and he's here to give a paper at the Hyatt Regency conference tomorrow."

"So why is he interested in you?"

"It seems I'm the only one able to provide information thought to be missing from a forty-year-old operational report held in the archive section, at the Los Alamos National Laboratory Library. That's all he told me."

"Well, that's rather thought provoking, isn't it? What time is he coming over tomorrow night?"

"We agreed on five thirty."

"I won't be able to shop after school. I'll make a list now of things we need, and you can go to the store tonight. Do think he would like barbequed salmon?"

"He said anything but pizza or hamburgers."

After dinner, Turner cleared the table and started washing dishes while Helen made up a shopping list. When she finished, she leaned back in her chair and asked, "Did he say anything about him having a family?"

"No, he didn't offer, and I didn't ask."

"Did you tell him about your family?"

"I didn't offer, and he didn't ask, but I did ask him to have dinner with me and my daughter. So he knows that much."

"You know, Dad, sometimes men don't seem to know how to ask the right questions."

The next day, he arrived home a little after 5:00 p.m. Helen was preparing dinner when he came into the kitchen. She looked up and said, "Hi, Dad. Our guest called and said he was going to be about fifteen minutes late. He seems to be very nice."

He thought, *How can a woman hear a voice over the phone, for a minute or less, and know the caller is nice?*

When the doorbell rang twenty-five minutes later, the table was set, the dinner almost ready, except for putting the salmon on the barbeque.

Turner went to the door, opened it, and standing with a big grin on his face and a briefcase in one hand and offering a bottle of wine with the other was their guest from Los Alamos National Laboratory.

"Come in, come in, Stephen." He accepted the wine and read, "Merlot, Sterling Vineyards, 1998. How very nice of you."

Turner took Brannen's coat and hung it over a chair. Brannen dropped his briefcase in the same chair, and they went into the kitchen-dining area.

"Helen, this is Stephen Brannen, a celebrity in our own home."

She gave a big welcoming smile, wiped her hands on a dishtowel, and shook his hand, saying, "We are always pleased to have a celebrity for dinner, Stephen Brannen."

"I'm really pleased to be here, and I'm not a celebrity, Helen."

Turner laughed and said, "Stephen, you gave a paper this afternoon at a very important conference. That, to us, makes you a celebrity."

"Dad, why don't you put the salmon on the barbeque while Stephen and I get to know each other."

After Turner went outside, Brannen commented, "You have your dad well trained."

"Actually, he always helped Mom in the kitchen and hasn't forgotten how."

She reached up to a nearby shelf, brought down three wineglasses, and handed them and a corkscrew to Brannen. "Let's start with your merlot."

He skillfully removed the cork and poured the merlot into two glasses. Giving one to Helen and taking the other, he said, "To new friends." They clinked glasses and took a sip.

Helen glanced at Brannen's left hand, saw a ring, and asked, "Is your wife at home, Stephen?"

"Actually, no. Martha is in an extended care home. She has Alzheimer's—the 'long good-bye,' you know."

"I'm very sorry. Dad told me it wasn't often you have a home-cooked meal."

"That's pretty much the case, but we have two grown children, and they invite me over often enough—of course, they have me over for holidays."

Helen continued the conversation, learning a great deal more about Stephen Brannen; his grandchildren, three boys and one girl, all teenagers; his looking forward to retirement from government service sometime in the next two years; and the possibility of moving from Los Alamos to Santa Fe to be closer to where his wife was being cared for. In turn, he inquired of Helen's background and what her future plans might be. She explained she had been married before, she loved teaching, and her relationship future was uncertain.

Brannen coaxed her a bit, and she went on to say, "Dad was finishing up his PhD at George Washington University in Washington DC when I was born. He stayed on as a postdoc in the medical school. When I was six years old, he took a teaching and research position at the University of California, San Francisco, Medical School. Mom worked for the federal government and was able to transfer to San Francisco. We lived in an apartment near Golden Gate Park."

She went on to say she was a mediocre student during her first eight years in public school, but when she graduated from middle school and entered Lowell High School, a high school with very strong academic standards, she blossomed. Her dad thought she needed the competition to find out what she could do academically.

"When I finished tenth grade, Dad resigned from UCSF and decided to accept a position at the Lake Tahoe College. I was sixteen. Mom, after twenty-eight years of government service, decided to retire. When I graduated from high school, I decided to go to college in Southern California and become a teacher. Dad tried to dissuade me."

"Why would he do that?"

"He felt the classroom was great, but parents, the administration, and politics take the life out of you."

"That's a pretty strong message, but it seems you ignored it."

"Well, I did. I left and enrolled at California State University, Long Beach, and majored in elementary school education. When I graduated, I found a fifth-grade teaching position at Gulf Avenue Elementary School in the LA harbor area. One night, five years later, Dad called and said Mom died of complications after surgery for ovarian cancer. Two years later, I decided to leave Southern California and come up here to teach fourth grade at Donner Elementary School."

Helen didn't go into her previous marriage and divorce.

"Well, you certainly got around. Very much like my kids when I was in the air force."

A few minutes later, her dad came in with the salmon, and they sat down to a very nice dinner accompanied by light and easy conversation. After dinner, Turner and his daughter cleaned up the kitchen while chatting with Brannen, who sat at the table, sipping the last of the merlot. When the dishes were finished, they joined him for a time, then Turner said, "Helen, Stephen and I are going up to the study and chat a bit. Don't wait up for me."

On the way, Brannen picked up his briefcase and followed his host up the stairs and into the study. He looked around and said, "This is the quiet kind of place a body could get a lot of work done, if they could keep from looking out the window."

"It is a nice place to work," Turner replied.

Brannen looked closely at two large seascapes occupying one wall.

"Real oils, they're beautiful. Are they from California?"

"No, they came from Naples. I bought them when I was in the navy."

"A long time ago, huh, Burt? Where are all your degrees? Somebody with your background should have a wall full."

"Well, over there is one from George Washington University, and next to it, a picture of me giving a paper at the medical school at UCSF. Those are the only academic things I feel are important."

Brannen looked at these, then saw a picture on Turner's worktable next to his desk. "Is that your wife and Helen?"

The picture was of two very attractive women, one older, the other younger, holding skis near a ski lift.

Turner replied, "Yes, taken about ten years ago at Diamond Peak over at Incline. We skied there once in a while."

Brannen turned and walked over to the wall by the doorway and studied a letter in a thin black-and-gold frame. The letterhead announced,

The Secretary of the Navy
WASHINGTON

In the upper left-hand corner was a flag with four stars, one at each corner, and a furled anchor all on a field of blue—the logo of the secretary of the navy.

Brannen read,

The President of the United States takes pleasure in presenting this letter to

LIEUTENANT BURT TURNER,
UNITED STATES NAVY RESERVE

FOR **services as set forth in the following**

CITATION:

"**For heroic conduct while serving at an undisclosed location in the month of November 1960. As Officer in Charge of Special Weapons/Explosive Ordnance Disposal Team Number ONE, Lieutenant Burt Turner (then Lieutenant Junior Grade) displayed exceptional courage and initiative while participating in an operation of a classified nature, involving**

great risk of injury to both himself and the members of his team. By his outstanding leadership and professional skill, he contributed materially to the success of an extremely hazardous assignment. His conduct throughout was in keeping with the highest traditions of the United States Naval Service."

Brannen continued,

Signed, for the President, by the Secretary of the Navy, Thomas Gates

"It would appear this was for a covert operation so highly classified a medal could not be awarded without compromising what the operation entailed."

Turner, pulling a second chair to the worktable, replied, "It's something like that." Then he added, "Stephen, let's talk."

Brannen put his briefcase on the worktable, and they sat down.

"What the hell do you want from me, Stephen?"

Brannen opened the briefcase and took out three official-looking papers and handed them to Turner.

Turner saw the first was a copy of a letter from the archives at Los Alamos to Stephen Brannen, asking him to contact Dr. Burt Turner after arriving at Lake Tahoe for the Hazardous Materials Transport Officers Conference.

The letter went on,

> Dr. Turner should be advised that he is the only source of extremely important information, which would be helpful in allowing the library archives of Los Alamos National Laboratory to complete its files on a classified operation in which Dr. Turner was involved while serving in the U.S. Navy at the Naval Air Station at Port Lyautey and attached to the Naval Ordnance Facility. You are directed to ask Dr. Turner if he would come to a meeting at Los Alamos National Laboratory to help clarify certain aspects of the operational reports on file in the library archives.

He noted that copies went to the United States Department of State and the Central Intelligence Agency.

The second and third letters were responses from the Department of State and the Central Intelligence Agency. They asked to be informed if Turner agreed to the request for his cooperation. If he did agree, the two agencies wished to be present and to later speak with Turner, separately, regarding particular issues germane to their agencies' interests and requested that Los Alamos provide a secure conference room for separate interviews.

When he had finished reading the letters, he laid them down, turned away, and looked out the window. The moon was partially obscured from time to time by clouds moving in from the west. He remembered hearing the weather report this morning saying there was a 40 percent chance of snow down to six thousand feet by midnight. He thought, *It seems too early for this sort of thing.*

Brannen, clearing his throat, asked, "Is there something you have read that you don't understand?"

There was no answer.

Brannen again asked, "Burt, is there something you have read that you don't understand?"

The question broke through Turner's preoccupation with the moon and forthcoming weather.

Turner turned back to the table and said, "I'm sorry, Stephen, I was thinking about something else." He looked at Brannen and said, "I understand the interest in filling in the gaps at the archives, but why are CIA and State interested in interviewing me?"

Brannen replied, "Shortly after the exchange of these letters, there was a meeting at Los Alamos. There was a representative from CIA, another from State, and one from Los Alamos. I was there as nonparticipant. From what I heard, CIA was interested in a series of terrorist activities involving groups in Algeria, Tunisia, and Morocco that led to the operation, or incident, you became involved with. Additionally, there are at least two of these terrorists who were part of a splinter group in the Front de Libération Nationale, the FLN, who the CIA feels cut their teeth in that operation. The two were teenagers at the time, not necessarily a unique age group in some terrorist activities.

"The Israelis say these two have continued to be active through the years and have survived to be senior players in the Al-Qaeda organization. CIA also suggested that you were involved in a covert operation called Scorpion Fish. Scorpion Fish, we understand, was intended to find out if the Russians were supplying weapons to the FLN by way of fishing boats along the Atlantic coast of Morocco. And it seems that somewhere along the line, you and your team did some work with the Foreign Legion."

"Look, I don't know if I can help you with what you are saying. It was a long time ago."

"Let me continue. State seemed to be mildly interested in what CIA was saying, but then State explained their interest was in the brief period between the French military and protectorate government finalizing exit from what was French Morocco and King Mohammed V's government's early stage of a Moroccan constitutional monarchy. It was at that time the so-called most noble experiment occurred."

At this point, Turner again turned toward the window and saw the moon had disappeared behind an advancing overcast and the Jeffrey pines were swaying,

After an uncomfortably long pause, Stephen Brannen said, "Would you be able to come to Los Alamos a week from today?"

Turner swung around and said, "I'm sorry, Stephen. What were you saying?"

Stephen Brannen repeated his question.

"I have a class on Friday morning, and usually there are faculty meetings in the afternoon."

Brannen replied, "I am sure your college administration would be pleased to know that the U.S. government has invited you to consult with the Los Alamos National Laboratory for a few days."

Turner, with extreme discomfort, replied, "That's true. Could I call you later about all this?"

Brannen took a card from his briefcase. "This phone number is a direct line to me at Los Alamos. Today is Friday. Call me Monday before noon, and we will make your travel arrangements."

They got up from their chairs. Brannen retrieved the letters and followed Turner out of the study and down the stairs to the front room.

As he put on his coat, he said, "Burt, I want to thank you and your daughter for your hospitality. The dinner and conversation with you two was wonderful. You made me feel at home." Then he said in a more formal way, "You are in a position to help your country once more. You can't imagine how important you are to us right now."

They shook hands, Turner opened the front door, and as Brannen walked out, Turner said, "Be careful driving tonight. It looks like it's going to snow."

He stood in the doorway and waved as Brannen drove away.

Saturday morning, the sun was just above the horizon in a cloudless sky. Turner was finishing shoveling more than a foot of snow from his sidewalk and driveway from the storm that had arrived a little after midnight. He looked up, saw Helen waiting to come up the driveway in his pickup truck, and got out of the way. She pulled into the garage, got out, and met her father with a big hug and smile.

"Good morning, Dad. I took your truck because of the storm warnings last night. I didn't know I would be spending the night over at Pete's."

"Well, when you didn't come down to breakfast, I thought you may have decided to go out last night. Have you eaten anything yet?"

"Not yet, have you?"

"Not yet."

They went from the garage into the utility room. As they took off their boots and coats, she asked, "How did it go last night? Are you and Stephen Brannen great friends now?"

"Let's go in and have breakfast, and I'll tell you."

Helen made waffles. There was a choice of maple syrup or Pete's mother's strawberry preserves. Her father had a glass of milk followed by Sumatra decaffeinated coffee, and Helen had the coffee; both added cream and sugar.

During breakfast, her father told of the meeting with Brannen. She didn't have any questions until he mentioned the State Department and CIA interests.

"Why on earth does the State Department and CIA want to talk to you?"

"During my tour of duty in North Africa, the French were being forced out of Tunisia, Algeria, and Morocco after seventy years of colonial rule. The Front de Libération Nationale, the FLN, and a few minor Islamic fundamentalist groups used terrorism in their drive for independence. We were concerned terrorist activities would be mounted against us, and we used diplomacy and small-scale covert operations to protect our interests. CIA and State Department may think I can add to what they already know, I guess."

"Why were we over there in the first place?"

"We established naval and air force bases in the area, with the permission of the French, as part of a cold war deterrent strategy to deal with Soviet expansionism. With the French leaving, the Arabs wanted all foreign infidels to leave, including the newly arrived Americans. Our policy was to be viewed as guests, not occupiers, which was acceptable to the newly independent country's governments, but not acceptable to all the people."

"This sounds like the British in the Sudan in the time of Chinese Gordon, and the jihad of the Madi," Helen replied.

"What makes it interesting is the Madi's jihad and the siege of Khartoum were about the same time in the 1880s that the French were colonizing North Africa. Eighty years later, the French were being forced to leave. That's when I was there."

"Do you think CIA and State are trying to establish a connection with what happened forty years ago, and what could be happening today in relation to Al-Qaeda, Hamas, the Islamic jihad, and what is euphemistically called the war on terrorism?"

"Yes." And smiling, he said, "I left out that your mother was involved in some of this." Changing the subject, he asked, "What time is Pete coming over for dinner tomorrow?"

She answered, "About five." And then she added, "Pete's making dinner for us."

Turner asked, "What is this all about, Pete making dinner in my house?" The emphasis was on *my*.

"Dad, it's going to be great. He really wanted to do this to impress you. He thinks the world of you."

"He probably is planning to move in with my daughter, or for her to move in with him."

"I'm not ready for that kind of relationship. Everything is fine the way it is."

Turner asked, "What sort of thing is he going to fix for my Sunday dinner, fish heads and rice, or maybe rats on a stick?"

Laughing, she said, "Neither one, Dad."

Turner saw an opening for a sea story. "After I left Officer Candidate School at Newport, Rhode Island, I had orders to Underwater Swimmers School and demolition training at the naval station in Key West, Florida. There were a number of senior enlisted men in our class. Two held the distinction of being first class divers. One night, these two were drinking quite a bit and stole two expensive ornamental peacocks belonging to the wife of the skipper of the naval base. They took the noisy peacocks out on Pier 3, wrung their necks, and, with blowtorches taken from their ship, burned off the birds' feathers, cooked them with the same blowtorches, and ate them. Someone alerted the Marine MPs that something strange was going on at Pier 3. The Marine MPs drove to pier 3 and caught the perpetrators as they were finishing their 'game dinner' and threw the sailors in the brig."

She laughed and said, "You are just making this up."

Turner, in a very serious way, said, "I am not making this up. A story like this could never be made up."

"What happened to the two sailors?"

"They went to captain's mast. The skipper gave them a week in the brig, on piss and punk, and told them to replace the peacocks."

"What's 'piss and punk'?"

"Bread and water."

"It sounds like they got off easy."

"Well, they were certified first class divers off a submarine rescue ship homeported at Key West. There were a number of subs also homeported there. The skipper of the base was a former submariner. Special people and special circumstances."

After a pause, Turner finished with, "You know, of course, Pete was a first class diver, so I am not sure what I am going to be asked to eat."

His daughter said, "Pete is going to try to get you Mackinaw trout." Turner smiled.

Sunday, Pete arrived at five sharp. Turner greeted him at the door, and before he could react, he found himself holding a raw eight-pound Mackinaw trout.

With both hands now holding a basket of vegetables and other things, Pete said, "I caught that beauty off Crystal Bay Point early this morning. He was down 475 feet."

They went into the kitchen, and Turner flopped the fish into the sink. Helen came in and, raising her voice, said, "Pete, what a beautiful fish. Did you just get it?"

"Caught it this morning. The conditions were perfect—cloudless sky after the snowstorm, quiet water, and a hungry fish. I'll cut it up for our dinner. You can put what's left in your freezer."

Pete expertly prepared the fish for baking, then set himself to preparing vegetables and salad things taken from the basket he had brought with him. Helen assisted when he let her.

"Your daughter told me you had a meeting with a guy from Los Alamos."

"Actually, I had two meetings. He has something to do with hazardous nuclear waste or something." Turner let it go at that.

Pete asked, "Does it look like you are going to be more involved?

"I don't know, I might be going to Los Alamos."

The dinner turned out to be quite good. Even the wine from Turner's hall closet was good.

———————————

Monday morning, between classes, Turner sat at his desk staring at Stephen Brannen's card propped up on his coffee mug. He thought, *I have to arrange being gone Friday. Maybe I should call Brannen first. There could be a change in his plans. But he would have called me by now. Wonder what would happen if I didn't call him? I wonder what he would say, or do, if I called him and said I wouldn't be able come? This is worse than deciding whether or not to call for an appointment for a colonoscopy or a root canal.*

He finally picked up the phone handset and dialed the number on the card. On the second ring, Stephen Brannen answered.

"Brannen speaking."

"Stephen, it's me, Burt."

"Good morning, Burt. Did you get any more snow?"

"Not after the night you left. Did you fly out the next day?"

"No, I hitched a ride on a Nevada Air Guard C-130 out of Reno that night. They were on their way to Texas and were nice enough to drop me off at Kirkland Air Force Base. I got a ride back up to Los Alamos from there."

"It was pretty windy here. How was your flight?"

"It was interesting. The snowstorm hadn't moved over the Sierras and into the Reno area yet, but the wind announcing the storm was fierce. I didn't think they would be taking off in that wind. They did, and I just held on. It was an E ticket ride. I'm way too old for that stuff."

Turner mused, *E ticket ride really dates Brannen. When Helen was a little girl, I used to take her on the E ticket rides at Disneyland in Orange County, California.*

"That night, we had winds over one hundred miles an hour at Donner Pass. It does get windy here," he said.

Brannen, changing the subject, asked, "Well, Burt, are you ready to come visit us?"

"Ah, I haven't made arrangements yet."

"Well, we made arrangements on this end, and it's all set. You will fly out on Southwest Airlines Friday morning at seven fifteen to Denver and arrive at Santa Fe about noon. I'll pick you up. Then on Sunday, you will backtrack to Reno, arriving at about 9:00 p.m. We have you staying at the Los Alamos Inn here in Los Alamos."

"Boy, Stephen, you guys really move fast. So Friday morning, I'm to go down to Reno-Tahoe International, check in with Southwest Airlines, and look forward to an enjoyable weekend?"

Laughing, Brannen replied, "Burt, it will be a stroll down memory lane. Don't bring anything but carry-on luggage, then you won't have to sweat security too much."

In a more serious tone, he added, "Burt, you don't know how important this is. I know you are uncomfortable, but I think everyone involved is going to do their best to make you feel at ease. See you Friday." Brannen hung up.

Turner held the phone for a bit, then put it back in the cradle and began the paperwork required for his absence from the college.

That night, he and Helen were in the kitchen getting ready for dinner when he said, "I called Stephen Brannen. He has already made reservations for me to fly to Santa Fe this coming Friday morning. He said he would meet me there, and we would drive up to Los Alamos. I would fly back Sunday evening."

"Evidently, he guessed you would commit to going to the meeting."

"I almost decided I wasn't going, and then he came on so fast with the arrangements he already made I just went along with it all."

"What time do you have to leave?"

"It's a Southwest flight scheduled to leave at 7:15 a.m. I would have to leave here about 4:30 a.m. to get through security. Could you take me to the airport?"

"But, Dad, it's so cold and dark," she joked. "I'm sure I can get Mary Thompson to cover my class Friday morning for an hour. What time do you come back?"

"Sunday night, at nine o'clock."

"Well, it looks like you are getting involved in something entirely new and different. Good for you!"

He was not happy to hear this declaration from his daughter.

For the remaining three days, he became more and more uncomfortable about going to Los Alamos. It was difficult for him to concentrate on his classes, and he was having fragmented dreams about people and actions from a long time ago.

Thursday evening, he sat in his study looking out the window. Feeling a chill, he pulled the zipper of his sweater up more tightly and glanced down at the indoor/outdoor thermometer in the corner of the window sill; it read fourteen degrees outside and inside sixty-seven degrees.

He hadn't bothered to turn on his desk light when he came in; the light from a gibbous moon was adequate enough. As he looked at this almost-full moon in the clear, cold sky, it made him think of another like it some forty years ago.

It was a gibbous moon when we were on our way back to Port Lyautey in the helicopter after the covert operation in the harbor at Larache. Petty Officer Cole lay on the floor dozing, and Chief Gallegos and I, too tired to sleep, were looking out the portside hatch at the white surf crashing on the beach two hundred feet below. The three of us were still in our UDT life jackets and dry suits, cold and tired after a long paddle down the coast, in our four-man raft, to a rendezvous with the helicopter and the sixty-five-mile flight back to the base.

He got up, stretched, and went to his bedroom across the hall. Inside, he went to the closet and took out an old blue nylon flight bag and began packing it in preparation for his trip to Los Alamos in the morning.

When his wife was alive, they had a matched set of expensive carry-ons when they traveled. After she died, he never used his again. Early on, his daughter had told him, "You dress nicely and are a very attractive man, but that damn old flight bag belongs in some landfill."

He would end the conversation by saying, "I like it because I can wedge it into the overhead bins more easily."

The next morning, after a quick breakfast, Helen drove her dad east on Interstate 80 in the pickup truck. It was brittle cold, and out of the front window, the stars were sharp points of bluish light. After passing Verdi and Mogul, Reno was just coming alive with traffic. She turned onto 395 South and, two minutes later, took the freeway off-ramp to Reno-Tahoe International Airport, drove on to the terminal, and found a parking space near the Southwest Airline passenger terminal entrance.

He opened his door and said, "I'll see you Sunday night." He leaned over and kissed his daughter on the cheek.

She gave him a hug and said, "I love you, Dad. Take good care of yourself."

He got out, took his flight bag from the truck bed, waved to his daughter, and then walked toward the terminal as she drove away.

After leaving the reservation counter, Turner counted eighty-seven passengers in line for the extensive security check for the flight. It took an hour and twenty-five minutes to go from security to his window seat over the wing of the Boeing 737-400. He usually chose this seat when he flew because he enjoyed looking out at the clouds and sky and watching the wing control surfaces operate during takeoffs and landings.

The entry hatch closed, and the safety belt sign came on. Turner snugged up his safety belt as the airplane tug pushed back the 737-400. Once clear and under its own power, the plane taxied out to the main runway.

On the way to the main runway, Turner, out of long habit, memorized the location of the escape hatches. He looked to see if there were any people sitting in such a way that they might block access to the escape hatches should there be a panic to get out. His wariness was the result of too many hours, as a passenger, in a low-flying navy helicopter and a navy twin-engine light aircraft under somewhat perilous conditions. The engines of the 737-400 spooled up; the aircraft turned onto the main runway, and as it accelerated, Turner was pressed back in his seat. They were off the ground in a matter of seconds. The aircraft gained altitude, banked slightly, and turned east into the rising sun. As he looked out the window, he had long thoughts about his tour of duty in Morocco, as a young naval officer, over forty years ago.

Chapter 2

1958-60

Recently promoted from ensign, Lieutenant, Junior Grade (LTJG) Burt Turner was sitting next to the window—seat A, row 39—on the portside of the Military Air Transport Service (MATS) C-121, the military version of the Lockheed Constellation commercial airliner.

Seated on his right was a young U.S. Air Force officer and, on the aisle, a solidly built middle-aged U.S. Army lieutenant colonel (LTC) with three rows of ribbons: Silver Star and Purple Heart in the top row, a combat infantryman's badge, jump wings, and a ranger patch.

They had been in the air for about an hour after leaving Maguire Air Force Base in New Jersey for the transatlantic flight to Orly International Airport, Paris, France. The sun was going down over the western horizon as the airplane flew east toward a night sky. Turner looked out the window and watched the blue flame from the engine exhaust stacks glow more strongly as the darkness increased. Then a few stars made their appearance.

He reached for a large brown envelope that earlier he had slid into the pocket located on the back of the seat in front of him. The envelope contained his official orders, officer service record, pay records, and medical file. He opened the envelope and took out the folder containing his official orders. He opened the folder and read for the fourth time:

> From: Chief of Naval Personnel
> To: LTJG Burt James Turner, 620554/1105, USNR.
> Subject: Change of Duty
>
> 1. At 1200 hours, 9 March 1958 you will be detached from Naval School, Explosive Disposal, Indian Head Maryland, and proceed

immediately to Maguire AFB, New Jersey, for further transport on 11 March to Orly International Airport, Paris, France, via Military Air Transport Command aircraft. Upon arrival at this destination you will report to the Navy Liaison Office at the Military Terminal. You will then make yourself available for immediate transport via VR24 to U.S. Naval Ordnance Facility (NAVORDFAC), Port Lyautey/Kenitra Morocco. You have been assigned a Priority Class I category for transport. You are required to wear appropriate uniform while en route.

2.   Upon arrival at the Naval Air Station, Port Lyautey/Kenitra Morocco, you will report to the Commanding Officer, Naval Ordnance Facility, for further orders involving primary duty involving the demolition of explosives.

Turner skipped over several paragraphs, enabling him to read paragraph 6. The preceding paragraphs were associated with authorized baggage weights, compliance to orders, accounting data, and other items. These paragraphs were written in official jargon with numerous lettered and numbered references (BuPers 68734, Bureau Contr. 174/1407, etc.), making the reading incomprehensible to him. He had been in the U.S. Navy eighteen months— initially at Officer Candidate School (OCS) at Newport, Rhode Island; then training in the volunteer special weapons/explosive ordnance disposal program at Indian Head, Maryland; and finally, a short tour of duty at the Hopkins Applied Physics Laboratory studying new approaches in delivering underwater ordnance. He had had a single two-week leave during the eighteen months.

Naval officers in his class at OCS who were assigned duty ashore or in the fleet would be familiar with this manner of communication by now. Other officers like Turner, who had been training in volunteer programs such as flight school, submarine service, and underwater demolition, for example, had yet to learn these skills. Turner would now have to learn these communication skills, and quickly. He liked reading paragraph 6.

It is certified that you hold a TOP SECRET/RESTRICTED DATA clearance from this command based on a BACKGROUND INVESTIGATION reported by ISO letter serial 91 of 18 December 1958.

The paragraph made him feel important. He scanned the official orders again and thought, *There is something odd here.* He looked more carefully and, smiling, thought, *There are hardly any commas in these paragraphs. Interesting.*

At that moment, the young U.S. Air Force officer seated next to him asked if he could turn on the overhead reading light. Turner said, "Of course." As the air force officer reached up and turned on the overhead light, Turner noticed that he was wearing the single silver bar of a lieutenant (LT). Turner thought, *He's the same rank as I am. I wonder where he is going.*

The air force officer introduced himself. "I'm Joe Logan. I couldn't help noticing that you were going over your orders."

Turner replied with a smile. "I think I understand what's important, but there's a lot here that I can't really decipher, like paragraphs 3, 4, and 5."

Logan replied, "The experts on this are the guys that write up orders. Almost always, they are middle-level enlisted men who have gone to a service school that teaches the art of unfathomable communication." They both laughed. "If you like, I could try to interpret what it says for you."

Turner passed the orders to Logan, who read through the paragraphs in question and said, "These paragraphs are not directed to you. They are directed to individuals responsible for covering the costs of your deployment and alerting other commands to expect you, that you are on your way."

Handing Turner's orders back, he continued, "You are a Category I for transport. They just want to get you to where you're going very quickly."

Looking for a set of wings, Turner asked, "Are you a pilot?"

"No, I'm what is called a loading officer."

"What do you load? Are you involved with MATS?"

Logan said with a smile, "I work for General Curtis LeMay."

"You're SAC!"

"Yes, I am."

When Turner was completing his training at the Explosive Ordnance Disposal School (EODS) at Indian Head, Maryland, he made the cut and was allowed to attend an additional six weeks of intense training in nuclear weapons and nuclear weapons rendering safe procedures. When he was in the nuclear weapons phase of his training, he learned that knowing about air force nuclear weapons, you also learned something about General Curtis LeMay and SAC.

Logan asked Turner, "What do you do? Are you going to some ship in the Med?"

"I just finished at the Explosive Ordnance Disposal School at Indian Head."

"I saw the diver's helmet on your belt buckle when you took your coat off. I thought you were a navy diver. I didn't think about EOD." He continued,

"A friend of mine has been admitted to one of the spring classes at Indian Head. I guess our air force guys don't go through all the underwater ordnance training and diving."

"Well, he will have a very interesting five months in the classroom and field learning the mysteries of surface and dropped ordnance, plus rockets and guided missiles, and—the special delight of all EOD guys and terrorists— biological and chemical warfare and booby traps."

"How long is the navy program?"

"Well, we have a few more phases. Initially, there's Underwater Swimmers School at Key West, Florida. We learned to use and maintain all the different types of self-contained underwater breathing apparatus, or the SCUBA, that the navy might have us use. Then there's demolition procedures, underwater and surface, and the use of a variety of explosives. This initial phase varied between five and six weeks. The next phase was about five or six more weeks of training in deep-sea diving at Indian Head in the Potomac River, a real joy in the winter. When we finished all of that, we integrated with army, marine corps, and air force students for the rest of our EOD training. We picked up a few CIA and FBI personnel in some of the later phases. Finally, some students go on to nuclear weapons, and a few of the naval officers go on to Advanced Underwater Weapons School if the command they are being sent to requests this additional training."

"That's a long training program. The beauty of a program like that is, you don't have to go to sea right away, or maybe never."

"Well, there are navy EOD teams on board aircraft carriers and ammunition ships, but most are at shore bases and deploy, usually by air, to where they have a mission or operation."

"I was almost a naval officer," Logan said and laughed. "I went to the Boat School. The Naval Academy at Annapolis, Maryland. During the summer cruises, I used to get seasick, awful seasick. So when I graduated, I wanted to get as far from a ship as possible and joined the air force."

"Sounds like Ulysses leaving his ship with his oar and walking inland."

"Exactly so."

"Why did you go to Annapolis?"

"I thought I would like to be a navy pilot."

The lieutenant colonel on the aisle looked over at Turner and Logan and said, "Gentlemen, it appears that our dinners from one of New York's finest restaurants are about to be served."

A cabin attendant with an apron of sorts over his air force shirt and trousers was passing out boxed dinners. A scoop of mashed potatoes, a puddle of gravy in a tiny paper cup, a leaf of lettuce accompanied by two slices of tomato, some sort of meat preparation (probably Spam derived), and for dessert, a kind of banana or apple cake with a maraschino cherry on top. Beverage: coffee, tea, or milk . . . to order.

The two lieutenants carefully emptied the contents of their boxes onto the drop-down tray in front of them. They ate their dinners with gusto. The lieutenant colonel, with a look on his face that betrayed his concern about an imminent chemical warfare attack, took out a package of antacids and placed it on his tray next to his dinner.

When the two younger officers had finished their dinners, they asked the cabin attendant if there might be more. There was, and they each were given another series of boxes, same contents as before.

After dinner, Turner and Logan continued with their earlier conversation. It was unusual for Turner to be so talkative with a stranger, but Lieutenant Joe Logan was one of those individuals who came across as the genuine article—sincere, unguarded in conversation, and unabashedly decent. He was also extremely bright.

Turner asked, "Where did you come from, Joe?"

Logan smiled and answered, "I am a product of the southwestern United States—Tucson, Arizona. My mom and dad lived there all their lives, except when they were both at the Arizona State University at Tempe."

"What do your mom and dad do?"

"My mom is a special education teacher at an elementary school. My dad is a middle school principal." He added, "And I have two sisters younger than me. What about you, Burt?"

Turner replied with an air of superiority. "I grew up in the heart of the Los Angeles Harbor District, in San Pedro, California. I am a product of the Los Angeles waterfront. I was raised by an aunt who worked at Van Camps Fish Cannery on Terminal Island. She passed away when I was in my first year at the University of Southern California."

Before Logan had a chance to ask the obvious question, Turner continued, "When I was a senior in high school, I worked part-time at Marineland of the Pacific in Palos Verdes. The chief of the technical staff helped me get a full-ride scholarship, in biology, at USC."

"Were you one of those surfer guys?"

"Not so much with the boards, but we did a lot of body surfing."

"Well, I can see why you entered into a navy underwater program. Why didn't you go on to grad school?"

"It was time to get away and do something different."

Turner noticed Logan wore a wedding band, so he asked how long he had been married and if his wife might be able to be with him at his new duty station. Logan said that he and his wife, Carolyn, had been married for two years and that she would be coming over, space available, in three weeks to stay for the length of his tour. He went on to say that they had their wedding at the U.S. Naval Academy after he graduated.

Turner asked how he had met her. Logan told him that Carolyn was from Roanoke, Virginia, and he met her at a dance at the Naval Academy when he was in his third year. The Naval Academy had an arrangement with nearby Mount St. Mary's College and Hood College, where girls were invited to dances held at the academy for the midshipmen. Carolyn had been a student at Mount St. Mary's College. He added that her dad was the retired admiral Fletcher Smith.

Logan asked Turner what his situation was. Turner told him that he was in love with a beautiful girl in the College of Engineering at the University of Southern California. They had been in a serious relationship for five months and two days. Her name was Joan, and she was studying chemical engineering.

Changing the subject, Turner asked Logan if he knew what the flight time was to Paris. Logan took a small notebook from his shirt pocket and said, "About twelve and a half hours, unless there is a headwind. If there is a headwind, we may have to refuel in the Azores at Lajes Airport." They had been in the air for seven hours; it was 1:00 a.m. New York time and 6:00 a.m. Paris time. The C-121 was flying into first light. Logan was just dozing off when Turner asked him where he was assigned.

Logan replied sleepily, "Morocco."

"I'm going to the Naval Air Station at Port Lyautey!"

"Doesn't that air base belong to the French Navy?"

"The French have been asked to leave by the nationalist insurgents with some haste. We have negotiated an agreement with King Mohammed V and the Moroccan government to use the air base, but for air transport purposes only—no fighters, no bombers."

"Well, you don't need the base for fighters or bombers. You guys have aircraft carriers out in the Med in the Sixth Fleet. We have three SAC bases in Morocco—Ben Guerir, Nouasseur, and Sidi Slimane. My orders are for Sidi Slimane."

Within ten minutes, the two junior officers in row 39, seats A and B, were asleep. Their ties and shirts loose at their necks, shirts bloused out at the belt. The older officer, in seat C, had fallen asleep somewhat earlier and was presenting gastric reflux activity (belching) periodically, but not enough to disturb his sleep.

About two hours later, Turner and Logan were awakened by the cabin attendant as he passed breakfast (boxes again) to the passengers occupying the seats in front of them. Turner said he had to go to the head. Logan said he had to go too.

They were just getting out of their seats when the army officer just returning from his head call said, "Gentlemen, it's all yours. Everyone else has addressed their needs or is still asleep." He allowed the two junior officers into the aisle, acknowledged their "Thank you, sir," then sat down.

The flight offered individual toilet kits (toothbrush, toothpaste, comb, towelette, and shaving gear) for the passengers. When Turner and Logan returned, they were nicely shaven and generally squared away with their bladders empty. The lieutenant colonel rose from his seat, letting them into theirs, and commented that the cabin attendant was going to be back shortly with breakfasts for the three of them.

He introduced himself as Lieutenant Colonel Pete Bennett, Regular Army. Turner and Logan introduced themselves. Bennett asked them what their destinations were, and they told him Morocco. There was a long pause, and then he said, "There are some very serious problems where you're going in relation to the FLN."

He went on to explain, "The FLN is the major group involved with terrorism activities against the French. They are not terribly interested in us at the moment, but there are a number of smaller groups of Arabs that are."

There was no doubt that he had the serious attention of the two junior officers.

"These smaller groups are more violent in their jihad, their holy war against all foreign infidels—that includes us, you know—and want all of us out of Morocco, Algeria, and Tunisia. I don't think we are going to be in these countries for very much longer, at least in Algeria and Tunisia. We may have a longer stay in Morocco, though."

Logan asked "Sir, are you going to North Africa?"

"No, I'm stationed at the American Legation in Paris as a military attaché."

Logan continued, "I know we have an air base in Tunisia, but are we in Algeria too?"

"Well, it isn't very well known, at least in the U.S." Looking at Turner, he said, "Lieutenant Turner probably knows about the weapons and ammunition we have stored at Oran and, in fact, in Tunisia at Bizerte."

Turner, in disbelief, said, "No, sir, I didn't know anything about that."

"Well, I overheard you say to Lieutenant Logan that you were EOD. The navy is responsible for the inventory at Oran and Bizerte, and I am sure you are going to be involved in some way with that responsibility, among your other duties."

Turner was about to ask more questions when the cabin attendant appeared with their breakfasts—in this case, scrambled eggs, bacon, toast (white), orange juice, and coffee. Turner and Logan asked for and were rewarded with seconds. This exhibition did not go unnoticed by Bennett, who said, "I envy you young men, with your appetites so large and ability to tolerate food that only a goat could digest. And you are able to stay trim and slender. I guess there was a time when I was like yourselves."

Logan said, "Sir, you look quite fit."

"Fit enough for what I do now, and unfit for what I used to do."

Turner and Logan were both tall and lean—Turner at six foot one and Logan at six foot two, both at about 170 pounds. Turner was in exceptional shape because of the demands of the underwater program he had recently completed plus working out daily with the marines on the obstacle course at Indian Head. Logan told Turner he ran track at the Naval Academy (440-yard and 880-yard) and still ran five miles a day.

The pilot came on the cabin speaker system and announced they were about an hour out from Orly, that they should be landing on time, and that it looked to be a beautiful summer day in Paris.

"Have you two young men been to Paris?"

They simultaneously said they hadn't.

"If you enjoy history and art and, of course, food, your visit will be well rewarded."

Turner said, "I don't know how much time either of us has between planes. I am supposed to fly out on VR24 for immediate transport to NAS, Port Lyautey."

"I've got a three-day layover before flying out on air force transport."

Turner looked at the colonel and said, "If there isn't any transport for me right away, maybe Logan and I could try to get into Paris from Orly. How much could we do in twenty-four hours or less?"

Bennett replied, "Well, you could do something, but I am sure you understand that Paris is not for quick visits. Do you have something to write on?"

Turner took a small tablet and pen from the envelope containing his orders, and wrote down Bennett's instructions.

"After you two do your paperwork at Orly, ask about a ride to the Orlyrail train station. There is a shuttle system set up at the Military Liaison Office.

Take the Orlyrail RER-C train. It runs every fifteen minutes to Gare de l' Austerlitz. It's about a thirty-five-minute ride. When you arrive at Gare de l' Austerlitz, it will only be a short walk to Place de L'Odeon and the Luxembourg Gardens. I would suggest you immediately get a room at the one of the small hotels nearby. From there, you can tour the Luxembourg Gardens. Down from the Place de L'Odeon is a small museum that is heavy into impressionist art. Farther on, if you have time, is Pont des Arts, leading to the Louvre. If time is a problem, just do the garden, walk around Odeon, and check out the outside market and cafes."

He paused, then added, "You must have dinner at La Mediterranee at Place de L'Odeon. In the morning, choose one of the cafes for breakfast. You might like *pain au chocolat* and *café crème* at Café Suisse." He couldn't help saying, Don't ask for Fruit Loops or Lucky Charms. He added, "Lieutenant Logan, you have time to do much more. I suggest you ask at the military liaison help desk for assistance. They have maps, suggestions for transportation, and places to stay."

"Lieutenant Turner, did you get all that?"

Turner read his notes back to him.

"It appears you got it the first time."

Bennett took a book and a pair of reading glasses out of a small bag he had under his seat. He opened the book to a page number he had memorized and began reading. Turner watched all of this and was interested to see an army officer reading Cagle and Manson's *The Sea War in Korea*.

He looked out the window at the morning sky. *It is so beautiful out there. Eighteen months ago, I graduated from USC and didn't have any idea what I was going to do next. Now I'm a naval officer flying over the Atlantic Ocean to Paris and then on to North Africa.*

I'm going to be officer in charge of an EOD team of two or three senior enlisted men. I wonder how they will feel about me, a college guy younger than they are. They have so much more experience. None of them has less than five years in the navy. I have never felt so out of place.

I should have gone to graduate school. I wonder if I should have asked Joan to marry me before I left. It would be awful if she found out she were pregnant. I wonder if I can physically keep up with my team. I wonder what sort of equipment they have where I am going. Why is there such a rush to get me to Port Lyautey?

His self-doubt wasn't unique for a new, inexperienced naval officer. He couldn't know how much the coming experience was going to cost him physically and emotionally. He couldn't know that he would be revisiting his coming experiences forty-odd years later.

Logan was reading a month-old *Life* magazine he had taken from a magazine rack nearby. Doris Day was on the cover. In the right hand corner, below the picture of Doris Day, was "Box Office Bonanza, Doris Day in a Shivery Role."

Turner turned away from the window and his thoughts. He asked Logan, "Why didn't you go to flight school and become a pilot?"

Logan continued to leaf through the magazine. He stopped after a bit and laid the open magazine in his lap. He closed his eyes, and Turner noticed that Logan's hands were turning white from gripping his seat's armrests.

"Joe, are you all right?"

There was no answer. Turner put his hand on Logan's arm and gently squeezed.

Logan was pale and, in a cold sweat, answered, "Just a minute, Burt. I'll be all right."

He stretched out his legs, brought his hands up to his face, and held them there for a few minutes. The magazine slipped away from his lap and onto the carpeted floor of the plane. Logan took his hands from his face, bent over, and retrieved the magazine.

Turner stuttered, "I'm . . . I'm, sorry I . . ."

"It's OK, Burt. Sometimes this happens. Not as often as it used too, though."

Logan relaxed and took a deep breath and began.

"After Annapolis, I was able to leave the navy and enlisted in the air force. I was admitted to the pilot training program and soloed, which ended primary flight training. The next step was jet-powered training. I was almost finished with this phase when my instructor and I were coming back from a crosscountry flight and had a flameout. The engine just went away on final approach. We were too low to eject and had to ride it out. We tried to stretch our glide and undershot the runway and crashed. The instructor was killed, and I woke up in the hospital with my legs burned and a head injury that screwed up the vestibular apparatus in my middle ear. That ended my chance to be a pilot."

Logan smiled at Turner and said, "I got to solo that once, so I guess I was a pilot."

Turner felt awful, and it showed.

A few minutes later, the pilot announced that they were on final approach to Orly and that they should please observe the sign to fasten the seat belt. Turner looked out the window. *Interesting coincidence. Logan just told me he went in on approach and here we starting ours.*

The C-121's engines had been throttled back, and Turner heard the whirring of electric motors as he watched the flaps being lowered. Then other sounds as the landing gear lowered and locked down into place.

Turner saw the perimeter fence come and go beneath the plane; then the black tarmac overrun section; then, almost immediately, the gray concrete; and finally, he heard the even screech of all main landing gear tires at the same time, designating a perfect landing. There was a short trundling as the plane settled, then reversal of the props slowing the plane. As the plane taxied along the main runway, it swayed heavily, lifting and lowering gently. It slowed and turned off onto a taxiway, then traveled another three minutes to the military terminal. Turner, Logan, and the colonel unsnapped their safety belts.

At the military terminal, the engines were shut down. There was an audible bump as the mobile airstairs were rested against the fuselage at the entry hatch. The hatch was opened by one of the cabin attendants, and an air force captain came up the airstairs and into the airplane. The captain was given a microphone. He cleared his throat and welcomed the passengers to Orly Airport, France. He then gave all the particulars germane to what the passengers of the various military services should do once they were in the terminal.

Logan asked Turner, "Did you get all that?"

"Fuck no, he talked way too fast!"

Bennett heard this and said, "Gentlemen, if you will, please follow me. I'll get you started." They made their way to the aisle then, trailing the colonel as he exited the plane.

Of the seventy-three passengers, Turner and Logan were two of only five junior officers who were on board the airplane. There were three generals (two air force and one army) and one admiral; a large number of marine, navy, and air force majors, colonels, and commanders; and a large contingent of senior enlisted men representing the different services.

Turner noticed that there were two civilians. One was a woman.

Turner, asked Logan, "What are civilians doing on board a Military Air Transport Service plane?

"They may be in the diplomatic service, or maybe they are spooks."

"What are spooks?"

"They are former students of Ivy League schools who have a history of being obsessed with minutia. They make up the membership of the Central Intelligence Agency. Most are analysts, very few are actual field workers, and they all collect information."

"Oh."

Once in the terminal, the colonel pointed out where to reclaim their bags and the general area where they could find the naval and air force liaison counters. The two shook hands with the colonel, thanked him, and saluted crisply. He returned the salute, and, reaching into the inside pocket of his jacket, withdrew his wallet and pulled out two name cards. He gave one to Turner and the other to Logan. They looked at the cards and saw, with his address and phone numbers, the following:

Lieutenant Colonel Pete Bennett
United States Army
Special Operations
United States Diplomatic Corps
Paris, France

Bennett looked at Turner and said, "Perhaps we will meet again, Lieutenant." He turned and joined the crowd of military uniforms going the other way.

After they picked up their bags, Turner with one seabag and one flight bag and Logan with two flight bags, both looked in the direction Bennett had indicated. Turner spotted a line of navy enlisted men in the distance and said, "Joe, navy's over there, and I can see air force farther down."

They hurriedly and awkwardly walked on with their baggage.

Turner said, "I'll meet you down the hall at the exit of this terminal," and left Logan for a line of officers next to the longer line of enlisted men at the navy liaison counter. Logan waved in acknowledgment and moved on to the air force liaison counter.

Turner was at the end of a line of fourteen other officers. He looked at the length of the enlisted line and thought he was glad he was an officer; otherwise, he would be here well into the afternoon. They had landed at 1150 hours, and it was now 1230 hours.

There were two enlisted men (yeoman first class and yeoman third class) at the counter trying to help a group of three sailors who had just come in from the naval station at Norfolk, Virginia. Turner overheard a heated discussion going on about how they had to get to Naples and meet their ship before it deployed.

Thirty-five minutes later, Turner was at the head of his line. The three sailors had left, on their way to catch a MATS flight that would put them in Naples in time to catch their ship.

There were other officers and sailors going to Naples as well as other places. Turner overheard several who were going to Port Lyautey but would have to wait three days for a flight out. He noticed that most of the officers going to Port Lyautey were wearing pilot's wings. Turner had no designator badge to wear showing his place in the navy; in fact, the only ribbon he had was for the not-uncommon marksmanship medal. It would take years before a badge designating the EOD volunteer program would be made available. Wings for aviators and dolphins for submariners were jealously guarded uniform designators by senior navy officers who wore them. The other volunteer programs would eventually have their own uniform designators.

Turner opened his brown envelope, took out his orders, and gave them to the yeoman responsible for officers' affairs. The yeoman read the paragraphs in the orders covering Turner's transportation to Port Lyautey, which he noted was to be expedited. He looked at Turner and the single silver bar on his collar and then picked up a nearby phone. At the same time, Turner saw Logan standing a short distance away and motioned him over.

Logan walked over and asked, "What's taking so long? I've been standing over there for twenty minutes."

"The mills of the gods turn very slowly, but very, very fine."

At that moment, an ensign appeared from one of the offices behind the counter. The yeoman gave Turner's orders to the ensign and pointed out the paragraphs that seemed questionable. The ensign read the paragraphs twice, turned, and went into another office next to the one from which he had come.

Logan said, "I bet it's the Priority Class One. It's a rare thing for a lieutenant jg."

Logan was right. A lieutenant commander with pilot's wings and ribbons came out of the office, followed by the ensign. He looked at Turner, then the air force officer next to Turner, then back to Turner, and said, "Mr. Turner, these orders are highly unusual. Do you have any idea why you have this travel priority?"

"No, sir."

He read the orders once more, took a clipboard out of the hands of the ensign, then asked the yeoman for a pencil. He used the pencil to cross out one name, and added Turner's.

"If the people want you this badly, by gosh, we will get you there, *toute suite.*"

He picked up the nearby phone, dialed, made a connection, and said, "Dispatch, this is Lieutenant Commander Bello. We need a seat for the flight to NAS, Port Lyautey. Bump Commander Jessup and, in his place, put in

Lieutenant JG Burt Turner." There was a pause, and Bello said thank you and hung up.

Bello looked across the counter at Turner and said, "Mr. Turner, your flight leaves in twenty minutes. Get you and your gear down to Gate 16. It's to your right." Handing Turner's orders back, he added, "Have a nice ride."

Turner stood looking at Bello, then Logan said, "Let's go, Burt."

When they were out of earshot, Turner said, "I have had three hours' sleep in the last twenty-four, I haven't had anything to eat in hours, and I don't get to see to Paris."

"But, Burt, you are a very important person, a real VIP. I have to stay here for three and a half days." He repeated, as he brushed a nonexisting tear from his eye, "Three and a half days of misery."

They arrived at Gate 16. The door was open with no passengers in sight. An enlisted man in a flight suit came from the flight line and said, "You must be Mr. Turner." And with a big grin, he said, "Sir, a commander just left the plane, and is he pissed. I'll take your gear. Our plane is the R-5D over there. We are loaded and will launch as soon as you are on board."

He turned to Logan, "Joe, you are one lucky bastard. Stay in touch."

Logan said he would, they shook hands, and Turner sprinted across the tarmac to the waiting airplane. They would meet again.

As he approached the airstairs going up to the entry hatch, one of the pilots was just finishing his "walk around," checking for any unusual fuel or hydraulic leaks or other evidence that might betray a problem. Following Turner up the airstairs, the pilot said, "We got word about you at the last minute. You must be a rather important junior officer."

Turner, looking back over his shoulder, said, with his face reddening, "I'm sorry, sir. I'm not sure what's going on."

Entering the airplane, the pilot hurriedly replied, "Well, that's how it is with most of us these days." He turned and went into the cockpit.

Turner turned the other way and, pulling aside a curtain that separated the entry from the passenger cabin, looked up the aisle and saw an airplane full of officers, enlisted men, and a number of women with children. The women and children were traveling as dependents of officers and senior enlisted men who had been ordered to two-year tours of duty at bases euphemistically called hardship bases. The armed forces encouraged families to be together under these circumstances. He felt quite awkward standing there. *They are all looking at me.*

A cabin attendant at the back of the airplane motioned for him. Turner, hearing the engines cough and begin to turn up, quickly made his way to the cabin attendant, who was pointing to an empty seat on the aisle just in front of the restrooms.

As he sat down, a little girl about six years old looked at him from across the aisle and said, "You better buckle your seat belt. We are going to take off." He smiled, took off his hat, put it under his seat, and buckled his seat belt.

The airplane turned slowly and started taxiing to the main runway for takeoff.

A young woman in uniform was sitting in the window seat next to him, watching the ground crew as they drove away in a jeep. Turner noticed that she was a lieutenant junior grade, and above the gold stripe and a half on her sleeve was a gold oak leaf emblem with a silver acorn in the middle—a navy nurse.

The R-5D slowed as it approached the main runway, then stopped. The pilots ran up each of the four engines and throttled each back, then waited for the control tower to give clearance for takeoff.

After about two minutes, the R-5D swung around to the main runway, paused, and then, with the engines coming up to full throttle, began its takeoff run. Turner pressed the button on his armrest and leaned the seat back so he could try to get some sleep.

The little girl across the aisle, seeing he had leaned his seat back, said, "You're not supposed to do that when we are taking off."

He turned his head slightly, opened his left eye, and said, "Oh, thank you, I forgot." And then, straightening up, he put the seat back in place.

The plane left the ground at 1350, five minutes late, and took a heading southwest over the Mediterranean. Turner was just dosing off when from across the aisle came an enthusiastic "You can set your seat back now, sir."

He groaned, turned slightly, and asked, "What is your name, miss?"

With a disarming smile, she replied, "My name is Judy Bello and my daddy is a pilot and he is on temporary additional duty in Paris and Mommy and I just visited him and he is coming home next week. What is your name?" This all in one breath.

Turner replied, "My name is Burt Turner. I am not a pilot and I just flew across the ocean and I am going to North Africa and I am very tired." Also all in one breath.

Judy Bello's mother had been listening to the exchange and, leaning around her daughter, said, "I'm sorry, Lieutenant. I'm Christine Bello. Judy doesn't act this way very often. She must see something special in you. I am sure she will let you alone now, won't you Judy?"

Judy, continuing to smile, said, "OK, Mommy."

Turner thought a moment, then asked, "Is your husband Lieutenant Commander Bello, and is he working at Navy Liaison at Orly right now?

"Yes, he is. Do you know my husband?"

"Only in passing. He got me on this flight."

"He must like you. You bumped a full commander. Are you going to NAS, Port Lyautey?"

"Yes, I am. Are you and your husband stationed there?"

"Yes, my husband is the operations officer at the NAS."

Judy Bello broke in with "I live there too. I'm in second grade, and I am learning French."

With that, Judy Bello's mother cautioned her daughter to let the nice lieutenant get some rest.

The navy nurse said, "It appears the little girl was very interested in your safety."

"I think she is a member of the seat safety patrol movement and has been alerted to be watchful for people like me."

She smiled and said, "I'm Mary Bianconi. I'm stationed at the NAS hospital at Port Lyautey."

He introduced himself and asked, "How long have you been stationed at Port Lyautey?"

"A little over a year."

"How do you like it?"

"It's great. The duty is interesting, and Morocco is wonderful."

"Are you returning from leave in Paris?"

"Yes, my girlfriend Kathy and I were there for four wonderful days. It was our third trip."

"It doesn't sound like it's difficult to get a hop to Paris."

"Well, we go when space is available. It can be difficult on weekends, though. During the week, there is a much better chance, but then you have to take leave."

"Is your girlfriend on board?"

Mary Bianconi leaned toward Turner and, looking through the space between the seats in front of them, pointed and said, "You can just see her two rows in front of us, in the window seat."

She sat back and asked, "Are you just coming off sea duty?"

Trying not to appear defensive (navy men belong on board ships, and ships belong at sea), he answered, "No, I'm not coming from sea duty. I've been in school, training."

"Are you going to be stationed at Port Lyautey, or are you going on from there?"

"I have orders to NAS at Port Lyautey and will end up at the Naval Ordnance Facility, also known as NOF."

"How long were you in school?"

"About eleven months."

She was incredulous and asked, "What kind of training takes that long?"

He took a deep breath and began to deliver an abbreviated description when she interrupted. "You must be taking Lieutenant Tom Goss's place. He's the EOD officer at NOF. We heard he was leaving."

"I guess I'm the guy relieving him. How is the BOQ here? Is it like most of the rest—smelly, old, and water stained?"

"Actually, it's really nice. It is well kept up and comfortable."

"How big is it?"

"Well, the BOQ houses about 95 percent of the seventy-five or so junior officers assigned to the Naval Air Station and the air station's tenant commands. Males and females in different sections, of course," she said with a smile. "The male to female ratio is about four to one. Nurses represent the largest group of females, the Women Naval Officers, are the second largest group. There are a small number of civilians, schoolteachers that teach at the base school, and a number of representatives from different companies in the U.S. that provide technical support for aircraft maintenance and other complex equipment maintenance."

"Do married junior officers have quarters on board the base?"

"No, the very few married junior officers live off the base, in what we call the American medina."

"The BOQ sounds like it could be a college dorm."

"Well, it is very much like a dorm. The residents for the most part have been out of college a year or more, but they don't seem to have trouble reverting to behavior characteristic of their undergraduate days. I speak mostly about the men."

"I suppose alcohol and everything else is very cheap here."

"Alcohol here is very cheap and very available."

"Does everyone get along with each other?"

"Actually, we do get along well with each other. Once in a while, it can get very loud when someone is playing the Kingston Trio, Fats Domino, or Elvis on hi-fi with their door open to the hallways. It's usually quiet, though, especially when the base is put on alert and everyone behaves professionally.

Of course, people gravitate to what they have in common: nurses, pilots, and those working at naval intelligence, Fleet Weather Central, operations, and all that."

He sighed and said, "Well, I'm not in the medical corps, I'm not a pilot, I'm not in naval intelligence—or any of the others you mentioned."

"I'm sure you will find people you will like."

Changing the subject, he asked, "What is the flight time to Port Lyautey?'

"Well, it depends. Sometimes the plane lands at the Naval Air Station at Rota, Spain, to let people on and off. I don't think we are landing at Rota this trip. By now, they would have let us know. If we don't land at Rota, the flight time should be about five hours."

"I suppose they will be giving us something to eat on a long flight like this."

"They always have a box meal of sorts. Actually, the dinner meal is pretty good, much better than the lunches."

At this point, she pressed the armrest seat button, reclined her seat, kicked off her shoes, stretched her legs out, and closed her eyes.

He looked at her, *She is really nice, really good-looking, and has great lips and eyes.*

The need for him to get any sleep had slipped away. He looked in the pocket on the back of the seat in front of him for reading material. Along with the usual flight safety information was a Welcome to Port Lyautey brochure. He lifted the brochure out and began to read:

GENERAL INFORMATION

Morocco, or the Sherifian Empire, is situated in the northwest corner of the African continent. Morocco occupies an area of 170,000 square miles, about the size of California. It is bounded on the west by the Atlantic Ocean, on the north by the Mediterranean Sea, on the east by Algeria, and on the south by the Sahara desert. There are long, sweeping beaches on the coast (Turner thought, *I wonder how the surfing is*), vast fertile plains, broad mountain ranges, and semi-desert terrains.

The climate throughout most of Morocco is moderate, much like Southern California. The air is generally clear and dry and affords excellent visibility. Humidity is low, and high temperatures are therefore not unbearable.

In summer, the northeast wind brings clear bright weather for weeks on end, broken only by local storms or dust brought by occasional east and southeast winds. From May to October, there are occasional Cherguis (Shergi)—hot, easterly winds sweeping in from the Sahara over the western slopes of the Atlas mountains. Temperatures near 100°F are common during this time for two or three consecutive days. The usual temperature range is between 40°F and 92°F with the lowest in January and the highest in August.

The population is composed of Berbers and Arabs, Jews and Europeans, presenting a diversity as broad as the landscape they inhabit. (Turner thought, *Nice line.*)

About 95 percent of the total population is of the Muslim faith. Jews and Europeans are present in relatively small numbers.

He skipped down to the historical information.

The Berbers, who are believed to have come from Europe several thousand years before Christ, are the native people of Morocco. Phoenician trading enterprises, Roman colonization, and invasions by Vandals, Goths, and Byzantines all preceded the arrival of the Arabs from the east in the seventh century AD.

Morocco's stormy history was thereafter marked by tribal wars, revolutions against the sultans, and conquest of foreign lands. The peak of the Sherifian power was in the twelfth century, when the country's rule extended from Tripoli to the Pyrenees. Several European countries were interested in establishing control over this strategic area, but France won out, following a series of international agreements. Under the Treaty of Fez in 1912, the sultan remained the supreme national authority in religious matters, but his civil control was assumed by the protectorate powers—France and Spain.

The port of Tangier, 115 miles to the northeast of Port Lyautey, was internationalized by separate agreement.

He thought, *Morocco has never been quiet. The French, after essentially colonizing Morocco, are being violently thrown out. It seems this cycle of invasion, colonization, resistance, then revolution has always been a part of human existence. Where there are human beings, there will always be fighting for turf and for cultural and religious reasons. Now the Americans have come and are leasing large amounts of land for strategic military bases that are targets, not only for the Russians, but also for Arab terrorists wanting all foreigners out. What's the difference between a nationalist removing foreigners by force and a terrorist?*

The first French resident general, Marshal Lyautey pacified most of the country, raised the economic level considerably and maintained many of the native values.

His policy of control through indirect administration was abandoned by his successors, and nationalistic opposition to the protectorate powers soon arose. This awakened nationalism led to the recognition of Morocco's independence by France and Spain in the early part of 1956.

But the French army and navy are still there. I am sure Lieutenant Colonel Bennett is right in his assessment that the Arabs want all the foreigners out and have been using terrorism to accomplish this in Algeria, Tunisia, and Morocco.

There are extensive contrasts in Morocco. On one hand, an indigenous population living in mud huts in the mountains, grass shacks in the plains, and tightly packed dwellings in the sprawling city medinas. In the rural tableland areas, there are acres of wheat, vegetable crops, orchards and vineyards.

Ah, the French and their wines. He continued reading.

Moroccans with wooden plows pulled by camel-donkey teams, in the midst of elaborate irrigation systems. On the rocky and barren slopes of the Atlas mountains, Berber tribesmen, dressed in flowing djellabas, shepherd sheep and goats can be seen. In the medina, artisans work at a variety of ageless crafts.

On the other hand, the European influence is in evidence at the commercial port of Casablanca, seventy-five miles south of Port Lyautey. Here are modern buildings flanking palm-tree-lined boulevards in the European sections of town.

The streets are traveled by sleek black Cadillacs alongside their much older counterparts, the well-laden donkeys hidden beneath their bulging loads. Rabat, the capital thirty-five miles to the southwest, on the coast, is much like Casablanca.

U.S. Naval Activities, Port Lyautey, is located on the Oued Sebou (Sebou River), about five miles from its mouth, which opens to the Atlantic Ocean. The U.S. Navy has been in Port Lyautey since the initial landings in North Africa in November 1942 and presently occupies the air base jointly with the French Navy.

The primary mission of U.S. Naval Activities, Port Lyautey, is to be responsible for maintaining and operating facilities for the logistic support of naval forces under the command of Commander in Chief, North Eastern Atlantic and Mediterranean (CINCNELM) and to provide the communications link between the United States and naval ships and stations operating in that area of responsibility.

Under this paragraph, Turner studied the fourteen activities listed, which included, the Naval Air Station (NAS), the Naval Ordnance Facility (NOF), Naval Communications Center, Fleet Intelligence Center, Fleet Air Intelligence, the U.S. Marine barracks, five naval air squadrons (patrol, heavy attack, transport, electronics countermeasures, and fleet air service) and the hospital dispensary. He fell asleep without reading about the town of Port Lyautey, the living conditions, and political situation.

Mary shook Burt Turner's arm gently and said, "Burt, they are beginning to serve dinner."

Rubbing his eyes, he sat up and said, "Gosh, I must have nodded off."

"Well, it was a long nodding-off. You have been asleep for almost five hours. It's 6:00 p.m., or should I say 1800 hours."

Turner looked at his navy issue watch (water proof diver's watch guaranteed to leak at one foot under water) and saw it was still on New Jersey time, 0600. He looked at her watch and changed the time on his.

He brought his seat back up, unbuckled his seat belt, and said, "Excuse me, Mary. I have to go the head."

He got up and started for the head five feet away. He was just passing Judy Bello when she said, "Did you know that you snore and sometimes you talk in your sleep?" He ignored the child and went into the head.

A few minutes later, Turner, with his bladder relieved and his face and hands washed, returned to his seat.

Mary said, "This might be a good time for a head call before they serve dinner." *I have never heard a woman use the word "head" for the bathroom. It sounds really coarse.*

She pushed herself up from her seat, worked her way around his legs, and went to the restroom.

Judy Bello was leaning over the armrest of her seat into the aisle waiting for Mary Bianconi to come out of the restroom.

When she came out the little girl asked, "Is he your boyfriend?"

Mary replied with a smile, "No, he's not my boyfriend, so you can have him if you want."

Judy Bello answered, "OK, then he's mine."

Turner looked up at Mary and quietly said, "I'm already taken."

The cabin attendant came by with their dinners. Turner carefully opened his box and found the main course, meatloaf and mashed potatoes on a moderate-size plastic plate, a small mound of coleslaw in a small plastic cup, fruit cocktail in another plastic cup, a small roll, packages of salt, pepper, and ketchup. Coffee to follow.

Mary started eating her dinner, paused, and said, "Here we are, a beautiful evening, flying at twenty thousand feet over the Mediterranean Sea and having a gourmet dinner. It's so romantic." They both laughed.

"Actually, the dinner tastes great. I haven't had anything to eat since this morning, when I was flying over the Atlantic, and I haven't had much sleep in the last twenty-four hours either."

Pulling her roll apart, she said, "I find it interesting you were able to bump the full commander that was sitting in the seat you're sitting in. You must be very important."

He almost choked on his meatloaf. "You know you're the third person that said this."

"You're lucky you have a nurse next to you. I could keep you from dying if you aspirated that chunk of meat loaf. How were you able to bump the commander?"

"All I know is that I have a set of orders that make these things happen. I don't have a clue why they were written up the way they were."

About an hour after they had finished their dinners, one of the pilots announced that they were about thirty-five minutes out from NAS, Port Lyautey. He added that it was another beautiful evening, like Southern California, only without the smog.

"When we land, what is the routine about checking in, Mary?"

"Usually, there is a representative from the command you will be reporting to at the terminal building. If there isn't anyone there for you, I'll take you to the BOQ. When we get there, all you need to do for a room is show your orders to the steward at the counter. You can call for a ride and report in to the Naval Ordnance Facility tomorrow morning."

"How do you get around the base?"

"Well, to begin with, it's quite large. Not including the fenced-off section that belongs to the French Navy, our side is still quite large. Some of us bought cars that have been passed down from those who have already gone home. A few bought new European cars locally. If you don't have a car, there is a navy bus, and there are vehicles attached to various commands. Off base, there are little Renault and Fiat minicabs—mostly old and held together with bailing wire. The drivers seem to always be racing to beat the next stop light—don't be surprised if they run the light on red from time to time. If you don't know the way, it is not unusual for the driver to tack on another five or six miles that you will pay for."

"It sounds a little like Washington DC, except the cars aren't old and small."

She thought a minute and added, "A minicab ride at night can be very scary. Often, the car generators are gone or don't work, and they drive without lights to conserve the car batteries. They only turn their lights on when they pass through intersections. Once through an intersection, the lights go off again. Some think they save gas when they do this sort of thing. Arab buses are available at the main gate for travel into and about town. Good way to immerse oneself in Arab culture."

The R-5D was coming around to its final approach to NAS, Port Lyautey. Turner straightened up his seat back and joined Mary Bianconi as she looked out her window. She pointed out the city center, the mosque, medina and brown-colored Oued Sebou winding alongside the NAS. The base administration buildings and principal roads slid into view, then, on a rise, a series of small buildings, several miles away from the main base. "That," she said, "is the Naval Ordnance Facility, your place of work."

Well beyond the buildings, Turner could see, was a large number of ammunition bunkers, surrounded by a perimeter fencing topped with razor wire. Well within the perimeter fence, there were two bunkers surrounded by double rows of heavy fencing and razor wire.

That could only be the exclusion area for nuclear weapons.

They were down at 1903 (7:03 p.m.). He felt the usual slight swaying, gentle rising and falling, and periodic bumping as the airplane taxied from the main runway to the taxiway and approached the terminal.

Along the way, Turner saw a large number of R-5Ds and R-6Ds of the VR24 transport squadron; two R-4Ds (military version of the old DC-3), one with "MARINES" painted on the fuselage; a number of P-2Vs from VP7, the antisubmarine warfare squadron; several A-3Ds that Turner thought were from the VQ squadron (electronic intelligence); an SNB Twin Beech, and a few air force C-124 Globemasters, heavy lift aircraft, and a smaller twin-fuselage C-119 "Flying Boxcar." There was a solitary A-4D tactical jet, probably from the Sixth Fleet, with its engine out. He was impressed with the variety and number of aircraft.

The R-5D parked near the terminal's main entrance. The engines were shut down, and the entry hatch opened at the same time the boarding stairs bumped into place and locked by the ground crew. Passengers rose from their seats, most groaning from the effects of the long flight, and worked their way into the aisle. Once in the aisle, there was the usual uneven starting and stopping a number of times before finally leaving the airplane. Turner and Mary, being in the very back of the airplane, let the aisle almost empty before getting up and taking their turn leaving the airplane.

As the last of the passengers bunched together for exit, he said, "Mary, have you ever seen a snake disgorge a bolus of food?"

She answered, "Not a snake."

They laughed, got up from their seats, went down the aisle, and left the airplane. The first thing Turner noticed as he went down the airstairs was the smell of the Oued Sebou, about two hundred yards distant from the runway. The smell of the river was occasionally interrupted by a saltwater breeze coming in from the west. Then, as they walked to the terminal, he caught the smell of charcoal, cook pots, and animal and human activities of an Arab port city over eight hundred years old. Everything else was reminiscent of the Southern California coast—the sky, the small rolling hills, the warm temperature, and the cool breeze from the sea.

"There's Tom Goss, your NOF representative, over by the luggage cart. He's talking to Kathy Roberts, my girlfriend."

Turner saw an officer in wash khakis and tie with two obviously new silver bars on each shirt collar. Lieutenant Goss was about five feet eleven inches tall, a little on the heavy side, and had a very red, well-trimmed, almost handlebar mustache. Seeing Turner and Mary approaching, he interrupted his conversation with Kathy Roberts and, with an enormous grin, extended his hand and said, "I'm Tom Goss, are you Burt Turner?"

Turner smiled and shook Goss's hand and replied, "Yes, sir. Are you ready to be relieved?"

Goss replied, "Burt, I'm more than ready. I fly out day after tomorrow and am out of the navy a week after that. Four years is enough."

Mary looked at Kathy Roberts and said, "Look what I found on the plane, Kathy. This is Burt Turner."

Kathy Roberts was a registered nurse, who graduated from the University of Texas, El Paso, 1954 and dropped out of Stanford University Medical School in 1957. She was tall, black haired, and beautiful. She smiled, extended her hand to Turner, and said, "I'm Binki's best friend." Giving Goss a withering look, she added, "And nemesis of obnoxious frogman, bare-chested warrior Goss."

Turner laughed. He shook her hand and said, "I am so glad to meet the Greek goddess Nemesis—punisher of extravagant pride, wasn't she? Or aren't you?"

She smiled and thoughtfully replied, "Well, it seems we have an intellectual here." Turning to Goss, she asked, "Tom, is this another person in your kind of work?"

"Be careful how you use 'your kind of work.' Play your cards right, and you could be one of us, Nurse Roberts. Yes, Burt is the new SW/EOD officer and will be taking over the team. In the future, when you see Burt, I am sure you will be thinking of me."

She looked at Turner and answered, "That, Mr. Turner, is an example of extravagant pride or gross stupidity."

Then Turner and Goss followed Mary and Kathy into the terminal. Goss said, "As soon as we get your gear, I'll take you to the BOQ. Binki, do you need a ride? I have a truck out in front."

"No, I have my car in the parking lot."

"Binki is your nickname?" Turner asked.

"Yes, it's after the name of my car—a Fiat Bianchina. Here comes the luggage cart."

They followed the cart to a long table and watched the ground crew unload flight bags, suitcases, and other bags and boxes. Turner and the two women waited until the majority of passengers had found their luggage, then Binki and Kathy found their suitcases (tan with green accents, Moroccan leather). Turner found his seabag and flight bag (olive-drab nylon and blue nylon). Goss helped the women with their suitcases.

As they were leaving the terminal, from out of nowhere came Judy Bello. She ran up to Turner, grabbed on to his flight bag, lifted her head, and quietly said, "I enjoyed meeting you. I think you are very nice."

Turner put the flight bag down, took her hand and said, "Well, thank you. I think you are very nice too."

She smiled and ran back to her mom, who stood next to a navy staff car. He waved to Christine Bello, picked up his flight bag, and walked on with his new friends. Approaching the parking lot, Kathy said, "That was Lieuteant Commander Bello's daughter. Believe it or not, she is very withdrawn. You must be something special."

He looked at Binki and said, "That's the fourth time."

She grinned and said, "That's my car over there, Burt. The Fiat Bianchina."

"That is a very small car for a very small nurse. Is it named after you, or you after it?"

"Actually, neither one, but it can hold four people."

Goss put the suitcases in the backseat; the two women thanked him and got in the car.

Just before driving away, Binki said, "Tom, when you get to the BOQ bring Burt by."

He gave a wave and led Turner over to an NOF pickup truck (Chevrolet, gray like every other navy vehicle). Turner threw his bags in the back.

They got in, and Goss said, "I know you're worn out from the flight, but do you want to see some of the base while there is still some light.?"

"Yes, I think that would be great."

Goss started the truck; put it into gear; and, as he left the parking lot, made a sharp turn; laid rubber; and drove off. Goss pointed out the various administrative buildings: the dispensary, navy exchange, slopchute (hamburger joint), senior officer's housing, chief's quarters, enlisted men's family housing, marine barracks, and enlisted men's barracks. He showed Turner where the U.S. Navy base perimeter fence ended and the French Navy base perimeter fence began.

Goss said, "It's getting dark, Burt. Let's go home. Tomorrow, after breakfast, I'll take you to NOF, and you can report in. After that, we can finish the grand tour."

When they arrived at the BOQ, a steward's mate first class was at the counter. "Well, Mr. Goss, is this the gentleman you asked us to have a room ready for?"

"That is exactly so. I am sure you are giving him the best room in the house."

"Second floor, room 214, a wonderful room with a view." He paused, then added, "Of the back side of Fleet Weather Central."

Turner took his orders out of the brown envelope and passed them to the steward. The steward did all the things necessary to make Turner's application for new residence official. He then went into a well-practiced monologue on dining room hours, laundry, and other things essential to the comfort and well-being of the new resident and his new neighbors. Finally, the steward welcomed him aboard and gave him a key to his new room.

Turner and Goss lugged Turner's bags upstairs to the second floor, and as they walked down hallway, Goss introduced Turner to everyone who had his door open. One officer stood out from the others. He was a navy physician and flight surgeon—Lieutenant Phil Pierce University of Chicago, Medical School, 1955, was a short, thin, prematurely balding young man with a few too many cynical remarks.

Walking on, Turner asked, "Where are the ladies housed?"

"They're in the other wing—segregated from the men, but not too segregated."

When they arrived at room 214, Turner was about to unlock the door when he heard from an open door, just down the hall, "That is total bullshit. You could have killed us both, and besides, Stravinsky's *Firebird* is a ballet.'"

"I made a very fine one-engine-out landing, and you fucking well know it." Then he added in a less strident voice, "I thought *Firebird* was a symphony."

Goss said, "Let's get your gear inside, and I'll take you over and introduce you to those two. Both these guys are unsuccessful pursuers of women and crazy as hell. Dr. Pierce hangs out with them. They are loners, and most of the other inmates avoid them. Binki and her friends seem to get along with them, though."

Turner unlocked the door; they went inside and put the flightbag and seabag on a narrow bed next to the wall. Turner took a quick look around, then followed Goss out the door and down the hall, to the room where the outburst had originated. The door was half open. Goss knocked twice.

A low voice said, "Yes, yes, come in."

Goss pushed the door open, and Turner saw two lieutenants junior grade, one sitting in a large leather easy chair, the other on a small couch. Both wore flight suits, frayed at the cuff and in need of washing, and both held glasses of red wine. Stravinsky's *Firebird* was being played on a very expensive hi-fi.

The officer in the easy chair said, "Ah, it's Mr. Goss. Who do you have there with you?"

"I have with me my relief. Lieutenant JG Burt Turner."

The two officers stood up. The nearest said, "Welcome aboard, Burt. I'm Bob Miller, and this is my copilot Ben Teipner."

Teipner immediately replied, "Miller is mistaken. He is *my* copilot."

Goss interrupted, "These two skillful navy pilots fly the air station's twin-engine Beechcraft, the SNB."

"And quite nicely too," Miller added. "Would you like to partake in a glass of Algerian wine we brought in this morning?"

Before Turner could reply, Goss said, "Burt has had a very long series of airplane rides in the last forty-eight hours, and I have the duty."

Turner added, "No, thanks. I'm really not wide awake right now."

On the way out, Goss said, "Don't keep Burt up too late, you guys. Burt, I'll come by at 0645 and take you down to breakfast."

Turner remained with Miller and Teipner for a half hour and found the two pilots immediately likable.

When he returned to his room, he looked around and saw the usual BOQ furnishings: a desk with lamp and chair, a single bed with small table and lamp adjacent, and a floor lamp—all steel and navy gray. To his left was a washbasin with cabinet and mirror above, and to the right of the washbasin a dresser of drawers. A well-worn easy chair was near the window; the window nicely displayed the security lights on the back side of Fleet Weather Central.

To the left of the washbasin was a closet. Opening the closet door, he saw on its back side a foldout of the 1959 Playmate of the Year, whom he thought well chosen for the honor.

He unpacked his bags, carefully stowed everything away in the dresser of drawers and closet, and took off his clothes down to his shorts. He pulled down the window shade, climbed into bed, and, after tossing around a bit, fell asleep.

The next morning, promptly at 0645, Goss knocked on Turner's door. Turner opened the door well rested, clean shaven, and dressed in a summer gabardine coat and trousers, a like-new shirt and tie, and spit-shined shoes. Goss couldn't believe what he saw.

"How did you do all this? Your room is squared away, and you look ready for captain's inspection."

"Well, I recover fast." He smiled and added, "I'll probably be on my ass by 1600."

"I'm sure you will." They both laughed and went down to the dining room.

The dining room was somewhat full, with men mostly in wash khakis and a few in summer gabardines. The women were in navy nurse uniforms or navy officer uniforms. There were a few civilians in summer clothes.

There were eight chairs at each table, all immaculately set with silver utensils and silver water pitchers. Stewards in white jackets were strategically positioned for service.

After a number of new introductions, they found Mary Bianconi and Kathy Roberts sitting with Bob Miller, Ben Teipner and Phil Pierce. Miller waved them over.

"Welcome, Burt Turner, to the table of never-ending gustatory joy and intelligent conversation."

Turner and Goss took their seats, and a steward came by and took their orders. Orange juice, fried eggs and bacon, a stack of toast (white), milk (reconstituted—fresh unavailable), and coffee for both men. There was small talk, mostly information that would be useful for Turner. The two nurses and the two aviators and flight surgeon finished eating and excused themselves. Five minutes later, Turner and Goss left the table. Twenty-five minutes after that, they pulled into the NOF parking lot. Goss parked the pickup, and they went into the building.

The NOF administration building was off-white, one story high, and quite long. The entrance opened to a hallway with offices on one side, and two heads (officers and enlisted men) on the other side. Farther down were conference rooms and general-use rooms.

Turner and Goss went into the main office complex. Sitting at a desk just inside the doorway was a yeoman second class.

"Hello, Jenkins. This is Lieutenant JG Burt Turner, my replacement. Can he give you his paperwork, and can we see Commander Hawkins?"

Jenkins rose from his desk smiling and said, "Welcome aboard, sir. We have been expecting you." They shook hands. "Can I have your orders and service record, sir?"

He gave the yeoman the brown envelope; the yeoman examined the contents, left his desk, and went into another section of the main office. A few minutes later, he returned with another yeoman.

"Mr. Turner, this is Yeoman First Class Bruce Fry, the commander's yeoman."

"I'm glad to meet you, sir. The commander and his executive officer are in a meeting and will see you and Mr. Goss in a few minutes. We can save some time if we can have your picture taken now so your security pass will be ready by the time you leave the office."

After Turner had his picture taken, he and Goss walked across the hall to a conference room and sat down at a long table covered with green felt.

Turner said, "Tell me about the commander and the exec."

Goss, tilting his chair back, explained, "Commander Gene Hawkins and his executive officer, Lieutenant Commander Donald Owens, came up through the ranks."

"So they were mustangs?"

"Yes, they were. During World War II, Commander Hawkins received a Silver Star for heroism during the battle of Corregidor in the Philippines and, shortly after that, was commissioned a naval officer. He has been in the navy for twenty-four years, the first five as an enlisted man. During that time, he became qualified as a first class diver. As an officer, he is an ordnance specialist rather than a command-at-sea-type officer. The commander is very demanding of his officers and enlisted men, but is fair in dealing with both. He is extremely intelligent and doesn't suffer fools easily. He is tolerant of junior officers if they show initiative and what he calls the can-do spirit." Then, looking at Turner very intently, Goss said, "He is well thought of at BuOrd, and there are rumors that he is becoming involved in operations associated with covert activities. I don't know what the hell that's about, and I don't want to know what it's about." He added, "I forgot to say that Commander Hawkins and the CO of the EOD School in Indian Head are buddies."

"What about the exec?"

"The exec has a Bronze Star for heroism, is real navy, and a very shrewd, bean-counter kind of guy. He is not as direct as Hawkins, but is what you might say 'correct' in relation to following the book. He's also an ordnance specialist. Hawkins and Owens work very closely together, and neither has a second agenda. They are real old-school navy." He finished with, "What you see is what you get with both of them."

Yeoman Fry appeared in the doorway and said, "The commander will see you two now."

The three crossed the hall, and Jenkins showed them to the commander's office. When they entered, the commander and his exec were sitting at a small conference table, studying the contents of a red folder. Turner glanced at the folder, saw TOP SECRET, and quickly looked away. The commander looked up, closed the red folder, and he and his exec rose to meet Goss's replacement.

The commander was a man in his late forties with a receding hairline; stood just under six feet; was solidly built, with short salt-and-pepper hair and a small paunch; and wore half-lens reading glasses, navy issue. The exec, pipe in mouth, was slightly shorter, thin, balding, and had bifocal glasses—also navy issue.

The commander said, "Welcome aboard, Mr. Turner. We are very pleased you were able to arrive when you did. Has Tom taken good care of you?"

Turner replied, "Yes, sir. Tom has been very attentive, and I am very glad to be here."

The commander continued, "Mr. Goss, since Mr. Turner will be taking your desk when you leave, would you familiarize him with the office spaces and people?" He added, "Has he seen the EOD spaces and met Chief Gallegos and Petty Officers Cole and Huwitt?"

"No, sir. I plan to show Mr. Turner the EOD spaces and give him a tour of the exclusion areas, the mine shop, and munitions bunkers when we leave your office."

The exec said, "Mr. Turner, Tom has done a good job for us, and we hope you will build on what he has accomplished so far."

"I'll try my best to do that, sir."

Hawkins said, "Tom, we need Mr. Turner back at 1300 for a meeting with a few more folks. You won't have to sit in with us. And, Burt, you can shift to wash khakis."

"Maybe I'll start packing to go home." They all laughed and shook hands. Then Turner and Goss left the commander's office.

Goss pointed out his desk, which was behind a partition that separated Goss's (now Turner's) desk space from the executive officer's desk space.

"There's a lot of paper on 'our' desk."

"Well, I'll have most of it taken care of before I leave. I'm not going to be a shit. Besides, everyone here knows you have no experience in dealing with navy paperwork." He added, "Have you ever worked in any kind of office before?"

"Never."

"Well, you're not just going to be thrown into this paper mill. The yeomen will help you get started and keep you from making a fool of yourself. They save me from embarrassing myself all the time. Nothing goes out of here without the exec checking the paperwork carefully before it goes on to the commander for his signature."

Just before they left the office spaces, Goss introduced Turner to Lieutenant Ted van Buren, the NOF supply officer. Van Buren was married, had one child, and lived off base.

Van Buren shook hands with Turner and said, "I understand you and I will be doing a lot of business together, Burt. I'll help you all I can."

Turner thanked him and was following Goss to the door leading out of the office spaces when Yeoman Fry called from his desk, "Mr. Turner, I have your security pass."

Turner walked over and was presented with a laminated pass. The pass, fastened to a clip, stated who Turner was and to what areas he had access at NOF (all areas). The picture was not too bad. He clipped the pass to his uniform as he and Goss left.

On the way down the hall, Goss said, "I wonder what Van Buren was talking about?"

Turner laughed and replied, "If you don't know, I'm scared."

"The only officer you haven't met is Lieutenant Commander Buckold, who runs the AUW shop in the exclusion area. You can meet him later."

They left the administration building, and walked along the length of a second building. Approaching the end of this building, Turner saw an older but like-new small utility truck—a weapons carrier. On the door, painted in red, was a horned mine crossed with a torpedo and bomb. The EOD symbol.

Turner said, "It appears we are at the EOD establishment."

The two officers went around the weapons carrier, went up a short flight of stairs to an open door, and went inside. A chief boatswain's mate in wash khakis turned from a workbench and greeted Goss. "I bet you have your relief in tow, sir."

Introducing Turner, he said, "This is the brains of the outfit—Chief Gallegos, Manuel Gallegos."

Turner and Gallegos were shaking hands when two enlisted men came away from another workbench at the back of the room. Gallegos introduced, "Mineman First Class Richard Huwitt and Aviation Ordnanceman First Class Jack Cole. These two have been overhauling our SCUBA gear. Both are mightily feared by sharks and evildoers of all stripes."

Turner shook hands with the two other enlisted men. Chief Gallegos asked, "Would you two officers like some coffee?"

They both nodded, yes. Cole brought over a coffee pot, and Chief Gallegos, five mugs, clean but stained by the effects of many years of experiencing coffee of great authority. The five men sat down at a clean but well-used table; the coffee pot made the rounds.

Turner asked, "Do you have cream and sugar?"

The enlisted men looked at each other, there was a long pause and Gallegos said, "The coffee mess."

Aviation Ordnanceman Cole left the table and went out the door in a hurry. Five minutes later, he came back with a half-mug of sugar and a jelly glass of powdered creamer.

The Gallegos smiled and said, "We will keep this on board for Mr. Turner."

Turner and Goss talked with the three enlisted men for almost two hours. It didn't take long for Turner to realized that Goss was, little by little, turning the team over to him. Gallegos noticed this too, and diplomatically explained what the EOD team's mission was at NOF and the NAS. Then, in a guarded way, he explained the political situation between the EOD team, the mine shop, the AUW shop, and the support groups at NOF. Turner realized very quickly that Gallegos appeared to be everything a junior officer in charge of an EOD team could want. He hoped Gallegos would have confidence in him, eventually.

"I'm going to take the weapons carrier and give Mr. Turner a tour of the area. From here on out, Mr. Turner is the officer in charge of the team."

Goss and Turner left the EOD spaces, got into the weapons carrier, and drove away from the buildings. Five minutes later, they drove up a small rise and followed a perimeter fence topped with razor wire to a gate and small guard shack, where a marine lance corporal stood with one of the new M14 rifles slung over his shoulder.

Goss stopped the weapons carrier at the guard shack and exchanged salutes with the marine; both officers showed their passes. The marine scrutinized the passes, compared the pictures with the officers in the weapons carrier, and waved them on.

After driving about one thousand yards, Goss said, "You probably know that NOF is responsible for providing a variety of ordnance, which includes underwater influence mines, depth charges, and antisubmarine torpedoes, to the Sixth Fleet in the Mediterranean." Pointing to his left, "That building's the mine shop. That's where the influence mines are serviced and prepared."

Turner, with an excessively authoritative air, recited, "Mines that could be triggered by sensing sound, presence of ferrous metal, or pressure wave of a ship passing near."

They both laughed, and Goss said, "Chief Mineman 'Frenchy' Douet, instructor, second phase, underwater ordnance group, EOD School, Indian Head, Maryland."

Farther on, Goss pointed out the advanced underwater weapons shop. Attempting to outdo Turner, he quoted, "Here we have weapons of antisubmarine warfare: antisubmarine torpedoes that are able to search and destroy submarines (hopefully not our own) and nuclear depth charges that destroy submarines—but without the elegance of the antisubmarine torpedo."

They both laughed. Neither could remember the instructor's name who used that same statement so many times to so many EOD School classes. Access to both the mine shop and advanced underwater weapons shop required a Secret, Need to Know clearance.

On the way back to the BOQ, Turner asked Goss, "What kind of physical shape are the guys in?"

"Pretty good, considering. The men haven't had to do anything physically demanding since Key West except to requalify every month for hazardous duty pay with a dive to one hundred feet and spend time in the desert blowing up unexploded ordnance from World War II. Actually, Chief Gallegos has the team swim in the surf for a half hour and then run about three miles on the beach three days a week, so I guess you could say they are in relatively good physical shape. I join them as often as I can, but there is a shitload of paperwork I can't get out from under. You're going to find that your requal dives and demolition work in the desert is the only break you get."

After lunch, Turner and Goss returned to NOF. Five minutes before the meeting, Turner left Goss at his (their) desk and went over to Yeoman Fry's space. He asked if the commander was ready to see him. Jenkins said they were in the conference room and were expecting him. Turner crossed the hall and knocked on the door. Commander Hawkins said, "Enter." Closing the door behind him, he saw Commander Hawkins and Lieutenant Commander Owens, along with a navy captain and a civilian, standing next to a conference table, talking.

Commander Hawkins motioned Turner over, "Mr. Turner, this is Captain Art Dillon, staff officer from COMNAVACTSMED, Naples." Referring to the other officer, he said, "And here, posing as a civilian, is Lieutenant Bruce Franklin, from our Fleet Intelligence Center."

Turner shook hands with Dillon and Franklin. He saw they were both "ring knockers," signifying graduates of the U.S. Naval Academy—real regular navy.

They sat down at the conference table with Commander Hawkins at the head, Captain Dillon at his right, then Lieutenant Franklin. At Commander Hawkin's left was Lieutenant Commander Owens, then Turner.

There were a number of file folders open on the table. Turner could see that the border of one of the covers was red, designating secret classification of the contents. Hawkins began the meeting by notifying Turner the information to be discussed was considered extremely sensitive, and because of this, the meeting was classified secret—not anyone's business except those at the table. He then turned the meeting over to Dillon.

Dillon was a very young-looking captain. He had two rows of ribbons, one ribbon designating the Navy Cross, the highest award the navy can give other than the Medal of Honor. The Navy Cross is usually give posthumously. This raised Turner's curiosity. Two of the ribbons indicated visits to Japan and Korea.

Looking at Turner, Dillon began, "Mr. Turner, you and your team will be playing an important role in a highly classified operation called Operation Scorpion Fish, which is currently in the planning stages. Your initial training at the Navy Underwater Swimmers School in Key West included insertion and extraction in the quite forgiving waters around Key West. We want you to be prepared to get in and out of areas a lot more demanding than Key West. We also want you to become experienced in reconnaissance and surveillance. In regard to that, on completion of your NOF/NAS orientation period, you and your team will accompany a highly skilled group on a mission, which will allow you to gain experience in reconnaissance and surveillance. Over time, you will be receiving further instructions, as necessary, in anticipation of your deployment."

Hawkins added, "As the SW/EOD officer assigned to NOF, you will carry out those duties as well as collateral duties to be assigned. However, allowances will be made in order for you and your team to prepare for your role in Operation Scorpion Fish."

With the inappropriateness that could only come from a young, very inexperienced junior officer, Turner asked, "Wouldn't it be more practical to assign one of the UDTs, the underwater demolition teams, to this operation?" Without waiting for an answer, he continued, "They have the experience and training in reconnaissance and surveillance that we don't have."

Hawkins and Dillon looked at each other. Then Dillon, with great disdain, replied, "Mr. Turner, of course what you say is true about the UDTs, but wiser individuals than you are planning this operation." He added, "You and your team have essentially the same initial underwater demolition training, but you have more potential for innovation because of your much longer and diverse training in ordnance and ordnance applications. For what we need right now, you bring more to the table." He paused and said indifferently, "No UDTs are available. They are all involved in amphibious training operations elsewhere."

Hawkins looked at his exec and asked, "What does Mr. Turner's timetable look like so far, Don?"

The exec leafed through a red file folder, found a calendar, studied it for a moment, and began, "Mr. Turner will have three days with us to learn what we are about and where he fits in, then three days at NAS for his orientation meetings. Immediately after that, he will be assigned temporary additional duty for six days as shore patrol officer off base, then will return to NOF for duty."

Turner was incredulous.

Hawkins began to gather up his file folders and asked, "Are there any questions?"

"I'm to be a shore patrol officer, sir?"

Hawkins answered, despairingly, "It's part of your orientation, Mr. Turner. All right, gentlemen, we are through here."

After the three senior officers left the conference room, Turner went over to a large map of Morocco on the wall. He examined the map legend and began randomly measuring distances with his thumb and forefinger. Franklin walked up and said sympathetically, "Burt, you just arrived on board, and I'm sure you are overwhelmed about all this."

He turned away from the map, looked at Franklin, and answered, "Yes, I am, Mr. Franklin, yes I am."

"It's Bruce, Burt." He smiled and said, "It looks like you are the chosen one.'"

"What do you mean, 'chosen one'?"

"Your predecessor, Tom Goss, evidently didn't make the cut. They could have held him over. In fact, they could have started all this earlier, but your service record and availability was enough to send Goss on his way."

"When I left Indian Head, I was told that when I arrived at my next duty station, I should keep a low profile until I got my feet on the ground. Fat chance of that happening here."

"Well, there is a positive side. You are going to be involved in situations your instructors and classmates would never have dreamed of, and it will be very much your show, for better or worse."

Changing the subject, Turner said, "Captain Dillon came across as a very serious kind of guy, all business."

"The captain is very smart and very well connected. Vice Admiral Erskin Horner, the COMNAVACTSMED, chose him personally to be on his staff."

"Do you know why Captain Dillon received the Navy Cross?"

Franklin thought about the question for a minute, then answered, "He was in UDT 3 as a lieutenant jg during the Inchon landing in the Korean War. All I know is, he saved a lot of lives and almost died of wounds received."

"That's amazing, he's the real thing."

"Yes, he is. I'll see you later, Burt." He turned and left the conference room.

Turner spent a few minutes more looking at the map of Morocco, then left the conference room and walked across the hall to the office spaces. As he came in, he saw Goss was not at his desk. He stopped and asked Yeoman Jenkins, "Where is Mr. Goss?"

"Mr. Goss left about a half hour ago. He had a chance to catch an early plane to Rota, and then a flight to CONUS."

Turner, in great surprise, asked, "How could that have happened? I still had a lot of questions."

"Commander Hawkins gave him permission to go and wished him well reentering the civilian world. Then Mr. Goss emptied his desk and left this note for you."

Jenkins took an envelope from his IN box and handed it to Turner. He thanked the yeoman, walked over to his new desk, opened the envelope, sat down, and read.

> Burt, had a chance to leave ten hours early and took it. The desk is ready for you, the team is ready for you and I wish you luck. Oh, the Sprite is yours. I'll leave the keys and registration at the front desk of the BOQ. I'll write you later about paying for it.
>
> Tom Goss (soon to be former Lt USNR)

He read the note twice, picked up his desk phone, and called the EOD shop.

Chief Gallegos answered, "EOD shop, Gallegos speaking."

"Chief, it's Mr. Turner. Are Huwitt and Cole still there?"

"Yes, sir, they are."

"We have to talk. I'm coming down." Without waiting for an answer, he hung up the phone and left the building.

When he entered the EOD shop, the three men stopped what they were doing and walked over.

Gallegos asked, "Do want some coffee, sir?"

"No, thanks, Chief. Let's sit down."

The three men glanced at each other, went to the table, and sat down. Turner joined them.

"What I am about to talk to you about is classified Secret, and can't be revealed to anyone else."

Huwitt and Cole went from nonchalance to rapt attention. Gallegos was already there.

"I just finished meeting with Commander Hawkins, the exec, an officer from the intelligence center, and a captain from COMNAVACTSMED. I was told the team will soon be required to start training in surveillance and reconnaissance in preparation for taking part in an operation called Scorpion Fish. I was also told to get used to working in waters more demanding than Key West."

Cole laughed and said, "Excuse me, sir. Surveillance and reconnaissance is one thing, but we are already used to waters far more demanding than Key West." He glanced at Huwitt.

Huwitt added, "Yes, sir, at Mehdiya Beach, and for some time."

Turner continued, "I'm glad to hear that." He looked at Chief Gallegos and said, "Chief, Mr. Goss told me about your conditioning program. I would like to have it increased to four days a week, a four-mile run, and forty-five minutes in the surf. In two weeks, increase to a six-mile run and an hour in the surf. And if you think we need more, I'll arrange for the time."

"Yes, sir, we will do that."

"Starting tomorrow night, I'm TAD for a week at shore patrol. I get off at 0630 and will meet you all here 0645. I'll be with you for the run and swim."

"Aye, aye, sir," Gallegos answered.

Turner continued, "I'm sorry I can't tell you more about this Operation Scorpion Fish business. I'm sure when I get back there will be more meetings, and as soon as I know something, I'll let you know."

Huwitt said, "Looks like Cole is finally going to lose some weight."

Cole answered, "Speak for yourself, old slug."

Turner got up from the table and was on the way out when he stopped and thought for a minute, then said, "Oh, you men should know that Mr. Goss left NOF for CONUS this afternoon."

Chapter 3

B y the time Lieutenant JG Turner finished his three-day NOF orientation, he was overwhelmed by the complexity and amount of paperwork he was going to be required to do, especially after Lieutenant Commander Owens notified him that his collateral duty would be as division officer of the mine shop.

He proceeded from his NOF orientation to the three-day orientation program at the Naval Air Station. He, along with fourteen other newly arrived officers attached to other commands, were taken on a tour of the base, which included: the Fleet and Air Naval Intelligence centers, Fleet Weather Central, squadron locations, officer's and enlisted men's housing, hospital dispensary, marine barracks, church and synagogue, school for dependent children, and, of course, the navy exchange, where everything imaginable could be purchased. After the tour, there was a long series of lectures, which included: chain of command, the French and Moroccan situation, Islamic religion, base rights and the status of forces agreement between the U.S. and Moroccan governments, and the importance of being a considerate "guest" of Morocco. Turner found the last part of the base rights and status of forces agreement lecture concerning the U.S Air Force Strategic Air Command (SAC) Forward Bases in Morocco and Algeria somewhat more interesting.

The most tedious lecture to endure was the first, "The Chain of Command from Local to General." It was filled with innumerable instructions and an impossible number of acronyms: NOF; the Naval Air Station, Port Lyautey; the commander of naval activities, Mediterranean (COMNAVACTSMED) in Naples, Italy; and the commander-in-chief, North Atlantic and Mediterranean (CINCNALM) in Paris, France, for example.

Guaranteed to command an individual's attention was the final lecture, actually a briefing given by an officer from naval intelligence and an officer from the French Foreign Legion. The doors to the room were closed, and marine guards were posted outside. The small audience was told the information to be presented was SECRET, in capital letters.

The officer from the Foreign Legion gave a detailed explanation of the current Arab/Berber uprising against French interests in Morocco and Algeria and gave examples of increasing attacks against French farmers and recent massacres of French civilians.

The naval intelligence officer read translations of communist Arab newspapers' inflammatory statements about French colonialism being replaced by American colonialism and Islamic values being threatened. And further, an important Imam (Muslim prayer leader) was calling for a holy war, a jihad against the new infidels.

The officer said that there was compelling evidence of emerging terrorist activity against Americans and American bases. And in response to this, American naval and air force bases were quietly developing additional security measures.

He also emphasized that Americans were to stay in groups of four, or more, when traveling off base during Ramadan, the ninth month of the Islamic calendar. During Ramadan, eating, smoking, and sex were prohibited starting from when there was enough light in the morning that one was able to tell a white thread from a black thread until nightfall, when there was not enough light to tell the difference. It was thought that fundamentalist Muslims could be more hostile during daylight hours because of the restrictions.

The briefing closed with questions from the audience.

Turner had trouble understanding why hundreds of Moroccans were allowed to work on American military bases when there was a security problem. If he had paid attention to the message being delivered during the base rights agreement and status of forces agreement lecture, he would have understood that providing jobs on base for Moroccans was one of the many requirements allowing an American military presence in this North African country. Morocco was a country striving to become independent of French influence and becoming a socialist democracy, and constitutional monarchy. He was put off by the number of times the term "compelling evidence" was used by the officer from naval intelligence. However, he was very sobered by the information.

With the withdrawal of the French colonial government and French military, Moroccan police, under the new Moroccan government, were now responsible for law and order. To cement relations with the new government and to try to win the hearts and minds of the local Arab population, a good neighbor agreement had been arranged, allowing a U.S. Navy Shore Patrol presence in the local gendarmerie. This was especially important with regard to Moroccan police arresting U.S Navy sailors for the many sins that sailors (and some officers) allegedly committed while on "liberty" or shore leave. The advantage, of course, was two-fold: first, if naval personnel were arrested, it would allow for comparable reports to be made up by the navy shore patrol officer and the arresting Arab law enforcement officer. Second, if there was a difference in point of view over the arrest, hopefully the navy shore patrol officer could prevent what he considered to be mistreatment of the alleged perpetrator prior to arraignment. Lieutenant Burt Turner found the two cultures having vastly different views of what was construed to be mistreatment.

For the most part, the Moroccan police had no problem turning navy personnel over to the shore patrol unless the alleged perpetrator harmed or stole from a Moroccan, destroyed private or public property, or behaved inappropriately toward women or the tenets of Islamic religion. Most importantly, the short assignment helped Turner understand the vast differences in Western and Arab culture and way of thinking.

He would later learn that the United States was looking beyond the cold war and the Russians. There was a second agenda, which was to ease into the vacuum created by removal of the French from Morocco and Algeria. Unknown to most, analysts in the U.S. State Department and Central Intelligence Agency were already anticipating that Arab nationalism and Islamic religious fundamentalism would eventually threaten Western Interests in North Africa and the Middle East.

Two enlisted men, Machinist Mate Second Class Adams and Aviation Electronics Technician Mate Third Class Peters were finishing their fourth month of six on TAD (temporary additional duty), as shore patrolmen when Lieutenant Turner arrived at the gendarmerie. Adams and Peters had a suspicion that this young and, in all ways, inexperienced naval officer would be like others they had to tolerate for six days to two weeks as part of "new boy on board" orientation. They found Turner to be unassuming, eager to learn, and knowing when to stay out of the way—a good officer. They actually liked having Turner as a "ride along" on patrol of the city twice a night: at 2200 hours and 0300 hours.

When they were on patrol, Turner rode on the passenger side of the navy shore patrol jeep. Peters and Adams and Moroccan police Sergeant Benebbou took turns at the wheel every half hour. Sergeant Benebbou and the two sailors were quite friendly with each other. The sergeant seemed to enjoy teaching the Americans a few important Arabic phrases. One in particular sounded to Turner like "shelley muk." He later learned that the mischievous sergeant had taught them a phrase that, when translated into English, was, "How much is your mother?"

At the gendarmerie, Turner spent most of his time sitting behind a desk (navy issue, wood, scuffed gray paint, and old) studying a map of Port Lyautey and its environs, and a map of Morocco. Both maps had been given to him by Lieutenant Commander Owens just before Turner went on duty as Shore patrol officer.

At the time Owens said, "The smaller map is the city of Port Lyautey. You will find it useful. The larger map is Morocco and western Algeria. Become familiar with central Morocco, the Anti-Atlas mountain area, and Western Sahara to the south. Commit to memory the Moroccan coastline, especially in the Larache area and south of Agadir at Cape Draa and the border area of Morocco and Algeria." Before Turner could ask any questions, Owens had looked him straight in the eye and said, "That will be all, Mr. Turner."

Turner's tour of duty as shore patrol officer wasn't as bad as he thought it would be. He became friends with the Moroccan police at the gendarmerie, with the exception of the assistant chief, Lieutenant Hamid al Karim. Al Karim disliked Americans far more than he disliked the French, and he wasn't subtle about it.

"Lieutenant Turner, the people of your country are arrogant, unsophisticated, and without embarrassment of being ignorant of cultural ways of others. You have no sense of history, have not bothered to learn more than your own language, and think yourselves better than others of different skin color." Seeing Turner completely bewildered, al-Karim paused, then finished with, "The French infidels, though often brutal and denying us liberty to govern ourselves, did not have your profound ignorance as a people."

Turner, not knowing what to say and how to say it, didn't say anything; essentially confirming al-Karim's criticism. He made a point to stay out of the way of assistant chief of police, Hamid al-Karim.

At 0645, he joined his team for the early morning run and swim at Mehdiya Beach. Mehdiya Beach was about four miles south of Port Lyautey and about three miles south of the mouth of the Qued Sebou. By the end his tour of duty as shore patrol officer, he was able to easily run the four miles at Mehdiya Beach, swim in the cold and dangerous surf and swell for forty-five minutes while garbed up with UDT life jacket, masks, swim fins, web belts, and knives. Gallegos called it extreme body surfing, and Turner agreed the surf was far more difficult than he had ever experienced.

During his six-day tour of duty at the gendarmerie, Turner had exercised the authority of his position by writing up and sending to the brig for later appearance at captain's mast twelve sailors for being drunk and disorderly; two for urinating in the street (one at a bus stop); four for fighting; four for being in a house of prostitution—two at Suzanne's off Rue du l'ecole and two at the Hotel du Seine bar on Rue Fort du Vaux; three for stealing a camel; and two for getting an airman from the SAC base at Nouasseur drunk, then, after stripping him naked, trading the young man's uniform to a hashish dealer for merchandise recently arrived from the Rif Mountains to the north.

Turner saw what Mary Bianconi was talking about when she explained the Arab predilection for driving with their lights off at night and only flicking them on as they sped through intersections, then off again after passing through. What he learned in his week as a shore patrol officer would have taken a year to learn if he had lived off base and "on the economy."

He was relieved of his position as shore patrol officer at 0900, Sunday, by a newly minted naval aviator who had just reported in to VR-24, the transport squadron. The two enlisted SPs drove Turner to the NAS and up to the NOF administration building in the jeep. Before the SPs left, they made a few jokes about working together, then shook hands, saluted Turner, and drove off. Turner smiled as he watched them go down the hill, make a turn and disappear from sight.

He went into the administration building, walked up the hallway, and entered the office spaces. Yeoman Jenkins said, "Welcome back aboard, sir." The yeoman glanced over at Turner's desk, with its accumulation of paperwork in the IN box, grinned, and added, "You were sorely missed."

"Gosh, I thought I would be long forgotten by now. How nice to be remembered."

He walked around to his desk and took off his hat and coat. He was just about to sit down when the exec, having heard him enter, called from his office, "Mr. Turner, please come in."

Turner was surprised the exec was working on Sunday. He got up and walked around to the exec's office and stood in the open doorway. The exec looked up from his desk and pushing his half-glasses lower on his nose said, "Come in, come in, Mr. Turner. Close the door and have a seat.

"Before we start, I want to let you know that Lieutenant Commander Franks, the officer in charge of shore patrol operations at the air station, called me yesterday and said you were quite the best young officer they had seen for some time. This is from a real hard-ass mustang. Congratulations."

"Well, thank you, sir, but how did he know about me?"

"Franks has spies everywhere. He probably got word from the SPs that you worked with. But enough of that."

To the left of the exec's desk was a rectangular work table within easy reach. In the middle of the table were three file folders, the middle one stamped SECRET. With his left hand, he slid the middle file folder to his desk, opened it, and removed a map along with three typewritten papers, all stamped SECRET. He pushed his glasses back into reading position and began to examine the map. From time to time, he glanced at one or another of the papers in front of him. Then with a red ink pen, he made a number of notations on the map. Turner was near enough to see the papers were all typed in single space and the notations the exec was making in red were often next to notations in blue and black, each by a different hand. Not wanting to be caught looking at something he shouldn't, he looked over to a picture of Owens and a middle-aged woman who may have been Owens's wife standing next to the mast of a large sailboat. Next to the picture was a sterling silver cigarette case with the engraving, "To Lieutenant Commander Don Owens, USN. The Greatest Authority on All Naval Munitions, From the Staff Officers, Hawthorne Navy Ammunition Depot."

Looking beyond the desk to the table, he saw a number of books held in place by bookends made out of 3.5-inch artillery brass casings. He read, from left to right, *Uniform Code of Military Justice* (the *UCMJ*, informally called *Rocks and Shoals*), *American Practical Navigator*, 1958, H. O. Pub. No. 9, *Knights Modern Seamanship*, thirteenth edition, Barnaby's *Some Ship Disasters*, *U.S. Navy Diving Manual*, NAVSHIPS 250-538, Potter's *Nimitiz* and Monsarrat's *The Cruel Sea*. He noticed minutia in the exec's office most others would miss.

When he had been studying genetics and evolutionary biology at USC, his major professor had given a lecture on how attributes many known, most unknown, may be responsible for forming an organism's strategy for survival. However, an attribute may or may not be elicited depending on circumstances of need during the individual's lifetime.

One of the survival attributes Turner was unaware he possessed was a unique, "quick look" sense of observation that delivered a large amount of information in an incredibly short period of time. This particular attribute, along with a not-as-well-developed ability to interpret the observed, would soon be tested by circumstances threatening his and his team's survival.

The exec, satisfied with what he had been doing, glanced at Turner and said, "Ah, you see my books. Are you familiar with any of them?"

"Well, actually I am familiar with all but *Nimitiz* and *Some Ship Disasters.*"

"You should read them both. They have to do with human success and failure when dealing with chance." Anticipating a question, "The diving manual helps me understand what Chief Gallegos is talking about when he is ordering parts for your team's diving gear. I understand that you and your team have been enjoying an early morning run and swim at Mehdiya Beach."

"Yes, sir. Before Lieutenant Goss left, I asked him what kind of physical shape the men were in, and he said not bad, but could be a lot better. I asked Chief Gallegos to set up a conditioning program for us because I didn't want to be surprised at what you and Commander Hawkins may be asking us to do."

"Well, you are very wise, Mr. Turner. Mr. Goss didn't have a very demanding physical conditioning program for himself or his team." Changing the subject, he continued, "I am sure you learned quite a bit while on shore patrol duty. However, in a few days, you and your team will be learning a great deal more about the situation here in Morocco. But let me tell you something about Mehdiya Beach. Perhaps you have heard of Operation Torch?"

"Yes, sir. It was the American invasion of North Africa on the beaches of Morocco during World War II. In 1942, I think."

"It's nice to see a young officer having a sense of history, a very nice thing these days, and not even a Naval Academy graduate. Anyway, yes—in 1942, there were landings at three beaches on the Moroccan northwest coast: Mehdiya, Fedala, and Safi. There were two cruisers, two carriers, and eight transports carrying about nine thousand men heavily equipped for combat waiting off the Oued Sebou for a night landing at Mehdiya Beach. The landing was delayed until early morning for some reason, and during the landing, something like three hundred young soldiers drowned because of heavy surf and undertow. Their life preservers were of no help. The weather forecast had called for slight breezes and low surf. However, the wind was up, and the surf was fifteen feet in sets of three and four."

"That's awful, sir."

"The message is, Mr. Turner, you are new to the sea conditions here, and you and your team are to always wear your swimmer's life jackets and swim fins in this surf. And don't always trust Fleet Weather Central."

"I get the message, sir."

The swimmer's life jacket issued to EOD and UDT personnel was actually a small collapsed floatation bladder covering the chest and continuing up and around the neck. Straps attached to the bottom on the left and right side tightened around the lower rib cage and held the preserver in place. There was a CO_2 cartridge that could fill the floatation bladder with gas when activated by pulling on a lanyard. There was also a tube near the diver's mouth that could be used to inflate the floatation bladder in the event that the CO_2 cartridge didn't work. It was comfortable, didn't get in the way, and was the only life preserver available that could be used with open circuit or closed circuit (no bubbles) self-contained underwater breathing apparatus. The equipment had only one real flaw—if one was to try to activate it below thirty or forty feet, the water pressure wouldn't allow it to inflate. Everyone using this equipment knew this limitation.

"This is a copy of the map I gave you when you left for shore patrol. Your map obviously didn't have all these colorful notations. The notations are associated with areas of great interest to Fleet Intelligence Center." Using his red-inked pen as a pointer he added, "Presently, the areas of interest are the port cities of Larache, Sidi Ifni, and Mogador—here, here and here. At a later time, one of these ports will be selected for a possible covert insertion and extraction mission to be undertaken by your team."

Without further comment, Owens took a small notebook from next to the silver cigarette case. Using the nail of his index finger, he opened it to a dog-eared page. Referring to the page, he said, "Monday morning at 0900, you are to meet Lieutenant Commander Frank Bello at NAS Operations. He will introduce you to the modes of conveyance that he will make available for you to carry out duties to be assigned. Although Frank Bello is an airdale—I'm sorry, an aviator—he is a fine officer who solves problems others walk away from in total confusion."

"I met Lieutenant Commander Bello at Orly. His wife and daughter were on the plane coming here. They are very nice people."

"They are that, although the daughter, Peggy—"

"Judy, I think, sir."

"Yes, of course, Judy. The child can be trying." Turning the page, he continued, "Monday afternoon, at 1400, you and your team will go to the marine barracks and meet Master Sergeant Forbes. Forbes, among other things, is in charge of field training for the marine detachment at the NAS. He will see that you and your men will be fitted and then issued field uniforms of a different kind than you have. You and your team will wear these uniforms during covert operations. You will not wear these uniforms at any other time. After the uniform fitting, you will be issued other field equipment and then taken to the armory, where you will be issued sidearms."

"Sidearms, sir?"

"Yes, Mr. Turner, sidearms. The marine detachment has an eight-man reconnaissance-capable team. Master Sergeant Forbes is taking this RECON team on a two-to-three-and-a-half-day field problem in the Rif Mountains, the variation in time depending on completion of the mission. Your team will accompany this team. You will fly out Wednesday at 0500 and land at an old airfield just south of Tangier at about 0600. You will be met by an officer in the French Foreign Legion and will then accompany this officer and his men to the field problem area in the Rif Mountains. Your team, along with Forbes's team, will be under the command of this officer from the time you land and until the time you arrive back at that airfield. This training is covert in nature and part of an operation classified Secret. On your return, there will be transportation waiting to immediately take you and your team to Fleet Intelligence Center for debriefing."

Seeing that Turner was about to ask a question, the exec raised his hand and continued, "You will participate in basic reconnaissance and surveillance procedures." His manner changed slightly as he continued, "Most importantly, we are interested in your observation and analysis of the procedures used to accomplish the task associated with the field problem. Take careful notes. You are to instruct your men that what they see and hear while you are with Forbes's RECON team and with our French military friends is Secret. There are a few more things I need to pass on to you, but since your eyes seems to be glazing over, I'll pause for a bit for your questions, if any."

"Thank you, sir. With all due respect, I feel that my team and I are being swept along into something we may not be prepared for. It would be helpful if I had some idea what you are going to ask of us."

The exec got up from his chair and walked over to the window on the other side of the work table. Using the fleshy part of his hand, he rubbed away something he saw on the glass, turned around and said, "Mr. Turner, it was your choice to join the navy. It was your choice to sign on to a volunteer program that demanded of its disciples discipline, intelligence, and resourcefulness. Your special weapons/explosive ordnance disposal training took almost a full year and cost the navy something like two hundred thousand dollars. It's payback time. When we have confidence that we have prepared you well enough for what we want you to do, then you will be told what this is all about. Meanwhile, step-by-step, we will see if you can meet or exceed our expectations."

"Yes, sir. I understand. May I tell the team what I know so far?"

"You may. But tell them that all navy and marine corps personnel are in a state of heightened operational readiness because of terrorist activities related to the French withdrawal from Morocco and Algeria. Honing their skills in insertion and extraction, coupled with gaining experience in reconnaissance and surveillance from Forbes's team is their part of heightened operational readiness. These activities are unclassified. Where you go and what you do when you get there is classified Secret/Covert Operations. You are not to mention Larache or Agadir at this time. The men will be put on twenty-four-hour standby when deployment of the team is imminent."

"Sir, I have a considerable amount of work on my desk. Is that work associated with what you are preparing us for?"

"Yes and no. The paperwork on your desk is associated with your collateral duty. You are the division officer in charge of the mine shop of thirty-six enlisted minemen. Warrant Officer Fulkerson and Chief Mineman Foss run the operation. The mine shop is responsible for supply of influence mines to the Sixth Fleet, as needed."

"Sir, the only thing I know about influence or other mines is how to render them safe when they are underwater or on the beach."

"You will sign paperwork Mr. Fulkerson forwards to you, such as that which is on your desk. As mine shop division officer, you will also represent, at captain's mast, any mineman accused of violating navy regulations. You will present the mine shop division to our commanding officer during inspections as well. You will find Mr. Fulkerson professional and extremely intelligent. Mr. Fulkerson and the yeomen in the office understand your level of competence in all of this, and"—the exec winked—"it is your cover for other things. There will be other paperwork you will be required to read and initial, mainly housekeeping items from the commander, myself, or other NOF officers, and of course, items forwarded from the NAS.

"Finally, because of your Top Secret/Restricted Data clearance level, you will be honored to be the other courier officer to receive and be involved with transport of materials associated with nuclear weapons or nuclear weapons themselves." The exec walked over to the door and called out, "Yeoman Fry, please bring in Mr. Turner's courier card."

Yeoman Fry replied, "It may not be ready yet. I'll check, sir."

The exec returned to his seat and explained to the obviously overloaded junior officer, "You have the duty Tuesday, day after tomorrow. An R-6 is flying in from Yorktown with four birdcages and three suitcases. The plane should be landing at 1300 hours. You will board the plane, show your courier card and introduce yourself. The onboard courier will ask you to inventory the shipment. After you do this to your satisfaction, he will sign off on delivery to you, and you will sign for acceptance. The NAS loading and receiving crew will offload the birdcages and suitcases and load them onto our weapons carrier. You will bring the shipment back up to the NOF exclusion area, where Lieutenant Commander Buckold or his representative will accept and sign for your shipment. Chief Gallegos has assisted others in courier transfers and will be your associate as needed. Understand that once in a while, the crew and courier you meet will be quite exhausted and occasionally rather shaken. The Atlantic crossing is long, the weather often very bad, and once they land here, they don't want to be in the airplane any longer than they have to. However, you are not to allow anyone off the airplane until you have received, accepted, and offloaded the shipment."

"Do others at the Naval Air Station know I will be doing this?"

"Operations is fully informed. Never underestimate the power of the courier card assigned you. Very powerful item, that. Chief Gallegos will show you how to acquire your sidearms. Do you have any other questions?

"Who is the other courier, sir?"

"I am. From here on, you will be the primary courier, another collateral duty." The exec called out again, "Yeoman Fry, are you there?"

"Yes, sir. We have the courier card."

Turner sat at his desk, thinking about his session with Lieutenant Commander Owens. He turned the pink courier card over and over. It didn't have much to say except that Lieutenant Junior Grade Burt Turner had a Top Secret/Restricted Data clearance and was authorized to accept and deliver items that fell under that clearance category. It further stated that others were to render assistance as necessary to expedite the delivery of the items. The picture on the card was the same as on his NOF ID card.

He put the courier card in his wallet and reached for the desk phone. There was a list of phone numbers on the handset base; including one for the EOD shop. He took the handset up and dialed the number of the shop. "EOD shop, Chief Gallegos speaking, sir."

"I'm in deep shit, Chief. Could you come over to the office?"

Recognizing the young officer's voice, Gallegos replied, "I'm on the way, sir."

Chief Manuel Gallegos had been in the navy for fourteen years, eleven of which were spent in special weapons/explosive ordnance disposal. Prior to being ordered to his present duty station, he had served a two-year tour of duty as an instructor at the Stumpneck field facility of the EOD School. He taught installation, detection, and rendering-safe procedures for booby traps and improvised explosive devices. Gallegos was married (Norma) and had a nine-year-old child (Alejandra). Since NAS, Port Lyautey was considered a "hardship" duty station and because he was a senior enlisted man, he was allowed to bring his family with him. They lived in base housing. Alejandra was in the fourth grade at the base elementary school.

Gallegos had seen many junior officers of varying ability during his career; the junior officers he had served with in the SW/EOD program were consistently several cuts above the usual. They had undergone careful screening before entering the program and were subject to intense scrutiny while going through the program. Even so, of the four teams he had been involved with, only three of the junior officers were competent and the fourth was, in his opinion, unsafe. All had the confidence that came with inexperience and youth.

Gallegos's service record was exemplary; he had been awarded the navy and marine corps medal for heroism and had several letters of commendation. He fired Expert with the rifle and pistol. He had been recommended twice for Officer Candidate School; he declined twice. The men who served on teams with Gallegos considered him a strong leader, able to get things done; and most importantly, he wouldn't get them killed.

Gallegos had yet to form an opinion of Lieutenant Burt Turner. Turner appeared to be adequate so far, rather serious, although when they were on the beach and in the water at Mehdiya, he seemed to be very happy at being where he found himself.

Chief Gallegos appeared in front of Turner's desk four minutes after receiving the phone call. Turner got up from his chair and, after offering his hand, asked Chief Gallegos to sit down in the chair next to his desk.

Chief Gallegos asked, "How can I help you, sir?"

"I just spent a rather bewildering hour and a half with the exec. It seems I am going to have a lot on my plate, and I'm going to need your help." He hesitated, then said, "Look, I know you and I are just beginning to know each other, and what I can offer isn't much. I just got off shore patrol, and I haven't even had a chance to go over the service records of the men on the team. I plan to do that right after you and I finish here."

Turner paused to allow a possible comment from the chief. Hearing none, he went on, "I was just informed that I have been appointed to be the primary courier at NOF and will be standing by for a classified shipment to arrive the day after tomorrow at 1300. You will be joining me. Did you know about that?"

"I knew a classified shipment was coming in. I thought the exec and I would be meeting the plane."

"Well, it seems I am taking the place of the exec. I think I know what to do in relation to the paperwork, but I don't have a clue about drawing a weapons carrier or sidearms. I don't even know where to meet the plane."

"Sir, I'll have the weapons carrier here at 1200, and we can get the duty yeoman to check out the sidearms to us at the same time. We can call Operations about the plane. It will all be a piece of cake."

Feeling somewhat relieved, Turner said, "I would like to be with you when you pick up the weapons carrier. I'd like to see how it is done."

Gallegos smiled. "Actually, we don't have to draw a weapons carrier from the NAS. The team has one."

Turner began to feel at ease with Gallegos. He said, "This is probably as good a time as any to talk with you about the meeting I had with the exec concerning plans for the team.

As part of the current state of heightened operational readiness, we are going to be involved in an operation involving insertion and extraction for reconnaissance and surveillance. The locations are to be named later. The operation is classified Secret/Covert. The operation sounds like it is still in the planning stages."

Turner briefly filled in the details for Gallegos regarding Marine Master Sergeant Forbes and the team's new clothing to be worn in the field. He further explained that they would be accompanying the marine reconnaissance (RECON) and French Foreign Legion teams on a two—to three-day field problem starting on Wednesday in the Rif Mountains.

Hearing this, Gallegos said, "This sounds very interesting. I know Master Sergeant Forbes very well. He will be good to work with. The French will be something new."

Respecting the chief's experience and position, Turner asked, "Would it be appropriate for you to tell the men what I just told you, or should I?"

"I suggest you should, sir."

"Would you set up a meeting with the men at 1600 today?"

"Consider it done, sir."

"The exec also told me I was to meet with Lieutenant Commander Bello at NAS Operations at 0900, Monday, to look, in his words, at 'modes of conveyance to be made available to us.' I would like you with me at the meeting."

"I'll be there at 0845, sir."

"Good. One last thing, Chief—the mine shop and Warrant Officer Fulkerson. I was informed that beside having a collateral duty as a courier, I'm also to have another collateral duty as mine shop division officer. I know nothing about administration, let alone running a mine shop."

Pointing to the stack of paper, he continued, "The paper on top has a note from the commander. It says I am to read and sign my name where appropriate, then pass it back to Yeoman Fry. Halfway through the stack is a memo from the exec asking me to generate a letter to BuOrd asking permission to use white paint instead of deck gray paint for the mine shop floor." He corrected himself, "I mean deck of the mine shop."

"Mr. Turner, the skipper has trained many junior officers who started out in the same situation you find yourself in now. He would never jeopardize the appearance of his command because of incompetence or inexperience in his junior officers. For that reason, he wants to bring you up to speed as rapidly as possible, so you will be able to competently assume the responsibilities that come with your position at NOF. I would suggest you start as soon as possible with a meeting with Warrant Officer Fulkerson. Let him know your concerns. You will find that you can be involved as much as you want in the operation of the mine shop division. He knows you are the SW/EOD team officer and will make allowances for your SW/EOD responsibilities. He is a good man. Mr. Fulkerson runs a tight ship, and the division consistently passes ORIs with high marks."

Gallegos paused for a possible response. Hearing none, he continued.

"The best friends you can have, as you learn to do official paperwork, are the yeomen. Get to know them, cultivate a respect for them, be considerate of them, and they will keep you out of trouble. Arrogance because you are an officer and involved in what you consider to be an elite group will find you out on your own and miserable."

"Thanks for the steer, Chief. I appreciate your words. I'll see you at 1600."

The two men got up, Gallegos left the office spaces. Turner went over to Yeoman Fry's desk and stood for a minute.

"Yes, sir. What can I do for you?"

"Yeoman Fry, I would like to look at Chief Gallegos and Petty Officers Jack Cole and Richard Huwitt's service records. Could you help me?"

Five minutes later, he was reading the chief's service record; a half hour after that, Petty Officer Jack Cole's; then twenty-five minutes later, Petty Officer Richard Huwitt's. By the time he was finished, he realized he was far out of their league. Chief Gallegos was simply incredible; he had seen it all and done it all, with honors.

The youngest, Jack Cole, was six years older than Turner and had been in the navy for ten years, eight on SW/EOD teams. Cole had the Navy Commendation medal and three letters of commendation. He was consistently ranked "Outstanding" on his yearly evaluations. One item in particular caught Turner's eye: "At times, Petty Officer Cole's initiative borders on taking risk(s) beyond reason. Petty Officer Cole's perspective on what is considered risky or dangerous is on a lower level of perception than most others."

Cole may need watching. He could get someone hurt, maybe me. But there is no evidence that Cole is reckless or behaves stupidly.

Petty Officer Richard Huwitt was eight years older than Turner and had twelve years in the navy, six years on SW/EOD teams, and two letters of commendation. He had been to the U.S. Army Parachute School at Fort Benning, Georgia, and was a qualified parachutist with twenty-four jumps. Evidently, he had requested the training, and the powers that be had thought it might be useful having a qualified parachutist in the EOD program.

Interesting.

Items in Huwitt's Enlisted Performance Evaluation included "resourceful, innovative, rock solid in reliability."

When he finished studying the men's service records, he gathered up a number of papers from the stack, and with the service records on top, he went to Yeoman Fry's desk. He gave the service records to the yeoman and said, "Yeoman Fry, I've finished with the service records. These are quite a group of guys."

Fry said with a big grin, "Well, sir, there are some that feel Petty Officers Cole and Huwitt have been exposed to too much pressurized air."

Turner laughed, started back to his desk, hesitated, then walked back to Fry's desk. Holding the papers out, he said, "I'm not sure where to begin with these. I think I need help."

Not really surprised, Fry said, "Let's start by getting your signature on this pad."

"How will that help?"

"At times, you will have a large number of repetitive items to sign. We will make a rubber facsimile stamp of your signature, supply you with an ink pad, and you will be in business. We can have it to you in a few days."

Turner signed on the pad with a flourish.

"Now, when someone puts a stack of papers on your desk or in your IN box, sort out the papers according to date, then deal with oldest first. If there is something needing careful study, put it in your HOLD box. We will help you to not forget anything that needs quick attention. If you get stuck, come and see me or one of the other yeomen. You will get the hang of it. Don't hesitate to ask Lieutenant Commander Owens about protocols. He really doesn't mind helping a new young officer."

"What do I do about mail?"

"The mail room is down the hall, next to the enlisted men's head. Local is every day and CONUS is once or twice a week."

Thanking Yeoman Fry, Turner went out the door, then down the hall to the mail room. He asked the yeomen on mail room duty if he had any mail. After a moment he was handed two *Time* magazines (international issue) and two *Science* journals from the weeks before, a USC alumni letter requesting money for a forthcoming building project, and three advertisements. No letters from Joan. He had written her four times since arriving at Port Lyautey.

When he returned to his desk, Turner found a telephone message slip (pink). It was from Lieutenant Bob Miller. Bob Miller, Ben Teipner, and Phil Pierce had rooms next to each other and across the hall from Turner's room at the BOQ. They were the only people he had become close to since his arrival at Port Lyautey.

He left work late at night these days. When he arrived at the BOQ, he usually ended up in Bob Miller's room. He and Teipner lounged on the couch (stolen from one of the rooms of the officer's club), Pierce on a Arab hassock, and Miller in the easy chair (rescued from a warehouse fire in town set by terrorists). The four would talk for hours about girls, the navy, places to go in Paris, geopolitics, terrorism, the Lebanon situation. When the opportunity presented itself, Turner would expound on the importance of special weapons/explosive ordnance disposal and why it was a more intellectual pursuit than driving airplanes and, in Pierce's case, far better than dealing with the BMW (bitching, moaning, and whining) of supposedly ill dependent wives and children.

They met in Miller's room because he owned the latest hi-fi radio-phonograph available, a Grundig. He had recently bought it on a flight to Paris. He and Teipner also had a nice collection of the latest Kingston Trio, Stan Kenton, and Ray Anthony albums and a number of classical music albums for balance. Miller and Teipner considered themselves connoisseurs of good music, Cuban cigars, and expensive wine and liquor from the best shops in Gibraltar and Paris. Donations were required from those who smoked and drank of these provisions.

Tuner dialed the phone number on the slip.

"Lieutenant JG Miller."

"What's going on, Bob?"

Recognizing Turner's voice, he said, "I want you to go with Teipner and Pierce and me to La Fennier's tonight. Teipner and I brought back eight Argentine steaks from Gib this morning."

"Sure, but what's is La Fennier's?"

"It's an outstanding French restaurant just south of town. They'll do our steaks for us. The place is safe. The owner is a communist and has made a deal with the bad guys so he can stay in business. Binki and Kathy are going to bring a couple of other nurses, and Pierce will be there to entertain. We'll take my car and Binki's. The guys will ride together and the women will ride together, at least going. Coming back, who knows? We leave at 1900, sharp. Did you buy Goss's piece of junk before he left?"

"No, but I'm going to. The check's in the mail. I'll meet you at your room before 1900." Turner put the phone down and left for the EOD shop.

The 1600 meeting in the EOD shop was the first time the team was to experience Turner as team leader. At Mehdiya Beach, the men considered him the new college guy—young, skinny, untested, and, though he tried not to show it, unsure of himself. He was a determined runner, not the fastest, but he was better than the others in the surf.

The men wanted to give him a good chance to show what he could deliver. They were receptive and respectful; they hoped this one was competent.

Though Turner felt hesitant and unsure of himself when he began talking, his confidence grew as he saw the information he was delivering was holding the men's attention. He talked for forty-five minutes. The men saw that he was well prepared, confident, and very much in charge. Gallegos was pleased.

After explaining what he could, he said, "I know we could talk for hours, second-guessing what the skipper and exec might be planning for us. I don't want to do that. As soon as they tell me anything, I'll tell you. To be absolutely safe, consider everything I have said to be Secret."

Gallegos said, "Sir, I think from now on, every time we go into the water, we put on dry suits, masks, fins, life jackets, web belts, knives, and smoke and night flares. We might as well get serious."

"I agree, Chief."

Dry suits were problematic. On the surface of the water, they made you float when you didn't want to. As the water pressure increased with depth, trapped air in the suit compressed, forming small wrinkles in the rubber, often pinching the skin painfully. When the suit was donned, no matter what the swimmer did to remove air, small amounts of it remained. The suit did prevent the swimmer from getting too cold in the low-temperature Atlantic waters off the coast of North Africa, but not for long. Divers' long underwear could be worn under the dry suit, but that could cause more problems.

Turner added, "At 0900 Monday morning, the chief and I will be meeting with the NAS operations officer. He will be showing us what equipment will be made available to us for insertion and extraction training. At 1330, I'll meet you here, and we will leave to meet Master Sergeant Forbes at 1400. Our deployment to and training in the Rif Mountains is Secret. If anyone asks why you were at the marine barracks, tell them that it's part of an interservice orientation program, or better yet, tell them we are preparing for the operational readiness inspection coming up next quarter. Do you have any questions?"

Huwitt asked, "Sir, we have never worked with the marines before. How are we supposed to fit in with them on their field problem?"

"We will fit in as a very interested and willing SW/EOD team, eager to learn as they try to teach us as much as they can about reconnaissance and surveillance. Are there any other questions?"

There were none. Turner got up and, just before leaving, asked, "Chief, what kind of watch are you wearing?"

"It's a Rolex Submariner. I see you're wearing a navy-issue diver's watch. They aren't very good. The Rolex is far better."

"Can I buy a Rolex at the Navy exchange?" Before the chief could answer, he added, "Are they very expensive?"

The chief laughed. "Yes, you can, and they are expensive, but less expensive here then anywhere else that I know of."

Turner thought he still had quite a bit of money in traveler's checks and said, "I think I'll get one." Then very seriously he asked, "Could you loan me some money, Chief?"

Gallegos opened his mouth to answer, but Turner laughed and said, "Just kidding, Chief." And left the EOD shop.

At 1900 in the BOQ parking lot, the four men in their civilian clothes met Mary Bianconi, Kathy Roberts and two women Turner hadn't met before. The women wore skirts and sweaters and looked wonderful. *Kathy Roberts especially*, he thought.

Binki said, "Burt Turner, this is Betty Armstrong and Sylvia Baxter. Betty and Kathy and I work together at the dispensary. Sylvia is the librarian at the base library." She turned to the two women. "Burt is the new EOD officer at NOF."

Betty Armstrong asked, "What is it you do there?"

"Currently, I ask a lot of questions, and they allow me to do elementary paperwork."

"Oh."

"Bullshit," replied Miller. "He's at the beach most of the day, while the rest of us are risking our lives for our beloved country."

Not letting that be the last word Teipner quipped, "Actually, Burt is here because he was unfit to go to the fleet. He doesn't have the requisite mechanical ability and eye-hand coordination to prevent him from putting a vessel and crew at risk."

Turner was about to say something in his own defense when Binki cut them all off. "It's time to go. We'll meet you at La Fennier's."

The men followed the women from the parking lot to Halsey Road, then to Spruance and the main gate. The stickers on their car windshields earned them a salute from the marine guard as they passed through.

As the cars headed south, Turner said, "That was a very badass thing you two guys just did. I try to make a halfway decent impression, and you fry me."

Dr. Lieutenant Pierce (as the other three called him in disrespect) said, "Burt, you must understand your two friends are classic cases of arrested development. There is constant competition as to which one can outdo the other in regard to unacceptable behavior." He added, "There is some question about their ability to drive airplanes as well."

The majority of officers in the BOQ found these three—Miller, Teipner, and Pierce—an obnoxious annoyance, ungentlemanly and disrespectful of their station as naval officers. Turner had at first been thought by others to be a "serious" naval officer, but now, seen in company of Miller, Teipner, and Pierce, was considered to be of the same ilk.

Actually, Miller and Teipner were exceptional aviators, well ahead of their peer group, and Dr. Lieutenant Pierce, flight surgeon, was a gifted physician who considered the physicians with whom he worked incompetent fools and most other officers the same. His snobbery overlaid a strong sense of decency and compassion for those in genuine need of medical care.

The nurses and other female naval officers in the BOQ were capable and professional in their duties. They behaved appropriately off duty and were discrete in their personal lives. The three or four women who liked Miller, Teipner, Pierce, and Turner enjoyed a strong sense of self-confidence and invulnerability and remained respected by other female and male BOQ officers, even though they were seen to be in the vicinity, from time to time, of the lesser-thought-of four.

After arriving at the La Fennier parking lot, Teipner opened the trunk of Miller's car and removed a helmet bag with still nearly frozen Argentine steaks, then joined the group and went into the restaurant. Once inside, they found one of three large round tables vacant and took possession of it. Recognizing Miller, Teipner, and Pierce, a rather corpulent waiter was immediately at the table and asked, "Will it be *bifteck a nuit?*"

Miller took the steaks from the helmet bag and, passing them to the waiter, said, "Mais oui, Monsieur Rochemont, bifteck a nuit."

Looking around the table, Miller asked, "Is there anyone who doesn't want their steak rare?"

Pierce called out, "Well done."

Turner called out, "Medium, please."

Rochemont made a note.

Teipner asked, "May I order the wine?" There was no disagreement. "Chaud Soleil, rouge, s'il vous plait, pour sept."

After writing up the orders, which included fried potatoes and salad, Rochemont exited for the kitchen.

Turner, sitting between Kathy Roberts and Pierce, said, "I didn't know Bob spoke French."

Pierce said disdainfully, "He doesn't."

Turner looked around. The restaurant was almost full, perhaps forty or fifty people, apparently French and upper-class Moroccan. There were a few couples on the small dance floor, dancing to a scratchy Harry James recording of "You'll Never Know." The building was constructed of cinder blocks painted light blue. Small lizards were on the walls and ceiling, mostly on the ceiling. He thought they were geckos (they were). There were two exits, one in the back of the building, one on a side wall. A sign on the opposite wall read "Femmes et Hommes" with an arrow pointed to a door opening to a short hallway. There were a number of plants he thought might be bougainvillea. The air smelled of extremely strong cigarettes, charcoal, and something like disinfectant.

Two tables away, four men were finishing their dinner. They appeared to be in their midthirties to midforties, wearing tan trousers and what Turner thought looked like paratrooper jump boots. Two had leather jackets on the backs of their chairs. One of the two wore a rough, long-sleeved, collarless green sweater; the other a sweatshirt with "11er Choc" printed on its back. The other two wore nondescript sweaters over off-white collared shirts. All four smoked cigarettes as they ate. Their faces and hands were very weathered, their hair was cut very short, much shorter than Turner's crew cut. Pierce saw him looking at the four men, and tilting his head toward the four men, he quietly commented, "Légion Étrangère."

"What does that mean?"

"Foreign Legion, the French Foreign Legion."

One of the men at the table was talking to the other three and pointed at Pierce, and a moment later, he rose from the table, walked over, and, with a heavy French accent, introduced himself. "Dr. Pierce, I am Captain Jean Salon." Extending his hand, he continued, "You kept my lieutenant from dying three nights ago. I wish to thank you."

All eyes at the table were on the captain.

Pierce stood up and, taking Salon's hand, said, "I am pleased to meet you, Captain. Your lieutenant didn't have an easy time of it." He gestured toward Binki. "Lieutenant Bianconi saved his life after everyone else left him to die."

The captain excused himself and walked around to where Binki was sitting; as she stood up to greet him, he took her hand and kissed it.

Continuing to hold her hand, he looked into her eyes. "Mademoiselle, you saved so much more than one life. I cannot tell you why I say this, but many people of importance are thankful."

"Actually, Dr. Pierce is a gifted trauma surgeon and came immediately when I called him. I only assisted."

At this point Pierce introduced Captain Salon to everyone. Before Salon left for his table, he called Rochemont over and said, "Give this table anything they want to drink and charge it to Captain Jean Salon of the 11er Regiment Etranger Parachutiste." He added, "I would hope we may meet again." And then he returned to his table. The young naval officers were astonished, except for Dr. Lieutenant Pierce. They were products of a rather unsophisticated culture that considered ignorance a virtue, consumption to be celebrated, and civility an afterthought—truly Americans.

The steak was served as ordered, the fried potatoes and salad were appreciated, and the six bottles of Chaud Soleil, greatly appreciated. With dinner over, the wine encouraged dancing. Bob Miller paired up with Mary Bianconi and Ben Teipner with Kathy Roberts while Harry James played "It Might as Well Be Spring." Pierce was having a third glass of wine. He and Turner were in serious conversation about what communism could offer Arab countries and capitalism could not. They were just getting into Islamic fundamentalism when one of the legionnaires from the other table came over. Addressing Pierce and Turner, he asked if he might introduce himself to mademoiselle over there for a dance. Pierce replied, "Mais oui." So did Betty Armstrong.

After several more songs, Teipner and Kathy Roberts left the dance floor. Teipner sat down and poured himself a large glass of wine. Pierce asked Sylvia Baxter for a dance, leaving Turner swirling what was left of the wine in his glass and watching the ceiling geckos. Kathy Roberts approached Turner and, putting her hand on his shoulder, said, "Dance with me, bare-chested warrior."

During "September Song," their second dance, Kathy Roberts asked, "Do you have a girl Burt?"

"I do. Her name is Joan, and she is a grad student in chemical engineering at USC."

"Is it serious?"

"Gosh, yes, it's serious." Then he started, "We started going together during our senior year. She waited for me when I was at Officer Candidate School at Newport. After that, I had two weeks we spent together before I left for Key West. It was tough for us when I was at Indian Head. I only saw her twice. After Indian Head, we had four days together while I was waiting for orders to Port Lyautey."

"I suppose you write a lot of letters?"

"We write often, but I haven't received anything from her since I arrived here."

"So in two years, you will go home, marry her, buy a house with a white picket fence, and have two children, a boy and a girl." She said this with derision.

He didn't answer. Right now he was holding a very attractive woman in his arms, and he liked it. And Kathy Roberts liked being held by Burt Turner. Turner danced with the other three women that evening, but ended up dancing again with Kathy Roberts. After the legionnaire danced with Betty Armstrong a few times, he chivalrously thanked her, joined his comrades, and left the restaurant.

An hour later, the Miller group left for the parking lot. The four women and four men, mostly sober—except for Pierce, who was not—got in the cars they came in and returned to the BOQ. Before entering the building, the women chastely kissed each of the men and retired to their rooms in the women's wing; the men, to their rooms in the men's wing.

A half hour later, Turner, in his tee shirt and shorts, was sitting on the edge of his bed, taking his socks off. There was a knock on the door. It was Teipner.

"Turner, are you abusing yourself, or are you asleep?"

"Neither one. Come on in."

Teipner opened the door and stood in the doorway, barefoot and in a tee shirt and shorts. "It is far too early to be hitting the rack. It would make good sense to go to Miller's room and discuss the events of the evening."

"Capital idea. Is Miller still up?"

"Oh hell I don't know. I'm sure he would rather chat than sleep, don't you think?"

Turner pulled on his socks, and they both padded out and over to Miller's room. Just before they knocked on Miller's door, they heard Pierce, in the head down the hall, apparently losing his dinner in one of the toilets.

Turner said, "My goodness, I think Dr. Lieutenant Pierce is in extremis. Perhaps we can help the fellow."

Teipner replied, "Yes, of course. Let us do what we can."

They went into the head, and there on his knees was Pierce, at the moment lifting his head from inside a toilet bowl. A toilet bowl that had, through the years, experienced many junior naval officers doing that very thing.

Teipner said, "Dr. Lieutenant Pierce, I presume you are considering how the siphon-jet toilet might be improved?"

Looking up at the two, he replied, "Well, yes, I was doing that very thing and thought it appropriate to test my glossopharyngeal reflex at the same time."

They helped Pierce up and to a washbasin. He was remarkably clean of vomit and only needed his face washed. They allowed him to do this.

"Perhaps you should join us in Mr. Miller's room."

The three made their way down the hall to Miller's room. The door was half-open, and Teipner pushed it open all the way. Miller was sitting in his lounge chair, reading a NATOPS manual on the SNB Twin Beech light transport aircraft.

As the three filed in, Turner said, "We saw your door open and thought you would enjoy company."

"How thoughtful of you. I was just reading a good book before going to bed."

Teipner looked at Turner and said, "He knows I am a much better pilot than he, and he thinks he can become a better pilot than I if he spends a lot of time with the owner's manual for our airplane."

Waving the SNB publication at his best friend, Miller said, "What bullshit. If you spent more of your time studying this, you wouldn't have to ask me so many questions when we are in a sandstorm at six thousand feet."

The two pilots were assigned to the NAS Twin Beech for short flights delivering small cargo and personnel. Often, other pilots not assigned to one of the squadrons on the base would use the airplane to get their flying time in. Miller and Teipner didn't like this. They felt the SNB was *their* plane. It wasn't. They flew it 80 percent of the time, but could be pushed aside by anyone senior to them who was qualified to fly the airplane. The important people at the NAS—the commanding officer, the exec, and operation officer—knew that Miller and Teipner were the most well qualified to fly the airplane, even though they were both lieutenants junior grade. They would be full lieutenants soon with two silver bars rather than one lonely one. This advancement in rank would automatically make them more credible to others who cared about such things. If there was a potentially difficult mission due to a marginal landing field or bad weather, the two junior officers were usually assigned that mission.

Teipner sat on the floor with his back to the leather hassock; Turner and Pierce sat on the lounge.

Pierce said, "Perhaps we could listen to *La Mer* as we chat. Not too loud though."

Miller got up, found *La Mer* in the nearby stack of albums, slipped the record out of the album cover, carefully put it on the Grundig's turntable, and turned the set on. After adjusting the volume, he returned to his lounge chair.

After a few quiet minutes Miller said, "You know, I think I will marry Binki."

Teipner groaned, "What bullshit. Three weeks ago, it was Sylvia Baxter. Before that, it was the French girl working at the navy exchange. You haven't a clue about serious relationships. You also have a problem going after girls smarter than you."

Turner asked, "What about Kathy Roberts? She's beautiful, a terrific conversationalist, and seems to be fun to be around."

Pierce commented, "She finished nursing school, was offered a full-ride scholarship at Stanford med school. She did a year and a half, got sick of being a second-class citizen among males, and quit. Then she decided to join the navy and see the world. She is a terrific OR nurse."

Then Teipner said, "She goes out with guys, but if they try to get her in the sack, she won't have anything to do with them. There is a rumor that when she first arrived, she had a very serious affair with a married guy from the VQ, the electronic surveillance squadron. His wife and kid were just coming over from the States when his A-3D was shot down by the Russians while on an electronic surveillance mission near the Turkish border. There were no survivors."

Turner asked, "How could that happen? We aren't at war with them. Why would they shoot down one of our planes?"

It was Miller's turn. "Mr. Turner, SW/EOD officer, what you just heard is not an isolated event. There is a lot of deception and bad shit being dealt out by bad guys and good guys. By the time you leave Port Lyautey, there is a good chance you will experience deception and bad shit, and in our national interest, you will deliver the same to others."

Pierce and Teipner responded together with, "And in our national interests, you will deliver the same to others."

Pierce, still not quite clear-headed, said, "That was sort of Gilbert and Sullivan, 'Policeman's Chorus,' don't you think?"

Turner said, "You guys are too much. I'm going to hit the rack." He left the room.

Halfway down the hall, he turned around and went back to Miller's room. Pierce and Teipner were just leaving, and he asked, "I forgot to ask. How do I buy Goss's car and get it registered?"

They took turns explaining. It came down to contacting a new ensign (Supply Corps) attached to the officer's club, who, as a collateral duty, would guide Turner in buying car insurance at a commercial insurance office at the navy exchange and then going to shore patrol headquarters at the main gate for transfer of ownership and new red license plates. Red plates signified a member of the U.S. military and allowed the car to be driven off base.

He then asked, "What kind of car is it?"

Teipner looked at Pierce, then at Turner, and replied, "An older Bugeye Sprite."

Turner asked, "What's a bug-eyed Sprite?"

Pierce replied, "A most unusual car you will find to be quite suitable for yourself."

With that, Pierce and Teipner went on to their rooms, and Turner returned to his.

By noon the next day, Turner had become the third owner of a light blue Austin-Healey Sprite. A very small two-seater 948 cc roadster, it was topless, had no side windows, and was essentially a cart with an engine. The seats were just OK, the floor mats cut from remnants of the new carpet in the officers' mess, and it had numerous dents, mostly in the front fenders, but most importantly, the car ran very nicely. Turner thought he had a great buy for the five-hundred-dollar check he had mailed to Goss.

During the afternoon, he explored the base more thoroughly in his "new" car. He found the navy exchange, where he bought a Rolex Submariner and received directions for a self-guided base tour. He started at the base gym. The gym was a very large Quonset building, and next to it was one of the two base pools. He drove on to the married officers' housing. First were duplexes for lieutenants and lieutenant commanders. As he drove by, he saw name plates on porch railings announcing the residence of Lieutenant Commander Don Owens and, farther on, Lieutenant Commander Charles Buckold's residence. Then commanders' row—elegant single-story homes with bronze plaques with the names of residents on the lawns. He passed by Commander Gene Hawkins's house; he considered calling on the commander and presenting his card, which was a protocol needing to be addressed, but thought, *Can't do this unannounced.*

Driving on, there was a slight hill where the base commander and his senior staff lived in two-storied French colonial mansions with large expanses of lawn. A number of Arab groundskeepers were mowing lawns and tending beautiful gardens.

He turned the Sprite around, and on the way out of the area, he saw Judy Bello playing hopscotch on the sidewalk with three other girls, in front of a duplex with Lieutenant Commander Frank Bello's name on the name plate. Her mother was sitting on the porch stairs reading a magazine.

Turner pulled up to the curb and parked at the curb where the girls were playing.

"Hello, small girl person, how are you?"

Judy Bello dropped her chalk, ran over to the car, and, hands on the driver's door edge, said, "Hello, Mr. Burt Turner." She turned to her girlfriends and said, "This is Mr. Burt Turner. He's a friend we met on the airplane from Paris. He isn't a pilot."

Obviously, Judy Bello didn't know many men who were not pilots. She was genuinely happy to see Turner. Her mother saw her daughter talking with Turner, got up from the stairs, and walked over to the car.

"Mr. Turner, how are you? Did you get settled?"

Turner pushed up from his seat to a sitting position on the cowling behind him. "I am well settled, well oriented, and very happy to be involved with my work."

"I see you've bought Tom Goss's car."

"I did, and I am enjoying a very fine Saturday afternoon run."

"Can Mr. Burt Turner stay for dinner tonight, mother?"

"Mr. Turner probably has other things to do, but of course he would be very welcome."

Showing some discomfort, he said, "I really do have to meet friends tonight, but thank you."

Christine Bello said, "Won't you come in and have some ice tea, lemonade, or something stronger? My husband is in the backyard, and I am sure he is ready for something cold."

"Actually, this afternoon, I'm trying to learn where things are on the base. But thanks for the invitation. How do I get down to the wharf? Is it very far from here?"

"It's about a mile and a half." Pointing down the street, she continued, "Go down to the first stop sign, turn left, and follow the curve of the road to the fence line of the French Navy's side of the base. Turn right, and it's a short distance down the hill to the wharf." He thanked her, slid back down into the seat, reached out and squeezed one of Judy Bello's hands good-bye, and drove off.

As he drove by the French Navy base, he was surprised by its size. It was enormous. He slowed the car and saw a large number of three-story buildings that looked like barracks. Farther on were a large number of one- and two-story buildings with open areas (parade grounds?) that may have had lawns at one time and a large numbers of French Navy and army personnel walking about. Farther on, he saw acres of French army trucks of various sizes, half-tracks, and tanks. He followed the road down the hill to the Oued Sebou and the wharf.

The wharf was about the size of a football field. Moored at the near end was a sixty-three-foot white-hulled, orange-decked U.S. Navy AVR (aviation rescue) crash boat, then a U.S. Navy YFR—a small refrigerator ship used to transfer refrigerated cargo from pier to ships or from ship to ship. Some distance from the YFR was a French Navy LST used for large-volume cargos such as tanks and trucks.

He parked the Sprite and walked over to the gangplank leading to the AVR. It looked like one of the old PT-boats without torpedo tubes or gun tubs. There was a well at the stern of the boat that ended with a drop-down ramp, very useful when bringing downed aircrew from the water and into the AVR. He spent some time looking the boat over. Seeing a sailor come up from a hatch amidships, Turner called down, "Why is the YFR tied up here?"

"I don't know. I have been here for almost two years and never seen it get underway. About once a month, a chief or officer form operations goes on board to look it over, that's all."

"Do you take the AVR out to sea often?"

The sailor looked up in disgust and said, "We haven't been out for six weeks. Got a bent propeller shaft, and there's no money to repair it, or something."

"Could I come aboard?" Turner, in civilian shorts and a NAVY sweatshirt, added, "I'm Lieutenant JG Burt Turner. I'm up at NOF."

"Sure, come aboard, sir."

Turner went down the gangplank, saluted the ensign at the stern, and asked, "Do you run the boat?"

"Yes, sir, I'm the coxswain, First Class Bos'n Mate Deacon, Bill Deacon." They shook hands.

Turner, looking around the boat, asked, "How many in the crew?"

"Two deckhands, an engineman, and myself."

"Is the bent propeller shaft the only thing keeping you tied up?"

"My boat is fully operational, except for the bent shaft. Would you like to look around?"

Turner smiled and said, "I would like that."

As they walked up to the bridge, Turner asked, "When the boat is laid up like this, what does the crew do?"

"We work at the NAS, doing odd jobs for Lieutenant Commander Bello, the Operations officer. The boat is assigned to the Operations Department."

After looking the bridge over, the coxswain gave Turner a tour of the boat. He was impressed with Turner's questions about the boat's engines, communications gear, and the boat's general capabilities. What should have been a fifteen-minute tour became a forty-five-minute tour of instruction and easy conversation.

At the end of the tour, Turner thanked the coxswain and asked, "Maybe I could get a ride if you ever get it running?"

"Well, if that ever happens, I'll offer you a ride."

Just before going up the gangplank, Turner said, "I think I'll go over to the LST and have a look."

"Don't look too close. The French are pretty testy about Americans looking at their ships and cargos these days."

Back on the wharf, Turner decided to walk to its far end. As he passed the gangway of the LST, he waved to the officer at the quarterdeck; the officer didn't return the gesture. From the far end, he could just see the navigation aid on the jetty where the winding brown Oued Sebou opened to the sea. He thought he could hear the crash of the waves on the jetty.

On the way back to his car, he again waved to the officer on the LST's quarterdeck. The gesture was again ignored. The sailor standing guard at the bow had seen Turner's gestures and the deliberate aloofness of the officer of the deck. As Turner passed by, he said, with a slight smile, "Bonjour, Americain."

Turner smiled back and said, "Bonjour, mon ami."

Driving up the hill from the wharf, he decided to go on to NOF and look over the mine shop. Eight minutes later, he showed his identification to the marine guard, was passed on through the gate, and drove the mile and a half to the mine shop.

A large door at the end was open. He pulled up to the entrance, got out of the Sprite, and went inside. Just inside were six influence sea mines in cradles. Farther on, there were three men using a hoist to drop an engine into a rather sad-looking jeep. One of the men was Yeoman Second Class Jenkins.

Jenkins was on the chain lowering the engine; the other two men were positioning the engine as it dropped into the motor mounts. The front of the jeep lowered with the weight of the engine. With the engine in place, Jenkins stepped back and saw Turner watching.

"Mr. Turner, you're too late. We could have used you ten minutes ago." He paused, then made introductions. "Warrant Officer Ron Fulkerson is the head man here, and Mineman Second Bud Townsend is one of his very talented crew."

Warrant Officer Fulkerson reached out and shook Turner's hand. "Welcome aboard, sir."

"Thank you, Mr. Fulkerson." He added, "Saturday is always the day to work on cars. At least where I grew up."

Fulkerson laughed, "So it is here. We are trying to bring this old wreck back to life. It was decommissioned a long time ago." He saw the Sprite parked at the doorway and said, "You bought Mr. Goss's car. He spent a few Saturdays in here with it."

"Well, it really runs great. I hope I don't break it."

Fulkerson wiped his hands on a gray cloth and addressed Jenkins and Townsend. "I'm going to show the new mine shop officer around."

They walked over to the mine shop office, went in, and sat down. Turner looked around the room. There were two desks, one for Fulkerson and one probably for a yeoman. On the wall was a large picture of an A-3D banking away after dropping a mine. The mine was deploying a parachute to retard its fall. There were great shelves on two walls filled with outsized mine maintenance manuals. Near the spotless window, with its view ruined by a steel grill, was a large safe with "CLASSIFIED Publications" painted in red on the door. Next to it was a small refrigerator and coffee pot (percolator, ancient) with no sign of creamora or sugar. There was a picture on Fulkerson's desk of himself, three small children, and his wife, taken at the swimming pool next to the NAS gym. There were three mail baskets on the desk, labeled IN, OUT, and HOLD. All were empty—a sign of efficiency in the world of paperwork? He was still looking around when Fulkerson said, "Mr. Turner, I know you have a strong background in sea mines from your training at Indian Head . . ."

"Please, call me Burt. And if it's OK with you, I'll call you Ron. About mines, I can take them apart and render them safe. I can't do what you do here, take them apart and put them back together so they work when they are supposed to. I have no experience managing people, and I know almost nothing about paperwork, as evidenced by the stack on my desk. Finally, the skipper has me doing a lot things for the next few weeks that have nothing to do with the mine shop."

Fulkerson, knowing that newly assigned junior officers frequently think that too much is expected of them too soon, replied, "Our senior enlisted men run the show on the floor, and I get involved as necessary. I do the paperwork and send it on to you for your initialing, then you send it on to the exec for his comments and initialing. If appropriate, he will send it on to Commander Hawkins. I will always add a page to help you understand what the paperwork is about. If you don't understand what I send you for initialing, call me, and we will work it out. The exec has already told me you would not be as available to the mine shop as Mr. Goss. We can work around that."

Feeling somewhat relieved, Turner replied, "Thank you, Ron. You're very generous. I am interested in the mine shop, and I will do whatever I can, when I can. I heard you have something like thirty men in the shop."

"Actually, we now have forty-two men, the largest division at NOF. Twenty-four of the men are married and live in enlisted married housing. The rest live in the enlisted men's barracks. The men are well trained and competent. We consistently receive a grade of Outstanding in operational readiness inspections. The men are proud of this. As far as discipline is concerned, we haven't had anyone at captain's mast for almost seven months."

Nodding his head toward the vastness of the mine shop, he continued, "We have two types of influence mines that we work on and store here for the Sixth Fleet in the Med. If the balloon goes up, the mines will be shipped out to the carriers to be air-dropped at ports and choke points, hopefully bottling up the bad guys. I'll take you up to the magazines where the mines are stored when we finish."

The conversation lasted for nearly an hour. Then, in Turner's Sprite, they went up to the conventional ordnance single-fenced enclosure and parked near the gate. They left the car and walked over to the guard shack at the gate. They showed their IDs to the marine, who saluted and waved them through the gate. After walking past a number of dirt-domed magazines, Fulkerson went up to the door of one. He selected a key from a large ring he was carrying and unlocked the magazine door, and the two men walked inside. It was dimly lit, cool, and clammy.

Fulkerson explained, "We have 172 influence mines here. The Sixth Fleet may have about forty on board each carrier. From time to time, they send us a certain number for routine maintenance. We send back 'ready mines.'"

When the tour was over, Turner dropped Fulkerson off at the mine shop and returned to the BOQ. He went up to his room, flopped on his bed.

How can a person like me be expected to have a collateral duty as mine shop officer? The navy must be crazy. The meeting went well, and Fulkerson seems like a good guy. Then he fell asleep a few minutes later.

Back at the mine shop, Fulkerson had told Jenkins and Townsend that Turner seemed to be OK. Jenkins in turn told Fulkerson that he heard Chief Gallegos felt Turner looked pretty good, so far.

About forty-five minutes after Turner had fallen asleep, Pierce opened the door to his room (hardly anyone locked their doors unless they were leaving for the day) and, accompanied by Miller and Teipner, went inside. Seeing that Turner was asleep, they took up station near his bed and began talking quietly with each other.

Pointing to the new Rolex watch on Turner's dangling wrist, Miller said with disdain, "Our special weapons/explosive ordnance disposal officer has a Rolex watch on. I think he's trying to make a statement here. He bought this watch because he thinks it is equal to our girl-magnet aviator's watches."

"He looks like he may be asleep, do you think he is?" asked Teipner.

Pierce answered, "This young officer appears to be not one of the living, I think. There is a certain odor about him, don't you agree, gentlemen?"

Miller said, "I think this young officer just farted in his snooze. Perhaps we should wake him before he does something really disgusting."

Teipner said, "I think we can cause him to do something disgusting. See how his hand dangles so nicely over the side of the bed? If we get a glass of warm water and dip his fingers in it, in a short time, he will piss his pants."

The three could barely keep from laughing. Pierce motioned for them to go out into the hallway. Once there, he said, "Teipner, you have come up with a method of diuresis that is unknown to science, let alone medicine. How will that make him wet his pants?"

"I don't know. It just will. One of the squadron ground crewmen told me he did it to a guy once."

Miller said, "We must do this. I'll get a glass of warm water. This is going to be just great."

A wineglass of warm water was forthcoming. Since it was Teipner's idea, he was chosen to carefully raise the wineglass of warm water up to immerse their sleeping friend's fingers and cause urination, if possible. Unknown to the conspirators, Turner had a substantial amount of urine on board which, if released, would cause considerable wetness.

Three minutes passed. Teipner, on his knees and with a fine sense of touch, was careful to keep three of Turner's fingers in the glass and the fourth finger and thumb outside and away from the glass. Pierce and Miller were watching with great anticipation. Possibly because he was dreaming, Turner jerked reflexively, and the wineglass fell.

The conspirators stepped back as Turner sat up and with great energy swung his legs from bed to the floor and said, "What the fuck are you guys doing?"

Before any of them had a chance to answer, he continued, "Are you guys fucking crazy?"

Pierce said, "It was a science experiment." Attempting to changing the subject, he said, "Why don't you get dressed, and we will go to dinner?"

Miller said, "Yeah, get dressed and we can go to dinner."

With great disgust he said, "I'm going to the head."

The four went to dinner at the officer's club. It was pasta Saturday night. After placing their orders with the steward, Lieutenant Turner delivered a series of comments about friendship, punctuated with the exclamation, "You fucking guys are fucking crazy."

During dinner Dr. Lieutenant Phillip Pierce explored with Turner the influence antidiuretic hormone (ADH) had on the collecting tubules of the kidney with regard to the formation of urine. The other two joined the conversation when it turned to discussing Syria's influence on Lebanon and Israel, and the possibility of the United States sending in marines and special forces, including SW/EOD teams.

After dinner, the four decided to go to Saturday Night at the Movies. On Saturday night, relatively new movies were shown in a large multipurpose room down the hall from the dining area. Tonight's movie was *The Big Country*, starring Gregory Peck, Jean Simons, Charlton Heston, and Carroll Baker. They were early enough to get seats together. The movie was excellent in that it held their attention, consequently keeping them from making obnoxious comments to the distress of the mostly family audience.

On Sunday morning, in the nearly empty officers' mess, Turner was finishing breakfast (glass of milk, two eggs over easy, bacon, four slices of wheat toast, and then coffee). A folded copy of the previous Friday's *Washington Post* was propped up in front of his plate. The newspaper had been courtesy of an aircrew that had flown in Saturday evening. As he read, he felt a hand touch his shoulder. He looked up and saw Lieutenant Mary Bianconi, RN, Medical Corps.

"Good morning, Binki. Why are you up and in uniform?" he asked.

She sat down across from him and replied, "Had the duty last night."

"Was it a peaceful Saturday night?"

"Two sailors and two French girls in a car versus telephone pole. The girls had a few bruises, but were otherwise OK. One sailor had a compound fracture of the right lower leg. The other sailor had a broken collarbone. A marine stabbed in the chest by an Arab who hates infidels, resulting in a hemopneumothorax. Got Dr. Pierce up on that one. A five-year-old male with severe tonsillitis and a thirty-seven-year-old female overdosed on sleeping pills." She paused and asked, "Why are you in uniform?"

"I have courier duty at noon today. A plane is coming in from CONUS with classified equipment on board destined for NOF. I have orders to receive and deliver the items."

Taking a leftover half piece of toast from his plate, Binki said, "Goss was a courier when he was here. He said he used to have nightmares about the responsibility."

"Chief Gallegos is going to be with me, so it should be a piece of cake."

Recognizing the name, she said, "Chief Gallegos has a nice family. His daughter, Alejandra, has asthma. We see her often."

Binki ordered her breakfast (fruit, bowl of oatmeal with brown sugar, slice of white toast, and coffee). After she was served, they continued to talk about their backgrounds, people they were working with, politics, and if they might be involved with the Lebanon-Syria situation. "Have you heard from your girlfriend? Joan, wasn't it?"

He picked up a cube of sugar and rolled it around between his thumb and forefinger. "Yes, it is Joan, and no, I haven't heard from her yet. Changing addresses can slow things down, and the mail is slow getting over here. I'm sure I will hear from her soon."

She thought, *This guy is dreaming. She should have written by now.*

"What are you going to do today, Binki?"

"Well, since I was up all night, I am going to go upstairs, take a hot shower, and take a long nap. Kathy, Betty, and Sylvia went out to the O club at Sidi Slimane for dinner and dancing last night, so they probably won't be up until noon."

They got up from the table, Binki went to her room, hot shower, and bed; Turner went to his car and drove up to NOF.

After ten minutes at his desk, he went over and asked Yeoman Jenkins for help. He found Jenkins to be a good teacher, and he felt like he was catching on. An hour later, Turner had suffered through five informational items—three unclassified and two classified Confidential—and items only requiring his initial to indicate having read them. A sixth item was a four-page report on the need for additional personnel in the mine shop (three men) written by Warrant Officer Fulkerson. Turner wrote a note to the exec (eight lines) asking for approval of Fulkerson's request, initialed the attached routing slip, and put the report with the previous five items in his outbox. He had started on another sheaf of papers when Chief Gallegos walked into the office. "Well, Mr. Turner, are you ready for your first courier experience?"

"I am. I'll call Operations this instant."

Turner called NAS Operations. The duty officer reported the R-6 from Yorktown would be landing at 1230 hours rather than 1300 hours; the airplane caught a tailwind. He passed the word on to the chief.

Addressing the yeoman, Chief Gallegos said, "Young man, would you please break out two .45s? We are going to meet an airplane."

The yeoman went to a safe in Commander Hawkins's office. He worked the combination lock, opened the door, and removed two .45-caliber pistols in leather holsters, each wrapped tight to a web belt. He also removed an eight-by-eleven-inch logbook. He closed and locked the safe and returned to his desk, where Turner and Chief Gallegos were waiting. He gave the pistols to the two men and had them sign the logbook as receiving them.

"Mr. Turner, let's you and I go in the conference room and check out the condition of these weapons."

In the conference room, the chief asked, "When was the last time you fired one of these?"

"About three months ago."

"Do you remember how to fieldstrip the .45?"

"I think so, but take me through it."

The chief passed one of the pistols to Turner. As he began to field strip his pistol, his voice changed to that of an instructor. "Sir, this is a Colt Model 1911A1, pistol, caliber .45 ACP, able to be worn in a shoulder holster or web belt and holster. The magazine holds seven rounds."

Turner watched with amazement at how smoothly and quickly the chief went through the movements of fieldstripping, examining the parts of the pistol, and reassembling it.

Then it was his turn. He popped the magazine, removed the slide, and, with minor hesitation, finished fieldstripping the pistol. All parts were neatly lined up on the table surface. He examined each part and, being satisfied, quickly reassembled the pistol.

"Mr. Turner, that was impressive. You must have had a fine instructor."

"I did, but it came easy for me, and I put in a lot of extra time on the marine pistol range at Indian Head."

"You should go after a pistol marksmanship medal while you're here. I would be glad to help you. I don't think Master Sergeant Forbes would mind you using his pistol range."

"I'd like to try it."

They went out of the building to the weapons carrier parked in the visitors' parking space and tossed the holstered pistols in the front seat.

Getting in the passenger side, the chief said, "Mr. Turner, why don't you drive so you can get used to this formidable minor truck?"

Turner got in, started the engine, let out the clutch, and, with a solid jerk, stalled the weapons carrier.

"You have to get used to the clutch, sir. We all did exactly what you did the first time."

Turner started the engine again, let out the clutch slowly, and drove down the hill and away from NOF.

They passed the Catholic church just when people were coming out of eleven o'clock mass. Binki and Kathy Roberts where getting into Binki's car when they both saw Turner at the steering wheel of the weapons carrier as it went by.

Kathy Roberts said with a laugh, "Do you suppose he turned the Sprite in for that truck?"

"He's playing courier today," Binki replied.

As they approached the NAS administration building, the chief directed Turner to turn left and go down a short street ending at the control tower. At the control tower, Turner parked the weapons carrier near a white-and-orange SNB Twin Beech aircraft. Just down from the SNB was a light gray twin-rotor helicopter. As they waited for the R-6 transport from Yorktown, a small dark blue jet aircraft was touching down.

Turner asked, "What kind of airplane is that? It looks like an old P-38 without props and with a jet engine."

"That is a de Havilland Vampire, a little twin-boom jet fighter designed by the British and built by the French for the French Navy. The French call it a Mistral. They have seven or eight of them here. Probably use them against the Arabs in some way."

"Chief, yesterday, I saw an AVR down at the wharf at the mouth of the river. A first class boatswain's mate came up out of a hatch, saw me, and asked if I would like to come on board. His name was Bill Deacon. Have you heard of him?"

The chief stretched his legs and said, "No, I haven't ever heard of him."

"He gave me a tour of the boat and said it hadn't been operational for a long time. He said the boat runs great, but it has a bent propeller shaft, and nobody seems to want to find the money to fix it. What do you think about having us dive on it, remove the propeller shaft, and then Operations could figure out about having it straightened out?"

"We could do that. The shaft would probably have to be sent to the shipyard at Gibraltar. It would have to be cleared by Commander Hawkins and the CO of Operations. You just want an AVR to play with."

"You bet. It would be perfect for us. I'll talk to Commander Hawkins."

The chief saw the R-6 was coming into the landing pattern.

"There it is, Mr. Turner. Shall we get out and 'weaponize' ourselves?" They dismounted from the weapons carrier and put on their side arms.

"Chief, after comparing the shipment with the invoice and making sure they are the same, is there anything else I should do?"

"Didn't anyone tell you how to accept a courier delivery?"

"The exec told me to be on time to meet the plane, and to make sure the shipment jibed with the invoice before I signed off as having accepted it."

"When the plane parks and they shut down the engines, the ground crew will have set the airstairs at the cargo hatch. At times, there may be a few passengers on a cargo flight. Let them get off the plane, then as we get on the plane, you show your courier card so they know what we are there for. The courier responsible for the shipment won't be hard to find, he'll probably be sitting on the shipment with a drawn pistol and be very eager to turn the shipment over to you.

"The airplane crew and courier will not leave the plane until we take possession of the shipment and leave with it. They know the drill, but sometimes you have to remind them. Oh, and carefully inspect the wire security seals on each item. Make sure they are secure and there has been no tampering. If any are broken or seem to have been tampered with, don't accept any of the shipment. Immediately call the duty operations officer and Commander Hawkins or the exec for instructions."

As the R-6 taxied up to the ramp he finished with "It's OK to act as though you have been doing this for a long time."

The R-6 parked, the four engines were shut down, the airstairs put into place, and four passengers (three officers and one enlisted man) exited from the cargo hatch. Turner and the chief went up the airstairs and into the plane. They passed forward through a narrow opening between large wooden crates to the front of the airplane. Near the cockpit bulkhead sat a nervous ensign armed with a Colt .45. As Turner and the chief approached, the ensign stood up, saluted, and said, "Sir, I'm Ensign Budner, the courier for this cargo."

Turner and the chief returned the salute, and Turner, looking at the birdcages and suitcases near where the ensign had been sitting, asked, "Mr. Budner, is that my shipment?"

"Yes, sir. Four birdcages and three suitcases." He reached down to a briefcase, opened it, and took out a clipboard with a number of pages attached. He handed the clipboard to Turner. Turner studied the invoice and passed the clipboard to the chief. He went to the shipment, tugged at the wire security seals, and examined them carefully. He glanced up and saw the cockpit crew, led by a lieutenant commander, waiting patiently at the doorway of the cockpit entrance.

He stood up, saluted, and said, "The chief and I will be out of here in a minute, sir."

"Take your time, Lieutenant. We understand what you need to do."

Turner walked back to the chief and said in a low voice, "It looks good to me, should I do anything else?"

"No, go ahead and sign the paperwork. I'll get the cargo ground crew to unload our shipment and put it in the weapons carrier."

Turner signed off for the shipment, and the ensign saluted him. He returned the salute and went to the rear of the plane to monitor the transfer of items used in setting off a nuclear weapon. With this accomplished, and with Turner at the wheel, they drove away from the ramp. He glanced back and saw the cockpit crew walking away from the plane with the ensign-courier in trail, dangling the web belt and with the holstered Colt .45 in his hand.

"Chief, how much money do you think we have in the back?"

"The detonators in the suitcases, about a hundred thousand dollars—or more. The three plutonium capsules in the birdcages, about a couple of million each."

"Maybe four million each."

"Maybe. No one ever told me."

Ten minutes later, they had driven by the NOF administration building, passed through the first gated checkpoint, and were now waiting to be admitted through a double gate leading to the advanced underwater weapons shop exclusion area. A marine came from the guard shack next to the first gate, saluted Turner, and asked for Turner's and Chief Gallegos's identification. They passed their courier passes and identification badges to the marine. The marine examined them closely, then passed them back, saluting Turner. He then waved to a second marine in the guard shack. The electronically controlled gates opened, then closed after they passed through.

Gallegos had Turner drive around to the double doors of the AUW shop. The two got out of the weapons carrier and walked to a secured side door nearby. The chief pressed a button on the right side of the doorway. There was a buzz, and a few moments later, the door was opened by a torpedoman first class. He recognized the chief and said, "Chief Gallegos, do you have the classified components for our Bettys and Lulus?"

"Just the Bettys, Roberts. Mr. Turner and I have them in our truck. Would you open the doors so we can unload?"

The torpedoman saluted Turner and said, "You must be the new SW/EOD officer. Welcome aboard, sir." Turner returned the salute.

The torpedoman closed the door as he went back into the shop. About the same time Turner and the chief returned to their seats in the weapons carrier, the double doors of the AUW shop began to slowly open. The doors stopped moving when the doors opened just wide enough to allow the weapons carrier to drive in. Turner drove in, parked, and shut off the engine. As he and the chief were leaving the weapons carrier, they were approached by a lieutenant commander wearing the golden dolphins of a submariner. Next to him was a chief electrician's mate with an advanced underwater weapons patch on his sleeve. Turner and the Chief Gallegos saluted, the officer returned the salute in a rather off-handed way, and the chief electrician returned Turner's salute in a more formal way.

Introducing himself as Lieutenant Commander Charles Buckold, he commented, "You're the new boy from Indian Head."

"Yes, sir. Lieutenant JG Burt Turner."

"Well, welcome aboard, Mr. Turner." He looked at the chief. "Did all go well with the transaction, Chief Gallegos?"

"Very well, sir."

Lieutenant Commander Buckold introduced the chief at his side. "Mr. Turner, this is Chief Electrician's Mate Oscar Eddings. He runs this place and, from time to time, shares beer and confidences with Chief Gallegos. Chief Eddings isn't a churchgoer."

The two chiefs glanced at each other. Gallegos was uncomfortable with the shares "confidences" part. Turner wondered about the "churchgoer" part.

Buckold then said, "Mr. Turner, let's get the paperwork out of the way." The two chiefs went to the back of the weapons carrier, let down the tailgate, and slid the birdcages and suitcases onto it. The two officers carefully examined the cargo. Buckold, satisfied, signed off as having received the shipment. Chief Eddings called over three enlisted men and had them take the cargo to the storage area in the assembly room.

Turner asked, "Sir, may I follow and see your shop?"

Buckold gave Turner a long look, then replied, "You may, but I would like to see you in my office when you are finished. Don't dally."

"Thank you, sir."

He caught up with Chief Eddings and his men as they passed through the assembly shop, where a group of torpedo men were testing electronic circuits on MK-43 ASW (antisubmarine warfare) acoustic homing torpedoes. Leaving this shop, they went down a short hallway, where a marine stood guard at a secured door. They showed the marine their IDs and passes; he allowed them entrance to the nuclear weapon shop. Two MK-90 Bettys and one MK-34 Lulu were in cradles. Both were nuclear antisubmarine depth charges, the Lulu, the most modern. One of the Bettys was partially disassembled the other was intact.

It was strange for Turner to see weapons he was trained to disarm in this place, over four thousand miles away from Indian Head. Looking around, the tool sets were the same and stowed perfectly in place, electronic test sets were neatly arranged, and lifting devices were sparkling clean with no rags adrift. Where nuclear weapons were maintained, there was extremely tight control of the environment—almost like a surgical suite.

After the tour, the torpedoman escorted Turner to Buckold's office. Turner knocked on the door.

"Enter."

He opened the door and hesitated. Buckold said, "Close the door and sit down, Mr. Turner."

He closed the door and sat down. He felt he needed to say something. "Your shop would easily please the folks at DASA. It looks perfect." (DASA, the Defense Atomic Support Agency, was the U.S. government agency responsible for all ready nuclear weapons and those in stockpile). He thought he was saying something appropriate. Seeing the look on Buckold's face, he realized he sounded condescending.

"It is perfect, Mr. Turner."

Looking around the office, he saw that it was scrupulously ordered and clean: numerous technical manuals were placed according to type and size, nothing adrift. There were two steelcase filing cabinets on the wall next to the doorway. On the filing cabinet nearest the door were three books held in place by simple steel bookends. He was unable to make out the titles of the books. Buckold's desk was clear except for one empty basket and a silver ballpoint pen resting on a pad of paper. On the wall were several commendations for outstanding practices in mission readiness and a large beautiful picture of a submarine underway on the surface.

"Sir, what sub is that?"

"It's the *Sea Robin*, my last boat. Have you been on a submarine, Mr. Turner?"

"Once, just for an orientation on how a swimmer might be able to 'lock in' and 'lock out' of the escape hatch for an insertion and extraction mission. The submarine was tied up at a pier. We were on board for about an hour."

"How interesting."

Buckold was uncomfortable with this young officer. But then Buckold was uncomfortable with most everyone. He asked, "Are you a religious man, Mr. Turner?"

Taken aback by the question, Turner had to collect himself. "Not since my aunt died a few years ago."

"Your aunt? You were close to your aunt?"

"Very close, sir. She was my guardian. I was alone after my mother died."

"What about your father?"

"I don't know anything about my father."

After a pause, he told Turner that he had been an enlisted man for seven years then became an officer while in the submarine service. He further explained that nine years ago, he left the submarine service for the advanced underwater weapons program. He talked about how strongly he felt that this command and other shore commands he was assigned to in the last few years were not "mission oriented" or "war ready." He hated communists and their atheistic form of government. He felt that the United States was not taking the cold war seriously and would not be prepared if it turned "hot." Turner felt awkward listening to Buckold's diatribe, but he didn't have any choice but to listen.

Buckold became more strident, and his face reddened as he went on, "When the *Sea Robin* became a hunter-killer boat, we were involved in finding and tracking the first ballistic-missile-capable Russian submarines. These submarines threaten the security of our nation. I wanted to kill them preemptively. The people at COMSUBLANT refused to understand the continuing threat of those malignant, atheistic communists. It is our mission to remove this malignancy from God's earth. We must use every weapon we have been provided with to do so. These damnable Satanist submarines are still out there."

Buckold seemed to pull himself together.

"Mister, someday you must go to sea. The sea is where a man can find himself. Good day to you."

"Good day to you, sir."

As Turner left the office, he was able to read the titles of the three books on the file cabinet: the Holy Bible, *The Prophet Zoroaster,* and *Moby Dick.*

Driving back to NOF, Turner was deeply concerned about Buckold. *What the hell is that guy doing in a nuclear weapons program?*

"How did the meeting go with Lieutenant Commander Buckold?"

"I have never met anyone like him."

"He's old navy, Mr. Turner."

"He is more than that, Chief. Let's leave it there."

Chapter 4

Turner and Chief Gallegos met outside of Lieutenant Commander Bello's office on the first floor of the NAS Operations building at 0845. The two went into Bello's office and introduced themselves to the yeoman working at the desk. After acknowledging their presence, the yeoman looked down at a sheet of paper with Monday appointments arranged according to time, name, and subject. Second from the top of the listing was for 0900, "LTJG Turner and Chief Gallegos, Orientation, HUP, SNB, AVR." The yeoman put a check mark to the left of 0900 and added, "arr. 0846." Pointing to a row of four chairs on the wall across from his desk, he said, "Have a seat. The commander will be here shortly."

At exactly 0900, Bello entered his office wearing wash khakis and a well-worn leather flight jacket with a VA-106 patch on the right side. Not noticing Turner and Gallegos, he stood in front of the yeoman's desk and asked, "Any phone calls, Adams?"

The yeoman stood and said, "No, sir, but Mr. Turner and Chief Gallegos are here, sir."

Bello turned around as Turner and Gallegos rose from their chairs. Turner introduced himself and Chief Gallegos. Bello looked hard at Turner, then said, "Mr. Turner, have we met before?"

"Yes, sir, at the military terminal at Orly."

With a frown, Bello said, "Oh yes, you were the one that required me to bump a commander for the Port Lyautey flight."

"Yes, sir, I hope it didn't cause a problem."

"It could have been a problem. The commander was scheduled to fly out to the aircraft carrier *Forrestal* from Port Lyautey the next day. Luckily, an hour after you flew out, I was able to get him a flight to Rota, then a COD flight out of Rota to the *Forrestal*. He arrived that evening quite pleased with our service." He added, "I need to make a phone call, then we can go on tour." He went into his office and shut the door. Ten minutes later, he came out.

"Let's go. All the players are accounted for."

The three went out the door and were just starting down the hallway when Bello's yeoman called from the office doorway, "Mr. Turner, you have a phone call from NOF."

Turner excused himself, returned to the office, and answered the phone.

"Turner speaking."

"Mr. Turner, this is Yeoman Fry. They want you at the dispensary at 1200, something about your health records. See the corpsman at the reception counter."

He replied that he would, left the office without a thought about the phone call, and caught up with Bello. They were about to leave NAS Operations for the flight line when Bello said, "Let's stop for a minute before we go out."

Facing the two, he lowered his voice and said, "Commander Hawkins and a couple of senior officers from COMNAVACTSMED in Naples had a meeting with Captain Travis the CO of the base. After the meeting, Captain Travis ordered me to provide you and your team with a helicopter, access to our SNB light transport and our AVR fast boat for some sort of insertion and extraction training to begin a week from today. We can do the helicopter and SNB, but the only fast boat we have isn't operational."

Turner, looked at his chief and smiled.

Bello continued, "I was also told that Commander Hawkins and Captain Travis, after agreeing on certain conditions, gave permission for you to work directly with me as to when and how this equipment will be used. Unfortunately—or maybe fortunately—I am not cleared for where the equipment is to be used. The pilots and boat crew involved will know what I know, but obviously they will be cleared on a need-to-know basis as to where the equipment will be going. This morning, I briefed the pilots and boat crew about who you are and who the members of your team are and the importance of the operation. I told them the operation your team will be undertaking is classified Secret and to help you all they can in carrying out your mission. Do you have any questions?"

After glancing at Chief Gallegos, Turner replied, "No, sir."

Bello added, "I'm sure there will be a lot of questions as we get into this."

They left the Operations building and walked out to the flight line where a gray navy helicopter was parked and, a little farther on, a small twin-engine two-tone white-and-red airplane—the SNB. As they approached the helicopter, a tall thin man with closely cropped gray hair jumped down from the helicopter's cargo hatch.

Seeing Bello, he said, "These must be the EOD personnel you were telling us about this morning."

"Yes, this is Mr. Turner, the officer in charge of the EOD team, and Chief Gallegos. And this is Chief Williams, Flint Williams, our primary helicopter pilot."

Williams took a clean rag out of one of the leg pockets of his flight suit, wiped his hands, and shook hands with Turner and Gallegos. With the introductions made, Bello asked Williams about the condition of the helicopter. This led to a technical discussion about the turnaround for ordering and receiving new replacement rotors for the helicopter. While Bello and Williams talked, Turner noticed on the left breast of Williams's flight suit a leather patch with navy wings stenciled in gold, and just below the wings was "CPO, Flint Williams," also stenciled in gold.

Turner thought, *This guy is one of the navy's Flying Chiefs. There can only be a few left.*

The navy was running short on aviators during WWII and for a time leading up to the Korean War. A temporary program was put in place for exemplary senior enlisted men with aviation ratings to attend flight school. Williams, it turned out, had earned his wings in 1950, had three tours of duty during the Korean War flying a rescue helicopter off the aircraft carrier *Bon Homme Richard* and, later, F-9F Panther jets off the aircraft carrier *Princeton*. He was awarded two Distinguished Flying crosses, and three Air Medals. He later attended Navy Test Pilot School at Patuxant NAS, Maryland. Currently, he was the only navy pilot qualified to fly any aircraft attached to NAS, Port Lyautey, which included jet fighters, helicopters, light air transports, and a Gruman air-sea rescue amphibian.

"Chief Williams will take you through the helicopter and explain its capabilities. He will answer any questions you may have." Pointing in the direction of the SNB, he said, "I'll meet you two at the SNB in about a half hour."

The three men saluted. Bello returned the salutes in an off-handed way and walked back to the Operations building.

Williams turned and placed his hand on the Plexiglas nose of the helicopter and began, "This is a HUP-3 *Retriever* made by Piasecki. It can carry a pilot, a crewman hoist operator, and up to four passengers—in a pinch, five. Depending on weight being carried, it has a range of 340 miles and a breakneck maximum speed of 105 miles per hour. It has an autopilot for accurate hovering and is the best helicopter in its class. Before we go inside, let's do a walk around."

He pointed to the forward and aft rotors and explained how the rotors were linked to the engine, housed in a compartment at the rear of the fuselage. As they walked around the helicopter, Williams explained at length how a helicopter could be flown without control surfaces such as rudder, elevator and ailerons of conventional airplanes. The walk around ended at the main entry into the helicopter, the cargo hatch. Williams climbed in first, then Turner and Gallegos. Inside, Williams and Turner crouched down just forward of the hatch entry. Gallegos sat down on a bench attached to the bulkhead separating the passenger compartment from the engine compartment. There were no other seats except the two in the cockpit about seven feet in front of where Gallegos sat.

Gallegos looked around and said, "This is a very small aircraft. It looks like you only have places for two passengers to sit. Where would the other two sit?"

Williams laughed and said, "On the floor. Actually, we provide a little padding when we have a crowd, so it isn't too uncomfortable."

Immediately behind the pilot and copilot seats was the rescue hoist and hoisting cable hanging from the overhead. At the end of the hoisting cable was a yellow "horse collar." The secured entry hatch was in the floor directly below the hoisting cable and horse collar.

Pulling the short length of hoisting cable and horse collar toward Turner, Williams said, "Here, Mr. Turner. Try it on."

Turner fumbled a bit as he worked one arm and then his head through the horse collar, then the other arm. Once in the horse collar, it formed a sling across his lower back and forward and up under his arms with the cable showing at about eye level in front of him. He found the apparatus to be relatively comfortable.

Williams watched as Turner took it off and said, "You and your team will become experts in this stuff very quickly."

Williams worked his way into the cockpit, then sat down in the left seat after removing a helmet with radio cables attached, which he put in his lap. He motioned for Turner to take the seat on his right and Gallegos to come forward and look over his shoulder. He then showed and explained the functions of the controls and instruments used to fly the helicopter.

When he finished he asked, "Do you have any questions?"

The two SW/EOD men, concerned about the adequacy of this so-called mode of conveyance and potential safety problems the team should be made aware of, began.

Turner: "Could the helicopter carry a team of four and four sets of double-bank SCUBAs?"

Answer: "It depends on the total weight and ambient temperature. If the ambient temperature is high, there is less lifting ability, and the range decreases to maybe only a thirty-mile operational radius; maybe we couldn't even get off the ground. We would have to calculate all this at the time of the flight."

Gallegos: "If we were working in the water at night, how would you find us for pickup?"

Answer: "Unfortunately, you would have to use your waterproof flares. Hopefully, we could find you and pick you up before bad things might happen."

Turner: "What bad things?"

Answer: "Hypothermia, drowning, hungry sharks, or your capture."

Turner: "Oh. If you lost power at altitude, is it catastrophic?"

Answer: "Not necessarily catastrophic. We could be autorotating down. The rotors continue to turn or windmill, keeping us from falling like a rock."

Gallegos: "What if we're flying close to the water and you lose power?"

Answer: "I'll put the helicopter in the water on my side, stopping the rotors. You will have to exit out the cargo hatch on the same side."

Turner: "Is there anything that might surprise us when you are extracting us from water?"

Answer: "The downwash from the rotors during hover. There is a kind of Bernoulli effect with high-pressure downwash hitting the water or any other surface of pickup. The air moves away from the center of the downwash at high speed, causing a drop in air pressure in the breathing airway of the person in the downwash. The pressure drop triggers a gasping reflex that can be a surprise, but it is no big deal."

Williams continued answering questions, and confidence grew between the pilot and the men he was to fly on missions.

Finally, with no more questions, Williams said, "Chief, if you go back to the bench seat and strap yourself in, I'll have Mr. Turner strap in to the copilot's seat, and we will go for a little ride."

Turner and Gallegos looked at each other wide-eyed, shrugged their shoulders, and went to their places.

Williams lifted the helmet from his lap, examined the cables to the earphones and microphone attached, put it on and secured his safety belt. After Turner sat down in the copilot's seat and secured his safety belt, Williams reached behind his own seat and lifted out a second helmet with the same earphone and microphone attachments as his own. He passed the helmet to Turner. After Turner put on the helmet, Williams showed him how to secure the helmet cables to the attachments leading to the radio. Both were now able to communicate with each other and the control tower. Williams looked back into the cabin and, satisfied that Gallegos was strapped in safely, started the engine and engaged the rotors. While the engine was warming up he called the control tower for takeoff clearance.

Over his earphones, Turner heard, "Lyautey tower, this is Pedro one-five. Request permission for takeoff."

There was additional exchange of information, then the rotor's *chop, chop, chop* increased as Pedro one-five slowly lifted from the ground, tilting forward, gaining speed and altitude. Seconds later, the helicopter was over the main runway. It veered to a southwest heading toward the wharf at the mouth of the Oued Sebou. Two minutes later, they passed over the AVR, YFR, and French LST, then out over the breakwater, and followed the surf line south. Turner noticed the altimeter steady at 175 feet.

Turner heard a click in his earphones. "How do you like this, Mr. Turner?"

"It's really great. I'm ready to do this for real."

Turner looked back at Gallegos, who was all grins and gave him a thumbs-up.

About fifteen minutes later, Williams returned low over the headlands, just above the deserted beach. He called in to the NAS control tower, asked permission to land, and received it. A few minutes later, the helicopter passed over the main runway and began to let down where a ground crewman was waiting to spot the helicopter for landing. As the helicopter lost altitude, Turner saw Lieutenant Commander Bello standing next to the SNB. Concentrating on directional gestures from the ground crewman, Williams gently landed Pedro one-five.

After the engine was shut down and the rotors stopped, the three men left the helicopter. Turner and Gallegos, smiling broadly, shook hands with Williams, thanked him, and walked over to the SNB.

Standing to one side and just behind Bello were Lieutenants Miller and Teipner, both looking very professional in their flight suits, leather flying jackets, and aviator sunglasses.

Bello said, "Well, I see you two have become well acquainted with the HUP." Then, to no one in particular, "I'm not sure that flight was authorized. I guess Chief Williams was checking out the engine." Actually, Bello had suggested Williams take Turner and Gallegos up for an orientation ride.

"Mr. Turner and Chief Gallegos, this is Mr. Miller and Mr. Teipner. They will be your pilots when you need to be transported in the SNB. Mr. Turner, have you met these two before?"

"Yes, sir, I have met Mr. Miller and Mr. Teipner before."

Gallegos said, "I haven't met the two young officers." He stepped forward, shook their hands, and stepped back.

Bello continued, "These two officers are under my command, and you will find them to be capable of safely flying this aircraft. I try to not know what they do off duty, but there are rumors. Which of you gentlemen will be showing this airplane to Mr. Turner and Chief Gallegos?"

Teipner stepped up and said, "I'll be doing that, sir."

"Very well, Mr. Teipner, get on with it. It is almost eleven thirty, and we are yet to visit the AVR."

Teipner said, "If you will both follow me, this won't take any time at all."

Bello and Miller watched from in front of the SNB's left wing as Teipner took Turner and Gallegos on a walk around, and then disappeared inside the SNB.

Inside, Teipner explained, "The SNB is a very straight-forward airplane. It has a crew of two, and we can carry up to six passengers for about 300 miles or three or four passengers out to 450 miles, the mileage being very dependent on weather conditions and additional cargo weight. Our cruising speed is about 140 miles an hour, but this can vary too, based on weather and total weight."

Turner thought, *This isn't much larger on the inside than the HUP helicopter. It's longer, but still a tight fit.*

Teipner went on to speak of icing on the wings, engine-out performance, lack of parachutes on board, and other things esoteric. Turner was not interested in hearing of these things. Nor was Gallegos.

After twenty minutes of show and tell, Teipner asked, "Do you have any questions?"

Turner and Gallegos looked at each other; there were no questions, and the three left the airplane.

They walked over to Bello and Miller. Bello said, "We have a date with an AVR gentlemen. Thank you, Mr. Teipner." Then, to Turner and Gallegos, "My jeep is in the hangar behind us. Let's be on our way."

As the three began to walk toward the hangar, Bello turned and said, "There appears to be hydraulic fluid coming from the left wheel well. Better check it out, gentlemen."

Miller replied, "We called maintenance this morning, sir. They will work on it this afternoon."

"Very well. Thank you, Mr. Miller."

Lieutenant Commander Bello was the only officer that Miller and Teipner respected. They respected his flying ability, intelligence, insight, and sense of fair play. Additionally, they admired his refusal to tolerate stupidity and junior officer sycophants obsessed with their yearly fitness reports. Miller often said that Bello was as close to being the Lone Ranger as one could be (Miller held the Lone Ranger in high regard). Bello, in turn, was the only one who could rein in the two officers' exuberance and cause them to act like professionals.

After a white-knuckle ride to the wharf, Bello parked his jeep near the gangway leading down to the AVR. They left the jeep and walked over to the gangway. First Class Boatswain's Mate Deacon and another man were working on the AVR's radar mast.

Bello called down, "Deacon, we're coming aboard to look over your boat. Is it shipshape, Bristol fashion, these days?"

Deacon laughed and called back, "It is that and more, sir."

They went down the gangway, and as each boarded the AVR, they saluted the ensign at the stern. On deck, as Bello was about to introduce Turner and Gallegos, Deacon said, "Good morning, Mr. Turner. Good to have you aboard again, sir."

"You two have met?"

Yes, sir. When I was getting acquainted with the base, I ended up here on the wharf. I saw the AVR, and Deacon was kind enough to show her off to me."

"Well, good. Chief Gallegos, this is Boatswain's Mate First Class Bill Deacon. This is Deacon's boat. Some call it the USS *Never Sail*."

They laughed, and Bello asked, "Would you show us around? Perhaps Mr. Turner might have some questions he may not have asked before."

Because there was a chief gunner's mate with Bello and Turner, Deacon delivered far more details about the AVR then he would have if it was just the two officers. When they visited the engine compartment, Deacon brought up the casualty of the bent propeller shaft.

"Oh yes. It's a damn shame the coxswain in charge of the boat before you was a lousy seaman, Petty Officer Deacon."

"Yes, sir. Our present crew has worked very hard to make the boat perfect. Can't do anything about the propeller shaft, though."

Turner took a deep breath, looked at Bello, and said, "Sir, Chief Gallegos and I were talking about the problem, and we think we could make a dive and remove the bent propeller shaft. Then perhaps the propeller shaft could be sent to the shipyard machine shop at Gibraltar for straightening. Once straightened, we could reinstall the propeller shaft, and you would have an operational boat."

Bello thought for a minute, then, "We could have it delivered by the SNB and could find money for the machine shop costs, but there is no money for a diving operation."

"I'm sure Commander Hawkins would let us do the removal and reinstallation as a training project, and there would be no cost to the Naval Air Station, sir."

"All right. You get permission from Commander Hawkins, and I'll do the rest," Bello replied.

The four men nearly lost their professional composure in satisfaction of a problem about to be solved. Actually, Turner did lose his when he elbowed Gallegos in the ribs, but the action was not noticed by the others. Turner and Gallegos asked how the AVR performed under a variety of sea conditions. Deacon answered their questions and the meeting was over.

Bello drove back to the NAS Operations building and dropped Turner off at his Sprite and Gallegos at the EOD weapons carrier.

It took Turner four minutes to drive to the base dispensary; he arrived at 1220. He was twenty minutes late. He parked the car and ran to the front entrance of the dispensary, through the double doors, and on to the reception counter, where a hospital corpsman reminded him he was twenty minutes late.

"Sir, you will have to wait for an opening." The hospital corpsman made a note on a clipboard and, pointing to an empty chair next to a woman with a very irritable baby, said, "Please take a seat over there."

At 1315, another hospital corpsman called his name from the reception counter. Turner went to the counter where the corpsman gave him his officer health record and told him to go down the hallway on the left to examining room 6, and in a short time, someone would be in to give him his cholera shot.

"Cholera shot? I had a whole series of shots before I left Indian Head."

"I'm sorry, sir. Your immunizations are complete except for cholera. There will be someone to help you in a few minutes."

He thanked the corpsman, went down the hallway, and found examining room 6 with its door open. He went in and sat down on a chair next to the examination table, leaned back, and emitted a barely audible, "Shit."

Ten minutes later, a corpsman came into the examination room, all smiles, and put down on a counter next to the small sink what looked like some sort of stainless steel butter dish with a bit of gauze showing over the side. He asked to see Turner's officer health record. Turner handed it to him.

"I see you are a diver, sir. When was your last dive to one hundred feet or more, and did you have any problems during or after the dive?"

SW/EOD divers must make a monthly requalification dive to a depth of one hundred feet if they have not been involved in an operational dive for thirty days. Because of the possibility of pulmonary problems showing up, it was not unusual to have a record of previous underwater activity noted in an individual's health record.

"About six weeks ago, I had a dive. I'm due for one now, and no, I haven't had any problem before."

Turner looked over at the stainless steel dish and saw a needle and syringe nesting in some gauze. He quickly looked away.

The corpsman made a note in the health record, put it on the counter, and said, "Well, sir, if you will sit on the examination table and roll up your sleeve, we'll get this over with quickly. Are you allergic to eggs or had any problems with immunization before?"

Trying not to think about what was about to happen, he replied, "No."

The corpsman picked up a ball of cotton from a glass container and wetted it with alcohol from a small bottle. He energetically swabbed down the injection site on Turner's upper right arm. With this done, he picked up the syringe from the stainless steel dish, pointed it toward the ceiling, tapped the glass to bring any air bubbles to the top, and pressed the plunger slightly. A minor amount of fluid squirted from the needle. Turner had turned his head from this exercise in hydraulics.

Kathy Roberts was coming down the hallway when she recognized Turner's voice. She stopped and looked into the examining room as the corpsman said, "Just a little stick, sir," expertly inserted the needle, pressed the plunger, and quickly withdrew the needle.

Turner passed out.

The corpsman said, "Oh shit," dropped the syringe on the examination table, and caught Turner just as he began to crumple and fall off the examination table.

Kathy Roberts came through the door and, shoving the corpsman aside, said, "I'll take care of this, Potter. Close the door as you go out, please."

The corpsman hesitated, then said, "Yes, ma'am." He reached for Turner's officer health record, made a quick note in it, put it back on the counter, and left the room.

She put her arms around his upper body and carefully laid him down on the examination table, then spun a handle at the front of the examination table raising his legs slightly. She put her right hand on his chest and lowered her ear near his mouth and nose to make certain he was breathing. At that moment, Turner came to and drowsily lifted his head touching his lips to her cheek. She slightly brushed her lips against his unintentionally as she turned away and straightened up.

She grinned, "Are you back with us, Mr. Turner?"

Lifting himself up with his elbows, he replied, "I thought I was Snow White and you were Prince Charming. You kissed me, and I woke up."

"I didn't kiss you, Burt. Don't flatter yourself. Do you usually faint when you get a shot?"

"Sometimes. I guess it depends on what's in the syringe."

"Let's see if you can stand up without falling down."

He slid off the examining table, stood up, walked toward the door, and opened it. He started out, thought better of it, turned, and sat down on the chair. She had seen all this before and stood, quietly watching Turner.

After a few minutes, he got up and said, "I'll be all right. Why don't you go on?"

Seeing that he had recovered, she picked up his officer health record and said, "I'll walk you to the front door."

As they walked down the hallway to the dispensary entrance, he took her hand and said, "Thank you, Kathy."

She squeezed his hand and released it. "I am glad I walked by when I did."

At that moment they both felt a warm pleasant excitement that quickly gave way to caution. Neither was prepared to cross a line that would lead to a complicated intimacy.

––––––––––––

At 1445 Turner, Gallegos, Cole, and Huwitt were at the marine barracks supply stores, being fitted with a type of uniform they had never seen before. The trousers were baggy and had extra pockets on the thighs and elastic on the cuffs. Shirts and light field jackets also had extra pockets. Completing the uniforms were floppy hats and soft tan boots. Everything was an odd shade of tan. After making sure the team was comfortable in their new field uniforms, Master Sergeant Forbes took them to a full-length mirror, where they took turns looking at themselves. They came away with mixed emotions.

Next, Forbes took the men into an adjoining room, where from a caged window, they were each issued: a web belt, a canteen, a small first aid pack, a dagger and scabbard, a compass, a mummy sleeping bag, a nylon poncho, and a knapsack. There was no indication of origin on the uniforms or equipment.

Then Forbes said, "Change back into your uniforms and put your field uniforms and other gear in your knapsacks. You can leave the knapsacks on the deck and pick them up after we finish at the armory."

The armory was a separate building surrounded by a cyclone wire fence with razor wire strung in loose coils at the top. After showing their ID cards, they were allowed to pass through a security gate and, after a short walk, entered the armory. Inside were racks of the newly issued M16 rifle, a number of Browning Automatic Rifles (BARs), a few shotguns, and light machine guns.

Forbes led them into a room with a long wooden workbench smelling of rifle—and small-arms-lubricating oil. Standing in the middle of the room, he announced, "I have been ordered to issue each of you a weapon and three magazines of ammunition." He turned and called over to a marine who was working inside a caged room where small arms were stored. "Sergeant Evans, break out the weapons assigned to the SW/EOD team and bring them over."

A few minutes later, the sergeant had four pistols, twelve loaded magazines, and four shoulder holsters laid out on the workbench in front of the group. Turner's men looked at him. Cole asked, "Sir, what are we supposed to do with these?"

Turner asked, "Yes, Master Sergeant, what are we supposed to do with these?"

"Sir, I have been told to tell you there will be times when you will be armed for contingencies, and I am to issue these weapons accordingly. When you go out with us on the field problem, there may be such contingencies."

Cole lifted one of the pistols and said, "I have never seen a pistol like this. It looks like a kid's toy."

Forbes took the pistol from Cole and began, "This is a Walther PPK 380. It holds six rounds of what you might call .38-caliber bullets. It is the larger

PPK. The PPK/S is smaller and fires .32-caliber bullets. The 380 doesn't come close to the shocking power of our Colt .45s. It seems that higher authority does not want you four identified as part of our group when you deploy with us, therefore your nondescript utilities and weapons. I am to also tell you, when you deploy with us, you will leave your dog tags behind."

The four men looked at each other. Huwitt said, "It looks like no one is supposed to know who we are."

Gallegos, addressing Forbes, asked, "Is that what's going on, Master Sergeant?"

"Yes, Chief. It appears they want to keep your team invisible. Now as to the weapon, the PPK, although small, has good short-range accuracy, handles nicely, and has been known to maim and sometimes kill. If you will each take one, I will show you how to fieldstrip the weapon and put it back together. Once you are comfortable with the weapon, we will go to the pistol range in back of the armory and shoot a few targets."

Thirty-five minutes later, Forbes was pleased to see that his trainees had quickly learned the fine points of the Walther PPK 380, and sufficiently enough so as to not harm themselves or the weapon. They would not have been admitted to the explosive ordnance disposal program if they did not have a high degree of mechanical ability and the intelligence to go with it.

After the familiarization session, they spent and an hour and a half on the pistol range. Forbes sent for additional rounds of ammunition to make sure the team was able to hit a target often enough to make the act of firing the PPK with accuracy credible. Gallegos was by far the best shot at twenty-five yards; Turner was second; Cole, a close third; and Huwitt, noticeably embarrassed, was fourth.

Forbes, surprised at their scores, commented, "You have all fired quite well. And you, Petty Officer Huwitt, scored better than most others who are acquainted with this weapon."

After they secured from the pistol range, they cleaned their weapons. Forbes then had them fill out a series of forms stating that they each would be responsible for the care and feeding of their Walther PPK 380.

"Let me have the form after you sign it," he directed. Then, pointing to a series of lockers on the back wall, he continued, "Over there, you will find a locker with your name on it. Put your weapon and ammunition in the locker. There is a key in the lock. Lock it and give the key to Sergeant Evans. I'll meet you here at 0430 Wednesday. You can pick up your keys and collect your weapons. We will go down to the plane from here."

The team left the marine barracks feeling pretty good about themselves, but were uncomfortable about the nondescript clothing and leaving their dog tags behind.

Turner decided to go back to NOF to see if he had received the long-awaited letter from Joan, his girlfriend. It was after working hours when he arrived, and Lieutenant Van Buren, the NOF supply officer, had the duty.

Van Buren looked up from his desk and greeted him. "Hi, Burt. I know you are here to relieve me so I can go home to my wife and family."

"Not a chance, Ted. You are far more qualified to deal with Russians and Arab terrorists."

"How can you say that?"

"Because you can snow them with catalogue numbers, references, and invoices that would overwhelm their mental circuits and cause them to forget why they are here."

"Well, that's true. I'm a virtual secret weapon."

"I'm only here to check my mail, then I'm gone until 0800 tomorrow."

"Before you check your mail, the exec wants you to call him as soon as possible."

Turner went to his desk and called the exec. The phone rang twice, then, "Lieutenant Commander Owens speaking."

"Sir, this is Mr. Turner."

"Mr. Turner, Commander Hawkins and I had a conversation at lunch today with the commanding officer of the NAS and Lieutenant Commander Bello, the Operations officer. It seems you have offered your services to Operations to help them bring their fast boat back to life."

"Ah, sir, I . . ."

"Mr. Turner, of course you know the navy has what is called a chain of command. It serves to keep those responsible for carrying out the mission of our navy informed. By being informed, loss of expensive equipment, injury, or even loss of life can be avoided. By following the rule of chain of command, a junior officer can avoid problems that emerge when thoughtlessly deciding to sail independently. Sailing independently has led to the departure of many who had promising careers in the navy. Do you get my meaning, Mr. Turner?"

By now Turner was standing at attention and with a catch in his voice, he answered, "Yes, sir, I do understand what you are saying."

On the other side of the office Van Buren was wondering why Turner was standing at his desk and what the exec was saying that caused his face to be so red.

There was a pause, then the exec continued, "Commander Hawkins has given you permission to dive on the AVR. You will be in charge of the operation that begins tomorrow. How much time do you think it will take to remove the propeller shaft?"

Having never done anything like this before, and knowing he was going to be watched closely didn't do much to restrain his inclination to take advantage of the opportunity to do something interesting. Most young naval officers would not put themselves in a position that Turner would. Most were trying hard to be regulation naval officers, and many of these simply didn't have an enterprising nature. Turner had an enterprising nature and found himself in an environment of unending opportunities waiting for his attention and exploitation.

Commander Hawkins and Lieutenant Commander Owens had seen both kinds of young junior officers and variations of each. Although Turner had recently arrived, they were experienced enough to have some sense of what he was about and were willing to give Turner enough rope to hang himself. They wanted to see if he was not only able to recognize a problem, but also able to take the initiative and deal with the problem successfully.

"Sir, depending on the condition of the bolts holding the clamp and clamp bearings to the shaft, it may take as little as an hour or as much as three hours."

He didn't have a clue how long it would take.

"Mr. Turner, start as early as you can. Keep us informed."

The exec hung up his phone.

Turner sat down in his chair. *What was that all about? I didn't have a chance to talk to the commander or exec about the AVR, and then the exec gives me a lecture on the chain of command. Bello must have told them I offered to make the dive and caught Hawkins and Owens by surprise. They thought I blindsided them. They thought I was sailing independently. I didn't have a chance.*

Turner just had his first experience in being caught in a "bight." It would take time for him to understand that if he was going to make himself vulnerable to criticism, hurt feelings, or physical harm, he had better be careful. Self-confidence works both ways: it can save you or sink you. Experience and maturity help prevent too many sinkings.

Actually, Lieutenant Commander Bello understood the sensitivity of the situation, and when he brought it up, he was very diplomatic in letting Hawkins and Owens understand that Turner didn't offer to dive on the AVR, but suggested it might be possible. This, of course, was a subterfuge by Bello. Turner did say, "Sir, I am sure Commander Hawkins would let us do the removal and reinstallation as a training project, and there would be no cost to the Naval Air Station." Bello was protecting an overenthusiastic young junior officer who overstepped his authority.

Van Buren interrupted Turner's angst. "Burt, are you OK?"

"I'm tired, I missed chow, and I just got a lecture on chain of command."

"Mr. Turner, every junior officer, if he is good, is overworked and tired. Every junior officer gets a periodic reminding of the importance of adhering to the chain of command. You can go check your mail and then go over to the hamburger joint and have something to eat, or you can stay awhile and listen to my problems."

"As much as I would enjoy listening to your problems, I would enjoy more getting something to eat. Thanks for your counseling and guidance, though. Can I have the mail room key?"

Van Buren pushed across his desk a large key ring, ten inches in diameter, with eight keys.

The size made it hard to misplace or lose. Turner picked up the key ring and went to the mail room. He found his box and took out two issues of the journal *Science,* a form letter from a drycleaning store in San Pedro, California, thanking him for his patronage, and a forwarded letter from the U.S. Army recruiting office in Los Angeles explaining the advantages of joining up. There was no letter from Joan. Returning to the office, he gave the key ring back to Van Buren, went to his desk, and called Chief Gallegos at his home. On the second ring, a young voice answered, "Chief Gallegos's residence."

"Is this his daughter?"

"Yes, sir, it is Alejandra."

"How are you? This is Burt Turner. Is your dad in?"

"Yes, sir, Mr. Turner. Just a minute."

The next voice was Chief Gallegos's. "What can I do for you, sir?"

"We just got word to dive on the AVR. The exec wants us to start as early as we can tomorrow and keep him informed. I told him we could get the job done in one to three hours, depending on whether the mounting bolts are frozen or not."

"One to three hours. Did you find out what the state of the tide is in the morning?"

"No, Chief, I didn't think of that."

"There is a pretty good current in the river when the tide changes. When it goes out, the current could be as fast as five or six knots, and because the water is so muddy, there is no visibility. The sewage in the water is at the max too. With an incoming tide the current is substantially less, there is some clarity in the water, and less of a sewage problem."

"Well, we can't use the SCUBA gear if the current is three knots or more. How long would it take to set up the deep sea gear?"

"We have to transport all the gear down to the wharf, then rig up the compressor and the telephones. We'll need to check out the helmet, life line, and air hose, so we may be looking at about two hours just to get ready for the dive."

"I'll check Fleet Weather Central and call you right back, Chief."

I may have bit off more than I can chew.

Turner was lucky this time. He called Fleet Weather Central and explained to the duty officer what he intended to do between 0900 and 1200 the next morning and requested information about the local tides and currents. The duty officer, not knowing there were divers on board the base, asked a lot of questions: "How deep can you guys go? What do you do when you see a shark? Do you get claustrophobia? What are the bends?"

Turner spent ten minutes patiently answering his questions.

Finally, with the help of a knowledgeable petty officer, the duty officer responded with the information needed for the dive. If they started the dive at 0920, they would have an hour and a half of relatively clear water and an incoming current of less than two knots. Turner thanked the duty officer and called Chief Gallegos.

Alejandra answered the phone again and put her dad on.

"Chief Gallegos."

Turner explained what he had learned from Fleet Weather Central and asked, "If you agree, I'd like to go with the SCUBA gear. Can you have us in the water by 0920?"

"Yes, sir. Who do you suggest for the dive?"

"I'd like Cole and myself, with you and Huwitt as standby."

"Good. I'll see you on the wharf at 0830."

"Thanks, Chief."

"No problem, sir."

Turner left NOF and, on the way to the BOQ, stopped at the little cafeteria and had a cheeseburger, french fries, and a beer. For dessert, he had a stale chocolate doughnut with coffee burdened with cream and sugar. He drove on to the BOQ, parked the Sprite, and went up to his room. He almost missed seeing a note thumbtacked to the door as he opened it. The note was from Miller.

"Mr. Turner, we are pleased that you and your team visited us on the flight line this morning. It is our understanding that from time to time, we may be flying you from place to place. This provides you and your closest friends and colleagues with an excuse to celebrate, so do come down to LTJG Miller's room when you return this evening."

Miller had signed his name with a flourish.

Turner took off his hat, tie, and shoes. He wearily unbuttoned his shirt and, in his stockinged feet, padded up the hallway to Miller's room. The door was open as usual, and he went in. Miller, Teipner, and Pierce were having wine (a Beaujolais) with crackers and Brie and listening to Beethoven's Violin Concerto in D Major (Yehudi Menuhin).

Teipner raised his glass to Turner. "Burt, you finally arrived. Sit down and enjoy this minor celebration with your brothers in arms."

Miller and Pierce raised their glasses with a "Hear, hear!"

He poured himself a glass of the Beaujolais and sat down in his usual place on the couch next to Pierce. "I understand these two introduced you to the expensive aircraft they have been privileged to fly. I also understand you and your team may be getting them to chauffeur you around on occasion?"

With some indignation enhanced by the Beaujolais, Miller replied, "We are not chauffeurs, Dr. Lieutenant Pierce. We are highly trained and skillful aviators."

"Yes, yes, I know . . . Highly trained and skillful aviators you are. So Burt, what did you think of their aircraft?"

"I think it is a really neat little aircraft, a beautiful little aircraft."

Miller said, "We are pleased to hear you say that. How was the helicopter ride?" He told them about the helicopter flight and how impressed he was with Chief Flint Williams.

Teipner became very serious when he said, "Flint Williams is without a doubt what all other aviators would like to be. He is the best of the best. No one on this base can do what he can do with an airplane. He's very professional and a good guy. He, along with Lieutenant Commander Bello, are the only people on the base who have taught us anything."

"It appears as though you like this fellow," Turner replied.

"It's more like hero worship," Miller added.

Changing the subject, Pierce asked, "Burt Turner, did I see you escorting Lieutenant JG—soon to be full lieutenant—Nurse Kathy Roberts to the door of our hospital this afternoon?"

"Actually, it was she who escorted me. I was at your place updating my shot records. When the corpsman was giving me a cholera shot, Kathy was walking by, looked in, and saw me. After everything was over, she walked me to the front door."

He didn't bother to give the other details.

"Kathy Roberts is a wonderful girl. Are you two interested in each other?" Miller asked.

"Of course not. She's is really nice, but I have a serious relationship with Joan."

"Yes, of course, you have a serious relationship with this girl Joan. Have you heard from her yet, Turner?" Teipner asked.

"Not yet."

They talked a bit about a recent terrorist attack on a French-owned television station outside of Tangier; Turner hadn't heard about the attack until Teipner brought it up. Four civilians had been killed: two women and two men. Three men had been seriously injured. The conversation shifted to the ever-present possibility of scandal developing in the senior officer ranks, especially about wives who were bored and husbands who seemed to be attracted to the bored wives of other men. When the conversation started to lag, Turner nonchalantly let his friends know what he was going to do in the morning. All three expressed surprise at hearing he was finally going to do something interesting. There were a lot of questions. Turner was happy to finally bring something to the table.

The next morning at 0830, Turner was standing on the wharf above the AVR talking with First Class Boatswain's Mate Bill Deacon as the EOD weapons carrier pulled up. Chief Gallegos climbed out of the drivers seat, walked over, and greeted Turner with a salute, then shook hands with Deacon. Cole and Huwitt had gone to the rear of the weapons carrier to let down the transom and begin unloading equipment.

"Great day for a dive," the chief said with a big smile. "No wind, no clouds, air is warm, and the Sebou River and ocean out there appear to be kindly."

Turner said, "Chief, our coxswain here said the stern ramp is down, the tools are laid out, and the boat is ours."

Gallegos added, "Deacon, we will be as careful and as gentle as possible with your boat. As soon as we unload, Mr. Turner and Cole will work on the propeller shaft."

Twenty-five minutes later, four aluminum double-bank SCUBAs with regulators attached were laying on the stern transom. Alongside were dry suits, masks, fins, UDT life jackets and weight belts. Turner and Cole stripped down and were struggling to pull on their dry suits. Gallegos was in his navy issue swimmer's shorts. He put on fins and mask and went under the boat to look for potential problems that might complicate the removal of the bent propeller shaft. He didn't see anything that would pose a problem and surfaced.

After hauling himself out of the water he said, "There's quite a bit of electrolysis (erosion caused by dissimilar metals in association with seawater) showing up on the blades of the propellers. They oughta be removed and cleaned up some time. The struts holding the shaft aren't bent, so the shaft should come away without too much trouble." He stood up and took a clipboard and pencil from Deacon. He drew a picture of the struts and bolts holding the shaft, showing they were easily accessible.

"The bolts might be frozen. If they are, be careful about rounding off the heads. Take off the propeller first and send it up, then go on to the propeller shaft. Huwitt, Deacon, and I will rig the cargo net and lines forming a cradle. We'll pass the cradle over the ramp, and you two can pull it under as we tend the lines on each side of the boat. Cinch the cradle close up to the propeller shaft and carefully release it into the cradle. The propeller shaft will weigh upward of one hundred pounds, so be careful. We'll lend a hand bringing the whole thing to the end of the ramp and hauling it aboard."

Half-jokingly, he added, "You'll both get a Sebou cocktail under there. The water will seep through the sides of your mouthpieces, so I hope you had your typhoid and cholera shots."

Cole added, "The water looks a lot like Mr. Turner's coffee."

Turner replied, "I'm sure it tastes like what you brew in the shop, Cole."

Huwitt put the tools Turner and Cole would need in a diver's tool bag and passed the tool bag to Cole. The two divers checked each other's equipment, then sat down on the end of the transom and slipped into the water.

The water was cool, and there was a slight tidal current coming up the river. Under the boat, the visibility was about four feet. Cole hung one loop of the tool bag over the end of the good propeller shaft and joined Turner in examining the problem propeller shaft. Turner pointed to himself, then pointed to the propeller shaft struts, then pointed to Cole and to the propeller. Cole gave a thumbs-up in understanding. They selected their tools and went to work.

Cole removed the propeller from the bent propeller shaft and, pulling himself along the good propeller shaft to the transom, surfaced and passed the propeller up to Gallegos. He slipped back under the boat and joined Turner, working on the fastenings holding the bent propeller shaft in place. The two men seemed to anticipate each other's actions and worked well with each other. The only problem they had was trying to gain leverage and stay in place while being almost neutrally buoyant.

After thirty-five minutes, Cole surfaced. "We're ready for the cargo net."

Gallegos answered, "We're ready to pass it to you. When you have it in place and slung, let us know. Then you can release the propeller shaft into it."

Cole gave a thumbs up and went back under the boat.

The two divers watched the cargo net appear in the light brown water as it came over the transom. With Turner on one side and Cole on the other, they wrestled the cargo net into position under the propeller shaft and secured in place. Cole surfaced.

"We are ready to drop the shaft, Chief."

"Drop the shaft."

Cole went back under and gave a thumbs-up to Turner. With the last few bolts removed, the propeller shaft settled heavily into the cradle formed by the cargo net. Suddenly, the unthinkable happened. A section of the cargo net gave way, providing an opening large enough to allow the propeller shaft to twist and hit Cole slightly on the side of his head, stunning him. Then the propeller shaft fell free, catching Cole across the stomach at the level of his weight belt. The propeller shaft rapidly descended forty feet to the bottom of the Oued Sebou and settled into the soft mud with Cole under it.

Turner hastily followed after Cole and nearly lost track of him as the visibility dropped off with depth. At the bottom, he used his hands to assess Cole's predicament. It was obvious Cole was not conscious enough to remove himself from underneath the propeller shaft, but Turner was relieved to hear Cole's rhythmic expirations coming from his SCUBA regulator. He was breathing normally. Turner tried to lift the propeller shaft off of Cole, but sank in the mud under its weight. He squeezed Cole's arm in reassurance and swam to the surface.

Gallegos, knowing the propeller shaft had fallen away, had a block and tackle rigged to retrieve it. He was unaware that Cole was on the bottom, pinned under it.

Turner surfaced, spit out his mouthpiece, and yelled, "I need a line. Cole is pinned under the propeller shaft. He appears to be OK so far."

Gallegos threw the line from the block and tackle and said, "Secure the line to the propeller shaft and give me two pulls when you are ready to haul up. We'll haul up slowly so you can free Cole."

Turner gave a thumbs up, and returned to the bottom. He found Cole and squeezed Cole's hand. To his relief, Cole squeezed back. Turner secured the line to the propeller shaft and pulled twice. The line went taut and began to slowly lift the propeller shaft, freeing Cole. Turner pulled Cole away, and holding Cole's arm, they swam to the surface.

At the surface, Gallegos and Huwitt were standing by and helped the divers onto the ramp and out of their gear.

Cole, fully conscious now, punched the young junior officer lightly on the shoulder as though nothing had happened. "Thanks for getting me out of the mud, Mr. Turner."

Turner, trying not to appear shaken by the experience, replied, "Are you OK? Is your head and everything OK?"

"My ears are a little sore, but I don't think I blew either one. It was a pretty soft landing in the mud. I might have a headache in the morning, though."

Deacon had called the dispensary about the minor diving accident to alert them that they were bringing Cole in for observation. Out of the corner of his eye, Huwitt saw three officers looking down from the wharf. He subtly gestured upward to the wharf and said, "Don't look now, but Commander Hawkins, Bello, and Owens may have heard and seen what just happened."

The three officers watched until they saw the propeller shaft landed. They were unaware of the diving accident. The dive had taken one hour and thirty-five minutes. *Not a bad guess,*

Turner thought. He was still a bit shaken.

Later, Commander Hawkins gave Turner a verbal "well done" with regard to the propeller shaft project. No one could figure out why a perfectly new cargo net would have failed in the operation.

––––––––––––

At 0430 the next day, the SW/EOD team was sitting on a bench in the Operations building with very large knapsacks on the floor in front of them. Each knapsack had a poncho in a tight roll strapped on the outside; inside were a sleeping bag, a minor first aid kit, a canteen of water and a dagger and scabbard attached to a web belt, a PPK in a shoulder holster with two spare six-round magazines, food rations for three and half days, a compass, a small roll of toilet paper, and a few other items—all courtesy of the U.S. Marine Corps.

Cole had been released from the emergency clinic after two hours of observation the previous afternoon. His only injury from the diving accident was a blown right eardrum from the rapid descent to the bottom of the Oued Sebou.

Chief Gallegos stretched his legs and commented to Cole and Huwitt, "Do you men find it interesting how, all of a sudden, things got busy for us when Lieutenant Goss left?

Huwitt answered, "I wonder if Commander Hawkins is encouraging Mr. Turner to do weird things for some reason."

"Well, it's our duty to make sure Mr. Turner doesn't hurt himself as he finds new things to do," Cole added.

The three enlisted men laughed. Turner's face turned red, but he felt good about being with these men.

It was 0450 when Master Sergeant Forbes came through the door and announced, "Mr. Turner, we're loading the plane. It's time to go."

The team got up from the bench, slung their knapsacks over their shoulders, and followed the master sergeant out of the building. They walked down the flight line to an olive drab R-3D with MARINES painted on the side. Eight marines, wearing utility caps but otherwise in full combat gear, were waiting to board the airplane at the open cargo door. Six had the new M16 rifles slung over their shoulders, and two had BARs (Browning Automatic Rifles—light machine guns). Forbes introduced the members of the SW/EOD team to the eight marines; they shook hands all around.

The left engine coughed a few times, caught, and began to idle, then the right engine did the same. A marine corporal stuck his head out of the cargo door and called, "Master Sergeant Forbes, we are ready to launch."

Forbes said, "OK, you men, in you go."

The eight marines boarded first, then the SW/EOD team, and finally Forbes went up the two step boarding stairs into the airplane. Inside, the SW/EOD team helped the marines to secure all the gear at the front of the airplane. Then, with the marines taking seats on one side of the airplane, backs to the fuselage wall, and legs stretching to the center, the SW/EOD team and Forbes took seats on the opposite side. The engines were run up, and the R-3D began to move, slowly at first then more rapidly, to the duty runway. Just before takeoff, the marine corporal came from his seat near the cockpit and made sure everyone had seat belts on. Five minutes later, they were in the air and headed north to Tangier.

Turner was sitting next to Forbes, Forbes next to Gallegos. Turner watched as one after another of the marines fell asleep. Motioning to the sleeping marines he asked, "Master Sergeant Forbes, did your men stay up all night?"

"No, Mr. Turner, they have a habit of catching a nap anytime they can. They never know when they may have to go without sleep."

"I noticed that all eight are older men and none of them are less than a sergeant. In fact, three are first sergeants."

Forbes turned to Gallegos and exchanged a few words above the noise of the engines. Gallegos shook his head no, then nodded yes.

Forbes glanced at Turner and said, "These men are volunteers in a special operations program. They have been carefully trained, have great experience, and are parachute qualified. They are very smart. Six were in Korea together. Those six and the two younger marines with them just returned from what was formerly part of French Indochina, but is now Vietnam. They were there for seven months. They were sent to Vietnam as observers to find out why the South Vietnamese government was unable to defeat or at least control the Communist National Liberation Front, the NLF insurgents, and Viet Cong. The French couldn't control or defeat the NLF and left four years ago. That was two full years after their humiliating defeat at Dien Bien Phu. Now the French are going through the same experience in North Africa."

Gallegos added, "And the British in Egypt. I'm not convinced any Western power can successfully defeat a nationalist movement these days, no matter if the nationalist movement is politically communist or religiously Islamic or driven by some other ideology."

The two talked quite knowledgeably about the early French, British, Italian, and Spanish colonization of North Africa and the Middle East and recent nationalist movements supported covertly by the Russians.

Turner thought, *It would have been interesting if these two could have lectured about this in my geopolitical science class at SC. I wasn't aware of what was going on in Indochina or this part of the world. I think they are both right. I hope we never get mired in a no-win situation in some foreign country like the French and British have in North Africa and the Middle East.*

Forbes turned his attention back to Turner. "These marines are part of a reconnaissance platoon. They have been in Port Lyautey for eight weeks and will leave in two weeks for who knows where."

"I have never seen the kind of equipment they are carrying."

"The communication equipment, rifles, and a few other things are new. The BARs have been around for a while. The eight men form two fire teams. Three riflemen and one BAR man make up a fire team. The concept of a fire team is not new, but how these two fire teams operate in the field is very new."

A half hour later, the marine corporal leaned into the cargo compartment and said, "We are landing in eight minutes. We will be on the ground for three minutes, enough time for you to disembark with your gear. There will be a French Foreign Legion officer to meet you. We will pick you up here on

Saturday morning." Using his arms to brace himself as the airplane gently pitched and yawed, he returned to his jump seat in the cockpit.

Turner looked through the small window just over his shoulder as the airplane banked in its final approach. A single small airstrip came into view, then a small L-shaped white building with radio antennas on its roof. Two troop-carrying trucks with light brown canvas covers were parked near an entrance of the building. A dirt road led away from the building, then disappeared in a forest of eucalyptus trees.

The landing was uneventful. The SW/EOD team and their gear were first off the airplane, then Forbes and the marines with their gear. The R-3D immediately swung around and went back down the runway. At the end of the runway, it turned into the wind, powered up with a roar, and took off.

While the men were organizing their gear, a large black man and a smaller white man left the building and walked over to the group. The two men wore tan desert uniforms without insignia, jump boots, and faded olive drab floppy hats. Turner's back was to the two men. In a low voice, Gallegos said, "We have company."

Turner turned around, and before he could say anything, the white man said, "*Bonjour*, Lieutenant Turner." It was Captain Jean Salon.

Turner was incredulous; he saluted and reached out and shook Salon's offered hand. He thought, *What is he doing here? I wonder if he's running this operation.*

"We are glad you and your team are with us these few days." He spotted Forbes. "Ah, Master Sergeant Forbes, it is good to see you and your reconnaissance marines again."

Forbes saluted and returned the greeting. Salon then introduced the black man. "Gentlemen, this is Sergeant Jules Mogangi. He is fluent in Arabic, Senegalese, and French, but not so fluent in English. He is my number one. We will go to our building now. When you enter, pass by the two rooms on your left. The third room will be where you will leave your weapons and other equipment. We will meet in the large room at the end of the other hallway in ten minutes for briefing. If you need to use the toilet, you will find it just before the large room. On y va, mes amis." Salon and the Senegalese led the marines and the SW/EOD team to the white building.

On the way, Cole looked at Chief Gallegos and said, "What does 'on mess a me' mean?"

Gallegos smiled at the butchered pronunciation. "The Captain said 'let's go, my friends.'" He added, "Didn't your French girlfriend teach you anything?"

"Well, yes, but not French." Then he said, "The captain called us his friends. That doesn't sound very regulation to me, Chief."

"The captain is used to working with small groups of men under extreme conditions. I am sure he is 'very regulation' at the appropriate times."

Salon led the group inside the building. Two fully armed legionnaires were standing guard on each side of the entrance to the hallway. As the Americans passed by the legionnaire on the left, he said, in perfect English, "Welcome. We are pleased you will be working with us for a short time."

As Turner walked by the first room, he saw five bunk beds and a desk. The door of the second room, with OFFICIERS painted in black, was closed. Turner and his team, followed by the marines, left their weapons and gear in the designated room and went to the meeting room. As they entered the room, a legionnaire gave each man a map. Turner looked around and counted eighteen folding chairs in two rows. At the front of the room, a podium stood next to a large table. On the wall behind the podium was a blackboard, a large map of northwest Morocco, and a smaller untitled map next to it. He saw the smaller map had great topographic detail. On the wall to his right was a long table with three coffee urns and four towers of disposable cups. On the other side of the room was a partitioned-off area with one side open to the meeting room. Within this space, he could see an older man wearing earphones sitting at a table in front of a radio. He was dressed in the same uniform as Salon and Mogangi.

After all the men had filed in and found seats, Salon went to the front of the room. He welcomed the men and pointed to the coffee table. "Gentlemen, the coffee is there. Perhaps you would like some on this rather cold and early morning."

The men rose as a group and left for the table and coffee. Turner was behind Cole when they got to the table. Cole turned his head and said, "It looks like there's plenty of coffee and sugar cubes, but no cream for you, Mr. Turner." Turner drew his coffee and put three sugar cubes in it. He tasted it, grimaced, and put in two more. Cole grinned. "Mr. Turner, you don't seem to be enjoying one of France's finest coffees."

"This is the worst coffee I have ever tasted, Cole." He looked around, and everyone else was slurping it down as though it was the best Sumatra blend in twenty years. He reluctantly sipped at his.

From the podium, Salon asked the men to return to their seats. When he was satisfied the men were ready to listen, he introduced four additional men.

"Will Corporal Karl Schepke and Corporal Petre Temirkanov please stand up?"

Schepke took off his earphones and stood. At the same time, from a seat in the back row, Temirkanov stood.

"Corporal Schepke is our radioman, and Corporal Temirkanov is our medical man. They and two more of my men, along with Sergeant Mogangi and myself, will be primary in this operation. We are all from 11er Regiment Etranger Parachutiste. Like many of you, we jump out of airplanes and manage to make beautiful women happy. Not at the same time, of course." There was scattered laughter as the two men sat down.

"Will Jules Denoeu and Antoine Delcasse please stand up?" Two men sitting together stood up. "Denoeu and Delcasse are from an agency in Oran." They lifted a hand in greeting and sat down. Nothing more was said of them.

Salon continued, "A week ago, five terrorists attacked and destroyed one of the French commercial television stations in Tangier. Two women and two men were killed and mutilated. The terrorists were young Moroccan Islamic extremists, trained and armed by the FLN and acting under the direction and planning of the FLN, and a cell of the Moroccan Communist Party ESPOUR. Attacks of this kind are not unusual in Algeria and have been going on for years. However, they are now beginning in Morocco.

"For those of you unfamiliar with our current situation, let me explain. The Moroccan-Algerian border runs through mountain and desert. It is long and largely unguarded. It has been easy for Algerian insurgents to find sanctuary on the Moroccan side, which allows them to rest, regroup, and recross to strike again our military and civilian populations. Now we find Algerian insurgents actively recruiting young Moroccan Arabs and Berbers to join in jihad to remove all foreign powers from Morocco, Algeria, and Tunisia. This is part of a movement to establish an Arab nation across all of North Africa, from the Atlantic to the Persian Gulf. Our experience in Indochina and Algeria has made us understand that terrorist attacks cannot be stopped, but we may be able to control the number of attacks by responding in kind and making terrorists pay dearly if caught.

"France gave Morocco its independence three years ago, in 1956. King Muhammad Cinq (the fifth) allowed France and the U.S. to continue to have a military presence here. However, because of his decision, Islamic extremists and the Moroccan Communist Party are threatening his constitutional monarchy. France and the U.S. want to protect their strategic interests in Morocco, Algeria, and Tunisia. To help protect these interests, France and the U.S. are undertaking a series of joint covert operations, which include reconnaissance, surveillance, and interdiction of arms to insurgents and the neutralization of terrorists. I need not elaborate on what I mean by neutralization. The Moroccan government has decided that it will be in its best interest to turn a blind eye towards these activities. This group has been selected to carry out a mission as part of the larger joint covert operation. We will use methods that have been found to be successful in operations of this kind in Algeria."

Turner began to see the big picture. Almost. He would learn more later with his loss of innocence.

Cole and Huwitt were shuffling their feet and nudging each other with their elbows. Turner heard them muttering "oh shit" a number of times. Gallegos leaned over to Turner and said, "Now look at the fine mess you got us into."

Turner thought for a minute and realized what Gallegos said, "Yeah, Laurel and Hardy would find a way out of this mess. So much for our new uniforms and little popguns, Chief."

Salon picked up a pointer from the nearby table and walked over to the map of northwestern Morocco. Turner was close enough to see that the pointer was made from a stick, with what looked to be a 9 mm or .30-caliber brass shell casting for a handle.

"We have found the five terrorists that attacked and destroyed the television station and killed our people. After the attack, they stayed in an Algerian sympathizer's house, east of Tangier, for four days, then started back to Algeria. They are presently in this area of the Rif Mountains." He pointed to an area of the larger map. "They are resting at the house of a hashish and kif grower who is also a member of the group interested in overthrowing Muhammad Cinq. It is not known how soon they will be continuing on their way to the border. We are going to, as you say in your CIA, 'terminate them with extreme prejudice.'"

He then described the route the trucks would be taking into the Rif Mountains. Tapping his pointer on the smaller map, he explained, "This is an enlargement of the area shown on the previous map. The map you were given is a copy of this one." There was a soft rustle as the men unfolded their maps. "We will transport from here to Chefchaouen, also called, Chauen. The distance is about eighty-five kilometers and at an elevation of about 2,133 meters. From Chefchaouen, we will go another eighty-two kilometers to an abandoned phosphate mine near Igsenen. We will meet a friend at the mine who will reward us with any last minute advice. The elevation of the mine is about 1,524 meters. You can see we have crossed over the summit of the Rif Mountains and are down the other side. We will be about 177 kilometers from the Algerian border. At 1,500 meters, the temperature will drop about 9.4° centigrade or more at night, so it will be colder at night than it is here."

Turner used the conversion table in his small notebook to work out the metric values: 2,133 meters was 6,825 feet; 85 kilometers was 51 miles; 82 kilometers was 49.2 miles; 1,524 meters was 4,876 feet; 9.4°C was about 15°F; and 177 kilometers was 110 miles.

"We will leave the trucks in a warehouse near the mine and remain inside until 0400 hours tomorrow morning. At that time, we will travel on foot 6.3 kilometers"—3.78 miles, Turner noted—"southeast to the hashish grower's house. The house is small. It has only two rooms. There is a large front door and a smaller back door. There is a window high to the left of the front door and another window about the same height also on the left side of the door in back. We expect to find the hashish grower, three men, and one woman inside.

"Sergeant Mogangi, Denoeu, and Delcasse will attack through the rear door of the house after the first marine fire team lays down ten seconds of heavy fire at that door and window. The second marine fire team, led by Master Sergeant Forbes, will back up Corporals Schepke and Temirkanov and myself as we wait at the front of the house for occupants, who have been encouraged, through the efforts of Sergeant Mogangi, to come out the front door. In the event they do not come out, we will assume they are all dead and wait for a sign from Sergeant Mogangi."

Turner thought, *He hasn't said a thing about giving them the option to surrender.*

"The navy team is here as observers and will not participate directly. Lieutenant Turner and his men will remain seventy-five meters to the rear of the marines deployed at the front of the house." Looking at Turner, he said, "If your team is discovered and fired on, you will return fire enthusiastically. Otherwise, your team's contribution to this field problem will be to not make the mission more complicated.

"The trucks will be driven by Corporal Temirkanov and Corporal Schepke. Sergeant Mogangi will ride in front with Temirkanov. The lieutenant and his men and I will ride in back with Denoeu and Delcasse. Master Sergeant Forbes will ride in front with Schepke, and the marines will ride in back. Corporal Schepke will take the lead. The communication and assault equipment is already in the trucks. We will not stop for a midday meal. We will have our evening meal at the phosphate mine warehouse. Do you have questions?" There were none. "We leave in ten minutes."

The men left the room, collected their gear, and went to the trucks.

Turner pulled his team together at Temirkanov's truck to give himself and Gallegos a chance to go over their notes with their men. After comparing notes, Huwitt had the only comment. "I hope these people know what they are doing."

As he put his notebook back in his pocket, Turner said, "I don't know how this thing is going to play out, but I want us to stay as far away from the players as possible. I want us close enough to each other to communicate, but not so close that we are bunching up. I don't have to tell you to stay under cover." Cole and Huwitt looked at each other as if to say, *Does he think we're stupid?*

"Remember, we are just observers and nonparticipants. Do you have anything else, Chief?"

"Captain Salon covered everything pretty carefully, but we better be prepared for surprises."

"Huwitt, do you and Cole have anything to offer?"

Cole replied, "Not a thing, sir."

Huwitt, asked, "Sir, what's *kif?*"

Turner looked at Chief Gallegos; Gallegos looked at Huwitt and said, "It's marijuana, Mineman First Class Huwitt."

"Oh."

Just before climbing into the truck, Cole said, "Don't worry, Mr. Turner. We'll take care of you." He was dead serious. The team was working with a new team leader without experience in the field and of unknown competence. The three men had been impressed with Turner on the AVR dive; this was different.

In the truck, Turner and his team were on one side, and Salon, Jules Denoeu, and Antoine Delcasse sat on the other. Cole asked Denoeu and Delcasse if they spoke English. Delcasse answered, "Un petit peu—a very little." Cole and Huwitt tried to converse, haltingly, but not for long. Five minutes later, the trucks were driving through the forest of eucalyptus trees that Turner had seen from the plane.

Turner, looking out the back of the truck, said, "Captain Salon, the smell of eucalyptus trees makes me think of home. We use eucalyptus for landscaping. This is a forest of hundreds."

Salon replied, "This is a eucalyptus tree farm. The Arabs grow the trees for a few years and then cut them down, form them into piles, and cover the piles with dirt. With that done, they set the wood on fire beneath the dirt. Over time, charcoal is produced, which they sell for cooking and heating."

"I suppose this method of charcoal production has been going on forever in North Africa," Turner commented.

Salon answered, "And in other places. The method is not unusual." He folded his arms and sat back with his legs stretched out and continued, "History tells us wars have been fought for many reasons, but usually a war is fought for resources one party has and another wants. The resource may be salt or gold or oil or fertile land or maybe Helen of Troy." He paused, and then continued, "Some analysts think that one reason for the insurgency in Algeria is the loss of trees native to the area in the south."

Where is he going with this? Then Turner asked, "What do trees have to do with insurgency or terrorism?"

"Ah, Lieutenant, let me explain. The native trees that supplied fuel and shelter are gone because of the needs of a human population that is rapidly expanding."

"Can't they tree farm eucalyptus in the south?" Turner asked.

"No, there is not sufficient water, and it is too late. Let me continue. With the trees gone, there is no protection for native shrubs and grasses, and the Sahara advances northward. What little agriculture there was has also been lost to this desertification. In fact, it may have caused the phenomenon. The population native to the area has been moving northward and is putting enormous pressure on the *pied noir*, the farmers of French descent who have been in this country for generations. The native Algerians want this land and want us out of Algeria. But we French are not living in a colony of France. We are the French of Algeria." He paused, "France without Algeria would not be France."

"All this because of charcoal?"

"Perhaps one could say that something as simple as the availability of charcoal may be one of the causes of insurrection. Do you find that interesting, Lieutenant Turner?"

"I find it very interesting. I couldn't have made that connection." Changing the subject, he asked, "Captain, how did you learn to speak English so well?"

"Our schools in France encourage us to learn English. I also spent a year at your Army War College." He paused and said, "You have been looking at our weapons, Lieutenant. Do you know of them?"

"No, sir. I have never seen weapons like you have. What are they?"

Salon passed his to Turner and said, "This is a nine millimeter MAT-49 submachine gun."

Turner looked the MAT-49 over carefully and handed it back to Salon. "I'm surprised how small it is. Is it reliable?"

"We had good experience with them in Indochina, and here in North Africa, we have found them to be quite good."

"The marines with us have the new M16s. I guess all the U.S. ground forces will be getting them soon," Turner added.

Salon lit a cigarette and said, "I would hope they don't. They kill people."

"Well, they are *supposed* to kill people."

"What I mean is that the person *using* one will get killed. That weapon jams over 30 percent of the time, giving advantage to an enemy."

Gallegos had been listening and joined in, "Master Sergeant Forbes was telling me the M16 jams often, even if it is well maintained. Makes you wonder why our government buys these things."

The trucks had left the eucalyptus grove behind and were driven southeast through arid scrubland. They then headed due east for the climb into the Rif Mountains. It wasn't long before everyone in the back of the truck except Turner was asleep, their bodies swaying in harmony with the movement of the truck.

The country they were passing through fascinated Turner. It was a little like driving up into the San Bernardino Mountains from Los Angeles. The landscape changed from arid land shrubs and grasses to shrubs and a few oaks, then the cedar-pine-fir community with its characteristic fragrance on the cooler air. He smiled as he watched the road traffic. There were donkeys with great thickets of sticks on their backs being herded along the side of the road, but very few cars or trucks. Not like the traffic going up to Lake Arrowhead or Crestline.

Salon jerked and woke up. He looked outside, then glanced at his watch.

"We should be coming into Chefchaoun about now."

Five minutes later, they passed through the scruffiness and unpleasant odors of Chefchaoun and were on the way to Igsenen. All the men were awake now.

It was early afternoon when the trucks left the poorly maintained two-lane asphalt road a few miles from Igsenen for a single-lane dirt road running south. Thirty-five minutes later, the forest gave way to a large clearing that ended at a cliff of an old abandoned rock quarry. There were several sheds, a small house, and a large warehouse. Near the warehouse were four old dump trucks with flat tires and broken widows. The mine looked as though it had not been in operation for some time.

The trucks pulled up to the warehouse. Salon and Mogangi climbed out of theirs, cautioned the men in both trucks to stay on board, then walked back to the house with their weapons at the ready.

Turner and the others watched from the back of the trucks as Salon approached the porch of the house with Mogangi a few yards behind and off to one side. The two stopped, and Salon called out, "Amid."

There was no answer. He called again, "Amid."

From around the side of the house, a rather short Arab in a brown djellaba came forward with an AK-47 slung over his shoulder. Turner heard him say, "La-bas, Salon."

Salon replied, "La-bas aalik, Amid."

To Turner's surprise, they started laughing and hugging each other, breaking into animated French. The three walked over to the trucks, and Mogangi called everyone out. The men climbed out of the trucks and stood by in their own groups. Salon introduced the Arab, who turned out not to be an Arab.

"Men, this is Lieutenant Pierre Tailliez, also known as Amid al Barc."

Tailliez greeted the men in English and said, "I'll open the large doors to the warehouse, and the drivers can pull the trucks inside. We will follow. Once inside, the doors will be closed and locked. There is a side door that we will use for the entrance and exit of two men who will stand guard in hidden positions on opposite corners of the warehouse. They will be relieved every two hours until the group deploys. The mine is a very secure place—we should not have any visitors, but we will be cautious and remain out of sight."

After a brief discussion, the guard duty was divided up between legionnaires and marines.

By 2000 hours, the men had eaten their field rations and settled down with coffee provided by the legionnaires. The only illumination was by two kerosene lamps and shaded flashlights. Turner drank his coffee slowly without comment. Salon called the men together, repeated the earlier briefing, and added, "Radio communication has been established with our intelligence unit at Targuis, which is about about eleven kilometers"—6.7 miles—"west of us. The most recent information about our subjects is that they are still in the house at the hashish farm. They are expected to leave early tomorrow morning. We will interrupt their departure and accomplish our task quickly. The marines and navy team will then leave the area immediately. My men will remain to search the house and deal with the bodies. We will then join you at the mine to load up and return to Tangier. Make sure all your equipment is in the trucks before we deploy to the hashish farm. Take with you only your weapons and ammunition."

He turned to Tailliez and asked, "Pierre, do you have anything to add?"

"You should know the window openings are opened and closed by heavy wooden shutters. If closed, it will be difficult to break in and attack with fragmentation grenades. The last few nights have been unusually cold, so expect the shutters to be closed. Which brings us to the weather. The weather report, received at 1100 today, revealed a body of warm, moist air slowly moving toward northeastern Morocco and northwestern Algeria. It will come ashore tonight at about 2300. We should be seeing misty rain or slight fog when we deploy. We will not be inconvenienced by what we intend to do."

Huwitt nudged Cole and said, "Poncho weather, ol' buddy."

Tailliez said, "If there are no questions, I suggest we get some sleep."

Forbes asked, "Just one question, sir. Will we form up in assault and assault support groups here or near the objective?"

"In the morning, we will form into the two groups here and travel separately. Sergeant Mogangi's group will lead us. As Captain Salon explained, on completion of our task, the marines and navy team will be first out of the area. They will travel as a group, in this case, with you, Master Sergeant, at the lead."

Turner looked around. Seeing no one else was going to ask questions, he raised his hand and asked, "If there are casualties on either side, how do we handle that?"

"If we suffer casualties, we will deal with that occurrence at the time." Tailliez left it at that.

The night was cold, the warehouse musty, and the floor the group slept on was a slanted, oil-spotted concrete slab. Turner finally fell asleep a little after 0100. He awoke and looked at his Rolex; it was only 0215. He pulled the top of the mummy bag down over his head and slept fitfully until 0320, when he awakened to the sound of Gallegos and Forbes sitting on their knapsacks, drinking coffee and joking about Cole and Huwitt, who found that the toilets in the warehouse did not work and had just come back in from the outside after relieving themselves.

The marines in ponchos and legionnaires in light field jackets had already loaded their gear in the trucks and were carefully checking the action of their weapons and loading them for the assault. Gallegos, seeing that they were going to be last to load up and be ready to go, said, "Lets go, men. Don't let them think we don't wanna go."

Turner worked his way out of his mummy bag, packed his gear, and followed his men to their truck. After loading their gear in the truck, they checked the action of their pistols, slammed home magazines, and slid their pistols snugly in shoulder holsters. He was wide awake now, and the hair on the back of his neck stood up as they went through these actions. It was the same feeling he'd had when he first strapped on his SCUBA at Key West, the same feeling he'd had the first time he placed and set off a demolition charge, and the same feeling he'd had in the copilot's seat beside Flint Williams in the helicopter. He was with special people and feeling special. This was the real thing, and he felt he was ready. After the team put on their web belts and ponchos, they waited for Salon to give the order to deploy.

Turner watched Temirkanov help Schepke strap on a radio pack. Schepke, in turn, helped Temirkanov strap on a large medical pack. Denoeu and Delcasse each had a large dark blue plastic bag slung over their shoulders. *Curious,* Turner thought.

Salon slung his submachine gun over his shoulder, said a few words, and ended with, "On y va mes amis." The group headed for the side door and exited the warehouse. As Cole went out, he looked over his shoulder at his teammates and said with a big smile, "Like the man said, let's go, my friends."

Tailliez led Mogangi, Denoeu, Delcasse, who were leading the first marine fire team, crossed the open space, and entered the cedar and fir forest. The others followed a short distance behind.

The weather along the route was exactly as forecast: misty rain with intermittent fog. But it was also cold. Moisture collecting on cedar fronds and fir needles formed droplets that fell onto impervious ponchos and light field coats. Exposed trouser legs became saturated, then socks in boots. But the men's thoughts were focused on another level, and the discomfort was ignored. By first light, they were at the edge of a small mountain meadow interspersed with clumps of willows.

The mist was clearing, and about two hundred meters away, just inside the tree line of the meadow, they could see their objective at the base of a large hill. Salon removed the lens covers from the binoculars hanging from a lanyard around his neck. He lifted the binoculars to his eyes and studied the house and surroundings. Mogangi and Forbes joined Salon with their binoculars.

Salon took the lanyard from around his neck and passed the binoculars to Turner. Looking through the binoculars, he saw a small sturdy-looking house with a roof of terra-cotta tiles supplemented with sections of rusted corrugated metal. At the front of the house was a dilapidated two-wheel cart with a tarp loosely hanging over one side. Light smoke coming from a makeshift chimney was the only evidence of anyone present. He handed the binoculars back to Salon without comment.

Salon brought the group together and said, "There doesn't seem to be a guard, but we will assume there is. They should be getting ready to leave soon, and we want this to be over before their transportation arrives.

"Tailliez, I want you to stay inside the tree line and cover the road approaching the house. We will stay and take our positions as planned. Synchronize your watches on my mark." They all readied their watches. "Oh-four-four-seven, mark. Sergeant Mogangi, commence the assault in ten minutes."

Seven minutes later, Mogangi, Denoeu, Delcasse, and the first marine fire team had settled in position on the slope behind the house when a terrorist with an AK-47 slung from his shoulder came from around the corner of the house to the back. He stopped, looked around, and, not seeing anything unusual, returned from where he came.

Addressing Denoeu, Mogangi said, "Deal with this man when the marine fire team opens fire at the backdoor and window." He added, "There could be another one somewhere."

A short distance from the front of the house, the second marine fire team took position in the high grass of the meadow, with the navy team about seventy-five meters behind—out of the way, but within good viewing distance of the action to come. Gallegos, seeing that Turner had not drawn his weapon, quietly advised, "Mr. Turner, we may not be shooting at anybody, but you may want to be ready."

Turner self-consciously reached under his poncho and drew his weapon. *I'm sitting here like a spectator getting ready to see a war movie. The Chief had to remind me to get my head out of my ass.*

Mogangi was right—there was a second terrorist on guard, waiting in a low clump of willows a short distance behind Turner's team.

Then it began. The second terrorist jumped up, shouted the alarm, and advanced, sweeping an AK-47 from side to side as he fired. Completely surprised, the team turned in the direction of fire. Huwitt stood up to return fire and was immediately hit. He dropped his weapon, grabbed at his right thigh, and fell to the wet grass. Cole ignored the shooter and crawled over to his friend.

At the moment Huwitt was hit, Turner got off four shots—three missed entirely; the last went into the terrorist's chest. As the terrorist slowly crumpled, Gallegos fired one shot, hitting him in the forehead.

Hearing the gunfire at the front of the house, Mogangi signaled for the marine fire team to lay down heavy fire. After firing for ten seconds, the wooden shutter protecting the window was shot away, and the backdoor was hanging by one hinge. The back wall of the house and part of the exposed sidewall was a mosaic of pockmarks from gunfire. The terrorist on guard lay dead with his upper body in shreds.

Mogangi, Denoeu and Delcasse got up from their positions, charged down the slope to the house, kicked the backdoor off its hinge, and stormed inside. They found two wounded terrorists fumbling for their AK-47s and killed them.

The last two terrorists, one recognized by Tailliez as the hashish farmer, were firing their AK-47s as they exited from the front door. Salon allowed them to live a few moments, then called for gunfire.

The assault ended in less than two minutes. Huwitt was the only casualty.

Turner and Gallegos joined Cole. Cole had cut away Huwitt's trouser leg with his dagger and was applying a pressure bandage from his first aid kit to try to stop the bleeding. Turner and Gallegos called for Temirkanov. Temirkanov looked around and, seeing one of the Americans down, immediately ran over, threw down his medical pack, knelt down, and began to assess Huwitt's condition. Turner knelt down beside him. Temirkanov removed Cole's hand from the wound on the inside of Huwitt's thigh and lifted the pressure bandage. Bright red blood spurted from the wound. He replaced the pressure bandage and put Cole's hand back on it.

Turner muttered, "Femoral artery."

Then Temirkanov felt around Huwitt's thigh and found a much larger exit wound. He turned and opened his medical pack and pulled out two large pressure bandages and a blood pressure cuff. He had Cole hold a pressure bandage to each wound as he wrapped the blood pressure cuff around Huwitt's thigh, just above the wound. He pumped up the cuff, and the bleeding stopped.

Salon arrived with Forbes, exchanged a few words in French with Temirkanov as Temirkanov bandaged Huwitt's wound, and said, "Master Sergeant Forbes, we have to get this man out of here, *now*. Please have your marines make a stretcher, and quickly return him to the trucks."

Forbes called the nearest fire team over and explained the situation. Within a few minutes, they had made a stretcher out of ponchos and tree limbs.

Salon took Turner aside and said, "Lieutenant, as you can see, your friend has lost a great deal of blood and is going into shock. After Temirkanov treats the wounds, he will start an intravenous line to add fluid and restore his blood pressure. He will do everything he can to help this man. Schepke will call Port Lyautey for a plane to meet us at our airstrip."

Turner hadn't recovered from the shock brought on by the events. Confused, he asked, "Isn't there somewhere for a helicopter or airplane to land near here?"

"We are out of range for a helicopter transfer. Ours is the nearest airstrip, and we cannot use the hospital in Tangier."

Becoming agitated, Turner asked, "Sir, why can't we use the hospital in Tangier?"

"This is a wounded American military person. The hospital in Tangier is a civilian hospital. There would be questions that would compromise American and French interests—I am sure you understand."

"Sir, he could die."

"Yes, I am sure he could. We will do everything possible to prevent this misfortune." Salon turned and walked away.

"Cole, I want you to stay with Huwitt. The chief and I will meet you at the truck."

Temirkanov and Gallegos gently lifted Huwitt onto the stretcher. The fire team lifted the stretcher and left for the trucks with Cole at Huwitt's side. Turner and Gallegos looked back toward the house. They saw that Mogangi, Denoeu, and Delcasse had dragged the five dead bodies together in front of the house, then lined them up side by side. Delcasse left Mogangi and Denoeu and walked back to the body of the terrorist killed by Turner and Gallegos. Turner and Gallegos joined him. Delcasse bent down and pulled away the kaffiyeh partially covering the face of the terrorist. "It appears we have the female here." He looped a short length of rope around her ankles, stood up, and began to drag the body away.

In horror, Turner touched Gallegos's arm and gasped, "My god, I've killed a woman."

Gallegos replied, "No, Mr. Turner, we killed a terrorist who has killed innocent people."

They watched as Delcasse placed the female's body next to the others. Denoeu and Delcasse then stripped the bodies of clothing. Turner looked on in disbelief as they cut off the genitals of each of the males and forced the genitals into each of their mouths. The dark blue plastic bags Denoeu and Delcasse had carried from the trucks were lying near the bodies. Denoeu pulled one over for himself and another for his partner. They opened the bags and, from them, poured animal entrails over the bodies. They then threw the bags aside, walked over to the house, and went inside. Turner clutched his mouth, trying to keep from vomiting. Gallegos steadied the young officer and turned him to walk away.

Salon came from around the back of the house. He was surprised that Turner and Gallegos had not left with the others. He walked over to them and said, "I'm sorry you had to see this."

Turner replied in anguish, "That was an atrocity your men just committed."

Salon replied, "This is an unusual war, Lieutenant. It is a war of escalating mutual atrocities, it is a war of imperialism, nationalism, and, in the Arab's case, of religion also. You were told to be the first away from this place, but you stayed too long, and you have seen something unpleasant. What you observed is the usual, not the unusual, and I might add, it was first started by our Arab adversaries. We are simply responding in kind."

"But the guts!"

"The entrails are those of the pig. If a person of the Islamic faith is buried with the entrails of the pig, they are considered doomed to hell. Very soon now, their friends will arrive and will see all of this. They will know that we will answer their terrorism with great force. Je ne regrette rien."

At this point, Mogangi walked up to Salon and said, "Lieutenant Tailliez is leading the others back to the trucks. Denoeu and Delcasse are finished with their work. We can start now, sir."

Salon replied, "Good. Was anything of use found in the house?"

"They found a few papers about kif and hashish business, nothing more."

"That finding may prove to be useful."

As the two legionnaires were talking, a pale and unsteady Turner quietly asked, "What does *je ne regrette rien* mean, Chief?"

"*Je ne regrette rien* means 'I regret nothing.'"

Denoeu and Delcasse joined them, and Salon said, "Lead us out of here, Sergeant Mogangi."

Thirty minutes later, under the supervision of Temirkanov and Gallegos, Huwitt was loaded on board one of the trucks. Temirkanov climbed on board and took station close to Huwitt. Then with Salon, Denoeu, Delcasse, and the three other navy team members on board and Mogangi at the wheel, they left for Tangier. The second truck was not far behind with Schepke and the marines.

With the IV fluid increasing his blood pressure, Huwitt became semiconscious and complained of great pain. Cole and Gallegos tried to comfort him with little success. Turner finally asked Temirkanov, "Can't you help him? Can't you give him a syrette of morphine?"

Temirkanov spoke to Salon in French. Salon replied, "Temirkanov has already given your friend a little morphine. Opiates suppress breathing. When we get to the aircraft, there will be oxygen available, and more morphine may be given."

The return to the airstrip took far less time than going up to the phosphate mine the day before. The R-3D had been on the ground for about twenty minutes, and when the cockpit crew saw the trucks emerge from the eucalyptus grove, they started the airplane's right engine. Mogangi drove onto the airstrip and, approaching the aircraft, quickly turned around, backed up, and stopped a short distance from the airplane's open cargo door.

Turner, looking out the back of the truck, saw Lieutenant Mary Bionconi in a baggy flight suit, standing on the gravel below the cargo door opening. She was holding a walk-around tank of oxygen with tubing attached to a mask. Seeing Turner, she opened her mouth in surprise. She hadn't known he was part of all this. He was disheveled and looked terrible. She lifted her free hand slightly in greeting. He returned the gesture.

The marine fire team that had carried Huwitt out of the forest quickly unloaded the stretcher from the truck. Then Salon jumped down, saluted the navy nurse, and said, "We meet again, Lieutenant, but under less pleasant circumstances."

She glanced at Salon, then put the oxygen mask on Huwitt and cracked open the valve on the oxygen tank. She made sure the flow was adequate, then placed the oxygen tank on the stretcher next to Huwitt's good leg. Then she took out a notebook and pen, looked at Temirkanov, and asked, "What have you done so far?"

Temirkanov explained his assessment and treatment in French to Salon, who translated the information to the navy nurse. She carefully examined Huwitt's wound, checked the intravenous line making sure the fluid was flowing properly, and ordered the marines to load Huwitt on board the airplane. When she was boarding the airplane, she noticed Cole had jumped down from the truck and was looking at her.

"Cole, come on board with me and stay close to your friend."

Salon saluted once again; she waved in acknowledgment, turned, and followed Huwitt's stretcher.

Turner and Gallegos jumped down from the truck and as they approached the airplane, Salon saluted the two Americans, and walked away.

On board, Turner sat next to Binki on one side of the stretcher, and Gallegos sat next to Cole on the other side.

An aircrewman secured the cargo hatch, checked the fastenings securing the stretcher to the fuselage deck, and went forward. The left engine coughed and started. The airplane taxied into position and, after engine run-up, took off and headed west. A few minutes later, they were over water and following the coastline south.

Binki administered antibiotics and morphine to Huwitt, who continued to slip in and out of consciousness. She monitored Huwitt's vital signs and tried to stabilize his condition as well as she could by adjusting his intravenous fluid and oxygen. Then she asked, "Are you all right, Burt?"

Ignoring her question, he answered, "When I first saw you with those overalls on, I thought you might be working on your car today."

She didn't understand at first. Then looking down, she said, "Oh, my flight suit. When we have a medical evacuation flight, we wear these." Then she again asked, "Are you all right?"

"I'm all right, Binki. Is Huwitt going to live?"

"I don't know. He's lost a lot of blood." She put her hand on Huwitt's forehead for a moment, then took his pulse and said, "He's not in shock. That's a plus right now. If we keep him from dying, we still have to worry about possible infection caused by the passage of the bullet going through his clothing and taking any fabric with it into the wound. I'm very worried about the exit wound. It's extremely large." She put her hand on Turner's. "Dr. Pierce and the surgical team are waiting for us. Your man will be well taken care of."

Turner was surprised to hear Mary Bionconi call their friend Doctor; none of their group called Phil Pierce Doctor except in jest.

She was quite worried about Turner's appearance and asked, "Were you hit anywhere, Burt?"

"No."

She squeezed his hand and turned back to Huwitt. Cole was holding Huwitt's hand.

From time to time, she glanced at Turner. She had two patients to be concerned about.

Chapter 5

As the R-3D touched down at NAS Port Lyautey, Turner closed the small notebook he had been writing in. The notebook was full of short statements detailing what he had experienced during the Rif Mountains mission. His objectivity was remarkable in spite of his mental state.

He looked at his Rolex and thought, *Three and a half hours ago, the assault began, and now we are back. Six are dead, and I killed one of them, a woman. Huwitt may die, and I witnessed an atrocity from a horror story . . . all this for what?*

The airplane left the main runway and taxied to an ambulance waiting near the control tower. After the cockpit crew shut down the engines, the ground crew opened the cargo door, and two medics went on board. The medics made their way forward and received orders from Lieutenant Bionconi, then they released and lifted Huwitt's stretcher and followed her to the cargo door entrance. Cole stood up and glanced at Turner. Turner quietly said, "Go on with Huwitt. I'll come up to the hospital as soon as I can. Leave your backpack with us."

At the cargo door, as Cole started to follow the stretcher out, one of medics asked, "Ma'am, is it OK for him to come along?

"Yes, of course," she replied.

Master Sergeant Forbes and his marines were waiting on the tarmac when Turner and Gallegos left the airplane.

"Mr. Turner, sir, we want you and Chief Gallegos to know how sorry we are that Mineman First Class Huwitt was wounded in the previous action. You and your men were outstanding in the way you handled a totally unpredictable situation." The eight marines mumbled in agreement.

"Thank you, Master Sergeant."

They exchanged salutes, and Turner and Gallegos, carrying Cole and Huwitt's gear and their own, trudged toward the terminal building. They were interrupted when a sailor ran up to them, saluted, and said, "Mr. Turner, Commander Hawkins's staff car is waiting for you and your men. You will be riding back to NOF with the exec."

"It will only be Chief Gallegos and me." He handed Huwitt's and Cole's backpacks to the sailor. "Here, you can take these. Let's go."

When they came around the corner of the control tower to the parking lot, they could see Lieutenant Commander Owens standing next to the staff car. Approaching the exec, they saluted; the exec returned their salutes and asked, "How is Petty Officer Huwitt?"

"Alive, sir, but in very bad shape. I sent Cole with him to the hospital."

"Good. The commander is waiting in his office for your report."

Ten minutes later, they followed the exec into the NOF office complex; all eyes were on Turner and Gallegos. As Turner walked by Lieutenant Van Buren's desk, Van Buren let out a gasp and said, "Oh shit Burt."

The exec looked over his shoulder and said, "As you were, Mr. Van Buren," and walked into Commander Hawkins's office. Turner and Gallegos dropped their gear next to Turner's desk and joined the exec in the commander's office.

Commander Hawkins said, "Pull up a chair, and let's talk. Do you want some coffee?"

Gallegos replied, "Yes, sir."

Turner said, "No, sir.

The exec went to the doorway and called out, "Yeoman Jenkins, bring us a pot of coffee and some mugs."

"Aye, aye, sir."

The commander asked, "What's the story on Mineman Huwitt? How bad is it?"

"He was bleeding from his femoral artery and the bullet's exit wound is massive. I am sure the French medic and our navy nurse did everything they could. I don't know, but I think we may lose him, sir."

"That's a damn shame. Keep me informed."

He slid a file stamped SECRET/COVERT to the center of his desk and said, "What I have here is a product of a cooperative agreement between Navy Intelligence and the Central Intelligence Agency with the Pentagon's imprimatur."

He opened the file and read from the first page:

Date/Time/Group, "Umpty Ump," Lieutenant JG Burt
Turner, USNR, was given verbal orders for his SW/EOD Team to

accompany Master Sergeant Russell Forbes, USMC, and a Marine RECON group of two fire teams on a field problem into the RIF Mountains of Northeastern Morocco. The SW/EOD Team and marines were to rendezvous with a French Foreign Legion Army group led by a Captain of the 11er Regiment Légion Étrangère Parachutiste. This Captain will be in overall command from the time they land at the airstrip south of Tangier and they leave from that same airstrip. The duration of the deployment will be between two and three and one half days, the variation in time is dependent on completion of the task associated with the field problem.

Lieutenant JG Burt Turner, USNR and SW/EOD Team 1's mission is to:

1. Train in basic reconnaissance and surveillance procedures.
2. Observe and analyze procedures used to accomplish the task of the field problem.

On return of Lieutenant JG Turner's team, Lieutenant JG Turner will report ASAP to Fleet Intelligence Center, NAS, Port Lyautey for debriefing.

Commander Hawkins looked up from the page he was reading and said, "This particular page is the preliminary and informal information that was given to you. The other pages include the official order requiring this command to undertake the operation in hopes of discovering important information that would prove useful politically as well as militarily. Additionally, there are possible scenarios added about what could happen if you and your team participated in this operation. One of the scenarios seems to describe what you experienced. Since the task associated with the field problem was accomplished so quickly, the participants that were to attend the debriefing at the Fleet Intelligence Center will not be here until tomorrow morning."

He leaned back in his chair and asked, "Now, what the hell happened out there?"

Turner had been watching a fly on the corner of the CO's desk. The fly had been rubbing its forelegs together, then it would stop and put its forelegs back on the surface, then it would pull them up, and smooth them over the back of its head, then over its eyes, then return them to the surface of the desk, pause, and then it ran through the same sequence again.

Gallegos nudged Turner. Turner said, "Yes, ah, what happened out there."

At this point he took his notebook out of his jacket pocket and read the entries. The commander and the exec asked a number of probing questions; Turner answered most of them, but also had to say, "I don't know, sir," a number of times.

Because Chief Gallegos was held in high regard by Commander Hawkins and the exec, they often asked, "Is this what you saw, Chief? Could this have been done another way?" And, "Do you agree with Mr. Turner?" The chief supported and reinforced Turner every step of the way.

They were interrupted by a knock on the door. With permission, Yeoman Jenkins came in with a well-worn silver tray weighed down with an equally worn silver coffee pot, creamer, and sugar bowl with small silver tongs and four porcelain mugs. He put the tray on a small table near the desk, asked if there was anything else. The commander replied, "Thank you, no. And please tell Yeoman Fry we do not want to be disturbed under any condition."

Yeoman Jenkins replied, "Yes, sir," and left the office.

Addressing his exec he said, "Don, why don't you and Chief Gallegos have some coffee? This may take a while."

It did take a while—two and half more hours. During the meeting, the commander and the exec were amazed at the degree of detail Turner presented. Altogether, the information proved to be much more than was expected from what was essentially a "let's see what we can get out of this" operation. As time went on, the commander saw Turner less and less capable of thinking clearly and decided it was appropriate to conclude the proceedings.

"Well, I think we have had enough for now—I must say, Mr. Turner, your conduct was exemplary." He looked at Gallegos. "Chief, outstanding as usual."

Turner gave his notebook to Commander Hawkins, hesitated, then said, "I am very concerned that I killed a woman. I do not—"

The commander interrupted him, "What you did was within the rules of engagement. There is nothing more to say. No one is going to make an issue out of this occurrence. You shouldn't either. Tomorrow at 1000, we will meet at Fleet Intelligence Center. Captain Dillon is flying in tonight from Naples, and representatives from the CIA field office in Paris will fly in early tomorrow morning. I am sure you will handle the question-and-answer period at the meeting just as well as you did here. Chief, you will not have to attend. Now, I would like you both to get some rest."

Turner and Gallegos replied in unison, "Aye, aye, sir." They were just going out the door when the exec said, "Oh, Lieutenant Commander Bello called. They didn't need to send the AVR propeller shaft to Gibraltar. The air station machine shop repaired it and sent it back down to the wharf. He said he would appreciate you remounting it when you are available."

Turner asked the exec, "When will I be available, sir?"

The exec looked at the commander, and the commander said, "After the meeting tomorrow, I don't want to see Mr. Turner or his team around here for forty-eight hours. I think we can leave the timing on that repair up to Mr. Turner. Don't you agree, Don?"

The exec replied emphatically, "Yes, sir, I certainly agree to that."

"Thank you, sir," Turner replied.

The exec said, "One last thing, Mr. Turner. Store all your gear in the EOD shop, including your weapons. No reason to bother Master Sergeant Forbes every time you deploy.

"Aye, aye, sir." Turner and Gallegos left the office.

The commander and the exec, frequently referring to Turner's notebook, spent the next hour discussing the meeting that had just ended. Finally, the exec remarked, "I think we have a winner here, sir. Turner's very bright, resourceful, and shows an incredible ability of observation. I liked the way Chief Gallegos supported Turner's explanations. Very unusual when one considers the short time they have been together. It would appear that the chief sees something of substance there."

The commander closed Turner's notebook and said, "I believe you're right. Anyway, I want to continue giving him more than the usual freedom of movement. We can always reel him in. I do appreciate his initiative. It will be interesting to see how soon he recovers from this experience—that is, if he does."

"Sir, I would suggest that we have Chief Gallegos tag along with Mr. Turner tomorrow morning. The young man is very worn out. He has never been involved in a formal debriefing, and of course, he is representing this command. He may be more confident with Chief Gallegos at his side."

"Good idea, Don. Have Fry call Chief Gallegos and let him know that he will appear at 1000 with Mr. Turner."

Turner and Gallegos had gone by Turner's desk and picked up their backpacks, and the two left by their driver. They were on the way out the door when Van Buren got up from his desk and walked over. "You OK, Burt?"

"I'm fine, Ted." And he wearily punched the supply officer on the shoulder.

They left the office complex and were halfway down the hallway when Turner stopped at the mail room.

"I'm going to check my mail, Chief."

"Good idea, sir. I'll see how many advertisements I've got."

They entered the mail room and went to their mailboxes. Gallegos took out a handful of envelopes, sorted through them, and dropped a number of unopened ads into a nearby trashcan. He ended up with two envelopes to take home, one a bill from the Sears mail order division, the other from his mother-in-law.

Turner quickly sorted through his mail, then with great disgust, dropped it all in the trashcan. One envelope caught his eye as it slid away from the rest. He reached down and retrieved it. The address was typewritten, and in the upper left-hand corner was the name Joan. There was no return address. His heart skipped a beat. He tore the envelope flap with his finger, slipped out a folded letter, and read:

> Burt, this relationship is not working for me. You are five thousand miles away, and I receive your letters intermittently. I know you are doing important work for our country, and I admire you for that. But I too have a life to lead. At the urging of my major professor, I have decided to go on to the PhD in chemical engineering. He has been a wonderful mentor, and to be honest with you, we have developed a relationship. You are a very special person, and I think you will come to understand this is best for both of us. Please do not write back to me. It's over.
>
> **Joan**

He leaned his back against the wall and slid down to the floor. He sat with his elbows on his knees, the letter dangling from the fingers of his right hand, and looked up at Gallegos.

"What's wrong, Mr. Turner?"

He handed the letter to Gallegos. He read it. "Well, a 'Dear John.' This sort of thing is not unusual in the navy. Give me your hand."

Turner took Gallegos's hand and pulled himself up.

Gallegos gave the letter back to Turner. "Now, sir, the drill is to get drunk. When you are through throwing up and your headache is about gone, do something physically demanding, then busy yourself intensely for a while. You have had a difficult twenty-four hours. You can handle this . . . I know about these things." He smiled at Turner and continued, "Perhaps after the debriefing tomorrow, we might do the surf at Mehdiya Beach. Right now, let's get rid of the gear and go see Mineman First Roger Huwitt."

Entering the hospital, Gallegos, with Turner in trail, went to the reception desk. Addressing the corpsman in charge, Gallegos said, "We are here to see Mineman First Huwitt." Before the corpsman could answer, Cole got up from a chair on the other side of the room, walked over, and said, "They won't let anyone see Huwitt."

Gallegos asked the medic, "Is that right? No one can see Huwitt?"

The medic replied, "Mineman First Huwitt came out of surgery an hour ago and can't be seen by anyone. I'm sorry, Chief, maybe tomorrow."

Turner stepped up to the counter and asked, "Is Dr. Pierce available?"

"I'll call and ask, sir."

The medic picked up the phone and dialed. The other phone rang a number of times, then a nurse answered, "Lieutenant JG Armstrong. Can I help you?"

"This is the reception desk. There is . . ." He put his hand over the mouthpiece and asked, "Are you marines or what?"

"Navy," Turner replied.

"There is a naval officer and two enlisted men to see Dr. Pierce."

"What is the officer's name?"

"What is your name, sir?"

"Turner, Lieutenant JG Turner,"

"His name is Turner, Lieutenant JG Turner, ma'am." There was a long pause, then the medic hung up the phone and said, "The nurse said to send you right back. Take the hallway on the left all the way to the end, take a right, and Dr. Pierce will be three doors down."

Gallegos thanked the medic and joined up with Turner and Cole, who were well on their way. Coming around the corner of the second hallway, Turner saw Betty Armstrong waiting next to an open door. She waved in recognition. As they approached, she said, "Dr. Pierce is waiting inside." They went in.

"I'm over here, Mr. Turner." Partially hidden by a bookcase, Dr. Pierce was sitting at a gray steel desk, writing a lengthy report regarding Mineman First Class Richard Huwitt's treatment. He looked up and, pointing at a number of chairs near a small table, said, "I'll be with you soon, have a seat."

Two minutes later, Turner got up from his chair and began pacing. Ten minutes after that, Dr. Pierce finished his report and fastened it to an aluminum clipboard. He got up from the desk and walked over. Gallegos and Cole stood up. Turner introduced them to Dr. Pierce.

"Is this the remainder of your team?

"It is. What's the story on Huwitt?"

"We had to remove Huwitt's leg. He remains in critical condition. We are sending him on to Bethesda Naval Hospital in Maryland. There is a flight to Yorktown in two hours. He will be on it."

Cole sat back down. He put his elbows on his knees, his head in his hands. Turner didn't know what to say. Gallegos asked, "Is he conscious? Can we see him?"

"He comes and goes. We have him heavily sedated." Because of Huwitt's appearance, Pierce was about to say no to the request, but reconsidered. "You can see him for a few minutes. Lieutenant Armstrong, take the gentlemen to see our patient. No longer than two or three minutes." He returned to the desk, sat down, and began writing in another chart.

After Betty Armstrong ushered the men into Huwitt's darkened room, she left them alone with their comrade. The window shade was down, and a lamp on a long flexible neck near the head of Huwitt's bed provided the only light. They were shaken by what they saw.

There were tubes in each of his arms, an oxygen mask on a face that was unfamiliar. Where they should have been able to see the outline of his right leg under his blanket, the blanket was flat. Running out from under the blanket on the left side of the bed was a catheter containing urine. The urine ran down to a plastic bag hanging from a hook on the bed frame.

They were standing quietly when Betty Armstrong returned. She walked over to Turner and whispered, "Its time to go, Burt." They followed her out of the room.

In the hallway, she gave each of them a small bottle and said, "Dr. Pierce wants you to take two of these tonight. It will help you sleep." The three started down the hallway. She touched Turner's arm and said, "Phil wants to talk to you, Burt."

Turner sent his men on and went to Pierce's office.

Seeing Turner come in, Pierce got up from his desk, looked over at Betty Armstrong, and said, "Betty, why don't you leave Burt and me alone for a few minutes." She closed the door as she left the office.

They sat down. "Burt, you look awful. When did you sleep last?"

"I slept about two or three hours on a concrete floor last night."

"I guess you can't tell me what happened."

"I can't tell you what happened. But it wasn't just what happened to Huwitt." He paused then said, "I participated in a horror story beyond belief. You can't imagine what's going on, Phil."

Pierce replied, "Huwitt was conscious just before we put him under. He was rather incoherent, but he said something about terrorists, drifted off, came around again, and said you killed the one that shot him."

Turner's voice was quivering when he said, "You can't repeat that to anyone. Did anyone else hear what he said?"

"No, I don't think so."

Turner couldn't keep still. He got up and began to ramble. "They sent us out to do things we weren't trained for, and under circumstances that were probably illegal. People don't know how military power is used fraudulently. There is senseless slaughter and atrocities going on here and in Algeria." He sat down and immediately got up again. "You know, greed, religion, and stupidity are the engines that drive humans to unspeakable behavior."

He became unsteady and Pierce helped him to a chair. He sat a minute; then in a state of utter exhaustion, he ended his monologue with, "And you know, the imperialism of economics and religion is as alive today as it was a hundred years ago, a thousand years ago." There were tears in his eyes.

Pierce replied, "Yes, yes, I understand, but I want you to get some rest."

Turner responded by pulling his former fiancée's letter out of his pocket. He unfolded it and said, "Fuck. Then I got this." He handed the letter to Pierce.

Pierce read the letter, passed it back, and said, "I'm sorry, Burt. This on top of every thing else is unfortunate. Is Commander Hawkins giving you some time off?"

"Yes, he told me and my men to take two days off. Before I can take advantage of that, I have to appear at a debriefing tomorrow morning at Fleet Intelligence Center."

"Do you want me to write you a time-off chit for medical reasons, say for five days?"

"No, I'll be all right."

Pierce wasn't so sure about that. "It's 1800. What are you going to do now?"

"I'm going to go to my room and crash."

"Take the pills Betty gave you."

He looked at Pierce with bloodshot eyes and said, "Bullshit." Then he crumpled up the letter and, with the bottle of pills, threw both in a waste basket and left the room.

Pierce retrieved the letter and bottle of pills, then made a phone call to the office of Lieutenants Bob Miller and Ben Teipner. Completing that call, he made another to Lieutenant Mary Bionconi, who, along with Lieutenant Kathy Roberts, was cleaning up after assisting in a hernia operation on a rather obese navy chaplain.

An hour and a half later, Turner was sitting at his desk writing a letter, fourth try, to his former fiancée. Address unknown. He remained in his filthy utilities and boots, his body stinking of odor characteristic of a person who encountered absolute terror overlaid with the smell of gunfire.

There was a knock on the partly opened door. Before he could answer, the door was pushed open. Pierce, Miller and Teipner came in. Miller carried two bottles of wine (Chateau Vignelaure and Chateau Petrus); Teipner had four wineglasses, which he placed on the small table next to the desk.

Pierce, with great sincerity, stated, "We are on the horns of a dilemma. We have a chance to get a case of one of these very fine wines for a song. We are unable to buy a case of each. We must decide quickly because the airplane transporting these wines to Naples for a change of command ceremony will be leaving within the hour. We have made arrangements with a colleague who is driving this airplane to purchase from him one of the sixteen cases on board."

Turner, too tired to make conversation or question what was going on, watched as Miller covered the label of one of the bottles and partially filled each glass with wine. He watched as they picked up glasses, swished, sniffed, and drank. Turner just drank.

Pierce commented, "Unpretentious, lush and fruity."

Miller replied, "Sweet oak and balanced tannins."

Teipner, "All that, and a smooth velvety finish."

Pierce and Miller looked at Teipner and smiled in agreement. Turner nodded.

Teipner gathered up the empty glasses, went over to the small washbasin, rinsed and dried each, then returned the glasses to the small table.

Miller announced, "This is bottle number 2. Perhaps Dr. Lieutenant Pierce would enjoy filling our glasses?"

Pierce replied, "Of course."

As Pierce prepared to pour, Teipner distracted Turner by reaching for the unfinished letter on the desk.

Turner pushed the letter aside and said, "Not for you, airdale."

At that moment Pierce dropped two pills from the bottle Turner had thrown away in Pierce's office into Turner's wineglass and quickly filled the glass to the brim.

This second tasting was followed by another, and with that, Turner began to drift off.

Addressing his coconspirators, Pierce said, "It seems our gallant friend is soon to leave us. Shall we prepare him for bed?"

His friends helped him stand up, then walked him to the shower room, helped him take his clothes off, turned on a warm shower, and put him under it. Then they stripped down to their shorts and got into the shower with Turner. They lathered, rinsed, and toweled off their barely-able-to-stand friend. Then they helped him to his room and to bed.

Pierce gathered up the four unfinished letters, Teipner the wine bottles and glasses. Miller turned off the light, and the good Samaritans left the room. It was 2040 hours.

They made their way to Miller's room and sat down in their usual places. After a short discussion, they decided that the Chateau Petrus was preferred. Miller and Teipner left for the Operations building to meet one of the pilots of the plane going to Naples. Pierce, after tearing up Turner's unfinished letters, went on to chat with Mary Bionconi and Kathy Roberts in their quarters.

Turner woke with a slight headache. He looked at his watch. It was 0915; he had forty-five minutes to clean up, get dressed, and get to the Fleet Intelligence Center. He didn't know why, but he felt well rested. The only thing he could remember was having a glass of wine with Pierce, Miller, and Teipner. He got out of bed, stood up, and wondered where his shorts had gone. He always slept in his shorts. He threw the bed covers back. No shorts.

He took a damp towel from the rack next to the washbasin and, just before leaving his room for the showers, saw his filthy field uniform in a pile with his boots on top in the corner. In one of the boots was a rolled up sheet of paper. He went over and withdrew the sheet of paper from the boot and read:

> These clothes (and boots) are odoriferous to the point of being a public health hazard. Send these objects of clothing for fumigation/laundering quickly, or we will take this matter up with the NAS biological and chemical warfare people. This is disgusting, Mr. Turner!

The notification was signed "Your friends and colleagues." He smiled and went on to the showers.

After showering, he put on fresh shorts, a tee shirt and socks, then shaved and brushed his teeth. He wasn't sure if he should be wearing his full uniform or leaving the jacket off. He decided to wear full uniform—"dress canvas," a good choice. He looked at his watch and saw that he still had a half hour and decided to try to get something to eat. He left his room and stopped at a full-length mirror at the head of the stairs going down to the officers' mess. He checked himself out. His eyes were showing the effects of the previous thirty-eight hours; otherwise, he decided, he looked pretty good. The mirror didn't reflect his emotional state.

At the officers' mess, he ordered two pieces of toast and a glass of milk. He ate quickly and left the BOQ feeling a little light-headed, and his stomach felt queasy. He felt somewhat better when he pulled into the Fleet Intelligence Center parking lot. He parked his car, got out, and walked around to the front of the building. As he was going up the stairs to the entrance, he was surprised to see Chief Gallegos, in full uniform, waiting at the top.

Gallegos met him, saluted, and said, "Good morning, Mr. Turner. You look much better than when we left you yesterday."

Turner returned the salute and said, "So do you, Chief. I thought you didn't have to come to the debriefing."

Gallegos smiled and said, "Fry called and said Commander Hawkins thought it would look good if we were both on board."

"Was there any word on Huwitt?"

"He was flown out at 1930 hours. The doc on duty said there was no change in his condition."

They went into the building and were stopped by a marine guard stationed in the lobby. They showed him their IDs and asked where the meeting was, received directions, and went on to the second floor.

There were two armed marines at the door outside the meeting room, one sitting at a table, the other standing. The marine at the table asked to see their IDs; Turner and Gallegos fished them out of their pockets and handed them over. The marine checked their IDs against a list on a clipboard and asked them to sign in next to their names. As Turner signed in, he counted eleven participants, including the commander and the exec. He also recognized Captain Arthur Dillon and Lieutenant Bruce Franklin's names. One name, an army lieutenant colonel's, seemed familiar. There was also a woman's name.

After signing in, the marine at the table reminded them to always wear their IDs clipped to shirt or jacket while in the intelligence center. The second marine opened the door, and Turner and Gallegos entered the room. Inside, the participants were standing in two groups.

In the nearest group, Turner recognized Captain Dillon talking with Commander Hawkins and Lieutenant Commander Owens. There was another commander he didn't recognize. The exec saw Turner and Gallegos and motioned them over.

"Captain Dillon, do you remember Lieutenant JG Turner?" the exec asked.

Captain Dillon extended his hand. "Yes, of course. How are you Burt?" Turner shook hands with Dillon and replied, "I'm fine, sir." He didn't look fine to Dillon. Dillon asked, "And this is Chief—"

The exec added, "Gallegos, Chief Gallegos."

Captain Dillon shook Gallegos's hand and said, "You are Mr. Turner's main man?"

"We are each other's main man, sir."

"Well said, Chief," Dillon replied with a smile. He then introduced Commander Peeta, the commanding officer of the Fleet Intelligence Center at NAS, Port Lyautey.

Captain Dillon said, "The first hour is yours, Burt. Try to relax. I understand you had a rehearsal yesterday with Commander Hawkins and Lieutenant Commander Owens."

"Yes, sir, we did talk a bit. I hope I can answer everyone's questions."

"I am sure you will do fine."

As the others continued to talk, Turner looked around. There was a conference table covered with green felt with name cards designating seating places. The conference table could seat fourteen. Between the head of the table and the back wall was a small table with an overhead projector on it. The overhead projector was trained on a pull-down screen fastened to the far wall. To the right of the pull-down screen was a series of roll down maps.

There was a group standing near a small table with a coffee urn and a number of small white cups and saucers, each with a small blue anchor on the side and a thin blue line circling the edge of the cup and saucer. He recognized Lieutenant Bruce Franklin, the intelligence officer who was with Dillon during their first meeting. On this occasion, he was in uniform. Franklin was listening to an army officer talking with a marine major, a navy captain, and a woman who had to be the one on the list. The major and captain were in the way; he was unable to see the woman very well.

He looked over and noticed two large paintings, one on each side of the door he and Gallegos had passed through. He excused himself and walked over to the paintings. The one on the left, he had seen before; it was of Steven Decatur's sea battle with the Barbary pirates in the Mediterranean, off Tripoli. *Rather appropriate,* he thought. The other he hadn't seen before and thought it might be a sea battle in the War of 1812—the *Constitution* versus the *Guerriere?* He walked over to it and saw on the lower frame edge a small metal plate that read "War of 1812, *Constellation* vs. *Cyane,* the Atlantic, west of Morocco." *Right war, wrong ship.*

He looked back at the group near the coffee urn. The army officer was looking at him with a smile. He remembered—it was Lieutenant Colonel Pete Bennett, the army officer he had sat next to on his flight to Paris. He walked across the room.

"Hello, Lieutenant JG Burt Turner. You appear to be somewhat more shopworn than the last time we saw each other."

They shook hands, and Turner said, "Good to see you again, Lieutenant Colonel Bennett."

Bennett was about to introduce Franklin when Franklin said, "Hi, Burt, old man." They shook hands, then Franklin introduced the woman to him. "Burt, this is Laura Brae. She works with Lieutenant Colonel Bennett in Paris."

"I'm pleased to meet you, Ms. Laura Brae." He shook her hand; she made the obligatory smile.

"And this is Captain Andersen, the naval attaché with our embassy in Rabat. Last, but not least, Major Larsen, commanding officer of the marine detachment here."

"Pleased to meet you, Captain Andersen," he said, shaking the hand of the unsmiling and aloof naval attaché; then he shook hands with Major Larsen. Before he could greet the major, the major said, "Mr. Turner, you did very well in the Rif Mountains. Sergeant Major Forbes told me you rose to the challenge and were exceptional."

Turner was astonished; some color returned to his face, and his voice broke when he said, "Thank you, sir."

The naval attaché looked away at this without comment. Captain Dillon broke away from his group and announced, "I would like to start the debriefing. Please take your seats."

Captain Dillon took a seat at the head of the table. On one side of the table were the naval attaché, Commander Peetz, Lieutenant Colonel Bennett, and Laura Brae. On the other side were Commander Hawkins, Lieutenant Commander Owens, Major Larsen, and Lieutenant Franklin. Turner and Gallegos sat at the end of the table.

Captain Dillon introduced the participants. Turner was surprised to hear that Lieutenant Colonel Pete Bennett and Ms. Laura Brae were from the Central Intelligence Field Office in Paris. Ms. Brae was an analyst for North African and the Middle Eastern Affairs.

With the introductions made, Captain Dillon continued, "I would also like to keep this debriefing to about fifty minutes. This will allow us to have a ten-minute break before we start the 1100 meeting. The second meeting will provide us with some background to the current situation in North Africa and what appears to be a developing threat to our naval and air force forward bases in Morocco, Algeria, and Tunisia. Two air force officers representing Strategic Air Command interests will join us for the second meeting. A reminder, this session is classified Secret. No notes will be taken. Shall we begin?"

There was some shuffling as the participants found more comfortable sitting positions. Captain Dillon continued. "When the Fleet Intelligence Center received authorization to participate in a French special forces action against the terrorist group involved in the recent attack on the television station near Tangier, our planning team was pressed to put together the mission objectives and plan of action rather hurriedly because of a limited window of opportunity. The terrorists were on their way to the Igsenen area in the Rif Mountains for a short rest before going on to their Algerian base. This became the first mission of Operation Scorpion Fish.

"The object of the mission, the planners noted euphemistically, was to 'train in reconnaissance and surveillance procedures.' Actually, the mission was to secure intelligence on procedures and equipment used by French special force personnel in neutralizing terrorist operations preemptively or in retaliation after a terrorist action. In this case, it was in retaliation. It was equally important to secure intelligence about equipment used by the terrorists and, if possible, to find out if the terrorists were citizens of Morocco, Algeria, Tunisia, or elsewhere.

"This morning, we have all had a chance to see copies of Mr. Turner's notes concerning his SW/EOD team's observations in regard to yesterday's action in the Rif Mountains. His notes provide very interesting information."

Handing Turner's notebook to Commander Hawkins, Dillon said, "Commander Hawkins, will you please pass Mr. Turner's notebook down to him so he will be able to reference his notes as needed."

After Turner received his notebook, the first question was from Commander Peetz of Fleet Intelligence Center. "Mr. Turner, did Captain Salon fully inform you of his objectives for the mission and how it was to be carried out?"

"Yes, sir, he did. The briefing given to all participants was detailed, and he made sure we all understood."

Peetz pressed on, "When the action began, why was your team first to be involved?"

"We were first to be involved because we were first to be fired on, sir."

"You were told to observe and record what you saw. Captain Salon essentially told you to keep yourself and your team out of the way, but you and the chief fired the first shots."

"Sir, we were told to stay seventy-five meters behind the marine fire team that was positioned near the front of the house. We did that. We were also told that if we were fired on, we were to return fire 'enthusiastically.' We also did that."

"I would say that you certainly did return fire enthusiastically, Mr. Turner."

Turner didn't know how to take the comment. He was uncomfortable revisiting what he was trying to put out of his mind.

Captain Dillon asked, "In your notes, you say that during the briefing, Captain Salon said there were five terrorists. After the action, you note there were six bodies. Was there an explanation given about six versus five?"

"The sixth was a hashish farmer in residence at the house."

Captain Dillon continued, "You say in your notes that the weapons used by the terrorists were five Kalashnikov AK-47 submachine guns, and in the house were four RPG-2 rocket-propelled grenade launchers and rounds and an American 4.2 bazooka. How did you know what weapons these were?"

"We were taught about the rocket-propelled rounds at the EOD School, sir. The AK-47s were mentioned in conversation at the briefing."

Lieutenant Colonel Bennett asked, "Mr. Turner, was there any indication of the country of origin of the terrorists?"

"I don't know the country of origin for the terrorists. I do know they were on their way back to Algeria."

Bennett followed up with, "Is there any chance you might have seen the condition of their teeth and what their ages might have been?"

Turner didn't understand that. Bennett was trying to establish if any of the terrorists were of the upper class, privileged group or were lower. This would help knowing who was being recruited for terrorist training and where they were from.

After a pause, he said, "No, sir."

After a time, the questions, especially those from the naval attaché, were moving beyond Turner's notes, and his underlying exhaustion began to show in his responses. Turner was in difficulty. Laura Brae noticed what was happening. She leaned over and spoke quietly to Bennett.

"This man is in trouble. Help him."

Addressing Captain Dillon, Bennett said, "Sir, perhaps we could take a break for a few minutes?"

"We will adjourn for five minutes."

Knowing exactly what was happening, Gallegos took the young officer's arm and said, "Let's get out of here, sir."

They left the meeting room and went up the hallway to the nearest head. Turner rushed to a toilet and vomited toast and curdled milk, then dry heaved a number of times. With this over, he croaked, "I'm OK, Chief. It must be something I ate."

Gallegos helped him to a washbasin. "Yeah, I know, sir. It must be something you ate."

After Gallegos helped Turner clean himself up, they made their way back to the meeting room. Dillon, seeing them come in, said, "Would you all return to your seats."

Laura Brae was following Bennett to their seats, and as they passed, she looked up at Turner and lightly put her hand on his arm. "Are you feeling better, Lieutenant?"

He looked down at her and was going to speak when Gallegos answered for him. "He's feeling just fine ma'am." She smiled and removed her hand.

When everyone had returned to their seats, Dillon said, "Well, we all needed some air. Are you ready to answer the colonel's question, Mr. Turner?"

Turner looked awful, but he answered, "Yes, sir. I'd like to go back to Colonel Bennett's question. All the men seemed to be in their mid to late twenties except one. He had a lot of gray in his hair and beard. The female appeared to be in her early twenties. The female and one of the young males, I remember, appeared to have excellent teeth. The others had very poor teeth."

Peetz asked, "In your notes, you mentioned that Denoeu and Delcasse were not wearing the same uniforms as the legionnaires. Could you tell us what they were wearing?"

"Their clothing was brown, and they wore tan floppy hats. There was no sign of rank or unit. They had web belts, knives, and pistols like the rest of Salon's men."

"Did they appear to be part of Captain Salon's command?"

Turner paused, then said, "Captain Salon was in command of the action, but now that I think about it, Denoeu and Delcasse didn't seem to have as close a relationship with the uniformed men as the uniformed men had with each other."

"Did the uniformed men assist Denoeu and Delcasse in dealing with the dead bodies?"

"Only in stacking the bodies. The mutilation and desecration was by Denoeu and Delcasse, sir."

"You said that Denoeu and Delcasse searched and found a few papers in the house and the papers were associated with kif and hashish accounting. Do you know who ended up with those papers?"

"Sergeant Mogangi took the papers from Denoeu and gave them to Captain Salon. Captain Salon looked them over and gave them back to Denoeu, sir."

As the debriefing went on, Turner's confidence grew. He knew he was doing well when he saw some of the participants glance at each other in a rather positive way after answering their questions. A few times, he saw Commander Hawkins and his exec nudge each other and smile after he successfully answered a question they thought he might not be able to answer.

Unfortunately, his confidence began to unravel when the naval attaché fired a series of questions in quick succession: "Mr. Turner, did you attempt to stop the mutilation of the terrorist bodies?"

"No, sir."

"Were you concerned that the terrorists were not given a chance to surrender?"

"I was concerned, yes, sir"

"Why didn't you intervene if you were concerned?"

Before Turner could answer, Commander Hawkins looked at Dillon and said, "Captain Dillon, with all due respect, Captain Andersen is completely out of order, and I want him to bring to an end this line of questioning."

Turner and Gallegos were shocked. This was a formal debriefing in the presence of officers junior to the rank of captain and with representatives of the U.S. Army and U.S. Marine Corps in attendance. Actually, Dillon, Hawkins, and Peetz knew Captain Andersen very well. Dillon and Andersen were classmates at the Naval Academy (class of '45). Hawkins and Peetz had sea duty with Andersen when all three were junior officers serving on board the destroyer *Fletcher* during the Korean "police action." Most officers who served with Andersen knew him to be incompetent and a fool. Unfortunately, Andersen did have strong political connections.

The attaché blanched and stuttered, "I, sir, represent the United States Navy in our embassy in Rabat. The questions I ask and will continue to ask are not out of order!"

Captain Dillon turned to Captain Andersen and said, "Paul, the questions really are out of order. It was not appropriate for Mr. Turner to intervene in the methods pursued by what we knew to be the French Foreign Legion and Douzieme Bureau."

Turner looked at Gallegos and quietly asked, "What is the Douzieme Bureau?"

"I'll tell you later."

In order to try to give Andersen a chance to save face, Captain Dillon diplomatically asked, "Captain Andersen, earlier you and I were talking about the large amounts of money the terrorists or insurgents had access to, and you were very smart in tying the kif and hashish trade to financing terrorist activities. Mr. Turner may have something to say about this."

The naval attaché puffed himself up and said, "Ah yes. Mr. Turner, was there evidence of large amounts of money in the house that was assaulted?"

"I didn't see any evidence of money that may have been in the house or that may have come from the terrorists' clothing, sir."

Commander Hawkins acquired Dillon's attention and asked, "My exec and I have a series of questions to ask of Mr. Turner, and I see we are almost out of time."

Dillon replied, "Please go ahead, Commander."

Hawkins and Owens then asked Turner a number of leading questions, allowing Turner's responses to gain strength and become more informative. The remaining time was quickly used up, and the naval attaché was unable to ask further questions.

Dillon said, "It's 1050. We have ten minutes before we start again. Mr. Turner and Chief Gallegos, your conduct in this affair was exemplary. Thank you both." He added, "It is important that you both stay for the next session."

The debriefing was over, and no reference was made in regard to Turner's or Gallegos's shooting of the female terrorist. Additionally, the senior participants (other than the naval attaché) were made to appreciate that this young officer was quite capable of carrying out missions suggested for the EOD/SWD team as part of Operation Scorpion Fish.

Most of the participants left for a head call; the few staying behind went over to the coffee table. Hawkins and Owens met Turner and Gallegos at the coffee table. The exec said, "You did a helluva good job, Mr. Turner."

Color had returned to Turner's face, and he replied, "Thank you, sir, and thank you, Commander Hawkins, for bailing me out."

The commander thought for a minute, then quietly said, "Captain Andersen behaved inappropriately."

The exec added, "We may be hearing more from those in high places who support Captain Andersen, sir."

"We have friends in high places too, Don. Andersen had better watch his ass." Turning to Gallegos, the commander said, "I'm glad you were standing by here today, Chief. Mr. Turner is new to these things."

"Well, it was looking uncomfortable at times, but I knew Mr. Turner would get us through all right, sir."

"If the chief had not been here next to me I wouldn't have made it."

The exec looked beyond Turner toward the door. "Air force arriving, a lieutenant colonel and a first lieutenant."

Turner looked around and, in great surprise, saw the lieutenant was Joe Logan. "I know him!" he said, a little too loud.

Logan saw Turner and spoke to the lieutenant colonel; the two walked over to the four navy men.

"Hey, Burt Turner."

"Hey, Joe Logan."

They shook hands, and Turner introduced Logan to Commander Hawkins and Lieutenant Commander Owens. Logan introduced Lieutenant Colonel Knox.

Logan said, "Turner, you look like Commander Hawkins is working you pretty good."

Turner, with a tired laugh, replied, "He's working me pretty good, all right."

Turner and Logan excused themselves and walked away from the coffee table.

"What do they have you doing, Burt? You look like hell."

"I just got back from a mission, no sleep, and a lot of bad things happened. I just got debriefed."

"Why don't you come out to Sidi Slimane? I can show you around, and we can chat."

"I'd like to do that, Joe. Maybe we could talk in a roundabout way about things. I'll call you."

Everyone had returned. Some had taken their seats; the rest were standing around talking. Dillon took his place at the head of the table and asked everyone to be seated. The air force officers found their seats, where their name cards were newly placed, near Bennett and Laura Brae.

Dillon began, "I want to welcome our air force guests who just arrived by camel from their base at the edge of the Sahara." Obligatory laughter at this point. "Lieutenant Colonel Knox is officer in charge of the weapons division at Sidi Slimane Air Force Base, and Lieutenant Logan works for him as a loading officer. Both are Strategic Air Command officers. I have known Colonel Knox for about a year, and we have shared a few whiskeys and branch waters after meetings in Rabat. He is held in very high regard by naval officers who know him. Lieutenant Logan is one of those highly talented officers who slipped through our navy's Bureau of Personnel and joined the air force after graduating from the U.S. Naval Academy at Annapolis. He graduated with honors, by the way."

Logan, with raised eyebrows, looked across the table at Turner. Turner shrugged his shoulders and formed "I didn't tell anyone" with his mouth.

Then Captain Dillon said, "This meeting is classified Secret/Need to Know." He looked over at Bennett. "Colonel Bennett, it's your meeting."

Bennett rose from his chair and walked to the podium. "Thank you, Commander Dillon. We all know that the Arabs are winning the war of insurgency against French rule in North Africa. Morocco and Tunisia have recently achieved their independence, although there are some serious issues between the French and the Moroccan king, Mohammed Cinq, yet to be worked out.

"The continuing French presence here in Morocco is important in dealing with Algerian terrorist activities, which include: attacks on French commercial and military interests in Morocco, recruitment and training of young Moroccan men and women to become terrorists, and to interdict military supplies coming from Moroccan ports and transported across southern Morocco to the Western Sahara and Algeria.

"With the war between Arab nationalists and the French winding down, there is increasing evidence that Arab communists and Arab Muslim extremists are turning their attention to the presence of our naval and air force bases in North Africa. To them, our bases represent the beginnings of neocolonialism and neorepression. It is important for us to understand as much as we can about Arab culture and Arab aspirations. It is also important to understand we are coming at this late and may live to regret the fact. With that said, I want to turn this over to our North African analyst, Miss Laura Brae."

Laura Brae took Bennett's place at the podium. Although she had been in the room for more than an hour, Turner had been too tired to really look at her; she had just been there. He looked at her now. She was wearing a tan suit, a white blouse, tan pumps, a pearl necklace, and pearl earrings.

She was a rather tall woman, maybe about five feet seven inches. She was thin—not as thin as his former fiancée, but not as well filled out as Kathy Roberts. Kathy Roberts was not heavy, just more filled out. Laura Brae's dark brown hair went well with her tan suit. She appeared very sophisticated, and her bearing conveyed a high degree of self-confidence. He thought, *This woman isn't awed by the audience or anyone in it. She looks young, but she acts older. She isn't pretty or beautiful, but she is extremely attractive.*

She opened a small briefcase, removed a sheet of paper and two overhead projector transparencies, and put them on the podium shelf near the lamp. Then she reached into the breast pocket of her jacket, withdrew a pair of stylish glasses, and put them on.

She began, "Gentlemen, this briefing is in two parts. The first will be an abbreviated historical review of important events leading to what the Arab culture in North Africa and the Middle East is today. Then I want to talk to you about how Arab nationalism coupled with the rise of radical Islamic fundamentalism may impact our national interests in this geographic area. I assure you, this second part will more than adequately hold your attention."

An aide from the fleet intelligence media center dimmed the lights. She placed a transparency on the overhead projector glass and turned the projector on. The transparency listed a series of years, followed by a short statement on which she would elaborate. Turner overheard the attaché quietly say to nobody in particular, "That's all I need right now—a history lesson."

She began. "Most people believe that the Arabs originated in North Africa. In fact, the Arabs and the Islamic religion came to North Africa from the Middle East.

"Between AD 610-680, the Islamic religion spread rapidly through Persia, Egypt, and a large part of eastern North Africa. Then, about AD 681, Oqba ibn Nafi left Damascus and struck out across North Africa to Carthage—now Tunisia. A short time later, after defeating the Byzantines and Berbers, Oqba drove on to the Atlantic coast of Morocco. The Arabs and Islam had arrived in Tunisia, Algeria, and Morocco. Unfortunately for ibn Nafti, he couldn't hold on to the lands he just overran, and he slowly retreated east. He was killed by the Berbers before he could make his way back through Algeria. The Berbers and Byzantines were able to repulse this first Arab invasion. However, a second Arab invasion occurred about seventeen years later; this time, the Arabs became established across all of North Africa except for the area just east of the Atlas Mountains, in Algeria and southeast of Algeria to Mauritania, which remains principally Berber today."

She paused, and asked, "Do you have any questions or comments so far?" There were none. She changed transparencies and continued on.

Turner, in bad shape to begin with, started to nod off. Noticing this, Gallegos elbowed Turner strongly in the left chest.

Startled, he said in a low voice, "Oh shit, Chief. I'm OK."

Major Larson, who was nearby, had trouble keeping from laughing.

Laura Brae sensed what was going on and said, "We are almost finished. Please bear with me a little longer.

"If we jump ahead, to the 1700s, the Spanish and Portuguese were constantly fighting with the Arabs in Morocco and Algeria. In 1787, something quite interesting occurred in relation to the United States. Does any one remember what it was?"

Dillon quietly asked Peetz, "Do you remember, Tom?"

"I don't know if I ever knew.

Dillon looked around and, seeing no one else ready to answer, replied, "Decatur at Tripoli?"

"No, Captain. That was 1804," she said good-naturedly.

No one else took a chance.

Then Turner blurted out, "The treaty of peace and friendship George Washington signed with Mohammed III of Morocco. Morocco was the first country to recognize the United States."

Laura Brae gave Turner a long look, smiled, and said, "You are a very rare person, Lieutenant Turner."

Peetz leaned over to Dillon and said, "He pulled that one out of his ass, didn't he?"

"The kid's smart, Tom."

At the same time, Gallegos whispered to Turner, "You are a very rare person, Lieutenant Turner," and quietly laughed.

The semidarkness hid Turner's embarrassment.

Christ, what if I was wrong?

Laura Brae continued, "By 1907, Britain, France, Spain, Italy and Germany were involved in varying degrees in North Africa. The Moroccan tribes in particular were not taking the presence of Britain, France, and Spain very well and were in revolt. I emphasize the word tribes. Everyone should understand that the people of North African and Middle Eastern countries are, for the most part, tribal societies governed by sheiks ruling through tribal law based on the Koran, as interpreted by a Moslem cleric or Imam. I will speak about the importance of the interpretation of the Koran a little later.

"With the Moroccans in tribal revolt, Britain and France signed a treaty giving over Morocco to Britain and Algeria to France. Spain was given a small part of northern and southern Morocco. By 1912, Britain bowed out of Morocco. France regained control by protectorate treaty with Sultan Mulay Hafid, who was having serious problems with disruptive tribesmen.

France appointed General Marshal Lyautey to become resident general of Morocco. Lyautey was a strong royalist and showed great respect for Mulay Hafid's position as sultan, which resulted in a good working relationship between the two. Because of this relationship, Lyautey was able to modernize the roads and railroad system, and improve phosphate mining and launch countrywide medical services. He left Morocco in 1925, highly respected by the Moroccans.

"By 1926, Britain and France had hegemony from the Persian Gulf across North Africa to the Atlantic Ocean and had arbitrarily set the boundaries for the nations of the Middle East. The boundaries of Iraq, Iran, and Syria, for example, continue to be rather difficult to enforce because so many of the tribes are nomadic and there is a long tradition in smuggling.

"About 1940, young upper- and middle-class intellectuals in Morocco became restless under foreign occupation. In 1944, the Istiglal party had been formed and began the fight for independence. Eight years ago, assassinations and bombings were common in Casablanca. France began returning large numbers of military, mostly Foreign Legionnaires from what was French Indochina to once again fight against Arab nationalists and Arab communists in Morocco and Algeria.

"Six years ago, French farmers and other civilians, along with Arabs and Berbers sympathetic to France, were being murdered wholesale in Morocco and Algeria; atrocities were common on both sides.

Independence was gained by Morocco and Tunisia four years ago, and the fighting and atrocities continue in Algeria, at great expense to France." She turned off the overhead projector and asked, "Are there any comments or questions?"

Dillon spoke up. "It appears North Africa is in a constant state of turmoil."

"Probably not much different from other geopolitical areas around the globe, sir. What becomes a problem for us in the future in regard to North Africa and the Middle East is our nation's need for a secure source of oil. Our need for oil is increasing exponentially. Unfriendly or unstable North African and Middle Eastern governments will threaten our access to this energy source. A number of analysts feel that governments of many of the oil-producing nations will probably become radical Islamic fundamentalist, rather than secular nationalist, as colonial governments retire. A government based on radical Islamic fundamentalism will have an autocratic head, probably clerical, and will prove to be very difficult to do business with, by Western democracies."

She paused, then said, "Game theory tells us that, within forty-five years, we will be at war with one or more North African or Middle Eastern nations because of our need for a secure source of oil."

Turner wondered if any of these professional military officers were keeping up with what she was saying. He wasn't.

"Well, we seem to be in the second part of the briefing. Let me explain. So far, the policies of containment and deterrence have been successful in holding the Soviet Union at bay. Unfortunately, this success is based on concentrating our attention on preventing the spread of communism beyond the Soviet Union at the expense of seeing a new threat coming over the horizon. This is much like what aviators call target fascination, the phenomenon of concentrating so completely on a target or so completely on a difficult landing that one loses situation awareness to other stimuli resulting in a catastrophe.

"This new threat is regional instability, a consequence of the rise of nationalism since World War II. North Africans have tired of repression, exploitation, and humiliation and are overthrowing colonial governments or protectorate governments, leading to regional instability. For example, Gamal Abdel Nasser, by forcing the British out of Egypt, caused the Suez Canal crisis four years ago. The French are being forced out of Libya, Tunisia, Algeria, and Morocco. Our military bases in these countries play a major role in our country's strategic doctrine of containment and deterrence of the Soviet Union. It will be interesting to see how long we will be able to hold on to these military bases.

"On the other side of the world, the French were forced out of Indochina by nationalist and communist forces two years ago. It is uncertain at this time if this event is important to our national interests. We have sent advisors to what is now called Vietnam to evaluate the change.

"In this part of the world, we are considered by Arab communists and Arab Islamic fundamentalists to be neocolonialists, infidels taking the place of the French. We have evidence that they are turning their attention to our naval and air force bases. For example, currently, Colonel Knox is investigating an incident where a bunker in the conventional ammunition storage area at Sidi Slimane was broken into and two cases of bomb fuses were taken. The individuals that did this cut through a perimeter fence and made their way to the only ammunition bunker that held bomb fuses. Obviously, they knew exactly where the bomb fuses were stored."

Addressing Knox, she asked, "Colonel Knox, would you explain how you found out about the break-in and theft?"

Turner looked over at Logan; Logan shrugged his shoulders as if to say he didn't know about the incident.

"A week ago, our security patrol found the door of the bunker in question partially open. On investigation, they found that the padlock had been sawed off. When they entered the bunker, they saw that a number of crates near the door had been opened and then pushed aside. The patrol sergeant called me immediately. When I arrived, I checked the inventory list of the bunker and found two conventional bomb fuse cases were missing. A short time later, the security petrol found a large hole cut in the perimeter fence. Our security officer contacted the Moroccan police and reported the break-in and theft.

"The day before yesterday, there was an explosion at a village about two miles west of Sidi Slimane. Three men were rushed to our base for emergency treatment. One was dead on arrival. The other two are in critical condition. The Moroccan police investigated the explosion and found the three men brought in for emergency treatment had been using the stolen fuses for improvising explosive devices for terrorist activities. We have not been able find out if they were planning to use the devices against the French or against us. We are acting as though they planned to use them against us, and we are adopting more adequate security measures."

Laura Brae then held up a picture and said, "This is a picture from a feature story on Morocco in the *National Geographic* magazine, dated August, 1955—three years ago."

She held up a picture for a moment, then passed it around. There were a number of gasps from the audience. The picture showed an Arab worker with a broom standing about ten yards away from the front of a Strategic Air Command B-47 Stratojet.

Laura Brae continued, "Colonel Bennett and I attended a meeting at our embassy in Paris just before we left for Morocco. A representative of the State Department held up this picture and said, 'I sure hope this airplane was not on ready alert with a thermonuclear bomb in strike configuration on board.'

"Gentlemen, what you see here continues today at our air force and navy bases in Morocco, Algeria, and Tunisia. Part of our base rights agreement requires us to provide jobs for native laborers. Fair enough, but native workers are compromising base security. This is a serious problem. I am sure the intent of this picture was to show the 'old Morocco' in juxtaposition to the 'new Morocco.' Moroccan insurgents have seen this picture and considered it patronizing and a good example of neocolonialism.

"The majority of native Moroccans and Algerians do not consider us neocolonialists. They do consider us as a provider of jobs and a source of a lot of money through direct lease payments and loan guarantees. We have not yet won their hearts and minds as President Eisenhower asked us to do. If we do not make an effort to understand the Arab culture, we will continue to have misconceptions about who these people are, and our problems will grow in this part of the world."

Captain Andersen said, "Ms. Brae, your history lesson was very informative, and the CIA's threat analysis, very interesting. But I think there is little that can be done except protect our local interests and carry out our part in support of strategic doctrine. The business of nationalism and regional instability is the business of the State Department and Pentagon."

Commander Peetz of the Fleet Intelligence Center offered, "Ms. Brae, the information you just provided will go a long way for us to better understand Arab culture and Arab aspirations. We will be in a better position to hope for the best and prepare for the worst as we negotiate with our Arab hosts. I have a few questions. Why do you think a radical Islamic fundamentalist government, a theocracy rather than secular national government, may be the kind of government taking the place of colonial or protectorate governments in the countries of the Middle East and North Africa?"

"To begin with, the radical Islamic fundamentalist movement is a movement by a splinter group of the already-in-place traditional Islamic religion. The movement is militant and growing. Its mission is to isolate or remove non-Muslims and their societies from Arab lands. The cleric leaders of the movement are very charismatic and are marshaling support against moderate or liberal interpretation of the Koran. Once installed in government, the radical fundamentalist clerics will govern through literal interpretation of the Koran. The clerics will try to accomplish all this through a corruption of the movement called jihad. This does not bode well for formation of a secular government."

Peetz continued, "I think you are losing us. Why do you think the people will prefer a fundamentalist theocracy to secular national government? And if I may, what is jihad?"

"The people associate the secular nationalist government to recent or ongoing occupation by foreigners. Their culture, their tribal government, is based on Islamic teaching. It isn't a great leap to a government based on radical Islamic fundamentalism for a people who have only known repression.

"As to jihad, I generalize here. Jihad, as explained by Muhammad, is a peaceful struggle for each Muslim to be obedient to God, to be a better human being, to improve himself or herself, to support his or her community, to exercise a high degree of moral discipline, and, if need be, to rebel against an unjust ruler. You will hear jihad means 'holy war.' It is not a holy war. Jihad as a holy war is a construct of Western society. Jihad is a peaceful struggle, according to Mohammed."

Marine Major Larsen asked, "If they want to remove non-Muslims from their countries, who will run their infrastructures, their factories, utilities, and healthcare facilities?"

"We may be seeing the answer to your question here in Morocco. As the French have withdrawn, electric utility service has become unreliable, telephone service varies from place to place, television stations are nonfunctioning, and transportation is unpredictable. But Morocco is a constitutional monarchy and will move quickly to deal with these problems. Foreign investment will then come in, and business and industry will modernize. In a radical Islamic fundamentalist theocracy this evolution will occur with difficulty.

"Finally, I will end this briefing with one last look. People becoming radical Islamic fundamentalists are taught by their clerical leaders, the imams and mullahs, that piety and purity is more important than worldly experience and Western education. Imams are sinless, infallible Muslim leaders divinely appointed, and mullahs are quasi-clerical Muslim teachers. The literal interpretation of the Koran by a radical fundamentalist imam or mullah is the only interpretation. It is not unusual for a radical fundamentalist cleric to teach, 'If you try to understand the Koran on your own, you have committed a crime.'

"Muslim extremism is rooted in the educational system and taught in schools called madrasas. The madrasas teach youths the literal interpretation of the Koran and anti-Western, antimodern fundamentalism. There is very little math, and culturally induced scientific ignorance, or agnotology, is practiced. The history and literature taught is only in context with the literal interpretation of the Koran. The status of women in radical Islamic fundamentalist societies is deplorable. A nation ruled by radical Islamic fundamentalists considers modern knowledge and technology unimportant. In turn, that nation will become noncompetitive economically and a problem in regard to global economy."

As Turner watched and listened to Laura Brae, he realized he was seeing a young woman different than any he had known. She was different than anybody he had known.

There were a few more questions. Some were more like statements than questions, and latent bigotry surfaced.

Captain Dillon ended the meeting by saying, "Thank you, Ms. Brae. You have given us a lot to think about. I want to emphasize the classification of this meeting is Secret / Need to Know. Good day to you all."

Gallegos looked over at Turner and said, "Have you had enough, Mr. Turner?"

"I don't know if I should be laughing or crying, Chief. I need to get away from all this."

As they started toward the door, Joe Logan met them. "I can't talk now, Burt. I have to leave right away. Call me in the next few days, and we can talk about you coming out to Sidi Slimane."

They shook hands, and Joe Logan followed Lieutenant Colonel Knox out of the room.

Turner and Gallegos were almost to the door when Bennett and Laura Brae intercepted them. The lieutenant colonel said, "We are going over to the O club for lunch. Why don't you join us, Burt?"

Gallegos looked at Turner and said, "I'll see you later, sir. Call me if you need me."

Bennett looked at Gallegos and said, "I had a long talk with Commander Hawkins about the Rif Mountain situation. Just know I'd want you at my back if I were active in special ops again, Chief."

"I would be honored to be at your back. I am sure you could still do the job, sir."

"I'm too old, too slow, too smart, and too scared to do that stuff again, Chief."

Gallegos shook hands with Bennett and Laura Brae and went through the door.

Bennett asked again, "Why don't you join us, Burt."

"I'm really worn out, sir."

"Well, maybe next time."

"Yes, sir, maybe next time."

They were just going out the door when Laura Brae said, "Mr. Turner, we have to fly over to Oran and then on to Bizerte for meetings. We'll be back in four days, then layover here a day before flying back to Paris. We'll give you a call when we fly back."

She smiled, then she and Bennett walked on.

Turner looked back and saw he was the last to leave except for the aide from fleet intelligence media center. The aide had just finished putting the cart and overhead projector in a corner at the far side of the room. The aide saw Turner and said, "I suppose I shouldn't say this, but I've sat in on a lot of debriefings, sir. Yours was riveting. I hope things go well for you."

"Thank you, Petty Officer."

Turner went out the door, down the hall, and out of the building. Going down the steps, he saw Commander Hawkins and the exec waiting next to the commander's staff car, parked at the curb. The commander waved him over, "We've been waiting for you. You did well today, Mr. Turner." Looking at Turner very intently he continued, "You look like hell. I meant it when I said I don't want to see you or your team around for two days, starting now, understand?"

"Yes, sir, I understand." He saluted, the officers returned his salute, then he stood by until they drove away.

He walked around the building to his car, climbed in, started the engine, and just sat. Five minutes later, Major Larson was on his way out of the parking lot and saw Turner sitting in his car. He pulled up and called out his open window.

"You look like shit, Lieutenant. Go get something to eat. And for God's sake, get some sleep." The marine officer waved and drove on out of the parking lot.

Turner sat up straight, put the car in gear, and headed out of the parking lot for the BOQ.

An hour later, after changing into a rather worn sweatshirt with USC on the front, Levis, and gym shoes, he grabbed his duffle bag with his swim gear inside and headed for Mehdiya Beach. Before leaving the base, he stopped at the base cafe and bought a cheeseburger, fries (large), and a bottle of beer (Heineken) and put it all in the duffle bag.

Twenty-five minutes later, he parked his car near a sand dune at Mehdiya Beach, got out, and looked around to make sure there was no one nearby who might be interested in stealing the car's wheels and tires, or anything else. Satisfied the car was safe, he walked down the beach for a distance, stopped, and dropped his duffle bag on the loose sand. He looked up and down the beach; there was no one as far as the eye could see, as usual.

He pulled his swimming gear and a blue baseball hat out of the duffle bag, took off his clothes, and stuffed them in the duffle bag. He put on his jock, swimmer's shorts, and baseball hat and lay down on the warm sand with his bag as a headrest. Looking out to sea, there was nothing in sight except three seagulls gliding over the crest of a northwest swell about to break into a monstrous wave. The surf was up and coming in sets of four, as usual.

His mind was wandering. *This is where our troops landed or attempted to land during Operation Torch in World War II. This is where hundreds drowned because of someone's carelessness or stupidity or incompetence. I guess, when they plan these things, they anticipate a certain number of casualties and compensate for the loss by increasing the number of troops to accomplish the mission. The military's concern for the loss of life didn't last. It was important only to the relatives and friends of those drowned. They were informed the men they knew and loved died as heroes in combat. They didn't know they died in the surf of Mehdiya Beach without firing a shot in anger.*

When a guy is drafted into the service or volunteers, he doesn't have any sense of what could really happen to him until it's shoved in his face. I think the guys that were in the act of drowning experienced real terror. But maybe just trying to survive overcomes terror. One of our instructors at Key West said, "Everyone gets scared, nobody wants to subject themselves to getting hurt or getting dead. But you do what you have to do to get the job done."

Maybe bravery or courage is trying to do what has to be done even when your mind and body rebels against the challenge. If a person doesn't have the common sense to survive, if a person doesn't have to deal with overcoming fear, that person can't be said to have courage or to have been brave. Maybe this is applicable not only to those going into harm's way in combat, but also to those facing and dealing with life's problems generally.

I wonder if the terrorists in the Rif Mountains were scared. Maybe if a person is deeply religious or some kind of fanatic, it simply overrides self-preservation. I didn't think about self-preservation. I just reacted. That's not bravery. After it was all over, I was physically sick and mentally sick. I still am. I can still see the girl's eyes when she attacked us. They were wide in anger. The moment she got hit, she looked so surprised and just crumpled to the ground.

He sat up and used the back of his sandy hand to wipe the tears from his eyes. After a time, he got up, took off his hat, pulled his swim fins out of the duffle bag, and walked down to the water's edge. He looked out at the breaking surf for a moment, then put on his swim fins, worked his way through the shallow, rough water and foam, then swam out and met the first breaking wave.

He dove deep under it and felt the familiar increasing then decreasing pressure as the wave passed over him. Surfacing in the quiet water left behind, he had just enough time to catch his breath before going under the next wave. He repeated the sequence for the third and fourth waves and finally surfaced just beyond the surf line. Rolling over on his back, he slowly flutter kicked as his body rode the rising and falling incoming swells.

It wasn't long before he began to feel the warning chill of hypothermia. He caught a swell, and as it picked up speed, he saw he was at least twenty feet above the calmer water ahead.

Then the swell broke. He tumbled violently for a time, then as the wave began to lose force, he found himself caught in a riptide. He struggled against the riptide for a time, then let the current take him back out beyond the surf line.

Shit. Here I am without life jacket. If I don't get out of this water, I'll be too cold and tired to get out. Then he did what he was trained to do. He swam along the surf line for several hundred yards, felt the current fade, and caught a wave that carried him all the way into shallow water. He stood up, took a few steps, and the outgoing surge of water took the feet out from under him. He rolled around in foam and turbulence, struggled to get back on his feet, and went down again. This time he stayed down and caught an oncoming surge that carried him to the beach. He weakly got to his feet, staggered, and fell to the warm sand. He lay still for quite a while, then got up and slowly walked back up the beach.

When he got to his duffle bag, he reached in and lifted out the cheeseburger, fries, and bottle of beer. He opened the bottle of beer, took a drink and a bite of cheeseburger, and promptly vomited. He kicked sand over the vomit, walked away a bit, and lay down with the duffle bag under his head. *I could have killed myself out there.* A few minutes later, he was asleep.

He heard voices coming up the beach. It was Cole and Huwitt. Huwitt called out, "Hey, Mr. Turner. Surf's up. The chief told us to come and get you!"
"You guys can't be here. Huwitt, you're at Bethesda!"

He woke up with a jolt, rolled over, and saw the sun close to the horizon. Looking at his Rolex, he saw it was 1920. He got up and slowly made his way back to the water. After washing the sand off, he dried himself; put on his sweatshirt, baseball hat, and gym shoes; and walked to his car in his damp swimmer's shorts. The beer, cheeseburger, and fries were left behind.

When he got back to the BOQ, he parked his car in the parking lot and went up to his room. The door to Miller's room was open, and his three friends were having a little red wine (Ait Souala) after dinner. They heard Turner unlocking his door. Teipner got up and went into the hallway; Miller and Pierce followed. They walked up to Turner just as he was going into his room.

Teipner took one look at Turner and blurted out, "Where the hell have you been? You look awful."

"Burt, you really do look like shit warmed over," Miller agreed.

They followed him into his room. Pierce said, "From all appearances, I think our colleague from the Rif Mountains may have gone for a swim."

"As a matter of act, I did"

Pierce continued, "You look quite cold and unkempt. Perhaps we should again help you to a warm shower, then a little good wine and some comradely conversation. Has our good friend eaten anything in the last twenty-four hours?"

With some irritation, he answered, "I don't need help taking a shower, and I'm not hungry, just pretty tired."

He grabbed a bar of soap from the sink soap holder and walked naked to the shower room, his friends following as they talked quietly about what to do about Burt Turner.

He went to the nearest stall in the shower room, turned on the hot faucet and then the cold—but only a small amount of cold—and stood with his eyes closed, letting the hot water cascade over him.

As they stood next to the washbasins talking, they decided that some wine and light conversation before bed would be most helpful for Turner.

Teipner, noticing Turner hadn't brought a towel, went back to Turner's room, took a towel from the towel rack, and returned just as he got out of the shower stall.

Turner looked around and asked, "OK, what did you guys do with my towel?"

Teipner replied, "Here, sir, is your towel."

Turner dried off, wrapped the towel around his hips, and started back to his room.

Miller said, "Burt, come with us first."

The four went to Miller's room and took their places. Miller poured a glass of what was left of the Ait Souala and gave it to Turner. He took a sip, it tasted good and was comfortably warm going down.

Miller asked, "Were you at Mehdiya Beach with your team?"

"Yeah, I was at Mehdiya, but alone. I had to do some thinking."

Then Miller asked, "My copilot and I flew a woman and an army lieutenant colonel to Oran this morning. His name was Bennett. Do you know him?"

Before he could answer the question, Teipner bristled. "You ass, I'm not your copilot. It was your leg! You were my copilot on the way back."

"OK, I was pilot-in-command on the way, and you were pilot-in-command on the way back."

Turner tiredly replied, "They were at my debriefing this morning."

Miller and Teipner looked at each other. They didn't know about the debriefing. They knew better than to ask.

Teipner continued where Miller left off. "The lady asked a lot of questions about you. I think she wants to get in your pants."

Turner didn't answer. The conversation changed to rumors of insurgents attacking military personnel off base, and Turner began to nod off.

"I'm going to crash. I'll see you guys in the morning."

He finished his wine, washed the glass, put it on the shelf with other glasses, and left. When he got to his room, he put the towel back on the towel rack, put on a clean pair of shorts, turned off the light, and got into bed. The security light from the back of Fleet Weather Central shone dimly through the window. He was too tired to get up and pull the shade down. He rolled over on his side and fell into deep sleep.

It was about one in the morning when Kathy Roberts, in bare feet and a light dressing gown, quietly unlocked the door to Turner's room. She went in and closed and relocked the door.

The key to Turner's room was made available to Kathy Roberts by one of the BOQ stewards. Kathy Roberts and Mary Bionconi had made an arrangement with this particular steward to forget placing a notation in his health record that he was receiving penicillin shots for sexually transmitted disease. In turn, he was happy to accommodate them if they asked him for such things as a better desk lamp, a rug, or access to the BOQ kitchen late at night. In this case, it was a borrowed key, given to Kathy Roberts, for Lieutenant Turner's room.

She walked over and pulled down the shade. Then she went to his bed, looked down at him as he slept with his forearm over his eyes. She loosened her dressing gown and let it slide down the curves of her body to the floor. Then she carefully lifted the bed covers and slid in beside him. He woke up with a jolt. "What the fuck are you guys doing now?"

Kathy Roberts laughed and said, "Its me, Burt."

He rolled over, put his arms around her and his leg between hers. She put her face next to his and kissed his forehead. Then she kissed each cheek and moved her lips and mouth to his. He lifted his head away slightly and said, "I'm so surprised you're here. I never believed this could happen, Kathy."

She replied, "When you were leaving the hospital, I didn't want to let go of your hand. It wasn't long after you left when I wanted to see you again."

"It was hard for me to just leave. I wanted to stay with you—I'm in love you, Kathy."

She put her finger to his lips. "Please don't say that. I just want us to enjoy each other when we can. I don't want a relationship right now." She held her mouth to his ear and whispered, "Take off your shorts."

He had trouble taking off his shorts. He finally sat up, pulled them off, and threw them to the middle of the room. He fell into her raised arms, pulled slightly away, and with his fingers began touching her lightly over her breasts and then lightly over her body. After a short time, they made love.

Afterward, with her lips close to his ear, she asked, "Do you feel better now?"

He whispered, "Gosh, Kathy, better than ever."

They lay quietly in each other's arms for a time. Then she withdrew slightly and softly said, "Binki told me you looked awful when you came out of the Rif Mountains."

He didn't answer right away, then, rather guarded, he replied, "It was very bad, Kathy."

"Do you want to tell me a little about it?"

He hesitated, then rolled over on his back and quietly began telling her what he had experienced in the Rif Mountains. From time to time, with her hand resting on his chest, she would say a few words, helping him work his way through the trauma of his experience. She carefully explained that when Huwitt was being put under general anesthesia, he had mumbled about the Arab girl. She put her lips to his cheek and tasted his tears.

With the story told, they made love again. The second time was far more wonderful for both of them. They were together until 0430. They parted with difficulty.

Chapter 6

Turner had been at his desk since 0700, trying to make up for lost time. Since he had been assigned as the mine shop division officer as a collateral duty, it was his responsibility to sign off on all paperwork before it was sent to Commander Hawkins for his final signature. Warrant Officer Fulkerson actually ran the mine shop and generated the paperwork. He finished using his signature facsimile stamp on the last of fourteen orders for parts and maintenance materials that were needed by the mine shop, three of which were stamped Priority. He then started reading, initialing, and piling into his OUT box everyday kinds of messages from various navy bureaus and commands. He didn't understand 90 percent of what he read and initialed. When it came to messages originated by Commander Hawkins and the exec, he understood about 40 percent. Thanks to Yeoman Fry, the percentage went up somewhat from there.

He was beginning to understand that a junior officer does paperwork. It didn't matter if the junior officer was in a navy volunteer program such as EOD or not. He had yet to find out that a junior officer had better know what he signed or initialed because someone in due course would ask about the item in reference to some other outgoing or incoming message.

Periodically, he would stop and think about Kathy Roberts. Late the night before last, he had discreetly visited her room in the women's wing of the BOQ. They had decided that it would be much safer for him to go to her room than she to his. He had arrived at a prearranged time and had silently entered her unlocked door. They enjoyed each other. He thought, *When I was involved with Joan, it was work. This is so natural. I just want to be around her all the time. I should call her at the hospital. No, if I didn't get her directly, someone would ask who's calling, then we would be compromised.* He returned to his paperwork.

Forty minutes later, his phone rang. He answered it. "Lieutenant JG Turner speaking."

"Do you have a car, Lieutenant Turner?" a woman asked.

"I'm sorry, ma'am, who is this?"

She replied, "I'm sorry, it's Laura Brae."

"Oh, of course. I didn't recognize your voice." Then he asked lamely, "How are you?"

Ignoring his concern about her welfare, she replied, "We just flew in from Bizerte. The colonel has a meeting this afternoon with the air station commanding officer, and I am in between things. About ten miles north of Port Lyautey, there are some Roman ruins at Thamusida. Farther on, there is a little town called Sidi Allal el Tazi. Would you like to go see the ruins and el Tazi with me?"

He was taken by complete surprise.

"Lieutenant? I asked if you would like go to see Roman ruins this afternoon."

Without thinking he said, "Yes, of course, but I have a lot of work I have been trying to catch up on. It would be inappropriate to ask my CO for an afternoon off."

She cut him off with, "Lieutenant, I'll call back in ten minutes."

Five minutes later, Commander Hawkins called from the door of his office, "Mr. Turner, would you come in please?"

"Yes, sir."

Turner picked up a pencil and tablet, pushed back from his desk and went to the commander's office door. He paused, then went to the front of the commander's desk. "Yes, sir?"

"Mr. Turner, I just received a call from the CIA woman that was with Colonel Bennett at our meeting. Apparently, they are interested in place called Sidi Allal el Tazi, north of Thamusida, for some reason. She asked if you could be released to escort her there this afternoon. You will do that very thing. I offered my staff car, but she said it would better if the visit looked like two people on tour. You have Mr. Goss's old car?"

"Yes, sir."

"Wear civilian clothes and keep track of your mileage. You will be reimbursed. Here is her phone number. Any questions?"

"No, sir."

Turner walked back to his desk and sat down. He didn't know what hit him. Yeoman Fry glanced up from his desk and said, "You OK, sir?"

"Yeah, I have to make a phone call."

He looked at the phone number and saw it was the transient officers' quarters. He was about to lift the handset when the phone rang.

"Lieutenant JG Turner speaking."

"Lieutenant, pick me up at the officers' club in about forty-five minutes. I'll pick up some lunch for us, then we can be on our way."

Without another word, she hung up.

Yeoman Fry asked again, "Are you OK, Mr. Turner?"

"Yes, yes, I am all right."

Turner got up from his desk and left the offices. Thirty minutes later, he drove out of the BOQ parking dressed in somewhat faded jeans, soft Desert Boots, and a long-sleeved black tee shirt with "Marineland of the Pacific," in white across the chest.

It was a short drive from the BOQ to the officers' club. When he arrived, she was waiting at the curb, dressed in brown jeans, boots, a white blouse, dark glasses, and a white visor. Her hair was pulled back in a ponytail. Hanging from a strap on her shoulder was a medium-sized canvas bag. He reached over and opened the passenger door; she smiled and thanked him as she got in the car. After closing her door, she turned and looked closely at him. "You look a lot better than when I saw you last."

"I feel a lot better, ma'am."

"She smiled and said, "My name is Laura, OK, Burt?"

"OK, Laura."

She unzipped the bag in her lap and drew out a map, studied it for a minute, then leaned toward Turner and explained the route to Thamusida. She was close enough for him to smell the light fragrance of her sun-warmed hair.

"Any questions, Burt?"

He put the car in gear, pulled away from the curb, and, as he made a U-turn, repeated out loud the directions he was given.

At the main gate, the marine saluted the sticker on the driver's side of the windshield. Being out of uniform, Turner gestured with his hand in return of the marine's salute. The marine waved them on, and they drove out of the gate and headed north.

After leaving the city, they passed through a forest of short trees. He asked, "Do you know what kind of trees those are?"

"Cork trees."

"You mean, like for bottles?"

"Yes. They harvest the bark. The cork is used for all sorts of things, including bottle stoppers."

Periodically, they passed an Arab leading a donkey carrying an unbelievably large load of wood branches used for cooking fires. The coastal overcast was just lifting, and the temperature was rising. By 1300, it was going to be hot.

Near the Roman ruins of Thamusida, they turned off the paved road and followed a narrow dirt road a short distance to a parking lot. Turner pulled in and parked the car in the shade of a date palm tree near the entrance to the ruins. When they got out of the car, Turner looked around and said, "Not much of a crowd today."

"The ruins here are not much of an attraction for tourists, Burt. The ones at Volubilis, east of here, are far more elaborate."

He took the canvas bag from the car, slung it over his shoulder, and followed her. Just inside the entrance was an old Arab man and a young boy sitting in the shade of a low wall.

Laura smiled at the old man and said, "La-bas aalik?"

From under a frayed kaffiyeh, a leathery brown face cracked a toothless smile. "La-bas, hamdullah."

As they walked on, Turner asked, "You know the language?"

"Yes, Burt, I know the language."

He thought for a moment about the self-confidence and knowledge base she had displayed at the briefing. *Miss Brae is quite a package. I wonder why she wanted me to drive her to this place.*

After walking through a few of the ruins, she said, "It's almost noon. Let's have lunch at the top of the small hill over there. We'll be able to see the layout of the ruins better."

When they arrived at the top of the hill, they sat down under an old oak tree. She pointed to their right and said, "From what I had read, the shops and living areas were over there, and over to the left were the military installations."

He watched her unzip the canvas bag and lift out a bottle of white wine. Then she brought out two baguettes, Brie cheese, what looked to be a roll of sausage, a jackknife with a large blade and corkscrew, two wineglasses, and one very large napkin.

Using the knife, she deftly sectioned one of the baguettes then passed the knife on to him. He extracted the corkscrew, and began to remove the cork. Halfway out of the bottle's neck, the cork broke in two. He was able to pull the upper half out; the lower half stayed deep in the neck. Perplexed, he looked around and found a small twig, stuck it in the bottleneck and forced the cork down into the wine. He poured a sizable amount of wine, accompanied by small cork fragments, into each glass. She glanced at the cork bobbing in the bottle, turned, and seeing the look on his face, said, "Perhaps it was a faulty cork from the local cork forest."

They looked out over the ruins as they ate and drank; they didn't speak for a while. Then she looked at his shirt and asked, "What about you? Did you work at Marineland in Southern California?"

"Yes, for about five years."

"What did you do at Marineland?"

"I fed the fishes and cleaned algae off the viewing windows. The job led me into studying marine biology and paid for my classes at USC."

"Why did you join the navy?"

"I wasn't ready for graduate school, and the navy had some interesting programs." He smiled and added, "Besides, a kid growing up near the beaches of Southern California is always looking for the perfect wave.

He knew what the next question was going to be.

"Why did you choose to go into a volunteer program like explosive ordnance disposal?"

"When I was at Officer Candidate School, I heard about the SW/EOD program and its initial twelve weeks' training in self-contained underwater breathing apparatus and deep sea diving . . . and you also got to blow things up. What else could a guy want?"

She smiled at Turner's sense of humor.

"Do you have a girl back home waiting for you?"

"No. Do you have a guy waiting for you at home, or a guy in Paris?"

"Not really."

Actually, she was seeing, two or three times a month, a British Royal Air Force flying officer attached to the NATO Headquarters in Brussels.

The conversation turned to North Africa; she said, "If I remember right it, was in the eighth century BC that the Phoenicians from the eastern Mediterranean established a number of trading sites on the Moroccan coast. They introduced an alphabet and writing and, along with other valuable things, iron weapons."

"So the Phoenicians were involved in an eighth century BC arms race and tribal wars?"

"I guess so. Access to the best weapons and the alphabet probably didn't change the way people behaved."

She had a bit of Brie, a sip of wine, and continued.

"Then in the fourth century BC, the Romans made their appearance and later secured their position in North Africa by defeating the Carthaginians in

146 BC. However, about AD 400, the Roman Empire was falling apart, and they left. The Byzantines came in next and established themselves in Ceuta and Tangier. They stayed until the seventh century, when the Arabs arrived."

"Well, the Romans were here a long time. I guess they came back when they were known as Italians in the early 1900s." He turned away from her and looked out over the ruins. "'Plus ca change, plus c'est la meme chose.' Or something like that."

She laughed and said, "If you mean 'the more things change, the more they stay the same,' you got it, Burt."

"Laura, how do you know all these things?"

"I really liked history and geography in high school. After I graduated, I was fortunate to get a partial scholarship at Harvard, and in my second semester, I decided to enroll in the international studies program. During the program, I became interested in North Africa and the Middle East. And since languages came easy for me, I also minored in Arabic and Farsi languages. Seemed like a good idea at the time. During my senior year, I attended a job fair, interviewed with the federal government, and later was offered a scholarship to the American University in Cairo. I accepted enthusiastically and later received a master's degree in Arab studies. I was immediately hired by the CIA. After additional training, I was sent to the Paris field office and have been there for two years as an analyst."

"You are a very interesting woman, Laura Brae."

"You are very interesting yourself, Burt Turner. And you have an unusually nice grasp of history."

"Thank you. I wasn't a history major, but I took a lot of history classes because I really liked it."

"Yes, I know." She smiled and continued, "Your grades at USC were mediocre the first two years, then you seem to have taken ahold. It was A's and a few B's from then on."

He was astonished. "How did you know all that?"

"I know a great deal about you, Burt. Shall I go on?"

"Well, yes," he replied with some consternation.

She continued, but became more formal. "At OCS, you were average overall. In navigation, you were outstanding in coastal piloting and marginal in celestial navigation. You did show a high degree of initiative and resourcefulness. At Key West, you excelled in your training at the Underwater Swimmers School. Your initiative and resourcefulness was rated as Outstanding in your fitness report. In the long course at the Explosive Ordnance Disposal School at Indian Head, you were in the top ten in a class of twenty-four in conventional weapons, and in the last phase of training—nuclear weapons—you were fourth in the class of twenty-one. Again, initiative and resourcefulness showed up in the field problems outside the classroom. Your ability to focus on a problem and your attention to details was a highlight of your overall evaluation."

"You didn't get this information from my navy background check for security clearance. What's going on, Laura?"

She looked at him and said, "After a more intensive background check of recent officer graduates from the EOD School, your name and the name of three others appeared at the top of a short list. The reason for the search was to determine the most well-qualified men for assignment to Port Lyautey and Operation Scorpion Fish. Of the three, you and one other officer were selected. So here you are, and we hope the other officer will be here in the next few weeks with a second team."

"Just who the hell are you, Laura?"

"I work for Lieutenant Colonel Bennett and a number of other people in the CIA field office in Paris. Lieutenant Colonel Bennett introduced me as the North African analyst there, which I am. However, from time to time, I may become involved in a few other things."

"OK, so you are who you are. Why are you telling me about these other things?"

"On our way back from Bizerte and Oran, Lieutenant Colonel Bennett explained to me how impressed he was with you at your recent debriefing. He decided that you should know more about your place in the big picture here so you will not feel blindsided next time. After we landed, he asked me to explain a few things to you, like why you received orders to report to Port Lyautey."

With growing anger, he said, "When I first reported in at Port Lyautey, I was given six weeks to prepare my team for covert reconnaissance and surveillance operations in coastal areas and the desert. Instead, we were put in the field four weeks early, totally unprepared, with lousy weapons and no plan B if things went wrong. The people that did this to us are irresponsible fools who wanted to show the can-do spirit and look good in the eyes of the officers and politicians at the top of the food chain. We came away with the possibility of one of my men dying, the knowledge that we were involved in an atrocity, and that we were expendable. What bullshit. And here you are assigned to tell me that things are going to be better next time. Fuck! All this bullshit about seeing Roman ruins. This is really a business meeting."

"Well, it does seem that way, doesn't it? Actually, you and your team are not expendable. You are an asset that has to be carefully used and not wasted.

I didn't mislead you. I believe Commander Hawkins told you that we were interested in a town called Sidi Allel el Tazi."

"So here I am, your escort to Thamusida, with a nice picnic and another history lesson. What this is really about is you being assigned to make me feel good by explaining what my part is in the 'big picture.'"

"You're right, it is. And the powers that be don't even have to do that. Lieutenant Colonel Bennett, however, feels naval intelligence misused you and your team because of political pressure from the naval attaché's office in Rabat. Therefore, he felt we should give you as much information as possible right now to help you understand why you and your team are important. I'm the messenger sent to deliver that information to you."

Turner softened a bit and said, "So the messenger is an attractive woman bearing wine, baguettes, and cheese."

"Are you ready for me to continue, Burt?"

"Do I have a choice?"

She gave him a hard look. "Listen to me, Lieutenant. Someone is trying to help you. Be careful. I will finish this conversation by telling you that the Pentagon and State Department are very concerned about our tenuous situation in Morocco, Algeria, and Tunisia. We don't know how long we will be able to hold on to our forward bases here. Our navy and air force aircraft do not have the capability to deliver nuclear or thermonuclear weapons over long distances into the Russian heartland. Aircraft carrier task forces can come close with their planes, but the task forces need logistic support from forward bases close to their area of deployment. That's why Port Lyautey is important to the Sixth Fleet here in the Mediterranean. Air Force Strategic Air Command bombers and their fighter escorts have to have forward bases in Morocco, Algeria, and Tunisia to accomplish their missions. It is critical to hold on to these navy and air force forward bases for as long as possible.

"It will be at least two years before we have intercontinental ballistic missiles capable of striking Russia from the U.S. Once the ICBM's are operational, we can withdraw from these forward bases."

"Can we get to the point, Ms. Brae?"

"It was decided that a small number of navy and marine corps personnel should be fielded to collect information to be used by the Pentagon and State Department for threat analysis and development of contingency plans. The part played by these navy and marine corps personnel, although small as far as the big picture is concerned, is very important."

"I have no idea how useful the team would be in collecting information useful for contingency planning." The cynicism in his voice was obvious.

Patiently, she continued, "We have to know more about the French government and the French Army situation. If President Charles de Gaulle attempts to pull France out of Algeria, there is strong evidence that the French Army's Foreign Legion is planning to mutiny, and the French people at home will head into a civil war between those that want to stay in Algeria and those that want out. Those that want to stay are supporting the millions of French who have lived in Algeria for several generations. Additionally, France cannot financially afford to continue its occupation in Algeria. If the French leave, all signs indicate we will have difficulty staying.

"We have to know more about how the Russians are able to supply weapons to Arab terrorists, insurgents, or whatever name one wants to give these people, and we have to learn more about the dynamics of terrorism and counterterrorism.

"Your premature deployment into the Rif Mountains was a chance for us to gain some understanding of what this unconventional warfare is about. It was unfortunate that one of your men was seriously hurt, but the information you brought back is extremely important. Finally, the role you will be playing in Operation Scorpion Fish is still evolving."

"So we are not to reason why, we are just to do or die. My team will be used like guinea pigs in the still-evolving Operation Scorpion Fish."

She almost struck back at his insolence but thought better of it; instead, she picked up the remains of the picnic, put them in her bag, got up, and left Turner to his thoughts.

Ten minutes later, he walked up to the car and saw her sitting in the passenger seat, studying her map. He got in, started the engine, looked straight ahead, and waited.

Folding the map, she said, "We have evidence there's a terrorist cell at Sidi Allal el Tazi. Let's take a few minutes and drive through the town."

She gave him directions. There was no conversation for the next forty minutes.

Sidi Allal el Tazi was a busy small town with narrow trash-littered streets and small, shabby stucco-and-wood single and two-story buildings. Overhead, electrical wires formed a confused webbing between the buildings. Near the town center, adjacent to a small unremarkable park, were a number of residences protected by six- or seven-foot cinder block—stucco walls with broken glass embedded in plaster on top. Inside the walls, orange trees, heavy with fruit, were visible.

They drove by a few open-air vegetable and fruit stands, and on the corner of one block, they saw three women in djellabas and scarves haggling with a butcher over cuts of fly-smothered meat hanging from a hook.

After driving through the town, he said, "I think we have covered all the streets. Do you want to go round again?"

"I've seen enough, Burt. We can leave now."

A few miles from Port Lyautey, they heard the hi-lo sound of a siren coming from behind. Turner looked into the rearview mirror and saw a Moroccan police car, a Citroën, with red lights flashing. The police officer driving violently waved for Turner to pull over to the side of the road.

"Now what?" He pulled over, stopped, and turned off the engine. He looked back over his shoulder and saw the police officer getting out of the car. Through the Citroën's windshield, he could see a second uniformed man sitting in the passenger's seat. The police officer walked over and stopped a few feet from Turner's door. Putting his right hand on the gun in his holster, he extended his left hand and demanded, "Votre papiers, s'il vous plait!"

Turner took out his wallet and passed his driver's license card (California) and U.S. Navy ID card to the police officer.

The officer looked at the cards, turned, and walked back to the passenger's side of the police car. The window rolled down six or seven inches, a hand came out palm up, and the police officer gave the identification to the hand. A few minutes passed.

The car door finally opened, and out stepped a tall handsome Arab wearing an expensive tan uniform with green-and-gold lapel and cuff accents. The bill of his hat partially covered aviator sunglasses. Turner recognized the man as Port Lyautey's assistant chief of police, Lieutenant Hamid al-Karim. Al-Karim walked leisurely over to the Sprite, the police officer followed.

Turner greeted the police officer, "Good afternoon, Assistant Chief of Police al-Karim."

"So we meet again, Lieutenant Turner." Al-Karim glanced over at Laura Brae and asked, "Is this your young lady?"

"No, sir. She is a tourist friend, and we are just returning from visiting the Roman ruins at Thamusida."

Al-Karim looked at Laura Brae and introduced himself. He then asked, "May I see your papers please, mademoiselle?"

She took a small folder out of the side pocket of her canvas picnic bag, drew out her passport and identification card, and handed it to him. The ID card identified her as an exchange student working at the Musee d' Histoire Archeologique in Paris.

"So you are a student and a tourist?"

"Yes, sir. Actually, more of a student, a student of Moroccan archeology."

"I see," he said, returning her papers. He turned his attention back to Turner. "Lieutenant Turner, step out of the car."

Turner stepped out of the car and followed al-Karim a short distance away.

"When I saw this small car moving very rapidly, I recognized you as the driver and had my man pursue you." He handed Turner's papers back. "Lieutenant Turner, your papers do not allow you to drive on our Moroccan roads."

"But Americans have permission to drive on Moroccan roads."

"Ah, but they must be in their military uniforms, *n'est pas?*"

"I didn't know that."

"It is your requirement to know the conditions by which you are allowed to be in my country. You Americans come to Morocco as uninvited guests. You do not leave your bad habits as you enter. You behave as if you are still in the United States—"

Turner interrupted, "I think you are being unfair, sir."

"It is you who are being unfair. Your proud arrogance prevents you from attempting to understand Arab culture and the religion of Islam. You Americans do not understand the oppressive conditions Arabs tolerated for a hundred of years of colonization and exploitation by the French and Spanish."

Turner stood looking at al-Karim as he took the abusive language.

Al-Karim ended his monologue with, "Arabs are not ignorant and insignificant in the plan of things. Americans will feel the same cut from the same sword as your Europeans friends. It would be good if you would leave in company with your French infidel friends—inshallah."

His delivery was calm, he didn't raise his voice, and he didn't waste words.

Turner's limited experience with al-Karim, while assigned to shore patrol, had given him an incomplete understanding of this man. He was now made to realize that al-Karim was a man not to be trifled with. Unfortunately, the inexperience of youth and poor judgment prevailed.

"Assistant Police Chief, I don't agree with what you say about us. I—"

Interrupting Turner, al-Karim gave him a hard look and said, "I am sure you understand. You are not welcome here." He added with utter contempt, "I suggest you acquire a Carnet de Passages en Douanes, then you will be allowed to drive on our roads. Otherwise, stay away."

He turned and walked back to the Sprite with Turner following. With a friendly smile, he said, "Mademoiselle, perhaps you would find the Roman ruins at Volubilis near the city of Meknes more interesting than Thamusida. There is much more to see. The tile mosaics are quite beautiful."

"Thank you, officer," she replied.

He saluted Laura Brae, returned to his car, and gave the order to drive on.

Turner got into his car and sat with his hands clinching the steering wheel.

Laura said, "His English is very good, and he gets right to the point. He's right, you know."

"What is a Carnet de Passages en Douanes?" He asked.

"It's a type of international license that is accepted by a number of different countries."

He started the car and drove back to the base.

When they arrived at the front of the transient officers' quarters, Turner didn't make an effort to help Laura out of the car; she in turn didn't make an effort to give any importance to his existence as she got out.

She closed the car door and said, "I suggest you go to the base library and check out T. E. Lawrence's *Seven Pillars of Wisdom*. It may help you understand the Arab way."

She turned and crossed the lawn to the transient officers' quarters. He put the car in gear, and as he was driving away, he thought, *Bullshit. If she was trying to make me feel like an ignorant fool this afternoon, she succeeded.*

He drove up to NOF, checked his mail—two *Science* journals and a brochure from of Southeby's of London offering mohair suits at lowest prices of the year—then walked down the hall to the office complex and to his desk. He lost himself trying to catch up with the work he wasn't able to do in the morning. Then he got an idea. He called a friend at Fleet Weather Central and asked, "What's the weather forecast for tonight?"

He received more than he asked for, but found what he was interested in. The moon was going to be full and going down on the western horizon at 2010 hours, and a few cirrus-stratus clouds were expected. He called the transient officers' quarters. The desk steward answered, "Transient officers' quarters, sir."

"Ms. Laura Brae, please."

A moment later, she answered. "Laura Brae speaking."

"Laura, this is Burt Turner. I want to apologize for this afternoon."

"Isn't necessary, Lieutenant."

"I behaved very poorly, and I would like to see you this evening."

She almost hung up the phone, then without thinking, she said, "I'm having a very early morning flight out tomorrow. If you want to come by to satisfy your need to apologize, come early." As soon as she said this, she wished she hadn't.

"I'll pick you up in front of the transient officers' quarters at 1745."

There was a long a pause, then, "All right."

That evening he arrived five minutes early and waited another twenty minutes before she made her appearance. She didn't apologize for being late; he didn't appear to be concerned. He helped her into the car, got in, and drove the three miles down to the wharf, passed the AVR and parked at the wharf's end.

He got out of the car and went around and helped her out. Then he took two folding chairs and a parachute bag from behind the seats of the car and set up the chairs with the parachute bag between. She had walked to the edge of the wharf and was looking down the Oued Sebou to the ocean.

She turned and said, "The view is very beautiful from here."

He opened the parachute bag and withdrew a bottle of wine (Pinot Noir, Taylor, from the navy exchange) and two very beautiful wineglasses—courtesy of Phil Pierce and wrapped in hand towels—then a baguette, a chunk of Spanish cheese, and a small silver plate, courtesy of NOF, and his KA-BAR knife.

This time, he expertly removed the cork from the wine bottle and partially filled the glasses. Then he skillfully cut and placed small pieces of bread and cheese on the silver plate, and put the silver plate between them. They sat quietly sipping wine and sampling the bread and cheese as the moon slipped below the ocean horizon and stars became visible overhead.

They talked for almost two hours, mostly about home and friends. She found him not at all the boorish young officer he had earlier appeared to be and rather likable.

"It's pretty late. I better get you back."

"Yes, you should."

When they returned to the transient officers' quarters, he accompanied her to the front door. He touched her arm gently and said good night, then turned and walked away without giving her a chance to respond.

———————

It was 1400 hours, two days later. Turner was at his desk, trying to figure out how to write an official letter to the BuOrd (Bureau of Ordnance) using all the necessary references he could find (four so far) requesting a full allowance of equipment for a second SW/EOD team to be based at the Naval Ordnance Facility, at Port Lyautey, Morocco. He had already taken three drafts to Commander Hawkins for signature; all came back with extensive editing. At the top of the first page of the returned third draft was a scrawl in red.

> Mr. Turner, perhaps it would be appropriate to run this by Yeoman Fry for format checking, etc., etc., before it comes to my desk.
>
> In the future, it would be very appropriate for the exec to have a look at your effort before passing it on to me for any thoughts I might have.

There was a barely decipherable **GH** near the margin. The phone rang; he picked up the handset. "Turner speaking."

"Hey, Burt, it's me, Joe Logan. What are you doing?"

"I'm being schooled in the art of writing official letters. I'm not having a happy time, Joe."

"Well, I'm about to bail you out. My boss is sending your boss an invitation for you to come out to Sidi Slimane at 1200 hours tomorrow. The message should be at your place within the hour. Have your commanding officer send your security clearance to us this afternoon, and I'll pick you up at the main gate. Carolyn will fix us lunch, then I'll dazzle and amaze you. Wear your wash khakis."

"What a nice fellow you are, Joe Logan. Let me have a number where I can call you in case there is a problem."

Logan gave his phone number to Turner, then they talked a few minutes more before agreeing to see each other the next day.

About forty minutes later, a messenger from NAS Operations stood at the front of Yeoman Fry's desk with an envelope. Fry signed for it and carried the envelope into the exec's office. A few minutes later, the exec carried the message to the commander's office. Five minutes later, the commander called out, "Mr. Turner, would you come in here, please?

Turner thought, *Here we go.*

Inside the commander's office, the commander was handing the message back to exec after reading it.

He looked at Turner and said, "We have just received an invitation from Lieutenant Colonel Knox at Sidi Slimane for you to meet Lieutenant Joe Logan at 1200 hours tomorrow for a tour of the weapons maintenance, loading areas, and the 'ready-alert' aprons at the airbase. This is quite a coup, Mr. Turner. No one has had a tour of these areas since Don and I have been here. This is a great chance to develop a good, nonpolitical working relationship with the air force people. It would be nice to put all interservice rivalry aside and be useful to each other during these uncertain times. Be your diplomatic best, Mr. Turner. Don, would you have Yeoman Fry forward evidence of Mr. Turner's security clearance to Lieutenant Colonel Knox at Sidi Slimane?"

"Yes, sir, I will." Then the exec said, "Mr. Turner, why don't you call Lieutenant Logan and ask him what the uniform of the day is or what he might suggest it should be for you tomorrow."

With an unusually great smile, or at least unusual for the commander and the exec to have seen before, Turner replied, "Yes, sir, I'll be in contact with Lieutenant Logan."

After Turner left the commander's office, the commander looked over at the at the exec and said, "He seems to be recovering OK. What do you think, Don?"

"I don't know, sir. I think we keep him busy, that may help him clear his head before he and his team are sent out again." The exec thought for a moment, "Yes, I think we keep him busy."

"Well, once he has the AVR and helicopter in hand, he will be very busy getting ready for Larache. Any word yet about the Russian trawlers?"

"Fleet intelligence center said one passed Malta heading west this morning, sir. They will let us know if it heads south after clearing the straits of Gibraltar."

"On another subject, Mr. Turner seems to have a great deal of trouble doing his paperwork properly. Do you have any suggestions, Don?"

"Friday he and Yeoman Jenkins have the duty. During their twenty-four hours together, I'll have Jenkins intensively school Turner on appropriate format choice and how to use appropriate references in official communications."

"Don't we have a plane arriving Saturday morning?"

"Yes, sir, at 0530. Four birdcages and two suitcases. Turner is the courier."

"Good, what is the latest on Petty Officer Huwitt?"

"Commander Olsen, senior medical officer at the Naval Air Station hospital, left a message this morning that Bethesda reported Huwitt was still critical and fighting sepsis. He will keep us informed."

It was a little after1600 hours when Chief Gallegos and Petty Officer Cole appeared before Turner's desk. Turner looked up and said, "Well, here I am trying to figure out how to ask for and get a complete allocation of equipment for the second SW/EOD team with great difficulty, and I look up and see you guys looking carefree, relaxed, and probably plotting to increase my workload in some way."

Gallegos answered, "Sir, you misjudge us. We would like to lighten your workload."

"How so, Chief?"

"Cole and I would like to put the propeller shaft back on the AVR tomorrow morning."

There was a long pause. "You and Cole would like to do that, huh? What about me?"

"Well, sir, Boatswain Deacon and his men are very capable of lending a hand as needed, and if you could get away, you could be topside and watch."

"So I get to watch."

"Yes, sir."

"What time are you going to start?"

"All our gear will be in place by 0930, so we'll begin about then."

Turner thought for a minute, then said, "I see no reason for us to do our early morning workout at Mehdiya Beach. Do you agree, Chief?"

"I think putting the propeller shaft back on the AVR requires energy that should not be squandered in running and swimming. Additionally, the work on the AVR demands a high level of concentration to prevent the kind of accident you and Cole experienced when you removed the propeller shaft."

At this point Cole couldn't hold back. He laughed and said, "We can't squander energy that could lead to the loss of concentration, no, sir!"

The three lost control, Turner doubled up laughing at his desk. Gallegos tried to maintain some dignity and finally said, "I think that's enough, Cole."

The yeomen in the office were surprised at the scene. Lieutenant Van Buren was heard to say, "Unofficerlike, if you ask me."

Turner pulled himself together and said, "Well, let's get back to the AVR. I'll be at the wharf at 0900. I'll stay out of your way and just watch for a while. Lieutenant Logan is showing me around Sidi Slimane tomorrow, so I have to be there at noon. It's your show, Chief."

"I'm sure we will have the job finished before you leave, sir."

After Gallegos and Cole left the NOF office spaces, Turner decided that he had exhausted his ability to refine his fourth draft attempt of his BuOrd request. He closed and pushed aside two four-inch-thick loose-leaf binders containing copies of former requests and answers to queries. He had been studying them as he tried to develop a workable format for his own request. He put his yellow pad covered with numerous notes written in no. 2 pencil in his middle desk drawer. He stood up, walked over to Yeoman Fry, and said, "I'm securing now, Petty Officer. If anyone wants me, I'll be at the hospital seeing Dr. Pierce, then I'll be at the BOQ."

Yeoman Fry replied, "Mr. Turner, you worked hard today. What you're trying to learn isn't easy, but you will be surprised how easy it gets once you get the hang of it."

"Thanks. I'll keep trying."

———————

Turner was sitting next to Pierce's desk leafing through the *Textbook of Obstetrics and Gynecology* he had just pulled off a nearby shelf when Dr. Lieutenant Pierce came into his office.

"Are you having licentious thoughts, Mr. Turner?"

"Actually, the text and pictures lack sufficient prurient value." He put the book back with the others and asked, "Have you heard anything about Huwitt?"

"Huwitt has a fulminant infection. He's in critical condition, and they don't seem able to get ahead of the problem."

"What's your prognosis, Phil?"

"He will die."

"That's it? He will to die?"

"You asked my prognosis. I said he will die."

"Pierce, you are such a cold ass."

"Your man had the very best treatment. He was injured badly enough that he should have died in the Rif Mountains, but he didn't. You and the rest of us kept him alive. Now his immune system is being challenged beyond its capacity to respond to the infection."

"What about antibiotics?"

"Antibiotics are able to do great things, but one needs a strong response from the immune system too. Huwitt has fallen too far behind the power curve to survive. Let's go join our friends and colleagues. I've had a long day."

Dinner in the officers' mess that night was Chinese—sweet and sour pork, egg rolls, and some sort of slithery vegetable combination spread over noodles. Carafes of a nondescript white wine accompanied the dinner. They agreed the dinner tasted quite good, but the wine was unremarkable.

When their dinner plates were cleared by the stewards, and coffee and dessert (brownies) were being served, Mary Bionconi, Kathy Roberts, and Betty Armstrong crossed the room from where they had just finished dinner and sat in the unoccupied chairs next to their male friends. During meals, it was not uncommon to find unoccupied chairs next to Turner, Pierce, Miller, and Teipner. Other junior officers preferred not to appear to be their associates because the behavior of the four was often considered to be unprofessional and embarrassing at times. A steward served coffee and dessert to the women as Miller asked, "Does anyone want to catch a hop to Rota (a U.S. Naval base on the southwest coast of Spain) Friday night and come back Sunday noon?" Without waiting for an answer, he continued, "We could take the bus to Cadiz and check out the sherry at Jerez de la Frontera."

Binki added, "And catch some flamenco dancing."

Pierce, suddenly enthusiastic, said, "What a capital idea. Cape Trafalgar is only about ten miles (*actually twenty-five miles*) south, and we could look out and see where Nelson got the better of the French and Spanish fleets in 1805."

Turner added, "He got his death too."

He sat back and listened to his friends as they pulled together the details of the trip to Rota and Cadiz. Miller and Teipner had been there before and explained how the very best sherry in the world came from the vineyards of Jerez de la Frontera. They considered the possibility of going to a bullfight in Cadiz Saturday afternoon.

Binki asked Teipner, "Can you and Bob get us seats on the flight Friday night?"

"Miller and I will set it up with VR-24 and make sure we can all get seats."

It was becoming obvious that Turner was not participating in the discussion. Finally, Binki asked, "Burt, what about you?"

"I can't go. I've got the duty Friday and have to meet a plane from CONUS at 0530 Saturday morning."

Miller slammed his hand on the table and said, "Shit, Burt. They really ought to let up on you."

Turner was surprised to hear mutterings of agreement. He answered, "Look, the commander just gave me three days off. They give me a free hand with my team, and they don't go nuts if I want to do something they think is off the wall."

Pierce commented, "I think anyone who signs up for a volunteer program in the navy stands to be used and misused. If people in command use these people inappropriately or unnecessarily put them in harms way, that's the chance the individual takes. It would be naive to think otherwise."

In light of Turner's recent experience, the others were stunned by Pierce's words. Pierce continued, "After all, to stay qualified as a flight surgeon, I put myself in peril once a month by flying an airplane."

This statement defused his awful gaff, as Pierce knew it would.

Teipner laughed and said, "You put *us* in peril because you are not allowed to fly the airplane by yourself. No one else but Miller and I will fly with you, and we rely heavily on our situation awareness and our considerable skills to keep you from hurting yourself. We should be getting double flight pay when we fly with you."

Kathy Roberts joined in. "This is a wonderful example of wrongful discrimination. Burt gets hazardous duty pay for working with explosives and diving. But if we treat patients under fire, we don't get hazardous duty pay. You three guys get flight pay because flying is considered hazardous, but when we fly with you on an evacuation flight with one or more patients, we don't get flight pay.

The other two nurses joined in, and the three proceeded to overwhelm the men with their verbal skills and considerable logic.

Miller interrupted, "I suggest that we change the subject. I would like to invite you three women to join us men in my room where we can continue to chat. We have recently purchased a case of Chateau Petrus, and there are too many bottles unopened. We would like to share this extraordinary wine with you."

Betty looked at Kathy and Binki. Binki answered for all three of them. "How very generous of you. Of course!"

Kathy said, "We'll go up and change and get something to go with the wine and be over in about a half hour."

Forty-five minutes later, the women arrived with two large trays heaped with crackers, chunks of sourdough bread, and three medium-sized bowls of three different kinds of dip (courtesy of the officers' mess kitchen). Turner and Teipner got up and sat on the floor at each end of the couch while Kathy and Betty took their vacated seats. Kathy's right leg rested against Turner's left shoulder. Betty's left leg wasn't anywhere near Teipner's right shoulder. Miller gave the lounge chair to Binki and sat on the floor next to it. Pierce stayed with the Arab hassock.

The conversation returned to the upcoming weekend in Cadiz and Jerez de la Frontera. When the conversation began to wind down, Pierce started talking about how important it was to visit Cape Trafalgar and the site of the battle for which Admiral Horatio Nelson was noted. Teipner demonstrated his lack of interest with an artificial yawn. Then Pierce said something about the death of Nelson that caught his attention. He asked, "When he died, did the crew *really* put him in a cask of rum so he wouldn't spoil before he got back to England?"

"Several accounts say rum, but some say 'spirits' and some say alcohol. Take your pick."

Miller asked, "Was he killed by cannon fire or cutlass?"

"He was mortally wounded by a musket ball shot from the mizzen top of the French ship *Redoubtable*, which the *Victory* was engaging."

"Do they know where he got hit?" Miller asked.

"After going through the fore part of his left epaulet, the ball entered his shoulder and then lodged in his spine. As he lay on the quarterdeck, he said to his friend, 'They have done for me at last, Hardy. My backbone is shot through.'"

Betty asked, "Who was Hardy?"

Pierce was pleased with the interest that seemed to be developing, but before he could answer, Teipner said, "Hardy was the captain of the *Victory* and the best friend of Admiral Nelson, or Lord Nelson. Nelson used the *Victory* as his flagship when he took his fleet to fight the French and Spanish fleets."

Turner added, "He should have been wearing his sword."

They all looked at him in confusion, and he repeated, "Well, he should have worn his sword."

This comment caught Pierce with a large chunk of sourdough bread in his mouth; he sputtered and almost choked as he attempted to beat Turner to an explanation.

Turner laughed and said, "You shouldn't try to talk with your mouth full." Then he explained, "As Nelson was leaving his cabin to go up to the bridge to engage the French and Spanish fleets, his sword was not in its usual place. He didn't stop to look for it. This was the only battle where Nelson didn't wear his sword."

Teipner asked, "Did he die immediately?"

There was a rush to answer, but Miller was first to say, "They took him below decks to the midshipmen's berth, and he died about three hours later. A great man, a gentle man."

Pierce interjected, "But a man with an enormous ego."

Binki asked, "Didn't he lose an arm and an eye in earlier battles?"

Miller answered, "That he did. He had one eye, one arm, one asshole—asshole not derogatory in this case."

Pierce added, "He lost his eye in combat on the Island of Corsica, and his right arm at Tenerife."

The session became a question-and-answer exercise, testing knowledge about Admiral Horatio Nelson.

"What was his last message by signal flag?" Pierce asked.

Kathy cut the three men off with, "England expects every man will do his duty."

Then she fired off a question. "Nelson was having an affair with Lady Hamilton. What was her first name?"

No answer. "Her name was Emma," she said with derision.

Then another question from Kathy. "Was Emma of royalty?"

Miller answered, "She was Lady Hamilton. Obviously, she was from royalty."

Teipner echoed, "Royalty, of course."

Pierce looked disgusted and said, "She was a former nursery maid and as a teenager worked in a dubious establishment."

"Well done, Dr. Pierce. Tell me, did Nelson have children?" Kathy asked.

"He had a daughter, Horatia, not by his wife, Fanny Nisbet, but by Emma," Pierce answered.

"Anyone else?"

"Horatia always denied Emma was her mother, but she was proud to say Nelson was her father. He did adopt Fanny's son Josiah, though, and gave him a good start in the British navy," Turner replied.

Teipner asked, "I'm curious. Nelson didn't die of infection when they cut off his arm, and there were probably thousands of others who lost arms and legs in combat or surgery who didn't die of infection. Why did some live and others die?"

Binki answered, "Back then, wine and different kinds of botanicals were used to treat open wounds. I'm sure this treatment worked to some degree, but you still needed a really great immune system to survive. Lister, in the 1860s, was using carbolic acid as a disinfectant preoperatively. That could probably be considered the point in time when Western medical societies began to see lives could be saved by using a disinfectant. Things didn't really get going until Koch, in the 1870s, developed the germ theory. Before Lister and Koch, you would have to have had a great immune system to survive."

Pierce added, "This is exactly what we are concerned about with Turner's man, Huwitt. We hope he has a strong immune response to go with the antibiotics he's getting."

The conversation became far more serious as it shifted to what was happening in Morocco, Algeria, and Lebanon. With regard to Lebanon, information was leaking out from various commands on board the base that marines were to be deployed to Lebanon, and probably soon. If marines were to go ashore in Lebanon, everyone in the room would become involved in some way. Turner and his friends were getting a crash course in geopolitics. They were certainly developing a knowledge base that was far broader and deeper than what was available to their friends back home—that is, if their friends were even interested in North African and Middle Eastern affairs.

About midnight, Betty got up to leave and said, "OK. I'm tired now. I'm going to bed."

Binki and Kathy followed. The three women thanked their male friends for the wine and conversation and were on the way out the door when Miller got up and said in a commanding voice, "Wait! We shall escort you to your rooms. There could be uncouth young naval or marine corps officers waiting in the shadows."

They left Miller's room and were well down the hallway when Kathy said, "I left my room keys back in Bob's room."

Miller said, "The room's open. We'll wait for you."

"Go on, I'll catch up," she replied.

Turner said, "I'll go with her."

When they were almost to Miller's room, Kathy stopped at Turner's door and said, "Let's go in."

He stopped for a second, fumbled for his keys, found them, unlocked, and opened the door. They quickly went inside. As he was closing and locking the door, Kathy went to the window and pulled down the shade. She turned around; there was just enough light to see him waiting in the middle of the room. She went to him and put her arms around his neck and then pulled him down and kissed him. He responded by pulling her closer. Their thighs and upper bodies pressed tightly together as he kissed her; then they gently pushed each other away and hurriedly took their clothes off. He put his arms around her waist and pulled her closely to him again. She giggled and said, "From what I feel against my thigh, I think you are glad I'm here."

He said, "Sorry."

"Oh, don't be sorry."

She took his hand and led him into bed.

The next morning, Turner reported in to NOF, and after checking his paperwork, he told Yeoman Fry he would be down at the AVR with Chief Gallegos and Petty Officer Cole for a short time, then he would be at Sidi

Slimane Air Force Base for an orientation tour with Lieutenant Logan, the ordnance loading officer, from noon on.

When he arrived at the wharf, Gallegos and Cole were putting on their dry suits. He climbed down the ladder to the AVR, saluted the flag, then exchanged salutes with the AVR coxswain Petty Officer Deacon.

"Good morning, Chief Gallegos and Petty Officer Cole."

Both said, "Good morning, sir."

"Cole, how are your ears?"

"Just fine, Mr. Turner. One of the corpsmen at the dispensary looked at them and said it was OK to dive today.

Turner gave him a funny look, turned to Petty Officer Deacon, and asked, "Deacon, anybody on board smoke?"

The boat crew looked at each other in puzzlement; Gallegos and Cole knew what was coming.

"Yes, sir, we all smoke."

"Could I have a cigarette and a light please?"

Deacon pulled a pack of cigarettes (Camels) and a Zippo lighter from his jacket pocket and passed them to Turner. He drew out a cigarette from the pack, put it to his lips, flipped open the Zippo and lit the cigarette. He took at drag on the cigarette and passed it on to Cole and said, "OK, Cole, you know the drill."

The "drill" had to do with a technique deep sea divers could use to check for a perforated eardrum. The person suspected of having a perforated eardrum would take a drag on a cigarette, then hold the smoke in their mouth while applying enough pressure to puff out their cheeks. This would enable the smoke to pass up the eustachian tubes in the back of the mouth and on to the middle ear and the eardrum. In the event of a perforated eardrum, smoke would pass through the hole in the eardrum and to the outside. The subject would literally have smoke come out of the ear. Spectators who didn't know about this phenomenon couldn't believe what they saw, of course.

Unfortunately this is not a reliable test. Examining the eardrum with an otoscope was the gold standard for detecting a possible perforation. Unquestionably, an otoscope had been used to examine Cole's ear after the diving accident, but Cole good naturedly went through the drill. When no smoke passed from his ears, Cole was cleared to make the dive.

Turner said, "Cole, I trust you, but not your hospital corpsman friends."

They all laughed. Turner knew he had come a long way in a very short time in gaining the confidence of his team. Through the Rif Mountain experience, they had progressed from being NOF SW/EOD Team No.1, in name only and had become a team in fact.

Turner stood out of the way and watched them for about an hour, then left for the U.S. Air Force Base at Sidi Slimane.

When he arrived at the main gate, he saw First Lieutenant Joe Logan sitting in a jeep just inside the fence. It was 1145. The gate security guard, an airman, saluted and asked for Turner's ID card. Turner returned the salute and passed his ID card over to the airman, who turned and went into the guard shack. After comparing the name on the ID card with a list of names on a clipboard, he took a plastic visitor's pass from a drawer and walked back to Turner's car.

He passed the ID and visitor's pass to Turner and said, "Welcome to Sidi Slimane Air Force Base, sir. You are cleared to go anywhere on the base as long as you are accompanied by Lieutenant Logan. Wear this visitor's pass at all times. Turn it in at this gate as you leave. It is good until 1700 hours. You may drive your car inside and park it next to Lieutenant Logan's jeep. Have a good day, Lieutenant Turner."

They exchanged salutes; Turner drove in and parked next to the jeep.

"Welcome aboard, Burt Turner! Get in, and we'll go see the greatest show on earth."

As Turner climbed into the jeep, he said, "Joe, I'm already impressed. I've never experienced such a display of courtesy in a gate guard."

"In SAC, we are all exceptional." They both laughed.

"I'm taking you home to meet my wife, Carolyn. She's making lunch for us. After lunch, I'll take you on the grand tour."

As they drove, Logan pointed out administration buildings, the large station hospital, recreation centers (two), movie theater, the enlisted and junior officer quarters (temporary-looking), the senior officer's quarters (more permanent looking), the BOQ, and officers' club (excellent food and dances held with a live band every Saturday night), and an enormous post exchange and attached commissary.

"The post exchange," bragged Logan, "has everything one could want. We get items from all over Europe and quite a bit from the U.S. On Thursdays, the commissary even has head lettuce and white bread flown in from the States."

Turner was impressed. Head lettuce and American white bread, neither to be found in Morocco.

"You air force guys really know how to live."

"Well, it's actually General Curtis LeMay and Strategic Air Command who know how to treat the men. He takes very good care of his troops. He asks a lot of us, but he delivers a lot of good things too."

"A lot of people say that his philosophy is 'everything for the mission,' and in trying to accomplish the mission, aircrews and planes are expendable. That's asking a lot, Joe."

"Yeah, you're right. But if the mission is accomplished, the cost-benefit is acceptable, I guess."

Turner remembered when one of his history professors had lectured on the "softening up" of Japan in preparation for the American invasion at the end of World War II. General LeMay had planned and carried out firebomb raids against major Japanese population and industrial centers, killing more civilians than were killed by the atom bombs dropped on Hiroshima and Nagasaki combined. The cost to the U.S. was over four hundred B-29s and most of their twelve-man aircrews.

During class discussion after the lecture, the students decided that LeMay could have been tried as a war criminal if the U.S. had lost the war because he was responsible for the deaths of hundreds of thousands of Japanese civilians. LeMay himself had said, "We scorched and boiled and baked to death more people in Tokyo . . . than went up in vapor at Hiroshima and Nagasaki combined." Turner didn't pursue the subject of General Curtis LeMay any further.

Logan and Turner drove about a mile to the perimeter fence separating the main base from the airfield, then turned onto the perimeter fence road. They passed the control tower, a number of smaller buildings, and several hangars. He counted fourteen B-47s on the flight line. Passing the end of the runway, there was a large grove of trees with an opening big enough to accommodate a large aircraft. The grove of trees seemed out of place; there was nothing else like it on the base. They obviously had a purpose.

"What is that grove of trees over there all about. Are you hiding something?

"Yeah, we are hiding things. I'll show you after lunch."

The base was set up like a country club, with lawns everywhere. Many of the lawns and yards were being attended by Arab workers. A few minutes later, they arrived at the junior officers' residential area, about twenty houses, small and repetitive. A right turn, then a left, brought them to Joe Logan's house. He pulled the jeep over and parked at the curb.

"Here we are, Burt. Let's see what Carolyn has whipped up."

They got out of the car and walked up to the front door. Logan opened it and announced, "Air force and navy arriving."

After closing the door, Turner followed him into a medium-sized room that did duty as a living room and dining area. A voice came from the kitchen around the corner from the dining area, "Just a minute."

Then the most beautiful girl Turner had ever seen came from the kitchen. Blond, blue-eyed, and with an amazing figure. She was wearing navy blue linen slacks, a crisp white sleeveless blouse, red beads, earrings, and sandals. She stopped in front of them and, with a smile, said, "Ah, two handsome officers, one navy, the other air force." She walked over to Turner, extended her hand, and, with a soft Southern accent, warmly said, "Burt Turner, I'm Carolyn. Welcome to our humble air force home."

Turner took her hand and blurted out, "Of course you are Carolyn. And you are incredibly beautiful, just like Joe said!"

His felt his face warm up, knowing he had just acted like a crude jerk right off the waterfront. Logan was all smiles. Carolyn looked directly into Turner's eyes and said, "Joe, I am glad you brought Burt home. He's just as you said—really special."

It didn't help Turner regain his composure.

"Let me have your hats."

She took them and put them on a sideboard near the dining room table.

"You two sit down, and I'll bring in lunch. We are having swiss cheese and ham sandwiches and a little potato salad. Is that all right with you, Burt?"

"It sounds wonderful."

"You can have iced tea or lemonade."

"I'll have iced tea, please," he replied.

Logan said he would have iced tea too. Carolyn returned to the kitchen.

After they sat down and Turner was sure she wouldn't hear, he said, "I'm really sorry I made such an ass out of myself."

With a big grin, Logan replied, "Look, you only stated the obvious. You came right out and said what you thought. Besides, Carolyn likes people who don't fool around, or should I say, are direct."

Logan had previously filled his wife in on everything he knew about Turner, based on the conversations they had on the long flight across the Atlantic, as well as a few things (unclassified) that the two had talked about a few days ago at the meeting at the Naval Air Station at Port Lyautey.

A few minutes later, Carolyn came in from the kitchen with three plates. On each plate was a sandwich made up of ham, swiss cheese, and lettuce. The sandwich was cut diagonally and each half was held together with a toothpick (with a tiny ribbon). There was a pickle (dill) and a hemisphere of potato salad. Logan got up and accompanied his wife to the kitchen. They returned with three glasses of iced tea and two small ceramic containers—one with mustard, the other with mayonnaise. A small bowl of sugar, napkins, forks, and knives were already in place on the table.

As they ate lunch, Carolyn was quite successful in making Turner feel comfortable. She was very interested in the navy special weapons/explosive ordnance disposal program and made him feel exceptional because he was part of it.

She asked him about growing up in Southern California and working at Marineland of the Pacific. She had a lot of questions about what it was like going to a large school like USC. She explained to him that Mount St. Mary's College, where she had attended, was very much smaller, very old (1808) and nowhere near as cosmopolitan as USC.

"What's it like being an admiral's daughter?" he asked.

"Well, before my dad retired, it was like living in a wonderland and I was a princess. There were official dinners and parties, and I, being an only child, was quite spoiled. My dad was away from home a lot, and it was my mother who insisted that I become well educated and self-reliant to enable me to survive in a 'man's world.'"

Her husband laughed and added, "Her mother did a really good job."

Changing the subject, Carolyn asked, "Joe told me you had a fiancée back home. Her name is Joan, isn't it?"

He was caught off guard, but decided he wasn't uncomfortable with the question.

"Joan seems to have become involved with her major professor at school. She wrote a while back and said she didn't want to continue our relationship." He shrugged. "So that's all over."

Logan was at a loss for words. It appeared to Carolyn that Turner was not very upset about the dissolution of the relationship and knowingly said, "I'm afraid this is not a very unusual occurrence in the military, especially in the navy. My dad used to say, 'Sailors belong on ships, and ships belong at sea.' It is very difficult to preserve a relationship when partners are away from each other. I guess it's all about mutual commitment." She added, "Is there someone else yet, Burt ?"

Turner was slow to answer. "Ah . . . no, not really."

The conversation turned to air force and navy life in general, then on to complex issues in North Africa.

Turner was very taken by Carolyn Logan's intelligence and sophistication. He thought Joe Logan would go a long way in the air force with a woman like Carolyn at his side. In turn, Joe and Carolyn found Turner comfortable to be around—smart and with an unusual sense of decency. The two officers left about forty-five minutes later.

As they drove out of the junior officers' residential area, Logan went over the tour ahead.

"We'll go out to the magazine area first. I'll show you where the terrorists broke through the fence and got into the conventional bomb fuse magazine. After that, we'll go on to the grove of trees you're interested in and meet a plane coming in from CONUS. The plane should be down in about a half hour. Then we we'll visit our weapon maintenance and assembly area and, finally, go down to the flight line."

Two airmen security guards stopped them when they arrived at the magazine area; one had a handheld radio. The guards looked at their passes and saw both had the highest security clearance category, then asked for their ID cards. Accepting the cards, the airman with the radio called for permission to allow two officers entry into the magazine area. Permission was granted, the cards were handed back, salutes were exchanged, and the jeep was allowed to pass through.

Logan said, "That was a first. Just about anyone could drive through with just a wave before the break-in."

They drove along the perimeter fence about a mile to the newly repaired section, stopped the jeep, climbed out, and inspected the repair.

Logan stooped down and traced over the repaired section with his finger. "The terrorists cut here, horizontally, for about three feet, then cut about the same length down to the ground. Then they folded back this small section and squeezed through. After they stole the fuses, they squeezed back through the opening and carefully folded the panel back in place. They did this well enough to prevent our unsuspecting young security guards, who are always driving too fast along the perimeter fence, to detect the incursion."

He straightened up, looked through the fence, and said, "See the smoke over there on the horizon? That, my friend, is where the perpetrators came from. It's also where a lot of the Arabs who work on the base live. How do we tell the difference between terrorists and 'friendlies'?" They climbed back in the jeep, drove along the perimeter fence, and then turned off on a road with a line of bunkers on each side. Waving his hand over the area as they passed through it, Logan said, "These magazines contain conventional bombs, fuses, assisted takeoff bottles, ATO bottles, for the B-47s, and photoflash canisters for night aerial photography."

Stopping in front of a magazine, he continued, "Here it is. They sawed off the padlock, opened the door, got two cases of bomb fuses, closed the door, carefully hung the padlock back in place so the door still looked secured, and left. If they hadn't been injured when they were improvising bombs and booby traps, we would never have known about them being here until security noticed the fence or discovered the sawed off padlock, or maybe we wouldn't have known until the bunker was inventoried."

They got back in the jeep, drove back to the perimeter fence and on to the gate. At the gate, the security guards inspected the jeep. There was an exchange of salutes, and they were waved on. It took about fifteen minutes to get to the other side of the base, where they turned onto a road leading into the grove of trees Turner had asked about earlier. Just inside the grove, they stopped at another gate. This gate was guarded by three airmen: two at the gate, the other about ten yards inside, standing behind a .50-caliber machine gun mounted on a jeep. They went through the same entry routine as before and were waved on.

After driving about a hundred yards, the road opened onto an enormous asphalt quadrangle that formed the center of the grove of trees. The opening to the airfield runway Turner had seen earlier was to the right of the jeep as they drove in. In the far corner of the quadrangle, a recently arrived C-124 Globemaster was shutting down its engines. A large flatbed truck and another jeep waited close by. They drove up and parked near the C-124.

"This is the biggest cargo plane I've ever seen."

"It is big, isn't it? We can sit here and watch."

The flatbed truck maneuvered into position under the open cargo door at the rear of the airplane. Six ground crewmen, three on each side of the truck, stood looking up into the cargo space ten feet above. There was a whirring sound, and a platform with a cable at each corner slowly began lowering. The cargo on the platform came into view. It was a brown half-round container about ten feet long and seven feet high. Turner and Logan weren't close enough to read the few lines of yellow stenciling denoting the cargo and other pertinent information.

"So this is how you transport weapons. A C-124 flies in from the U.S., unloads here, and you strap them on board the B-47s. Why not just carry them in the B-47s when they deploy from the U.S.?"

"The B-47, even though it has six engines, really becomes a medium-range bomber because of the weight of the weapon it carries. It can't fly a very great distance without air-to-air refueling. There are also other limitations that make it impractical. When you said, 'strap on,' you don't know how close you were." Logan left it that.

They watched as the ground crew loaded and secured the cargo to the flatbed truck. With that accomplished, the flatbed truck, with the ground crewmen following in another truck, began to drive away.

Logan said, "They're going to my shop. We'll trail along."

They arrived at the weapon maintenance and assembly administration building, went inside, showed their credentials, and started down the hallway.

"Let's make a courtesy call on Lieutenant Colonel Knox first, then go to the shop."

They made their way to Lieutenant Colonel Knox's office complex, where an airman, recognizing Logan, announced their arrival. A few minutes later, they were shown in to his office. As they entered, Knox was ending a conversation with a warrant officer and a sergeant standing in front of his desk.

"Well, here is our visitor from the naval establishment."

He then introduced the warrant officer and sergeant as being important in the scheme of things in his weapons maintenance shop.

Then he asked, "Have you enjoyed your tour so far, Lieutenant?"

"Yes, sir. Lieutenant Logan has been a fine host. I have never been on board an air force base before and I appreciate your hospitality. Commander Hawkins sends his regards and would like to return the honor."

"Well, I would like to see his operation, or at least have Lieutenant Logan visit. Interservice rivalry is a serious problem at home. There is no place for it here. The environment is far too volatile. You never know when we might be able to help each other. Please tell Commander Hawkins we are interested in promoting a good relationship."

"Yes, sir, I will tell him. I am sure he will be happy to know how you feel."

"You might also tell the commander that we do not have an EOD team or officer on base. The nearest air force team is south of here, at the Nouasseur SAC airbase. Since you're so close, we may need you sometime, God forbid."

"I'm sure Commander Hawkins would be happy to send us to help in any way we could, sir."

"Well, I'm busy here. Lieutenant Logan, please continue the tour."

They left the building and walked over to the weapons maintenance building and went inside. With another showing of cards and passes, they walked through the office spaces where Joe Logan had a desk. They continued down a short hallway and through a door to the very large weapons maintenance and assembly area.

Turner stopped and said, "This is so much larger than our shop." Then he saw the weapons. "My god, you have TNs here!"

TN was the abbreviation for thermonuclear bomb, the so-called H-bomb in public vernacular. TNs produced explosive yields in the megaton (Mt) range through fusion reaction. The atomic bombs dropped on Hiroshima and Nagasaki were fission atomic bombs with yields in the kiloton (Kt) range. A one megaton yield is equivalent to a million tons of TNT; a one kiloton yield is equivalent to a thousand tons of TNT. The Hiroshima "Little Boy" had an explosive yield of about 15 Kt; the Nagasaki "Fat Man" had an explosive yield of about 18 Kt.

"Well, you guys have them on your carriers in the Mediterranean."

"Well, yes, but they are on carriers, not in a foreign country. And none of them are anywhere near the size of the MK-36s like you have here."

"Well, you guys have MK-28s on carriers, right? What else?"

"Maybe MK-39s. But MK-34 Lulus and MK-90 Bettys, for sure."

"What are Lulus and Bettys?"

"Depth charges. For antisubmarine warfare. They aren't TNs like the 36, 39, and 28."

"So you know a few of our air force weapons?"

"We know all that needs to be known about all our nuclear and thermonuclear weapons: navy, air force, and army."

"All?"

"All. Even a little about the Russian nukes."

Logan looked at Turner closely and asked, "How many detonators, what is the weight, and what is the explosive in the primary of the MK-36?"

"Forty-eight, seventeen thousand pounds, and a cyclitol combination."

"What's the yield and damage radius?"

"Depends on who you talk to. Could be between nine and ten megatons or nineteen megatons. Damage radius could be up to nineteen miles."

"Geez, Burt, you really know this stuff. They're taking the lid off the cargo that just came in. Let's go over and have a look."

They walked over and stood a short distance from where a crane was lifting the top off the container holding the weapon. A second crane lifted the weapon, attached to a heavy steel cart, out of the container and gently lowered it to the floor.

Turner said, "Well, you have another MK-36 for your stable."

Logan took Turner around his shop. They spent most of the time watching technicians test radar and barometric sensors associated with the fusing and firing systems, and in-flight insertion (IFI) systems for the plutonium capsule.

Tiring of this, Logan said, "Let's go out to the flight line and see airplanes."

Before being admitted to the flight line, the two officers went through yet another security check, this one more thorough than the previous ones. Finally, they were allowed to proceed. There were a number of aircrews dressed in blue flight suits closely examining their airplanes as they did their "walk-arounds."

Turner commented, "Their flight suits are different from navy flight suits."

Logan replied, "SAC crewmen have special flight suits and boots in case they have to walk out. They also have special maps and gold coins as part of their survival gear. The crews understand the missions could be one way."

"One way?"

"One way—'everything for the mission,' Burt. These B-47s are on alert, carrying thermonuclear weapons in the 'strike' configuration, and could be airborne in minutes. The bomb bay doors are open on that one over there. Let's take a look."

They walked over, stooped down slightly, and looked up into the bomb bay. Inside was an MK-36 thermonuclear bomb suspended by what look to be a wide, heavy chain mail belt around its middle.

Turner said, "That's an awfully tight fit. It looks like there's only an inch of clearance at each end and on the sides of the bomb. How do you get it in the bomb bay?"

"Very carefully, with a very large jacking system."

They bent down slightly and backed away from the bomb bay. Turner pointed to the underside of the fuselage near the tail, where a rack of assisted takeoff rockets were attached. He asked, "What's that all about?"

"Well, you know how heavy that bomb is, and you know how hot it gets here. The only way the B-47 can get off the ground in this heat and with that load is with the help of the ATO rockets. The rack is called a horse collar, which holds thirty ATO rockets, fifteen on each side. Once in the air, the rack and used-up ATO rockets are jettisoned."

They walked to the end of the flight line and stopped at a rather different-looking B-47. Turner asked, "What are those bulges on the wing tips, fuselage, and tail?"

"This airplane's an RB-47 Raven. The Raven collects electronic intelligence. Inside the bulges are sensors that detect radar emission frequencies produced by Russian radar sites. If we know the radar frequencies, we might be able to jam them, allowing our attacking planes to fly in and not be threatened by their fighters and surface to air missiles. It's risky business. A Raven has to get close into the Russian border and trigger the Russian radars. We have lost Ravens."

"How big is the crew on a Raven?"

"A B-47 has a crew of three, an RB-47 Raven has the three crewmen plus three electronic warfare officers."

"Where do the electronic warfare officers sit? There's no room."

"Ah, but there is. They sit with their electronic suite in a highly modified compartment that used to be the bomb bay. It's a very tight, uncomfortable fit, especially for an eight- to fourteen-hour mission."

"We have what we call a VQ squadron, flying A-3Ds, at Port Lyautey that have the same mission as the Ravens. I heard they lost one flying along the Turkish-Russian border a while ago."

Logan looked at his watch. "Well, this finishes the tour, Burt. I better get you back to the gate before they start looking for you."

Ten minutes before Turner's pass expired, they arrived at the main gate. Turner climbed out of the jeep and said, "You gave me a great afternoon, Joe. I owe you."

Logan smiled and replied, "I really enjoyed showing you around, Burt. Maybe you could take me for a boat ride or something."

"I can do that if you promise not to get seasick." They shook hands, and as he walked away, he looked back and said, "Give my best to Carolyn. She was wonderful."

At the guard shack, he gave his pass to the airman security guard; they exchanged salutes, he went to his car, started it, and drove out through the main gate.

On the road to Port Lyautey, he thought long and hard about a nuclear war.

The training I went through was as realistic as they could make it. But there is still such a disconnect between that training and being here, where everything is real, deadly, and ready to destroy and kill. Civilians have seen pictures of the destruction of Hiroshima and Nagasaki. Those bombs were small. The fireball and blast of thermonuclear weapons we have now will totally destroy everything out to ten or more miles in every direction. The radiation will be unimaginable. Targets are supposed to be military or maybe political, not populations of innocent people who die by tens of thousands or hundreds of thousands. Maybe the populations are not totally innocent—they support a war machine in one way or another. The firebombing and atomic bombing of Japan, the bombing of Dresden, of London and other cities, destroyed military targets along with killing enormous numbers of noncombatants—people in their homes and neighborhoods—collateral damage. I guess war has always been this way . . . we just use different weapons to get the job done. Life is cheap. I wonder how Huwitt is.

He passed near the village where they caught the terrorists that had stole the bomb fuses.

Now there is another kind of war. Unconventional, they call it. From the Atlantic to the Persian Gulf, insurgency by terrorism is the method of political change, and it's coming our way. The action of terrorism is only limited by the imagination of the terrorist. How do you get ahead of that? Captain Salon said that counterterrorism doesn't work—he may be right. If he is right, we can never get ahead of the problem. It's cost-effective for them in bodies and money and not cost-effective for us in trying to control it. The terrorists have control. That's why the French and British are losing in North Africa and the Middle East.

At this point, his thoughts turned to Kathy Roberts.

Chapter 7

Early Saturday morning, a light rain was falling as a weak weather front came in from the North Atlantic. Fleet Weather Central forecast mostly sunny with scattered clouds by late morning.

Chief Gallegos had the SW/EOD weapons carrier, with its windshield wipers grinding away, parked in front of the BOQ at 0445. At 0447, Lieutenant JG Burt Turner, carrying a clipboard and dressed in wash khakis and foul-weather jacket, bounded out of the building's front entrance, ran to the passenger side of the weapons carrier, opened the door, climbed in, and promptly sat down hard on a web belt and holstered Colt .45. The web belt and sidearm would complete his uniform as courier.

"Good morning, sir. I see you have found your sidearm, and are dressed for the weather."

"Good morning to you, Chief. I am dressed for the weather and I have a bruise on my left cheek that wasn't there before I got in this rattletrap. Thanks for picking up my sidearm."

Gallegos laughed and, as he pulled away from the curb, said, "In our business, we must always know where our butts are, or going to be, in case we have to find it with both hands. What precious cargo is coming in from Norfolk this morning?"

"According to my clipboard, four birdcages and two suitcases." He finished adjusting the web belt and holster around his waist and asked, "Did you get an estimated time of arrival?"

"I called Operations just before I left NOF. They said there was no word of ETA yet. How did you and Yeoman Jenkins get along yesterday?"

Turner took in a deep breath and let it out with a sigh and said, "Jenkins doesn't fool around. At 0800, he helped get me started on my stack of paperwork. Every so often, he would come back and look over what I had done, and after making suggestions, he would tell me, diplomatically, to do it over again. As the day wore on, he visited my desk less frequently, and I seemed to begin to understand the basics. By 2030, I was all caught up. He is a great teacher."

"So in twelve and a half hours, you learned the basics?"

"Well, actually I spent about forty-five minutes making the two mandatory patrol rounds in the magazine area and checked to see if any marines in the exclusion area guard towers were taking a nap."

"Those young kids do nod off at times. It is a long, boring four-hour watch," Gallegos replied.

"I did take a break to see some friends off as they left for a weekend in Spain."

Ten minutes later, Gallegos drove through the Operations building parking lot out onto the tarmac and parked next to the control tower. They sat in the weapons carrier for about twenty minutes, then Turner said, "It looks like there is no one around, Chief. Let's go over to Operations."

They left the weapons carrier and walked over to the Operations building. Once inside, they went down the hall to preflight and saw Captain Sid Travis—the Naval Air Station CO—the CO and exec of VR24 (the Europe and Mediterranean naval transport squadron), and Lieutenant Commander Bello at a large table, intently poring over a chart of the western North Atlantic and a second chart of the area west of Morocco, out to the Azores, and south to Madeira and the Canary Islands.

Turner quietly asked one of the enlisted men standing nearby, "What's all this about?"

"The R-6 that was inbound from Norfolk has not been heard from for over ten hours. Evidently, the plane may have been involved in a serious hurricane south of Nova Scotia."

Turner and Gallegos walked over and sat down in chairs near a large rain-streaked window that looked out at the flight line. The nearest aircraft that could be seen were the HUP helicopter, the SNB Twin Beech, and, almost lost in the dim light, a P-2V Neptune from the antisubmarine warfare patrol squadron.

A side door opened, and a lieutenant, accompanied by a gust of wind and rain, came in. Protruding from his raincoat was the end of a rolled-up chart. Turner recognized the officer as being attached to Fleet Weather Central. They exchanged nods, and the lieutenant took out the rolled-up chart, walked over, and stood quietly near Lieutenant Commander Bello. Bello looked up, took the chart, and said, "I have the most recent weather map of the area, sir."

He thanked the lieutenant and asked him to standby for questions. Then he unrolled the weather map and placed it on the table in front of Captain Travis. Travis pointed to a very large counterclockwise swirl of cloud cover moving east-northeast about eight hundred miles south of Greenland.

He asked the lieutenant, "How old is this map?"

"About fifteen minutes, sir."

"Compared to previous weather maps, the hurricane has moved well away from Newfoundland and has weakened considerably in the last two hours. Hopefully, our airplane flew southeast out of this mess and should be making landfall near us soon. They may have had radio transmission problems and couldn't contact us earlier." He looked at Bello and asked, "How much fuel do they have left at this juncture, Frank?"

"It depends on the headwind they may have experienced. Worst case, enough for about thirty minutes. Best case, enough for about an hour and fifteen minutes, sir."

"So if we or NAS Rota haven't heard from them by 0700?"

"We may have to presume they are lost."

The CO of VR-24 said with some hope, "They could have BINGOed (diverted) to the Azores or maybe to the Canaries."

Captain Travis answered, "We can hope so." He straightened up and asked, "How many souls on board, Frank?"

"A crew of five and a courier with nuclear material, sir."

"I'll be in quarters. Call me immediately if you hear anything."

"Yes, sir," Bello replied.

The captain left the building. The two VR-24 officers went to the other side of the room, where there was a coffee urn and mugs. They drew their coffee, sat down on a lounge near the plotting table, lit cigarettes, and prepared for a long wait. Bello dismissed the lieutenant from Fleet Weather Central and walked over to Turner and Gallegos; they stood up as he approached.

"I am sure you overheard the news. I would suggest you stick around until 0700. We will know for sure by then."

"Yes, sir, we will," Turner replied.

Bello turned and left the room. Turner and Gallegos looked at each other, then sat down.

"Shit, Chief, this is awful. You know they're gone."

"Yes, I suppose they are." He paused and thoughtfully said, "I don't think many young naval officers ever experience in a four-year enlistment what you have experienced in the last few months."

"I've had enough, Chief. I don't need any more."

"Mr. Turner, there are very few like you. What you bring to the table opens the door for things to happen. The military loves that characteristic in a young officer and will take advantage of it."

Turner didn't like what he heard.

Gallegos continued, "Here is the good news. The AVR is all squared away, fueled, and ready for sea."

Turner's outlook on things changed in a rush; he asked, "We should take it out this afternoon. Do you think we can arrange it?"

"It's Saturday, sir. We would have to find out if the crew is available. I don't know who they have on watch, but I can find out."

Turner backed up a bit and said, "I apologize, Chief. It's Saturday and you don't have the duty. I'm sure you have plans with your family."

"We didn't have anything planned until after 1500." His professionalism suppressed his own eagerness—almost. "Let's try for some sea duty, Mr. Turner."

At 0715, Turner and Gallegos left flight planning and went to Lieutenant Commander Bello's office down the hall. Bello and his yeoman were standing in front of the yeoman's desk, talking about a sheet of paper the yeoman was holding. Bello noticed the two men standing in the doorway and asked, "Is there something I can help you with?"

"Yes, sir. We are going to secure now unless there is something more you might need of us."

"No, Mr. Turner, you can secure." He turned away.

"Sir, there is something else."

Bello looked back over his shoulder, sighed, and asked, "And what is that, Mr. Turner?"

"The AVR has been repaired and is ready for sea. Next week, we will be using it for insertion and extraction training along with the HUP. Would it be possible for the chief and I to take it out for familiarization today?"

"Mr. Turner, it's Saturday."

"Sir, it would help us a lot to know what the boat's characteristics are before we begin to use it."

Bello turned around and looked at Turner, then with a wry smile, answered, "I admire you and your chief's dedication to duty." He turned back to his yeoman. "Who has the AVR duty today?"

The yeoman went to a large bulletin board on the wall near his desk, ran his finger down a list of names and places, stopped at AVR, and said, "Petty Officers Deacon and Jackson and Seaman Reed, sir."

"Well, you are in luck. Petty Officer Deacon will run the boat and you, Mr. Turner, are officer in command. Beach it or put it on the rocks, and it will be your ass."

"Yes, sir, I understand. It will be my ass. I'll be careful."

"What time do you plan on getting underway, Mr. Turner?"

"About 1100, sir."

Addressing his yeoman, he said, "Call Petty Officer Deacon and tell him Mr. Turner and Chief Gallegos will be taking the AVR out at 1100." Looking at Gallegos as a fellow professional, he added, "Don't let this young officer break my boat, Chief."

"I'm sure he will do fine, sir."

By 1045, the sun was out and the sky was scattered with fair-weather cumulus clouds, just as Fleet Weather Central predicted. The temperature was 78°F, and there was a slight breeze. After Gallegos parked the weapons carrier, he and Turner went down the gangplank to the AVR. They saluted the ensign at the stern and exchanged salutes with First Class Boatswain's Mate Deacon. As they boarded, the AVR's engines were idling, producing a powerful low rumble from the exhaust blowing out underwater.

With a great smile that exposed a gold tooth and large diastema, Deacon said, "Well, Mr. Turner, it's a fine day for a shake-down cruise. She hasn't been out for quite a while, but we have her engines running smooth, and we can shove off when you give the order. Hopefully, the propeller shaft won't fall off midchannel."

"The propeller shaft was installed by experts. We guarantee installation for a thousand miles, Petty Officer Deacon," Gallegos replied proudly.

The three men went up to the cockpit's open bridge. Deacon stood at the helm, Turner stood at Deacon's right, and Gallegos stood somewhat farther to the right of Turner. Deacon looked at Turner expectantly. Turner cleared his throat and ordered, "Lets get underway, Coxswain."

"Aye, aye, sir." And called out, "Cast off, fore and aft."

Jackson and Reed hauled in the fore and aft lines. Deacon opened the throttles slightly, turned the helm to port, added more power, and started down the Oued Sebou at five knots.

"The tide is coming upstream, and the sea condition out there is very friendly. I'll take her out and give you the helm after a bit, sir."

Turner was more than flattered. He, with no seagoing experience, was going to be at the helm of a sixty-three-foot fast boat just slightly smaller than one of the old PT boats of World War II fame.

The Oued Sebou opened to the sea about two miles downstream from the wharf. As they closed to the mouth of the river, swells from the sea became more pronounced, and the AVR yawed and rolled increasingly. Once out at sea, Deacon carefully opened the throttles by increments, making sure the engines responded properly after their long period of inactivity. Finally, the hull speed was fast enough to lift the bow and cause the AVR to plane, and the yawing and rolling came to an end. Turner felt the power of the boat through his feet and legs as it picked up speed. He tightened his grip on the grab rail just below the windscreen and broke out in a big grin.

Deacon took the AVR well beyond the surf line, then turned north. After running the boat at different throttle settings for a time, he opened the throttles wide and, yelling above the wind and engine noise, said, "Mr. Turner, the top speed of the AVR is twenty-eight knots. We are doing thirty knots!"

Deacon put the AVR in a series of turns and varying speeds, straightened the AVR out, and asked, "Mr. Turner, is there any particular place you would like to go?"

"I'd like to cruise just outside the surf line and see what the conditions are, just as if we might be getting ready to get dropped off and swim in to the beach. I'd like to do the same thing off the rocky shoreline just ahead."

After about forty minutes, Turner asked the chief, "Do you think we have seen enough, Chief?"

"We should have a look at the point just ahead. Wind and current around a point like that could be a problem with a small raft or if we have to swim near it."

Deacon, overhearing the request, took a bearing on the point, and added speed. A few minutes later, he put the AVR just off the point. He slowed the boat until it was barely underway and it began to yaw and roll. Turner almost lost his footing several times and began to feel queasy.

Gallegos lifted a set of binoculars from the shelf under the windscreen and studied the current going around the point. He lowered the binoculars, looked at Turner, and said, "I think we could handle this sort of thing if we had to. Are you all right, Mr. Turner?"

"I'm OK. Can we get closer and get a better look at the current going around the point, Coxswain?"

"Aye, aye, sir."

Deacon came up in the lee of the point, throttled back, and let the current take them backward. Then he powered forward. As they began to round the point, Deacon had to add more power to overcome the wind and current.

Gallegos said, "We don't need to scare ourselves trying to swim or paddle our way through that."

Just as they rounded the point, they were surprised by three sea lions that began barking loudly at the intrusion of the AVR. The sea lions were just in front of a shallow cave five feet above the water. Deacon throttled back and, after everyone had a good look, said, "Why don't you take us home, Mr. Turner?" and moved away from the helm.

Turner took over the helm. He advanced the throttles too quickly and jerked the AVR's bow up.

Deacon called out, "Easy, Mr. Turner, we aren't going to the moon."

Turner, embarrassed at his inexperience in boat handling, throttled back and cruised at a lower speed, still fast, but acceptable. As he began to get the feel of he boat, his queasiness disappeared. He made wide turns, then sharper turns, then wide circles, then tighter circles and figure eights at various throttle settings. Deacon and Gallegos looked at each other with raised eyebrows, surprised at Turner's determination and sharp learning curve.

Forty minutes later, the wind was stronger and generating a significant chop with whitecaps. Turner made an approach to the mouth of the Oued Sebou and turned the helm over to Deacon. A short time later, the AVR was secure at its moorings wharf side. It was 1345. Everyone was well pleased about the AVR's performance, especially Coxswain Deacon.

Late Sunday night, Turner was sitting in an the easy chair next to his desk reading Steinbeck's *The Log from the Sea of Cortez*. It was a quiet night, and he left his door open to catch the cross breeze from the hallway. He put the book down in his lap and was thinking about what he had just read when he heard the unmistakable voices of Miller and Teipner echoing up the hallway. They had returned from their weekend in southern Spain.

He heard Pierce say, "You two should quiet down. There are people trying to sleep."

Teipner replied in a lowered voice, "Miller is displaying his usual arrogance and disrespect for others."

Turner got up from his chair and met them at his doorway. "Welcome home, my good friends. Did you bring me some expensive souvenirs?"

Miller replied, "Why would we do that, old sock?"

"Because I am the only one standing between you and Arab terrorists and their Russian friends."

Actually, he was very close to being right about what he said, but didn't know it.

Miller laughed and said, "After my fellow travelers have dumped their gear, I'd like to invite everyone to my quarters and we can tell our esteemed courier, frogman, and overworked naval officer of our adventure in the land of Don Quixote."

There was agreement all around.

A half hour later, they were sitting in their usual places in Miller's room. They all wore yellow leather Arab slippers—heel flap turned down, as was the custom. Miller and Teipner had changed into tight-at-the ankle baggy Arab pants and loose-fitting long-sleeved cotton shirts. Pierce wore black-and-white checked pajamas buttoned to the neck. Turner remained in his dark blue sweat pants and USC sweatshirt.

Miller got up and, with great ceremony, presented Turner with a bottle of sherry, saying, "We really missed you, damn it. This bottle of sherry is from Jerez de la Frontera. It is the finest sherry in the world."

Taking it, he said, "My gosh, Bob, this really is nice."

Teipner got up and said, "You have to be with us next time, Burt." And gave him a cut glass decanter. "It's for the sherry, from both of us."

"Thank you."

Pierce reached over and gave Turner a leather bota bag. "I wouldn't put sherry in this, Burt—too sweet. Cheap wine would be just fine."

"Thanks, Phil."

Seeing that Turner was displaying some awkwardness with the friendly gestures, Pierce said, "I must tell you about Cape Trafalgar. We rented a car in Cadiz and drove about forty miles south to a place called Vejer de la Frontera."

"It was Barbate de Franco, Dr. Pierce," Teipner said.

"Yes, of course, Barbate de Franco. Anyway, the sun was bright, the wind was up, and the ocean was showing some turbulence. The scene reminded me of Debussy's *La Mer*. The first part, 'De l'Aube a Midi sur la Mer.'"

Teipner interrupted, "Daybreak and Afternoon on the Sea."

"We all know that, Ben," Miller replied.

Pierce continued, "Looking out over the water, it was difficult to believe there was once a sea battle fought out there with an enormous loss of life and ships. A sea battle that changed the course of history."

"What about the girls? Did they enjoy the scene with you?"

"They stayed in Cadiz and spent lots of money shopping and watching flamenco dancers," Miller replied.

"Saturday, we saw a bullfight," Teipner added.

A discussion ensued concerning the art of bullfighting, how toreadors do not want for female companionship because of their lifestyle, and whether or not poor people actually receive the dead bull carcasses.

Changing the subject, Pierce said, "Probably the best part of the trip was going through the wineries in Jerez and seeing how they make sherry. Now that was really remarkable."

With a big grin, Teipner reported, "Miller and I brought back a case of assorted sherry: Oloroso, Amontillado, and sherry Bobadil."

"Well, I was pleased to return with three bottles of Pescador, a white wine, and three bottles of Cazador, a red wine," Pierce added.

Miller said, "I would like to open an Oloroso and share it with you all."

Matching Miller's generosity, Pierce said, "I will go to my room and bring back a bottle of Cazador."

Twenty minutes later, each of them had a small glass of Oloroso next to a larger one of Cazador. They began with the Cazador and the conversation turned to Turner.

"Did you have an exciting weekend, Burt?" Miller asked.

Turner hesitated, then, "The morning was very bad, the afternoon, much better."

"Well, start with the bad morning," Teipner replied.

"The R-6 from Yorktown that was supposed to arrive at 0530 didn't arrive. It went down."

Teipner sat up straight, almost spilled his wine, and said, "What do you mean it went down?"

"They think the plane got caught in a hurricane a few hours out of Newfoundland and went down at sea. They figured that by 0700, the plane would have been out of fuel. There hasn't been any word, and the plane is presumed lost."

Miller, with his head in his hands, said, "Fuck."

Pierce quietly said, "I'm sorry. What a tragedy."

The two pilots began to work their way through all the possibilities. They asked a few more questions of Turner, then they sat quietly. Pierce tried to change the subject.

"What about your afternoon, Burt?"

"We got the AVR running, and I asked Lieutenant Commander Bello if Gallegos and I could take it out for a familiarization cruise. He gave permission, and we did."

Miller said, "You did it all by yourselves? I mean did you run it?"

"No, we had the duty crew run the boat. We just rode along. But I did take the helm for a few minutes."

"Where did you go?" asked Teipner.

"We went north of the Sebou about ten miles and checked out where we will be insertion-extraction training with the HUP and AVR."

"That sounds like an adventure," Miller said with some amazement.

"Hey, for us, it's just another day at the beach."

Pierce got up, stretched and said, "I think its time to hit the rack."

The others got up to leave, and on the way out, Teipner asked Turner, "Maybe you will give us a ride in your boat soon?"

"I think that can be arranged. I'll try to work on it."

The four friends left each other in a very somber mood.

Turner woke up at 0130, went to the head, and returned to bed. He lay awake and thought, *Life's too short*, got up, put on his pants and tee shirt, and, in stockinged feet, padded on to the women's wing of the BOQ. He looked around to make sure no one was about, then knocked softly on Kathy Robert's door twice and twice again. He waited, then started leave when the door opened slightly. Kathy Roberts whispered, "Oh, it's you, Burt. It's very late, but come in. I have something for you."

He went in and quietly closed the door. His hands found her in the dark. He pulled her close and felt that she had a pajama top and panties. She pushed him away and went over to her bed and turned on a small lamp.

"Come and sit down, Burt."

Then she went to her desk, picked up a narrow paper package, and sat down next to him on the bed.

"I found this in Cadiz and thought you would like it." She kissed him on the cheek and gave him the package. He put the package down on the bed and drew her close. He kissed her, and she drew away.

"Open the package, Burt."

He opened the package. It was a beautiful wood carving of Don Quixote, about nine or ten inches tall. The details were remarkable, the cooking pan hat, the excuse for sword and lance, and the extreme gaunt look of the body overlaid with cheap armor.

"Kathy, this is wonderful. Thank you."

He kissed her again and tried to lay her back on her bed. She resisted and said, "It's late, Burt, and I have to get up early."

She got up from the bed, took his hand, and led him to the door, opened it, gave him a hug, and sent him on his way. He sheepishly made his way back to his room with his Don Quixote.

Before he fell asleep he remembered the girl's name—Dulcinea.

Monday morning after muster, Yeoman Fry went up to Turner and said, "Sir, the commander wants you and your team to meet with him and a number of other officers in the conference room at 0900."

"What's it about, Petty Officer?"

"I don't know, sir."

This was not exactly true. Yeomen in the navy know all things, and most know when and how to act dumb if need be.

At 0900, Turner, Gallegos, and Cole walked into the conference room and stood at attention. Sitting at the long green table were Captain Dillon, Commanders Hawkins and Peetz, Lieutenant Commander Owens, and Lieutenant Bruce Franklin.

Commander Hawkins said, "Mr. Turner, you and your men sit down, and we will start."

The SW/EOD team took seats four chairs down from the group. Commander Hawkins thoughtfully introduced Petty Officer Cole to the officers Cole had not met before.

Then he asked, "What is the status of your team, Mr. Turner?"

"We are ready to start our insertion-extraction training. The AVR is operational, and we have a green light for using the HUP—the helicopter, sir."

"How long will it take for the team to be mission capable?"

"With your permission, sir, we had intended to work with the AVR today and tomorrow, and Wednesday with the HUP. Thursday we'll work with both AVR and HUP at night." He cautiously added, "We should be ready after that."

Commander Hawkins looked at Captain Dillon. Dillon looked at Turner and asked, "Would it be possible for you to be ready by Thursday?"

Turner looked at Chief Gallegos and Gallegos, in a low voice, said to Turner, "We could do the AVR today. The HUP tomorrow and both on Wednesday night." He turned to Cole. "What do you think, Cole?"

"We can do that."

Turner was very uneasy. He thought, *Here we go again. We are going to be sent out unprepared. Even here, it's 'everything for the mission.'*

"We can be ready by Thursday morning, sir."

Captain Dillon took over the meeting.

"From here on out, this briefing is classified Secret." Addressing the SW/ EOD team, he began, "Let me bring you up to date about a few things. As you know, in the last number of years, Arab nationalism has forced British and French colonial governments to leave Iraq, Syria, Lebanon, and Egypt. What you probably don't know is that Russia supplied arms and advisors to help this happen.

"Now Egypt, under Nasser, has nationalized the Suez Canal by breaking the treaty allowing Western interests to control the canal. Most folks don't realize that oil destined for Western Europe and the U.S. is transported through this vital waterway. If the relationship between Nasser and the Russians becomes too cozy, the Suez Canal could be used to threaten the economies of the Western world.

"In regard to Algeria and Morocco, the French are struggling to hold on to Algeria and the constitutional monarchy of King Mohammed Cinq is threatened by communist insurgents. Intelligence informs us that the Russians are currently involved in supplying arms and advisors to insurgents in these two countries.

"It is in our national interest to neutralize and reverse this situation through making it too expensive, politically and militarily, for Russia to continue to curry favor by supplying arms and advisors to insurgents. Russia's adventure in the Middle East and now North Africa, if not challenged, could lead to the brink of nuclear confrontation."

Turner thought, *This is the 'brinkmanship' that newspapers said John Foster Dulles practiced at meetings with the Russians before he died last year. The secretary of state wanted the Russians to 'roll back' their growing sphere of influence in central Europe and North Africa. He wasn't afraid to threaten use of nuclear weapons.*

Captain Dillon continued, "The French are trying to interdict the supply of arms going to Arab Insurgents In Algeria, by way of the Mediterranean, to Tunisia and Libya. The problem is, as one line of supply is shut down, another takes its place. Now, the Russians are probing ways of arms delivery to Algeria through Morocco. We are going to help frustrate this probing in a number of ways. The NOF SW/EOD team will be part of this enterprise. Your mission has been one of reconnaissance and surveillance. We now add deterrence."

Turner and Gallegos glanced at each other; Cole seemed preoccupied.

Captain Dillon sat down, looked over at Commander Peetz and asked, "Tom, what is the latest from naval intelligence on the trawlers?"

Commander Peetz got up and went to a wall where two nautical charts were fastened. One was an enlargement of the Strait of Gibraltar; the other, the western Mediterranean. He pointed to an area just east of the Strait of Gibraltar.

"As of last night, one of the Russian trawlers is here. The other is two and a half days east . . . about here. If the first trawler, code-named Hot Dog, remains on present course and speed, it will pass through the Strait of Gibraltar sometime Wednesday afternoon. The second trawler, code-named Ketchup, could make its approach to the strait three or four days later.

"Turkish intelligence informed us that one trawler's destination is Larache. The other trawler's destination is about 350 miles south of Larache, in the area of Cape Draa, down here. The Turks didn't know if both were carrying arms and explosives or only one. However, one of their informers, a sponge diver, reported a trawler with a highly modified hull passed through the Dardanelles fifteen days ago. The hull, rather than being round bottomed, was flat bottomed and much deeper in draft. This trawler may be our arms and explosives carrier. Unfortunately, we don't know if it is Hot Dog or Ketchup."

Commander Hawkins asked, "Are these trawlers any different from the trawlers the Russians are using to shadow the Sixth Fleet?"

"They are about the same size as the trawlers being used to collect signal intelligence. They don't have antenna arrays and appear to be genuine fishing boats." Referring to the large nautical chart, he continued, "Hot Dog took on a load of fish off Benghazi two days ago. Ketchup did the same off the island of Pantelleria four days ago."

Commander Hawkins then asked, "How are you able to separate these trawlers from all the others in the Med?"

Not being ready to reveal very much about how this particular information was obtained, the intelligence officer paused, then carefully continued, "As you know, every vessel has a different propeller signature. The Turks have the same ability to record propeller signatures as we do, and they have a data bank of all vessels that have passed through the Dardanelles in the last thirty days. Because Hot Dog was observed to have a highly modified hull, Turkish intelligence thought we might be interested in tracking this vessel. We were, and we did.

"We found the communication traffic between Hot Dog and the other trawler, Ketchup, was 86 percent more than what would be expected between other trawlers or other fishing boats, and we began monitoring their communications in earnest. Because of their unique propeller signatures, Hot Dog and Ketchup were easily tracked by one of our subs. The longer we followed the two trawlers, the more obvious it became that they were involved with something other than fishing."

Commander Peetz returned to his chair.

Captain Dillon got up from his chair and went to the smaller chart of the Strait of Gibraltar. He put his finger on the port town of Larache, about sixty miles south of the Strait of Gibraltar. Looking at Turner and Turner's team, he said, "Thursday night at 2330, you will be inserted by rubber boat just south of Larache."

Commander Peetz slid a folder over to Dillon. He opened the folder and took out a number of glossy black-and-white pictures. He glanced at each one, then slid them down to Turner.

"This first picture is an aerial of the small harbor. The other pictures were taken from different points near the harbor."

Turner looked at each one and passed them on to Gallegor and Cole.

"You will paddle around the point protecting the small harbor, then up the channel about a hundred yards. At that position, you will haul out, secure the raft, and proceed under water about hundred and fifty yards into the harbor. As you can see from the photos, there's a pier coming off the wharf that's about two hundred feet in length and about thirty feet in width. It is anticipated that our trawler will be there. We have been told to expect a large tank truck to be parked on the pier next to the trawler. At this time of night, the harbor should be crowded with fishing boats, but moored some distance from the trawler. When you arrive at the trawler, you will carefully examine the hull. If you find the trawler is the one with the modified hull, you will disable it. Tom, please show Mr. Turner and his men the device they will be using to accomplish disablement."

Commander Peetz reached down and lifted a small brown nylon sack from the floor and put it on the table. He unzipped the sack and lifted out a round device that was dark green. The team immediately recognized a limpet mine.

He explained, "You men have been trained to recognize the large variety of limpet mines that you might have an occasion to discover if you had to do a ship bottom search. You also have been trained to render them safe without blowing up the vessel or yourselves. You have never seen this particular one. It cannot be rendered safe once fastened to the hull of a ship.

He passed the limpet mine down the table to Turner. With the mine in his hands, reality set in, and Turner experienced a wave of unease. He carefully examined the mine. It was about eight inches in diameter and four inches thick. There were four curved heavy magnets spaced about an inch apart and fastened at the outer curve of the mine. On the side edge, there was a recess about the diameter of a pencil that ended at a slotted face a quarter-inch down. The limpet mine felt like it was about five or six pounds in weight.

On the side of the mine, near the recess, was what he thought to be Arabic characters. He passed it on to Gallegos and Cole.

Commander Peetz continued, "This device contains 3.6 pounds of tetrytol for a total weight of 4.9 pounds. It will effectively disable the trawler, especially if placed near the engine room."

Gallegos looked at the mine and said to Turner, "It has Arabic characters."

Commander Peetz heard this and replied, "Actually, it's Israeli. They would like to send a message to the Russians."

Gallegos passed the mine to Cole, who, after looking the mine over, found the recess and slotted face. He looked at Captain Dillon, and Dillon said with a smile, "Go ahead, Petty Officer."

Cole took out a small utility knife from a scabbard fastened to his belt, opened it to a screwdriver blade, unscrewed a short column of steel, and lifted it out of the recess. He turned it up and saw two brass electrical contacts.

He passed the fuse to Gallegos and Turner and said, "Interesting fuse, Chief."

Commander Peetz continued, "This limpet mine is designed to open steel hulls on merchant ships or patrol boats. It will do nicely for a Russian trawler. If you look closely, you will see a coarse ring near the base of the fuse. This is the timer adjustment. When it is turned there will be an audible click. A click represents a half hour. There are a maximum of six clicks—three hours. Trying to unscrew the fuse or remove the mine after it is fastened to the hull will set it off. There is no turning back. This mine is inert. Please take it with you when you are training for the mission. The bag I have here is designed to carry the mine under water. The straps are adjustable for shoulder or waist."

He slid the bag down to Turner. Dillon said, "You have the equipment and resources to enable you to plan the mission. It is important that you submit your plan for approval to Commander Hawkins by 1600 tomorrow. The only caution we have, other than for your safety, is to make sure the trawler at Larache is the one with the modified hull before you place the limpet mine."

Commander Hawkins registered his concern. "I'm not sure Mr. Turner can develop a plan for carrying out the mission by 1600 tomorrow. He has yet to see the limitations of using the AVR and HUP under the best conditions during the day, let alone for a night problem and under poor weather conditions."

Dillon asked Peetz, "What did Fleet Weather Central have for the five-day forecast?"

Lieutenant Franklin handed the commander a sheet of paper.

He read, "Monday, clear with fifteen- to twenty-knot winds coming up in late afternoon from the northwest. Tuesday, the same. Wednesday, overcast with chance of rain in the afternoon, winds from the northwest at fifteen to twenty knots beginning early afternoon and dropping off in the early evening. Thursday, morning showers with winds from the northwest five to fifteen knots. In the early afternoon, clearing with wind from the west fifteen to twenty knots with gusts to thirty for a short time. Thursday night, clear with slight breeze from the northwest and gibbous moon. Temperatures vary from a low of 50°F to a high of 75°F for the next five days, and sea state will change with the wind, but conditions for the mission Thursday night should be ideal, based on the five-day forecast at this time."

Commander Hawkins turned and spoke quietly with his exec, then asked, "Mr. Turner, are you sure you can be ready to deploy Thursday night?"

Fuck, how do I know? He replied, "Yes, sir."

"Very well. Submit your plan of action to me on or before 1200 Wednesday."

There was no doubt that Hawkins and Owens were very concerned about Turner and his team. They did not want to see a repeat of the Rif Mountain mission, which they thought was planned by fools in Dillon's and Peetz's offices. They also thought Captain Andersen, the naval attaché in Rabat, had his fingerprints all over the last-minute plan.

Dillon said, "If there are no more questions or concerns to be considered, we are adjourned."

Turner and his team remained behind as the others left the room.

"Chief, I'm going to call Lieutenant Commander Bello for permission to use the AVR. Get the gear together you think we are going to need. We'll dress in the EOD shop, then drive down to the wharf. I want to be in the water by 1100."

"Aye, aye, sir."

Gallegos and Cole left for the EOD shop, and Turner crossed the hall to his desk and made the phone call. He was granted permission to use the AVR, then he called Petty Officer Deacon. After explaining what he wanted to do, Deacon said the AVR would be ready when the team arrived. He hung up the phone and left the office spaces. On the way out of the building, he passed the open door of the conference room.

"Burt, wait a minute."

Turner walked back and looked in the door. Franklin was sitting at the conference table with a pad of paper in front of him.

"Yeah, Bruce?"

"Come in for a minute."

Turner went in and stood across the table from Franklin. Franklin put down his pen, stood up, and said, "That weather report—there was more. There's a pretty good storm coming in early Friday morning and lasting until Saturday afternoon. You know weather forecasting gets pretty iffy beyond three days, especially here. Check Fleet Weather Central every day before you go, OK?"

"Thanks, Bruce. I'll do that."

He started to leave when Franklin added, "You are getting into some pretty scary shit, Burt. If I can help you from time to time, call me.

"Are you trying to tell me something?"

Franklin seemed to be struggling with how to begin. Then he said, "There are some things you should know. My boss, Commander Peetz, is straight arrow. So are Commander Hawkins and his exec. I'm not sure about Captain Dillon yet, but right now, he doesn't seem to have a second agenda. Watch your six o'clock in relation to Captain Andersen, the naval attaché in Rabat. You caught his eye at the Rif Mountain debriefing. Andersen doesn't like your boss or his exec because they are mustangs. He doesn't like you because you are SW/EOD and not in his navy."

"But Andersen isn't important. We take our orders ultimately from the commander of naval activities, Mediterranean, in Naples, by way of Dillon and others. Andersen is not in our chain of command."

"We do take our orders from COMNAVACTSMED, but Andersen, as the naval advisor to the American embassy staff in Rabat, is privy to a lot of information, and at times, he may exchange information with COMNAVACTSMED. He is well known for using classified information like Operation Scorpion Fish to better position himself for a future meeting with a selection board for admirals."

"How could that help him?"

"Well, the American ambassador to Morocco and his immediate staff are political appointees of the president of the United States. It wouldn't hurt Andersen's self-serving interest if he passed classified information to a few high-placed advisors who do not have a Need to Know clearance, who might later be in a position to smooth the way for his promotion. Quid pro quo, you know."

About now, Turner didn't want to hear any more. He wanted to get ready for Thursday night.

Franklin finished with, "The CIA field office in Paris is working with us in planning and implementing Scorpion Fish. With Andersen in the loop, CIA is very concerned about him compromising current and future Scorpion

Fish activities. You should know about this because your team is one of the few assets we have that can provide us with in-field information during a very volatile time. The Rif Mountain mission was politically driven. We can't afford to use the team the way it was used in the Rif Mountains. It is too important an asset. You are not expendable. The point is, only you can tell us if your team is capable of carrying out what is asked of it."

Assets and expendable are the same words Laura Brae used a week ago. How nice to hear people are concerned about us after the fact. Interesting. Maybe Franklin can help us.

"I won't know until tomorrow afternoon if we have the capability to do Larache. A lot depends on how we work with the AVR today and the HUP tomorrow. Right now, we plan insertion and extraction just south of Larache Point, protecting the harbor. We need to know if there are any people living on the headlands of the point. If no one is living in that area, how far away is the nearest habitation? Can you help us with this, Bruce?"

"I'll try. If I find anything useful, I'll get it to you right away."

"I owe you, Bruce. Thanks."

"Oh, the monologue I just delivered didn't occur."

Franklin sat back down, and Turner left the building.

The next morning, when Turner arrived at the EOD shop, Gallegos and Cole were pulling on their light green dry suits. The team didn't like the new wet suits sent out for field testing because the neoprene tore easily, and if they were going to be in cold water for a while, they trusted the uncomfortable dry suits, anyway.

Cole was cussing about his suit being too tight under the arms. After Turner undressed, Gallegos began helping him pull on the upper part of his dry suit.

"Better try using more talcum powder on your arms next time, Mr. Turner."

They sprayed aerosol graphite on their steel watchbands to prevent shimmering that could attract sharks or barracuda. They taped an orange smoke flare to each side of their knife scabbards, strapped on their swimmer's life jackets, and made sure their wrist compasses and wrist depth gauges, along with their masks and fins, were in the net 'go' bag. Gallegos and Cole had already checked the regulators and pressures on the SCUBA bottles and loaded them in the weapons carrier. Each member checked the team's equipment checklist and initialed it. They were ready to go.

On the way to the wharf, Chief Gallegos pulled around and parked at the back of the chiefs' club. He left the weapons carrier and went inside.

Turner looked at Cole. "He's not dressed to go in there—what's he doing?"

Cole smiled and said, "He's going to take advantage of his seniority and popularity."

A few minutes later, the chief came out, carrying a box. He went around to the back of the weapons carrier and returned empty-handed.

"What was that all about, Chief?"

"We are going to get hungry out there, Mr. Turner. We now have ham and cheese sandwiches and a gallon thermos of hot coffee."

Turner had no idea the chief made arrangements for provisions.

"You are really something, Chief."

Cole added, "Yes, you are, you devil. I don't know how you get away with it."

"I get away with it because I am nice to little old ladies, children, and other chiefs besides being very good-looking in dress canvas and lesser gear."

Turner had another reason to hold Chief Gallegos in awe.

At 1035, the AVR was at sea, heading north from the mouth of the Oued Sabou. There were great swells coming at an angle to the AVR. The boat would go up one side, and on the way down the other, skid somewhat, settle heavily in the trough, climb up, and repeat it all over again.

Raising his voice over the sounds of the engine exhaust, wind and sea, Turner called out, "Chief let's try the beach ahead—from just off the surf line—then come back out to the AVR for pickup. Then we will go for five hundred yards off the surf line. No SCUBA.

"That's a good start, sir."

The coxswain acknowledged what he overheard and put the AVR on course to the target beach. A few minutes later, he checked the nautical chart of local coastal waters, came in close to shore, and, after several range and bearing sights with the pelorus, he throttled back and gave Turner a thumbs-up. Then he added, "Sir, we can't let the transom down on the stern and put you in from the well. The swells are running too high, and the transom would take a real beating."

"OK. we'll go over the side."

"I'll rig a rope ladder over the side for your recovery."

The team had already put on their wrist compasses; the depth gauges they wore out of habit. They put on fins and masks, took a compass bearing on a point at the beach, and, with Turner leading, jumped from the deck on the windward side of the AVR into the water. The AVR quickly drifted away from the team.

The squeeze of water pressure forced a small amount of air into the upper part of their dry suits; they vented it through a tube attached to the upper left side of the suit.

Gallegos asked, "Are you ready to go in, sir?"

"I'm ready."

They took a quick look at their compasses; flipped over on their backs; and, rising and falling with the gentle swells, made their way toward the beach. Every few minutes, they flipped back over and checked where they were relative to each other and checked their bearings and distance to the breaking surf ahead. Five minutes after leaving the AVR, they were close to where the swells began to break.

They came together, and Turner said, "You guys ready for an E ticket ride? It looks like we have three surf lines at a time going in, and they are all the same size—big!"

Gallegos answered, "Let's see where the rip ahead takes us. You ready, Cole?"

Cole laughed and said, "I'm ready!"

They bent over and dove deep to avoid the turbulence of the swell as it broke. Turner felt the familiar pressure on his body and in his ears as the breaker surged over him. As it carried him forward, it began to roll, and Turner, caught in the roll, rolled with it. Finally, almost out of air, he surfaced in the turbulence and foam of the expired wave. He looked around and saw Cole surfacing ten yards in front of him. Cole waved and got in position for the second wave.

Turner looked back and up; it was one of the fifteen or twenty footers they saw once in a while at Mehdiya Beach. He twisted back around and headed for the bottom. He felt the enormous pressure of the second wave as it passed over his body; then as it rolled up, it lifted Turner's legs, and his whole body followed the arc of his legs into a series of backward somersaults as the wave rushed forward. He surfaced in the second wave's turbulence and foam.

The last of the three waves was the smallest, but now he was caught in the riptide. He let the riptide take him back out, then he swam parallel to the beach until the riptide weakened and rode the surf to the sandy beach.

He saw Gallegos sitting in the distance about where they planned to come ashore. He took off his fins and walked unsteadily up to Gallegos and sat down beside him.

"Did you have a nice ride, Mr. Turner?"

"I had a nice ride—90 percent somersaults, 10 percent surfing. What did you get for lapsed time from our start?"

Gallegos looked at his Rolex and said, "Seventeen minutes."

"I got twenty-one. Let's call it nineteen. Where's Cole?"

"He was first ashore and climbed up the rise behind us. He's coming back now.

Cole came down the rise, kicking sand in every direction. "Not a land mine in sight."

"There are land mines here?" Turner asked

Gallegos answered, "In 1942, the Vichey government in France ordered the French Army here in Morocco to resist the American landings here at Fedala, and Casablanca. One of the things they did was plant land mines behind the beaches. Unfortunately, most of the land mines are still here."

"Every so often, somebody's dog gets blown up back there," Cole added.

"I would say this is a very unsafe place to be. Let's go back out," Turner replied.

They returned to the water. Swimming, then diving underneath each wave as it broke, they worked their way back out through the surf. Finally, they were beyond the surf line and as they rose and fell with the swells, they could see the AVR circling much farther out at sea. They checked their watches and decided that if they went on for another four minutes, they would be in the general area where they were dropped off.

Four minutes later, Turner said, "Show some smoke, Cole."

Cole cut the tape on a smoke flare, lifted it high, and set it off.

The crew on the AVR saw the orange smoke, and three minutes later, the coxswain put the AVR close by the SW/EOD team. The rope ladder was put in place over the side, and the team climbed back aboard.

Turner called up to the coxswain, "OK, now make it a thousand yards."

"Aye, aye, sir."

When the coxswain had the AVR a thousand yards from the beach, Turner said, "Deacon, log our time to the beach for five hundred yards at eighteen minutes, and back out at twenty-two minutes."

The three men went to the windward side of the AVR and returned to the water. Making sure he was clear of the swimmers, Deacon swung the AVR around, advanced the throttles, and roared off to sea. The swells continued to be gentle and very large. Periodically, they checked their bearing and compass heading. The additional five hundred yards changed the visual perspective of the shoreline, but as they came closer, it became comfortably familiar. By the time they approached the surf line, they physically knew they had traveled a thousand yards. There was no surprise going through the three surf lines; it was as demanding as before.

Turner, fins in his hands, slogged his way through the turbulence of the shallows and saw Gallegos sitting on the sand above the high-water mark. He looked around and couldn't see Cole. It was Cole's turn to enjoy being last man.

"What did you get for this leg, Chief?"

"I read twenty-eight minutes."

"I have thirty minutes. I guess we should be using the maximum time."

"We can use Cole's time. He is just breaking the last wave."

Three minutes later, Cole flopped down next to Turner and Gallegos.

"I took the long way this time. I didn't want to show you and the chief up, OK?"

Cole laid back and looked up at the sky. "God, I love this stuff." A minute later, he said, "I wonder how Huwitt is doing."

Turner replied, "As soon as we get back, I'll check with Dr. Pierce. I'm sure Bethesda sent something by now."

It was a hard swim back out. They had the benefit of a current tending toward shore for the first five hundred yards going in. Now, after coming back out through the surf, they had to work against the current.

"I think we are damn close to where we started, what do you think, Chief?" Turner asked.

"I think it's time to show some smoke. Next time, we get the AVR to spot for us."

Turner cut loose a smoke flare, held it up, and lit it off.

After they were aboard the AVR, Turner had Deacon add to the log, "One thousand yards, thirty-two minutes to the beach objective. Return from objective to AVR, forty-five minutes."

The coxswain then asked, "To the sandy beach area, sir?"

"Do that very thing, coxswain. When we get there, we will take a half hour rest and have some chow before we go back in the water."

Forty minutes later, the SW/EOD team had eaten their sandwiches—Turner and Gallegos three, Cole four; coffee, hot and black, Turner two mugs, Gallegos and Cole three mugs each. Turner jokingly made an issue about no powdered creamer and sugar and was glad to feel the warmth of the coffee going down. The AVR crew had their own provisions; the provisions didn't include powdered creamer or sugar.

Using the numbers that were logged, they calculated the amount of air they would need to duplicate the distances made earlier on the surface.

Turner said, "Under average conditions, we would anticipate using 600 pounds of air for five hundred yards at a maximum depth of twenty-two feet and about eighteen minutes under water."

Cole added, "A thousand yards under these conditions, we would use over 1,200 pounds. So round trip, we would use over 2,400 pounds in sixty to seventy minutes. We can't do two legs of five hundred yards and two legs of a thousand yards with twenty-five hundred pounds of air in our tanks."

"Not in these waters. It's too cold, and there is some current. We already know that we take too much time to go those distances," Gallegos added.

"Turner said, "We might as well just do the thousand to and from."

The three men continued to stare at the numbers, then the chief said, "You're right, sir. Let's get it over with. I suggest we stay between ten and twenty feet to conserve air.

Turner replied, "Between ten and twenty feet it is. I'll take the point. Chief, you stay in trail on my right and Cole in trail on my left for the first ten minutes. Then we will rotate and Cole can take the point and I'll rotate to his position for ten minutes and so on. At rotation, the new point will surface for a bearing. If visibility goes to hell, we go to the beach independently. Any questions?"

There were none.

Cole said, "Let's go for a swim!"

Turner looked at the coxswain and said, "Take us to the one-thousand-yard mark off the beach. After we go in, stay at a thousand yards so we know how far we have to go on the way back. Begin to expect us after an hour."

"Aye, aye, sir."

When the AVR was at the insertion point, the three swimmers helped each other strap on their SCUBA gear. They checked their regulators and took a bearing on the same object on the shoreline, then went over the side.

After a few minor adjustments in gear, and with Turner leading, they descended to fifteen feet and started to the beach. The water was light blue, clear, and cold. The surface of the water formed a wavering mosaic ceiling above, and below, rays of sunlight penetrated at an angle to great depths.

Swimming underwater without a visual cue for depth always made Turner uncomfortable. When he could see the bottom, no matter how deep, he was comfortable. It was one of the many things he had to learn to put out of his mind. Early on, he was surprised at how many divers, under differing circumstances, had to deal with claustrophobia—even though they had made it through a screening process before being admitted to underwater training.

Gallegos was at the point when Cole grabbed the chief's fin. Gallegos turned and saw Cole, with eyes as big as saucers, pointing at two hammerhead sharks—the first about eight feet long, the second about ten feet long—lazily swimming slightly below and to Cole's right about thirty feet away. Turner saw Cole gesturing to Gallegos and looked down at the sharks. He saw the claspers on each side of the anal fin of the larger shark that identified it as a male. The smaller shark without claspers was a female.

Gallegos gave a come-on sign, and Cole returned to his position. As they approached the surf line, the visibility dropped off rapidly as turbulence stirred up the sandy bottom. Gallegos gave the signal to surface.

When they broke the surface, they dropped their mouthpieces and Cole said, "Those hammerheads were so great!"

Turner said, "They were," and, absently, "I wonder if there are many more here."

Gallegos asked, "Are you two as cold as I am?"

They nodded yes.

Turner asked the chief, "I don't know if it's a big deal to go under the surf and to the beach. We are already at the thirty minute mark. I think we should head back to the boat."

"We still have to do the four-man raft at the point. Let's go back," Gallegos replied.

The wind was coming up, and former swells became waves with spray blowing off as they crested. The swimmers each took a quick bearing on the distant AVR, tucked forward, and with a last fin slap at the surface, drove down to the quiet of the fifteen-foot level and rhythmically flutter kicked toward their target. Passing through the area where they earlier saw the hammerhead sharks, they saw three more—two males about eight feet in length and a six-foot female. Turner was surprised at the shark's disinterest.

When they arrived at the boat, they were extremely tired. Turner looked at his Rolex; the return took them forty-two minutes. The boat was rocking, and it was impossible to climb up the rope ladder with their diving gear on. One at a time, they took the equipment off and passed it up to the crewmen on deck. Then, aided by the crewmen, Cole first, Gallegos second, and, finally, Turner climbed aboard.

"Coxswain, put us in the lee of the point ahead."

Coxswain Deacon was concerned about the team's condition, but replied, "Aye, aye, sir," and, at full throttle, made for the point and its lee side.

Around the point and away from wind and waves, the coxswain throttled the engines back and the boat settled and rocked gently

Turner and his two men were sitting in the four-man raft in the well at the stern. Seeing Cole nodding off, Gallegos said, "I think we've had enough for the day, Mr. Turner. What do you say?"

"I say we secure and go home. Tomorrow morning, we can do the point. When we get back to the base, I'll call Chief Williams and set up the HUP. Maybe he can pick us up from the AVR after we challenge the point a few times."

"That sounds just right," Gallegos said with a sigh.

Cole jerked awake as Turner yelled out, "Coxswain, take us home."

"Aye, aye, sir."

A half hour later, the last of the diving gear was on board the weapons carrier and, with Turner at the wheel, headed for NOF and the EOD shop. As they passed by the airstrip, Cole said, "Look at all the cargo planes. I have never seen so many here at one time."

Gallegos looked over to where Cole pointed and said, "There's a lot of air force cargo planes there too. Something's going on."

When they arrived at the EOD shop, they took turns hosing the salt water off each other in their dry suits, then hosed off their gear and stowed it away. Then they stripped off their dry suits and hung them on the drying rack in back of the shop. After they got dressed, they stood looking at each other, in total exhaustion, for a few moments . . . then Gallegos and Cole went over to the SCUBA tanks, picked them up with a grunt, and carried them to the air compressor volume tank. They took off the regulators and began to recharge the tanks—this time to twenty-eight hundred pounds.

Gallegos saw Turner was looking around for something to do and said, "Mr. Turner, why don't you shove off. We're going to secure right after we charge the tanks."

"OK. I'll call Chief Williams about tomorrow. I'll see you two here at 0900."

As he went out the door of the EOD shop, he was still shivering from the effects of the cold water. It was 1730. Arriving at the NOF office spaces, everyone seemed to have secured except Petty Officer Jenkins, the duty yeoman.

"Good afternoon, sir. Did you have a good day?"

He couldn't mask his shivering and stammered, "It-t-t-t w-was a hard d-d-day, Jenkins."

He went to his desk and called Chief Flint Williams's office. The yeoman on duty answered and said, "Chief Williams is at Operations. I'll transfer your call, sir."

A few minutes later, "Is that you, Mr. Turner?"

"It is, Ch-ch-ch-chief. C-c-c-can we get the HUP tomorrow for f-f-f-five or six pickups?"

"I have been told your team has priority over anyone else for the next three days. Where do you want to go?"

"We will be w-w-w-working with the AVR off the first point n-n-n-north of the mouth of the Oued Sebou at 1030. We should be ready for you at 1230. You could pick us up near the AVR and initially drop us about f-f-f-f-five miles offshore. Once we learn how to use your equipment, I w-w-w-w-want to do a few drops and pickups just outside the surf line, then in b-b-b-between the breakers."

"Why do you want to do this in between breakers? That can get hairy."

"I want us to h-h-h-have the experience of being p-p-p-picked up during rough sea conditions. I don't want to be surprised l-l-l-later."

"My hoist guy and I can get the cable and horse collar down near you, but it is going to be jerking up and down and whipping around with the surge and wind from the surf."

"We n-n-n-need the experience, Chief. We also h-h-h-h-have to experience doing a drop and pickup with the SCUBAs."

"How much do they weigh?"

"They weigh about s-s-s-seventy pounds each, and there will be three, one for each of us."

Chief Williams didn't answer right away, then said, "Let's do this. I'll give some idea of our capability, and you see if you can work within that envelope."

Turner picked up a pencil and slid over a pad.

"OK, I'm ready."

"Range depends on load and temperature. Me and my hoist operator and two riders, about 340 miles, maybe. Maximum speed, about 105. Usually, I fly about seventy-five miles per hour. If the distance is less than 340 miles and at low altitude, we can carry more weight, possibly four riders, at best, under one hundred miles. Hovering really cuts into distance and weight possibilities. You can see right now that you three men and 210 pounds of SCUBAs limits you severely."

"I'll w-w-work with these numbers t-t-tonight and call you tomorrow."

"Why are you stammering? You sound like you had a scare."

"I was in cold water too long."

"Oh."

Flint Williams had a few interesting things to say about young junior officers who stayed in cold waters too long, but thought better of it.

"I'll be in my quarters tonight. Call me if you need help."

"Thanks, Chief."

At the same time Turner put the phone down, Yeoman Jenkins called over from his desk, "The exec wants to see you in his office, sir."

Turner wasn't surprised the exec was working late; it seemed to be his habit.

He got up from his desk, walked over, and stood in the doorway of the exec's office.

"Come in and sit down, Mr. Turner. We should chat a bit."

Turner went in and sat down in a chair in front of the executive officer's desk.

"Well, before we start, how did it go for you today?"

"It-t-t-t w-w-was d-d-difficult, sir, but we came close to f-f-f-f-finding our limitations."

"My god, Burt, are you cold?"

"J-j-j-just a b-b-bit, sir."

The exec rose from his chair, walked over to his doorway, and called out, "Jenkins, I want a hot mug of coffee for Mr. Turner, quickly now!"

The exec turned and lifted off an old and well-worn foul-weather jacket from the coat rack next to the door, walked over to Turner, and draped it around his shoulders.

Turner was incredulous. He stammered, "Th-th-thank y-y-you, s-sir."

Petty Officer Jenkins came in and pressed a large mug of steaming coffee into Turner's open hands. Before Turner could thank him, he was gone.

The exec sat down at his desk and just looked at Turner for a few minutes. Then, he asked, "Do you want cream and sugar?"

"Th-th-this is fine, sir."

After Turner had stopped shivering somewhat, he repeated, "How did it go for you today?"

"To begin with, sir, we worked very well with the AVR and its crew. They were capable, cooperative, and interested in making it work for us. We selected two different areas for time and distance calculations, both with heavy surf conditions. We went in with SCUBA on one."

He took a small notebook from his shirt pocket and read the time and distance with and without SCUBAs and amount of air used during the SCUBA swim. The exec unleashed a number of questions and was satisfied with Turner's answers.

"It sounds like things are going your way so far, Mr. Turner. What are your plans for tomorrow?"

"Yes, sir. Tomorrow we will see how we do when we deploy from the AVR with a four-man raft and work our way around a point north of the Oued Sebou. It's a good place to see how we handle rough water and wind. After that, we will switch to the HUP for pickup and drop orientation. Tomorrow night will be our dress rehearsal. We will launch from the AVR and recover with the HUP."

"It sounds very challenging. Tell me how you are going to manage recovering with the HUP when you have SCUBAs and a four-man raft?

"I won't know until we finish tomorrow. I know I was told to have my plan of action ready by 1200, day after tomorrow, I would like to have permission to turn it in on or before 1500, sir."

"I guess you would. I'll take care of it. Understand there has to be enough time for the commander and I and fleet intelligence and the embassy in Rabat to review and OK the plan. Get it to us on or before 1500, Wednesday. Is there anything more I should know about?"

"Well, sir, the cold water combined with long distance is a problem. We can get to the beach or the objective, but the amount of energy left to do anything else is pretty limited. We have to be careful about how much more you ask of us other than attaching the limpet mine. I'm sure you understand that if there is a problem in getting back out for pickup by the HUP and we are discovered . . ."

"Heads will roll, Mr. Turner, heads will roll."

"Finally, I would like to schedule the SNB to fly us up the coast and have a look at the general area on Wednesday, early afternoon."

"Do it. If you have any problems getting what you need, let us know immediately."

"Yes, sir, I will."

"By the way, this is the time of year hammerhead sharks seem to spend a lot of time just off the surf line. Did you see any?"

"We saw a few. They are there, sir."

"Now, I want to bring you up to date about a few things. The second SW/EOD team that was on its way to us has been diverted to the Sixth Fleet. We have no idea if and when they will be ordered back to us. Besides this interesting item, a replacement for Petty Officer Huwitt has been put on hold."

"On the way back from the wharf, we saw a large number of navy and air force cargo planes parked on the ramp. Is something going on, sir?"

"Last night we were put on twenty-four-hour alert to be ready to supply and load large amounts of ammunition on transport aircraft that will be coming in to the Naval Air Station from the U.S. Once loaded, these transport aircraft will go on to an undisclosed site in the eastern Mediterranean. The ammunition will be in direct support of Sixth Fleet operations off Beirut, Lebanon."

"That sounds very serious, sir."

"Lebanon is coming apart at the seams, Mr. Turner. A Maronite Christian-Muslim civil war is imminent. Pro-Nasser anti-Western Muslim groups,

Sunni, Shia, and Druze, all want to bring down the president of Lebanon, who is Maronite Christian. Palestinian refugees from Israel are adding to the confusion. The Russians are siding with the Muslims by providing arms and advisors."

"Do you think we might go to war over this?"

"I don't think so, but one never knows, with our secretary of state at the helm."

Turner stopped shivering.

"Will there be a problem for us if we don't get the second SW/EOD team?"

"The second SW/EOD team was to cover EOD requirements as needed while you were deployed. Without that second team, it could be a problem for NOF." He thought for a minute. "I'm sure the people running Scorpion Fish are not overly concerned about NOF's problems."

"Sir, we have been concerned about Huwitt. Has there been any word?"

The look on the exec's face said it all. "We received word this morning that Petty Officer Huwitt died four days ago. The commander wanted to tell you himself tomorrow morning. I'm sorry."

Turner was shaken. After a moment, he asked, "Would you excuse me, sir. I would like to see if my men are still on board."

"Yes, of course. Tell your men the commander and I feel very bad about this and plan a memorial service for our shipmate."

He stood up, handed the foul-weather jacket to the exec, thanked him, and left. Just before leaving the office complex, he stopped by Yeoman Jenkins's desk to return the drained coffee mug.

The yeoman said, "I'm sorry, sir. Huwitt was a good man."

"He was a *very* good man. Thank you for the coffee, Jenkins."

On the way to the EOD shop, he thought, *How am I going to tell them about Huwitt? Do I do a monologue about what a good shipmate he was? Do I talk about his professionalism? Do I talk about Cole's and Gallegos's relationship with Huwitt? Do I talk about how thoughtful he was, helping me learn how to be officer in charge of the team? I was never told how to handle something like this.*

He ended up doing none of these.

When he arrived at the steps going up to the EOD shop, Gallegos and Cole were just locking up.

Gallegos and Cole came down to where Turner was standing, and Gallegos said, "We thought you were long gone, Mr. Turner."

"I was with the exec I have bad news."

Cole said, "I know, the AVR sank and we are not going anywhere."

Turner let that go by.

"Dick Huwitt died four days ago. The skipper will arrange a memorial service. They will let us know when it will be."

Gallegos wasn't surprised; he didn't expect Huwitt to live. Cole was afraid his friend would die from the start. They knew of men from other teams that died in the line of duty, but this was one of their own.

Turner couldn't get it through his head that Huwitt was gone . . . forever.

Gallegos touched Cole's shoulder and asked, "Do you need a ride?"

"I have the bike."

Cole and Huwitt had an old British Triumph motorcycle parked in the NOF motor pool; it belonged to Cole now.

Lieutenant Turner, not knowing what to say next, turned and walked away.

Chapter 8

By the time Turner got to the officers' mess, the last serving was almost over. He found his friends sitting in their usual places having afterdinner coffee, and sat down in his usual place. As he put a napkin in his lap, Miller said, "Where the hell have you been, Turner? We waited almost five minutes for your arrival and decided you had better things to do."

The other two made their snide remarks; Turner ignored them and motioned the steward over. It was Italian night, and he ordered spaghetti and meatballs. When the meal arrived, he poked his fork around a bit, causing a small meatball to surface from the gooey, glutinous noodles, then chose instead to have a chunk of sourdough bread and a glass of characterless red wine. When he didn't become engaged in table conversation, it became obvious to the others that something was wrong.

Pierce thought that Turner probably found out about Huwitt. A few hours earlier, Pierce had been told by the chief surgeon that word had been received that Mineman First Class Richard Huwitt had died at Bethesda Naval Hospital in Maryland.

Miller and Teipner made a few awkward tries for conversation, then Teipner said, "OK, Burt, what's going on?"

"I just got word my man Dick Huwitt died at Bethesda four days ago."

Teipner said softly, "Oh fuck, Burt, I'm sorry."

Miller pushed away from the table and said, "OK, I suggest we go up to my quarters and chat over some very good *vin rouge*."

They all got up, and on the way out, Turner glanced over at the table where Kathy Roberts and her friends usually sat. Betty Armstrong was with a number of women he didn't know; Kathy Roberts and Binki Bionconi were not there.

He asked, "Where are Kathy and Binki?"

Pierce answered, "They left for Rota this morning. They are giving a short course on trauma to the nurses and X-ray folks at the base dispensary there. They will be back tomorrow."

When they arrived in Miller's room, Miller went to his closet and brought out two bottles of Chateau Petrus; he opened one. Teipner brought over glasses from the shelf above the washbasin, gave one to Pierce, gave another to Turner, put one on the floor next to Miller's lounge chair, and kept the last for himself. Miller opened the bottle of wine and made the rounds.

"You know, we really made the right decision when we bought this very fine case of Chateau Petrus from that enterprising pilot who was transporting it and others to Naples for the change of command ceremony," Pierce remarked.

"We do all things well," Teipner replied.

Turner looked over at Pierce and said, "You were right about Huwitt. I thought he might have a chance."

"He did have a chance, but it was very slim."

Miller and Teipner had heard that Huwitt had been shot. They were able to piece together what might have happened, but knew enough not to ask questions. If Turner wanted to talk about it, OK; otherwise, the subject was out of bounds. Turner didn't want to talk about it.

Pierce said, "I want to make an announcement!"

"What could be so important that you want to make an announcement, Dr. Lieutenant Pierce?" Miller asked.

"Well, to begin with, you men are so caught up in your testosterone-driven military activities, you would never know."

"Never know what?" Teipner asked.

"Kathy Roberts made full lieutenant, and she can put her double bars on tomorrow," Pierce replied.

"That is so outstanding. We must have a wetting-down party tomorrow night," Miller added.

They all agreed.

Then Turner said, "We need to start at seven. I have to be someplace at nine."

Miller asked, "Do you have a young lady that you haven't told us about, Mr. Underwater Warrior?"

"No, I have the duty."

The other three just looked at each other.

"I do have a request, though. I need you and Teipner to give my two guys and me a ride north along the coast up to the strait and back. I'd like to fly out at about eleven on Wednesday. I'll clear it with Bello."

"We would be glad to do that, but there is a catch," Teipner said.

"OK, what's the catch?"

"You are to give us SCUBA lessons in the pool, soon."

Pierce said, "Don't include me!"

Turner said, "I can do that." He looked at Pierce and said, "If we do this, I want you there. You don't have to get involved, but I want you with us." He smiled and added, "One of these guys could get a pulmonary embolism."

"I'll think about it," Pierce replied.

With the second bottle of Chateau Petrus opened and poured, the four men became more relaxed. For Turner, it was good to be with his friends.

Turner asked, "What do you guys know about what's going on in Lebanon?"

Miller replied, "Bad shit. The Sixth Fleet is going in to land marines on the beach at Beirut with the carrier *Forrestal* ready to give close air support with its air group."

"I wish we were going with them. We are checked out in the A-4. It would be way more fun than chugging around in the SNB," Teipner added.

Pierce said, "I'm not sure why we are going in there."

"We are going in there because it is in our national interest. The place is loaded with bad guys that don't like us," Miller replied.

Turner said, "It's a Muslim-Christian problem." He went on to explain what he just learned from Lieutenant Commander Owens.

"Well, if the Russians are trying to destabilize a place like Lebanon, it is in our national interest to go in and establish a military presence," Miller said.

Then Teipner added, "The world of Islam hasn't forgotten the time when the crusaders carrying banners of Christianity invaded their lands. They are getting a handle on running their own countries after being colonies of France, England, and Italy, and now we make a very noticeable appearance off Beirut."

"Don't forget, the U.S. has been siding with Israel against the Palestinians, and that sets us up for an eventual confrontation with the Muslim Arabs of Syria, Egypt, Jordan, and Iraq," Turner added.

The conversation became more thoughtful as it went on. It was the first time Turner realized that the two pilots had some intellectual depth.

Pierce had been quiet as the three others tried to work their way through a religion-driven geopolitical conundrum. Finally, he said, "Do you gentlemen have an understanding of the Eisenhower Doctrine?"

Miller said, "The Eisenhower Doctrine has to do with preventing the Russians from taking over the Middle East."

"It's a little more sophisticated than that. The Eisenhower Doctrine commits the U.S. to providing help to Middle Eastern countries threatened by communist aggression or subversion. There is concern by some diplomats that the doctrine doesn't apply in this case, but the Sixth Fleet is on its way to the eastern Mediterranean and will stand off from Beirut and land marines to try to keep the peace. So where do we go from there?"

"What do you mean, where do we go from there?" Teipner asked.

"Do we have an exit strategy? How long do we stay and at what cost?" Pierce asked. Before anyone could answer, he added, "If we stay for any time at all, the Arabs or whoever will consider us neocolonialists and start attacking us. Also remember, Muslims call us infidels for a reason."

The discussion shifted to why women become incomprehensible after they form an emotional relationship with a man. At this point, Turner caught himself as he began to nod off.

He got up and said, "Gentlemen, I'm going to hit the rack."

The others agreed they were ready too.

The next morning, while having breakfast, the four men worked out the details for Kathy Roberts's wetting-down party. Turner would reserve a room at the officers' club. Miller and Teipner would order finger food and make arrangements for a portable bar; Pierce was assigned the task of inviting only those few males that were agreeable to him and his three friends, but all the nurses not having the duty were to be asked to attend.

When they were in the thick of planning this joyous occasion, a lieutenant in full uniform and wearing a set of wings came up to their table and asked, "Is one of you Mr. Turner?"

"I'm Turner."

"We just flew in from Paris. I have an envelope for you." He handed the envelope to Turner.

Turner thanked the aviator and invited him to their table. The aviator said he was going to have breakfast with his cockpit crew, thanked him, and walked away.

Turner looked at the envelope. In the upper left-hand corner, the return address was, "Musee d' Histoire Archaeologique, Paris." The envelope was addressed to Lieutenant Burt Turner, NAS Port Lyautey.

Teipner asked, "Well, what was that all about?"

He showed them the envelope.

"So you are also involved in archeology, Mr. Turner?" Pierce asked.

"I am a man of many interests, and now I must leave. I have an engagement with the crash boat and the HUP."

As he left the table, Miller called out, "Check in with Lieutenant Commander Bello about the SNB."

"I'll do that very thing."

When he got to his room, he sat down at his desk, opened the letter, and read:

> Things are going well here at the museum. I continue my research and the outing to the ruins at Thamusida proved to be invaluable. I would like to examine the ruins at Lixus soon. The ruins are about two and a half miles north of the fishing port and town of Larache. Lixus is one of the oldest Phoenician trading posts in the Western world. It's located on a hill overlooking the Loukkos River and estuary. Larache, I understand, is a tranquil, no-hassle town that is rather scruffy, but good for a short visit.
>
> South of the point protecting the port, my friends tell me, are headlands and cliff faces—an area not much good for swimming and therefore without any people. No one seems to live on or near the headland, but from time to time, sheep may be found grazing there. I guess there is a beach for swimming below Lixus, but there are people nearby, so no nude sunbathing, which some of us enjoy.
>
> I attended a meeting the other day, and one of my colleagues said a more important archeological site associated with my research is near a minor fishing port south of Agadir near Cape Draa. Oh well, the people with the grant money (the power, you know) get to choose where to do research. I'm not one of those.
>
> I seem to be meandering. My partner and I wonder how you are doing. Please take good care of yourself; you are very special. Hope to see you again soon.
>
> Laura Brae, MS

To begin with, he was surprised to receive anything from this Laura Brae. He thought, *Why did she send me something like this?* He read the note again, put it back in the envelope, and dropped it into the trashcan next to his desk. Then he reached over and spread out a coastal navigation chart of the area from the Strait of Gibraltar to Rabat that he brought from his office.

He carefully examined the coastline between Port Lyautey and Larache. Taking a legal-size pad from the center drawer of his desk, he took a pencil and started to outline his plan of action for Thursday night.

Using the data collected from today's swims and a set of navigational dividers that he wrongfully appropriated from the navigation department at OCS Newport, he worked out the time and distances for a number of different approaches to the port of Larache.

Knowing the AVR had radar, he thought there should be no problem getting down the Oued Sebou and going out to sea in darkness. He figured by about 2300 hours, they should be at the point of insertion where the four-man raft would be deployed and then would follow a two-mile track bearing 75° east-northeast to the point protecting the port of Larache.

He thought about Captain Dillon's aerial pictures of the surrounding area and the strong suggestion Dillon presented about taking the four-man raft around the point and up the channel to the long pier and came to the conclusion that the risk of discovery was too great.

He came up with two options: either paddle north around the point and haul out on the lee side, sending two swimmers underwater to the pier where the trawler was tied up, or paddle and haul out on the rocky shoreline under the cliffs on the south side of the point, then send two swimmers underwater around the point to the trawler.

Paddling around the point and hauling out would make the time and distance underwater shorter, but there would be a chance of being discovered before putting the swimmers in the water. Hauling out south of the Point would be a much longer swim around the point under very turbulent water, but there would be less chance of being discovered.

Coming back out, his calculations showed there would be plenty of air left in the tanks if they went around the point in the four-man raft and then put swimmers in the water. If the swimmers were put in the water south of the point, they would probably have to surface on the way back and swim several hundred yards to the beached four-man raft.

He would work this out with Gallegos and Cole tomorrow morning.

He began trying to work out the HUP helicopter plan. After a few tries, he got up from his desk, went down the hall to the phone, looked up the number of Chief Flint Williams, and dialed. After four rings, the chief answered. "Chief Williams."

"Chief, this is Burt Turner. I need help."

"I thought you might, Mr. Turner. I waited up until 11:30, and then went to bed."

Turner was surprised hearing Williams using the civilian time of 11:30 instead of the military time of 2330. He looked at his Rolex and saw it was 0145.

"I'm sorry, Chief. I didn't know what time it was."

Williams thought, *Another junior officer who doesn't have a clue about the time of day or night.*

"I guess I told you to call me. What's the problem?"

"I have my proposed plan of action pretty much finished, except for the HUP. I don't even know where to start."

Williams didn't answer. "Chief, I don't know if you heard me—"

"I heard you. I was thinking. What can you give me to work with?"

"Three men, two SCUBA rigs, two cylinders each, at seventy pounds each rig. Distance to Larache one way, seventy miles." Turner had already worked out the distance and bearing from the point at Larache for the pickup. "Pickup rendezvous will be two miles off the point of Larache at a bearing of 85° east-north-east. We will each have two flares. Hopefully, we will not need more than two or three."

"You said three SCUBA rigs when you told me before. I glad you are down to two. That sounds manageable. Three would be taking a chance. I'll call you tomorrow morning about nine. Will you be in your office?"

"Yes, I will, Chief. Thanks."

Williams hung up the phone without further word.

Turner went back to his room and worked out the team's rendezvous position for the HUP. It was the reciprocal of 85° or 265°, two miles from the point where the HUP, hopefully, would be orbiting as it waited for the four-man raft.

The real problem would be their retrieval by the HUP at 0100. Tomorrow, he would find out if they had the ability to work with the HUP at night.

At the bottom of his proposed plan of action, he wrote, "Determine weather, tide, and current status."

After quarters the next morning, Turner and his two men were at the long table in the NOF conference room. He had carefully gone over the nautical chart of the area and explained the options with regard to the team's insertion.

Chief Gallegos said, "I think taking the four-man raft around the point, hauling out, and swimming from there makes more sense than swimming around the point. If I remember the aerial photo correctly, it would be a very difficult swim to get around and back in the amount of time necessary, especially if we have to surface on the way back."

Cole said, "I agree with that. Instead of coming in south of the point and paddling around it, why not save time and go more directly toward the channel entering the port, and then hug the lee side of the point?"

"What do you think about that, Chief?" Turner asked.

"It would be shorter, but we would be open to discovery for quite a while. I think we need to come in from south and stay under the cliffs as we work our way around the point."

"That sounds about right. Cole, how about you?"

"I think the chief is right."

"We will do it that way, then. I didn't get far in working out the extraction with the HUP, so I called Chief Williams and gave him all the information I had. He said he would pull it together and call me here early this morning."

Gallegos asked, "What was your plan for the four-man raft when we meet the HUP?"

"I didn't think of that, Chief."

"How about, after coming back around the point, we put into shore and put a load of rocks on board, then paddle out to the HUP rendezvous point. The last man to be lifted out by the HUP will slice open the air chambers of the raft and let it sink," said Cole.

Gallegos looked at Turner and said, "I think that would work fine, sir, if the rocks don't spill out on the way down."

"Then we'll plan to do that—if we can't come up with anything better."

Yeoman Fry came from across the hall, poked his head in the doorway, and said, "Mr. Turner, Chief Williams is on the phone for you."

Turner thanked the yeoman, rose from the table, and left the room.

Ten minutes later he returned and said, "Chief Williams said he could do it, but it won't be a piece of cake. Based on the three-day weather report and the weight calculations, he could orbit our pickup point for maybe twenty minutes. Any longer than that, and we could say good-bye to recovering our SCUBAs. Five or ten minutes after that, we'd better have a plan B because he would have to abort."

Gallegos said, "We better work on plan B, a contingency plan."

For the next forty-five minutes, they worked on some possibilities. If the AVR broke down, they would stay with it and radio for rescue. If the AVR was sighted but not caught, they would abort the mission, sink the four-man raft and limpet mine in deep water, swim south for a time, then go ashore and continue to work their way south. Hopefully, at daylight, the HUP would find them. If caught, they would have previously dumped the limpet mine, would plead they were training, and let the embassy and navy bail them out.

After the three agreed on the plan of action and the added contingency plan, Turner said, "I'll have the yeomen type this up, and I'll meet you in the shop. Chief, would you call Operations and tell them to alert the AVR that we are on the way."

They left the conference room. Gallegos and Cole went on to the EOD shop, and Turner walked across the hall and stood in front of Yeoman Fry's desk.

The yeoman looked up and asked, "Yes, sir? What can I help you with?"

"I'd like to have you go over this with me, make suggestions, and type it up. I have a meeting at 1500 tomorrow and would like to pick it up, in the 'smooth,' at 1400."

The yeoman looked in at Turner for a moment, then pushed aside what he was working on and said, "Sit down. Let's see what you have."

After going over the plan of action draft and adding a number of editorial suggestions by Fry, the draft was ready to be typed up. As Turner got up to leave, the yeoman said, "The exec wants to see you before you leave, sir."

Turner walked over to the exec's office, stood in the doorway and announced, "Yeoman Fry said you wanted to see me, sir."

The exec picked up his phone, dialed, and said, "Mr. Turner is here, sir. Yes, sir, we will come right in."

As they entered Commander Hawkins' office he stood up from his desk and said, "An hour ago, I received word that your plan of action is to be completed and ready for review at 0900 tomorrow morning at the Fleet Intelligence Center. Captain Dillon will be flying in tonight from Naples and will run the meeting. The naval attaché from Rabat will sit in."

"But, sir, I requested that I be allowed to turn in the plan of action in at 1500 tomorrow!"

"Mr. Turner, these are times that try men's souls. Bring your plan of action to my office at 0800 tomorrow, and you and the exec and I will make it ready for my signature. We understand you will be working with the AVR and HUP today and the HUP tonight. With that background, we are sure you will be able to deal with any questions the review board will have in regard to your overall capability to carrying out your plan of action.

"A cover letter signed by my executive officer and me recommending additions and deletions will be appended to your plan of action. I hope there are few additions and deletions necessary. Don, do what you can to help Mr. Turner. That will be all."

After leaving the commander's office, the exec asked, "Mr. Turner, do you have your plan of action at your desk?"

"I just turned the draft in to Yeoman Fry for typing, sir."

"Well, let's have a look at what he has so far."

They walked over to the yeoman's desk. "Yeoman Fry, let me see what you have done so far with Mr. Turner's plan of action."

The yeoman passed two completed pages to the exec.

He read through the pages and then said, "Let me see the smooth copy when you are finished. Mr. Turner, if you think of any possible changes to your plan of action after you finish with your exercise today with the AVR and HUP, get back here immediately." He quickly added, "Oh, I am sure you have cleared how you plan to deal with insertion and extraction with Lieutenant Commander Bello. If you haven't, do so."

"Yes, sir."

By the time the team left the NOF, Gallegos collected lunch from the chiefs' club, and the AVR was underway, they were thirty-five minutes late. The swells were running six or seven feet, there was a slight chop with the wind coming from the northwest at about fifteen knots. As they approached the point immediately north of the Oued Sebou, the coxswain asked, "How far off the point do you want us to be when you launch, sir?"

"Put us off about two hundred yards."

"Aye, aye, sir."

When they arrived at the drop-off point, Turner told the coxswain, "Stand off here while we try for the point. If we do it without much trouble, we will try it again to make sure we know what we are doing. After that, we will paddle back out to the AVR and get ready for the HUP. If we swamp and are able to get back aboard, we will keep paddling. Otherwise, we'll swim the raft around the point. If we get in real trouble, we will let the raft go its own way, and we'll swim around the point. You can follow and pick us up in the lee of the point."

"Aye, aye, sir."

The coxswain put the AVR in position, throttled back, and let the boat drift. The team, with their fins on and facemasks around their necks, secured the paddles to the raft, lifted it, and with Turner holding the raft's bowline, they sent the raft over the side of the AVR.

Gallegos and Cole followed the raft into the water, grabbed on to it as it bucked up and down, and pulled themselves aboard. They untied the paddles and quickly gained control of the raft. Then Turner jumped in the water with the bowline, pulled himself aboard the raft, grabbed the third paddle and, using it as a rudder, steered the raft toward the point as Gallegos and Cole paddled.

Close to the point, the combination of wind and current made paddling increasingly difficult. Then, as they rounded the point, the force of wind and current caused the seas to rebound with great strength from the rocks at the base of the cliff. The raft bucked violently and slewed around, with water coming over the bow, sloshing about, then spilling over the side. Finally, they were on the other side, in the lee of the point.

Cole, laughed and said, "That wasn't so bad. Let's go back and do it closer."

Turner had just really scared himself.

As they rested, Gallegos said, "I think we began this exercise too close in. If we go any closer, we are going for a swim."

Turner answered, "Well, we know what to expect here, but not at Larache. I think we should try worst-case."

He was sorry he said this as soon as the words were out of his mouth. He was still pretty uneasy.

Cole answered, "Why not? Let's go for it!"

They turned the raft around and started paddling hard as Turner steered closer in. They did well until they were almost around the point, then in an instant, the raft was upside down and getting blown toward the surf crashing against the rocks. The three men were close enough to get ahold of the grab lines on the raft and swim it away from the point.

Once in quieter water, they turned the raft back over and climbed aboard. Turner looked at the chief and sheepishly said, "I guess I should have listened to you, Chief."

He laughed and said, "Well, we live and learn, Mr. Turner, we live and learn."

Cole added, "Yeah, but if we didn't try it, we would never know if we could. Besides it was great!"

Starting somewhat farther out than the first attempt, they went around the point again easily, then repeated the experience two more times before recovering at the AVR. Turner was confident that they could deal with the point at Larache.

After they came aboard and hauled the raft out of the water, the coxswain reported, "We just got word from Operations. The HUP will be about forty-five minutes late."

With that salutary message Gallegos said, "Cole, break out our gourmet luncheon."

The lunch from the chiefs' club was excellent. Ham and swiss cheese on rye with American head lettuce, pickles, chocolate chip cookies, and some sort of grape drink. They had an hour to eat lunch and rest.

At 1315, the AVR radio was loud enough for them to hear, "AVR four-four-three, this is Operations. Over."

One of the crewmen answered, "AVR four-four-three. Go ahead, Operations."

"Pedro one-five has just launched and will be in your area at 1325."

The crewman answered, "Pedro one-five just launched and will be in our area at 1325. Thank you, Operations. AVR four-four-three out."

Eight minutes later, they heard the *chop-chop-chop* of the HUP. Turner looked to the south and saw the helicopter rapidly coming toward them at a height of about fifty feet. Just before passing over the AVR, Chief Williams slowed the helicopter and gave a hand signal to follow him out to sea. The coxswain jammed the throttles forward, swung the AVR around, and, slamming up and down in the swells, followed the HUP. About two miles ahead, the HUP began to orbit. The AVR closed the distance, and the coxswain throttled back and let the boat drift. With a wave of their hands, the SW/EOD team jumped into the water and swam away.

When they were a good distance from the AVR, Turner called out to his men, "I'll go first, then Cole, and then you, Chief."

The HUP swung around, and as it came into position to hover, water spray from the rotor downwash struck the glass of the team's facemasks, obliterating their vision. They lifted their facemasks to their forehead and squinted in the direction of the HUP. A split second later, they each made a series of gasps, trying to catch their breaths as they experienced the full downwash from the rotors. Even though Chief Williams told them earlier that this was going to happen, it was still a startling experience.

Looking up, the team could see the hoist operator in the entry hatch lowering and guiding the hoisting cable with its yellow horse collar toward them.

A swell lifted Turner up toward the horse collar, but before he could grab it, the swell passed on and he was down in the trough with the next swell coming on. He rode the oncoming swell up and tried again to catch the horse collar and missed. After two more failures, he finally timed the rise of the next swell with where the horse collar was going to be and caught it. Chief Williams put the helicopter in a climb and swung away as the crewman hoisted Turner up. Then with Turner safely on board, he headed back for the next pickup.

Gallegos and Cole learned a lot by watching Turner's initial attempts. They both had the horse collar on in two tries.

They made four more drops and recoveries before heading for the surf area. They were fifty feet above the water on the approach to the surf when Chief Williams turned around in the cockpit and yelled above the engine and rotor noise, "I'm going to fly along just outside the surf line for a few minutes. If you look down, you will see something interesting. I'll find a gap between groups before I drop you off."

They looked down and saw hammerhead sharks in twos, threes, and fours milling around just out from the surf line.

Cole said, "Jesus, is that what we have been swimming through?"

Gallegos answered, "Oh yes."

Turner said, "I think they are too busy mating to be concerned with us . . . I hope."

One of the things Turner was required to do when he was employed at Marineland of the Pacific was to periodically sit on the bottom of the large oval tank in his diving gear and hand-feed the smaller fish for the amusement of the audience. There were a few five-foot blue sharks that would swim by, which didn't prove threatening, but the hammerheads gave him some concern.

Chief Williams turned around again and yelled, "This looks good. I'll go down to ten feet, and you can drop in. How many drop and pickups do you want to do?"

Turner raised three fingers and yelled back, "After the last one, drop us near the AVR.

Williams saluted and put the helicopter in hover. Just before the team launched themselves through the bottom entry hatch, Turner looked at Gallegos and Cole and said, "When we get in the water, let's try to position ourselves between the breaking first and second waves in the set of three. If we can't hold position, let's go all the way in, where the third wave is breaking up."

Turner dropped through the hatch first, then Cole and Gallegos. In the water, Turner looked down, was pleased not to see any hammerheads, and followed the first wave in. Gallegos and Cole preferred not to look for hammerheads and followed Turner.

They tried to hold position in between the first and second waves, but only Cole was able grab the horse collar, put it on, and be hoisted as the HUP lifted and swung away. Turner and Gallegos were swept on toward the beach. When they were in the turbulence of the breaking third wave, they were able to hold their position, and Gallegos was hoisted on board, then Turner.

The second and third cycles of drop and pickup were uneventful. The team's success in learning to work with the HUP was primarily due to the skill of Chief Williams and the hoist operator.

On the way back to the AVR, with the HUP bouncing around a bit, Turner gingerly worked his way to the cockpit and asked, "Chief, can we meet in Operations at 1600? I want to go over the plan of action with you. We have to make some changes."

The chief looked at him, smiled knowingly, and gave a thumbs-up.

The recovery with the AVR and ride back to the wharf was uneventful. After offloading their gear, their adrenaline was still up and drove them to joke about each other's ability to work with the AVR and HUP. Cole was at his best with his fantasy about fighting off hammerhead sharks snapping at him as he dangled from the end of the hoisting cable.

When they were back in the shop getting dressed, Gallegos said, "I think you are wise to make changes in the plan of action, Mr. Turner. Even if we find out we can handle the drop and pickups tonight, it will be entirely different working with our raft and diving gear off Larache at night, especially if the sea conditions change for the worse—even slightly."

"My learning curve is giving me a real headache, Chief."

"My best advice to you is to continue to talk to people who have information that will help you get the job done. It could also help you avoid a visit to the long green table. Now that would be an even bigger headache."

(*The long green table is a table covered with green felt where an officer accused of professional misconduct and/or moral misconduct would be sitting at one end, and at the other end would be a senior officer or officers sitting in judgment.*)

Cole thoughtfully said, "What if we get picked up on land instead of water. There must be a remote place where Williams could set down and retrieve us."

Gallegos looked at Turner and said, "When we were looking at the aerials, wasn't there a cove and broad beach south of the point at Larache?"

"It was about five miles south of the point. We could paddle that far. Let's go talk to Chief Williams."

Before leaving NOF, Turner went by the office and picked up a copy of the plan of action draft he had in the middle drawer of his desk. When they arrived at Operations, Williams was talking to Lieutenant Commander Bello. Bello saw them and waved them over.

"I understand you three enjoyed working with our AVR and HUP today. I guess I should thank you for allowing our air-sea rescue team to have some extended realistic practice."

"A good time was had by all, sir. We appreciate you making the AVR and HUP available to us. We need all the practice we can get," Turner replied.

"Well, some very important people have told me to do everything possible to get you and your team ready for a mission—one I am not cleared to know about, except for date, time, and that it will require the HUP and the AVR for your insertion and extraction. Your CO asked me to sign off on that section of your plan of action. I understand you are to submit the whole plan for approval early tomorrow morning?"

"Yes, sir. It seems they moved the review for the plan up, and I am scrambling to finish it."

"Let's go into my office and talk."

Inside Bello's office, Turner looked around and saw the usual navy-issued gray steel desk, bookshelf, and chairs, but in addition, under the only window in the office, was a drafting table, slightly tilted, with a world aeronautical chart (no. 420) of northwestern Morocco.

Looking more closely at the bookshelf, he saw a variety of reference manuals put out by different navy bureaus—Bureau of Aeronautics, Bureau of Ships, and others—and flight manuals of the Douglas A-4 Skyhawk attack fighter and the new McDonald F-4 Phantom fighter aircraft. On his desk, to one side of a stack of official papers, he recognized Bello's wife and daughter in a picture. On the wall opposite the window was a moderately large picture of Bello, in a flight suit and holding his helmet, standing next to an A-4 Skyhawk with an older man in civilian clothes. *Bello's dad?* he thought.

Bello broke Turner's 'look around' with, "Mr. Turner, let's have a look at the section of the plan I'm to sign off on."

Turner leafed through the plan, found the section, and gave it him. As Bello finished a page, he passed it on to Chief Williams to read.

When reading, he said, "The ideas you have here are plausible, Mr. Turner. How the HUP is to be used during the extraction phase is damn near catastrophic."

Williams laughed and added, "It was a good first try, though."

Turner took the criticism easily and said, "We have worked out an alternative for your consideration, sir. Do you have a nautical chart of the area we could look at?"

Bello went to the door and called out, "Mr. Dohr, would you please bring me a nautical coastal chart that has the area between Rabat and Tangier?"

Dohr was a newly arrived lieutenant jg who had recently won his wings and was on TAD until being transferred to the aircraft carrier *Forrestal.*

A short time later, Dohr came into the office with the rolled up chart and gave it to Bello.

"Thank you, Mr. Dohr. Pease shut the door on your way out."

Dohr did as requested.

Then Bello gave everyone a big smile and added, "I couldn't help that. I could have asked someone else for the chart, but then I wouldn't have been able to ask Mr. Dohr to shut the door, don't you see?"

They all tried not to laugh but they couldn't keep from it. Turner wasn't sure if they were laughing at Lieutenant Commander Bello or at his setting-up of Lieutenant Dohr.

Bello gave the chart to Turner, who unrolled it and laid it out on the drafting table.

He began, "Chief Gallegos, Cole, and I realized after working with Chief Williams and the HUP today that the extraction in the plan was unreasonable. So after thinking about it, we considered being extracted by the HUP here."

He pointed to a cove on the chart just below Larache and continued. "There is a broad sandy beach backed up by tall cliffs in this cove. The cliffs are consistent in height going south of Larache for about fifteen miles. Because the HUP would land on the beach and not have to hover, our weight and the weight of our gear would not be a penalty in the amount of fuel needed to get us home."

Bello asked Williams, "Flint, would wind or rotor downwash bouncing back from the cliff faces be a problem?"

"I have flown over that area. I'm sure we could pull it off and probably with fuel to spare. Of course, it would depend on the weather."

Turner asked, "Sir, we would like to schedule the SNB for an 1100 reconnaissance flight tomorrow. Perhaps Chief Williams could ride along for a look?"

"Work out the SNB scheduling with Miller and Teipner. It would probably be a good idea, Flint, if you went along."

Chief Williams nodded in the affirmative.

Turner continued, "We have a four-day weather report, which will be periodically updated. For now, Thursday night is clear, with a gibbous moon and a breeze from the northwest."

He forgot to add, *Early Friday morning, storm continuing through Saturday afternoon.*

Bello looked at Chief Gallegos and asked, "What do you think, Chief?"

"We have talked it over pretty carefully. I agree with Mr. Turner."

"And you, Petty Officer Cole?"

"We can do it, sir."

"About an hour ago, I was informed by Captain Travis to be at the meeting tomorrow. Chief Williams and I will work on your insertion and extraction section and present it at the meeting. Understand that we will go along with the AVR insertion and, probably with some variations and qualifications, go along with your proposal."

Feeling greatly relieved, Turner said, "Thank you, sir. You have been of great help."

Chief Williams said, "I'll see you tomorrow at the SNB. If Mr. Miller and Mr. Teipner are driving, I may go over to the parachute loft and check one out."

The SW/EOD team left Operations feeling upbeat and confident.

That evening, Turner and his friends, dressed in civilian casual, arrived early at the officers' club for the surprise wetting-down party for Kathy Roberts's promotion to full lieutenant. Miller and Teipner had selected a room just off the larger banquet room. As they entered, they were pleased to see how well the stewards had set up the room for the occasion. There were two long tables of food adjacent to one another, and on the other side of the room, a bar on wheels. There were two stewards, one posted at the tables, and the other at the bar on wheels.

At the first table were varieties of cheese—Brie, swiss, fontina, cheddar, and a few only Dr. Lieutenant Pierce was able to recognize—plus sliced meats and a variety of olives. The little space that was left was occupied with a variety of breads, crackers, dips, and salads. The second table was more substantial: chicken breasts with broccoli and ham, next to boeuf a la bourguignon. For those with more pedestrian tastes, there were mashed potatoes and a very nice meat loaf.

After sampling the first table, there was a quick approving look at the second, and then the four made for the bar on wheels.

Pierce was the first to ask the steward, "May I have a martini with two olives, please?"

The steward quickly produced the drink and passed it to Pierce with a smile.

Then Miller asked, "Do you have Pilsner Urquell or Stella Artois?"

"We have both of those fine beers and one American—Pabst—sir."

Miller and Teipner asked for Pilsner Urquell.

Turner ordered a martini. "One olive will be fine."

Fifteen minutes later, Turner was nursing his martini and his friends were on their second rounds when Binki Bianconi, Kathy Roberts, and Betty Armstrong arrived with four other nurses, the hospital director (Commander Berry Roscoe, orthopedic surgeon), and two other physicians, all in uniforms worn while on duty at the hospital.

Turner, Miller, and Teipner held back a little as Pierce greeted the medical group. Then, very correctly, Pierce introduced his three friends to his coworkers, except for the three women who were already known to them (one known in the biblical sense to Turner). One of the physicians, an anesthesiologist who assisted Pierce during Huwitt's surgery, recognized Turner and waited behind when the others went to the tables and bar on wheels.

He approached Turner and said, "I haven't heard anything about Petty Officer Huwitt. How is he doing?"

Turner took a sip of his martini and answered, "They let us know yesterday he died four days ago."

The anesthesiologist was obviously upset. "I am so sorry. We really worked hard. I thought he had a good chance. Bethesda works miracles, but not in this case, I guess. I'm so sorry."

"Thank you for trying to save him. I know you and Phil did your best."

They shook hands, and the anesthesiologist went on and joined the others at the bar on wheels.

Turner walked over to his friends and joined in their conversation. He tried not to look directly at Kathy. Finally, the subject turned to Kathy and Binki's trip to Rota. The two women talked about the navy exchange and how much more of a selection there was compared to the navy exchange at Port Lyautey and the background of constant flamenco dance music from radios.

Betty asked, "Did you see any cute guys?"

Binki answered, "There was one cute doc that gave a lecture on chest trauma, but he didn't know as much as we did. Kathy, with great sensitivity, helped him out."

Kathy Roberts was making an effort to catch Turner's eye and finally said, "What's been going on with you, Burt? Have your three friends been leading you astray?"

Before he could answer, Miller said, "We haven't been able to misguide him very much. He appears to be very busy."

Teipner added, "We think he may have something going on in town."

Binki asked, "Burt, do you have something going you are not telling us about?"

Kathy Roberts had a big smile and raised her eyebrows and said, "You would tell us, wouldn't you, Burt?"

He looked into her eyes and was completely thrown off balance; his face turned red, and he almost dropped his fontina and cracker. Miller and Teipner were elbowing each other; Pierce was waiting for Turner's response.

Only Binki noticed how Turner and Kathy were looking at each other. She had thought there was something going on between the two; now she was sure.

He collected himself and replied. "I wish I had time to develop something in town. While you guys have fun, play games, and are shopping here and there, someone had to stand tall against potential evildoers."

There were a few more jokes, mostly about Miller and Teipner. Pierce was always the butt of jokes, yet able to hold his own. Finally, it was time to mix with the others. The group broke up, except for Turner and Kathy Roberts.

"I see you are having a martini, Burt, just like me."

"Jesus, Kathy, why did you do that?"

"I didn't do anything. Why are you so sensitive?"

He started to turn and walk away. She grabbed his arm, looked in his eyes, and said, "I think you are wonderful, and I enjoy being with you. I'm sorry if I made you uncomfortable."

"Let's go outside. I need to hold you."

"I need you too, but we can't."

From the other side of the room, Commander Roscoe tapped a spoon against a wineglass and called out, "Ladies and gentlemen, ladies and gentlemen."

Having their attention, he continued, "We are here to celebrate the promotion of Lieutenant Junior Grade Roberts, Kathy that is, to lieutenant. I have here double bars to take the place of her single bar." He held up the double bars and continued. "Before I bestow this symbol of her new rank, I want to say a few words about our colleague." The three not involved in the medical corps had never heard naval officers refer to each other as colleagues. "Lieutenant Roberts is the finest operating room nurse and trauma nurse that it has been my pleasure to work with in my twenty years as an orthopedic surgeon."

Genuine and well-deserved clapping and cheers.

He continued, "We all work long hours and without the best of equipment. We are experts at improvising in the clinics and operating rooms. In the two years I have been here, Lieutenant Roberts has provided leadership by showing how magnificent medical treatment can be delivered through dedication, inspiration, and resourcefulness. Kathy, would you please come up?"

She came forward and stood to one side of Commander Roscoe. He turned and removed the single silver bars from her lapels and fastened in their place the double bars of a full lieutenant. Cheering and clapping, the guests gathered around Kathy Roberts hugged her or shook her hand, whichever was appropriate.

When Turner hugged her, he whispered in her ear, "I love you so very much."

She smiled and squeezed his hand.

Then began the eating and drinking. It was a very friendly group; the aviators were comfortable with the medical folks, and the medical folks, with the aviators. Miller was trying his best to make himself likeable to Mary Bionconi. The attempt was marginally successful.

Teipner found a new nurse, Juniper Cooper; actually, she found him, and he was happily telling her what a fine airman he was.

Pierce was chatting on a professional level with the other physicians. Turner stood next to Pierce, listening. He was careful to limit himself to his one martini, two pieces of bread, and a slice of fontina.

At 2045, he went up to Miller and said, "I've got the duty, I have to cut out. See you later."

Miller gave him a punch on the shoulder and, surprising Turner, said, "Watch out for the hammerheads, old buddy."

He looked around and found Kathy Roberts. He discreetly took her aside and said, "I have to go do a few things. Can I see you later?"

She pressed up against him, squeezed his hand, and said, "Yes, I would like that."

He left the party, went to the BOQ, changed into his wash khaki uniform, and left for the NOF and EOD shop.

When he came through the door at the EOD shop, Cole laughed and said, "We didn't think you were coming, sir."

"I wouldn't miss this for anything. Besides, I will probably have to rescue you old men."

Cole laughed and said, "Did you hear that, Chief? This young officer may have to rescue us, and he called us old men."

"Just humor the young man. He knows who he is working with."

By 2115, they were dressed in their dry suits with webbed belts buckled on, two flares taped to their knife scabbards, and their life jackets on; and they had completed the inventory list check off

Going out the door, Turner said, "I'll drive. You older men should get as much rest as you can."

Gallegos laughed. Cole said, "Actually, you need the time behind the wheel, sir. This is another check ride before we allow you to solo."

Turner drove the weapons carrier down to the wharf without slipping the clutch or missing a gear. By 2145, they had transferred their gear to the AVR and were on the way out of the Oued Sebou.

At 2150, they heard Chief Williams call in from the HUP.

"AVR four-four-three, this is Pedro one-five. I'll be two miles west of the point to your north in ten, over."

The coxswain replied, "Pedro one-five, this is AVR four-four-three, roger you're two miles west of the point to our north in ten, out."

The weather was clear, with the moon showing through a light haze as it rose just above the horizon, the wind at about ten knots from the west, and the sea showing six-foot swells with a slight wind chop.

Five minutes after they arrived at the drop-off and pickup site, those in the AVR could see the navigation lights of the oncoming helicopter. The coxswain pulled the throttles back and let the AVR drift, then over the loudspeaker came, "AVR four-four-three, this is Pedro one-five. How many cycles of lift and drop are we to do tonight?"

The coxswain looked over at Turner and gestured for him to take the microphone. Turner reached over, took the microphone, and said, "This is Turner, Chief, let's go for two. Each man has two flares. One man will light his flare at a time. The second man will light off after the first man is up and away, then the third. If for any reason the operation goes sour, we will recover on board the AVR. If that goes sour, we will swim to the beach south of the point. Over."

"Roger that. I should warn you. From the air, all we see is the flare under the best conditions. If we could get a light on your head, it would appear about the size of a volleyball. If the sea is running at all, we begin to have difficulties finding you. Over."

"I understand, Chief. We are going in now. Out."

"Pedro one-five, roger. Out."

Gallegos, Cole, and the coxswain heard the transmission.

Just before entering the water Turner said, "Cole, you get the first lift, then the Chief, then I'll go." They saluted in acknowledgment. He gave a big grin and said, "Let's get wet."

They entered the water and swam away from the AVR.

When the running lights of the AVR appeared to be about a hundred yards away, Cole cut loose one of his flares and tried to light it off; it didn't light. On the third try it did.

The HUP was a hundred feet up and about two hundred yards away; Williams saw the light immediately and swooped down and into hover. Three minutes later, Cole was hoisted on board, and the HUP swung out and around for another pass.

When Cole loosened himself from the horse collar, he looked at the hoist operator and said, "It is a beautiful night isn't it?" Then with his fins flip-flopping on the deck of the HUP, he went to the passenger bench and sat down.

"You guys are fucking crazy, you know that," the hoist operator said, shaking his head.

Cole answered, "We just like to have fun, man."

Williams saw Gallegos's flare far to the left of his flight path, banked left, dropped down, and went into hover. Turner had drifted a considerable distance away from Gallegos and could only see the navigation lights of the HUP from where he was. When the HUP pulled up and away, he was able to catch a glimpse of the cabin light showing from the entry hatch beneath the fuselage. He couldn't see if the chief was being hoisted up.

He had drifted so far away from the AVR that he was now unable to see its running lights. He pulled the hood of his dry suit back so he could better hear the HUP if it came near. A few minutes later, he heard the *chop-chop-chop* of the HUP's rotor blades, then the sound faded away in the distance. Turner began to feel very much alone.

He reached down, slid his knife out from its plastic scabbard, and cut away the first flare. When he was putting his knife away, the flare slipped from his fingers. His hand hit the flare as he groped for it in the water; he was lucky enough to grasp it.

Next time, I'll wedge the flare in my web belt before I start screwing around with the knife. Lose a flare, lose the HUP, maybe.

He checked his Rolex; twelve minutes had gone by since he last heard the HUP.

Then, in the distance, he heard the HUP's rotor blades. The sound came up and began to fade away again, then came up and faded away again. The HUP was searching. He lit off the flare and held it up as high as he could.

The hoist operator was sitting in the copilot's seat next to Chief Williams. He called out, "We have our last fish at three o'clock, Chief!"

Williams swung the helicopter around to where the hoist operator was pointing and saw the faint flicker of the flare as Turner rose and fell with the swells.

Three minutes later, Turner had been brought up to the cable stops in the HUP and was slipping out of the horse collar.

The hoist operator saluted and yelled out over the rotor and engine noise, "Welcome aboard, sir!"

With a look of some relief, he returned the salute and replied, "Glad to be aboard and out of the embrace of the sea, Petty Officer."

Gallegos and Cole made room for Turner on the passenger bench, and as he sat down, Cole remarked, "And you were going to rescue us. The chief and I were almost ready to start looking for you, Mr. Turner."

"Well, Aviation Ordnanceman First Class Cole, it ain't over yet."

The HUP was beginning to shake like the wind might be coming up and the sea state could be changing. Williams told the hoist operator to have Turner come up to the cockpit. The hoist operator looked back at the passengers, pointed at Turner and waved him forward.

When he arrived in the cockpit, Williams yelled, "I just called the AVR. The wind is coming up a bit and I'm going to drop you close to the AVR so I won't lose you. It will be a high drop and pickup so you will know what it's like. Get ready to go."

Turner went back to his men and told them about the drop. They stood up and made their way to the hatch below the hoist. As Williams moved the HUP slowly forward, they dropped out one at a time and about thirty feet apart. Turner was last.

Because of the height and darkness, they couldn't see the surface of the sea and were unprepared when they hit. The shock of hitting the water caused their fins to break away from their feet and ride up their legs to their thighs. If they had not been holding their facemasks tightly, they would have lost them.

After sorting themselves out, they could see the AVR's running lights dimly in the distance. Cole lit off his last flare, and the HUP came in with its search light on and hovered at a much higher altitude. Cole looked up and was surprised to see how far above the entry hatch was. He was barely able see the hoist operator, outlined by the cabin light, as he tried to hold the hoisting cable steady.

When the horse collar was in reach, Cole quickly grabbed it and was able to get one arm through as he felt the cable tighten pulling him up and out of the water. The HUP quickly gained altitude and flew away, with Cole safely secure and dangling far behind.

Gallegos called over to Turner, "That looks interesting. Before he disappeared into the night, Cole looked like a spider at the end of a long strand."

"You're next, Chief, enjoy it. I'm swimming to the beach," he kidded.

"What about the hammerhead sharks? I think they eat at night."

Turner was losing sight of Gallegos and yelled, "I changed my mind Chief."

Gallegos's flare was spotted quickly, his high pickup uneventful.

When the HUP moved into position to pick up, Turner, he waited for it to drop down closer to the water. It didn't, it remained very high. Correspondingly, the cable and horse collar took more time to lower from the added height. When it was down and within reach, he was floating at the crest of a swell, then he was down in the trough with the horse collar ten feet above his grasp. After several crest-to-trough, trough-to-crest cycles, he was finally able to grab, hang on, and pull himself into the horse collar.

At the same time he was being hoisted up, the HUP was climbing away. He looked down and became very uncomfortable when he saw how quickly he was rising above the running lights of the AVR that had just come into view. He looked up and saw the cable he was hanging from strung out a great distance behind the HUP. He didn't like it at all. Unable to control his situation, he became apprehensive and close to panic.

If I don't get hauled up faster, I'm going to drop back in the water. I don't like this high pickup shit.

Finally, there was nothing to see below; it was too dark, and he was too high up. He looked up and saw that he was approaching the entry hatch. Getting ready to come aboard, he felt back in control of his situation. A minute later, he was aboard the helicopter. He got out of the horse collar, worked his way to the passenger bench and sat down next to Gallegos. Gallegos could see that Turner was a bit rattled and said, "Well, I hope we don't have to do that very soon again."

Turner replied quietly, "Me too, Chief."

On the other hand, Cole said, "That was so great, I wish Huwitt was here."

A few minutes later the team was dropped close by the AVR. The wind was up, and there was some chop along with heavier swells. Knowing the change of sea state was going to make recovering the team difficult, the AVR crew put the four-man raft in the water on the leeward side of the AVR and secured it.

With a searchlight on the swimmers, the coxswain carefully brought the boat in close enough for them to climb aboard the raft, then from the raft, the AVR crew was able to help them aboard and then haul up the raft. With the exercise completed, the coxswain turned the AVR and headed back to the wharf.

By the time the team returned to the EOD shop, utter fatigue had taken the place of the adrenaline rush. The usual banter was absent as they put away gear and changed clothes. On leaving, there were only half-hearted "see you tomorrows."

It was 0120 in the morning when Turner wearily went through the front door of the BOQ and was going upstairs. When he got to the top of the stairs, he tripped and almost fell. He stood up, pulled himself together, turned down the hall, and walked to his room. Standing in front of his door, he fumbled for his key and promptly dropped it. He picked it up, unlocked the door, went inside, shut the door, and turned on the light

From his bed came a sleepy voice. "Burt, shut the light off, and come over here."

He whispered, "Oh, Kathy, it's you!"

"Who else would it be, Burt Turner?"

He shut off the light and was taking off his clothes when he said, "Gosh, it's really late. I didn't know you would be here."

"When the party was over, I went back to my room and waited for you. An hour later, I decided that I didn't want to miss you, so here I am."

When all his clothes except for his socks were thrown in the general direction of his closet, he said, "I need to take a shower, I'm kind of smelly."

"Come to bed, I'll decide how smelly you are."

He sat down on the edge of his bed and pulled his socks off, and as he turned toward her, she lifted the covers in invitation. The dim light through the drawn window shade enabled him to see her naked body. She was on her side propping herself up with her left arm and holding the covers up with her right, her breasts tending a little downward. He rolled in next to her and gently pushed his left leg through her slightly open legs. They put their arms around each other and shifted their positions in such a way as to allow as much of their naked bodies to touch as possible. She turned her head and pressed her partially open lips just below his ear and tasted salt.

She quietly said, "My god, Burt, have you been in the water tonight?"

"We had to try a few things with the AVR and helicopter."

She hugged him more tightly and said, "I feel you, but you must be pretty tired. I would be happy if we just held each other."

"Not a chance."

Their lovemaking was gentle, passionate, and without limits. An hour later, after the second time, they fell asleep in each other's arms.

Shortly after 0400, she eased herself away from her lover, got out of bed, lifted her light dressing gown from the nearby chair, and put it on. With a last look at Turner, she quietly left his room with tears in her eyes and went on to her own room.

There was little to no chance that he would ever see Kathy Roberts again.

Chapter 9

At 0620, the only officers having breakfast at the officers' mess were a few cockpit crews scheduled for early morning flights and Burt Turner. He was sitting by himself at the table where he usually had meals with his friends and had just finished a hasty breakfast of two bear claws, a glass of milk, and a cup of coffee. Getting up from the table, he saw Bruce Franklin come in; Franklin saw Turner at the same time and walked over.

"Good morning, Burt. Are you ready for the meeting?"

"Just about, Bruce. I'm on the way up to NOF for a final review. Do you have anything for me?"

"I checked the areas immediately north and south of Larache. North, for about two or three miles, there's a lot of human activity near the ruins at Lixus and in the vicinity of a sandy beach used by the fisher folk called Plage Ras r' Mal. To the south, the only activity on the headlands above the cliffs appears to be sheep herding. This time of year, the sheep are found farther to the east. That's all I have. I hope it's useful."

"You're a good friend, Bruce. Maybe I can do something for you someday."

"Maybe you could give me a ride in your boat sometime."

I seem to be owing more and more people a boat ride. "I'll try to arrange it. Will you be at the meeting?"

"I'll be there with Commander Peetz. It should be interesting."

"I'll see you there, Bruce."

Franklin went over to a table where some friends were having breakfast. Turner left for NOF.

On the way to NOF, Turner thought about the note from Laura Brae. *She was trying to help me. She had information that I might not have gotten from anyone else. I wonder what that's all about.* He put that subject out of his mind; he had other things to think about.

At 0640, he walked into the NOF office complex. The yeoman on duty, Petty Officer Third Class Castello, greeted Turner.

"Good morning, sir. Commander Hawkins said he wanted to see you in his office as soon as you came in."

"Good morning to you, Petty Officer Castello. Is the exec in with the commander?"

"Yes, sir. They have been in there together since about 0600."

"Thanks."

He went to his desk, got a clipboard and pencil, and walked over to the commander's open door. Looking in, he saw Commander Hawkins and Lieutenant Commander Owens sitting at a table near the commander's desk. Within easy reach was the silver coffee pot, four mugs—two with varying levels of black coffee—and a plate of plain cake doughnuts. The two officers were comparing Turner's plan of action draft with papers stamped "SECRET" in red. He knocked twice on the frame of the open door.

The commander looked up. "Come in and sit down, Mr. Turner."

He went in and sat in a chair next to the exec. The exec pushed an empty mug and the silver coffee pot over to Turner, followed by the plate of doughnuts. There was no cream or sugar in sight.

"Perhaps you might fortify yourself?" the exec asked.

"Thank you, sir, but I just finished breakfast."

The commander looked up and said, "We are almost finished going over the final copy of your plan of action, less the insertion and extraction section. Lieutenant Commander Bello called this morning and said that section is ready and he will bring it to the meeting. It seems there wasn't much to add." He took a sip of coffee. "He said you did a good job."

"Thank you, sir. Chief Gallegos and Petty Officer Cole helped out quite a bit."

"We have made a few changes in form, somewhat less in substance. Don, pass the pages you have finished to Mr. Turner."

Turner read the pages and waited for the others. Finally, after the exec finished proofing the remaining pages, he passed them on for Turner to read.

When the commander saw Turner had completed comparing and reading all the pages, he asked if he had any questions.

"No questions, sir. It's in far better shape than when I finished with it."

Ignoring the compliment, the commander looked at his watch; it was 0815. He said, "We have forty-five minutes, just enough time to get copies made up and get over to the review board."

When they arrived at Fleet Intelligence center, it was 0850. At 0906, everyone who was supposed to be at the meeting was seated. Captain Dillon was at the head of the table; to his left was Commander Hawkins, then Lieutenant Commander Owens. To Dillon's right was Captain Andersen, the naval attaché from the American embassy in Rabat, then Commander Peetz; next to him was Lietenant Commander Bello, then Lieutenant Franklin. Turner was at the end of the conference table with several empty chairs separating him from the others, adding to his feeling of being completely out of place in the presence of the senior naval officers.

Dillon called the meeting to order, then said, "I want to remind you all that the classification of this meeting is Secret. Commander Hawkins, will you give each of the members a copy of the plan of action for the mission."

Hawkins complied with the request.

Dillon continued, "If you would like to make notes for discussion, please use the stenographic pads we have provided that are on the table. When we finish here, leave your copy of the plan of action and the stenographic pad with your notes on the table."

The participants pulled themselves up closer to the table and began to read Turner's plan of action. About ten minutes later, Captain Andersen, the first to finish, looked over his half-glasses at Dillon and asked, with an air of self-importance, "Where is the insertion and extraction section, Commander?"

"I have copies here," Bello answered, and passed them out.

When all participants had finished reading the complete plan, Dillon asked, "Lieutenant Commander Bello, what is the status of the AVR and HUP?"

"The AVR and HUP have been carefully checked out by maintenance and repair personnel and are ready for the mission, sir."

"And the crews?"

"The crews have been working with Mr. Turner's team under a variety of sea conditions during daylight and at night. The crews are ready and standing by for orders to go."

Dillon and Peetz asked Turner a number of questions about time and distances during the surface and underwater phases of the mission. Without hesitation, Turner answered their questions in detail and with confidence.

Captain Andersen pressed Turner about contingencies that could lead to aborting the mission. Turner answered the naval attaché's questions carefully and with respect. When his questions began to become absurd, Turner would answer, diplomatically, "I don't know, sir, but I'll find out."

As time went on, Turner gained confidence and showed himself to be well-grounded in the details of a complicated mission. Hawkins and Owens were surprised at Turner's first-rate performance.

Perhaps an hour and a half went by without Captain Andersen asking any questions. Then he said, "There are a number of questions that were not answered adequately. I am having doubts that Mr. Turner and his team are capable of carrying out this mission successfully."

Everyone was frankly bewildered by Andersen's statement, everyone except the officers representing the Fleet Intelligence Center, Commander Peetz and Lieutenant Franklin. They knew exactly what was going on with this man; he was getting cold feet. If the mission went sour, Andersen would be caught up in the resultant mess because of a commitment he had made at a cocktail party.

It was a month ago when Commander Peetz was required to attend a cocktail party for two senior senators and a representative from the Department of State at the American embassy in Rabat. One of the senators was the chairman of the Senate Intelligence Committee; the other was a member of the Senate Foreign Relations Committee.

Peetz was sampling hors d'oeuvres when he overheard a conversation between the two guests, the U.S. Naval attaché, the U.S. Air Force attaché, and a French official. The French official was bemoaning the ease by which the Russians were delivering arms to Arab insurgents in Morocco and Algeria. The chairman of the Senate Intelligence Committee commiserated with the French official and explained that he would like to help, but wasn't sure how he could do so. Peetz was watching as Andersen said, "Excuse me, sir."

The chairman of the Senate Intelligence Committee looked at him and said, "Go ahead, Captain Andersen."

"Thank you, sir. I think we might have an asset that could be used to interdict a Russian shipment or two, which might cause them some discomfort or worse."

The Department of State official asked a few questions, and then the chairman was heard to say, "You do the planning, Captain Andersen, and I'll take care of the navy red tape."

The French official thanked the chairman, and the conversation went on to other things.

It was clear to Peetz that Andersen, ever the opportunist, would use the offer and acceptance of the offer as a sure way to gain selection board recognition when his number came up for promotion to flag rank (admiral).

Later, Peetz related what he had overheard to his second in command in the presence of Lieutenant Franklin. Both were told to cooperate if asked, but forget how and where the mission idea originated.

As time went on, Andersen did apply pressure on Peetz at Fleet Intelligence Center and was in touch with a few well-placed contacts at COMNAVACTSMED in Naples, and came up with the Russian trawler gambit.

Now, at this meeting, Peetz and Franklin watched as Andersen tried to put obstacles in the way of the mission.

Dillon, exasperated by Andersen's statement of doubt, asked, "Could you help us understand your concern, Captain Andersen?"

"I'm concerned about detection before and after the event. For example, I know SCUBA equipment produces a large amount of detectable bubbles."

Turner and his team forgot to consider this when they were working up the plan of action. Turner wasn't prepared to interrupt with an answer right away. Franklin did it for him.

Addressing Dillon, Franklin said, "If I may, sir."

"Go ahead, Lieutenant."

"As part of my responsibility to provide Mr. Turner with information that might be useful in carrying out his mission, I had a weather update I was going to pass to him immediately after this meeting. The updated forecast includes a light shower at the time of his team's insertion, which would begin to taper off about the time of their extraction. The effect of the shower on the water surface would more than hide bubbles coming to the surface from the SCUBA equipment. Additionally—"

Captain Andersen rudely interrupted. "Look, young man, those of us who have seen a lot of sea duty know that last minute weather changes are not unusual. If air bubbles exhausting from the regulators are detected, the game's up."

Actually, Captain Andersen, a naval aviator, was expected to have considerable time at sea on board aircraft carriers. However, he didn't like aircraft carrier takeoffs and landings, especially at night, and had successfully pulled innumerable strings to keep from having orders to aircraft carriers. Consequently, he had many shore duty staff assignments. He flew once a month on any available two-place airplane as a copilot to continue to receive his flight pay. Everyone at the table knew about Captain Andersen's professional situation, except Turner and Franklin.

Dillon, trying to take the edge off Andersen's strongly delivered assertion, said, "Lieutenant, the Captain has a serious point there."

"Sir, if I may. I was going to add that we have found the lights on the piers are turned off at 2200, probably to save money. There is only a navigation light high above the point of entry to the harbor of Larache. This light will not pose a problem for the team as they paddle close to and around the point.

"There is another brighter light on a stanchion above a warehouse on the main wharf. This light illuminates the main wharf and very dimly illuminates the long pier. If there is a watch on board the trawler, we feel there is no chance for air bubbles to be seen."

Turner, without anyone's notice, breathed a great sigh of relief.

Addressing Dillon, Andersen said, "Because of the gravity of this situation—I would like to talk with the members without Mr. Turner being present."

Hawkins was about to explode. The exec put his hand on the commander's arm, cautioning him. Dillon glanced at the others, who were looking down at their hands.

Then, looking at Turner, he said, "Mr. Turner, please wait outside."

"Aye, aye, sir." And he left the room.

Addressing Andersen, Dillon asked, "Now, Captain, what was your concern?"

"Everyone at this table knows how that young, inexperienced officer made a mess of the Rif Mountain mission."

Lieutenant Commander Bello was surprised to hear this, he didn't know about the Rif Mountain mission.

"I will be sending Commander Hawkins a letter of reprimand to be appended to Mr. Turner's next report of fitness. The letter of reprimand will report Mr. Turner's demonstrated lack of leadership leading to one of his team members being mortally wounded and hazarding the lives of the other team members during the Rif Mountain mission. This officer is not competent to embark on the Larache mission."

The other officers looked at Captain Andersen in disbelief, then at Commander Hawkins. Commander Hawkins, barely holding down his rage, looked at Captain Dillon and said, "I think we covered this ground before at the Rif Mountains debriefing. I would like to move on."

Dillon quickly said, "Are there any more comments about the Larache plan of action?"

Seeing none, he added, "Then we will proceed with the plan of action for the mission. Mr. Franklin, please show Mr. Turner in."

Franklin went to the door, opened it, and saw Turner leaning against the wall across the hall. "Come on in, buddy." And the two returned to their seats.

Captain Dillon looked at Turner and said, "Mr. Turner, the mission will be undertaken as planned, with one addition. There will be a second limpet mine, which will be attached to the opposite side of the trawler's hull from where the initial one is attached. The second limpet mine is exactly like the first, except it is a dud. It will not explode."

Everyone at the table was surprised at what Dillon just said, except Captain Andersen. Before anyone could ask questions, Dillon continued, "The second mine is meant to be found. I will say no more about that." Addressing Commander Hawkins, he added, "The mines will be delivered to Turner and his team at the AVR at 2015 tomorrow night." He turned to Commander Peetz and asked, "Finally, what can naval intelligence tell us about the disposition of the trawlers?"

Peetz replied, "The trawler code-named Hot Dog, if it remains on course and speed, should be transiting the Strait of Gibraltar at about 1500 tomorrow and should put into the harbor at Larache at about 2100 tomorrow night. The second trawler, code-named Ketchup, remains three to four days behind."

"Thank you, Commander. This meeting is over." He looked at Turner and added, "Good luck, Mr. Turner."

The first out of the room was Capt Andersen. Commander Hawkins and his exec were in a heated discussion with Captain Dillon. Commander Peetz and Lieutenant Franklin walked over to Turner. Peetz said, "Looks as though you were blindsided, Mr. Turner. One must watch their six o'clock, at times."

"I'll be watching my six-o'clock from now on, sir."

Peetz turned to Franklin and said, "Bruce, do everything you can to help Mr. Turner," and went over to where Hawkins and Owens were talking with Dillon rather heatedly.

With Peetz gone, Turner said, "Thanks, Bruce, you really saved my ass. I didn't even think about bubbles."

"You would have eventually. I'll call you if anything new develops."

Turner looked at his Rolex; it was 1105. "I have to catch Lieutenant Commander Bello. I'll see you later, Bruce."

Bello was just going out the door of the building when Turner caught him.

"Sir, it's 1105, and I scheduled the SNB for 1100. Could we change the flight to 1300?"

"Go ahead and call Operations. Tell them I want the change."

"Thank you, sir."

Turner was about to follow Bello out of the building when he glanced back and saw the exec standing in the hallway motioning for him.

He walked back and the exec quietly said, "When you return from your flight to Larache, come to the commander's office immediately."

"Aye, aye, sir."

The exec went back in the conference room and rejoined the group.

On the way out of the Fleet Intelligence Center, he stopped at the front desk and called Operations. The yeoman answered. "NAS Operations, Yeoman Second Class Peterson. Can I help you?"

"This is Lieutenant JG Turner. I would like to speak to Lieutenant JG Miller or Lieutenant JG Teipner, please."

"Neither one is here, sir. They may be over at hangar 3. I'll transfer your call."

Turner heard the call going through, then, "Hangar 3, Aviation Machinist Mate Lincoln speaking."

"This is Lieutenant JG Turner. I need to talk to either Lieutenant JG Miller or Teipner, please."

"Mr. Turner, how are you? I was your hoist operator last night on board the HUP."

"I'm fine. Thanks for your work last night." He couldn't think of anything else to say about last night.

"Mr. Teipner is right here, sir."

Teipner came to the phone, "Is that you, Burt? Where the hell have you been? We're ready to go."

"I just got out of a meeting from hell. Bello was there, and he is going to call Operations and reschedule the flight for 1300. I thought I would call you guys and give you a heads-up."

"Got it. We'll see you at chow."

Lunch at the BOQ was tomato soup and grilled cheese sandwiches and tapioca pudding. Turner, Miller, and Pierce, not liking what they saw, pushed their puddings over to Teipner, who decided the tomato soup was not to his liking, quickly ate the puddings, and asked the steward for more.

"So you three gentlemen are going for an airplane ride this afternoon?" Pierce inquired after watching the puddings quickly disappear.

Miller replied, "We would ask you to go, but you are probably indispensably occupied this afternoon with a major surgical event."

"Yes, I am, but not in surgery. I am talking to the Officers' Wives Association this afternoon about the importance of washing vegetables bought off base in 10 percent Clorox before eating because of the possible use of human excrement for fertilizer. I will also address the importance of not buying ice cream off base because it could have been melted and refrozen and the continuing tuberculosis problem and anything else that comes to mind."

Turner asked, "Why don't the nurses do this? They could do a better job."

"They could do a much better job, but the officers' wives want a doctor. And since I am both a very fine physician and a fine aviator, I feel I do have something to offer."

With that, Miller let slip the last of his grilled cheese sandwich into his tomato soup. As he tried to retrieve it with a fork, he said, "You are not a very fine aviator. You are a very awful aviator."

Turner said, "The good doctor is a very fine surgeon, historian, counselor, and friend. I would let him take my tonsils out, if I still had my tonsils."

Miller said empathically, "But he said he was a very fine aviator!"

"Look, if he isn't one now, then you and Teipner should be making him into a very fine aviator."

Pierce dabbed his napkin about his mouth, carefully put it back down on the table, and, as he got up, said, "Lieutenant JG Turner is now the only one with good sense at this table. I bid you adieu."

He walked away to meet with the Officers' Wives Association.

At 1315, Miller and Teipner were in the cockpit of the SNB with Chief Flint Williams and the SW/EOD team in the passenger compartment. Teipner was the pilot in command on this leg of the flight. After getting clearance from the control tower, he turned the airplane into the wind on the main runway, pushed both throttles forward, and started down the runway. The airplane gained speed, the tail came up, the landing gear tires scuffed a bit as they left the pavement, and they were airborne.

Miller raised the landing gear, and Teipner put the airplane in a climbing turn coming around to a northerly heading. A few minutes later, they were cruising at six thousand feet.

Gallegos and Cole were looking out the windows, Chief Williams was asleep, and Turner watched Miller and Teipner fly the airplane. He was surprised at how businesslike they were. It was a real disconnect from their behavior on the ground.

He looked out the window on his left. The airplane was flying about two or three miles inland from the headlands, overlooking the sea. The land below was dry and treeless, with few signs of habitation. Here and there, there were a few small herds of sheep grazing on sparse grass close to the edge where the headlands dropped off to the rocks and sea below. There were dirt paths and a few dirt roads meandering here and there.

Chief Williams woke up about ten miles from Larache and went up to the cockpit. Looking out through the windshield and at times pointing to where he wanted Teipner to fly the airplane, he said, "Take us east of town, then pick up the Oued Loukkos and follow it to the estuary."

As they approached the estuary, he continued, "To the right, on the hill above the beach, you can see the ruins at Lixus. Go north about five miles, then do a 180. Stay offshore so we can look at the point protecting the harbor. Then take us farther south so we can have a look at the cove." He took a last look out the pilot's side window, then returned to the passenger cabin.

As Teipner flew the route, Williams pointed out landmarks that could prove important to the team tomorrow night. After flying by the cove, Turner went up to the cockpit and said, "I'd like to make another pass from the harbor to a few miles south of the cove, but I don't want to attract anyone's attention down below."

Miller looked over at Teipner and said, "Maybe we would be less obvious if we took a ride up to Tangier and then out over the strait and came back down instead of circling around here.

"Good idea. I'll give the plane to you when we are over the strait."

Teipner gave Miller a thumbs-up and flew the airplane out to sea, then headed north to Tangier and the Strait of Gibraltar.

Cole was at one of the port side windows as they approached Tangier; he called out, "Over there, a big passenger ship is coming in."

They flew over Tangier and out into the Strait of Gibraltar; Teipner brought the SNB down for a closer look at the ship as it began its transit through the strait.

Chief Williams said, "I think it's the *Constitution* from the States on one of its Med cruises."

There was no other vessel in sight. Teipner circled the majestic ship, then climbed back up to cruising altitude and turned the airplane over to Miller.

On the way back, Turner and his team had a good look at the harbor, the point, and the cove south of Larache where they would visit tomorrow night. There was no sign of a trawler along the coastline or in the harbor at Larache.

After they landed at the Naval Air Station, Turner waited until Williams, Gallegos, and Cole exited the SNB, then he went up to the cockpit. Miller and Teipner were finishing their after-landing checklist when Teipner noticed Turner. "Well, Burt, did you enjoy the ride?"

"The ride was terrific. I really enjoyed watching you guys work together. You are very professional."

The two pilots were moved by what Turner said and it showed, but just for a moment, then they started.

Teipner said, "I am sorry that 'Pilot in Command' Miller made such a lousy landing. He comes close to breaking this airplane much too often."

"The landing was smooth, actually, exceptional, considering the crosswind. There are those that takeoff and fly an airplane, and those that fly and land an airplane. The act of landing an airplane properly has a greater degree of difficulty than just flying about. My copilot does a lot of flying about."

"You great ass, I am not your copilot."

Miller changed the subject, became serious, and said, "Commander Bello told us this flight was part of a secret operation and not to ask questions about it or talk to anyone about it."

Teipner added, "If they got you doing some crazy shit, be careful. Don't do anything dumb and hurt yourself, Burt."

They were concerned about their friend. They thought it too soon for him to go out again after the traumatic experience he had recently gone through that included the loss of one of his team members. The two pilots got up and followed Turner out of the airplane.

It was 1530 when Turner walked into the office spaces at NOF. He stopped at Yeoman Jenkins's desk and said, "The commander asked me to see him and the exec when I came in. Would you tell him I'm here?"

Jenkins lifted the handset from the phone cradle and dialed the exec's number. The exec answered, and Jenkins reported, "Mr. Turner just came in, sir."

"Tell Mr. Turner we will see him in a few minutes. I'll call him when the commander is ready."

"Sir, the exec said to standby and he will call when the commander is ready for you."

Turner went over to his desk and found a stack of papers waiting for his signature. Most were informational only, requiring his initials after reading. He conscientiously read the first few and carefully initialed each one, then began scanning and initialing, and finally scribbling his initial after a quick glance at the remaining stack in his IN box. When he came to mine shop paperwork, Warrant Officer Fulkerson had clipped notes to each page carefully explaining what the paperwork was about, and where Turner was to sign before forwarding to the exec and Commander Hawkins. Turner appreciated this immensely.

Twenty minutes later, the exec came out of his office.

"Mr. Turner, let's go see the commander."

He got up and followed the exec to the commander's office. The commander was on the phone and waved them to sit down in the two chairs in front of his desk. After taking his seat, Turner made an effort to deliver the impression he was not overhearing the commander's conversation by avoiding looking in his direction. What he did hear was a heated discussion between the commander and "Tom"—Tom being Commander Peetz—about how the recent meeting was conducted. He and Peetz appeared to be in agreement about a number of things Turner couldn't make out. He overheard nothing that could be considered classified information.

The commander finally said, "Thanks for your support Tom. I think our friend may have gone too far. Maybe his meddling will soon be over," and hung up the phone.

"Well, Mr. Turner, did you find your flight informative?"

"Yes, sir, very informative. Getting around the point may not be as big a problem as we thought—we have experienced worse. The cove is a little farther south than we thought and secluded from anyone peering down from the headlands. If the helicopter were sitting on the beach, it would be difficult to detect it from offshore because the opening to the cove is so narrow."

"Was there any sign of the trawler?" he asked.

"No, sir. We flew all the way up to the strait. There was no sign of the trawler."

The exec asked, "What about the harbor interior?"

"When we first flew by, there were five small fishing boats tied up at a short pier. The long pier had a dredging barge tied up close by the wharf and nothing else. When we flew back from the strait, a tank truck was parked at the end of the long pier where the trawler is expected to tie up."

The exec looked at the commander and said, "According to naval intelligence, the local fishing boats come in during the evening. There should be about ten or twelve of these boats tied up at the short and long piers unloading their catch."

The commander asked, "Mr. Turner, I know your plan of action has been accepted, but are you sure you remain comfortable with the timeline? Let me read to you." He put on his half-glasses and read from the plan of action.

"Mine delivery to the AVR 2015 and AVR deployment at 2030." He looked up and said, "I added the mine delivery to that statement." Then he resumed. "Your estimated time of arrival and insertion at Larache, 2330. Around the point and to objective at about 0015, and at the cove for extraction, 0130. Detonation of the limpet mines, 0145."

He raised his head and looked over his half-glasses expectantly.

Turner answered, "The team and I, along with the AVR crew, Chief Flint Williams and Lieutenant Commander Bello, worked out the timeline. If we arrive at the haul-out position inside the harbor at about 2400, ten minutes either way, we should be in good shape for the rest of the mission."

The commander took his glasses off and gave Turner a long and hard look. "Mr. Turner, if this timeline breaks down before you get to the trawler, or if you are uncertain if the trawler is the one with the modified hull, you are to abort the mission. Is that understood?"

"Yes, sir."

"That will be all, Mr. Turner. Don, let's go over tomorrow morning's munitions shipments to Beirut."

Turner left the commander's office and went to his desk to finish his paperwork. Forty-five minutes later, he had used his facsimile stamp with his name eighteen times, stamping basic supply requests (toilet paper, two cases; swabs, three; paint brushes, three; etc.). He put the stamped supply requests in his OUT box, leaned back and thought, *During the Uniform Code of Military Justice class at OCS, the instructor told us that as young naval officers, we would often be put in positions of responsibility, on board ships or elsewhere, that was far beyond our years and experience, and that lives and equipment would be at stake. We were expected to measure up to the challenge. Well, I hope I can.*

He started to get up to leave and said out loud, "Oh shit, I forgot the tide and current and weather update for tomorrow night."

Across the way, Yeoman Fry heard this and, with a knowing smile, asked, "Excuse me, sir, did you need something?"

"No, no, I just thought of something I should be doing. Thanks."

He called Fleet Weather Central and wrote down, "south-southeast, current approaching three knots." *Nothing unusual here, might get our attention going around the Point on the way in, but on our way south to the cove . . . a nice help.* "High tide in that area at 2235." *Looks good. We might catch a little downstream current from the Oued Loukkos on the way back out to the point.* The weather forecast didn't change from the last forecast, except for light rain beginning before midnight, turning to heavy rain with winds of twenty to thirty knots from the northwest, beginning about 0200 Saturday morning and lasting til Saturday noon.

Just as Bruce Franklin told me.

He thanked the petty officer on duty, hung the phone handset back in its cradle, waited a few seconds, then lifted the handset again and dialed the EOD shop.

"EOD shop, Chief Gallegos speaking."

"Chief, I just got the tide, current, and weather reports for tomorrow night. I'll read it to you."

"That's all right, sir, I called in earlier and wrote it all down for us. Do the commander and exec have anything more for us to do before tomorrow night?"

"No, Chief, I think it is now our show. I'll meet you and Cole at the shop tomorrow morning at 0800 to check over our gear, then we can pack and load it on board the weapons carrier. Once we get all that out of the way, I want us to go over the mission one last time. We will secure about noon and come back at 1900 to dress for the occasion. At 1930, we'll get underway for the wharf."

"Aye, aye, sir. Sounds good. See you then."

They hung up their phones simultaneously.

Turner wasn't surprised the chief had already checked out the weather and water conditions for tomorrow night. He didn't know that Gallegos and Cole had already pulled together equipment they would need for the mission and laid it out for Turner's inspection.

He left his desk, checked out with the duty yeoman, and left for the BOQ.

The dinner that evening was fried pork chops, fried potatoes, green beans, and tossed salad. To wash it all down, the choice was between water, milk, or coffee. Turner had milk, and his three friends had coffee (black). Midway through dinner, he looked around and over to where the nurses usually sat. Kathy Roberts, Mary Bianconi, and Betty Armstrong were missing.

"Where are the three main women?"

Pierce answered, "If you mean Lieutenant Roberts and Lieutenants JG Bianconi and Armstrong, if I understood correctly, they are having a girls' night out."

Teipner said, "Ah, but the lovely new nurse, Ensign Juniper Cooper, is at the end of the second table looking with longing eyes at *moi*."

He had a pork chop in his hand and waved it in her direction. She opened her mouth in surprise and promptly looked away.

Turner said, "I'm not sure if she cares for you demonstrating your lack of fastidiousness. About all you need is a bearskin and a club to complete your caveman image."

Miller added, "A beard and a bone through your nose would be good too."

They finished their dinner with dessert—apple pie a la mode. Pierce was satisfied with one helping; his friends received a second helping each after pleading with the steward. After coffee, they retired to Miller's room for their usual afterdinner wine and conversation.

Settling in their places, Miller chose the last two bottles left from the case of Chateau Patrus.

Miller opened the first bottle and said, "As I come around, I am going to pour each of my friends, then myself, a full glass of this precious wine. A full glass, not a half or two-thirds, but a full glass."

Pierce asked, "Is this a celebration?"

"It is. This wine has served a much better purpose with us than it would have if poured and slurped down at some change of command ceremony."

He went around the room and poured a full glass of Chateau Petrus to each.

Teipner took a drink and said, "You know . . . you are right. The participants said their good-bye to some former commander and hello to some new commander. They wouldn't have appreciated the wine as we do. The wine would have been theater, you know, show business."

Turner replied, "It would have been exactly so. What a shame."

There was some discussion about drinking good wine at ceremonies and how people miss what good wine could deliver when preoccupied with ceremony and superficial talk.

Pierce had been quiet, then he said, "When a person leaves a place of duty after truly meritorious service and goes on to something else, have you noticed how quickly they and their work are forgotten?"

"I have never experienced anything like that. I mean, I have never been in a situation where a person has done good things and was celebrated," Turner explained.

Miller erupted, "Oh, for God's sake, Turner, haven't you been to a change of command ceremony?"

Teipner added, "A Boy Scout merit badge or Eagle Scout ceremony?"

"I wasn't a Boy Scout, and I've never been to a change of command ceremony."

Miller asked, "Have you ever seen a movie of an old guy retiring and being given a gold watch or something like that?"

"Yeah, I guess so."

Pierce went on, "Look, the point is, when a person is recognized for doing something great, how soon is the recognition for the accomplishment lost to everyone except the recipient?"

Turner said, "I guess it has to do with the size of the monument."

Pierce said, "Exactly. We extol people of power and accomplishment. We perpetuate the memory of these individuals by erecting various size marble statues, brick buildings, parks, schools, or ships in their names. But what happens to people that do not have monuments to their lives or efforts?"

Teipner replied, "They and their works are forgotten. That happens even if they have a monument of some sort."

"Of course. So perhaps the point is, if you want to be remembered during your lifetime, you have to keep doing meritorious things that will make people notice til you drop dead. Of course, if you have a good public relations person available, it would be most advantageous. So after death you will not be remembered for long unless you have a substantial monument. Gravestones do not count, you know."

Turner offered, "Biologically speaking, an organism has not successfully lived unless it has reproduced itself. It's a biological imperative. A female, depending on the species, has a huge investment in energy in relation to her part in the production of offspring. She must select her mate carefully to provide the best possible genetic complement for the new offspring and maybe to help raise the offspring successfully. So the male has to be able to sell himself to the female through his accomplishments and should be able show a sense of responsibility.

Miller, in exasperation, asked, "What the hell are you talking about, Turner?"

Pierce explained, "Burt is absolutely right. A successful reproduction is much like a monument to oneself. The genetic disposition will go on and on and on, probably will be significant longer than anything made of marble, don't you agree?"

Teipner said, "But what about fame and fortune and position, for right now?"

Turner answered, "That is what I am talking about. It doesn't last. It's ephemeral. But it may help you score with Juniper Cooper. Besides, the biological imperative may cause Juniper to make a bad decision."

Pierce said, "There it is. What our friend and colleague just said so simply is what is important. The fact is, we are here to make babies. Everything else is driving us to that end."

Teipner reasoned, "So then meritorious accomplishment is ephemeral, mate selection is important for the long run, and sex is not for the fun of it. That's quite a reach. I think I prefer to live life more simply. Sex is fun and may be part of mate selection, and I would be happy to accept an award for meritorious accomplishment if it were offered."

The other three happily agreed with Teipner's philosophy.

With that discussion out of the way, Pierce asked, "Burt, did you tolerate well your airplane ride with our two compatriots?"

"It was great. We went up in the air, flew around, and landed successfully. Actually, we flew up to the Strait of Gibraltar and back, it was a beautiful ride. However, it made me realize how hard a country it must be to live in. From what I saw, there is a relatively small amount of arable land to raise crops and livestock. It is much like Southern California before they brought water in from the Owens Valley. As to the quality of airplane driving, I'd fly anywhere with these two guys."

Miller replied, "You may have to."

It was close to midnight when Miller started to doze off. Teipner nudged him and said, "We're leaving. See you at breakfast."

Turner went to his room, took his clothes off down to his shorts, and brushed his teeth. With that done, he crawled into bed and thought about going down the hall to Kathy Roberts's room, but fell asleep.

At 0500 Thursday morning, Lieutenant Kathy Roberts was going up the boarding stairs and into an R-6D bound for Anacostia Naval Air Station near Washington DC. In the side pocket of her flight bag, she carried advanced orders for her to report to the U.S. Naval Hospital, Bethesda, Maryland, for temporary duty and to be detached from the U.S. Naval Service three months later. Her close friend, Lieutenant Junior Grade Mary Bianconi, was wiping her eyes as she walked away from the plane after a tearful good-bye. Twenty minutes later, the R-6D was in the air and heading northwest for the long flight to the United States.

There were only a few others in the officers' mess at 0640 when Turner finished a breakfast of scrambled eggs, bacon (two strips), fried potatoes, and glass of milk. He usually had breakfast with his friends at 0700; today, he wanted an early start.

At 0710, he stood waiting in the hallway outside the NOF office complex after pressing the buzzer button on the wall next to the door. He could see Lieutenant Van Buren through the security window approaching the door with a mug in hand. Recognizing Turner, he pressed a button on the yeoman's desk next to the door, releasing the door lock with a noisy, low-pitched *brackkk*.

As Turner entered the office complex, Van Buren said, "Ah, Mr. Turner, what on earth are you doing here? Working hours for most begin at 0800."

"I am here to check on you and your duty officer duties. Have you been dutiful?"

"I am a regular navy lieutenant in the U.S. Navy Supply Corps. I take pride in doing my duty dutifully. Are you here to relieve me? And would you like some of last night's coffee?"

"I'm sorry, Ted, I'm not here to relieve you. I just need to pick up a folder from my desk. No coffee, thanks."

He went over to his desk, opened the top drawer, and took out the folder containing his plan of action. He started for the door, and Van Buren asked, "Is there anything of a classified nature in the folder, Burt?"

Realizing he was about to violate classified document security, he said, "Yes, I'm sorry. I forgot."

Van Buren picked up a clipboard from the yeoman's desk, handed it to Turner, and said, "Give the classification, title, and number of pages, time removed from the premises, and where the document is to be taken."

Turner printed, "SECRET, Plan of Action—Larache, eleven pages. Out at 0715, destination EOD shop."

He handed the clipboard back to Van Buren and then handed him the folder. Van Buren checked the folder contents against the clipboard and handed it back to Turner.

"Thanks, Burt. You sure you don't want some coffee?"

"No, thanks." Then, going out the door, he asked, "Twenty-four-hour duty officer here gets pretty boring, Ted?"

"Actually it is quite pleasant after everyone secures. Hope you have an interesting day, Burt."

He answered, "I'm sure I will, Ted," and walked out the door.

At the EOD shop, he unlocked the door and went in. He was surprised to see the display of equipment Gallegos and Cole laid out the night before. He went over to the table near the chief's desk, put down the plan of action folder, and picked up the clipboard with the equipment check-off sheets attached. He flipped over the pages and saw his teammates' initials for each item on display.

At 0730, he was just finishing his inventory when Chief Gallegos and First Class Petty Officer Cole entered the EOD shop.

"Good morning, sir. How does it look?" Gallegos asked.

"Good morning. It looks like we are about ready to go. I'll be finished in a minute."

Gallegos walked over and sat down at the table. He took a small notebook and pencil out of his jacket and carefully added a few words on the page margin near penciled-in text. Cole went to the workbench and prepared a pot of coffee. A few minutes later, the three men were sitting at the table with mugs of hot coffee.

"I stopped by the office and picked up my copy of the plan of action." He opened the folder and continued, "I met with the commander and the exec yesterday afternoon. They wanted to make sure I knew what we were doing tonight and the gravity of it all. They made one addition. He pointed to a lower paragraph on the ninth page. "Mine delivery to the AVR, 2015. There are no changes otherwise. Let's go over tonight's adventure from the beginning."

Two pots of coffee later, they were finished. The only uncertainties were weather and rendezvous for extraction with the HUP.

Finally, Turner said, "I want to emphasize what the commander emphasized. If the timeline breaks down or the configuration of the trawler hull is uncertain, we abort the mission. That means we make for the cove and the HUP. If we miss the HUP, then it's plan B. We begin paddling south, hoping for a later recovery by the HUP."

Cole took a deep breath and said, "One last thing."

"Go ahead, Cole."

"Who is going for a swim, and who stays with the raft?"

"The chief and I swim. You stay with the raft."

"Aye, aye, sir." Cole was obviously disappointed.

"Do either of you have anything else about the plan of action?"

Gallegos looked at Cole, Cole shook his head no, and Gallegos said, "I think all we have to do is get on with the mission."

"OK, let's go down and visit our friends at the AVR, and then visit the HUP. After that, we will call it a day."

The drive down to the wharf was unusual for the lack of conversation. At the AVR, they had coffee with the crew; Turner, uncomfortable with the amount of caffeine he already had on board, diplomatically denied the offer. Once again, they went over the AVR's state of readiness, and the only thing the crew was to know was their part in carrying out the mission: loading, 1930; deployment, 2030; and time and place of the team's insertion, 2330, two miles off the point at Larache. The estimated time of return to the AVR's mooring was 0230.

The team and boat crew had become quite comfortable working together, and the boat crew had grown to like the young and unassuming SW/EOD officer. Probably because he was "straight up," listened to the coxswain, and didn't let his rank get in the way.

After the meeting, the team drove up to Operations and tried to find Chief Williams. The Operations duty officer told them the chief was testing a recently reengined A-4 and wasn't available.

On the way out of Operations, Turner said to Gallegos and Cole, "Let's go out to the flight line. I'm sure Chief Williams wouldn't care if we looked over the HUP."

They walked down the flight line to the helicopter, walked around it, then climbed inside. They examined the hoist and horse collar even though they didn't expect to use it and looked into the cockpit. Just before leaving the HUP, Gallegos and Turner sat down on the passenger bench, and Cole sat on the floor. They just sat for a time.

Then Turner said, "The next time we are in here, we will be on our way home. Let's get back to the shop, Chief."

It wasn't Turner's plan to go down to the AVR or to the HUP. He simply did it on the spur of the moment. Psychologically, it was a very smart confidence builder, especially for him.

When they arrived back at the EOD shop, Turner looked at his watch and said, "It's 1215. I'll see you back here at 1900. Get plenty of rest, and we will have a good time tonight."

Gallegos and Cole laughed, and Cole said, "You get plenty of rest too, sir. We might need you to carry us home."

Turner blushed and said, "I'll always be ready to carry you old guys home."

He drove back to the BOQ, went up to his room, pulled the shade down, took off his shoes, and lay down on the bed. After a few minutes, he got up, took off his clothes, and put on his sweatshirt, swimming shorts, gym shoes, and baseball hat, then on the way out of the room, he grabbed a towel, his sunglasses, and bottle of suntan lotion and headed for Mehdiya Beach.

Once there he put suntan lotion on, sat down on the sand, and looked out at the surf. After a while, he got up and walked down the beach. When he returned, he sat down on the sand again. He couldn't relax, so he got up, took off his sweatshirt, baseball hat, and gym shoes and went into the water. After twenty minutes in the surf, he left the water and walked back up to where he had been sitting, dried off, and spread the damp towel on the sand. He sat down on the towel, put his hat and sunglasses on, lay back and fell asleep.

He heard people talking quietly next to him. He lifted his head and saw Gallegos and Cole talking to Huwitt.

Noticing Turner had awakened, Gallegos said, "Well, Mr. Turner, we were wondering when you were going to wake up. We were just telling Huwitt about our mission tonight."

Huwitt pointed to where his right leg would have been and said, "I'd go with you guys, but I might slow you up. Besides, Cole can paddle the raft for both of us."

Cole laughed and said, "You candy ass, I would be paddling for both of us if you still had your leg."

Huwitt said, "I can't figure out why they want you guys to blow up that boat in an Arab port. I bet the Arabs are going to be pissed."

Gallegos and Cole helped Huwitt get up and to his crutches. Then the men walked up the beach.

"Wait, you guys, I wanna talk to you!"

They disappeared in the distance.

On his other side, he heard, "Burt, are you all right?"

He rolled over in the direction of the voice and saw Kathy Roberts, in her hospital uniform, kneeling next to him. She held a syringe.

"Just a little pinch, Burt."

"Nooooo."

He sat up straight, wide awake, and he cried out, "Jesus, what was that all about?"

He looked at his watch and saw he had been asleep for an hour and a half and got up. He put his sweatshirt on and immediately felt the pain of sunburn in the area of his back where he couldn't reach with sun tan lotion. He put on his gym shoes and baseball hat, picked up his sunglasses and towel, and left for the BOQ.

After taking a shower, he was crossing the hall with a towel around his waist when Miller and Teipner came into the hallway from the stairwell. They stopped and looked with some curiosity at him.

"Look, you guys, can't a fellow take a shower before dinner?"

"Yes, of course, but how come?" Teipner asked.

"Yes, of course, but why?" Miller asked.

"I took the afternoon off, OK?"

He was just opening his door when Pierce came up the hall behind Miller and Teipner.

"Ah, Burt, it is so refreshing to see a fellow officer getting scrupulously clean before the evening meal. You two might do well to emulate our friend once in a while."

Miller said, "How come you took an afternoon off without telling us. We could have all gone to the beach or something."

"It was a last-minute thing. I'll get dressed and go down with you guys."

Dinner was fried chicken, mashed potatoes and gravy, zucchini, and tossed salad. Coffee or milk or water, no wine was in the offering. Dessert was jello with a dab of imitation whipped cream.

During dinner, Turner looked around twice for Kathy Roberts. She wasn't sitting with Binki and the other nurses. He thought she must have the duty and was working late at the hospital.

After dinner, they were having coffee and a deep conversation about the significance of dreams. Turner had brought the subject up.

"So, Dr. Pierce, you feel it is the body's way of clearing refuse from the mind. And, Miller, you think it's associated with clairvoyance. What about you, Teipner?"

"I don't know. I never thought about it. I guess dreams are dreams. What do you think?"

"I think I would go along with the good doctor. Dreams are refuse, litter left over from incomplete or fractured thoughts based on some experience."

Miller added, "Maybe so, but I still think they could provide messages about the future."

This went on for another twenty minutes. Turner glanced up at the clock on the wall and, as he got up, said, "Gentlemen, I have to leave you. I have a few things to do."

Pierce said, "Sometime, you must tell us if there is a certain young lady in town you are seeing."

"Sometime, maybe I will."

As Turner walked away, Teipner said, "Don't stay out too late. They say it's going to rain later tonight."

He didn't look back; his mind was focusing on the next number of hours.

At 1850, he was sitting at the table in the EOD shop with Gallegos and Cole. Cole was talking about how there were increasing numbers of incidents between enlisted men who were on liberty off base and small groups of militant Arabs. Gallegos said, "I think Islamic fundamentalists will always have a problem with us 'infidels' from the West. I guess we could start loading the weapons carrier. What do you think, Mr. Turner?"

"Let's do it."

At 1905, their equipment had been rechecked and loaded on board the weapons carrier, and they were pulling on their dry suits.

At 1915, they were dressed for the mission and on the way to the AVR. Turner was feeling very uneasy.

At 1925, they had arrived at the AVR and were being assisted by the AVR crew in loading their equipment on board. When the loading was finished, Gallegos and Cole were on board the AVR, and Turner was still on the wharf. He looked down at the AVR. *I don't want to do this. How can I get out of it?* Then he began to walk mechanically down the gangplank. By the time his foot hit the deck of the AVR, he was back in focus for the mission.

A little later, when they were checking and securing the SCUBA gear on the four-man raft in the stern well of the AVR, a Citroën sedan pulled up near the gangplank. Two men in civilian clothes got out, went to the back of the car, and unlocked and opened the trunk; and one of the men lifted out a leather suitcase. The other man closed the trunk, and both men walked over to the gangplank and looked down at the men working on board the AVR. The man with the leather suitcase asked, "May we come aboard?"

The coxswain looked up and asked, "Who are you and what are you carrying?"

The man with the leather suitcase answered in perfect English. "We are messengers carrying two devices to be turned over to a Lieutenant Turner for further delivery to the port of Larache."

"Come aboard."

They came aboard, and the man with the leather suitcase asked, "Which of you is Lieutenant Turner, if you please?"

Turner came up from the stern well, Gallegos and Cole followed. "I'm Lieutenant Turner."

"I'm Mr. Black, and this is my coworker Mr. Smith." He and Smith extended their hands; Turner shook hands with them both.

"Could we talk privately with the men who will be making the delivery?"

Turner looked at the coxswain and said, "Deacon . . ."

The coxswain replied, "I understand, sir. The crew and I will prepare to get underway." He turned and went below deck.

Mr. Black put the leather suitcase on the deck of the AVR; Mr. Smith knelt down with a key, unlocked and released two catches, and opened it. Nestled in individual soft plastic forms were two limpet mines. He lifted one out and said, with a slight accent, "This one is inert. Otherwise, it is the exact replica of the other, except for these three characters on the side. We understand you and your team have already been advised as to how these weapons work?"

"Yes, we have, but please go over it once more."

Mr. Smith went over the fusing and timing system, emphasized that once the timer was set on the live limpet mine, there was no turning back; it would explode at the precise time as set.

He added, "It is important that both limpet mines are to be set at the same time even though one is inert."

He put the limpet mine on the deck, lifted the second one out, and placed it on the deck next to the first. He then lifted out the soft plastic form from the suitcase, revealing two small carrying sacks with adjustable straps.

"These are the carriers for the limpet mines. I'll show you how to strap them on."

He put an arm through a loop of strap attached to each end at the top of the carrying sack and pulled each loop tight at a draw-through buckle. He then put the strap attached to the bottom of the sack around his waist, passed its end through another draw-through buckle, and tightened it up the same way.

"As you can see, the sack with the limpet mine will fit comfortably on the chest, and will not interfere with your type of SCUBA straps or any of your movement."

Turner thought, *These guys are familiar with the type of SCUBA gear we're using.*

Mr. Black asked, "Do you gentlemen have any questions?"

Turner looked at Gallegos and Cole; there were no questions.

Mr. Black returned the limpet mines and their carrying sacks to the leather suitcase and closed it without locking it. "Mr. Smith and I will be on our way. *Bonne chance*, gentlemen."

The men shook hands all around, then Mr. Black and Mr. Smith quickly went up the gangway, got in the Citroën, and drove away.

Turner put his toe on the edge of the suitcase and asked, "Do you guys know what the three characters etched on the edge of the inert limpet mine might be about?"

Cole shrugged his shoulders as if to say he didn't know. Gallegos answered, "I don't know what they mean, but they are Hebrew characters, and the suitcase was delivered by two Frenchmen. Kinda interesting, don't you think?"

At 2027, the crew was readying the AVR to cast off. The coxswain yelled out, "Heave around handsomely there." At exactly 2030, the last line securing the AVR to the wharf was cast off, and they were underway.

The sun had set an hour before, and the coxswain used the radar to navigate down the winding Oued Sebou then out onto an unusually friendly sea that presented an unusually gentle swell. The throttles were advanced to two-thirds; the boat's hull rose with the increase in speed, and planed along trailing a turbulent white wake across the dark waters.

After ten minutes on a westerly heading, the coxswain brought the AVR around to the north and set a course for the port of Larache. On the new heading, the starry skies began to give way to early evidence of the storm forecast for the area. At the moment, it was a beautiful night at sea.

Gallegos and Cole were lying comfortably in the four-man raft, and Turner stood with the coxswain on the bridge, enjoying the experience. He yelled above the rumble of the boat, "Deacon, this is just absolutely beautiful. It's a wonderful feeling having a boat like this under your feet with the engines throbbing and be just flying along."

The coxswain almost made a snide comment to the young officer, but also enjoying the experience, he yelled, "It *is* great, sir."

An hour later, the coxswain motioned Turner close. He yelled, "Why don't you take the helm for a while, Mr. Turner? Try to keep it on the compass heading we have showing."

With obvious pleasure, Tuner took the helm.

Forty minutes later, they were coming close to the position of insertion. The coxswain pointed to himself and then at the helm. Turner moved aside, and the coxswain took control. When they arrived at the position of insertion, they were fifteen minutes early. It was raining slightly, and the sea was presenting a slight chop. It would be getting worse.

The coxswain throttled back to idle, the wake subsided, and the boat began to wallow a bit as it moved in large circles at low speed. After a few minutes, Turner said, "Let's go ahead. If we get in the water ten or fifteen minutes early, it may give us an advantage against the current from the north."

To the east, a little over two miles away, they could just barely see through the rain a flashing ten-second light above the point that guarded the entry channel leading into the harbor at Larache. Using the binoculars, Turner didn't see any other boats at sea or in the channel.

He joined his team as they made the four-man raft ready for launching, and then put on masks, fins, life jackets, and weighted web belts with knives. Turner's adrenalin was up. The last time Turner felt this way, he was getting ready for the mission in the Rif Mountains. This mission was different; he was better prepared and in control. The mission was his to fail.

The coxswain turned the AVR into the chop, allowing the transom at the stern to be lowered into relatively quiet water, easing the launch of the raft.

As the team slid the raft into the water, they jumped on board, released the paddles, and, with Turner using his as a rudder, Gallegos and Cole started paddling for shore. The AVR crew watched until the raft was lost in the haze of rain; then with a soft muffled sound of the engines, the AVR turned west, cruised quietly at very low speed for a time, then turned south and slowly came up to cruising speed for home.

The team found the coastal current was setting the raft south of the point. They compensated for this by setting a more northerly course and paddled more strenuously against the current and slight wind. When they were in the lee of the point, they rested. Cole said, "If we hadn't put into the water earlier than we planned, we probably wouldn't have been able to make up the time, Lieutenant."

Turner replied, "We were just damned lucky. Chief, do you think we should get in closer to the point before we try to go around?"

"I don't think so. The wind is picking up, and we could get slammed against the cliff. Let's stay out where we are. Once around the point and in the channel, the wind may help us some."

Gallegos was right; when they finally made it into the channel, the wind did help them for a time, then the wind dropped off with the rise of land on each side. They paddled on in the darkness, then after a bit, Cole quietly said, "Just ahead, I can see a masthead light."

They followed the curve of the channel as it opened into the harbor. Then a few more masthead lights appeared dimly in the light rain. About a 150 yards away, on the right, a masthead light much higher than the others appeared. It was the trawler.

"Well, there she is, sir. I think this would be the place to put into shore."

"Let's put into shore, Chief."

They changed course and quietly paddled in the direction of the nearby shore. When the bow of the raft gently nudged bottom, the team slipped over the side and immediately sank in mud up to midshin. They struggled for a minute, then reached for the grab lines running from bow to stern on each side of the raft and pulled the raft from the water, then up to the base of a small rise about ten yards from the water's edge.

They stood listening, then Turner whispered, "Shall we get on with it, Chief?"

He whispered back, "I hate to leave Cole behind. He just might take off without us."

"I'm not going anywhere without you guys. But you know what? When we were in the Rif Mountains, it was raining."

Turner didn't need to be reminded.

Gallegos replied, "This time, the rain is on our side, fella."

They released the lines securing the SCUBA gear and lifted them out of the raft. Then Turner and Gallegos fished out the luminous compasses and depth gauges from the knit bag and put them on their wrists. The carrying bags with the limpet mines were last out of the raft. They opened the bags and removed the limpet mines.

"Chief, you take the dud, and I'll take the real one."

Gallegos grabbed Cole and whispered back, "This one here?"

"No, that's Cole. The other little round one."

"You guys are so funny," replied Cole.

Gallegos took out a small tool kit from the knit bag, opened it and took out a utility knife. He pulled up the screwdriver blade and passed it to Turner, saying, "Here, sir. You first."

Turner took the utility knife and unscrewed the fuse from the fuse recess on the side of the limpet mine, then passed the utility knife back to Gallegos. Gallegos picked up the inert limpet mine with the characters etched on the edge and removed its fuse.

Looking at his Rolex, he said, "If your watches don't say 0009, set them to 0009."

They didn't need to reset their watches.

"Chief, let's set the mines for 0150."

Both fuses were set for 0150, then screwed back into the fuse recesses before the limpet mines were returned to the carrying bags.

After Turner and Gallegos put on their fins, Cole helped them put on their SCUBAs. They opened the air valves and checked their regulators. Finally, Cole helped them strap on the limpet mine carrying bags.

"Chief, there is no visibility, and I think we are going to quickly lose track of each other."

"Let's meet at the trawler's rudder."

Turner thought for a minute. "OK. Whoever gets there first waits for no more than five minutes for the other guy to show up. If he doesn't show up in that amount of time, we abort the mission and meet back at the raft. If the missing diver doesn't show up at the raft in ten minutes, Cole and the returned diver will leave for the cove and the HUP."

"Aye, aye, sir. I'll see you at the rudder in fifteen minutes."

Cole patted both divers on the head, and they clumsily made their way into the water. When the water was waist high, the two divers took compass bearings on the trawler's masthead light, glanced at each other, and then quietly disappeared beneath the surface.

The water was cold and dark. At the edge of Turner's mouthpiece, he could taste the weak salinity of the river water as it merged with the tidal outflow. At ten feet, there were no visual cues, and he began to experience vertigo, then claustrophobia. His training took over, and he overrode the problem by concentrating on the luminous dials of his compass, depth gauge, and his Rolex. Eight minutes later, he surfaced with just the top of his head and the upper part of his mask showing above water. The rain had increased. He made a compass correction, taking into account the slight current with the tide going out, and went back underwater.

Five minutes later, he surfaced, made a second course correction, which would bring him to the stern of the trawler, and slipped back under the water once again.

Approaching the trawler's hull, he heard the hum of generators in the engine room spaces. He surfaced a few yards from the trawler, looked around, and saw a few small fishing boats anchored some distance away. He slipped back under and swam to the trawler's rudder. Gallegos was waiting and signaled him to follow.

They surfaced under the wharf a short distance from the rudder.

"Did you have a nice swim, sir?"

"For a dark and stormy night, it was OK. What's going on?"

"There's two men under a bulkhead lamp on the main deck having a smoke, and there's a tank truck just above us." He steadied himself at the piling and added, "I think we're lucky to be covered by the rain."

"Let's have a look at the hull. Do you think we should search the length of the hull, Chief?"

"I don't think we have to. We'll know pretty quick if this is the one with a modified hull."

"OK, you take portside, I'll take starboard. I'll meet you back here."

Beginning at the stern, they felt along the hull for a short distance then descended to the keel; satisfied with what they discovered, they swam back to the wharf. Gallegos arrived first then Turner.

"I think it's the modified trawler. Chief?"

"It's the modified trawler, all right. The hull is deeper than it should be, and below the bilge keel, the hull squares off. It looks like it is only a short time out of the yard, and there's not much marine growth. Where the generators are loudest should be the engine room spaces. We'll place the mines in that area, just above the bilge keel."

Turner looked at his Rolex. "We have four minutes to place the mines and meet back here, Chief."

Gallegos made sure his watch was synchronized with Turner's. Then Turner said, "OK, here we go. I'll meet you back here in four minutes or less. Whoever gets back here first will wait an additional three minutes beyond the four minutes, then go on without the straggler." Gallegos looked curiously at Turner.

"I mean it, Chief?"

"OK, let's get it done and get the hell out of here."

They slipped under the water. Turner swam under the trawler to the starboard side, and Gallegos to the portside, which was next to the pier.

Turner positioned himself at the bilge keel where the generator's hum was loudest. He was essentially neutrally buoyant—weightless—and had to work to hold his position in the current. He opened the carrying bag and lifted out the limpet mine. He was almost ready to attach the magnet side of the mine to the steel hull when the mine slipped from his hands. He grappled for it, but it dropped away and went to the bottom of the channel.

"Oh fuck."

At the same time he heard a light *thunk* as the magnets of Gallegos's limpet mine fastened to the steel hull of the trawler.

Tuner let the air out of his lungs and, twenty feet later, was at the bottom with no visibility, cold, and mud. During the winter on the Potomac, when he was learning rendering safe procedures on varieties of underwater mines and other ordnance, the trainees were told by the master diver topside, "If you lose your tools or tool bag in the mud, don't come up empty-handed." Because of the cold, if someone lost a tool or tool bag and didn't find it quickly, the trainee would lose all feeling in their fingers and hands, and the search would get much more difficult. Turner didn't lose tools during that phase of his training, but he lost a limpet mine in the harbor at Larache.

He moved his foot to steady himself and felt the mine. He reached down into the mud and brought the mine up, and holding it tightly, took a deep breath of air and letting it out slowly moved toward the surface. His head bumped lightly against the hull close to where he tried to place the limpet mine the first time. This time, he successfully placed the mine. But as he did so as quietly as possible, there was still a *thunk* as the magnets took hold.

As he felt his way to the keel of the trawler and to the other side, his SCUBA regulator unexpectedly started a high-frequency squeal. He reached over his shoulder and turned off the main air valve, stopping the noise, but also stopping the airflow to his mouthpiece. He made his way under the hull, then up the other side and under the pier. He surfaced a few yards from where Gallegos was waiting.

"Well, there you are, Mr. Turner. Glad to see you again. I was about to leave."

"I'm in deep shit, Chief. One of the pressure stages in my regulator just went away."

"I thought I heard a pig squeal," Gallegos said.

"Well, if you heard it, others heard it, I'm sure."

Others did hear the noise. Lights were going on all over the trawler, and a small boat was being launched.

"Let's get out of here now, Lieutenant. I'll swim alongside you."

"No, you won't, Chief. You go on underwater. I'll probably make it back to Cole before you. Get going."

Gallegos went under and headed downstream to the raft and Cole. Turner swam in the dark of the pier as long as he could then went into open water. The trawler's small boat, with one crewman rowing and the other with a flashlight, searched along the trawler's waterline. A small searchlight on board the trawler swept the area farther out.

Turner took off his mask so there would be no reflective surface if the lights came his way. He kept as low in the water as he could. All of a sudden, he felt a strong bump at his left shoulder. Then something moved along his leg and away. He was paralyzed with terror.

Oh fucking shit, what was that?

Then, not more than two feet from his face, up popped the glistening head of a seal. The seal's big round eyes above its bristled muzzle looked directly into his eyes, and the stench of recently eaten fish on the seal's breath was overwhelming. A little farther away, the head of a second seal popped up for a look. Then, curiosity satisfied, both seals slid beneath the surface and were gone. Turner pulled himself together and thought, *Those guys probably heard the high frequency sound from my regulator and came to investigate.*

He was about fifty yards downstream from the trawler when he heard loud voices between the crewmen on deck and those in the small boat, and then laughter. The seals were periscoping the larger curiosity. When the trawler's crew saw the seals, they assumed the seals were responsible for the noises they heard and abandoned the search.

The swim back went without further incident. When Turner came ashore, he saw that Gallegos had arrived earlier and was helping Cole move the raft to the water's edge for launching. They stopped what they were doing and helped Turner out of his SCUBA gear, then the three divers quickly secured the SCUBAs and other loose gear to the raft, and at the moment of launching, jumped in and began paddling with the current toward the mouth of the channel and the open sea. Turner would not be telling his teammates how two marine mammals might have saved his life until later.

The wind at the mouth of the channel was coming from the north strongly now, and they made several tries before successfully rounding the point and picking up the strong coastal current running south. With the wind at their backs and the favorable current, they were able to make up for time lost after Turner's SCUBA failure.

The rain was decreasing, but the wind was increasing; as a result, the following sea came close to causing the raft to broach a number of times. Finally, at 0120, they were in the lee of a low hook of land protecting the cove. They could see the HUP on the sandy beach a hundred yards away, engine idling, the rotor blades turning lazily.

They paddled on and beached the raft as close to the HUP as they could. The HUP hoist operator-crewman jumped down from the cargo hatch, ran down, and helped pull the raft out of the water. After their gear was loaded on board, Turner went around to the front of the helicopter, where Williams had his head out the side window.

"Just in time I see, Mr. Turner. Come aboard, and let's get out of here."

"Chief, I'm going to slash the raft open and load it on board. Do you have a problem concerning the weight?"

"We should be all right. We have a tailwind. If fuel gets critical, I'll simply drop you and your team off in the water or on a nice sandy beach."

Turner called back to Gallegos and Cole, "Slash the raft, roll it up, and put it on board, ASAP."

Cole looked at Gallegos, and the chief said, "You heard the young officer. Cut and slash, me hardy!"

Cole laughed and replied, "What would the taxpayers say about this?"

At 0143, the HUP was in the air, heading south at seventy-five miles an hour. At 0150, Turner and Gallegos were sitting on the passenger bench, looking out the open cargo hatch. Cole was sitting on the floor with his back against the rolled up raft—almost asleep. To the north, there was a flash and, a second later, a lesser one. Turner and Gallegos looked at each other for a moment and smiled.

Cole looked at the two of them and said, "I think you guys did something very bad." And then he nodded off.

Chief Williams looked back from the cockpit and yelled out above the engine and rotor noise, "That was an interesting flash back there. We should be home in about forty minutes."

The HUP had gotten ahead of the rainstorm and was bouncing around a bit from the tailwind. A gibbous moon illuminated lines of white surf two hundred feet below. Cole was asleep, and Turner and Gallegos were enjoying a beautiful night.

A while later, the hoist operator-crewman unbuckled his safety belt and gingerly made his way from the cockpit back to the passengers.

Swaying with the HUP, he said, "We are five minutes out, and Chief Williams just received word you have a reception committee."

Chapter 10

When the helicopter was letting down at the Naval Air Station, there were two staff cars waiting. Standing near the staff cars were four officers being buffeted by the helicopter's downwash.

Chief Williams landed, shut the engine down, and, turning around from the cockpit, said, "Welcome to NAS Port Lyautey. We hope you had a good trip and will fly with us again. The people you see standing out there are waiting for you. I would suggest you hurry along."

Turner was the first out, followed by Gallegos and, rubbing his eyes, Cole.

They walked over to the waiting officers, who turned out to be Commanders Hawkins and Peetz, Lieutenant Commander Owens, and Lieutenant Franklin.

Without a greeting, Hawkins said, "Mr. Turner and Chief Gallegos will ride with Lieutenant Commander Owens and me. Petty Officer Cole will ride with Commander Peetz and Lieutenant Franklin."

Turner hesitated before he got into his assigned car and said, a little a too loudly, "Sir, our gear is on board the HUP and the weapons carrier is at the wharf."

"Mr. Turner, this will all be taken care of by others. Get in the car." He got in the car. With Commander Hawkins at the wheel of the lead car, they left the apron and at great speed drove on to the Fleet Intelligence Center. When they arrived, the cars parked in the "Senior Officers Only" slots, and the group went in the building.

The duty officer at the counter couldn't believe what he was seeing—his boss, his friend Bruce Franklin, two other officers, and what seemed to be three navy frogmen with their hoods pulled back on their necks. He wisely didn't ask for identification as they all hurriedly walked by.

The group ended up in the conference room where Turner made his plan of action presentation forty-three hours ago. He saw four tables arranged differently than before. Two tables were pushed together at their ends facing two tables pushed together at their ends, with a gap separating them of about ten feet. The four officers took their places at one set of tables; the team sat opposite at the other set of tables. A yeoman was standing by a large corkboard easel.

Pinned to the easel were the aerial photographs of the harbor at Larache and the nautical chart used during the presentation of the plan of action yesterday morning.

With everyone seated, the yeoman walked over and gave the officers what Turner thought were copies of his plan of action. The yeoman then went over and sat down at a separate table where there was transcribing equipment.

Commander Peetz began, "We are glad the team is safely home." Verbal agreement from the others. "Mr. Turner, this is the first of what may be a series of debriefings concerning your mission. We would like you to start at the time the AVR arrived at the position of the team's insertion."

The officers flipped ahead a few pages. Turner got up and went to the aerial photos and nautical chart. "To begin with, it was understood the mission was time critical. We were fortunate to have a calm sea from the Oued Sebou to the point of insertion, allowing the AVR to go at a better speed than planned. We arrived at the point of insertion at 2320, fifteen minutes early. The time saved helped us when we experienced a stronger wind and current than anticipated paddling to and around the point here," he said, referring to the aerial photos and chart.

Using time, distance, and compass headings, he explained where they beached the raft and swam up the channel and into the harbor, then to the Russian trawler. He noted the water and bottom characteristics encountered, and other details that could have proven rather much, but his presentation held the attention of the four officers.

Ten minutes into the presentation, the team's dry suits became extremely uncomfortable because of body heat build-up.

"Excuse me, sir. We are very uncomfortable in our dry suits. Could we have permission to take the tops off?"

Commander Peetz answered, "Yes, of course."

Gallegos and Cole stood up and helped each other pull off their skintight dry suit tops, revealing tee shirts wet with sweat. After helping Turner with his, they sat back down, and Turner returned to the aerials and chart with his tee shirt clinging to his skin.

"When we entered the harbor, the visibility above water was extremely poor due to rain and lack of harbor lighting." Again referring to the aerial photo, he said, "As expected, the Russian trawler was tied up here. The tank truck was on the pier, next to the trawler, also as expected."

He asked, "Are there any questions so far?" There were none. He was surprised.

He continued with the assault on the trawler. Then the questions came.

"How can you be sure this was the target trawler, code-named Hotdog?" asked Peetz.

"Chief Gallegos and I examined both sides of the hull from amidships to stern and then to the keel."

Then Commander Peetz asked, "Chief, are you absolutely sure this was the target trawler?"

"I absolutely agree with Mr. Turner. This vessel was the target trawler, sir."

Commander Hawkins asked, "Was there any trouble transporting and placing the limpet mines?"

Turner looked at Gallegos, Gallegos made a small face and shook his head no. Turner answered, "No, sir, we didn't have any problems transporting and placing the limpet mines."

Commander Hawkins then asked, "The individuals that delivered the limpet mines, did they speak with you about how to ready them and use them?"

"Yes, sir, they made sure we knew how to use them."

"We are interested in the nationality of these men, was there any evidence of who they might be?" Peetz asked.

"When they spoke to us, one had perfect English. The other had an accent. When the two were some distance away, Chief Gallegos thought they may have spoken to each other in French."

"Is there any chance that you and the chief could have been detected?"

Turner looked at Bruce Franklin and said, "Not a chance. The weather was on our side. The rain hitting the water masked our bubbles, and when we surfaced, we were under the pier.

Bruce Franklin smiled.

Turner answered a number of other questions, then Commander Hawkins asked, "Did you see or hear anyone onboard or near the trawler?"

Turner looked at Gallegos, Gallegos answered, "Yes, sir. There were two crewmen on board standing under a bulkhead light amidships. What they were saying was unintelligible."

Turner then explained the swim back to the raft, and the long paddle to the cove, and extraction by the HUP. He also explained with some hesitation how he ordered the destruction of the raft.

The four officers began collecting themselves, signifying the debriefing was over. Turner asked, "Sirs, is there any word about what happened?"

Commander Peetz answered, "Mr. Franklin, please inform the team what we know so far."

"Our contact at the scene reported that the trawler was listing heavily on its port side and there was a significant fire. There was a secondary explosion that may have been caused by the tanker truck blowing up due to diesel fuel on board or possibly other explosive material on board. The pier was on fire, but the fire was confined to the trawler and tanker truck area. The fire provided enough light to see an enormous number of dead fish that may have come from opening up the port side of the trawler."

"Oh shit!" Turner said quietly.

Commander Peetz heard him and replied, "Oh shit is an understatement, Mr. Turner. If you are right about the target, it is someone else's problem. We are adjourned, gentlemen."

Commander Hawkins walked over and said, "I'll take you and your men back to the EOD shop in my car."

It was raining by the time they arrived. Just before the team left the staff car, the commander turned and said, "The air station people have probably unloaded the HUP by now. I'll send a crew down for your gear. They can bring up the weapons carrier at the same time. In regard to the raft, have Lieutenant Van Buren order another ASAP. Tell him I said it is in support of Operational Readiness."

They got out of the staff car and were walking toward the stairs of the EOD shop when he lowered the driver's side window and called out, "You men get some sleep. I don't want to see any of you in the area until early afternoon." He rolled the window back up and drove off.

When they were inside the EOD shop getting out of their dry suit pants, Cole said, "It smells real bad in here. I'm glad it ain't me." The three men were very tired, but still laughed.

The smell was of sweat, waste products of adrenaline and urine. The smell of urine was not unusual. It seems when a swimmer dons a dry suit and finishes gearing up for a mission, they often have an uncontrolled need to pee—even after going to the head immediately before donning the dry suit. If not right away, they will pee some amount in it eventually. Turner thought the phenomenon complex and hormonal. One day, he would use the experience as a tool in teaching his physiology classes about the endocrine system.

After cleaning up a bit, Turner, in his Sprite, and Gallegos and Cole, in Gallegos's Ford station wagon, left NOF.

Back in the BOQ, Turner was in his room drying himself after a long hot shower. There was a suggestion of light coming through the window from the east. He pulled on clean shorts and sat down on the edge of his bed and thought about going down to Kathy Roberts's room. He decided not to. He crawled under the covers, rolled over to his right side, and fell into a deep sleep.

At 0700, Miller and Teipner went to Turner's door. Miller knocked and said, "We know you are in there." Then he more forcefully knocked again and said, "We know you are in there, goddamn it!"

No answer.

Teipner said, "Maybe he stayed in town last night?"

Down the hall, Pierce was standing outside his room, waiting for Miller and Teipner. He said, "I think I heard him come in earlier this a.m. A very hard night, I expect. This woman of his must be very demanding."

The three went on to breakfast.

At 1100 Turner was wide awake, looking at the ceiling thinking about a dream that awakened him a few minutes before. The only thing he could remember about the dream was Laura Brae lying naked on the sand at the beach below Lixus.

What was that all about? Her note said there was no nude bathing on that beach because there were people around, and why her?"

There was a knock at his door. "Mr. Turner, Mr. Turner, it's me, Alcade, the steward."

Turner got up, went to the door, and opened it. "What's going on, Alcade?"

"Commander Hawkins wants you to call him immediately, sir."

"Thank you, Alcade."

He left the door partially open, put on his trousers and socks, then went out and down the hall to the phone and dialed for NOF.

"NOF, Yeoman Jenkins speaking, sir."

"Jenkins this is Mr. Turner. I was told to call Commander Hawkins."

"Wait one, sir."

A minute later. "Is this you, Turner?

"Yes, sir."

"Get your blues on and come up here. You are going to Naples on the 1230 flight. I'm sending my car for you right now."

"I'm going to Naples, sir?"

The other phone clicked off.

He hung up the phone, stood for a minute, then ran back to his room, dressed and packed his flight bag. Before he left his room, he wrote a note to Kathy Roberts.

Kathy, I have to be gone and want to see you as soon as I get back, I think early next week—but I can't be sure. I miss you so much, Burt

He put the note in an envelope, sealed it, and on the way out of the BOQ, he gave it to the steward at the reception desk, saying, "Please put this in Lieutenant Roberts's box."

"Oh, she left something for you, sir."

The steward reached around to Turner's box, removed an envelope and gave it to Turner. He took the envelope and put it in the inside breast pocket of his coat, and as he ran out the door to the waiting staff car, the steward called out, "Sir, Lieutenant Roberts isn't here anymore."

He didn't hear what the steward said.

Twenty minutes later, he was standing in front of Commander Hawkins's desk.

"Admiral Horner, COMNAVACTSMED, has sent for the officer in charge of the NOF SW/EOD team—that's you, Mr. Turner. It seems there is a flap developing about last night's mission." He called out, "Yeoman Fry, bring in Mr. Turner's orders."

Fry came rushing into the office with Turner's newly typed orders and gave them to the commander. He carefully looked the orders over and signed them.

"Mr. Turner, these orders are for you to attend a meeting at COMNAVACTSMED tomorrow, Saturday morning, at 0900. You have a Priority air transport designation, in case there is a need. Your clearances are noted. You will stay at the transient officers' quarters on board the Naval Air Station, meals are covered, etc., etc. You will catch the Monday morning flight back here. Have a good time. I know you will enjoy Naples."

"But, sir, I—"

"Don't worry about a thing, Mr. Turner. It's going to be a great experience. Please shut the door on the way out."

"Aye, aye, sir."

The commander's staff car took Turner to the Operations building. He went into the departing passengers' counter and showed his orders to the duty officer, a Lieutenant Junior Grade Agnes Ryan. She examined the three pages, initialed where appropriate twice, and said with a smile, "Have you been to Naples before, Mr. Turner?"

"No, this is my first time."

"You will enjoy it." She looked at her watch. "Your plane leaves in seven minutes. It's down the flight line a bit. Better hurry."

He was running down the flight line when he passed the SNB; Miller and Teipner where getting out of the plane after a flight. When they saw him, Miller yelled out, "Where are you going, and where have you been?"

"I'm on the way to Naples. I'll be back next week, and I'll tell you all."

Up ahead, at the foot of the boarding stairs, Lieutenant Commander Bello was laughing with one of the pilots who was on his way back up the air stairs, obviously a friend. Turner ran up to the airstairs, stopped, and saluted Bello.

"Well, Mr. Turner, what a surprise. How good it is to see you healthy and whole. You must be on your way to Naples for a well earned bit of shore leave, I hope?"

"Yes, sir, and no, sir. I have to go to a meeting."

Bello knowingly stated, "I heard there was an awful accident in the harbor at Larache last night." The pilots started the airplane engines, and Bello continued above the noise, "Better get on board. They are waiting for you." As Turner started up the stairs, Bello patted him on the back and said, "Take care of yourself, Burt. My daughter thinks a lot of you."

Going on board the R-6D, he showed his Priority designation to the cabin attendant in the doorway, then made his way down the aisle. The airplane was half full, and on the port side, he found three empty seats next to each other over the wing. He put his flight bag on the middle seat and sat down in the window seat. Twelve minutes later, the R-6D was in the air, flying northeast toward the Rif Mountains and the Mediterranean.

At 1940 hours, the R-6D landed at NAS Naples. As the airplane taxied to the terminal, the cabin attendant announced over the intercom, "Remember, Naples is an hour ahead of Port Lyautey. You may want to check your watches. For those of you staying over, there will be a bus in front of the Operations building to take you to the transient officers' and transient enlisted Quarters. Those going on, check in at the counter just inside the door of the Operations building."

On his way down the boarding stairs, he noticed the air. There was no evidence of the Oued Sebou; there was no evidence of charcoal burning or other smells he was used to. It was humid like Port Lyautey, but the smell of the air was different and hard to describe. Overhead, he could see a few stars through the haze. The moon was up and still gibbous. As he walked with the other passengers to the Operations building, he thought, *I wonder what the people around me would think if they knew what I was doing under that moon last night. I look like just another insignificant Lieutenant JG with a gold stripe and a half on each sleeve, with no ribbons and passing through on the way to a ship.*

Once inside, he passed the counter for those going on. There were already ten or more officers and enlisted men lined up. He wondered where they were going and what they were going to do when they arrived. He wondered the same thing about those in his group as he walked with them through the building and out to the waiting bus.

The bus ride was short, and inside the transient officers' quarters, the check-in line for a room was long. As he stood in line, an ensign behind him attempted to start up a conversation. Just in time, another steward opened a second registration line, and Turner was saved. He wasn't interested in talking with anyone. Checking in, he was given a room—first floor for two nights—and meal chits for the officers' mess in the building across the street. He found his room, put his flight bag on the bed, and left for the officers' mess.

After 2000 hours, the officers' mess was closed except for a serve-yourself buffet. This night there was gnocchi alla romana garnished with basil or a layered meat loaf (with cheese-flavored pasta inside) and a large tossed salad. There was bread in large chunks in a warmer. He looked around hopefully for something familiar other than what was in front of him. Sensing there were a number of others behind him waiting for him to make a selection, he chose the layered meat loaf and carefully lifted away a small slice. Then he served himself a large amount of salad and selected the largest of the chunks of bread in the warmer. He took a seat at the only table with few officers and sat down with a "good evening" to the officers nearest him. There was a carafe of wine (Italian) nearby. He looked around for a wineglass and, finding none, he took the carafe and poured the wine into an empty water glass, filling it halfway. The officers nearest him were a lieutenant and two lieutenant commanders. They seemed to know each other and, thankfully, didn't attempt to include him in their conversation.

He cautiously tried the layered meat loaf; it was wonderful. The salad and bread were far superior to what was available at the officers' mess at Port Lyautey. After eating all the layered meat loaf on his plate, he went up for seconds, but took much larger portions. He had another half glass of wine, then another. By the time he finished dinner, he was quite full, but not uncomfortably so, and the wine was enough to cause him to feel pretty good, but not buzzy.

On the way to his room, he stopped by the reception counter, "Excuse me, I just arrived and wonder if there happen to be any messages for me. My name is Turner." He showed him his ID card. The steward looked at the card and said, "Just a minute, Mr. Turner."

He turned to a series of alphabetically arranged boxes on the wall to his right and slid out the one with a T on the front. After sorting through a number of envelopes, he found one with Turner's name on it. "Here you are, sir."

Turner took the envelope, thanked the steward, and went to his room

After undressing, he sat on the bed and opened the envelope. There was a short message on COMNAVACTSMED stationery:

FROM: COMNAVACTSMED, Department of Security
TO: Lieutenant (JG) Burt Turner, 610554/1105, USNR
SUBJECT: Meeting Concerning NOF/Port Lyautey/SW/EOD
TEAM No. 1

He skipped down to the body of the message.

. . . at 0830 a van will take you from the Transient Officers'
Quarters, NAS Naples, to Headquarters, COMNAVACTSMED
where you will report to the Department of Security for further
orders.

Etc., etc.

He fell asleep after reading chapter 11, the March 20 entry from *The Log from the Sea of Cortez.*

After breakfast (scrambled eggs, milk, and toast), he waited near the curb in front of the transient officers' quarters for ten minutes. The van showed up at exactly 0830. He walked over to the van and opened the front passenger door; the sailor at the wheel asked, "Mr. Turner, sir?"

"Yes, I'm Turner. Are you my ride to COMNAVACTSMED?"

"Aye, aye, sir. Hop aboard."

After a five-minute circuitous ride, the driver pulled up to an imposing two-story granite building and stopped. He took a pack of cards held together with a rubber band from the dashboard, slid one out, and gave it to Turner. "Sir, if you need a ride back, call the number on the card."

He thanked the driver and went up the stairs to the building's entrance, saluting senior officers as they were coming down the stairs. At the entrance, he pushed through double doors, walked through a short hallway and into an enormous marble floored atrium. He looked up and saw a massive crystal chandelier hanging from a domed ceiling, and across the atrium, he saw a large staircase with wrought iron railings gracefully following a curving wall, going up to first- and second-floor balconies fronting offices and hallways.

In the atrium, navy and a few marine corps officers were standing in small groups in serious conversation or, in some cases, talking and laughing. Others were going and coming every which way, some in considerable haste. Because of the marble floor, the atrium was quite noisy. He asked a marine guard standing nearby the location of the Department of Security and was directed to the right side of the atrium. He carefully made his way across to the glass doors of the Department of Security and went in.

He looked around and finally saw a Visitors sign hanging by a chain over one section of a long counter. He walked over and presented his orders to one of the marines. The marine looked at Turner's orders, made a note on a clipboard, and said, "Could I see your ID, Mr. Turner?" Turner took out his wallet and ID and gave the ID to the marine.

"Thank you, sir." The marine looked at the ID, opened a drawer, took out a badge fastened to a chain, and presented it to him. "Wear this at all times while in the building, sir. Your meeting is in Vice Admiral Horner's office on the second floor." He returned Turner's orders.

Turner put the chain, with the badge dangling, around his neck and went back out to the crowded atrium. He went up the staircase to the second floor and easily found Admiral Horner's office and went in. It was 0850. There were four desks in the reception area. The yeoman at the first desk asked, "Can I help you, sir?"

"I'm Lieutenant JG Turner." He gave his first and second set of orders to the yeoman.

The yeoman looked at the orders, made a note, and pointed across the room to a great oak door with a brass plate at eye level announcing Vice Admiral Erskin Horner.

"There are a couple of lounges near his doorway where you can wait, sir. The admiral's aide will come out for you when they are ready."

He walked between the desks and saw the lounges set up across from each other and selected the one nearest the admiral's door and sat down. There was a very expensive oak coffee table between the lounges with an institutional plastic coffee carafe (gold with black trim), cups, and saucers. There was no cream or sugar. Five backdated *Naval Institute Proceedings* journals were stacked neatly with the titles showing.

He was watching the WAVE yeoman at the desk nearest him; she was quite pretty and concentrating on a handwritten page that she was typing up. Suddenly, he heard a loud voice through the oak door. "Goddamn it to hell, how could this have happened without me knowing about it! Who in the goddamn hell put this goddamn operation in action? I want to know now! No more of this 'It didn't happen on my watch' bullshit!"

Then Turner was amazed to hear Captain Dillon's voice. "Sir, the operation stemmed from an initiative that surfaced during a meeting at the U.S. embassy in Rabat."

"Who in the goddamn hell came up with this so called *initiative?*"

"Well, sir, it seems to have been part of a discussion that involved the naval attaché, some congressmen, and a French Army officer."

The admiral's voice became louder; the yeomen at the desks looked at each other with a smile. The WAVE stopped typing, looked at Turner, and said, "They have been in there since 0800, and I think he has finally lost his composure."

Turner said, "The admiral sounds like he doesn't take prisoners."

"I have never heard that phrase before. If you mean the admiral doesn't tolerate excuses from people who have proven themselves incompetent in carrying out their duties, yes, he doesn't take prisoners." She began typing again and added with finality, "I have never heard him so upset. Something must have gone very wrong."

Turner had been uneasy since he was told that he was going to COMNAVACTSMED. When the marine downstairs told him the meeting was in Admiral Horner's office, he went from uneasy to growing dread. Now the WAVE's message gave him a feeling of impending doom.

He leaned more closely to the door and heard Dillon say, "Sir, we understand the mission outline was in support of Operation Scorpion Fish. A copy of the mission outline was sent to COMNAVACTSMED and up the chain of command to my office. I showed the mission outline to Captain Showalter, who said he would forward it to the admiral's staff for consideration."

"Is this true, Captain Showalter?" he heard the admiral ask.

"Yes, sir, what Captain Dillon said is true. However, our investigation found that the mission outline was mistakenly routed to CIA in Paris and not to your staff."

"Oh my god!"

"Sir, the officer responsible explained to us that other departments had trouble making a decision about routing, and the decision ended up being his. He based his decision on what he understood was civilian authority requesting a mission outline—"

"Civilian authority? What civilian authority, for God's sake?"

"Civilian authority in our embassy in Rabat, sir. He thought there was a link to the State Department in Washington and/or to a congressional representative. He said it seemed logical to send the mission outline to the CIA in Paris because the CIA was a civilian authority."

"This is an incredible breakdown of the chain of command and outrageous misuse of authority. The naval attaché in Rabat gets a wild hare up his ass, develops a mission outline, sells the idea to an unknown civilian authority and God knows who else, and starts this snowball rolling downhill. Then the folks at Port Lyautey get pulled into this because of some incompetent officer's decision. Of course, the response is in the can-do spirit and ends up risking assets we can't replace and causing an international incident."

The admiral's aide was sitting to one side and behind the admiral. The admiral turned and softly said, "Lieutenant, have what's his name, the SW/EOD team officer in charge, come in."

"Aye, aye, sir. His name is Turner, Lieutenant JG Burt Turner."

The admiral's aide got up from his seat and went to the door.

When the door opened, Turner looked up and saw a lieutenant wearing an aiguillette, the braided cord around the right shoulder and under the arm, designating him to be the admiral's aide.

"The Admiral will see you now, Mr. Turner. Better two-block that tie."

Turner pulled up his tie, tightened the knot, and followed the aide into the admiral's office. The first thing he saw was a green felt-covered rectangular table; his heart skipped a beat.

Oh shit, the long green table.

He saw the admiral at the head of the table, a short, thin man with a moustache who appeared to be in his fifties. He wore naval aviator's wings above five or six rows of ribbons on his coat. Sitting at his right was a captain, also a naval aviator, and on his right, a commander, then a lieutenant commander, and, to Turner's astonishment, lieutenant colonel Bennett and Laura Brae. On the admiral's left was Captain Dillon and, on his left, another lieutenant commander. All the officers had multiple ribbons from World War II and the Korean War. In front of each officer was an open red file folder containing a sheaf of pages.

The admiral's aide said, "Admiral Horner, sir, this is Lieutenant JG Burt Turner, the officer in charge of SW/EOD Team One at NOF Port Lyautey."

The admiral said, "Sit down, Mr. Turner."

Turner sat down at the opposite end of the table from the admiral, two empty chairs away from Laura Brae, who was wearing a dark blue business suit, white blouse, and pearl earrings. He thought, *She wore a pearl necklace with those earrings at the Rif Mountains debriefing.*

Dillon commented, "Glad to see you are all right, Mr. Turner." Lieutenant Colonel Bennett smiled and said, "Good to see you again, Burt." Both acknowledging previous familiarity.

Burt smiled weakly.

Laura Brae gave him a warm smile.

He just looked at her.

The admiral said, "Mr. Turner, I want to congratulate you on accomplishing a very difficult mission. Unfortunately, your skill in carrying out this mission has put a large number of very important people in great difficulty."

The captain sitting next to the admiral was looking down at a pencil he was fiddling with and mumbled, "Sorta like the operation was a success, but the patient died."

The admiral looked sharply at the captain.

"Uh, sorry, sir."

The admiral continued, "I would like to go over the plan of action that you developed for the mission."

There was a sound of ruffling pages as the admiral and the other participants sorted through the sheaf of papers in their open file folders and brought out Turner's plan of action.

"We have already looked at this plan of action very carefully, Mr. Turner, and I for one cannot understand how you could have pulled the mission off. There are an incredible number of things that could have gone wrong during every stage. What was most disturbing to us was your confidence in a weather forecast announcing an important weather change to begin close to your anticipated time of completion of your mission. Let me see here." He found the weather forecast section in the plan of action and read, "Forecast—heavy rain and wind twenty to thirty knots from the north beginning at 0200." He put the plan of action aside and, looking intently at Turner, continued, "According to your timeline, you were to be extracted by the HUP at 0130?"

"Yes, sir. It was 0143, actually."

The captain sitting next to the admiral noticeably cleared his throat; Dillon lifted his head slightly and raised his eyes to the ceiling; the lieutenant commander next to Dillon grunted and shifted his position in his chair.

Raising his voice, the admiral said, "Let me reiterate, what disturbed us was your confidence in a weather report forecasting an important weather change at 0200. Do you get my meaning, young man?"

"Ah, yes, sir. The weather change could have occurred earlier."

The admiral's tone of voice softened. "It seems you had an enormous amount of luck."

"Sir, if I may."

"Go ahead, Mr. Turner."

"I would refer to the section on our contingency plan, sir. We understood the timeline was critical and there was not very much room to deviate from it. We also understood it was critical for us to abort the mission if the timeline broke down or the trawler's hull configuration was uncertain. If either was the case, we would have immediately initiated the contingency plan."

The admiral ignored Turner and looked at the captain. "Fred, do you have any questions?"

"Yes, sir." He turned and looked down the table and said, "Mr. Turner, I commend you and your team on the accomplishment of a very difficult mission."

"Thank you, sir."

Then he asked, "Can you help us understand why the choice was Larache?"

"Sir, I was not aware of a choice. I was told the Russian trawler putting in at Larache was expected to be the one with the modified hull. I was also ordered to be absolutely sure it was the trawler with the modified hull. After examining the hull, Chief Gallegos and I both agreed that it was the right trawler, and we proceeded to carry out the mission."

The captain turned to the admiral and said, "That's all, sir."

"Chief Gallegos . . . Chief Gunner's Mate Manuel Gallegos?" the admiral asked.

"Yes, sir, Chief Gunner's Mate Manuel Gallegos."

"If I remember correctly, we served together in the aircraft carrier *Princeton* in 1953. He was a second class gunner's mate then. A good man, a very good man indeed."

The admiral picked up a few pages and a number of aerial photographs he had put aside earlier. Giving the aerial photographs to Captain Dillon, he said, "These aerial photos were taken by an RF-8 Crusader this morning. Pass them down to Mr. Turner. I also have the damage assessment from a reliable source at the scene. I'll read you a few of the highlights."

He began, "The Russian trawler was seen to be listing heavily on its port side. Fish from the vessel's hold were evenly dispersed over approximately half the harbor, along with a large amount of diesel fuel." Skipping over a number of paragraphs he continued, "Near the stern and below the bilge keel on the starboard side was a large opening caused by a device that exploded when an attempt was made by a crew member to remove it. Prior to the explosion, the device was examined, and a series of characters were noted on its edge. The characters were thought to be Hebrew characters."

Someone wanted the Israelis blamed for all this. How stupidly transparent.

"The tank truck on the wharf, adjacent to the Russian trawler, was consumed by blast and fire. There was little other collateral damage. The tank truck was probably empty of fuel at the time of the second explosion. Known casualties: one dead, five crewmen with varying degrees of burns, two of the five with broken bones (one leg, the other an arm), one of the five severely burned. No native Moroccans were in the vicinity."

I killed another person, and severely injured others. It was the first time Turner had thought about casualties.

"Well, there you have it. The aerials reflect very much of what I have just read. Do you have any comments Mr. Turner?"

Turner pushed the aerial photos away he had been looking at and said quietly, "No, sir."

The admiral asked, "If there are no more questions, we are adjourned. Mr. Turner, remain seated."

As the participants were leaving the room Capt Dillon unobtrusively patted Turner's shoulder.

The admiral's aide was the last to leave and closed the door on his way out.

Pointing to the chair on his left the admiral said, "Mr. Turner, come up here and sit down."

Turner, confused and feeling sick to his stomach, got up and walked to the chair. He took his seat, sat at attention, and asked, "Yes, sir?"

"Young man, you have done something quite exceptional. Your attention to detail in developing your plan of action and adherence to the timeline in that plan of action was quite an accomplishment. And am I presuming that you were the one who took the initiative to make the AVR operational earlier?"

How does he know all this?

"Sir, the AVR only needed the propeller shaft straightened, and we were available to help out. Later, we thought the HUP might be useful and Lieutenant Commander Bello, the NAS Operations officer, made the AVR and HUP both available to us. Commander Hawkins and his exec, Lieutenant Commander Owens, encouraged us to pursue using the AVR and HUP."

I just said too much.

"I think Commander Hawkins and his exec gave you enough line to hang yourself. Chief Gallegos and, what's his name, the First Class Aviation Ordnanceman . . . the one in the report I received."

"Cole, sir, First Class Aviation Ordnanceman Cole."

"Well, Gallegos and Cole did their job in keeping you from hanging yourself, and in turn protected their own well-being. I want you to understand clearly that your team is an important asset to us in regard to Operation Scorpion Fish, and do pay attention to advice Chief Gallegos may offer from time to time."

"Yes, sir. I will do as you say."

"In this mess, the only people I have confidence in are Commander Hawkins and the Fleet Intelligence Center at NAS, Port Lyautey. You may go now."

As Turner was going out the door, the admiral said, "Give my best to Commander Hawkins. We were shipmates a long time ago. And tell him thanks for the heads-up. He will know what I mean. Shut the door on the way out."

"Aye, aye, sir."

Leaving the admiral's office, he closed the door, turned, and saw Laura Brae as she got up from the lounge where he had previously sat. She wasn't wearing her glasses.

How could she be so good-looking and be so awful otherwise?

"Hello, Laura. I was surprised to see you here."

"Hello, Burt. Well, it appears that someone on the admiral's staff misrouted a message that ended up in our office instead of his. We were sent to help clear up the mess."

As they walked out of the office complex together, he said, "When I was waiting outside the door, I couldn't help but hear a lot of what was going on. The admiral was pretty upset."

"It's a very bad situation, Burt."

In the hallway, she asked, "When do you have to return to Port Lyautey?"

"I have a 0615 flight out tomorrow."

There was no conversation as they went down the stairs, but as they entered the atrium, she asked, "Do you have any plans for tonight?"

"No, I—"

"Burt, I don't have time to fool around. We didn't part company very nicely in Port Lyautey. Shall we try again?"

He was taken completely by surprise. Without thinking he answered, "OK, do you want to go to the cafeteria here, if there is one?"

She gave him a puzzled look and said, "I know a place you might like. Are you at the transient officers' quarters?"

"Ah . . . yeah."

"I have a rental car. I'll pick you up at seven."

He stood watching her as she hurriedly crossed the atrium and went out the double doors to the street. He pulled himself together and made his way to the Department of Security and turned in his security badge, then went to reception center, picked up the courtesy phone and, using the card that was given to him earlier, dialed the number on the card for transportation.

When he got to his room, he took off his clothes and lay down on the bed in his shorts and tee shirt. He looked at his Rolex. It was twelve noon. He thought about getting up for lunch, but fatigue was catching up with him and he fell asleep.

He woke up at 6:30, went into his bathroom, and took a quick shower. As he toweled off, he looked in the mirror closely and decided not to shave. He put his flight bag on the bed, took out and put on fresh underwear, a pair of wash khaki trousers, and a gray crew neck sweater, then put on the shoes he wore with his uniform. At 6:55, he was waiting at the curb when Laura Brae pulled up in a Fiat 500. She reached over to the passenger door, opened it, and said, "Hey, sailor, want a ride?"

As he got in he replied, "I'm easy. Take me out to dinner."

She pulled away from the curb and quickly began to wind her way through traffic. With one hand on the dashboard and the other on the handhold over his door, he said, "This traffic is terrible. Aren't you going kinda fast?"

She ignored him and drove on. Thirty-five minutes later, she drove up a hill overlooking Naples Bay, pulled over to the side of the road, and parked under an olive tree.

"We get out here and walk up the hill ahead of us a bit. There's a little restaurant just before we get to the top."

The neighborhood was made up of small apartment houses, single-story and two-story old stucco buildings. They were predominantly off-white, some tan, and with combinations of yellow, blue, or orange trim. Most had a small balcony with wrought iron railings. Flowers were everywhere—in boxes, on shelves, in every nook and cranny. As they approached the restaurant, he could see it was a small stucco building two doors down from a grocery store. The grocery store had an open-air display of fruits and vegetables like nothing he had ever seen. Behind the front window was a crowded display of breads, cheeses, and wines.

Laura asked, "Would you like to have dinner inside or outside?"

"It's still warm. Let's eat outside."

There were four small oilcloth-covered tables. An older couple sat next to the doorway having wine, cheese, and bread. On the other side, a young couple was sharing a plate of food foreign to Turner. Laura chose the table just in front of the older couple but still away from the road. As soon as they sat down, a young man with an oversized apron approached their table with menus. Guessing from their appearance that they were American, he greeted them in English. Laura answered in Italian, and he gave them each a menu.

She glanced at the menu and asked, "Do you like Italian food, Burt?"

He smiled and, putting his menu down, said, "I have only recently been introduced to real Italian cuisine. You are going to have to help me."

"Is there any kind of food you don't particularly like?"

"Liver dishes, just liver dishes, so far."

"Do you care if I order for us?"

"Please do."

She looked at the menu and said in English, "We will start with the pancetta and pecorino." She paused and added, "and will then have the tagliarini."

The waiter wrote the order down. Then she asked, "Please bring us a bottle of Chianti."

"Of course, signorina."

"What did you order for us?"

"I ordered pancetta and pecorino cakes on a bed of farfalle for starters, then we will have tagliarini with meatballs in red wine and oyster mushroom sauce. With the pancetta and pecorino cakes, you will have a choice of pesto or anchovy sauce for a topping."

He gave her a helpless look and said, "You have the advantage of me, Laura."

Across the street, there was a sizable gap between olive trees, opening up a view of the Bay of Naples below. There was a great variety of vessels—mostly small fishing boats, a number of large yachts and merchant ships. At anchor in the distance, he could see the monotonous but concealing gray of several destroyers and a guided missile cruiser, probably American; if so, they were part of the sixth fleet.

"Do you wish you were out there, Burt?"

"No, I really like what I do. I work in a small group of very smart guys doing interesting and, at times, unusual things. I guess if I had to go to sea, I would like to be on one of those destroyers, one of those 'tin cans.' They are small, fast, and, at times, are able to sail independently without having to escort a carrier or something—but I know I would get seasick a lot, probably, and it would be pretty regimented. I bet it would be great being a tin can skipper though."

Without being annoying she said, "I think you would make a great destroyer skipper. You are smart, you think clearly when challenged, and you have a lot of initiative. You would be great."

They continued looking out toward the bay. Then he said, "It's so beautiful out there. I'm glad you brought me up here."

"It's my favorite place to see the bay." She paused, then added, "It's hard to believe that almost two thousand years ago, Mount Vesuvius erupted and the air here and over Naples Bay was transformed into a hundred-mile-an-hour hurricane of superheated poisonous gases. It incinerated Pompeii over there and, up the coast, the town of Herculanium. The whole area was buried under hundreds of thousands of tons of rocks and ash."

"It sounds like a scenario for the end of the world."

"It was the end of the world for four or five thousand of the very rich and privileged that chose to live there. Over the years, archeologists have unearthed magnificient frescos, gold and silver plates, and jewelry."

"But what an awful way to die."

"Burning to death has to be an awful way to die."

It made him think about the men who were injured and terribly burned two nights ago. Without realizing it, he was clenching his napkin in both hands.

She glanced at what he was doing. "Are you angry with your napkin, Lieutenant Turner?"

He looked down at the napkin and said, "Oh. Not really. I guess my mind was wandering."

Filling their glasses with Chianti again, she said, "Here come our starters."

The waiter carefully placed the pancetta and pecorino cakes, first in front of Laura, and then Turner.

He cautiously sampled, then quickly finished. "Is there more Laura?"

"Burt, you eat far too fast. Did you get to taste what you were eating?"

"Of course I got to taste what I was eating. It was so good. We should order more."

"I don't think it would be wise. There is still the main dish coming."

His plate was empty, his hand was folded around a glass almost empty of Chianti, and he was looking at Laura.

Her face reddened a bit. She asked, "Are you trying to make me feel uncomfortable, Lieutenant Turner?"

"You were trying to warn me, weren't you, Laura?"

She used her fork and spoon to take the last morsel of food from her plate, looked at it for a moment, put it in her mouth, closed her eyes, and swallowed it. Then she lifted her glass to her full lips and finished the small amount of wine remaining, put the glass down, and sighed. "That was very good. What did you ask me?"

He quietly said, "You know what I asked you."

"Yes, I tried to warn you."

"When I read your note, I didn't understand why you sent it to me. I realized later you were trying to help."

"We had access to information you might need, and I thought we would pass it on."

"Did you guys know the trawler we dealt with probably wasn't the one carrying weapons?"

Her voice changed a bit as she asked, "What do you know about the Spanish enclaves at Ceuta and Ifni?"

"Almost nothing, except Ceuta is north near Tangier, and Ifni is south toward the Western Sahara."

"Moroccan nationalists are trying to force the Spanish out of their holdings in northern and southern Morocco, just as the French are being forced out of the rest of Morocco. The French are geographically adjacent to the Spanish in the north and south, and they are covertly cooperating with each other in fighting so-called irregulars. These combined operations, which are euphemistically called police actions, have recently killed at least six hundred of these irregulars—actually nationalists—in the area south of Ifni by using heavy armor and ground attack airplanes.

"This is the same general area that Russian arms are going to the Algerians by way of the Draa corridor in the Western Sahara. A large number of arms are being siphoned off to weaponize the irregulars. There are a lot of things going on in the Western Sahara we have to know about, and we have very few reliable indigenous assets who are able to keep us informed about such things as the how and when of delivery of Russian merchandize.

"And Andersen, the naval attaché, doesn't know about all this?

"He has a habit of misinterpreting the information he has access to. He seems to have a second agenda that overshadows the reality of a particular situation. Correspondingly, he is known to make mistakes, and because of his political position, others end up being blamed."

"So the other trawler probably has the arms."

"Actually, the other trawler is unloading arms as we speak. That trawler came through the Strait of Gibraltar thirty-six hours before yours did."

"How could that have happened?"

"There was a problem in the hand-off during shadowing, and the second trawler was lost before transiting the strait. Once through the strait, the so-called second trawler stayed on a westerly course for a time to prevent easy observation, then changed course to the south and east to Cape Draa."

"Oh fuck."

"I can't tell you any more. I shouldn't have told you this much, so forget all of it. I mean it, Burt. Forget all of it. A lot of good people could get hurt professionally and physically."

Turner was astonished; he just looked at Laura.

Laura motioned to the busboy standing inside the doorway; he came over and quickly gathered up their empty plates. The waiter, seeing this, brought out the main dish and served it with a flourish. Burt ordered another bottle of Chianti.

Having recovered to some extent from Laura's monologue, he took his fork, selected one of the meatballs, tasted it, and proceeded to eat it, then ate another and another.

He paused and said, "Laura, this is wonderful. Thank you."

"I'm happy you like it, Burt. I'm having fun introducing you to new things."

"When we were at Thamusida I told you about my background. You didn't tell me much about yours."

"What do you want to know?"

"What about before Harvard?"

She went on to tell him about her high school years in Alexandria, Virginia, being on the swim team for three years, and working at her father's pharmacy in the summer. She told him about the family excursions with her sister and parents to the museums and historical places in the Washington DC area and, because of this exposure, her interest in Arab culture and language.

By the time she completed the story of her early years, Turner was mesmerized. She was the original girl next door, the one he never had a chance to date because of guys who were better looking, could dance better, and were first-string athletes. Laura Brae was a decent, very bright, and sensitive young woman. He hadn't forgotten her demonstrated sharp edge during their first meeting, though.

They finished dinner and most of the second bottle of Chianti, declined dessert, and were having coffee—Italian coffee, a second pot.

It was almost eleven o'clock when Laura put her hand on his and said, "Look, Burt, over the mountain. The moon is rising."

He felt her warm hand on his. He turned his hand over hers and held on.

There were a few more words, then she said, "Burt, I have to get you back. You have an early morning flight, and I fly out a little later for Bizerte, Tunisia, with Lieutenant Colonel Bennett."

He sighed, pushed away from the table, and replied, "Yeah, I guess we should go."

He motioned to the waiter, looked at the bill, ignored Laura's attempt to pay it, and paid the bill with too many of the lira he bought at the transient officers quarters.

When they arrived at the car, Turner opened and held the driver's door for Laura. She got in, and before he closed the door, he bent down low and kissed her. She put her arms around him and pulled him in close and returned his kiss enthusiastically. He pulled away, closed her door, went to his side of the car, got in, and they were immediately in each other's arms.

Forty minutes later, as Turner wiped off the steamed up windows, Laura started the car, then drove down the hill and delivered a well-spent Lieutenant Junior Grade Turner to the transient officers' quarters.

The next morning, Turner was riding in the back seat of the courtesy van on the way to the Naval Air Station with two other passengers on board.

The driver looked in the rearview mirror at Turner and asked, "Did you have a good time in the storied city of Naples, sir?"

Without breaking his gaze out of the window, he answered, "I had a very good time."

After checking in at the terminal, he was sitting near the passenger-loading door as his plane taxied up and parked. One of the pilots came down the airstairs and followed passengers into the terminal. Turner and the pilot saw each other at the same time. The pilot was an acquaintance of Miller and Teipner.

"Hey, Burt, you coming home with us this morning?"

"If you are going my way, I'd sure like a ride!"

"We leave in about five minutes. I have to pick up a package at Operations."

"I'll be on board!"

Turner picked up his flight bag and started for the door when there was a tug on his sleeve. He stopped, turned, and saw Laura.

"Gosh, I'm glad to see you, Laura."

"Well, I'm glad to see you too."

"My plane leaves in five minutes." He paused, then said, "I enjoyed last night."

"I did too, Burt. I'll be in Rabat next week. I'll call you."

The pilot came toward the couple and said, "Time to go, frogman," and proceeded out the door.

Turner and Laura put their arms around each other and had trouble letting go.

"I have to get going, Laura. I'll be waiting for your call."

She put her hand on his cheek for a moment, and then he was gone.

Lieutenant Colonel Bennett was a short distance away and saw the two young people saying good-bye. When she walked back, he greeted her with a knowing smile and said, "It appears you have a new young man, Miss Brae."

"I do, and he is something I'd like to hold on to, Lieutenant Colonel Bennett," she said in a determined voice.

"I think you're right, Laura. You look good together. Be careful. You are both doing very serious work in a very serious time." They sat down and waited for their plane to Bizerte.

Turner's plane was at cruising altitude when he took off his coat, and as he folded it, Kathy Robert's envelope fell from the coat's inside breast pocket to his lap. He picked it up, opened the envelope, and slowly read the note. Then he put the note back in the envelope and let it slide through his fingers to the floor. He sat back, looked out the window, and thought about Laura Brae.

A few days after Turner returned to Port Lyautey, the officers and men of the Naval Ordnance Facility, Fleet Intelligence Center, and marine detachment attended a memorial for Mineman First Class Richard Huwitt of Special Weapons/Explosive Ordnance Disposal Team No. 1. The ceremony was held Sunday evening in the Protestant church on board the base.

Price, Miller, Teipner, Mary Bionconi, Betty Armstrong, and Juniper Cooper were also in attendance in support of the team's loss of their shipmate. The six friends sat in the pew behind Turner, Gallegos, and Cole.

Commander Hawkins gave a thoughtful eulogy that reflected the contribution Huwitt made to the U.S. Naval Service. The eulogy was appropriate for both those who knew the how and why of Huwitt's death and those who thought his death was due to an accident.

While the Protestant minister delivered excerpts from the often-used "Order for the Burial of the Dead," Turner was in deep thought about what Commander Hawkins had said about Huwitt. He came back to the present when the minister raised his voice and said, "Man that is born of a woman hath but a short time to live and is full of misery. He cometh up, and is cut down, like a flower. He fleeth as it were a shadow and never continueth in one stay."

What the minister just said caught his attention. He thought, *Man that is born of a woman hath but a short time to live and is full of misery. What an awful comment on life.*

On the following Friday, Laura Brae called Turner from Rabat and asked him if he would be able to meet her at the American embassy at eleven on Saturday morning. After letting the exec know where he was going to be for the weekend, he left the BOQ the next morning at 0945 with a small navy-issue off-white laundry bag slung over his shoulder. The laundry bag was just the right size for his toilet articles, change of clothes, and his swimmer's shorts—he always had his swimmer's shorts with him. He drove down Highway P2, and approaching Rabat, he was held up by a traffic jam on the bridge crossing the Bou Regreg River, between the town of Sale and Rabat, but still was able to arrive at the embassy at 1050.

After going through security, a marine guard showed him into a small conference room. At precisely 1100, Laura Brae walked into the conference room, escorted by a very young looking marine corporal. She was wearing a gray skirt, white sweater and flats. She carried a moderately large light blue Moroccan leather bag.

She gave Turner a hug and said, "I'm really glad to see you, Burt." The marine escort discreetly looked away. She turned to the marine and said, "Thank you, corporal." And with her arm in Turner's, they walked back out through security and on to Turner's car.

"Boy, the marines are recruiting young kids now," he said with some derision.

"He likes to escort me to the gate when he is on duty. He's cute, don't you think?"

"I've never seen a 'cute' marine. Where are we going, Laura?"

"We are going to Tamara Beach, just south of Rabat. We are going to take advantage of one of the available rooms set aside for embassy guests at an apartment house close to the beach."

She gave him directions as he worked his way through traffic, and they arrived at the apartment house at 1130.

The Arab superintendent at the desk saw them come in and, holding up a key, said, "Ah, Mademoiselle Brae, your room is ready."

She smiled, accepted the key, and gave it to Turner. Then said, "Thank you Abdulla. Is the water at the beach warm today?"

"The sea water is especially warm today. I recommend bathing this afternoon."

She smiled and said, "We will see how warm soon enough. Thank you."

Turner thought, *The water is never warm on this coast.*

When they arrived at the door to their room, Turner unlocked it; they went inside, closed the door after them, and tossed their bags on the bed. The room was quite small—very European, but large enough for a double bed and a night stand on each side. Laura walked over to a windowed double door and opened it to a very small balcony that overlooked another apartment house nearby. The smell of blooming geraniums in a plant box hanging from the wrought iron railing came into the room.

"Isn't this wonderful, Burt? And it's ours for two nights!"

"Is this where you stay when you are in Rabat?"

"Yes, but not in a room as nice as this."

She went to her bag, pulled out a white bikini and said, "Let's go to the beach."

She went to the balcony doors, closed them, kicked off her shoes, took off her dress, then her brassiere, and was slipping out of her panties, when she saw Turner staring at her. "Are you going to the beach with me, Burt Turner?"

"Yes, but I have never seen you without your clothes. You're beautiful."

"Well, when we were in the car in Naples, you felt what you're looking at now. Let's go to the beach."

He turned his back, took his clothes off, pulled his jock and swimmer's shorts from his laundry bag and put them on. It was Laura's turn to stare at him as he did these things.

The surf at Tamara Beach was substantial, but far friendlier than the one thirty miles north, at Mehdiya. With a little instruction from Turner, Laura quickly learned how to body surf.

He was in the water long enough to get cold, caught a sizable breaker, and rode it in. He shuffled up the beach, and sat down on the warm sand. After a while, he stood up to get a better view of Laura surfing. He was fascinated by how comfortable she was in the turbulent water. She was easily the strongest female swimmer he had ever met.

Twenty minutes later, she caught one last wave and rode it into shallow water. Pressing her hands against the sandy bottom, she got up laughing, stumbled a bit in the undertow, and ran up to where he stood. She threw her arms around him and pulled her cold body tight against his and said, "That was the most fun I have had in a very long time, Burt."

He held her tight and, pressing his face against her wet cheek, replied, "You are truly amazing. You are just terrific in the water. You are really smart, and you have a beautiful body."

He almost commented on her erect nipples showing through her bikini top.

She gave him a long look and replied, "Well, thank you, Lieutenant JG Turner, those were very nice words, especially when you said 'really smart' before you said I had a beautiful body."

He didn't understand what she meant.

She kissed him on the cheek and said, "You're pretty amazing yourself. You're a little on the thin side, but I like that."

He reached down, picked up her towel and put it around her shoulders. She looked up at him and said, "Is it time to return to our room?"

"Yes, I believe it is."

During that weekend at Tamara Beach, they spent more time in their room getting to know each other in all ways than on the beach or in Rabat.

With regard to the Larache Affair, Vice Admiral Erskin Horner handpicked three officers and one senior enlisted man to make up an in-house Board of Inquiry to investigate the background for and steps taken to implement the Larache mission.

In early fall the Board of Inquiry produced an eighty-one page document:

-SECRET-
For Limited Distribution Only
A Report on the Larache Mission

Most of the document concerned itself with a section titled "Examination of the Proposed Plan of Action Outline," which included the finding that "the proposition a booby trapped limpet mine, with three Hebrew characters on its edge linking the mission to the Israelis, was conceptually irrational, unreasonable, and politically perilous. The originator of the proposal considered this action reasonable because Russians were supplying arms to Palestinians, Syrians, and Egyptians for use against Israelis."

This and other dangerous assumptions in the "Examination of the Proposed Plan of Action Outline" section continued to be scathing as it addressed the "irresponsible endangerment and potential loss of an irreplaceable asset" (Turner's team). The team garnered three lines at the end of this paragraph recognizing: "resourcefulness," "professionalism," and "courage leading to successful accomplishment of the task assigned."

In one of the last paragraphs of the document: "The Board regretfully states that the Larache mission could yet evolve into an incident with far reaching implications, internationally."

"The Proposed Plan of Action Outline wholly originated in the Naval Attaché's Office at the U.S. Embassy in Rabat" was the last line in the document.

With regard to the junior naval officer at COMNAVACTSMED who wrongly routed the attaché's outline for the Larache mission, he was ordered to a U.S. naval weather station on Adak Island in the Aleutian Island chain. This would be his last duty station as a member of the U.S. Naval Service. He would not be allowed to reenlist when this tour of duty was up.

A few French officials had a little something to smile about, but not for long. The insurgents continued to gain ground.

By fall, the political flap precipitated by the Larache mission was quietly laid to rest through the efforts of the chair of the Senate Intelligence Committee and his friend on the Senate Foreign Relations Committee. The Israeli and Moroccan governments received compensation from the United States government, by way of the CIA, for an incident that never happened.

Chapter 11

Tafas "the Lizard" was one of many abandoned children living in small gangs on the waterfront in the port of Algiers, Algeria. A gang was able to survive by taking advantage of what the waterfront and the surrounding environment provided, and the survival of a member within a gang depended on the member's contribution to the gang's well-being. All gang members were accomplished thieves; some were skillful fighters. The gang leaders had both attributes and were politically skillful in intra- and inter-gang politics. Gangs, and especially their leaders, had become fertile recruiting grounds for insurgents, especially in Algeria.

When he was nine years old, the Lizard was caught stealing a chicken from the chicken coup of Mullah Mohammed al Kahdi. Al Kahdi was a native of Saudi Arabia, a Sunni Muslim and a graduate of Al-Azar University in Cairo, Egypt. His later preparation was in strict interpretation of the Koran and the extreme Wahhabi doctrine as practiced in Saudi Arabia. He hated infidels.

The mullah's purpose in life was to bring into being young Islamic radical fundamentalists who would take up the fight against infidels, through jihad. The method of jihad the mullah preached was one that sanctioned killing non-Muslim men, women, and children as a method of removing infidels from Arab countries and regaining lands taken away, and if necessary, killing Muslims of different ethnicity or sect who did not practice Islamic radical fundamentalism.

The mullah had been quietly observing the sacrilege of the boy, stealing eggs from his chicken coop, for a number of weeks. When the thief became careless by coming to the chicken coop at the same early morning hour every third day, the mullah decided to end the enterprise.

Just before sunrise on the day of the next expected visit, the mullah placed a small stool in a corner of the chicken coop and sat down in the darkness. Soon the boy pushed open the back window of the chicken coop, pulled himself up on the ledge, and dropped down inside. He pulled a bag from a string holding up his pants and quietly padded over to the chicken hutches, reached into the nearest one, and carefully removed a hen. With a quick twist, he wrung the hen's neck and dropped the hen in the bag. Then he reached into the hen's bed of straw, took two eggs and put these in the bag with the lifeless hen. He turned and was about to leave when the mullah stood up and said, "Allah could strike you blind for what you do."

The boy froze in his place.

The mullah grabbed the bag with one hand, a handful of the boy's hair with the other, and dragged him out of the chicken coop, across the yard, and into the small whitewashed decrepit but spotlessly clean madrasa. The boy, squirming and screaming, was dragged through the empty classroom, and down the hall to a door that opened into a small windowless room with a single chair. On the chair was a book, a Koran. The mullah shoved the boy into the room, pointed to the book, and told him to read it. Then he turned, walked out of the room, slammed the door shut, and locked it.

Two hours later, the mullah returned and opened the door, the boy was asleep on the floor in the far corner of the room. The Koran was untouched. The mullah kicked the boy awake; he scrambled to his feet and stood in his filthy clothes looking up at the mullah in grand defiance. The mullah picked up the Koran, opened it and, as he handed it to the boy, pointed with a leathery finger at a passage and said, "Read this, you excrement of a jackal!"

Holding the book first one way then the other, he looked up at the mullah with a puzzled look on his face. The mullah snatched the Koran back, knowing the boy could not read. He sat down on the chair and, with the boy at eye level before him, began to talk with him. The boy's vocabulary was enough for his survival on the streets and no more. In time, the mullah became impressed with the boy's quickness in trying to answer questions, his obvious intelligence and spirit.

The mullah rose from the chair, twisted the boy around, and roughly sat him down on the chair. He stood looking down at him for a time, then said, "If you come here every day, I will give you food and drink. If you do not come here every day, I will find you and take you to the authorities. They will beat you and confine you forever!"

He then sent the boy away.

The next morning, before any of the students appeared in the madrasa classroom, the boy walked in, sat down on the floor in the back of the room, and waited. A short time later, the students filed in, each with a bag over their shoulder. They quietly slid sideways into three separate benches, one bench in front of the other, ten students to a bench. In front of each bench, facing the students, was a structure with a tilted shelf running the length of the bench, which was designed to hold the students' reading material. At the front of the room was a podium made up of a single length of wood, about five feet high, held in place with cinderblocks and topped with a tilted plank.

A few moments after the students were seated, the mullah appeared, said a few words, the students took Korans from their bags, opened them, placed them on the tilted shelf in front of them, and began memorizing the writings by chanting out loud and rocking in unison. The boy in the corner in the back of the room fell asleep.

He came to the madrasa every day through fear of what would happen if he didn't and the guarantee of something to eat. When he entered the madrasa, he always sat in the same place on the floor in the back of the room and listened to the students as they memorized the Koran. Periodically, the mullah stopped the students to explain what they were memorizing and emphasized the importance of not questioning what was written.

Over time, the boy became fascinated with the mullah's spoken word. Sometimes the method of delivery was strident and scared the boy, especially when the mullah looked at him in particular. Other times, the delivery was quietly thoughtful and caused the boy to think about what was said; almost always, the information held the boy's interest.

The boy began to come to class long before the other students arrived. He would search out the mullah and shyly ask questions he thought of the night before. He usually stayed long after the other students departed, seeking out and asking more questions of the mullah.

Eventually, the mullah said, "I will answer your questions, but the answers are within the Koran. Learn to read, and the world will be yours."

It was very difficult for the boy to learn to read. The Mullah assigned students who read the best to help. It was still the boy's self-discipline, curiosity, and innate ability that would eventually find him sitting on the bench with the best readers.

He learned the Koran was the summit of all things, the basis of moral character, social order, unity, dignity, and pride. The Koran made him understand the importance of sobriety and self-control, to be uncomplaining as one accepts the hardships and limitations of life. He was transfixed by the stories the mullah told of the prophet Mohammed. He learned about the great struggle of the people of Islam, who were killed, maimed, and stolen from for thousands of years by infidels from other countries, especially infidels who practiced the religions of the Jews and Christians.

He learned of the Catholic pope Urban II, who started the movement called crusade, and recruited people from all of Europe to attack and kill Muslims, who he said stole Jerusalem from the Christians. His "crusade" became many crusades against Muslims and lasted over two hundred years.

The boy progressed physically and mentally under the care of the mullah, and by the end of the boy's third year at the madrasa, the mullah decided to adopt him. The boy's adopted name was Owdi ibn Zahwahiri.

Zahwahiri was never made to understand that the prophet Mohammed did not explain a jihad of killing as a way of becoming a better human being, improving himself or herself and one's community in obedience to God. He wasn't to know that the majority of Muslims believe that a militant jihad was a perversity of what jihad really means and stands for.

Over time, young Zahwahiri learned of the historic spread of Islam fourteen hundred years before, from North Africa into Spain and from the Middle East to as far north as Austria and Poland, of Suleiman and Saladin and martyrdom.

When Zahwahiri was seventeen, he left the madrasa and Mullah Mohammed al Kahdi and joined a splinter group of the Front de Libération Nationale (FLN), who were radical Muslim fundamentalists in jihad against the French colonialists in Algeria and Morocco. He became an expert in explosive demolition, improvised booby traps, and the use of rocket-propelled grenade (RPG) launchers. He then was assigned to a group specializing in blowing up local police stations and French colonial government facilities. He later became a leader of a group that was assigned to destroy French-operated electrical delivery systems and French military communication facilities. He became a killer without remorse and soon was recognized as being among the most dangerous of the insurgents operating on the Algerian/Moroccan border. He was an important target for neutralization by the Deuxiem Bureau and Légion Étrangère.

In time, Zahwahiri joined a cell of the jihad organization Ikhwan-ul-Muslimeen (Muslim Brotherhood). The cell was beginning to study ways of attacking U.S. Navy bases and U.S. Air Force Strategic Air Command bases. The bases were recognized as a new colonization threat by the United States to take the place of the French, who were being forced out of their holdings in Morocco and Algeria. Zahwahiri was to be a principal player and was sent to a safe house in the little town of Sidi Kacem near the Roman ruins of Volubilis.

Two and a half weeks had gone by since Turner and Laura Brae had met in Rabat. During that time, they talked to each other twice on the phone and exchanged three letters. Most recently, they were trying to work out a plan to meet in Paris. They were having difficulty because of her schedule and, at times, unscheduled travel requirements, and of him being in the required six-day rotation as duty officer on twenty-four-hour watch at the Naval Ordnance Facility, coupled with periodic standby alerts for his team. There was no provision in the oaths they took, with regard to their military and intelligence service, that provided for nurturing of what began in Naples and intensified in Rabat.

It was midnight before Turner finally got to bed after a long discussion in Miller's room concerning the United States assuming the role of international policeman in geopolitical affairs. Initially, the discussion was intellectually interesting, but deteriorated to total nonsense because of too much of an unremarkable Algerian wine.

He was half-awake when there was a knock on the door.

"Mr. Turner, Mr. Turner, are you there?" Then two more knocks on the door in quick succession.

"Just a minute, just a minute." He rolled out of bed, padded over to the door, and opened it. It was Yeoman Second Class Jenkins.

"I'm sorry, sir. Commander Hawkins wants to see you right away. I have his car downstairs."

Turner looked at his Rolex. It was 0320.

"Let me get something on. I'll be right down."

Jenkins left the room.

As he put on his wash khakis, he thought, *It's oh-dark-hundred in the morning, and a message like that could only mean something serious.*

When he was about to leave his room, he looked in the mirror, rubbed his chin, and reached for his electric razor. He thought better of it, shut off the light, and ran out the door.

In the car he asked, "What's going on, Yeoman Jenkins?"

"There was an explosion at the communication site at Sidi Yahia."

(The U.S. Navy communications site at Sidi Yahia was one of the main communications links between the U.S. and naval ships and stations in the eastern Atlantic, Europe, and the U.S. Navy Sixth Fleet in the Mediterranean.)

When they arrived at the NOF office complex, they were met by the duty officer, Warrant Officer Fulkerson. "Good morning, Mr. Turner. The skipper is across the hall in the conference room. You're expected."

Turner went across the hall to the conference room door, knocked twice, and just as he put his hand on the doorknob, the commander called out, "Enter."

He went in, looked around and sat down at the long green table with the exec, Commander Peetz, Major Larson of the marine detachment, and a French Army officer.

"Yes, sir. You called for me?"

"I did. This is Lieutenant Lafort of the French Army. He has a small detachment about eight miles northeast of Sidi Allal el-Tazi."

He reached over and shook Lafort's hand, then sat down next to the exec.

"I think you know everyone else. Commander Peetz, would you fill Mr. Turner in on the Sidi Yahia situation?"

Peetz looked over at Turner and said, "At about 0215, an attack was made on our communications site at Sidi Yahia. Three of the five towers were blown up, and one fell over on the high-voltage line feeding the station. The site will be down a few days. This is the first attack on an American base in North Africa."

Laura had given a warning that something like this could happen, he thought.

Peetz looked over at Lieutenant Lafort and asked, "Lieutenant, would you please tell Mr. Turner what you told us earlier?"

In almost perfect English, he replied, "We had not experienced an insurgency event in this area before, and last week, we received a message saying there could be one forthcoming. Two nights ago, one of my four-man patrols stopped a Fiat 500 sedan and a petite taxi following the Fiat 500 sedan. Both appeared to be coming from the direction of Sidi Allal el Tazi. The patrol inspected the Fiat 500 sedan first and found two young men who had been drinking. When asked what they were doing out past curfew, they explained they were on their way to their homes after a party. Their homes were about six kilometers south. One of my men stayed with this car, and the other three went back to inspect the petite taxi and question the driver, who turned out to be alone. When my three men came near the car, the driver called out, 'Allal Akbar,' and the car blew up, killing the driver and my men. The soldier detaining the first car ran back to try to help, and the first car sped away. The two men who got away may have been responsible for the attack at Sidi Yahia this morning."

"Thank you, Lieutenant," Peetz replied. Then addressing Major Larson, who was in charge of base security, he asked, "Is this a possible continuing threat that's manageable, Bill?"

"We don't have anywhere near the marines necessary for base perimeter security here or at Sidi Yahia."

Peetz said, "In a few minutes, Captain Travis is going to ask me and you a lot of questions. We had better have some answers, Major."

"Well, I will have to say the marine corps has a lot of obligations—Lebanon and the far east, for example, and that I have been told there is no way to augment the number of marines we currently have here. I would suggest that perhaps something might be worked out between our embassy in Rabat and the Moroccan government where the Royal Army of Morocco personnel could help provide security."

Commander Hawkins said, "I would be careful about saying something like that, Major. I'm sure we wouldn't want to compromise King Mohammed's situation by asking his government to do something on that order, especially so soon after the removal of the French." He glanced over at Lieutenant Lafort and said, "No offense, young man."

"None taken, sir. I understand."

"Well, this is not what Mr. Turner is here for." Commander Hawkins replied. He turned his attention to his SW/EOD officer. "Mr. Turner, I want you and your team to get out to Sidi Yahia and see what happened and how they got away with it. Get down to Operations. The helicopter is waiting for you."

Commander Peetz added, "When you get there, look up Lieutenant al Karim, the assistant chief of police for this area. He will be on site. We have found him to be helpful and honest, although abrasively nationalistic at times."

Oh shit, al Karim.

He almost asked if he could go back to the BOQ and shave, but caught himself and said, "Aye, aye, sir."

He went back across the hall to his desk, picked up the phone, and called Gallegos. His wife answered, "Chief Gallegos's residence."

"Mrs. Gallegos, this is Mr. Turner. I need your husband."

"Just a minute, Mr. Turner."

A minute later, "Chief Gallegos speaking."

"Chief, we are flying to Sidi Yahia. There's been an explosion. Commander Hawkins wants us to get out there and find out what happened. Get Cole, and I'll meet you at the EOD shop in twenty minutes. I'll tell you more when you get here." He hung up without waiting for a response.

Twenty-five minutes later, the team's weapons carrier pulled up near the HUP; the HUP's rotors were wind milling. They got out of the weapons carrier and, with Cole carrying a medium-sized canvas satchel, ran to the open door of the helicopter. Once inside, a familiar face looked around from the cockpit; it was Chief Flint Williams with a mug of coffee in his hand.

"Welcome aboard, you guys. You too, Mr. Turner. I'm covering for another pilot. He became sick for some reason. Probably had a premonition about you. Fasten up, and away we will go."

Because there were no crewman on board, Turner went forward and strapped himself in the copilot's seat next to Williams. Turner yelled above the engine and rotor noise, "Sorry to get you out of the rack, Chief."

"Mr Turner, you always have interesting things to do, and I can sleep anytime." He added, "I'm not going to put you on report for not being shaven."

Williams lifted the helicopter and set a course for Sidi Yahia. It was 0432, first light.

Williams had grown to like Lieutenant JG Turner because of the way he handled himself with regard to his team and the respect he showed for other enlisted men. He was especially impressed with Turner's ease in taking the initiative, sticking his neck out, and his resourcefulness after taking it.

Fifteen minutes later, they landed on the Sidi Yahia communications site parking lot. As the team left the helicopter, Williams shut down the engine. "I'll stay with the HUP and monitor the radio while you guys go do your thing."

A marine officer and a navy chief warrant officer met the team. The marine said, "Welcome aboard. I'm Second Lieutenant Richards, the security officer here. This is Chief Warrant Officer Donnelly, who runs this place."

The officers shook hands. Then Turner asked, "We are supposed to talk with a Moroccan Police lieutenant by the name of al Karim. Is he here, Lieutenant?"

"He and two Arab policemen are over looking at one of the downed antennas. I'll take you over."

As they walked along, Turner counted eight battle lanterns substituting for the downed lights that previously illuminated the area. "If there were security lights on, how did the intruders get in and set charges without the marine sentries seeing them?"

Second Lieutenant Richards replied, "We have two marines on duty at the main gate and one marine at a desk just inside the main building. The few lights in the antenna area are primarily for equipment maintenance purposes. Unfortunately, it would be difficult to see anyone if they didn't want to be seen. We don't have enough marines to provide adequate security. Orders are for keeping a low profile in terms of numbers and to not appear to be taking the place of the French."

"Why is al Karim here, Lieutenant?"

"The higher ups asked him to examine what happened. I think it's a courtesy. Maybe they are thinking to ask if it would be possible for some of his police force to help provide security here."

That's Major Larsen's line. It's exactly the kind of thing that would really piss off the insurgents. Commander Hawkins had it right. Laura would call this kind of thinking a case of cultural blindness.

Lieutenant al Karim was kneeling down at the base of the downed antenna nearest the perimeter fence. This antenna was also the farthest from the only building at the communications site. Seeing the group approaching, al Karim got up and brushed his trousers off. Lieutenant Richards saluted al Krim and said, "This is the special weapons/explosive ordnance disposal team from NAS Port Lyautey. The team leader is Lieutenant Junior Grade Turner."

Turner reached out to shake al Karim's hand and said with a touch of irony, "I think we have met before, Lieutenant al Karim. Last time, you were wearing dark glasses."

Al Karim looked hard at Turner, then recognizing him said indifferently, "Oh yes, Turner. The American that permits himself to drive automobiles in our country without knowing our customs." Then with real derision he added, "I see you are growing a beard. Are you trying to become Arab or Berber?"

Cole and Gallegos were standing behind and to one side of Turner, listening to this exchange. Cole worried that Turner was going to lose his head and say the wrong thing. Gallegos wasn't sure what would happen next; it could be very bad.

Turner surprised them both when he said with real interest and in a tone of camaraderie, "Lieutenant al Karim, how do you think they did it?"

Al Karim was completely unprepared for the question and the way it was asked. He considered the question contrived and patronizing and almost said so. He looked at Turner's face for a moment, then answered, "Let us walk over to where they entered."

The marine officer started walking away and said, "I have to go back inside, my sergeant is in the process of interrogating the marines that were on outside duty. If you need anything, come and get me."

Al Karim spoke in Arabic to his policemen, sending them toward the parking lot, then led Turner and his team to where the fence was cut open. Looking at the entry point, Turner thought it was much like the entry through the perimeter fence Joe Logan showed him at Sidi Slimane—cut on three sides and bent back, providing a small and not easily observable hole.

Al Karim got down on one knee and pointed at the disturbed dirt in the hole of entry.

He carefully lifted two wires from the loose dirt that were coming from the antenna tower area and going through the fence to the outside and showed them to Turner. He dropped the wires, got up, and, pointing to a small scuffed-up area a little farther on, said, "There were two fellagha. They went to the farthest antenna tower, established their charges, and then, on the way back to the entry, continued to unwind their wires and to establish charges at the other two antenna towers."

There was now enough light to allow Turner and his team to see the wires trailing back from the entry hole and into desert shrubbery.

He turned and exchanged glances at Gallegos and Cole. All three knew the people who did this were very well practiced. They used a remotely controlled electrical firing system to detonate cutting charges, which went off in split second delays, to efficiently take down guy-wires and the three antenna towers.

Turner asked, "Excuse me, Lieutenant al Karim. What are fellagha?"

"They are Algerian insurrectionists. It is they who are driving the French out of Algeria and Morocco by force."

"But this is not a French communications site!" Turner replied.

"The fellagha want all infidels out of Algeria and Morocco," he replied.

They walked over and stopped at the first downed antenna tower. Gallegos and Cole examined the cut guy-wires that braced the antenna tower in position, and Turner and al Karim examined the tower base that had been blasted away, toppling the antenna tower.

What was left of the wires of the electrical firing system provided evidence of branching off a main line from each antenna tower base and going to guy-wires supporting each antenna tower.

Gallegos and Cole walked over to Turner and al Karim.

Gallegos said, "From the way it looks, they probably used Primacord."

(*Primacord looks very much like clothesline. The core is high explosive— PETN—the covering is textile or plastic, and waterproof. Primacord is used in variety of ways, such as an explosive wrapping or stretched out in an explosive line.*)

Turner said, "From the way the tower base looks, they probably used C4 (a plasticized high explosive) as a cutting charge."

The group looked at the other two towers. They agreed that the tower toppled over the high-tension electrical power lines serving the facility wasn't done by accident; it was part of a very sophisticated demolition plan.

Turner asked, "Lieutenant al Karim, shall we follow the electrical firing wires and see where they lead?"

"Yes."

They went around to the security gate entrance; a marine guard opened the gate, allowing them to pass through, and they followed the fence line to where the electrical firing wires came through. They followed the wires snaking through about a hundred yards of desert brush and came to a stop at tire tracks.

As Turner and al Karim discussed the attack, Turner found al Karim's terminology hard to follow, but he understood enough to know that al Krim had a great deal of experience in this sort of thing. Gallegos and Cole were watching Turner and al Karim interact with much interest.

As they walked back to the communication site, the marine officer came out of the main building and yelled, "The helicopter got a call to return to the NAS. The chief wants you guys to hurry."

Turner stopped and extended his hand to al Karim and said, "I really appreciate working with you. Thank you, Lieutenant al Karim."

They shook hands, Turner saluted al Karim and said good-bye. As they parted, al Karim paused and said, "Maybe another time, Lieutenant Turner." And putting his hand to his heart, he added, "Bi s-slaama."

Through mutual respect, a friendship was being formed.

Gallegos and Cole were standing just away from the two officers and couldn't believe what they were seeing and hearing. There were very few Americans who showed such openness and respect to an Arab.

When they were in the air on the way to the NAS, Gallegos and Cole took their small notebooks from their foul-weather jackets and gave them to Turner.

Gallegos said, "You might need these, sir, but get em back to us?"

When Turner realized what he was handed, his face immediately reddened, and he sheepishly said, "I guess I forgot mine."

Cole laughed and said, "You do realize that we are here to keep you out of trouble and not get ourselves hurt, among other things."

Gallegos added, "You did a good job with Lieutenant al Karim, Mr. Turner, a very good job."

"Thank you, Chief."

The helicopter landed near the Operations building and, as Turner made his way to the cargo door, Chief Williams turned around and called out,

"They just called from the Admin building. You're wanted at the base CO's office right now."

"Did they want all of us?"

"Just you, Mr. Turner."

Turner and his team began walking to the rear entrance of the Operations building when a jeep drove up and almost slid sideways as the brakes took hold. The sailor driving the jeep asked, "Mr. Turner?"

"I'm Turner."

"Sir, I'm to take you to Admin. Captain Travis's orders."

Turner glanced at Gallegos and Cole. "You guys go on. I'll get a ride back later."

"Aye, aye, sir," Gallegos replied.

When they arrived at the base Administration building Turner jumped out of the jeep as it was rolling to a stop, ran up the sidewalk, skipped the three stairs at the entrance, and went through the open doors and into the lobby. The officer of the day at the counter, a lieutenant junior grade recently arrived after a tour of sea duty, waved him over, observed his scruffy appearance, and asked, officiously, "Do you have business here at this time?"

"Yes, I do. I am here to see the commanding officer of this base, Captain Travis."

A first class yeoman at a desk to the rear of the lieutenant junior grade said, "Sir, I think that is Lieutenant JG Turner. The skipper wanted him upstairs as soon as he came in the building."

"Do you have an ID, Mr. Turner?"

Turner pulled his security pass out of the pocket of his foul-weather jacket and handed it to the officer of the day.

He looked at it and said, "Thanks, please wear this while you are in the building." He handed back the security pass and said to the yeoman, "Call upstairs and let them know Mr. Turner is on his way."

On the way up the stairs, there were a number of officers who commented on Turner's scruffy appearance. He went into the CO's outer office, and a very attractive female yeoman first class stood up from her desk and said, "You must be Mr. Turner. Captain Travis said to show you in when you arrived." She pointed to the CO's door.

He went to the door, knocked twice, and heard, "Come!"

He took off his hat and walked in. Captain Travis was sitting at the head of a table near an expanse of windows that looked out over a number of eucalyptus trees to the base golf course. Next to Captain Travis was Commander Felix, the CO's exec, then Commander Peetz, Commander

Hawkins, and Lieutenant Commander Owens. On the other side of the table were Lieutenant Commander Bello from Operations, Major Larson of the Marine Detachment, and Lieutenant Franklin.

Pointing to the end of the table, Captain Travis said, "Take off your jacket and sit down, Mr. Turner."

As Turner took off his foul-weather jacket, his hat fell from his hand to the floor, his shirttail came out on one side, and his tie became out of true. Commander Hawkins smiled, and Lieutenant Commander Owens rolled his eyes. The others watched with some expectation of something more to follow.

Turner draped his foul-weather jacket over the back of his chair, picked up his hat, and put it on the table. Tucking in his shirt as he sat down, he said, "Excuse me, sir."

Captain Travis smiled and said, "The fact that you are unshaven completes your Chaplinesque performance, young man."

The group good-naturedly laughed.

Then he continued, "The officer in charge at Sidi Yahia radioed a report concerning the attack. What did you see out there, Mr. Turner?"

Over a period of forty minutes, Turner expanded what he remembered from Gallegos's and Cole's cryptic notes, coupled with what he remembered while working with al Karim. His ability to remember details and explain his interpretation of events in a compelling way proved him to be much more substantial than his appearance as a disheveled junior officer that entered the room earlier.

Captain Travis asked, "Do we know how the insurrectionists got demolition equipment and how they learned to use it with this level of sophistication, Commander Peetz?"

What did the captain think has been going on here for the last five years? They had plenty of time to steal it or win it in combat from the French Army. Once they have it, it doesn't take long to learn how to use it, especially if they have Russian advisors.

Commander Peetz answered, "They buy it from the international market. They get a lot of their weapons from the Russians, and they certainly have ways of taking it from the French Army. They have been at it long enough to become quite expert, sir."

The captain seemed to think about this, then asked, "Why did they attack an American Navy facility when we mean them no harm? After all, we are neutral in respect to what they are attempting to do."

Peetz again answered, "Intelligence sources, especially in the last few months, have been reporting that the insurrectionists in Morocco, Algeria, and Tunisia are well on their way to winning the war of independence against the French. There are indications that a radical Islamic movement within the insurgency is turning its attention to the presence of American military bases in North Africa. They consider these bases another Western neocolonial adventure, taking the place of the French. The same intelligence sources strongly advise this movement will soon surface as terrorist activity against our bases."

"Well, it certainly looks as though they have started with Sidi Yahia," the captain answered. Then looking at Major Larson, he said, "I have a base to run here, Major. What can you do to beef up our security?"

"Frankly, sir, not much. To begin with, we have no systematic vetting procedures to vet indigenous worker applications, and we must rely on the Moroccan police. We have asked each facility attached to this base to hold security review sessions for their personnel. Our marines are at a heightened state of alert at all entrances to the base and while on roving patrol at exclusion areas, such as at the Naval Ordnance Facility, the Fleet Intelligence Center, and air operations."

"What about the perimeter fence and checkpoints, Major?"

"Roving patrols at the perimeter fence are limited because of lack of personnel, and we can't afford to take personnel from other areas. We do not have personnel to man checkpoints."

Commander Felix asked, "What is the total length of the perimeter fence, and how much of the length is close by the airport runway, Major?"

"The total length is somewhat over twelve miles. About three miles of the fence is parallel to the south bank of the Oued Sebou, and the airport runway's closest point of approach is about fifty yards along that section of fence."

"What is the distance from the river to the perimeter fence?"

"It varies between five hundred and about one thousand yards."

"If you were planning to infiltrate this base where would you do it?"

Without hesitation, Major Larson replied, "Two miles from the mouth of the river, the base perimeter fence abruptly curves inland to the south. The closest point to the Naval Ordnance Facility's perimeter fence protecting twelve ammunition bunkers is about fifty yards before the curve begins. I would cut through the base perimeter fence at that point, and then the NOF perimeter fence, and go after the conventional ammunition bunkers, sir."

Captain Travis asked, "What about the nuclear weapons in the exclusion area?"

"The exclusion area, with its own double fences and two watch towers, with a marine in each tower, is about a hundred yards farther in. I would consider going after the nuclear weapons magazines rather than spending time on the conventional weapons magazines if I knew nuclear weapons were there, sir."

Turner was incredulous; he looked over at Bruce Franklin, who was staring with his mouth half-open in disbelief at Major Larsen.

Then, addressing Commander Hawkins, Captain Travis asked, "What do you think about what the major said, Gene?"

"I totally agree with the major. My staff and I have worked with him on the problem, and he has done his utmost to provide us with the best security possible based on the number of marines at his disposal. We will continue to work hard to improve our security situation, sir."

No one had anything else to say; the room became uncomfortably quiet

Captain Travis broke the silence. "It appears the requirement of keeping a low military profile in this country is compromising our base security."

Major Larson replied, "Sir, I would like to add, the marine corps is currently maxed out in manning requirements of the fleet both ashore at home and overseas, and now small units are finding themselves as advisors in places like Indochina. Even without the low military profile requirement, there are not enough marines to go around."

Ignoring the major, the captain said, "I want a proposed contingency plan from each of your commands within five days, addressing additional measures to prevent terrorist infiltration as well as what is to be done in case infiltration occurs. That will be all, gentlemen. Commander Felix, stay, please."

Turner, the last to leave the office, saw the captain and his exec standing and looking out over the eucalyptus trees to the golf course. He heard the exec say in a low voice, "I wonder how many paid attention and, if they did pay attention, understood the importance of what that woman from CIA was talking about a while back?"

He heard the captain reply, "I don't know, I don't know. But bad things this way come, George."

Two nights later, after dinner, Turner, Miller, and Teipner were waiting at Operations for Lieutenant Phil Pierce to come in from Paris via U.S. Navy Air Transport Squadron VR24, Flight 241. Pierce was returning from a conference at the Academie de Medecine, where he had been invited to give a paper on the "Outcome of Surgical Intervention in Lower Extremity Trauma Due to Military Action." His presentation included the treatment of wounds of an anonymous patient who later died. The patient was Mineman First Class Richard Huwitt.

The loudspeaker announced the landing of Flight 241, and the three officers walked out to the air station terminal and waited close by to where the airplane would park.

Four minutes later, the R-6D trundled toward them, swung around, and stopped. At the same time, the pilot shut the four engines down, the ground crew pushed the boarding stairs into place at the passenger entry/exit hatch, and a large cargo lift towed by a small tractor was set in position at the cargo hatch.

As the last of the passengers exited the airplane, Teipner said, "It looks like Pierce didn't make the flight."

Then from the opened cargo hatch, "Hey, you three, I need some help."

They walked over and stood near the cargo lift. Pierce looked down and said, "Wait 'til you see what I have!" He stepped back into the airplane and, when he returned, he was holding what appeared to be a case of wine that he placed on the platform of the cargo lift that just moved into position. He backed in again and returned with another and again for a third. Then he stepped onto the platform, and the lift operator lowered Pierce and the three cases of wine. Pierce stepped off and pontificated, "I have here three cases of wine from the Loire Valley, one case of pinot noir and two of sauvignon blanc. I know your tastes are quite pedestrian, but hopefully, through my continuing mentoring, you will become more interested in taste and bouquet rather than a wine's ability to inebriate."

Miller replied, "It would have been better if you had stayed in Paris and sent the wine on to us, you snob."

Turner and Teipner laughed, and Turner said, "Actually we are very happy to see you back. Even if you hadn't brought what seems to be very fine wine, we would still be happy for your safe return."

Teipner echoed, "Oh yes, we are still happy for your safe return."

An air crewman called out, "Lieutenant, here's your flight bag," and dropped it. It landed with a thump next to the cargo lift.

Pierce picked it up and thanked the air crewman; the others each picked up a case of wine, and they proceeded to the Operations parking lot and Miller's car.

On the way to the BOQ, Miller asked, "Seriously, Phil, how was it in Paris?"

"My paper was well received, I think. At least, they were very nice to me—they gave me a small certificate. But politically, things are going very badly for the present government. The newspapers are full of questions about what President de Gaulle is going to do about Algeria: stay and continue to fight the FLN guerillas or what some are calling insurgents, grant independence to Algeria—after negotiating access to oil, natural gas, and agricultural products—or just flat get out. In Algiers, there is house-to-house fighting. The Sahara is a massive killing field, and unspeakable atrocities are common on both sides. I'll tell you more over a glass of the very fine wine I brought."

After leaving the car in the BOQ parking lot, they went inside with the precious cargo and on up to Miller's room. They put the cases of wine in the middle of the room, sat down, and settled up how much they owed their friend and physician. It came to thirty-six dollars each. Miller paid in full, then loaned Teipner twelve dollars to pay his share, while Turner gave two twenties and told Pierce to keep the four. All paid in 'script,' since no American currency was allowed in Morocco. They opened a case of pinot noir and sauvignon blanc and thought it sensible to open one bottle of each for tasting purposes.

Ritualistically, Pierce poured the white wine; they swirled and noted the bouquet, sipped, and then, with new glasses, did the same with the red.

Pierce said, "I tried a bottle of each in Paris and thought it wonderful. What do you beer and taco lovers think?"

The three made jokes about the wine but finally expressed their pleasure. Pierce was quite pleased.

Miller said, "We should ask the girls if they would like to join us in sampling this Loire Valley wine and hear the latest news from Paris from Dr. Pierce."

Teipner replied, "They might not be here."

Miller asked, "Why not?"

"They might be at the gym. They have been spending a lot of time there."

Turner asked, "What are they doing at the gym?"

"Yoga and lifting weights or something. They're doing it maybe two or three times a week."

Miller put down his glass, went to the phone, and called Lieutenant Junior Grade Mary Bionconi.

"This is Miss Bionconi."

"Binki, it is I."

"I'm sorry, who is I?"

"Come on, Binki. It's me, Bob!"

"Oh yes, Bob."

"Phil Pierce just got back from Paris with some terrific wine and interesting news. Can you get Betty and Juniper and come over?"

"We just got back from the gym, and we decided to catch up with writing letters home tonight." She hesitated and continued, "I don't know. Why tonight?"

"Because I love you and want to marry you, Binki!"

There was a long pause, then, "Yes, well, Phil may have something new and interesting. I'll ask Betty and Juniper, just a minute."

After a few minutes, she returned to the phone. "OK, but this isn't going to be a late nighter. We will be over in a few minutes."

They arrived in Levis, navy sweatshirts and Arab slippers (yellow). Miller had put a record on, Erik Satie's *Gnosiennes* for mood, and was in his easy chair. Turner and Teipner sat on the floor with their backs against Arab leather hassocks. Pierce was sitting in the desk chair. The three women sat on the lounge.

Betty Armstrong opened the conversation with, "How very nice for the two aviators, our good doctor, and our underwater warrior to invite us to wine and news of the outside world."

Miller, in a rather plaintive way, said, "You know, we haven't been together this way since Kathy Roberts left us."

Binki replied, "Well, Bob, perhaps you might have invited us over."

He answered, "Your social calendar seems to be rather hard for us to break into these days."

"You and the other aviator are always gone, Phil is tied up in meetings, and who knows what or where Burt is."

"Well, I'm glad we are all together, finally," Juniper said.

They were surprised at her intervening statement. Being new to the group, she had been slow to establish herself. However, she and Teipner had been spending some time together, which may have boosted her self-confidence.

Miller gave the women glasses; Pierce poured them sauvignon blanc.

Betty was the first to comment. "This is unusually good, better than most whites I have ever tasted. What makes it so good?"

The others agreed with her, opening the door for Pierce to explain. "The Loire Valley is just south and east of Paris. The weather for growing a delicate-skinned grape like sauvignon and pinot noir is quite good, but also, the soil is exceptional. There are combinations of chalk, flint, and clay that prove to give the grape and resultant wine this wonderful color and taste." Everyone lifted their glasses and tasted again, registering a pleasure that was facilitated by what Pierce just said.

"Now I'm going to give you a real surprise." He went to the unopened case of sauvignon blanc, opened it, and in the space where there should have been a bottle was an elongated package that he lifted out.

"Mr. Miller, a knife, please."

Miller went to his desk drawer, opened it and took out a navy utility pocketknife and gave it to Pierce.

Pierce added, "And a saucer, please."

Miller and the others had, over time, brought from the officers' mess, cups and saucers and glasses for their postdinner periodic get-togethers. Miller handed Pierce a saucer. Pierce untied the brown string holding the wrappings together, folded it back, and said, "This is Crottin de Chavignol, goat cheese."

He cut pieces away from the whole and placed them on the saucer.

"Now, I will pass this around, and please have some with your wine."

Teipner asked, "Is this a science experiment?"

"Well, actually it is, a study in biochemistry."

Binki was the first to comment on the combination of wine and cheese. "This is wonderful!" Again, general agreement.

More wine was poured, and cheese passed around. There was inconsequential conversation for a time, then Turner asked, "What about Paris? You said things were going very badly."

Pierce put down his glass and became very serious.

"Well, France is on the edge of civil war because of awful economic problems brought about by inflation, noncompetitive industry, inefficient small farms, the cost of staying in Indochina and Morocco too long, and now the unsustainable cost of the war next door in Algeria. So to try to resolve the situation, the parliament just brought de Gaulle back as prime minister after his absence of eleven years.

Binki said, "A couple of weeks ago, there was an article in *Time Magazine-International Edition* saying they were trying to convince him to come back."

"Why don't they just leave Algeria to the Algerians?" asked Juniper.

Miller replied, "Because they think Algeria is France. When we are in Oran, you can't find a wall that doesn't have *L'Algerie est La France* painted on it."

"What does '*L'Algerie est La France*' mean?" she asked.

Teipner answered, "Algeria is France."

"The French colonized it in the late 1880s," Pierce added. "They have been administrators, business people, technicians, farmers, and fishermen for six generations. They own almost all of the arable land, and Arabs are hired to work it. They have a vested interest in Algeria and are calling themselves the Pied Noir, the Black Feet. They say they are the French in Algeria, not Frenchmen in Algeria. They also insist that France without Algeria isn't France."

Binki asked, "How could Algeria be French if the millions of Muslim Arabs are not Frenchmen with equal rights?"

Betty added, "The Algerian Arabs live in poverty and are not equal partners in their own country. Are the French racist as well as imperialist?"

Before Pierce could attempt to answer their questions, Juniper in a more forceful then usual voice said, "A nation that colonizes another nation doesn't permit self-determination and never gives equal rights to the inhabitants."

Teipner asked, "Is there any Arab nation that allows self-determination and gives equal rights to its inhabitants?"

"I don't know if there is any Arab nation that hasn't been colonized by a Western country," Pierce replied.

Turner thought, *If a colonial government is forced out through insurgency, the new government would probably be a theocracy based on the Islamic religion or a dictatorship with Islamic underpinnings. If there's a strongly conservative interpretation of the Koran, like Wahhabism in Saudi Arabia, Teipner is on the right track. Laura would know.*

There seemed to be a feeding frenzy developing, and Turner loudly said, "It sounds like you guys are putting the screws to Phil. He's just telling you the way things are." Then he asked, "Phil, what else did you find out?"

"As I said, it is very bad. In France, the people are putting pressure on their government to get out of Algeria. The French in Algeria, the Pied Noir, are putting pressure on the government to stay. The last newspaper I saw before leaving Paris said the government is close to making a decision to leave Algeria. There is talk that if the decision is made to leave, there are a number of French Army and Foreign Legion generals in Algeria who will side with the Pied Noir, which means there is a possibility of a mutiny against the current French government.

"The newspaper also said De Gaulle is attempting to get permission from parliament to negotiate with the FLN. The Pied Noir has found this out and charged the present government in Paris with committing treason. Add to this a growing number of army and Foreign Legion personnel who are deserting the ranks in Algeria to join a secret military force supporting the Pied Noir. I think the force is called the OAS. I don't remember what OAS stands for."

Miller asked, "What about the atrocities you said were being committed?"

"Atrocities are being committed on both sides. In the villages, huts are burned, many times with the inhabitants inside. If there are crops, they are burned. Sheep, goats, and chickens are slaughtered along with suspected insurgent sympathizers. In the cities, suspects are taken from their homes in the middle of the night, never to return. Torture is common. It is thought that a unit in the French Army called the Deuxiem Bureau is responsible for most of the atrocities. There are rumors of decapitations."

Miller said, "I have never heard of the Deuxiem Bureau."

The others agreed they never heard of the Deuxiem Bureau. Turner broke out in a cold sweat and became nauseous. It wasn't the wine and goat cheese. He excused himself and said, "I have to go to the head."

As he went out the door, he heard Pierce say, "I think the way the newspapers described the group, it's something like our CIA, maybe."

When Turner got to the head, his stomach felt better. He went to the wash basin, splashed cold water on his face and neck, dried off with paper towels, and returned to Miller's room.

The group was so engrossed in Pierce's account of what the Paris newspapers and television reported that Turner's return was unnoticed.

Betty asked, "All this has to do with the French. What about the other side?"

"The other side? Well, their preferences are bombing market places, cafes, and dance halls—generally, wherever Europeans collect. Some of the bombings are suicidal. Police stations, government facilities, radio and television stations are routinely bombed. What is very interesting is the insurgents inform the media, at times with film, when they kidnap and kill civil servants and technicians."

Teipner said, "Terrorism on both sides. I can't understand how the French, with their modern weapons, including airpower, could be losing a war against undisciplined, loosely organized tribal Arabs. Don't the French have enough men to deal with these guys? And where the hell do the Arabs get weapons to use against the French?"

"From what I read, there are about 150,000 French Army troops in Algeria. About thirty thousand are Légion Étrangère—Foreign Legion. They say the number of insurgents representing the FLN, the National Liberation Front, are far less than the French military. The FLN comes by their arms by buying from international arms dealers, recovering arms from combat, or clandestine delivery of arms from other Arab countries sympathetic to their cause. Russia is very interested in what is going on in Algeria, and rumor has it they have secretly set up a pipeline for arms supply to the insurgents."

Teipner, in exasperation, said, "Jesus, this is a mess. The only word we have heard here is the Arabs are kicking the French out of Algeria, just as they did here and in Tunisia. We are neutral to what's going on between the French and insurgent Arabs, and it shouldn't matter to us."

"Well, it does. What about Sidi Yahia?" Turner asked.

Teipner answered, "A propane tank blew up, big deal."

From the look on Turner's face, Pierce knew Turner had more to say about the subject. He took a chance and asked, "Burt, are you going to tell us what happened?"

Turner was caught off guard. There was a pause; he said, "I haven't heard the event was classified, so I guess its OK. The fellagha blew up three of the communications towers at Sidi Yahia."

They were all astonished.

"How do you know, Burt?" Miller asked

"We were called out at four this morning to investigate the situation. When we got there, three of the towers were down, and there was plenty of evidence of how it happened."

"Who the hell are the fellagha?" Teipner asked.

"The fellagha are Algerian insurgent terrorists."

"If they are Algerian, why are they attacking one of our bases here in Morocco?" Binki asked.

"They probably made a mistake—they thought it was a French communications site," Miller replied. "But why would they cross the border to do this?"

Turner said, "I don't think they made a mistake at all. They knew what they were doing. I really believe they want us out. And borders? Borders in North Africa don't have much meaning, especially when you consider a large number of Arabs and Berbers lead a culturally nomadic life."

As the conversation continued, Turner became more an observer than a speaker and noticed the irony of how the designation of the people responsible for the explosion at Sidi Yahia changed from "insurgents" to "terrorists." Soon, supposition took over from known specifics about the occurrence at Sidi Yahia, and interest in the discussion ended.

Pierce said, "Now, with that wake-up call that our world isn't as safe as we thought, does anyone know how Kathy Roberts is?"

Binki replied, "In Kathy's last letter, she said she was leaving Bethesda and the naval service for Stanford Med School on the first of next month. Earlier, the med school invited her out for an admission interview. Because of her unusual background, especially in the treatment of trauma, she was recommended for admission. She thought they really wanted her enrolled to show that the med school held no prejudice in regard to women becoming physicians. She said at least two of the seven on the interviewing board were very obvious about what they thought was the appropriate role a woman should play in medicine."

Pierce interrupted, "Only two out of the seven. That's interesting. Usually, most of the board are faculty, and it would be interesting to know how they treat female students these days."

Miller added, "Kathy probably wowed them with her looks."

Binki gave him a dirty look.

"Well, she is really good-looking you know," he said with some small sign of embarrassment.

Binki continued, "There is more. After the board approved her admission to the med school, she applied for a scholarship. The scholarship committee was also impressed with her background and need, and gave her a full-ride scholarship and campus dorm privileges."

The room went quiet and then erupted in cheers and clapping.

Pierce asked, "Did she ask about us?"

"Kathy said to especially thank Dr. Phil Pierce for his letter of recommendation. It carried a lot of weight. She had a few nice remembrances of you others." She glanced at Turner and added, "Some quite touching."

Miller laughed and said, "She could only be talking about me, no kidding."

Betty Armstrong ended the session with, "Well, with that, I'm going to bed."

Only two people in the room would ever know of the affair.

The next morning, Turner, being very much behind in his paperwork, walked into the office complex at NOF forty-five minutes early. He was surprised at the aroma of fresh coffee so early.

"Good morning, Yeoman Fry."

Fry looked up from his typing, greeted Turner, and said, "The commander wanted to see you as soon as you came in."

The commander always seems to want to see me as soon as I come in.

"What's going on, Fry?"

"He and the exec were here most the night and came back early this morning. They have been working on a proposal for the base CO. It's very serious business, sir."

"I'll go right in."

Passing by his desk, he dropped his hat in the OUT basket and went to the commander's open doorway. The commander and his exec were sitting at the worktable near the desk, examining a series of typewritten pages and making notes on yellow pads. Within reach of both officers was the institutional gold-and-black plastic coffee pot and ceramic mugs. The mugs steamed with hot coffee. In the middle of the table was a large map of the Naval Ordnance Facility, showing in detail perimeter fences, administration and warehouse buildings, ammunition bunkers, the advanced underwater weapons exclusion area, and the mine shop building.

Turner knocked on the doorframe. "Good morning, sir. Yeoman Fry said you wanted to see me?"

The commander looked up. "Sit down, Mr. Turner."

He took a seat at the table and waited.

Five minutes later, the exec made a last notation on his yellow pad and put his pencil down. He then carefully tore off the pages with his notes, attached them to typewritten pages he earlier examined, put them all in a nearby file folder with "SECRET" on the cover, and pushed it over to the commander. He sat back, folded his hands, and looked up at the acoustic ceiling. Turner thought the exec was studying a water stain. A few minutes later, the commander took off his half-glasses, tore off his pages of notes, and placed his work in the Secret file folder. Then he acknowledged Turner's presence by saying, "Mr. Turner, have Yeoman Fry come in."

"Yes, sir."

Turner got up, went out to the outer office and returned with Yeoman Fry. The yeoman asked, "Do you have more corrections, sir?"

The commander passed the file folder to the yeoman. "Add these corrections to the others. There will be more later. Please close the door as you leave."

"Aye, aye, sir."

With Yeoman Fry gone, the commander looked at Turner in a rather guarded way and said, "Yesterday, as you know, Captain Travis asked all the commands to draw up contingency security plans, which will address strengthening defenses against terrorist infiltration and adding procedures to deal with terrorist infiltration, if it occurs.

"We are firming up NOF's plan with input from Lieutenant Commander Anderson in the advanced underwater weapons shop and Warrant Officer Fulkerson in the mine shop. The exec and I started down this road some months ago, primarily because of the presentation by Lieutenant Colonel Bennett and that woman analyst from CIA . . ." He looked over at his exec.

"Brae, sir, Miss Laura Brae."

"Thank you. We should have the contingency security plan in the smooth and on the way to the captain in the next forty-eight hours."

"Probably before the other commands," added the exec.

"That's great, sir."

The two senior officers frowned in unison at the unsolicited approval provided by this very junior lieutenant junior grade.

The commander continued, "Mr. Turner, last night, we received a message requiring this command to add an additional section to our contingency security plan. The section to be added is a zero-defect demolition plan for the destruction of our stored nuclear and thermonuclear weapons."

"Jesus, Commander!"

"That's enough, Mr. Turner," said the exec.

The commander made a gesture toward the exec, as if to make the comment less wounding, then continued, "When we received orders to make the destruction of these weapons part of the contingency security plan, our comment was somewhat more vigorous. There is little chance of terrorists gaining access to the exclusion area and the nuclear weapons storage magazine. However, this is a contingency plan, and we have to plan for worst case."

"But, sir, research hasn't proven a nuclear weapon won't produce a nuclear yield if detonated by an explosion or fire initiated externally."

"Yes, Mr. Turner, we know nuclear weapons have yet to be proven one-point safe," the commander replied, using the lingua franca of the nuclear weapons program.

Turner pressed on, "Even if there wasn't a nuclear yield, sir, there would be enough plutonium and uranium released from those warheads to contaminate and possibly deny use of large areas of northern Morocco and Algeria for thousands of years!"

"Actually, include southern Spain and, if the winds are right, the southern coast of France, Mr. Turner," the exec added thoughtfully.

Growing tired of the discussion, the commander said, "You and your team will develop the demolition plan for the destruction of our stored nuclear and thermonuclear weapons. You have thirty-six hours."

"Thirty-six hours, sir?"

"Thirty-six hours."

The commander continued, "There are fourteen Mark-28s in one magazine and four Mark-101 Lulus and two Bettys in the other magazine. As I said, the possibility of these weapons falling into terrorist hands is almost impossible. But if only one of the Mark-28s were taken and detonated under the right circumstances in a city, the thermonuclear yield would result in a radius of total destruction of over one mile. The overall nuclear radiation effect would be far more extensive. We are not talking about just one weapon here."

He got up, went to his desk and picked up a two-foot square blueprint with "SECRET" printed in large letters above the margin at the top. He returned to the table and, handing the blueprint to Turner, said, "This is a blueprint of the exclusion area and the magazine holding the nuclear weapons. Use it in your planning. You will find the blueprint quite complete, with dimensions and distances noted and where electrical services and water services are located. We have added outlines to the magazine floor plan, designating where each individual weapon is located on its carriage. This blueprint is not to leave NOF. During your planning, if you find equipment you need that isn't already on board, let us know immediately. We will expedite ordering and request emergency delivery."

"Yes, sir."

"Are there any questions?"

"No, sir. We will start on this immediately."

As Turner got up to leave, the commander added, "If there is anything you have pending at your desk, let Yeomen Fry know about it. He will handle it."

Turner left the commander's office, went to Yeoman Fry's desk, asked to sign the classified document log for the blueprint, signed for it, and went to his desk. He sat thinking for a few minutes, then picked up the phone and called the EOD shop.

———

The Hizb-i-Islami terrorist cell at Sidi Allal el-Tazi lost its leader, Sherif Nasir, earlier than planned when he delivered himself to martyrdom and paradise at 2234 hours, while stopped at a French Army checkpoint on the outskirts of Sidi Allal el-Tazi. He was at the wheel of a petite taxi with eighty-eight pounds of melinite (picric acid) explosive located under the backseat. The explosive was provided by Russian advisors located in the Draa Valley in the Western Sahara of southern Morocco. The detonating apparatus for the explosive was wired to a switch located on the car's dashboard near the heater controls. The petite taxi, with its explosives, was scheduled to be placed and detonated at the main gate of the Naval Air Station at Port Lyautey early the next morning.

Stopped a short distance in front of Sherif Nasir was a Fiat 500 sedan driven by Owdi ibn Zahwahiri, accompanied by his close friend Ali el Kader.

On the floor of the second seat of the Fiat 500 sedan were two moderate size cardboard boxes labeled, *"Aicha Confiture D'Abricots—Pur Fruit, Pur Sucre, Product Du Maroc."* There were ten blocks of the plastic explosive Composition C4 in one of the cardboard boxes and one hundred feet of detonating cord on a spool in the other.

On the seat were two more cardboard boxes of much larger size and with the same labeling. One cardboard box contained a "hell box" (electrical generator), the other, a five-hundred-foot reel of electrical firing wire and electric time-delay blasting caps to be used to detonate the C4 and detonating cord. Ibn Zahwahiri and el Kader used this equipment to successfully attack the U.S. Naval Communications Site at Sidi Yahia the night after the martyrdom of Sherif Nasir.

Three days after the attack on Sidi Yahia, the two surviving members of the terrorist cell at Sidi Allal el-Tazi received the following message:

> In the name of Allah, the Most Compassionate, the Most Merciful.
>
> A message from your political council: Sherif Nasir has made a splendid sacrifice in our Jihad to free our people from the tyrannical French government and to establish an Islamic nation founded upon the Koran and Hadith of our noble prophet Mohammed.
>
> You, Owdi ibn Zahwahiri and Ali el Kadar, are congratulated for your strike against the emerging threat to our Islamic movement, the imperialist infidels of the United States. Now they will feel the sword used against the infidel French who humiliated and spilled our blood. The infidel Americans must leave Morocco, Algeria, and Tunisia!
>
> The political council directs you to renew your efforts against the infidel Americans. A strike against one of the American air bases at Nouasseur, Bunguerir, or Sidi Slimane is now your work.
>
> Allah is great and the honor is for Islam!

Chapter 12

After his meeting with Commander Hawkins and the exec, Turner left the office complex for the EOD shop carrying a notepad in one hand and the rolled-up blueprint of the exclusion area in the other. When he entered the shop, he was met with the familiar smell and dampness of diving gear accompanied by the smell of coffee brewed to near-toxic levels. He walked over to the table where Chief Gallegos and First Class Petty Officer Cole were sitting with almost-empty coffee mugs close at hand, reading what looked to be new technical bulletins from the EOD Technical Center at Stump Neck, Maryland.

Almost in unison, Gallegos and Cole said, "Good morning, sir."

"Good morning. Actually, it's not a good morning." He put the notepad and rolled-up blueprint on the table and was about to sit down when Cole said, "Well, sir, it sounds like you better start with a cup of coffee. The pot is fresh and hot, guaranteed to establish a sense of well-being, no matter what."

He straightened up and walked over to the end of the workbench, took the mug from the hook below his stenciled name, and, from the shelf, took powdered creamer and sugar. A small sign attached to the edge of the shelf where the powdered creamer and sugar resided warned, "When Placed in Coffee, Will Inert"—obviously a message from First Class Aviation Ordnanceman Cole. He drew coffee from the small urn at the end of the workbench, added powdered cream until black became blond, and added an overfull teaspoon of sugar. Stirring the solution, he walked back to the table and sat down.

Cole put down what he was reading and said, "You really know how to ruin a good cup of coffee, Mr. Turner."

"I'm just civilized, Petty Officer Cole. What did we get from the tech center?"

Passing what he had been reading to Turner, Gallegos said, "The Turks found a Russian submarine-launched homing torpedo in one of their fish nets, one we didn't know about. Cole has a report on a new North Korean influence mine that the South Koreans got for us. Both items pretty sophisticated." Seeing that Turner was very upset, he asked, "What's going on, sir?"

Turner unrolled the blueprint of the exclusion area and began, "People are pretty upset about the infiltration and destruction of the radio antenna towers at Sidi Yahia."

"I bet they are," Gallegos replied.

"Yesterday, when I left you two and went to the admin building, I went up to the air station CO's office. When I went in, Captain Travis, his exec, and all the officers in charge of tenant commands on board the air station were sitting at the captain's conference table, talking about current security measures. When the discussion got around to Sidi Yahia, the captain asked me to give a report on what we found there. I explained the extent of damage and how we thought the insurgents did it. When I finished giving the report, he didn't say anything about me leaving, so I was able to listen to what they were talking about. They seem to think that reasonable security measures had been taken, based on the information received from intelligence sources and availability of marine corps security guards. The CO of marine corps personnel assigned to the air station explained that the number of marines on board is limited by marine corps' obligations worldwide and the limited number of U.S. military personnel allowed in Morocco by the king and his government."

Gallegos said, "Well, the attack on Sidi Yahia makes it look like our reasonable security measures are not reasonable enough."

"Exactly. So Captain Travis told each command to come up with a more realistic contingency security plan that would prevent insurgent infiltration and attack. In fact, he ordered all commands to present their contingency security plans to him within five days. Commander Hawkins and the our exec have decided to demonstrate their can-do spirit and submit their contingency security plan in forty-eight hours."

"That sounds like the skipper," Cole replied with a smile.

"Actually, after coming away from the big meeting with the CIA analyst and Lieutenant Colonel Bennett a couple of months ago, Commander Hawkins and the exec began to prepare a contingency security plan for NOF. Because nuclear weapons are stored here, Lieutenant Commander Buckhold was involved to some extent. Now, orders have come down from higher authority concerning additional security for the nuclear weapons, and Commander Hawkins wants us to come up with a worst-case plan for the nukes."

Turner had finished his coffee and was toying with the grounds with his spoon. He asked "I wonder if you can read a person's fortune in coffee grounds like they do with tea leaves?"

Gallegos stretched his arms and asked, "What do they want us to do?"

Turner sat back, folded his arms, and explained what the team was ordered to do. The content of what Turner explained elicited no interruption. When he finished, Gallegos and Cole were staring across the table at each other; Cole was biting his lip.

Then, in disbelief, Cole looked at Turner and said, "Jesus, Mr. Turner, do they know what they are asking us to do? Even if there is no nuclear yield or partial yield, the fallout of uranium and plutonium particles in the smoke and debris downwind will be catastrophic. The footprint could be for hundreds of square miles or more."

"And for twenty thousand years," Gallegos said. After a moment, he added, "The commander and the exec have the background to know exactly what the implications are, and I am sure they didn't come up with this business at the O club after a few drinks."

Turner replied, "Well, I'm sure when the chief of naval operations in Washington received word about the terrorist attack on Sidi Yahia, he met with the joint chiefs of staff and came up with contingency security recommendations that included a worst-case situation for nuclear weapons stored overseas."

Gallegos added, "It seems there should already be plans in place to evacuate nuclear weapons stored at advance support bases, especially if a host government is known to have possible insurgency problems."

Turner replied, "I'm sure there is a plan to evacuate nuclear weapons, but . . . if there isn't time, then the demolition plan is put into operation."

There was nothing more to say. Turner went back to studying his coffee grounds. Cole absentmindedly was turning his now empty mug in his hands; Gallegos had his elbows on the table and his face in his hands. The only sound came from a periodic burp of the coffee urn. Abruptly, Gallegos sat back and said, "Let's get to work."

Turner pushed his mug aside and unrolled the exclusion area blueprint. From that moment on, there was a singleness of purpose that overrode previous concern about the task.

They studied the layout of the perimeter double fences, entry points, and location of the two guard towers, then worked out the distances of the magazines from each other and to the nearest fence. Turner took a pencil and, using it as a pointer, described the location of the various nuclear weapons on their carriages in the magazines.

"I think we better have some tools to get us started," Gallegos said.

The chief got up and went over to the old two-pedestal Navy-issued desk and brought back a pair of dividers, a fifteen-inch English and metric metal ruler, a yellow pad of paper, and a slide rule.

Cole swung around on his chair to a bookcase near the table and selected two books—*FM 5-25, Explosives and Demolitions* and the DuPont *Blasters' Handbook*—for references.

Because of long experience in the field, often under extraordinary conditions, it was Gallegos and Cole who moved the planning along at this point. Out of deference, they asked Turner's input from time to time and were rewarded with his contribution from his recent demolition training at Key West and Indian Head.

By early afternoon, they were well enough acquainted with the blueprint of the exclusion area to work out several possible electrical circuits that could initiate the explosion, destroying the nuclear weapons. Final calculations would be worked out after visiting the exclusion area.

Turner ended the session by saying, "I think that's enough for now. Let's go to chow. I'll make arrangements for getting into the exclusion area, and we'll go up this afternoon. Any questions?"

Gallegos said, "What about keys to the magazines?"

"I'll talk to the commander about getting them. Let's meet back here in an hour."

He picked up the blueprint and notes, went to the back of the shop, opened up a small safe, and put them inside. He closed the door, spun the combination lock and walked out of the shop.

By the time Turner got to the officers' mess, there were only three officers present. He knew he was late, but decided to take a chance anyway. When he sat down, a steward who had been standing near the kitchen door walked over and said, "Mr. Turner, your friends came in early and left early. They asked for you and I told them you hadn't come in yet."

"Gosh, Franklin, my guys and I have been really working our tails off. I just lost track of time. I guess the kitchen is closed?"

"Yes, sir, the kitchen is closed. Perhaps I might find something for you though."

Franklin was one of the stewards who liked Turner and his friends. Unlike most of the other officers, they never gave the impression of being privileged plantation aristocracy when dealing with the stewards.

A few minutes later, Franklin returned from the kitchen with a chicken salad sandwich, pickle, potato chips, and a Coke.

"I'm sorry, Mr. Turner, this is all we could stir up," he smiled as he served Turner.

"I really appreciate this, Franklin. You are very good to do this."

"Well, it's really a small thing, but we do appreciate you and your friends."

A half hour later, Turner was at Commander Hawkins's open door and knocked on the doorjamb.

"Come in, Mr. Turner. How is your doomsday plan coming?"

Turner was surprised by the cavalier attitude of his commanding officer toward an action that, if undertaken, would lead to a catastrophe beyond belief.

"It's coming along, sir. We need to go up to the exclusion area and work out measurements to help us decide on a demolition firing system. We'll also want to go inside the magazines. Would it be possible for us to check out the keys to the two magazines?"

"Wait one."

The commander picked up the phone, dialed, and, a moment later, said, "This is Commander Hawkins. Let me have Lieutenant Van Buren." Among other collateral duties, the NOF supply officer, Lieutenant Van Buren, was also in charge of the NOF limited-access key locker.

After a pause, "Lieutenant Van Buren, sir."

"Lieutenant, I want Mr. Turner and his team to have a look inside magazines one and two in the exclusion area. Have him sign out for a set of keys. He will need them for about an hour or so."

There was a quick, "Aye, aye, sir."

He pressed down on the phone cradle switch, released it, and dialed again.

"This is Commander Hawkins, Charles. We have Mr. Turner and his team working up the demolition plan I spoke to you about. They will be entering the exclusion area shortly, and I have authorized Turner to check out keys to open and enter magazines one and two. Could you meet them up there?" He looked at Turner and asked, "How soon will you be going up?"

"About fifteen minutes, sir."

"In fifteen minutes, Charles. Fine, I'll tell him. Yes, yes, there will be no reason for him or his men to touch any of your items." He looked at Turner as he said this, then with the call completed, hung up the phone.

"Lieutenant Commander Buckhold will meet you at the exclusion area. Know that the nuclear depth charges are his turf, and he has strong feelings about that."

"I understand, sir."

He was on his way out when the commander said, "One minute, Mr. Turner."

"Yes, sir?

"We have been asked to shoulder a very heavy responsibility. None of us take the responsibility lightly. You do understand?"

"Yes, sir, I do understand."

He met Lieutenant Van Buren, accompanied him to the vault, signed for the keys, and went on to the EOD shop.

Gallegos and Cole were finishing a lunch of cheeseburgers, fries, and 7 Up.

Turner asked, "So you were too late for chow?"

Picking up a sliced pickle that had escaped from the last bite of his cheeseburger, Gallegos answered, "We were too late, but I was able to buy these outstanding burgers at the chiefs' club for the two of us. Of course, now that Cole has moved into his half-French, half-Berber girlfriend's apartment, he says he's not used to this kind of food anymore."

"Actually, Celeste has really spoiled me. I have never eaten so good."

Turner went to the safe, dialed the combination, opened the door, and removed the blueprint and notes, then secured the safe again.

They left the shop and, with Cole at the wheel of the weapons carrier, drove up to the exclusion area and pulled up to the first of two gates. A marine security guard walked up to the driver's window and, even though he recognized them, asked for their IDs. They passed their ID badges with photographs to the marine. He carefully examined each badge and its photograph, noted that all three badges were uniquely color coded, allowing the bearers access to any area of the Naval Ordnance Facility. Satisfied with their credentials, the marine exchanged salutes with Turner and waved the weapons carrier on through to the second gate.

At the second gate, the marine security guard carefully went through the same procedure again, but went to the back of the weapons carrier and looked inside and, seeing it empty returned to the driver's window, exchanged salutes with Turner and waved the weapons carrier into the exclusion area. Cole drove in a short distance, made a sharp left turn to the front of the first magazine, and parked next to a jeep. Lieutenant Commander Buckhold was standing in the open door of the magazine.

They climbed out of the weapons carrier and, with Turner in the lead, walked up the driveway to the magazine and Lieutenant Commander Buckhold.

Approaching the officer in charge of the advanced underwater weapons shop, they saluted in unison. Buckhold returned the salutes with a well-practiced, parade ground salute, rather unlike most submariners.

"Before you men go in, these are the ground rules: Do not touch, in any way, my underwater nuclear depth charges. They are 'war shots' and ready to go. You may spend no more than fifteen minutes inside. You may not ask any questions about how my weapons are to be used or their capability. Is this understood?"

"Yes, sir," Turner replied.

They followed Buckhold inside. As Turner and his men made notes and measurements of the six nuclear depth charges, from each other and the door of the magazine, Buckhold began a monologue much like the one he delivered to Turner the first time they met. This time, his monologue was oriented around the destruction of *his* nuclear weapons.

"These weapons were given to us by the Lord to be used in his name for the destruction of the godless communists lurking under the sea. The devil incarnate is waiting in the guise of Russian submarine crews under the seas of the world. The devil wants to destroy our manhood and all the good and wonderful things that our Lord has enabled us to do with our manhood. America is all there is between heaven and the hell that comes from communism. I don't understand why these weapons are to be destroyed, when our Lord gave them to us to carry out his will."

Turner and his men worked quickly and tried not to be distracted by this very strange religious radical fundamentalist who was in charge of weapons of incredible destructive power. Fifteen minutes went by, and Buckhold continued to hold forth as he followed the men while they collected the information needed for their demolition plan. He was oblivious to what they were actually doing.

Finally, Turner said, "Sir, we are finished."

"Ah, yes, of course you are."

"Thank you, sir, for allowing us to collect this very important information. We will be on our way now."

Turner and his men saluted Buckhold and left the magazine. When they were out of earshot, Cole said, "Hoo, boy, I have never seen him in such bad shape. Did you hear him call those depth charges 'war shots.' That's what the sub guys call their torpedoes."

Gallegos said, "I understand he is being watched very closely, and a request for his replacement is in. He wasn't always like this."

"Well, I'm sure the Russians have their Buckholds too," Turner replied.

After Turner unlocked the second magazine, they went inside and saw the fourteen MK-28 thermonuclear bombs in two rows of seven each. They stood quietly, looking at the bombs, for a time. They were three of the very few military EOD graduates who had studied the rendering safe procedures and applications of all known nuclear weapons systems used by the United States as well as by other countries, whether air dropped, jet/rocket launched, artillery projectile, or placed as mines. During their training, they only saw one of each type of nuclear weapon—never before so many of one type in one place.

Cole said, "My god, this is like looking at a garage full of Ferraris."

"Diameter, twenty inches. Length, eight feet. Weight, 1700 pounds," Turner recited from memory, then added, "And very sleek looking."

"It's hard to believe these are fourteen of the thousands of nuclear weapons we have. It's hard to believe we need so many," Gallegos added.

Cole walked over to the nearest MK-28, put his hand on it, and said, "Each of these babies has a thermonuclear yield equivalent to a million tons of TNT, one megaton—all in this small package!"

Turner had his notebook and pencil out and did the arithmetic. "Each one has the equivalent yield of 67 Hiroshima bombs."

The three were behaving much like some people behave in a very expensive automobile show room—then they got down to business. Forty-five minutes later, they decided they had all the raw data they needed, Turner locked up the magazine, and they left the exclusion area. On the way to the EOD shop, they dropped Turner off at the NOF office complex, where he returned the keys to the nuclear weapons magazines, and then he left for the EOD shop. It was 1830. They had spent almost two hours in the exclusion area.

As he walked along the perimeter fence road parallel to the NOF buildings, he stopped to look through the fence at a shallow draft cargo vessel in the distance as it slowly went down the Oued Sebou toward the sea. He was just able to see a few deckhands working amidships.

I just came from a storage area where there are examples of nuclear weapons produced by the application of some of mankind's greatest scientific discoveries. But out there, there's a small insignificant cargo vessel that is contributing more to mankind through its service. I guess the principle of mutually assured destruction as a deterrent to nuclear war allows that cargo vessel to ply its trade. But if nations with unstable governments get nuclear weapons, what is going to become off us?

When he walked into the EOD shop, Gallegos was on the phone, and Cole was using the slide rule to work out a possible electrical firing circuit.

Gallegos held the phone away from his ear and asked, "I have the chiefs' club on the phone, Mr. Turner. What do you want to eat?

"Whatdya got?"

"Hot pastrami sandwiches, spaghetti and meatballs, or fried chicken and mashed potatoes, and you can have coleslaw salad on the side."

Without much thought, Turner said, "Fried chicken and mashed potatoes and coleslaw."

"Pete, we will have one more order of fried chicken and the fixins. Call us when you leave for the NOF gate."

Genuinely surprised, Turner said, "Another example of the initiative and drive of our chief." Then he added, "How much do I owe you?"

"Two bucks should do it."

Turner took out his wallet, drew out two dollars in script, and gave it to Gallegos. A half hour later, the phone rang while Cole was trying to explain why Gallegos's plan for a firing circuit was too complex to be reliable.

"I'm going out to the gate to get our chow. Please help our first class aviation ordnanceman of ten years' experience to see the light."

After Gallegos left the shop, Cole said, "You understand what I mean, don't you, sir?"

"Yes, I do. But from where I'm sitting, I think you are both right."

Gallegos returned with an insulated box that held the dinners inside. He put the insulated box on the table and carefully lifted out three hot porcelain dishes covered with plastic domes, then spoons, forks, and knives wrapped in napkins (gray), three small covered bowls of coleslaw, and, finally, a jar of chutney.

Cole said, "There are all sorts of soft drinks in the fridge, Mr. Turner."

When they were eating their dinner, Turner wondered out loud, "I don't know why the officers' mess can't do chicken like this."

Gallegos answered, "It's because they use frozen chicken over there, and we use fresh."

They worked on Gallegos's firing system throughout dinner, and finally, after a few minor changes, Cole was satisfied with its reliability. They had a viable plan.

The next task was the selection of the explosives and equipment to apply the plan. They had an inventory of demolition explosives and electrical equipment stored at NOF that they could choose from, which listed everything they would need for the operation. But a zero-defect plan was still a question. By this time, they had been working for more then ten hours and were very tired.

Turner offered, "Instead of putting one bag of tetrytol blocks on one bomb in each magazine, which will light off the rest of the bombs in the magazine, why not two bags of tetrytol blocks, one bag on one bomb, the other bag on the bomb next to the first and with modified separate firing systems?"

They considered the possibility for another hour, found a way to make it work, and ended by having a somewhat more reliable system. At 2245, the demolition plan was completed for the destruction of the nuclear weapons being stored for the Sixth Fleet at the U.S. Naval Ordnance Facility at Port Lyautey, Morocco. Thirteen hours of the thirty-six hour limit set by Commander Hawkins had lapsed.

Before the team left the EOD shop, Cole said, "We forgot something. If this plan goes into action, who is going to set it off?"

Gallegos answered sarcastically, "Well, you are. You are the most junior person on the team, so you have the honor. You have a thousand feet of firing wire between you and the nuclear weapons you will be blowing up. What else do you need?" They left the EOD shop laughing at the thought of Cole's chance of survival—or anyone else's.

The next morning, at 0800, Turner gave Yeoman Fry the rough draft for typing. At 0920, Turner received the plan in standardized format. At 0950, he finished editing. Before sending it back to the yeoman, he had Gallegos and Cole review his edited version. At 1035, Yeoman Fry was typing the final draft. At 1200, Turner knocked on the exec's door.

"Enter," the exec replied.

"Well, Mr. Turner, what can I do for you?"

"We just finished the demolition plan for stored nuclear weapons, sir." He handed the plan to the exec.

"Sit down, Mr. Turner." He read a few lines of the first page and went on to read more carefully the remaining pages. Examining the diagrams concerning placement of the explosives and the electrical firing system, he leafed back to other pages and made a few notes on a nearby pad.

"I'll go over this with Commander Hawkins this afternoon. Be close by."

"Aye, aye, sir."

He left the exec's office somewhat deflated.

He thought, *The plan is outstanding. We worked our asses off, got it done way before expected, and he says, 'Be close by.' Fuck!* He went to his desk, shuffled through some papers mindlessly, got up, and, as he left the office, said, "Fry, I'm going for a walk." The yeoman, knowing Turner thought the meeting with the exec was unfairly perfunctory, replied, It's a good plan, sir. Have a nice walk."

Turner didn't pay attention to Yeoman Fry's words.

He walked along the road he usually followed while patrolling in the NOF security pickup truck when he had the duty. The air was cool, and a slight breeze coming from the northwest brought the pungent smell of eucalyptus trees from somewhere beyond the perimeter fence.

He thought about how long and hard he and his team worked to develop the demolition plan that ended up being accepted as no big deal. He walked up the hill to the exclusion area, stopped near one of the guard towers, and looked up at the marine. The marine gave a salute and called down with a smile, "Did they take your pickup truck away from you, Lieutenant?"

He returned the salute and said, "No, I don't have the duty—I just needed a walk. Do you know that, right now, you probably are doing the most important thing you will ever do in your lifetime?"

"Yes, sir, we know what we are guarding, and we take the duty very seriously."

Turner gave a wave and went on. He stopped again before leaving the area and looked through the double fences to the magazines holding the nuclear weapons. He and his men had discussed the implications of carrying out the demolition plan in a rather clinical way. Now, as he stood alone, looking at the subject of an action that would lead to a horror beyond imagination, he experienced great sadness. As he walked away, he also knew he and his team and hundreds of thousand of other human beings would certainly not be around to tell about it.

A little later, his mind turned to the night before last and the knowing look Binki gave him when she was telling about the letter she received from Kathy Roberts. How much did Binki know of what went on between him and Kathy? He really thought he loved Kathy Roberts, but she always seemed to want to hold him off. Then she was gone. Then Laura Brae came along. Initially, he couldn't stand her, and now he found himself in a strongly committed relationship with her. Laura didn't hold him off. He hadn't realized how naive he was and how complex life could be until he left home. Being in the navy was his introduction to the real world. He was changing and could see that what went on before in his life was uncomplicated child's play.

When he arrived back at the office complex, Yeoman Fry greeted him, saying, "Did you have a nice walk, sir?"

"I did, and I am ready to deal with whatever comes my way."

"Good. The commander and the exec want to see you at 1330."

"I'm on the way to the officers' mess for lunch, and I'll be back by 1300."

He went to his desk and phoned the BOQ.

"Lieutenant JG Miller speaking."

"Hey, Bob, wait for me, and I'll go to lunch with you guys."

"Who the hell is this? Is this Lieutenant JG Burt Turner, you shit? Don't you eat with us anymore?"

"I'm on the way. Wait for me." And he hung up the phone.

When he got to the BOQ, Miller and Teipner were waiting for him downstairs.

As he came through the door, Teipner said, "We are incredibly fortunate that you have decided to break bread with us this noon hour."

He answered, "It is I who is fortunate. Let's go."

The steward at the counter said, "Before you go Mr. Turner, one of the VR24 officers brought this envelope for you."

The steward handed the envelope to Turner. Miller and Teipner did their best to look over his shoulder and find out what the envelope was about. Teipner had a good enough look to read in the upper left-hand corner, "Musee d' Histoire Archaeologique, Paris" and "L. Brae" under the address.

"So what's going on at the museum in Paris, old friend?" Teipner asked.

"I don't know. Some advertisement, I guess."

"What bullshit! Obviously, a pilot from VR24, out of courtesy to you and someone else, delivered this envelope to you," Teipner said with a laugh.

"Yeah, that's bullshit," Miller added.

Turner shoved the envelope in his pocket, and the three went on to the officers' mess.

Pierce was already sitting in his place, eating a toasted, melted cheese (American) sandwich with a bowl of chicken soup and a nearby glass of milk (usual reconstituted). They took their seats, and when the steward came, they all requested to have what Dr. Pierce was having, except Miller and Teipner asked for coffee in place of milk.

The subject of the lunch hour was the movie at the officers' club this night. Pierce led off the conversation with the importance of seeing this particular movie.

"Even though *The Maltese Falcon* is a rather dated movie, it is a classic. We should go and enjoy Humphrey Bogart and Sidney Greenstreet as they deal with this black bird."

Miller added, "What about Peter Lorie? He was terrific in it."

Pierce replied, "Of course, I erred."

Turner asked, "Did any of you guys read the book?"

Pierce and Miller said they had.

Then he asked, "Who wrote it?"

"Dashiell Hammett wrote it," Miller answered.

"That's what I was going to say," Pierce added. Then he asked, "What year was the book written, and who was the hero?"

Turner said, "Sam Spade was the hero—"

Miller interrupted with, "1930."

"How do you guys know all this stuff?" Teipner asked.

Pierce answered, "Because we paid attention in high school English class."

This started a discussion about other movie classics, allowing Turner to unobtrusively take out the envelope and slip out the note. Holding the note in his lap, he read,

> Burt, I'll be in Barcelona this coming Friday and will be taking five days leave from there. Saturday, I plan to fly down to Gibraltar and take the ferry from Algeciras to Tangier. When I get to Tangier, I'm going to rent a car in preparation for driving down the coast on Sunday morning. If you could get away Saturday and meet me in Tangier, we could drive down to Port Lyautey together. I don't know where I am going to stay in Tangier Saturday night, so I can't give you a way to contact me. But what I can do is drive to the Tangier airport, south of town, and take a chance you might have found a way to get there. I'll try to be there between one and three; if you don't arrive, I'll drive back to Tangier and start for Port Lyautey early Sunday morning. I'll call you at the BOQ when I arrive at the transient officers' quarters.
>
> Laura

Pierce said, "Burt, you are not paying any attention to what is at hand. Can you share with us what you are reading?"

Miller said, "He just got a letter from the archaeological museum in Paris."

This got Pierce's attention. "What is your interest in the archaeological museum in Paris?"

"Actually, I have a friend who works there."

"Male or female?" Teipner asked.

He was studying the note.

"Male or female?" Teipner asked again.

He folded the note, put it back in the envelope, and slid the envelope back into his pocket. Then he began to study the swirl pattern forming as he slowly stirred his tomato soup with his spoon.

His three friends knew they were on to something and quietly watched for his next move.

He looked up, and addressing Miller and Teipner, he asked, "What are you guys doing Saturday afternoon?"

Miller and Teipner looked at each other. Teipner said, "We got the duty."

Miller added, "Yeah, we have to fly some stuff up to NAS Rota. Why?"

"Do you have enough room for me to hitch a ride to Tangier?"

"Tangier! What's going on at Tangier?" Before he could answer, Teipner added, "I don't know if we can file a flight plan to include a stop at Tangier."

Miller asked, "What have you got to trade?"

"I'll get you a ride on my yacht, and Pierce too."

Miller and Teipner put their heads together for a moment, then Teipner said, "We will try and get you to Tangier, but you have to eventually give all of us a SCUBA lesson in the pool as well as a boat ride in the ocean."

"Done," Turner replied.

Pierce said, "I'll pass on the lesson. I'll just watch. But I will go on your boat."

"OK. Now, what's going on, Burt?" Miller asked in a low voice.

"The note from my friend in Paris said they are traveling in Spain and will be taking the Tangier ferry from Algeciras Saturday morning and will rent a car in Tangier for a trip down the coast. If I could meet the car at the Tangier airport early Saturday afternoon, or at least before 1500, I could ride down too."

"For Christ's sake, Burt, why are you avoiding gender?" Teipner asked.

Knowing that they weren't fooled, he came clean. "It's a woman."

All three exclaimed loudly, "It's a woman!"

Other officers nearby looked over at the always troublesome table that seemed to again be displaying a level of offensiveness, demonstrating why others refused to sit with, or near them.

On the other side of the mess, near the back, where the hospital nurses usually sat as a group, Betty Armstrong said in a low voice, "They're at it again."

Juniper replied, "Isn't that why we like them?"

"Tolerate them is more appropriate," Binki despairingly replied.

Pierce, Miller, and Teipner were ecstatic, not because Turner had a girlfriend, but because they finally got him to admit it.

At 1315, Turner walked into the NOF office complex and sat down at his desk. Under a paperweight in the middle of his desk were three "While You Were Out" phone message slips requiring return phone calls and an overflowing IN box. The OUT box was empty.

He took the paperweight off the phone message slips and laid them out in order of importance. He picked up the phone and dialed the first, the personnel office. After talking to the yeoman who left the phone message, he was told that if he did not deliver the paperwork signifying each team member's monthly dive and explosives requalification by 1600 tomorrow, they would not be eligible to receive their hazardous duty pay for the month. He said the paperwork would be in before 1600 tomorrow.

The second call was from Petty Officer Deacon, who advised him that the AVR would be down for two days for general maintenance. Turner told Deacon he needed the AVR for about two hours in the morning for requalification dives for him and his men. Deacon told him they would not be starting work on the boat until early afternoon and to come aboard about 0900.

The third call was from Master Sergeant Forbes of the marine barracks. Forbes wanted Turner and his team to come down to the armory, get their locker keys from Sergeant Evens, retrieve the Walther PPK pistols from their lockers, and turn them in to the sergeant. Tomorrow afternoon would be fine. Forbes told him that the team would be issued Smith & Wesson .38 Specials, as needed. When Turner asked why the .38 Specials were not issued for the Rif Mountains mission, Forbes said "higher ups" wanted to see how the Walther PPKs worked out. At that point, Turner exclaimed, "Shit!" and slammed the phone down. Yeoman Fry was startled by Turner's exclamation; the other two yeomen grinned, and fortunately, the office doors of the commander's and exec were closed.

He removed the stack of papers from his IN box, looked them over, and found that all but two were official letters sent from BuOrd (Bureau of Ordnance), BuPers (Bureau of Personnnel), and others less significant, to Commander Gene Hawkins. The commander forwarded the letters to the officers in his command as "Information Only," requiring their initialing on a slip after reading. Turner read, initialed, and put them in his OUT box.

Of the other two, one had to do with a request by the commander with regard to security measures currently in place for the EOD shop and its contents, and the second, a request from the exec regarding the status of the SW/EOD team's radiation detection equipment and protective clothing.

At 1335, the commander opened his office door and asked Yeoman Fry to have Turner come to his office. Fry went over to Turner's desk and said, "Your time has come, Mr. Turner. The commander is ready to see you."

Turner thanked him, picked up a pad and pencil, and went to the commander's office. The door was open, and he saw a quite large new aerial photo of NOF that had been put on an easel next to the small conference table. The commander and exec had stuck red pins in different places of the aerial photo.

"Excuse me, sir. Yeoman Fry said you were ready to see me."

The commander turned and said, "Yes, Mr. Turner, sit down please. How do you like our new aerial photo?"

"I think it is remarkable, sir. Even from here, the detail is amazing."

"Lieutenant Commander Owens and I finished going over your demolition plan for the nuclear weapons magazines, and we're using this aerial photo in regard to clarifying some of the points you covered in the plan. How much time would it take to set up the system, and where would you, or whoever, fire it from?"

Turner replied, "After receiving word to put the plan into action, it would take less than ten minutes to set up the system after the team arrived at the exclusion area. Once the system is set up, only one man is required to activate the electrical firing system and set off the charges. That man would be located outside the exclusion area, about where you have just placed that red pin. The other men would have left the area."

"Did it dawn on you that the men who left the area would have about the same chance of survival if they just stayed and sat on top of one of the magazines?" the exec asked.

"Yes, we know that, sir."

"We have gone over your plan, and except for a few editorial changes, you have done a good job. Now, a few questions. Is there any demolition equipment that is needed that isn't already on board?" the commander asked.

"No, sir. We have checked the inventory, and everything we need is on board."

The exec asked, "How are you going to get the tetrytol explosives from their magazine and electrical blasting caps from where they're stored, then transport them to the nuclear weapon magazines, put everything together, and accomplish all this in less than ten minutes?"

This caused Turner to wonder how well the exec had read the plan.

"Sir, our plan is to stow two M1-Tetrytol bags, or satchel bags, in each of the nuclear weapons magazines. The firing wire reels and electrical generators will be in the magazine closest to the gate. As you know, the electrical blasting caps cannot be housed in the same place as the M1-Tetrytol explosives. We plan to stow them in the EOD shop or in a secure place within the exclusion area."

Additional questions asked of Turner reminded him that he wasn't the only one who knew something about demolition by explosives.

It was a little over an hour later when the commander told his exec, "Don, I think we are finished here. Do you have anything else?"

"I think Mr. Turner and his men produced a very impressive plan under rather severe time constraints."

Turner self-consciously said, "Chief Gallegos and Petty Officer Cole were primarily responsible for the plan." And he added, "They are exceptional men, sir."

"Well, hopefully we will never have to ask you or someone else to implement the plan. Good job, Burt, thank you."

Turner got up to leave and thought, *Good time to ask,* and addressing the CO, he did ask, "Sir, I have accumulated a lot of leave, and I have a chance to meet a friend in Tangier Saturday morning and drive down with her—"

The exec interrupted, "How much shore leave are you requesting, Mr. Turner?"

"Out to Wednesday morning at 0800, sir."

The exec looked at the commander, and the commander said, "Make sure you have your responsibilities covered here, and work out with Yeoman Fry how we can find you if you are needed. These are very uncertain times, Mr. Turner."

With a smile he could hardly contain, he said, "Aye, aye, sir," and left.

As he walked back to his desk, he thought, *The commander called me Burt!*

Yeoman Fry glanced up from his desk and asked, "Your plan was well received?"

Still grinning, he answered, "Very well received, Yeoman Fry, and I want to thank you for your help in editing the smooth copy."

"I'm here to serve, Mr. Turner. I'm here to serve."

He sat down at his desk and began to answer the commander's request for information regarding security measures currently in place for the EOD shop. An hour later, he had finished that and was well into the exec's request for the status of the team's radiation detection equipment and protective clothing. When he finished the report to the exec, he thought long and hard about the radiation detection equipment on board and decided to add two more paragraphs:

"The two radiation detection devices, AN/PDR-27s, mentioned in paragraph 3b as part of the NOF SW/EOD team equipment allowance are designed for the detection of gamma radiation produced by a nuclear or thermonuclear explosion. The AN/PDR-27 is of no use in detecting alpha radiation contamination from plutonium (Pu^{239}) resulting from the destruction of a nuclear or thermonuclear weapon by mechanical means or burning. Terrorist infiltration leading to destruction of a nuclear or thermonuclear weapon by mechanical means or burning is more probable than a nuclear or thermonuclear weapons attack by an adversary at this time or in the foreseeable future."

"Since the NOF SW/EOD team does not have equipment for the detection of alpha radiation, it is requested that at least one of the new PAC-3G alpha detection devices be ordered to increase the operational readiness of the NOF SW/EOD team."

He gave the two handwritten memos to Yeoman Fry for typing and left the office spaces.

That night after dinner, Turner and his friends went to the officers' club, sat in the front row on folding chairs, and enjoyed *The Maltase Falcon*. Turner and Miller were representative of many college students in the 1950s who claimed this old movie as their own, and they had seen it a number of times. Memorizing significant parts of the movie was de rigueur, and tonight, when Humphrey Bogart and Sidney Greenstreet were exchanging veiled threats, Turner and Miller mimicked them, causing Teipner to break out laughing and Dr. Lieutenant Pierce to caution the three that their actions were annoying to the rest of the audience.

When they were walking back to the BOQ after the movie, Turner said, "Commander Hawkins gave me permission to take leave and go up to Tangier. I don't have to be back until next Wednesday at 0800. If you guys can fly me up Saturday, it would really be great."

Miller replied, "We think we can explain to Lieutenant Commander Bello that flying into Tangier on the way to Rota would be for familiarization purposes in case we are ever required to land there. He will probably say OK, but who knows?"

At 0900, the SW/EOD weapons carrier pulled up and stopped at the gangplank leading down to the AVR. The team climbed out wearing their dry suits and went around to the back. Cole dropped the transom and pulled out the net bag with their masks, life jackets, web belts, knives, fins, weighted belts, and other odds and ends, then stepped aside, allowing Gallegos to pull out a smaller net bag containing their air regulators and a canvas haversack that he passed to Turner.

The canvas haversack contained three combination flare/smoke signal flares and three waterproof packs. Each of the waterproof packs contained a half-pound block of TNT, fuse lighters, a length of powder train time fuse cut to burn for two minutes, and a blasting cap. With Turner at the lead, they started down the gangplank.

Looking up from the AVR, Petty Officer Deacon called out jokingly, "EOD team arriving." At the moment Turner set foot on the AVR, he saluted the flag at the stern and then exchanged salutes with Deacon, who said, "Welcome aboard, Mr. Turner."

"Thank you, Petty Officer Deacon, it's good to be back on one of the finer vessels in our navy."

Gallegos and Cole arrived on board and saluted the flag at the stern; then Gallegos asked, "Do I smell the odor of fine coffee, First Class Petty Officer Deacon?"

Deacon shook hands with Gallegos and Cole and replied, "As soon as we get underway, you will have the best coffee served on the Sebou River. Do you want some help bringing down your air tanks, Chief?"

"If you have a couple of seamen that need exercise."

Deacon called over to two crewmen on deck, "Jackson and Reed, lay up to the weapons carrier and bring down our guests' air tanks."

With the team's gear stowed on board, Deacon took the helm and got the AVR underway.

A few minutes later, they passed through the mouth of the river, and Deacon advanced the throttle. The engine exhaust went from a low rumble to a roar, the hull rose from the water, and the AVR planed along at twenty knots.

Deacon throttled back a bit and asked, "Where do you want to go, sir?"

"Let's go south about ten miles, Coxswain. After we get the dive out of the way, we'll get back on board, and you can take us to about a hundred yards off from the surf line and drop us off. We'll swim in to the beach, light off some half-pound blocks of TNT to requalify for explosives, and swim back out for retrieval. We won't be using our SCUBA gear on the swim."

"How deep do you go for a requalification dive Mr. Turner?"

"Hundred feet. If you can have one of your men put a hundred feet of line over the side with a weight on the end, we'll use it for a descending line. All we need to do is go down to the weight and come up, and we are requalified."

"And that's how you earn your monthly hazardous duty pay—blowing something up and making a dive to a hundred feet?"

"I'm embarrassed to say, yes, it is, Coxswain."

Coxswain Deacon answered, "I'm sure there can be more than that involved from time to time. Wanna take the helm for bit, Mr. Turner?"

—————"You bet, Coxswain!"

The water was smooth with a gentle swell, the air was cool and clear, fair weather cumulus interrupted an otherwise blue sky, and the AVR's engines were in full song. Turner thought, *I'm the luckiest guy in the world.*

A half hour later, the AVR's engines were stopped. After the descending line was rigged with a fifty-pound weight and tied to a cleat at the stern, the deck crew threw the line and weight over the side. Then Turner and Gallegos, with their SCUBA and other underwater gear on, walked across to the edge of the AVR's lowered transom and plunged into the cold water. They floated for a minute, checked the flow of air from their regulators, moved over to the descending line, and started down feet first. Periodically, they slowed to equalize the air pressure on their ears, then continued down.

Rays of sunlight penetrated the light blue crystal clear water to depths far below the weight at the end of the descending line. Turner tilted his head back and exhaled. He watched the bubbles from his regulator glinting in the sunlight as they rose to the surface. The bubbles expanded with lessening water pressure, and many combined to form much larger bubbles that expanded and exploded into smaller bubbles as they approached the surface. Turner thought, *There is real beauty in Boyle's Law.*

They paused when they arrived at the weighted end of the descending line, then Gallegos gave a thumbs-up. Breathing easily and not exceeding the rate of rise of his bubbles, he returned to the surface, leaving Turner behind. A few minutes later, Cole descended and met Turner. Cole took a minute to adjust his tank straps, and they slowly returned to the surface and the AVR, the requalification dive completed.

When they were underway again, Turner said, "Coxswain, when we get to the drop-off point, we will go over the side at ten second intervals and swim to the beach. After we light off our demolition blocks, we will swim back out. Once beyond the surf line, we will make orange smoke so you can recover us."

"Aye, aye, sir. We will get you to drop off and then wait for orange smoke."

Without the encumbrance of their SCUBA and weight belts, the swim in to the beach with their waterproof packs was more recreational. However, Cole caught a rougher-than-usual breaking wave and came to the beach with his mask hanging around his neck. Otherwise, the swim was uneventful.

They came ashore about fifty yards apart, took off their fins, and walked up the sandy slope and into scattered shrubbery. They opened the waterproof packs with their knives, primed their explosives, and each yelling, "Fire in the hole," pulled the fuse lighter retaining pins. With the fuses to the explosive charges burning, they ran back into the surf, pulled on their fins, flipped over on their backs, and watched for the fireworks. They were rewarded with three explosions throwing up black smoke, dirt, and shrubbery. They made their way through the roaring surf and, once beyond the surf line, found that the wind had come up and the previously smooth water had given way to a moderate chop that was increasing in strength.

The AVR was cruising slowly in large circles in the distance. The coxswain and deck crew saw two plumes of orange smoke; there was no evidence of the expected third. With the increasing chop, the transom at the stern couldn't be lowered, and a rope ladder was rigged to the side of the AVR. The coxswain brought the boat close by the nearest swimmer; it was Cole. Two crewmen helped him grab the rope ladder and pull himself up. Gallegos was the second swimmer and received a few bruises when the AVR heeled over, and, swinging back, slammed the rope ladder and Gallegos against the hull. There was no sign of Turner. A half hour later, Third Class Petty Officer Reed, using binoculars, saw Turner's head in the chop. The coxswain swung the boat around and quickly came alongside the last swimmer. It took somewhat longer to recover Turner, but once he was on board, they headed for home.

The three swimmers were grouped together on one side of the open bridge when Cole laughed and yelled above the noise of the boat, "Did Mr. Turner lose his flare?"

Which was entirely possible.

Turner pulled the flare out from where he had wedged it in his web belt, "The damn thing didn't light off; I tried both ends, and neither end worked. I knew if I dumped it, some wise guy would say I lost it, so I kept it with me. Here, see if you can get it to work." He handed the flare to Cole, who took the flare, looked it over, and tried to light it. Nothing happened. Then he said, "I guess this is why we take two flares."

Coxswain Deacon waved Turner over and, as he approached, stepped aside of the helm, "Why don't you take us to the mouth of the river, sir?"

"Very well, Coxswain." He took the helm with authority.

———————

Friday afternoon, three days later, Turner was sitting at his desk when Yeoman Fry walked over and handed him a memorandum from the commander and said, "I think you will be pleased with this, sir."

Seeing the subject, he skipped down to the body of the memorandum and read:

> I want to congratulate you and your team for producing an extremely important segment of the new NOF contingency security plan. The segment of the plan you were responsible for was one of complexity and demanded a sound understanding of ordnance disposal technique. Additionally, you and your team were able to complete the assignment within a very tight time frame. Because of your efforts I want to say, "Well done."
>
> You and your team are of great value to this command. This memorandum will be appended to the team members' personnel files.

> Commander Gene Hawkins, USN

Having felt unappreciated for his teams' work on the demolition plan for NOF nuclear weapons, he was more than pleased. He was already feeling good about being caught up with his paperwork and pleased with a memorandum earlier from the exec OKing the team's security measures regarding the EOD shop and giving him permission to pursue a request for PAC-3G alpha monitoring equipment. Receiving the commander's memorandum made him feel especially good. He got up from his desk and was about to take the commander's congratulatory message down to the EOD shop to show his men when the exec, coming from the commander's office, saw him.

"Mr. Turner, will you come in my office for a minute?"

"Yes, sir."

The exec sat down and motioned Turner to sit down. He was putting the papers he had brought with him from the commander's office in a manila folder on his desk and took a moment to look at something that caught his eye.

Turner was thinking about the first time he was in the exec's office almost ten months ago, and how uncomfortable he was . . . not so much anymore. It was odd that nothing ever seemed to have been moved out of place since his first visit: the picture of the exec's wife standing next to the sailboat, the silver cigarette case, paper pads, and writing implements were all located in exactly the same place. He glanced at the nearby table, where the exec had his books dressed tight against each other between the brass casting bookends. He thought one book was missing, but couldn't remember which one. Actually, he was right. The exec recently loaned Monsarrat's *The Cruel Sea* to Lieutenant Van Buren.

The exec finished with what had caught his eye, closed the folder, and took the time to lay it about eight inches from, and perfectly parallel to, the middle edge of the desk.

"Mr. Turner, we have a problem, and I thought you and your team might be able to come up with some kind of solution."

"We will do anything we can to help, sir."

"Yes, of course. We have a large amount of outdated conventional ammunition, which includes 250- and 500-pound bombs, mortar rounds, and hundreds of cases of .30- and .50-caliber ammunition. We also have a large number of .30- and .50-caliber machine guns still wrapped and crated up as if they had just arrived from the manufacturer. The Bureau of Ordnance doesn't want to transport any of this back to the U.S. for disposal. We have been asked to find a way to dispose of it here, which means finding a place and a method of disposal that's also secure from insurgent terrorists." He paused and added, "Do you have any ideas?"

Turner thought for a minute. "Sir, there's an old YFR, a small, in-port refrigeration/cargo vessel, tied up at the wharf near the AVR. Maybe it could be used for dumping the ammunition at sea. I don't know if it is operational or could be made operational, but I could try and find out. Another possibility is burning the .30 and .50 caliber ammunition and blowing up the bombs . . . if we could find a demolition range, a secure demolition range."

The exec, not too surprised with Turner's quick demonstration of initiative, smiled and said, "Well, ask around and see what might be possible. On another subject. In one section of the your EOD shop security plan, you mention equipment currently being carried at all times in the weapons carrier for rendering safe procedures. You didn't detail the equipment."

"Yes, sir, there is a minimum of equipment, based on what we might expect to see. Recently, we added gas masks, chemical and radiation protective clothing, and our AN/PDR-27 radiation detector."

"That is exactly what I wanted to know. Before you go on leave, let me have a supplement to your plan detailing the equipment carried on board the weapons carrier."

"Yes, sir."

"Oh, and have a good time in Tangier and the drive down the coast with your friend."

"Yes, sir. Thank you, sir."

He left the exec's office and returned to desk. He sat thinking for a minute, then lifted the phone and dialed a series of numbers. He heard the phone buzz intermittently on the other end and then, "Sidi Slimane Air Force Base."

"This is Lieutenant JG Burt Turner calling from the Naval Ordnance Facility at the Naval Air Station, Port Lyautey. I'm trying to get hold of Lieutenant Joe Logan. Can you help me?"

"One minute, sir."

About four minutes later, "Weapons maintenance, sir, can I help you?"

Turner went through his introduction again, then asked, "I'm trying to find Lieutenant Logan."

"Just a minute, sir."

Then a familiar voice, "Hey, Burt, how are you?"

"I'm real good, and careful of what people are asking us to do."

"I'm sure you are. What do you need?"

"You have an awful lot of empty land way beyond your ammunition magazines. Is there any chance we might use some of it to blow up outdated ammunition?"

"I thought this was a social call, Burt. And you ask if you can blow up stuff on a SAC base?"

"Well, it is a social call. If you give us access to your wasteland to blow up stuff, I could stay over and have lunch or dinner with you and Carolyn."

"You know, you might be in luck. I think we might be able to help you. We have some outdated photoflash canisters you could help us get rid of too. I'll talk to my boss. Give me a couple of days, and I'll call you. Why don't you come out this weekend? We could play some golf. Carolyn and I would be happy to see you."

"I don't know how to break this to you, Joe, but I don't play golf. Thanks anyway. I have to meet a friend in Tangier this weekend, but maybe later I could come out and watch you and Carolyn play golf."

"We would be glad to see you, Burt. Have a good time in Tangier. I'll call you about using some of our land for a demolition range."

"Thanks, Joe, you are a good friend."

He hung up the phone, got up to go, thought a minute, then sat down again, picked up the phone, and dialed."

"Air station wharf, Reed speaking."

"Petty Officer Reed, this is Mr. Turner, is Petty Officer Deacon around?"

"No, sir, he's at the machine chop. Can I help you, sir?"

"Maybe you can. What do you know about the YFR?"

"Well, about once a month we go aboard and try to start the little ship's engine. We fiddle around with it a bit, get it started, and let it run for a couple of hours. There isn't money to keep the YFR up proper."

"Is it seaworthy?"

"I don't know, sir. I have been here a year and a half, and it's never left the wharf."

"Tell Deacon I called. Tell him I'm interested in taking the YFR out to sea about thirty miles and dumping outdated ammunition."

"I'll do that very thing, sir."

"Thanks, Reed."

He hung up the phone and went to the EOD shop, where Gallegos and Cole were overhauling the team's SCUBA air regulators.

"If you two gentlemen come over and sit down with me, I have something to read to you."

They put down their tools and ambled over.

"Are they sending us to Paris, sir?" Cole asked.

"I'm sure there are reasons why they would never think of something like that."

He read the citation to them. Then let them each read it for themselves. They were more than pleased and proud.

Friday was fish night at the officers' mess. There was a buffet of shrimp salad, clam chowder (Boston), and grilled John Dory (locally caught). The two pilots, the flight surgeon, and SW/EOD officer took one look at the buffet and decided that there would be better luck in town. They changed into civilian clothes and drove to town in Miller's car.

The Hotel des Princes, located on Rue Fort du Vaux, was about ten minutes from the base. It was a small hotel of six rooms, and in the back, on the first floor, was a small restaurant. Some time ago, Pierce had introduced the other three to the excellent Moroccan and French cooking this delightful restaurant provided.

Across the street from the Hotel des Princes was a number of French-owned shops that catered to the small French population and the few Americans who ventured off the navy base.

The owner and operator was a French family, the staff was Arab, and because of decent working conditions, the staff turnover was very low, which was the primary reason the service was far above standard.

The owners, Mr. and Mrs. Mauritz, like the French in Algeria, considered themselves to be French in Morocco. Both born in France more than fifty years ago, they were more native to Morocco than France. Also, analogous to the French in Algeria, they represented French colonialism and were threatened from time to time by Moroccan insurgents. More than once, the front windows of the hotel had been broken, but because the Mauritzes were well thought of in the community, Arab friends and neighbors were quick to help replace them.

The Mauritzes had a thirty-two-year-old daughter, Bernadette, who trained as an engineer in France and was on the staff running the electrical power plant that served Port Lyautey and the surrounding area. She had been employed by the Oran Electrical Power Company in Algeria, but because the Power Company was a frequent target of terrorists, she left two years ago and came to the less politically turbulent Port Lyautey. Bernadette was very tall, almost six feet, and somewhat thin, but with subtle curves just where they would be expected to be. Her hair was jet black and "poodle cut," in current Parisian style, and with green eyes, she was quite striking. She was fluent in Arabic and English, well-read, and a Marxist.

Bernadette lived in one of two small suites on the second floor at the rear of the hotel; her parents lived in the other at the front. Her suite looked out over a large well-tended vegetable garden and four producing apricot trees. To deter thievery and terrorists, a nine-foot cinder block wall with broken glass embedded in the cement on top protected the premises. Additionally, a noisy family of storks nesting at the top of a telephone pole in the corner of the yard provided an early warning system.

At one time, Miller and Teipner had told Turner they thought Bernadette was the woman Pierce was romantically involved with, although they couldn't prove it. Giving weight to this, though, Turner had noticed Mrs. Mauritz treated Pierce far differently than she treated Miller and Teipner and himself, although she treated them very nicely too.

Mr. Mauritz was at the reception desk reading *Le Moroccan Courier* when the four walked in through the open door of the hotel. He looked up and said, "Ah, the four American naval officers. How good to see you again. You are here for a nice Moroccan dinner, no?"

Miller said, "Yes, sir, we are here for a nice Moroccan dinner."

He came from behind the reception desk, gave each one a warm handshake, and led them down the hallway to the restaurant. There were five tables. One was occupied by two middle-aged women and an elderly man; the other tables were vacant. Mr. Mauritz led his guests to a table near the center of the room.

When they were seated, he called to his wife, "Suzette, we have four friends for dinner." Through the swinging door from the kitchen came a thin, white-haired woman wearing a spotless, crisp white apron. Seeing the four young men, she burst out laughing and said, "Mon dieu, les jeune officiers naval sont arrivees!" The four men stood up to receive her as she rushed toward them. She hugged each one, but seemed to hold on to Pierce somewhat longer. This demonstrated affection for Pierce wasn't lost on the other three. Her greetings completed, she stepped back to her waiting husband. Standing together emphasized their difference in height; she was several inches taller than he.

In accented English, she said, "It is so good to see you young men. We have only the older families anymore. Your presence makes us remember being young so long time ago." Turning to her husband, she said, "Maurice, bring two bottles of wine!" He hustled away for the wine.

There was the usual small talk: the weather, gossip about how the local French viewed General—now President—De Gaulle and his attempt to solve the Algerian problem. Then the four naval officers were surprised to hear that the French technicians who ran the TV stations and public utilities in Morocco were joining those French who had formerly run the civil service infrastructure in departing for France. Now, a myriad of problems began to surface because they didn't train the Moroccans to take their place.

Mr. Mauritz returned with four glasses and two bottles of Algerian red. With the wine poured and sampled, it was agreed that the wine was more than quite good.

Then Mrs. Mauritz was pleased to inform them, "Tonight you may have *bastela* (light pastry covering shredded pigeon, chopped hard-boiled eggs, and ground almonds, cinnamon, and saffron) or tajine with lamb (a kind of meat stew with peas, squash, carrots, favas, prunes, onions, chickpeas, and saffron)."

With no hesitation, they all ordered the bastela.

"Mais rien avec des yeux, s'il vous plait." Teipner had made it a point when eating Moroccan fare to say, "Nothing with eye balls, if you please." His friends rolled their eyes. Mrs. Mauritz, having heard this before from him, said, "Not tonight, *mon cherie*, not tonight." She left for the kitchen; her husband returned to the reception desk.

They talked a bit about the French technicians leaving Morocco, and when this conversation died away, Turner, acting as though it was unimportant, said with a sigh, "I suppose the flight to Tangier didn't work out. Otherwise, I would have heard something?"

Miller looked at Teipner, "Didn't you call him?"

"I thought you did."

Being above this conversation, Pierce concentrated on the color of wine in his glass.

Then Miller, addressing Turner, asked, "Why didn't you call one of us?"

"I didn't know I was supposed to."

The two pilots, with a dejected look on their faces, slumped down in their chairs, arms stretched out on the table and hands slowly turning their wineglasses.

Then Turner said, "Look, it's OK, you guys. Thanks for trying."

Teipner looked at Miller and said, "I guess we could tell him now."

"Yeah, I guess so."

Teipner took a deep breath and said, "We are going to drop you off at Tangier."

Turner sat up and loudly said, "What!"

The two middle-aged women at the other table looked over, then turned away; the elderly man didn't appear to hear Turner's outburst.

"We told Lieutenant Commander Bello that Flight Surgeon Pierce was due for his flight check ride, and since we were going to Rota, on the way, he could do some touch and goes at Tangier. There is essentially no traffic there, and it would be ideal. He said it was OK. We asked if Mr. Turner could go along. He said that was OK too. So we launch at 1230 tomorrow." Teipner was grinning as he finished.

"You assholes, how could you lead me on?"

Looking shocked, Miller said, "Our flight surgeon, Lieutenant Dr. Pierce told us to do it."

Pierce looked up from his glass and said, "What a gross canard. You two should be ashamed of yourselves."

Turner at first was very annoyed, but his anger quickly turned to relief. "You know . . . I will get even."

Miller said, "You are too nice to even think that."

Dinner was served, and it was delicious. They were finishing when Miller looked up and said, "Gosh, look who's here." Bernadette was coming from the hallway toward their table.

"Hello, gentlemen, I just came in, and my father said you were here."

They stood up and greeted her.

Turner said, "Why don't you sit down with us? There's plenty of room."

"You are very nice, but I have to freshen up. I'm going back out soon." She smiled and went back the way she came.

When they finished dinner and were having coffee, Teipner suggested they go back to the club. They worked out who was paying what, left a generous tip, and as they walked by the reception desk, Turner commented, "It was a wonderful dinner. You and your wife always take good care of us. Thank you." The others said much the same.

As they were going out the door, Pierce said, "I'm going back to talk to Mr. Mauritz. Don't wait for me." He turned and went back. When they were driving back to the base, Miller said, "Teipner, this is very bad. Pierce and Turner have girlfriends, and we have personality and style, and no real girlfriends."

Teipner replied, "It is a pitiful situation."

At 1215 the next day, Turner, in his wash khakis and carrying his blue flight bag, walked out on the flight line to the SNB. His cohorts were finishing a walk around, examining the airplane for any indication of hydraulic fluid or oil leakage or anything mechanical that might be significant enough to cancel the flight for safety reasons. Being naval aviators at work, they wore tan flight suits, navy-issue leather flight jackets, and rough-side-out boondockers.

Turner joined them and said, "OK, you airplane drivers, I'm here to further my experience in the romance of flying."

Pierce, addressing Turner with the authority he displayed when beginning a complex surgical procedure, said, "The flight plan I filed has Teipner in the cockpit with me to Tangier, then Miller and I to Rota, and Teipner splitting with Miller on the way home." The take-charge tone of the delivery went right by Turner, but not Miller. He elbowed Teipner and was going to make a sardonic comment to their very inexperienced doctor/pilot/friend, but didn't.

The flight surgeon went on board the SNB first, then Teipner, Miller, and Turner. Pierce entered the cockpit and took the left seat; Teipner followed, taking the right seat. Turner sat in the left seat just in back of the thin bulkhead separating the cockpit from the cabin; Miller sat across from Turner on the right side. The small cockpit door was open, and Turner was able to see and hear what was about to take place. The cockpit crew fastened their safety belts; Pierce looked over his shoulder and asked, "You gentlemen have your safety belts fastened?"

The two passengers gave him a thumbs-up.

Turner noticed Pierce was looking around the cockpit as if he had misplaced something and heard Teipner say, "You may have forgotten a few steps for starting, Dr. Pierce. Follow what I do." With Teipner's help,

Pierce started the left engine, then the right, and as the engines idled, they went through the cockpit checklist. Then, very professionally, Pierce called the control tower for clearance, received it, and taxied the airplane to the duty runway. He ran up the engines, made a final cockpit check, advised the control tower of his intention to take off, advanced the throttles, and began the take-off run. As the airplane reached take-off speed, Pierce eased back on the control column (too much), and the airplane struggled to get in the air. Then he rather abruptly pushed the control column forward then back again.

"Christ, Phil, you're porpoising the airplane. I've got it,"

Turner looked over to Miller and saw Miller had his head resting against the cabin window and was fast asleep. Teipner took over the controls, regained control of the airplane, and as he put the airplane in a climbing turn, said, "OK, Phil, it's all yours."

The climb out to altitude and setting course for Tangier was uneventful. Thirty-five minutes later, they were flying over Larache, and Turner strained to see if there was evidence of the fiasco four months ago. There was none. A few minutes later, he unfastened his seat belt and, standing up as much as he could in the aisle of the compact passenger compartment, opened his flight bag, and took out a white shirt, gray crew neck sweater, and Levis. He took off his uniform and carefully folded the trousers, shirt, and tie and packed them in the flight bag. Because of some turbulence, he had trouble dressing, especially when it came to pulling on his Levis.

Approaching Tangier, Pierce requested and received permission for touch-and-go landings. He descended into the landing pattern and began his approach. On the final leg of the approach, he lowered the landing gear, lined up with the runway centerline, and at touchdown, slammed the left wheel down first, resulting in a sickening swerve that put the airplane in extreme peril for a "wing over" and crash. Teipner called out, "I got it," and Pierce took his hands off the control column. Teipner shoved the throttles forward, regained control of the airplane, and put it in a climbing turn. Miller didn't wake up, and Turner watched all this in fascination. Teipner gave the controls back to Pierce and said, "Shall we try again?"

Pierce answered, "Of course, that was just a minor miscalculation on my part."

He brought the little transport plane around again, bounced back in the air at touchdown, and climbed out again. Teipner didn't touch the controls. The third pass was much better. Pierce bounced the airplane once and put it down somewhat off the centerline—the landing was acceptable otherwise.

Miller, now awake, said, "That was like a carrier landing! Good show! I'm ready for a cup of coffee."

Turner said, "That was a controlled crash, my friend."

"That's what I said, just like a carrier landing. Let's get some coffee."

Pierce taxied to the small rather neglected terminal and parked next to a very old Royal Air Maroc DC-3, shut down the engines, and stated, uncharacteristically for him, "I guess I need more practice."

Miller said, "Any landing you can walk away from is a good landing, Phil."

They walked through the sleepy reception area and into a small café and bar with windows looking out over the airport runway. Turner looked around for Laura and saw her sitting at a table next to one of the windows. She was wearing dark slacks and a white sweater set, and she was beautiful. She smiled and waved to him. Not taking his eyes off her, he said to his friends, "Come on, and I'll introduce you to someone." They walked over to the table, and Laura stood up and met Turner with a kiss on the cheek. He gave her a long hug.

"Laura, I'd like you to meet Phil Pierce, our flight surgeon, and Bob Miller and Ben Teipner, aviators supreme, who usually drive the airplane. Gentlemen, this is Laura Brae."

They shook hands with Laura Brae. Pierce somewhat reserved; Miller and Teipner just beamed.

Teipner thought for a minute, then said, "Did you fly with us a couple of months ago, from Oran to Port Lyautey?" Before she could answer, he added, "I remember you asked us some questions about Burt."

"Yes, you're right—in both cases."

"You were doing some sort of archeological study in Oran, I think."

"You have a good memory, Ben." Changing the subject, she said, "When you were coming in, I thought the plane was in a lot of trouble. Then I knew you were in trouble when you went around a couple of times. What went wrong?"

Miller and Teipner looked at Pierce.

Pierce, with some discomfort, began, "Ah, Miss Brae—"

She interrupted, "Please, Phil, it's Laura."

"Ah, yes, of course. Well, I'm one of those physicians usually attached to a Naval Air Station or air group on board an aircraft carrier. The navy feels it important for physicians assigned to aviation to know as much as possible about flying to better serve naval aviator health needs. So they send a lot of us to flight school, where we learn the basic elements of flying, and at the end of our training, we are allowed to solo in a very simple training aircraft. Having accomplished this task, we are awarded a set of wings with an inverted acorn in the middle, rather than the usual anchor in the middle, and bumped up to the rank of full lieutenant or higher. Because we have been awarded wings and want to stay on flying status, we have to fly once a month to stay qualified. So under the watchful eye of a qualified pilot, I try to fly at least once a month. You should know that I was trying to land the airplane and not doing it very well."

Teipner, feeling Pierce's pain, said, "Laura, Phil soloed in a very easy-to-fly aircraft. Our SNB out there is a twin-engine airplane that is much heavier and much more demanding. Dr. Pierce did just fine."

It was a rare moment for Pierce; he was at a loss for words.

Miller said, "We have to be on our way, but let's have some coffee first." He called the waiter over; coffee was ordered and delivered to their table. Turner was the only one who added cream and sugar.

A half hour later, Turner and Laura, holding hands, watched from the tarmac as the SNB bounced twice, then took to the air and set course for Rota, Spain.

Laura looked up at Turner and said, "Shall we start our weekend?"

He took her in his arms and said, "I really missed you."

"I missed you too, Burt." She stepped away and said, "I was able to get a room at the Hotel Continental. It's on the edge of the medina, near the waterfront. Let's get the car."

They walked around the terminal to the parking lot, where four cars were parked at odd angles. Laura led Turner to a small two-door Renault and unlocked the car's trunk. He lifted the lid, dropped his flight bag inside, and closed it. She had some trouble locking it again, but the latch finally caught. After unlocking the car's doors, she slid in on the driver's side with Turner on the passenger's side. She was reaching to start the car when Turner put his arm around her shoulder, leaned over, and kissed her; at the same time, he moved his free hand up and under her sweater.

Pulling his hand down and away, she quietly said, "OK, this can wait until we get to the hotel. Sit back and enjoy the ride." He did as he was told. After starting the car, she pulled out of the driveway and began the eleven-mile drive to the port of Tangier and the Hotel Continental.

"I didn't know if we were going to be able to meet each other here. When I saw the plane, I hoped you would be on board, and I was relieved when I saw you get out. How did you do it?"

"I have friends in high places."

"No, really, how did you make this happen?"

"Well, to begin with, I hadn't taken shore leave since we were in Rabat, and I had just finished a contingency security project for the commander and the exec that was well received, and I thought I would take advantage of the timing. I made a deal with Miller and Teipner—if they could get me up here, I would give them some pool time with the SCUBA and a ride on the AVR. They worked up a flight plan with NAS Operations to fulfill Phil Pierce's flight time requirement, which enabled me to get a ride."

"I would say your friends are expert in working the system."

"I would say they are enterprising."

"Well, I enjoyed meeting them. They have a rare sense of humor, and it shows up when you four play off each other. Individually, Phil Pierce seems extremely intelligent, but a bit full of himself."

"That's pretty much true. But Phil can also be very compassionate at times."

She continued with her unsolicited assessment. "Bob and Ben are also very bright, but they hide it by clowning around. I bet they're a handful for their superiors."

"Everything you just said is true, Laura. They also don't hold their peer group in very high regard. But then the feeling is mutual."

"And you, Burt, you're so different, but you do fit right in with them. I wonder how you managed to find each other."

"It just happened, I guess. They were about the first people I met, along with a few nurses."

"You will have to tell me sometime about 'a few nurses.'"

There was a pause, and then he said, "The nurses would hang out with us once in a while as a break from their monotonous life, I guess."

"I think if you didn't have those three for friends you probably wouldn't choose to be hanging out and drinking at the O club with the usual run of officers right out of college or the naval academy. You probably would be doing something else by yourself."

"I'm not antisocial, OK?"

"No, but I don't think you would have much discomfort sailing independently. You're not the type that hangs around at the bar. You're not the type that stays very long at a party."

"Laura, I'm not reclusive, either."

"I'm not saying you're antisocial or reclusive. I do think you're careful about who you choose to spend time with. I have seen how you behave when you appear before groups of very important people dealing with very important problems. You're well thought of, maybe not by all, but by most. Your profile made a point about how you work well with small groups—as long as you are the leader, and not so well in large groups, probably because you think faster and your impatience with others is not well masked. You are a very different kind of person, very unique. I guess that's why I find you attractive."

He didn't know whether to be flattered or disappointed. She could have added, "You don't tolerate ignorant people easily."

The Hotel Continental, although not five-, four-, or three-star quality, had a large pleasant terrace that overlooked the port of Tangier to redeem itself. It was a two-story building and appeared to be recently painted—white, with doors and window shutters painted red, and like the small apartment balconies and storefronts nearby, had window boxes jammed with geraniums and other flowers.

Laura pulled into the almost-empty parking lot, and parked near the hotel's front entrance. After retrieving their luggage, they walked across a struggling-to-survive lawn, then up well-worn wooden stairs to open double doors and a lobby.

She left Turner standing near a potted palm that had seen better days, walked over to the reception counter, went through the reservation formalities, was given the key—"Down the main hallway, turn right at the second hallway to room 104, mademoiselle."

Turner followed her with their luggage. Arriving at room 104, they found a typical small clean European room with a window view of a narrow back alley. Laura closed and locked the door, the luggage fell to the floor, and they were in each other's arms. It was five minutes after three. At ten minutes after seven, they surfaced for dinner and a quiet evening.

Early the next morning, they had breakfast on the terrace of warm croissants (four for Turner, two for Laura), fresh fruit, and coffee (milk and sugar available). They checked out of the hotel, went down to the parking lot, and loaded their luggage in the Renault's trunk. Then Laura took a map from her bag, spread it on the roof of the car, and traced out the route they would be following along the coast. They spent a few minutes in conversation about things to see along the way, and then she folded the map and put it back in her bag. Turner had earlier noticed the bag was the one she brought with her on the not-so-joyful picnic at Thamusida eight months ago. She handed the keys to Turner; they got in the car and headed south. As they drove down the coast, they talked about home and how people were quite uninformed about what was occurring in North Africa and the Middle East.

Turner, offering himself up as an example, said, "I knew about the Israeli-Palestinian problem and something about Nasser and the British in Egypt. But I didn't know anything about Arab culture, and I certainly didn't know Nasser's ultimate goal was to establish an Arab empire from the Middle East westward to the Atlantic—the concept of Al Magreb. You're the one that opened my eyes to this."

"Well, I think one has to have a desire to know things, a curiosity, and the drive to take advantage of what's out there in pursuit of knowledge."

"I wonder if the drive to know things is innate or learned."

"Probably both. I guess it has a lot to do with the subject matter and access to it," she replied.

"You know, I just thought about how there is a similarity between Nasser and the Mahdi who took Khartoum during the siege of 1884 and killed General Gordon, Chinese Gordon."

She looked at him and smiled. "That's a good comparison. The Mahdi's jihad was religious. He wanted to kill all infidels—Christians, Jews, and Muslims who didn't interpret the Koran the way he did. The Mahdi wanted to retake Sudan, Egypt, and Syria, then go on into Greece and who knows where else. In Nasser's case he doesn't claim to be the Mahdi, the 'Chosen One,' but he could certainly use his Islamic religion to help his drive to Al Magreb."

"Well, the stakes are much higher today than in the 1800s. Nasser controls the Suez Canal and access to the oil reserves of the Middle East. I don't think the majority of American people understand this. They are too tightly focused on the threat of the Soviet Union and communism and what Castro is doing in Cuba," Turner replied.

"Do you think Americans understand or care about the possibility of civil war in France over the insurgency in Algeria and the loss of Morocco, Burt?"

"Of course not."

They agreed; complex issues reduced by the media to uncomplicated stories are just about enough to satisfy the information appetite of the American people.

They also agreed that the U.S. military's policy of "everything for the mission" was leading to a growing Arab apprehension about an American military presence, which was an anathema to their culture and religion. Real trouble could be coming.

"Are we intellectual snobs, Laura?"

"Only when we are together, I hope."

They were twenty-five miles south of Tangier and approaching the coastal town of Asilah when Laura asked, "Do you know anything about the town of Asilah, Burt?"

"Not a thing. Like most Americans, I'm a big picture guy."

They both laughed at this.

They stopped in Asilah and picked up bread, wine, and cheese for a later lunch, then continued on their way.

"As your tour guide, let me begin. Most history buffs know about the influence of Roman occupation, and later, Spain's and Portugal's occupation of this area. However, few know of the outlaw Raisouli, who was from Asilah."

"Who was Raisouli?"

"In the late 1800s, Raisouli terrorized Tangier and Tetouan and accumulated an enormous fortune by exacting tribute from nearby tribes, kidnapping wealthy merchants, and general plundering. He even kidnapped Ion Perdicaris and his stepson."

He sighed and asked, "OK, who was Ion Perdicaris?"

"Ion Perdicaris was a wealthy Greek-American businessman who lived near Tangier. In 1904, Raisouli kidnapped Perdicaris and his stepson and held them for ransom. He demanded almost a hundred thousand dollars from the American consul in Tangier and to be given the title Pasha of Tangier. The American president at the time was Teddy Roosevelt, and when he was made aware of the kidnapping, he sent seven warships and a force of marines to Tangier and told the American consul, 'I want Perdicaris alive or Raisouli dead.' There was no negotiation, and father and son were released."

"That's right up there with Steven Decateur and the Barbery pirates off Tripoli. Someone in congress said, 'Millions for defense, not one penny for tribute.' These days, when terrorist insurgents kidnap someone and they don't get what they want, they mutilate the hostage, kill them, and send the head back. Sending in marines or tactical aircraft, or both, to teach a lesson to the group responsible for the offense is a kind of gunboat diplomacy that isn't going to work anymore."

"Well, scale it up to insurgency movements against the British in Jordan and Egypt and the French in Syria, Lebanon, Algeria, and Morocco. I'm sure they're finding it isn't cost-effective anymore to try to reestablish control by military occupation," she replied.

For the next three days, there would be no more talk of geopolitics.

They turned off the coastal route and traveled east to the Sais Plain and to Fes, the spiritual capital of Morocco.

As they approached Fes, she explained, "During the 1800s, Muslims, persecuted in Spain and a number of North African cities, came to Fes in large numbers. Most of them were craftsmen, merchants, and academic scholars who then built mosques and libraries and established a university. Along the way, they pushed the Berbers, who they considered to be barbarians at the time, farther into the Atlas mountains and to its eastern slopes.

"Fes has seen a lot of foreign Islamic dynasties through the ages, and the French not Islamic of course—established Morocco as a protectorate in 1912. General Lyautey was appointed governor, and one of his many projects was building a new town over the old one here."

"And their dynasty is coming to an end now," Turner quietly said.

She took Turner on a tour of the remarkable Islamic monuments, standing among blue agave and olive trees. On the way to the medina, they passed a number of stench-producing leather tanneries that caused Turner to wonder how the people could stand to live so near.

When they arrived at the medina, they left the car outside the walls and walked over to a gate that opened to a web of extremely narrow passages. Turner was quickly lost. Laura knew the area and continued as his tour guide.

"This place looks like it's falling apart, Laura."

"Well, there has been a flood of poor families that have moved in from the Rif, and there isn't any work for them. The wealthy merchants left for better markets in Casablanca and the rest of the world, and there just isn't money to keep the place from going downhill."

Periodically, the narrow passages opened to wider areas paved in stone, where men squatting in doorways were selling fruits, spices, and goat legs. They stopped at a shop Laura knew about that sold varieties of wild honey produced by feral bees in the Atlas Mountains. Delicious. They bought two bottles.

The signs of abject poverty were softened by flowers in splintered bowls and tiny gardens. By the time they returned to the gate where they entered, he had mixed feelings about Fes. Incredible beauty, fascinating history, and abject poverty.

After Fes, they traveled west to Meknes, then on to Rabat. After checking in at the American embassy, Laura was able to get a room for the night in the same apartment where they stayed before. After fresh fruit, cheese, and wine, they swam in the surf of Tamara Beach until they were tired and cold, then they stretched out on the warm sand. They talked until the late afternoon wind came up, then gathered up their towels and blanket and returned to the apartment.

After showering together, they toweled each other off and held each other, skin-to-skin, on the bed.

"I've had a wonderful weekend, Burt."

"I don't want it to end, Laura. I wish we could be together more often."

"I'll try to be with you every chance I get, as long as you want me."

"I'll be with you every chance I get, as long as you want me, Laura."

Early next morning Laura took Turner to the railway station in Rabat and put him on the train to Port Lyautey. Then she drove to the airport, turned in the rental car, and caught the late morning plane for Paris.

Chapter 13

Three months passed. Once Laura flew into Rabat or Port Lyautey for a RON (remain over night) before returning to Paris, and they had a short time together. Otherwise, they corresponded by mail or through the auspices of a couple friends of Turner's who were pilots in VR24, the transport squadron.

During their time apart, he was saved from dreary office routine when he and his team took the initiative to deal with the Naval Ordnance Facility's vexing problem of outdated ammunition disposal. The ammunition was left over from the Allied invasion of North Africa in November 1942, and there was great concern that it had become chemically unstable because of inadequate storage facilities at an earlier time. Even though the storage facilities were now modernized, the problem was worsening. The preferred transport by U.S. Navy ammunition ship to the U.S. for disposal at sea or demolition on land was now out of the question because of the monetary cost and potential hazard to the ammunition ship and crew.

Possible alternatives were dumping at sea locally or by explosive demolition in a remote area. The small arms ammunition, .30- and .50-caliber rounds, could be destroyed by burning with intense heat in a steel chamber if not disposed by sea.

The initial planning began with a meeting on board the AVR with Turner and his team and First Class Boatswain's Mate Deacon and his crew. Because Turner's team had developed a comfortable working relationship with the AVR crew, it was not out of place for him to ask if the AVR crew could make the YFR that was tied up just aft of the AVR seaworthy, so the little freighter/refrigerator vessel could be used for dumping outdated ammunition at sea. Deacon and his crew were very agreeable to taking on the task, but there was a problem. The Operations Department was not interested in spending money to make the YFR seaworthy.

When told this, Turner impulsively asked, "If I get the money, could you do the repairs and crew the YFR?

Deacon replied, "We could do the repairs with some of your help. If we got it running, this crew could take it to sea. But you have to get clearance for all this from Lieutenant Commander Bello, and he would have to get an OK from the air station commander."

Gallegos asked, "What if there was an emergency requiring the AVR, and your crew was at sea?"

Deacon replied, "The AVR standby crew could deal with it."

Turner asked Gallegos, "Could you and Cole help the coxswain?"

Gallegos smiled and said, "I'm sure we could lend a hand to help make the YFR seaworthy. Let's go aboard and have a look at the old girl."

Deacon went below deck and returned with a clipboard, paper, and ballpoint pen; then he and his crew, along with the team, left the AVR and went aboard the YFR. Two hours later, Turner and Chief Gallegos were in Commander Hawkins's office and began to explain how the YFR could be used to dump the outdated ammunition at sea if money could be found to defer cost of repairs.

The commander said, "Whoa, before you go any farther, Mr. Turner, I want my exec to hear all this."

He lifted his phone, dialed, and, a moment later, said, "Don, will you come in? I want you to hear Mr. Turner's and Chief Gallegos's possible solution to our outdated ammunition problem."

When the exec arrived, the commander said, "OK, gentlemen, sit down, and let's have a go at this."

For the next hour, Turner and Gallegos made a very convincing case for using the YFR for dumping the outdated and dangerous ammunition at sea. When there were questions, most were answered by Gallegos, who had a better technical grasp of the situation. Finally, the commander looked at the exec and asked, "Heard enough, Don?"

"Sir, I'm very concerned about not knowing the degree of instability of much of the explosives. Moving tons of it from the magazines to trucks, then transporting the load to the wharf, hoisting it on board, and storing it in the cargo holds is dangerous and difficult. At every point of loading and unloading, there is a chance of explosion. At sea, hoisting the explosives out of the cargo hold and dumping it over the side is high-risk business, even if there isn't much of a sea running. However, we don't have much of a choice, sir."

Commander Hawkins replied, "We don't have much of a choice, so it will be necessary to find out if the YFR is indeed seaworthy. Mr. Turner and

Chief Gallegos, I want you to come up with an outline for the operation immediately."

Turner and Gallegos gave a simultaneous "Aye, aye, sir," and left the office.

Because of the urgency of the situation, Commander Hawkins had no difficulty finding a way to ready the tired old vessel for sea by using money already allocated by the navy Bureau of Ordnance for disposal of the outdated ammunition. Unknown to them and others locally, the YFR was soon to be slated for decommissioning and sent to the ship breakers. The YFR would be giving its all during its last days at sea.

An agreement was made between the Naval Ordnance Facility and the Naval Air Station's Operations Department, saying, in part, "the YFR will be made available for transporting and dumping at sea outdated explosive ammunition, light weapons (machine guns, .30 and .50 cal., thirty-eight in number, crated), and other items of ordnance."

The proposed agreement, later to be signed by Lieutenant Commander Bello, representing the Operations Department, and Commander Hawkins, was written by Lieutenant JG Burt Turner and Chief Gunner's Mate Manuel Gallegos. Lieutenant Commander Owens did the editing, which was extensive.

Carrying out the logistics of the operation was through the efforts of the exec and the head of the NOF Ammunitions Division, Chief Gunner's Mate Humphries. After studying the inventory of outdated explosives, Humphries would provide the crew to load, transport, and then transfer the explosives to the YFR for disposal at sea. Lieutenant JG Turner's team, in an advisory capacity, would accompany the explosives to the designated dumpsite at the 1,500-fathom curve thirty miles west of Port Lyautey.

Ten days after the meeting, the first dumping-at-sea operation, including .30- and .50-caliber machine guns, was completed successfully under the close supervision of the exec, Lieutenant Commander Owens.

On the way back from the second dumping-at-sea, Turner decided the thirty-mile ride back to the wharf on a very slow boat that wallowed around a lot wasn't much fun. It occurred to him the team's physical training program could be augmented by helicopter pickups while at sea. From the third trip on to the fifth, the last one, arrangements were made with the air station Operations Department that when the operation was completed for the day, the YFR would radio Operations for the HUP to rendezvous with the YFR, recover the SW/EOD team, and return to the Naval Air Station.

With confirmation, the HUP was on the way. Turner, standing on the bridge with binoculars, would search the horizon. When the HUP was sighted, he joined his team on the main deck, taking off uniforms, stowing them away, and putting on dry suits and other swim gear. When the team was ready, they went over the side one at a time and swam away from the YFR. If the water was rough, they would light off the orange smoke end of their signal flares to help the HUP crew spot them more easily.

Once recovered, it was a twenty-minute flight to the air station. Most of the time, it took longer because of the need for recreational sightseeing or dropping in the water off the surf line to surf into the beach, and being recovered. The exercise would be repeated four or five times. The Operations Department considered this unexpected opportunity of great value for ramping up training of the helicopter air-sea rescue crews. The team considered the exercise far better than being at work in the NOF office and EOD shop.

During planning for disposal at sea, Turner called Lieutenant Joe Logan at the U.S Air Force Strategic Air Command (SAC) Base at Sidi Slimane and asked if he had any outdated ordnance he would like to get rid of. He did. There was a very large number of outdated and surplus night photo-reconnaissance flight photoflash canisters. The fourth dumping-at-sea deployment had Lieutenant Joe Logan and four of his enlisted men on board the YFR, sending thousands of photoflash canisters over the side. When finished with the task, the air force Lieutenant made an unsteady passage to the fantail of the YFR and lay himself down on a bench.

Turner, looking for his friend, asked one of Logan's men, "Where's Lieutenant Logan?"

"He's somewhere in the back of the boat, sir."

Turner walked aft and found Logan. "Hey, Joe, you taking a nap?"

Shielding the sun from his eyes with his hand, he looked up and said, "I'm seasick, especially after Chief Gallegos and that crazy Cole began to pass out 'lard' sandwiches."

"I guess you were serious when we were on the plane to Paris and you told me you didn't stay in the navy after Annapolis because of seasickness."

Logan groaned and said, "Of course, I was serious!"

Turner felt terrible about his friend's condition and kindly said, "Look, you will be back at the wharf soon." Then he added, "If you would like to get in the water with us, we can get you back to the wharf in twenty minutes."

"No, thanks. I have read about bad things in this water that eat people, my friend. I'll just stay here, thank you."

A few weeks later Lieutenant Joe Logan's report was sent up the chain of command, telling of the successful disposal at sea of the air force photoflash canisters, and it included a recommendation in the last paragraph: "Since there is a large portion of empty land some distance away from the air base conventional ammunition magazines, it is suggested that this area be designated an explosive demolition site. The site could be made available to the navy for disposal of outdated explosive ordnance."

A month later, the recommended site became an important location for disposal of the navy's outdated ammunition, a nice piece of interservice cooperation.

Because of good planning and execution, the YFR operation ran its course smoothly. It was then thought that truck transport of explosive ordnance to Sidi Slimane for demolition would be a piece of cake. It wasn't. The American military "can-do spirit" and "everything for the mission" disregarded the host country's cultural way of doing things and ignored their politically cautious transition from colonial government to a constitutional monarchy. Additionally, the possibility of an American military truck convoy transporting ammunition to Sidi Slimane and being intercepted and highjacked by insurgent terrorists wasn't considered by the navy planners. Because of these oversights, an unpleasant political confrontation was inevitable.

The plan was to have a convoy of two five-ton trucks and the weapons carrier travel the thirty-eight miles between the naval base at Port Lyautey and the air force base at Sidi Slimane twice a week for four weeks. The SW/EOD team, in the weapons carrier, would lead the convoys. A week before the first convoy, Naval Air Station security sent a letter to Lieutenant Hamid al Karim of the Moroccan police for Port Lyautey and the surrounding area, informing him of the intent to transport explosive material from the U.S. Naval Station at Port Lyautey to the U.S. Air Force Base at Sidi Slimane. Date, time, and route was given.

Al Karim reported the message to his superiors in the Moroccan police and the Royal Moroccan Army, who, after studying the message, wrote their own message in return, which included the following (when translated): "Because of known fellagha activity in the area, an assignment of Moroccan police escorts to the American navy convoys will be required." Followed by, "Agreement to the order of all trucks in convoy will have no insignia or identification markings of any kind is required and two-week advance for permission to travel in convoy with explosives from Naval Air Station, Port Lyautey, to U.S. Air Force Base, Sidi Slimane, is mandatory. If permission is granted, permission can be recalled at any time."

There was no arguing the point. A letter of apology and agreement to requirements, as put forth by the Moroccan authorities, was sent from

Commander Hawkins to al Karim and his superiors, with copies to Naval Air Station security, the commander of the Naval Air Station, and the COMNAVACTSMED. A few days after the letter was sent, Commander Hawkins decided to take advantage of the relationship formed when Turner and al Karim successfully worked together at Sidi Yahia. To make sure there was no misinterpretation of the tone of the official U.S. Navy letter, especially after the letter was translated into Arabic, he sent Turner to al Karim's office at the gendarmerie in Port Lyautey.

When Turner arrived at al Karim's office, it was late afternoon. He went inside and walked across the concrete floor to a Formica-surfaced counter and identified himself to a young police officer. The police officer wrote down his name and time of arrival on a clipboard, then motioned him to follow. They went down a short hallway and stopped at an open door. Turner looked in and saw al Karim at his desk reading a newspaper. The police officer knocked twice on the doorframe and announced, in Arabic, the presence of Lieutenant Turner. From behind the newspaper, al Karim said something in Arabic in return, and the police officer waved Turner inside and then departed.

Turner looked around the spotlessly clean but rather bare office. On the floor in front of al-Karim's desk was a moderate-sized black rug with a red-and-white trim; he thought it might be like a smaller one he had seen in Pierce's room in the BOQ. Pierce said his was a *shashawa*, one of the brighter Arab rugs. On his right, next to the wall, was a large multicolored, overstuffed couch with a number of large colorful pillows. In front of the couch was a brass meter tray on a hexagonal wooden table. Behind the couch, rather high up, was a window where one could see a stork nest at the top of a telephone pole a short distance away. Overhead was a slow turning fan between two metal shaded lights that hung from the ceiling. He glanced to his left and saw a small bookcase with all three shelves filled with books, and a display of Arab curved daggers on the wall above. There were two wooden chairs in front of al Karim's desk. On the desk was an old-fashioned French telephone handset and cradle, two other newspapers, one in Arabic, the other in English—he couldn't see the titles. A desk lamp with a green glass shade provided moderate light, and on the wall behind the desk was an imposing portrait of King Mohammed Cinq.

Al Karim put the newspaper down, stood up, and, as if the police officer hadn't already announced Turner's presence, said with some surprise, "Well, Lieutenant Burt Turner, it is you!" He reached over his desk and shook hands with his guest. They exchanged respectful greetings, and al Karim motioned

Turner to sit down on the nearest chair in front of his desk; he in turn sat back down on a well-worn leather chair.

Moving his chair closer to al Karim's desk, Turner said. "Hamid, the reason I am here is to let you know that the intent of my superiors is to be a good neighbor and to be more thoughtful in working with you and your superiors. You have already received their message saying they will comply with all the requirements set forth in the message they received from your superiors for transport of explosives from the Naval Air Station to the air force base at Sidi Slimane."

Al Karim listened thoughtfully, then said, "The American navy has no choice but to comply. The show of cooperation is acknowledged, but with some lack of enthusiasm." His delivery was sharp and professional. Leaning forward, he continued, "You stay here for a short time, maybe two years. When you leave, you take with you your bad manners, disrespectful behavior, and ignorance of a culture a thousand years older than yours." He waved his hand as if to say "that's enough" and said, "We must have some tea, don't you agree?"

Exercising his limited French, Turner replied, "Oui, s'il vous plait."

Al Karim reached over, picked up his phone, dialed one number, and, in rapid Arabic, gave an order.

A few minutes later, the same young police officer who ushered Turner to al Karim's office came through the door with a silver tray with a blue globular, long-spouted porcelain teapot and what looked like two small jelly glasses and a small plate of dates. Al Karim motioned him to put the tray on the low table in front of the couch.

Al Karim got up and, waving Turner over from his chair, said, "Let us be more comfortable." Turner followed him to the couch and sat down in the soft pillows. The meter tray in front of him was elaborately engraved with geometric designs; the table supports, also carved in geometric designs, were inlaid with mother-of-pearl.

Holding the teapot quite high, al Karim expertly poured a stream of hot green mint tea in one glass, then the other. They sat quietly, enjoying the aroma and taste of tea for a time; then Turner put his glass down and said, "I'm a rather insignificant naval officer in all of this, but don't you think the act of providing escort for the trucks would draw attention to something of value being transported?"

"Lieutenant Turner"—he paused and corrected himself—"Burt, do you not think convoys that have never been seen before on the road to Sidi Slimane are going to draw attention?" Without waiting for an answer, he added, "The escort will be quite modest." He reached over, picked up the teapot, refilled Turner's nearly empty glass, then his own. After returning the teapot to the meter tray, he took a sip from his glass and changed the subject. "How is your tourist friend from the Musee d' Histoire Archaeologique, the student of Moroccan archeology?"

Turner was very surprised al Karim remembered Laura.

"The last I heard, she was fine."

"The woman is very attractive woman. I think she is more sophisticated than she appears to be, *n'cest pas*?

"Yes, I agree with you."

"Perhaps you might see more of her?"

"It would be difficult, Hamid."

The conversation became less guarded and turned to the political situation in North Africa and the Middle East.

"Why are you Americans so concerned about the Russians?"

"Well, they seem to be determined to obtain hegemony in North Africa and the Middle East."

Almost jokingly, al Karim replied, "Why do you say that?"

"They are helping Gamal Abdel Nasser build up Egypt's economy, and they are helping Nasser build up military forces that will be used against Israel. They are doing the same for Hafez Assad in Syria. We know that Russia is sending arms and advisors to Algeria and Tunisia to be used against the French. We also know that Russian advisors and arms were important in the Moroccan insurgency against the French."

"Much of what you say is true."

"Doesn't it bother you that an increasing Russian presence in the countries of the Middle East and North Africa would get in the way of a movement toward self-determination and a democratic form of government? And what about atheistic Russia threatening the religion of Islam?"

"My friend, you have a lot on your mind. You must remember, we have endured for nine hundred years the French, British, and other European friends . . . they all come and go."

The irony was not wasted on Turner.

Al Karim continued his instruction. "Did you know 90 percent of Muslim countries were under colonial rule by European nations, and others, until as recently as thirty years ago?"

"No, I didn't."

"During this time, foreign infidels came and went. Some stayed longer than others, but our culture remains. Islam prevails. The establishment of an enduring hegemony, or even a temporary one, in Arab nations is not possible, my good friend. We will always be happy to send you and others home, along with the exploiters of our land and people. It is written."

Turner was sitting back in the couch cushions looking at his folded hands as he thought about the Arab phrase, "it is written," which is all about the inevitable.

Al Karim got up from the couch, went to his desk, picked up the phone, and dialed. After receiving a response, he said a few words in Arabic and returned to the couch.

Turner, deep in thought, was interrupted by, "What have you been doing to help you to understand our Arab culture while you are with us?"

Turner sat up, reached for his glass, saw that it was empty, and set it back down on the meter tray. He answered, "I recently finished reading *Seven Pillars of Wisdom* and—"

Before he could finish, al Karim said, "Ah, the writings of the British man, Lawrence, his time in what is now Saudi Arabia. A presumptuous adventurer, but a start to his and your understanding of the Arab culture." He emptied his cup with a last sip, savored it for a moment, and said, "It would be helpful if you could find time to read our Koran."

"I found a copy in English in our library. I just started reading it."

"What have you learned thus far?"

"It's like the Bible. Its message is to seek high moral and cultural value, to promote social order and unity, prevent cruelty, seek sobriety and temperance, and to help the less fortunate have dignity and pride."

"That's very good."

"I think one of the most thoughtful messages had to do with the uncompromising acceptance of the hardships and limitations of life."

At that moment, the police officer who had earlier brought in the tea entered the office with a large tray piled high with fresh fruit and another pot of green mint tea. Turner was overwhelmed.

"This is all from our land. Did you know of the great variety of fruit we have?"

"No, I didn't."

Al Karim took a large beautiful fresh peach from the collection of fruit and gave it to his guest. "You will find this to be quite excellent."

"Thank you," he said, and, trying to be as fastidious as possible with the succulent fruit, devoured it.

Returning to the subject, al Karim said, "I am impressed with your search, Lieutenant Burt Turner. You are quite different than most infidels."

"What I can't understand is how those who follow the Koran treat women so poorly and commit terrible atrocities in the name of Allah."

"Consider this. You have a variety of religions in your country, and Christianity is one with many churches, with many interpretations of your Bible, and many ways to worship. There are many interpretations of the Koran, and Islam is made up of many approaches to worship, but all worship only Allah. Islam has the prophet Mohammed, Christianity has the prophet Jesus.

"As for women . . . our history shows an interpretation of Islamic Law—Sharia, allowing women to keep their own name in marriage, seek work and education, take custody of their children after divorce, and own money. There are those that follow the Wahhabi interpretation of the Koran, which is most strict and allows for none of these permissions.

"So you see, an action interpreted to be permissible by Islamic law by some could be considered an atrocity by others. It is written: Anyone who attacks you, attack him in a like manner. If you feel the attack was an atrocity, you can commit the same against the attacker. Islamic law also tells us, 'Who so defends himself after he has suffered wrong, there is no blame against him. Fight in the way of Allah against those who fight against you, but begin not hostilities. Allah loveth not aggressors.'"

"I didn't know these things."

"I must remind you, Americans have visited atrocities on others and each other. Before and after your unpleasant civil war, you Americans committed atrocities against the people you call Indians in what was their land. During your civil war, you committed atrocities against each other. I recall reading of the man Quantrill and his terrorists committing atrocities against the people in your province of Kansas. Your Christian people tied ropes around the necks of black American Christian people, hung them, and committed other atrocities against them. So you see, we are not unlike you in your interpretations of the words of your Bible."

"I guess all world religions have different interpretations of a basic message. Some are radical fundamentalist, some are more moderate, and some are liberal in their interpretations."

"I believe it so," al Karim replied. He paused and said, "As for the Russians, 'the enemy of my enemy is my friend.'"

There was some talk of families and more fruit and mint tea before Turner left Lieutenant Hamid al Karim's office. He had much to think about as he drove back to the base.

During the four-week ammunition disposal operation, the convoys safely transported almost sixty tons of explosives to the demolition site at Sidi

Slimane. Insurgent terrorists made three attempts to interdict the convoys. Lieutenant Al Karim's men successfully crushed each attempt.

Because the air force base commander was concerned about excessive noise, his staff stipulated that no more than one thousand pounds of explosive was to be detonated at any one time. After the first few detonations, Lieutenant JG Turner and his team considered it appropriate and expeditious to incrementally increase to two thousand pounds of explosive for each detonation, lessening the overall number of explosions per day—but only if the sky was clear. An overcast would multiply the distance by which the sound could be heard. No complaints were registered.

At the end of the fourth week, the last of the outdated ammunition was ready to be detonated. The day before the last detonation, Turner invited Lieutenant Joe Logan to participate in the final act, and in turn, Logan invited Turner for lunch afterward.

The temperature was hovering in the low nineties—unusually high for mid-March. There was no wind, and the only clouds were far to the east over the Moyen Atlas Mountains. The airborne dirt and dust from the last detonation was settling as Logan drove up and parked his jeep next to the navy vehicles; it was 1100 hours. At 1117 hours, after instruction from Turner, Logan called out, "Fire in the hole," and, rotating the handle of the electrical blasting machine sharply, successfully detonated six 250-pound general purpose bombs. The normally staid Naval Academy graduate, now U.S. Air Force officer, turned and, in great delight, yelled out, "That was incredible, 1500 pounds of explosives! That was really neat."

Turner slapped him on the back and said, "Good job, Joe!"

Gallegos shook the lieutenant's hand. "Expertly done, sir!"

Cole, all smiles, said, "You sure put a fine hole in that North African dirt, sir!"

After Gallegos and Cole reeled in the electrical firing wire, Gallegos joined Turner and Logan in front of the weapons carrier. Cole went around in back and stowed the equipment, then reached under a tarp and came away with a wooden ammunition box.

He dragged it out of the vehicle and carried it to where Turner, Gallegos, and Logan were congratulating each other on the successful end of a difficult project.

With a look of contrived incredulity, Cole said, "Hey, look what I found in the back!"

He put the box down on the desert floor, swung back the lid, and sticking out of a bed of crushed ice were four bottles of Heineken beer.

Gallegos reached in and pulled out a bottle. "I can't imagine how this could have happened. I guess we shouldn't ask questions and just enjoy the moment."

Cole, still holding the open box, said, "I sure don't want to go to captain's mast for drinking while on duty, Chief."

Turner replied, "We have worked very hard, it is a very hot day, and we deserve a reward for our efforts. As the chief said, let's enjoy the moment."

After finishing the beer, Turner sent Gallegos and Cole back to NOF with the two empty trucks, then in the weapons carrier, followed Logan off the demolition site.

When they arrived at the Logan residence, Turner parked close behind the jeep, got out, and joined his friend, who was standing on a postage stamp—size lawn in front of his house.

"Every time I come on board your base, I think I'm visiting a country club far beyond my means."

"It's one of the perks that help retain officers and enlisted men who are thinking about going back to civilian life. We have to keep everyone we can, Burt."

As they walked up to the house Turner asked, "Do you sometimes think about bailing out and doing something else?"

"I did at first. Then I got hooked when I was screened and selected to be in the SAC nuclear weapons program. It's a great career field, and when long-range ballistic missiles come along, it will be something to behold."

Changing the subject, Turner asked, "Will your neighbors be curious about my navy olive drab truck being parked in back of your air force blue jeep?"

"I'm sure they will be curious about your vehicle, Burt. The phenomenon will be grist for the weekly officers' wives' tea."

Logan opened the screen door, and as they crossed the small front room to the kitchen, he called out, "Navy arriving."

Carolyn Logan replied from the backyard, "I'll be right in."

Logan went to the refrigerator, opened the door, and looked inside. "Burt, we are in great luck. I see a bowl of coleslaw, a platter of club sandwiches, and a pitcher of iced tea. I think we should have lunch here, don't you?"

Carolyn Logan smiled as she opened the screen door, came in, and saw Turner. She gave him a big hug and said, "Hi sailor, welcome aboard!"

She was as beautiful as she was when he first met her some months ago. With her blond hair and blue eyes, she was absolutely striking. She wore brown slacks, white tennis shoes, and a tan short-sleeved blouse with the second button open, showing a hint of cleavage. She stepped away from Turner and, after hugging her husband, she stood back with arms folded and looked at the two disheveled young men and said, "I sent my husband to work this morning in a clean uniform. Look at you two! You look like you have been playing in the dirt!"

Self-consciously, the two young officers brushed themselves off. Logan looked at Turner, then back at his wife and replied, "Burt made me do it."

"Burt didn't make you do any such thing. You two go and wash up. I'll set up lunch outside."

They went down the hallway to the small but efficient bathroom, took turns at the wash basin, left a soiled towel, and went outside to the backyard. Carolyn was sitting under an awning at a circular wooden table with three place settings. She was reading the international edition of *Time* magazine. The platter with the club sandwiches had been put in the middle of the table, the bowl of coleslaw to one side, and the pitcher of ice tea on the other side. In addition, there was a small plate of sliced pickles. Logan sat down close to his wife, and Turner, still standing, was looking around.

There were two rows of prefabricated houses, twelve in each row on this particular block. The front of the houses looked out on narrow streets; the back of the houses faced each other across about forty feet of common lawn running the length of the block. There were a few small shade trees and no fences. It was a pleasant parklike setting. A few houses down, four children were playing.

Logan said, "Sit down, Burt, and enjoy this." He picked up the pitcher of iced tea and, as he filled each of the three glasses, asked, "What's going on in the real world, Carolyn?"

She put the news magazine down on the lawn next to her chair and replied, "Things in France are getting worse because of the economy and the Algerian problem. In Algeria, the Foreign Legion is in a state of mutiny, in support of the Pied Noir—the French farmland owners and business people who want France to hold on to Algeria, and a lot of legionnaires are deserting and joining a new group called the OAS."

Taking another club sandwich from the platter, Turner said, "Well, there is something new that just went on in our real world."

She answered, "What is that, Burt?"

"You should know your husband did something today no one else on this base could do, or will ever do."

"Oh dear, I don't think I'm going to like this. What did he do?"

"My friend and colleague, your husband, had the honor of setting off the final explosion ending the outdated ammunition disposal operation. He detonated almost two tons of explosive ordnance."

"It sounds like you endangered my best friend, lover, and husband."

Before Turner could reply, Logan said, "It wasn't dangerous, Carolyn. It was really incredible. It was just incredible."

She put her hand on his arm and said, "Don't make it a habit, Joe. I mean it."

Turner took a larger than usual bite out of his sandwich and the tomato between the leaf of lettuce and Monterey Jack cheese lost its integrity, the juice ending up under his Rolex watch band. Carolyn passed a second paper napkin and asked, "What's been going on in your life since I last saw you, and don't tell me about office politics."

"Carolyn, I'm embarrassed to say nothing much except getting rid of outdated ordnance from World War II."

"Have you found time to develop a new relationship, Burt?"

Without hesitation he said, "I've been seeing a girl who is doing grad student studies at the Museum of Archaeology in Paris."

Carolyn asked, "How on earth did you meet her?"

A little too quickly, he came up with, "She and her supervisor were being sent here to do an archaeology research project. There was some sort of U.S. embassy connection passed down from command to command until it ended up on someone's desk who would provide a helping hand. The helping hand ended up being my CO. I was told to give her a tour of the Roman ruins at Thamusida. I did, and then we became involved."

Logan looked at him in total bafflement. A grad student in archaeology making a connection with the CO of a Naval Ordnance Facility, who in turn would ask the officer in charge of a special weapons/explosvie ordnance disposal team to take this grad student on a tour of Roman ruins? That was quite a stretch.

Caroline continued, "Is she French? What is her name?"

"She is an American. Her name is Laura Brae."

As soon as he said her name, he thought, *Oh shit. A year ago, right after the Rif Mountain debriefing, Joe and his CO came into the meeting room and sat in on Laura's CIA briefing on Arab history and current problems. He might remember her name.*

Logan didn't make the connection between then and now.

Carolyn asked, "Isn't it rather difficult, you being here and Laura being in Paris?"

"It is. We managed to spend a short time with each other in Naples, then later in Rabat. Most recently, we met in Tangier."

"That sounds very romantic."

Logan asked, "How did you like Tangier?"

"We only stayed overnight. The next morning, we rented a car and drove down the coast, stopped at a number of historical places, then went inland to Fes and Meknes for a few days."

Logan smiled and said, "Alone, overnight, romantic intimacy, and—"

Carolyn interrupted, "OK, Joe that's enough." She looked at Turner and said, "I'm very happy for you, Burt. Sometime when you and she are in the neighborhood, it would be nice if you brought her by."

"That would be great. I know she would really like you and Joe."

Bits of cheese and a few crumbs of bread were all that remained of the club sandwiches. The bowl of coleslaw was empty, and Logan was finishing the last pickle when Turner asked, "How many personnel are on board the base, Joe?"

"Close to four thousand, not counting the B-47 crews on three-week deployment from CONUS."

"I didn't think there would be that many," Turner replied.

"A little less than half are dependents of officers and enlisted men."

"Carolyn, how are the dependents adjusting to being so far from home?"

"Actually, pretty good. Once they settle in here, it's just another base, although couples with children seem to do better."

"Why is that?"

"Boredom. Boredom is the enemy of women without children. It's not unusual for these women to leave for home before their husband's tour of duty is up. Two years away from home can be a very long time for some. Even with athletic fields, swimming pools, all sorts of activities, and a commissary with just about all the foods available that one could find in a good supermarket in the U.S., we are still in a foreign country far away from friends and relatives. Unfortunately, family problems surface more often here than we see at an air base at home, and our religious leaders stay busy administering counseling and guidance."

"That all sounds pretty awful."

"I don't mean to mislead you, Burt. Far more people adjust to the situation than not, and the career-oriented take it in stride."

"We probably have the same problems, I guess. All of us that are single, at least those I know of, don't seem to be bored. There's always something to do. My friends and I hang out on the base or go into town to the medina to eat or simply look around. We try to get out and see the country, and almost everyone tries to take advantage of space-available flights to Paris, London, or Naples. Of course, we are pretty busy taking care of things we are here for."

Logan thoughtfully added, "There are families and single air force men and women who never leave the base for the eighteen months to two years they are here. They never get to know the country and the people, let alone the history and cultural attributes." He paused for a moment and continued, "Even though we have tours available to introduce our people to Morocco, not many take advantage of the experience. Those that do really like it."

Turner added, "It probably has to do with a lack of curiosity or being insecure. I'm sure some just don't care about knowing things outside their immediate situation."

Logan said, "It's hard to believe there's a sizable population in the most powerful country in the world that fits into that category. It's kinda scary. I think John Adams or Thomas Jefferson said, 'The only way a democracy can work is if there is an educated electorate.' I don't think we have an educated electorate in the U.S. these days."

"You two are getting a bit snobbish, don't you think? What evidence do you have in relation to what you are pontificating about?"

Her husband replied, "Think about your college friends at home. Most were academically talented, coasted through classes, and were essentially intellectually vacant. It was exactly the same at the Naval Academy—academically talented, technologically educated, and intellectually vacant. Now think about the officers you have met here. They are super goal oriented, know only enough about geopolitics to think there is a communist under every bed and anyone thinking otherwise is part of a great communist conspiracy."

"I don't think what you just said is intellectually noteworthy." Turning her attention to her guest, she asked, "Burt, you have been in North Africa for, what is it, a year or so?"

"A little over fourteen months."

"Is it anything like you thought it would be?"

"Is it anything like I thought it would be—not in a million years. What about you two?"

Logan replied, "Actually, they did a good job of getting me ready. The nuclear weapons training program was rigidly standardized to match exactly what we would be doing in the field, so we could hit the ground running when we arrived at our assigned air base. Consequently, there have been no surprises."

Carolyn added, "We were married for two weeks when Joe was selected for weapons school. I was able to go with Joe, and we lived in married student officer housing. He was all day in class and lab, came home for dinner, and went back to study until ten. He couldn't tell me a thing about what he was learning to do. After he graduated, we had to get to know each other all over again." She reached over and gently touched her husband's cheek.

Thinking of Lieutenant Commander Buckhold Turner asked, "Have you ever met anyone in the program you felt didn't belong, Joe?"

"You went through the screenings. You know how selective they are. No, I haven't met anyone I thought didn't belong. Have you?"

"I have. Others recognize the situation and are dealing with it."

Carolyn shifted her chair more into the shade and said, "Tell me, why it hasn't been anything like you thought it would be?"

"Well, that's a long story, Carolyn."

"Well, indulge me, Burt Turner."

He thought for a minute, then said, "I went through almost a year of training at Key West and Indian Head and, loaded with self-confidence, considered myself prepared for anything. About six weeks after arriving at Port Lyautey, my team and I were tasked to do things we weren't trained for. We went through what one might call on-the-job training. The experience exposed me to a world I didn't know existed and it led to things . . . uncomfortable."

Sounding rather indifferent, Logan said, "Those in the military are encouraged to be resourceful, sorta like the Boy Scouts."

Turner found himself on the edge of white-hot anger and thought, *If he was in the Rif Mountains with us or at Larache, he wouldn't be saying that.* He cooled down a bit and said, "I guess I just felt not fully mature for the demands of the real world of the military."

"Actually, Burt, I was just kidding. What happened?"

"Can't tell you."

Carolyn asked, "Was there anything else that took you by surprise?"

"After sitting through the Welcome to Morocco lecture during orientation week, I thought I was quite well informed about the Naval Air Station's mission, its surroundings, and the dos and don'ts while off base. The political situation between us, the Arabs, and the French was well covered too, I thought. Then a few months later, your husband and I sat in on a meeting that included a lecture on the history of Islam and Arabs in North Africa, from about 1,300 years ago to the present withdrawal of the French from Tunisia, Morocco, and soon from Algeria. We were told an anti-American movement was developing. All this was missing from the initial orientation lectures. There were other things we were told that we can't tell you about."

"Joe told me about that conference. He said it was long, academic, and disturbing."

"It was. But although we were told of a developing anti-American movement, we weren't told why this was happening, except that the Arabs see us as neocolonialists."

Logan replied, "It's hard to believe there is an anti-American movement here. Moroccans are employed on our air force bases and your navy base, making more money than they ever could have imagined. A lot of American families hire Arab women to take care of their children, do laundry and cleaning. We help their economy when we buy things in the medina and the marche. Add to that the big money paid to the Moroccan government for allowing us to have American military bases on Moroccan soil. All of this has a big impact on Morocco."

"All that is true, of course. Economically, we are having a positive impact. But when we behave like we are still in the U.S., and we believe the assertive Arab bargaining in the marketplace represents Arab society as a whole, we show our ignorance and disregard for Arab society and culture. When we are in town getting drunk, getting loud, and using profanity, when we show intolerable familiarity with Arab women, we are showing ignorance and disregard for Arab society and culture. All of us were told the Arabs consider the way American women dress to be immodest and provocative when they come into town, yet we don't do much to enforce the dress code as they leave the base. Then, on top of all this, we often treat Arabs as second-class citizens in their own country. They don't like it. It reminds them of the French."

Carolyn answered, "We are a very diverse population here. We come from different economic, educational, and racial backgrounds, and the air force tries very hard to make all personnel and dependents understand what it means to be guests in a foreign country, especially in regard to what you have just said. But there will always be some who just don't get it."

"And that's the problem. Recently, I made friends with a man by the name of Hamid al Karim. Al Karim is a police lieutenant in the Port Lyautey Area Police Department. He's very well educated, well spoken, and doesn't particularly like Americans or other foreigners in his country."

Turner went on, at length, to tell of the thoughtful and, at times, very uncomfortable conversations he had with al Karim. When he finished, Logan said, "That's remarkable. You are one of the very few, I am sure, to have an experience like that."

"I know. Lately, I was thinking one could know too much. Another thing I was unprepared for was how a few in the upper echelons of the chain of command take advantage of their position and substitute dishonorable self-interest for leadership with honor."

Carolyn said, "That is very strong stuff, Burt."

"It is very strong stuff when unscrupulous civilian politicians and equally unscrupulous senior military officers put important military assets needlessly in harm's way for personal gain. Those farther down the chain of command go along because they think the officers above appear to know what they are doing, or they go along because their careers could be threatened if they question the concept."

Logan replied, "Historically, not unusual I'm afraid. I hope you haven't experienced something like this personally."

The look Turner gave his friend said it all.

The conversation was interrupted by the sound of jet engines. Turner looked up, and in the distance saw a number of B-47s coming in from the west on final approach for landing.

Logan looked at his watch. "A little late, must have had some weather on the way over the Atlantic."

"It looks like quite a few coming in. They're really beautiful airplanes, Joe."

"It's the new rotation from MacDill Air Force Base in Florida. There should be twelve of them. We expect three more later. Usually fifteen or so are deployed from each air wing in the U.S. The rotation is part of the SAC Reflex Action operation."

Carolyn got up and started clearing the table.

Turner got up to join her.

"Burt, you and Joe talk for a while. I'll do this."

With some reluctance he sat down. Shading his eyes, he watched the silver six-engine swept-wing B-47s as they gracefully let down, and asked, "What's Reflex Action, Joe?"

With obvious pride, Joe answered, "Reflex Action is the alert system code for deploying B-47s and crews for three-week rotational periods from Air Wings in the U.S. to a forward base, and then return home."

"Where are the forward bases besides here in Morocco?"

"In the UK, Spain, Guam, and Alaska. After arrival, all aircraft are refueled, put through routine maintenance, and armed with weapons in the strike condition. Here in Morocco, because the air and ground temperatures are so high, a rack of thirty ATO bottles, or what you navy guys call JATO bottles, are attached; then the aircraft are put on fifteen-minute alert. If the klaxon horn sounds, they have to be ready to launch within fifteen minutes. Just to keep the crews on top of things there is a periodic unannounced Coco exercise."

"And . . ."

"The klaxon horn sounds and the Coco alert begins. Crews rush to their aircraft, start engines, and taxi to the main runway. Then, with full throttle, they start their takeoff, but without firing their ATO bottles. At the last minute, the control tower calls it all off, and the aircraft return to their pre-Coco positions."

"So the object is not only a fifteen-minute alert, but being called out any time, and they don't know if it is for real or not?"

"Exactly, they don't know if it is for real or not. It's the same in the U.S. with one third of each Bomber Wing, who are on fifteen-minute alert, ready to answer a Soviet strike on the way."

"That's a lot of airplanes with thermonuclear weapons on fifteen-minute alert."

"Yes, it is. Don't forget the planes on your aircraft carriers would get in on the show too."

"And the SAC intermediate range Thor and Jupiter missiles in Trieste and Turkey. But I wonder how many planes would actually get through to their targets?"

Logan replied, "Just before I came over here, I was talking to one of the instructors at the weapons school about that. He said he attended a conference where a speaker said the attrition rate would be about 68 percent because of Russian fighters, ground-to-air anti-aircraft missiles, and mechanical failures. The intermediate range Jupiter and Thor missiles probably wouldn't get off their launching pads. The Russians would take them out right away."

"I guess 32 percent would be more than enough to send Russia back to the Dark Ages."

"We would be right there with them. That's the deterrent, Burt."

The screen door slammed shut, drawing their attention to Carolyn carrying a tray with three long-stem goblets, vanilla ice cream in each one. Putting one goblet at each place setting, she warned, "Don't touch anything, there's more," and went back in the house. She returned with a bowl of previously frozen strawberries and said, "Please serve yourselves, gentlemen."

Logan pushed the bowl of strawberries over to Turner. Before taking any for himself he spooned out several servings onto Carolyn's vanilla ice cream. "Would you like more, Carolyn?"

"You are such a gentleman. No, that's fine."

A short time after they finished dessert, Turner said a warm good-bye to his friends and left for NAS Port Lyautey.

With Turner gone, Logan said, "Burt has really changed since I saw him last. He looks tired around the eyes, and he seems older. I think some unpleasant things may have happened to our friend."

"I think you are right. I was surprised how intense he became during the conversation. And I don't know anyone as interested in the Arab situation as he is. He is such a bright guy and so nice."

"He is. When he was talking about sending important military assets in harm's way, don't you know it was him and his team?"

"Of course it was. I feel sorry for him. I hope he is able to spend time with his girlfriend. I'm sure he couldn't talk about what he and his team are going through, though."

"Why talk about anything? There are a lot better things to do, actually."

"I'm sure they both understand that, Joe."

As Turner drove through the heat of the late afternoon, he thought about Joe and Carolyn. One of the things he really liked about Joe was he never knocked his ring (a trait common to graduates of the Naval Academy) or came across as a regular air force officer status vis-á-vis Turner, a lesser sort, being commissioned through the naval officer candidate school at Newport, Rhode Island, and a reserve naval officer. Joe was really smart and a nice guy all around. Carolyn, without doing it intentionally, made him remember his position on the social ladder. She was warm, intelligent, quick, and inordinately gracious. In some ways, she reminded him of Laura. He wondered if they all might spend some time together in the future.

It was overcast Tuesday morning, three weeks after the last detonation of ammunition at Sidi Slimane. Turner and his team were in the EOD shop putting on their uniforms after returning from their morning run and swim at Mehdiya Beach when the phone rang. Cole was closest and answered, "EOD shop, Petty Officer Cole speaking. Yes, sir. Yes, sir. Right away, sir." He hung up and said, "It was the exec, Mr. Turner. You are wanted in Commander Hawkins's office right now!"

"Did he say anything else?"

"No, sir."

Turner finished tying his shoes, stood up, took his hat from a nearby hook, and hurried out the door. When he got to the NOF administration building, he was walking down the hallway to the office complex and met Yeoman Fry coming the other way.

"What's going on?"

"The commander said to have you go right in, sir." He paused and smiled, then added, "It seems you are hopping a plane tomorrow." Before Turner could ask another question, Fry was on his way down the hall.

He went into the office and, as he went by his desk, took off his hat and dropped it in the half-full IN box as he passed. He knocked twice on the commander's door, waited, then was about to knock again.

"Come in!"

Turner opened the door and stepped inside. The exec was sitting in one of the two wooden armchairs in front of the commander's desk, reading from a file folder.

"Shut the door, Mr. Turner." The commander waved him to the second armchair.

Remembering Turner's and his team's early morning workouts at Mehdiya Beach, he asked, "What was it like at Mehdiya Beach this morning, Burt?"

Oh, this is going to be bad. "Overcast, surf was down quite a bit, sir, water temperature the usual—cold—and fish were jumping all over the place farther out. We don't see fish activity like that very often, sir."

Looking at his exec, he said, "Don, you and I should go out and do some surf fishing this afternoon."

The exec looked up. "That would be just fine with me, sir."

Turner knew this empty dialogue was preliminary to something unpleasant.

The commander got up from his desk, tucked his shirt in the back, and walked over to the window. He put both hands in his pockets and looked out over the cyclone fence to the Oued Sebou in the distance.

Then said, "Mr. Turner, we have just received word from COMNAVACTSMED that Operation Scorpion Fish is being reactivated."

Turner sat back in his chair, put his hand to his mouth, and uttered a barely audible, "Oh shit!"

The commander slowly turned and looked at the exec, who had looked up from the file folder on hearing Turner's comment. They both knew the expletive was well founded in Turner's experience with previous missions in support of Operation Scorpion Fish. They ignored his muted remark.

The commander continued, "Commander Peetz and I will be attending a background briefing tomorrow at COMNAVACTSMED. You will accompany us. The briefing will include the part we will play in support of the operation."

"Excuse me, sir. With all due respect, do you think this will be any different than previously?"

"Unlike our previous experience, naval intelligence at COMNAVACTSMED will be running the show. We have been informed the people assigned to the mission in support of Operation Scorpion Fish will be given background on the required mission and the reason for the necessity of the particular mission and will have the opportunity to comment on the plan. Evidently, Vice Admiral Horner has tightened up his rein on his chain of command after the political fallout from the Larache mission. That's all I can tell you right now."

"Sir, can I tell the team about this?

"You can tell your team you are going to Naples. That's all. The plane leaves for Naples at 0830 hours. The briefing is at 1500 hours. You can pick up your orders this afternoon."

"Aye, aye, sir."

The evening meal at the officers' mess was Chinese. The four officers sat at their usual table, close by the swinging door from which the stewards brought in servings. They all made up a joke—or jokes, in the case of Teipner—about the navy's understanding of what Chinese food was. The jokes seemed to be centered on how the navy continued to prepare Chinese food the same way they had attempted to prepare it on board U.S. Navy gunboats patrolling on the Yangtze Kiang River in China during the 1920s. When they finished the main dish, the fortune cookies came out.

"I can't believe this." Miller read, "'You will be in high places'! I'm an aviator. Of course I will be in high places."

Pierce read, "'Somebody waits for you.' Doesn't mean a thing."

"Of course it does, it's perfect. Somebody is really some body. You are a physician, a body is always waiting for you," Turner replied.

"Well done, Turner!" Miller replied.

Pierce laughed and said, "I guess that's true."

Turner read, "'She will see you soon.' I hope so!"

Finally, Teipner read, "'You will be first.' Always better than last! Let's go upstairs and drink some interesting wine."

They got up from the table and were on their way out of the dining area when Pierce said, "It would appear there are two nurses in distress or something. One of them is trying to get our attention."

It was Betty Armstrong, waving a napkin. Teipner said, "It's obvious they are in extremis. We are obligated to be of assistance."

They walked over to the table informally reserved for the NAS hospital nurses in the back corner of the dining area.

Folding her napkin Betty Armstrong said, "We have a proposition for you."

Miller couldn't contain himself. "Yes, yes, of course you have. It's about time, you know."

Betty Armstrong gave Miller a hard look and said, "It will never be time for what you are interested in, Mr. Robert Miller, airplane driver." She looked across at Mary Bionconi and said, "Binki, I don't know if we still want to ask them."

Turner said, "Binki, you do understand, Bob is not representative of our group. Please give us your proposition."

Teipner interrupted. "Since we have not spoken for quite a while, perhaps you might come over and enjoy an interesting wine we have newly obtained, and we could discuss your proposition?"

Binki glanced at Betty, then replied, "It would be better if you came to my room with your wine."

"What time?" Miller asked.

"Forty-five minutes should be just fine."

With great smiles, Miller, Teipner, and Turner lightly pushed and shoved at each other. Pierce, in a rather casual way, said, "It will be our pleasure."

Binki's room was somewhat larger than the usual BOQ room because of its location in the corner of the building at the end of the hallway. With her bed pushed against a wall, the room would just hold the couch and chairs from her and Betty's rooms. No one would have to sit on the floor.

After the men left, Binki and Betty talked to one of the stewards they had recently treated for a social disease acquired in town. Treatment for sexually transmitted diseases could lead to disciplinary measures if reported. He was pleased to find a way to give them a small amount of American cheddar, Monterey Jack, and Spanish Manchego cheese, and three freshly baked loaves of sourdough bread.

In Binki's room, the women cut the cheese into small cubes and put each kind on a midsized plate. The bread was cut in regular chunks and put on two larger plates, and the plates, with napkins from the officers' mess, were put on a brass meter tray.

Forty minutes later, the men showed up with the wine. Teipner sat on the couch next to Betty, and Turner sat next to Teipner. On the chairs, Miller, straining to be as unobtrusive as possible, sat next to Binki; Pierce sat at Binki's right. A recording of the Ray Coniff singers was playing on the Phillips hi-fi at low volume.

With everyone seated, Teipner opened with, "The wine we have brought has no labels. My copilot and I"—Miller winced at "copilot"—"bought this wine from a merchant in Oran. He let us know that if the Algerian insurgents caught him selling wine produced by the French, he would be killed. Without labels, he felt safe. We have sampled this wine and found it to be more than superb."

At this point, Pierce produced six wineglasses; Teipner filled them halfway.

Binki asked, "How did you find Oran?"

Miller answered, "We weren't allowed to go much beyond the airfield, but those we talked with said things were very bad. It appears both sides are finding more and more awful ways to kill each other, mostly by small arms fire from ambush on narrow streets and apartments. Booby traps and placed package bombs are common, and there have been a few car bomb explosions. The killing has become quite indiscriminate on both sides."

Binki replied, "Bruce Franklin was in for a tetanus booster today, and he told me the French Foreign Legion captured an insurgent by the name of Ben Bella a few weeks ago on the Algerian/Tunisian border—"

Pierce's relationship with Bernadette Mauritz allowed him to know about Ben Bella, which in turn allowed him to hold forth, "He is one of the most important individuals in the Algerian insurgency and very much responsible for the violent radical movement in the insurgency."

Ignoring the interruption, she continued, "Anyway, Bruce said they brought him to Rabat for trial, and a French lawyer was defending him. Last Sunday, the lawyer, on his way to mass at the local Catholic church, left his apartment building for his car in the parking lot. Arriving at his car, he looked up at the balcony, where his wife and daughter were waving good-bye. He waved back, opened the door, and got in the car. When he sat down on the seat, the car blew up, killing him."

Turner thought, *A pressure release device between the pavement and car floor probably set off the explosion. Very easily done.*

Betty quietly said, "That's so awful, and his wife and child saw it happen." Then she asked, "Why would he have a French lawyer, and who would want to kill him?"

Turner took a large chunk of bread and two cubes of Spanish Manchego to go with his "no name wine." Miller and Teipner poured themselves more wine, full to the top.

Pierce answered, "An Arab lawyer defending Ben Bella may be a problem. Even though it is a Moroccan court, most of the important judges here are still French. Besides, it might look better, internationally, if it was a French lawyer providing a strong defense for Ben Bella. Who would have wanted him killed? Why not have the French kill the lawyer as a warning to those who would appear to side with Arab insurgents?"

Turner thought, *Deuxiem Bureau.*

Teipner replied, "I guess that's possible, but with the French on the way out, unclassified reports say different groups led by communists, socialists, and Islamic radical fundamentalists are showing up. If that's true, there's going to be a real fight for political power between these guys. Ben Bella in prison is one less player in the fight. Kill the lawyer and a lesser lawyer would lose the case and Ben Bella goes to prison."

Turner replied, "It's a tribal society. The group that controls the largest number of tribes will control the government. Even then, there will be violent disharmony from time to time, with frequent government turnover."

Miller asked, "How do you know that?"

"During World War I, when the Turks were on the side of the Germans, the Brits sent T. E. Lawrence to Arabia—now Saudi Arabia—to organize the Arab tribes to fight the Turks. It wasn't easy, but he pulled it off, and the Arabs won. With that success, he tried to get the tribes to work together and form a national government. It didn't happen because of generations of uncompromising intertribal animosity. He found Arab tribes willing to join and fight outsiders but having real trouble joining together to form a national government. So the British moved into the vacuum, at least for a while."

Everyone except Pierce was staring at Turner. They were all products of American higher education, and they didn't know what he was talking about.

Pierce said, "You found *Seven Pillars of Wisdom* in our library, didn't you?"

"Matter of fact, I did."

Pierce smiled and replied, "I checked it out four of five months ago, and I agree with everything you just said."

At 0835 the following morning, the R-5D was in a banking turn as it climbed to cruising altitude on its way to Naples. Turner was sitting in a window seat over the wing, next to a seat conveniently unoccupied. Commanders Hawkins and Peetz were seated behind him, chatting. He took off his hat and coat, put the hat in his lap, folded the coat carefully, laid it on the unoccupied seat, and put the hat on top. He slid off his Wellington half boots, adjusted the seatback slightly, and stretched out. Just before drifting off to sleep, he heard Hawkins and Peetz beginning to talk about their early days in the navy.

Peetz didn't have an enlisted history like Hawkins; he entered the navy through the NROTC program at Brown University and spent most of his early years at sea, initially on an ocean-going minesweeper, then a destroyer in the Atlantic and an ammunition ship in the Pacific. Finally, he was serving his second tour of duty in the naval intelligence community.

Hawkins told Peetz he enlisted in the navy just before World War II; he was seventeen, fresh out of high school, and there were no jobs. Three weeks after Pearl Harbor, he was a torpedoman second class on the AS-9 submarine tender *Canopus* stationed in Manila Bay, the Philippines. On board the *Canopus*, he first met Don Owens, a bos'n mate third class who later became his executive officer at NOF.

Just after Christmas, the Japanese were attacking Manila Bay and its surroundings by land, sea, and air. All U.S. Navy ships in Manila Bay were given sailing orders to leave except the *Canopus*. It was considered too old and slow to save herself. Even though the crew fought bravely, a number of air attacks took the ship out of operation; then there was a direct hit. The crew scuttled the ship and went ashore to fight. Hawkins explained that he was the only one left who was an expert on submarine torpedo guidance systems and was selected, along with a few other enlisted men with special technical skills, to board the submarine *Seawolf* and be evacuated to Darwin, Australia. Owens was left behind and escaped to fight with the Philippine guerrillas against the Japanese. The rest of the crew was captured by the Japanese and died on the way to prison camps.

Turner had great respect for his CO and exec, and now hearing their stories, he developed enormous admiration. Unfortunately, he was unable to continue listening because of prior self-imposed sleep deprivation.

He woke up to, "Sir, sir, we're five minutes out from Naples," from one of the crewmen.

"OK, OK, thanks." He went to the head, filled the stainless steel washbasin, splashed water on his face, washed his hands, and dried off.

Looking in the mirror, he retied his tie, buttoned up his coat, and said, "You are so dashing."

As he left the head there was a strong, prolonged rumble indicating the lowering of the landing gear. Three minutes later, they were on the ground, taxiing to the military air terminal. It was 1315 hours.

After checking in at the military air terminal, the three officers were transported by van to the transient officers' quarters. They had just enough time to drop off their bags in their rooms and return to the van for transport to COMNAVACTSMED; it was 1428 hours. After going through security and obtaining temporary photo-security badges and passing two more security checks on two different floor levels, a marine carefully examined their photo-security badges, thanked them, and passed them through the entrance to the conference room.

Turner followed the two commanders in, then stood for a moment and looked around. It was a different conference room from the one he had been in months before. In the middle of the room was a highly polished wooden conference table with four armchairs on each side and one at each end. At the far end on the right side was the usual tripod easel covered with a black cloth. Next to the easel was a sizable wooden-framed blackboard on wheels. To his left was a large window bordered by heavy dark blue drapes pulled to the sides with a view over terra-cotta tiled roofs to a hillside of olive trees. At the far end of the conference room was a dark blue door matching the drapes. On the wall to his right was a large gilded frame painting of men-of-war exchanging cannon fire—probably the War of 1812 era. Covering the floor was an elaborate oriental rug he thought unremarkable.

He caught up with Hawkins and Peetz as they joined Captain Dillon, Lieutenant Colonel Bennett, and two other officers near the window.

Dillon smiled and said, "Ah, the Port Lyautey contingent. You of course know Lieutenant Colonel Bennett." They took turns shaking Bennett's hand. "And this is Commander Foster, Admiral Horner's intelligence officer, and Lieutenant Commander Alvarez from the aircraft carrier *Forrestal's* photoreconnaissance detachment." He saw Alvarez was wearing a set of gold wings. They shook hands with Foster and Alvarez. As conversation started, Turner took his place a step to the rear of the group and became invisible.

Dillon gave the group a few minutes, then looked at his watch and said, "Gentlemen, the admiral should be with us shortly. We should take our seats."

While they were seating themselves, Bennett inconspicuously put an envelope in Turner's hand and took a seat next to Capt Dillon. Without looking at the envelope, Turner put it in his coat pocket.

At precisely 1700 hours, Vice Admiral Erskin Horner entered the conference room, followed by his aide, who was carrying a folder. All officers stood to attention. The admiral went to the chair at the head of the table and sat down. The admiral's aide stood a respectful distance behind and to one side.

"Gentlemen, please sit down." Looking to his right, he asked, "Captain Dillon, have these officers been introduced to each other?"

"Yes, sir."

The admiral looked around the table, then back at Turner for a moment in slight recognition, then he began. "Gentlemen, this meeting is classified Secret. There is a substantial sea change going on in regard to how the insurgency, formerly benign to our presence, is now beginning to pose a demonstrated threat to NAS Port Lyautey and our Sixth Fleet conventional ammunition storage sites at the ports of Oran, Algeria, and Bizerte, Tunisia. The French military presence in Morocco is essentially at an end, and we are fortunate the constitutional monarchy is friendly to us. With the French military close to defeat in Algeria and Tunisia, the insurgents are in the process of forming new governments to take the place of the French colonial governments. The evolving new governments may not prove to be friendly to us. For example, we have learned a formerly unimportant radical Islamic fundamentalist group called Ikhwan-ul-Muslimeen has become very important in the politics of government formation, and the cleric leaders of this group are currently proselytizing the importance of forcefully removing all Americans from bases in Tunisia, Algeria, and Morocco."

He turned to his aide. "Let me have the pamphlet, Lieutenant."

The aide opened the folder, withdrew a folded light brown paper clipped to a single sheet, and passed it to the admiral.

"This is one of the pamphlets handed out two weeks ago at Mosques in Oran and Bizerte and a few days ago in Casablanca and Rabat. The translation is attached."

He passed the pamphlet and translation to Dillon, who read it and passed it on.

"As you can see, the message is couched in extremely inflammatory language, with an emphasis on American infidels being the 'new crusaders, in collusion with Jews.' In the last paragraph, there is a warning that a Muslim who works for or becomes a friend of an American is an apostate and must be 'taken from their houses and sent to hell.' We have a very large Arab population working on our North African bases, and if a sizable number heed this warning, it could be a real problem for us, let alone the Arabs' local economy. We have also been informed that militant mullahs in their madrasas, especially in Morocco and Algeria, are drilling their students to understand that American infidels are the new occupiers of Muslim countries, taking the place of the hated French."

When Turner received the pamphlet and read the translation, he was not surprised. The message was well grounded in the history of the Arab experience with the West that Hamid al-Karim had talked to him about.

"In Morocco, the Istiqual, a political group with ties to the communist party, is out to topple the throne of Mohammed V, and is well along in developing a movement to get us out of Port Lyautey and Sidi Yahia."

Turner studied the officers around the table. The only officer he noticed not giving rapt attention was the admiral's intelligence officer. He thought this officer was already well aware of what the admiral was saying.

"All of you know our mission is to support the Sixth Fleet and its activities in the Mediterranean. To do this, we have to protect our forward bases until it is time to leave, based on our schedule, not the schedule of the Istiqual party or a small group of Islamic fundamentalists.

"We have received orders from higher authority to do what we can to help protect the throne of Mohammed V. I am sure you all realize this isn't just because we are nice folks. It's because if he goes, we are gone.

"We have been informed that the king's son, Moulay Hassan II, has raised twenty thousand troops and is going after the Istiqual. A plan is being discussed for us to help the prince by collecting information on the transport of weapons along caravan routes heading north along the Moroccan/Algerian border. Most of the weapons are slated for use against the French military and the Organisation Armée Secrète, commonly known as the OAS. A significant number of these weapons are slated for the Istiqual and those supporting the Istiqual in Morocco.

"Where along the route the weapons for the Istiqual will be split off from the main caravan and sent west is conjecture. Best evidence we have is in the area of Bou Afra. Information on the routing of a weapons caravan and the location of border entry would be most valuable to Moulay Hassan's intelligence people in time for interdiction after entering Moroccan territory.

"Because of tight operational obligations, we are severely limited in our ability to undertake this task. For that reason, the mission is a one-shot deal for us. It is up to the Moroccan military to plan and deploy interdiction patrols at the newly identified location of weapon entry."

"Sir, why can't the Moroccans collect the information on caravans and find the border entry?" Peetz asked.

"The caravan routes often crisscross the Algerian/Moroccan border. If the Moroccan military is found to be on Algerian soil, it could lead to a dangerous confrontation. On the other hand, it is difficult for the Moroccans to patrol their side of the lengthy border with Algeria because of topography and lack of personnel and equipment.

"The proposed plan is to covertly insert the Port Lyautey SW/EOD team into the Western Sahara to meet what is left of a contingent of French Foreign Legionnaires and accompany them as they continue in their attempt to interdict Algerian insurgent weapon supply lines. The team's mission is to collect information in regard to the legionnaires' tactics in interdiction and to be the on-the-ground element of an aerial reconnaissance plan to find targets for the legionnaires.

"We will use our aerial reconnaissance assets from an aircraft carrier to collect intelligence on weapons transport, whether by camel, truck, or jackass, when and where delivered, and amount."

He bit his lower lip for a moment and added, "Some would say helping the French is a subterfuge at this point in time. You can see the conundrum here. Historically, we have been allied with the French in North Africa and elsewhere when it was in our national interests. It is now in our national interest to keep our forward bases in Morocco, Algeria and Tunisia. To that end, we must develop a good diplomatic relationship with the insurgents or nationalists as they form sovereign nations. Complicating this, as I already noted, is the situation of the Istiqual receiving weapons from the Algerian side of the border by way of the insurgents' weapon supply line from the south."

In a low voice, Commander Hawkins said, "Sir, it sounds like we are sailing through a mine field."

"I used that particular phrase at an earlier discussion. However, the mission as planned has been gamed out at the joint chiefs of staff level and at the Department of State. Commander Foster, would you give us the outcomes?"

"Yes, sir, the joint chiefs' analysts gave the mission an 86 percent chance of success, the Department of State analysts, 88 percent—if the mission is no longer than three weeks. Longer than three weeks, the mission has less than 37 percent and 41 percent chance, less than three weeks, 91 percent and 93 percent chance."

Addressing Foster, Commander Peetz asked, "What's 'success' based on?"

"The team not being discovered."

Turner thought, *Oh fuck!*

The admiral continued, "Commander Foster will now explain the background and proposed plan we intend to put into action. Commander Foster."

The admiral got up from his chair, the officers at the table rose to attention, and with his aide trailing him, he left the conference room. The officers sat back down and began to talk to each other. It was now obvious to Alvarez why the lieutenant junior grade was sitting at the table. He looked at Turner and said, "I'm Pete. I bet you wish you had chosen sea duty instead of a volunteer program."

"I'm Burt, Pete, and yes, sometimes I do wish I had gone to sea."

Foster said, "Gentlemen, let me begin. Operation Scorpion Fish has been resurrected. A number of months ago, the initial missions within Operation Scorpion Fish didn't work out so well. Some say it was because of miscalculation, and others say it was incompetence in concept leading to the useless endangerment of very valuable assets. I might say those responsible have been relieved of any activity associated with Operation Scorpion Fish."

His eyes were on Turner when he said this. Turner smiled weakly.

"We are determined not to underestimate the Istiqual and the more dangerous growing Islamic fundamentalist splinter group, or groups, such as the Ikhwan-ul-Muslimeen. The covert operation plan will be based on proven capabilities of those ordered to carry out the plan and those providing intelligence, logistical, and communication support."

He went to the nearby tripod and slipped off the black cloth cover, revealing a five-by-five chart of Morocco, Algeria, and Western Sahara. Taking a pointer from the sill at the bottom of the easel chart, he began.

"This is Zamora. It is about 240 miles northwest of Fort Tindouf, located here." He pointed to the lower right. "Zamora is geographically at the base of the section of the Anti-Atlas where the intermittent Oued Draa has given up most of its water before moving down and into the Hamada du Draa."

Aware there might be a question, he added, "*Hamada* means wind-stripped rock, a geological characteristic of the Western Sahara. There is enough soil to support a variety of xerophytes scattered about, however."

Turner wondered if anyone knew what a xerophyte was.

"When you see *Erg* on a chart, the word denotes a landscape like Hamada, but at lower elevation. In the Zamora area, there are caves and man-made tunnels called *faggaras* that were dug at an earlier time for water used in irrigation. The insurgents store weapons temporarily in the caves and faggaras and later send them along the Moroccan/Algerian border to

Bou Afra. Bou Afra is about 330 miles to the north. As the admiral said, Bou Afra is thought to be the final weapons storage and staging area before sending them on to northeastern Morocco—the Rif Mountains—and north to Oran and Algiers.

"About ten days ago a shipment of weapons was transported through Mengoub, thirty miles southwest of Bou Afra, from there to Kar es Souk, then northwest through the Middle Atlas to Azrou, Meknes, and ending at the small town of Sidi-Allal-el-Tazi, where it is known an Ikhwan-ul-Muslimeen cell located. The weapons delivered included twenty-eight Russian RPG-2s. Over the years, the French Army and Foreign Legion have not been able to interdict and shut down this weapons delivery system."

Commander Hawkins asked, "What makes this so difficult?"

Foster turned to Lieutenant Colonel Bennett. "Colonel Bennett?"

"Unfortunately, the caravan routes are quite varied, the weapon storage sites at Zamora and Bou Afra are well defended, and there is evidence the weapons are randomly shifted between caves and faggaras, making it difficult to know exactly where weapons are stored at any one time. Added to that are terrain restrictions which make it difficult or impossible to accurately bomb or rocket the storage positions.

"Fielding personnel is a problem. The French Army is currently withdrawing troops to France, and large numbers are deserting their regiments to join with the Pied Noir and OAS against the Arab insurgents. Additionally, large numbers of Foreign Legion troops have mutinied in support of the Pied Noir and joined the OAS. More are expected to do the same. We are unsure if the remaining legionnaires in the Sahara—at Fort Tindouf, for example—are siding with the Pied Noir and OAS or are Gaullists ready to follow orders and return home to France. For the moment, there is a small number of legionnaires in the Western Sahara, particularly along the Moroccan-Algerian border, committed to destroying weapons in transit and weapons at the storage sites."

"Can't the French use their Mistral aircraft at Port Lyautey for reconnaissance and interdiction?" asked Hawkins.

"The aircraft you speak of are now being ferried back to France, along with heavy equipment. When they were here, the Mistrals didn't have the range or ability to loiter over the caravan routes. For example, there are a large number of caravans traveling north and south, some with as many as sixty or seventy or more camels. Most of these caravans are legitimate. It is difficult to know from the air which caravans or groups of camels within a caravan are carrying weapons. Add to that the variety of caravan routes and nocturnal travel to avoid the heat of day."

Foster continued, "We have been working with senior legionnaire staff on this venture, and they are quite enthusiastic about a combined operation of this kind. They fully understand our ground element will only be interested in collecting information and assisting in the aerial reconnaissance mission. The team will not be joining the legionnaire group in combat."

Turner and Dillon looked at each other; they both knew the mission was very similar to the disastrous Rif Mountain mission, "to observe and learn only." The mission similarity was not wasted on Hawkins and Peetz.

Turner asked icily, "What are the rules of engagement, sir?"

Without hesitation, the intelligence officer replied, "Return fire if directly fired upon," and returned to discussion of the proposed plan.

Not joining in combat, but returning fire if fired on—is that an oxymoron?

"The Port Lyautey team would be flown to Fort Tindouf, where they would join up with a detachment of legionnaires. The combined group would deploy, by half-tracks and jeeps, northward to search for camel and/or truck caravans thought to be carrying weapons. This is a frequent undertaking by the Fort Tindouf Legionnaires. The legionnaire staff call this 'harassment and making mischief.' It would be more accurate to call it annihilation without remorse."

Dillon asked, "How far north will the navy team accompany the legionnaires?'

"All the way to Bou Afra."

"My gosh, that looks like a long way."

"Depending on the caravan route selection, the distance could be about 740 miles. We have been told a deployment of this type, which includes setting up ambush sites, chases etc., could be on the order of two to three weeks."

Peetz asked, "What if there is mechanical failure of a vehicle or vehicles? What if there are casualties? What about water? What if there are more hostiles than thought? Remember George Armstrong Custer and the Seventh Cavalry at Little Bighorn."

There was some laughter.

"Colonel Bennett?" Foster asked.

"The group will be self-sufficient and very well equipped for contingencies. The legionnaires have great experience dealing with vehicular problems in the desert. If the problem is insurmountable, the vehicle may be towed to one of the resupply outposts along the way or be abandoned. There will be a legionnaire medic deployed, very much experienced in combat trauma. A gallon a day of water per man is standard this time of year. Depending on the caravan route, there could be water available every

20 to 40 miles this time of year, but don't depend on it. As far as large numbers of hostiles, the legionnaires are heavily armed with jeeps and half-tracks mounted with .50-caliber machine guns and the best available personal automatic weapons. They will also have mortars and land mines. If overwhelmed, their strategy, based on long experience, is to run away and live to fight another day."

"Going back to Beau Geste days," added Hawkins.

Grunts and smiles—except for Turner.

Foster continued, "From here on out, the combined operation group will be called Scorpion One."

It dawned on Turner what Operation Scorpion Fish was about. *Scorpion was associated with the desert, and Fish . . . there it was—Larache, a sea mission.*

"An RF-8 photoreconnaissance aircraft from the aircraft carrier *Forrestal's* air group will make contact with Scorpion One every other day, beginning on the first day of deployment from Fort Tindouf. The time of day is still being considered. The RF-8 will be taking aerial photos of caravan positions and movements within a strip fifty miles on each side and one hundred miles ahead of Scorpion One's last reported position along a yet-to-be-decided-upon route running northeast from Fort Tindouf. The navy team will have radio equipment for communicating with the RF-8. The legionnaires will have their own radio equipment for communicating with Fort Tindouf and outposts to the northeast. They will not have the capability to communicate with the RF-8.

"The RF-8 will relay information to Scorpion One, advising location of possible targets prior to leaving the area. Aerial photos will be taken of these targets and again, later, if the target is attacked. Along with pre-and post-attack aerial photos, possible weapons storage sites, identified by Scorpion One will be photographed. When the aircraft returns to the *Forrestal*, all aerial photos will be processed and immediately interpreted, along with information from Scorpion One, sent to COMNAVACTSMED. Photo-interpretation information will also be communicated from the RF-8 to Scorpion One on subsequent flights. In the event photo-interpretation information reveals a possible danger or other information needing immediate attention, a return flight from Forrestal will be scheduled to alert Scorpion One."

"Sir, where and how will we be extracted?" asked Turner.

"The team will be extracted by air at an improvised airstrip near Bou Afra. The date and time will be based on your estimated time of arrival at Bou Afra. Are there any other questions?"

Hawkins asked, "With Mr. Turner's team ordered to the Western Sahara, what do we do about a replacement team? And when will Mr. Turner's team deploy?"

"Let me answer the last question first. We anticipate the final plan to be finished in about a week and the team to deploy about ten days later. In regard to a replacement team, there's a class graduating from the EOD School at Indian Head in two weeks. A special team will be made up from that class of an ensign and two enlisted men and a chief who is currently finishing a refresher course. This team is scheduled to arrive a few days before deployment of the Port Lyautey team. Are there any other questions?"

There were none.

"Finally, a week before the Port Lyautey team will be deployed, it will undergo a three-day desert survival training period, led by . . ." He took a card from his jacket pocket, looked at it, and said, "A Lieutenant Hammad Bajda of the Royal Moroccan Air Force. Date and time is yet to be determined. Tomorrow morning at 0830, Commander Hawkins and Commander Peetz will meet in this room for a briefing on the situation in Oran and Bizerte. You both will be able to catch the flight back to Port Lyautey at 1100. At 0800 tomorrow, Mr. Turner and Mr. Alvarez will have a briefing on radio equipment and communication procedures to be used on the mission. Mr. Alvarez will be the primary RF-8 driver for the mission. There'll be other pilots, but he will be responsible for planning the photorecon segment of the mission. Is there anything else?"

Turner answered, "Yes, sir. The name for the RF-8 is *Crusader*. Arabs of any political leaning would take offense if they knew this." He lightened up his comment by adding, "I hope Pete doesn't have a forced landing for some reason."

"Well, with Mr. Turner's philosophical comment and concern for Mr. Alvarez noted, we are adjourned."

As the others left the conference room, Turner remained seated. He took out the envelope and read:

> The colonel said the meeting would be over about five or so.
> I'll be waiting in the lobby. Your friend and admirer,
>
>   L. Brae.

He jammed the note in his pocket, got up, and left the room with some hurry.

Arriving in the lobby, he was surprised to see her standing and talking with Lieutenant Colonel Bennett, Commander Hawkins, Commander Peetz, and Lieutenant Commander Alvarez.

He thought Alvarez was standing rather close to Laura; his naval aviator wings seemed four or five times larger than they should be.

As he joined the group, Commander Hawkins said, "Mr. Turner, look who we found here. Do you remember Miss Brae?"

"Why, yes, sir." He extended his hand; she took it, held it a bit too long, and said, "Mr. Turner its been too long!"

His face immediately turned red, and he replied, a bit too strongly, "Yes, it has."

Before Turner joined them, they had been talking about Naples. They resumed complaining about heavy traffic and the difficulty of getting from place to place. Laura was quite expert, having visited Naples often, and was explaining how to find the nearest decent eating places and where there might be a bar with good jazz to go with Italian wine. A decision for the evening was made, and Alvarez turned to Laura Brae and asked, "Miss Brae, would you like to go to dinner this evening?"

Turner looked down at his shoes.

"Well, thank you, Pete Alvarez, but I have a dinner engagement already," she paused purposely, looked at Turner, and said, "with Mr. Turner. But thank you."

Turner looked up and smiled at her.

Hawkins and Peetz took notice of the exchange and looked knowingly at each other. Hawkins said, "Well, the commander and I have other fish to fry. Alvarez, you want to come along?"

"Yes, sir, I believe I will."

Hawkins added, "Well, good day to you two." And the three men started making their way through the crowded atrium.

Laura tugged on Turner's sleeve and quietly said, "Burt, tell Commander Hawkins you want Friday off."

"I can't do that!"

"Sure you can."

He caught up with the others just as they were approaching the double doors going out. Addressing Commander Hawkins, he asked, "Sir, could I speak with you for a moment?"

Hawkins stopped and waved the others on. "Yes, Mr. Turner, what is it?"

"Sir, it may be difficult for me to catch a flight out tomorrow afternoon, and—"

The commander interrupted and said, "Yes, it may be difficult for you catch a flight out tomorrow afternoon, and Friday is always chancy. You may end up in Rota, you do understand that?"

The commander was having his fun. Turner didn't realize his CO and exec thought him to be a very exceptional young officer, deserving of exceptional consideration, because of what they had asked of him these last seventeen months.

"Yes, sir, I could end up in Rota, and it could be difficult to get a seat to Port Lyautey over the weekend."

Looking over Turner's shoulder he said, "Well, I'm sure you will be busy here for a while. Just be sure you catch the flight on Monday."

"Aye, aye, sir!"

They exchanged salutes, and Hawkins joined Peetz and Alvarez leaving the building. Then he turned; standing behind him was Laura with a big smile.

"Were you standing there all the time?"

"Not all the time. Wasn't that nice of him? I think he likes you."

"He should, I'm a cool kind of guy."

She laughed and said, "Yes, you sure are. Let's go to dinner. I've got a rental car a couple of blocks away."

After picking up the car, an almost-new Fiat 600, Turner quickly became completely lost. He didn't know which direction Naples Bay was or the quite large building complex they just left. Fifteen minutes later, she turned into a narrow one-way street at speed. He expected to hear scraping of both sides of the little car against the antiquated buildings, but it didn't happen; she was a very skillful driver.

After a short run, the street opened to a piazza with a number of shops and two small restaurants somewhat opposite each other. She pulled over to restaurant on the right and shut off the engine. They looked at each other for a moment and fell into each other's arms. He took his right arm away and moved his hand down the side of her suit coat, then under and up to her breast. An old man and woman walking silently past smiled as they saw the proceedings.

Laura pushed away and said, "Its time to eat. We have plenty of time for this later."

"It seems I've heard that before."

They got out of the car, and as they walked to the restaurant, she glanced down at his trousers. "Do you have something in your pocket, or are you just glad to see me?"

"I think Mae West said something like that, but I am very glad to see you. We should sit down right away. This is embarrassing."

They went inside, took a seat next to the window, and almost immediately, a heavyset middle-aged woman was at their table with a very large smile and menus. After looking at his menu, he put it down and said, "I don't know what I'm looking at. What I had last time would be OK."

"Let's try something else." She scanned her menu, ordered for them both, and asked for a small bottle of Chianti. When the Chianti came, they sipped and then . . .

"Oh, I meant to tell you. Tomorrow morning, I'm the one giving the Oran and Bizerte briefing to Commander Hawkins and the others. I've scheduled it for about two hours."

"And at 0800, I'll be attending a briefing with Alvarez and I don't know who else," he answered.

"I know. Yours is about communications with the RF-8 on the mission in the Western Sahara."

"You know about that?"

"Yes, I do. I sit in with a couple of other analysts during mission planning. Our role is to give information when asked or offer advice when we think it's needed."

"You know about it, then?"

"Yes, pretty much. I think it has a high degree of risk. But I know the people doing the planning have excellent reputations and have the resources to make the plan credible. Admiral Horner is very aware that the mission could threaten our developing relationship with Arabs, who are going through the first political steps of nation building. They agreed that if any facet of the plan was the least bit questionable, emphasizing putting your team at unnecessary risk, the plan would be a no-go.

"I'm glad to hear the last part."

Topping off both glasses, she said, "Colonel Bennett warned me about having a relationship with you. He reminded me that I'm considered to be a well-thought-of professional, and I don't take avoidable risks. But I have fallen in love with you. The colonel suspects the depth of our relationship. Fortunately, he is the only one." She paused, then continued, "Another thing. I just found out my tour of duty here is over in three months. I'll probably be assigned to CIA Headquarters outside of Washington, at Langley."

He put both hands on the wineglass in front of him, swished the wine inside ever so gently, and said, "My tour of duty is up in five months. I don't know what they will do with me after Port Lyautey. I owe them a year more."

The mood was somber at best.

"Burt, when I first met you at the Rif Mountain debriefing, you were exhausted and very shaken. I was amazed how you were able to give such a remarkably lucid and detailed report on an extremely traumatic combat situation. I had never seen anything like it in my career. I knew you were special."

"Then there was the business picnic at Allal-el Tazi, Laura."

"That was a business meeting, OK? Even so, I found you very attractive." She smiled and reached over and put her hand on his and added, "The night you took me to the end of the wharf and we talked under the moonlight and stars, were you trying to make up with me?"

"No. I wanted to show you there was more about me than you may have thought."

She withdrew her hand from his. "Oh, I see . . ."

He reached over and took her hand. "Then we were in the car, after dinner in Naples."

"I guess the chemistry began to work for both of us."

"And here were are."

The waitress came back to their table with two enormous plates filled with a variety of food, followed by a young boy with a larger bottle of Chianti. After serving the food and wine, they smiled and quickly left the Americans.

Turner asked, "What is all this beautiful food?"

"You are having spaghetti alla bucaniera. It is sole and hake fillets skinned and chopped with shallots, crushed garlic, cider, a few other things, and, of course, spaghetti. I'm having saffron mussel tagliatelle. It's mussels, chopped onion, cloves, heavy cream, saffron powder, olive oil, egg yolk, and, of course, tagliatelle."

They ate slowly. Then he put both elbows on the table and began to push his food around his plate with his fork.

She asked, "Don't you like it?"

"I like it very much. It's just I have a lot to think about."

They finished dinner, the table was cleared, and coffee was ordered in place of dessert. He had been looking out the window for a while, when Laura, tired of the hiatus in conversation, said, "We have a place to stay just north of here."

He turned and said, "How did you manage that?"

"A girlfriend of mine and her husband have a small villa near Pozzuoli. I told her about us, and she said they were going to be in Tuscany this week and offered the place to us. I thought we could drive up after your briefing.

We could stay through tomorrow afternoon and until you have to leave for Port Lyautey on Monday, OK?"

He smiled and said, "That sounds wonderful."

He paid the bill, she left a sizeable tip, and they left the restaurant.

At 1100 the next day, Turner was waiting in the lounge in the transient officers' quarters when Laura came down with her luggage. He picked up his flight bag, they went to the registration desk, and after checking out, they went on to the parking lot and the Fiat 600.

Once out of the heavy traffic, Laura asked, "How did you sleep last night?"

"I almost got up and knocked on your door."

"I'm glad you didn't. If we were caught it, would have been terrible for both of us. Think about it."

"Yeah, I know."

On the way to the villa, they stopped at a small market and bought fresh bread, cheese, eggs, vegetables, fruit, sausage, a few fish filets, olive oil, and several bottles of wine. After trying a variety of olives, Turner made a selection that added up to more than they would ever eat in two and a half days.

Time seemed to slow as soon as they entered the villa. They found the kitchen, put the groceries away, and made a tour of the villa. The floor was travertine, the ceilings quite high, and the rooms quite spacious. A bathroom separated two bedrooms, and each bedroom opened onto a balcony also shared by the living room/dining area. The balcony looked over a precipitous drop to a small cove and out to the Tyrrhenian Sea.

After choosing one of the bedrooms, they left their bags on the bed, and Laura opened the folding glass doors and went out on the balcony. Turner followed her to the railing—with some hesitation. He looked down and thought, *That's a long way down. It's not like being in a plane, or the HUP. This is really scary.* He backed away a few feet.

Looking out to sea, she put her hand around his waist and said, "We are so lucky to be here and have each other." He hugged her, and began to unbutton her suit coat. She gently pushed him away, took his hand, and led him back to the bedroom. They hurriedly undressed each other and fell into bed.

Later, as they lay side by side, looking out to sea, they saw the shadows were lengthening over the cove below.

"I think we should get married before you leave for Washington, Laura."

"I think we should too."

That night, he had his first Mediterranean meal prepared by Laura; it was excellent. He had no idea she could cook, and when he asked her about her cooking skills, she explained, "My mother made it clear to me that someday I would be selecting food and cooking it for myself, and I might as well learn to do it properly."

Laura ran the kitchen, he did the dishes, pots, and pans, and the meals continued to be excellent. They didn't leave the villa for the next two and a half days, except to go down an infinite number of stairs to a very small beach. Their time together at Pozzuoli would be unforgettable.

Chapter 14

Kahlid ibn Zuweid, also known as Abu Diraa—"Father of the Shield"—was a seventy-one-year-old Algerian Arab and leader of the Ikhwan-ul-Muslimeen cell located at Sidi Allal el Tazi. He was quite thin, walked with a limp, and appeared to be just another old man in old clothes. For the last eight months, he had been living in one of a small group of mud-walled shanties belonging to a family who farmed a few hectares of oats and barley about a three and a half miles north of the U.S Air Force Strategic Air Command air base at Sidi Slimane.

He had been employed at the air base for almost six months and was assigned to one of the crews responsible for clearing weeds and brush from the area between the air base perimeter fence and security fence. Recently, his crew had been working where the security fence came very close to a number of large aircraft hangars at the northeast end of the twelve-thousand-foot air base runway. From this vantage point, he saw that the perimeter fence came within forty yards of the end of the runway, and beyond that, the distance of separation between the perimeter fence and the security fence increased quickly.

From time to time, when he was working with his rake and shovel, he would hear a klaxon horn that started a chain of events leading to the movement of a long line of aircraft from their parked position in front of the hangars to the runway for possible takeoff. However, since activation of the klaxon horn was random, it was difficult to know when it was going to sound. To try to solve the problem, he recorded in a small notebook with a calendar on the inside of the back cover the time of day, week, and month when the horn sounded. He recently added weather conditions. He kept the notebook and two pencils, one pencil more well-chewed than the other, in an inside pocket of his oversized threadbare French Army field jacket.

Adding weather conditions to the notebook, especially wind direction, was fortuitous. For the last few weeks, the exercise was most often between six and eight in the cool of morning and with a relatively stronger than usual wind from west of southwest. Additionally, he noted how long it took air base security to complete a perimeter fence patrol cycle in their jeeps.

Collecting and analyzing this information allowed the members of the Sidi Allal-al-Tazi cell to form a simple plan of attack against one or more airplanes taxiing by the closest point of approach to the perimeter fence.

Two days before the attack, Owdi ibn Zahwahiri and Ali al Kadar came to stay with ibn Zuweid; they brought with them their RPG-2 launchers and AK-47s.

The night before the attack, there was a heavy overcast helping to conceal Zahwahiri and Kadar as they carefully made their way to the section of fence where the attack was to take place. The fence was well lit by flood lights, but by staying low in the dry shrubbery outside the perimeter fence, they couldn't easily be seen. When they arrived at the perimeter fence, they carefully cut open and bent back a section of fence at ground level large enough to crawl through to get to the security fence. At the security fence, they cut a smaller opening the same way, and about two feet up from the ground. The opening would provide enough room for the mounted warhead of a rocket-propelled grenade launcher.

They closed the opening and, with very fine wire, carefully fastened the free sides of the cut fencing, making it almost impossible to see where the fence had been cut. Returning to the perimeter fence, they crawled back through, then repaired the opening as they did in the security fence, and left the area.

At first light the following day, they were in position for their attack on the expected aircraft.

At 0520, the klaxon horn sounded. Crews ran from the alert shack to twelve B-47 aircraft parked in the "cocked" position in front of the hangars. Each aircraft carried a thermonuclear weapon, full ammunition belts of 20 mm HEI (high explosive incendiary) rounds for the radar-controlled tail turret's twin cannons, a jettisonable "horse collar" carrying thirty assisted take-off (ATO) rockets, and full fuel tanks.

Engines were started, and the aircraft, in orchestrated unison, began a short forward movement, then a ninety-degree left turn, moving slowly, then more rapidly as they made their way up the taxiway parallel to the runway. At the end of the taxiway, two right turns put an aircraft in position on the runway for a minimum interval takeoff (MITO), allowing for the largest number of aircraft to become airborne in the least amount of time.

When the first of twelve aircraft reached takeoff position on the runway, the pilot advanced power to 100 percent, began the takeoff roll, but then immediately retarded the throttles and slowly began to taxi down the runway for return to its "cocked" position on the flight line. Each of the following aircraft would go through the same sequence.

The sixth aircraft was about a third of the way down the runway when the pilot retarded the throttles and the seventh turned onto the runway. No one could hear the cry "Allah Akbar! Allah Akbar!" accompanied by a flash of a rocket-propelled grenade launched toward the seventh aircraft. The rocket-propelled grenade went low and under the left wing of the aircraft, then sputtered out and skidded harmlessly to stop in the dirt some distance off the runway.

Then a second "Allah Akbar! Allah Akbar!" and flash. The second rocket propelled grenade was also low, but hit and shattered the casting of one of the two wheels of the rear-wheel assembly located at the fuselage centerline. What was left of the rear-wheel assembly could not continue to support the enormous weight of the aircraft. The fuselage buckled aft of the failed rear-wheel assembly, raising the nose and starting a fire. The three-man crew, with some difficulty, escaped through the aircraft entrance hatch just below the cockpit and dropped down to the runway. Knowing the aircraft fuel could explode at any moment, they ran to a ditch some distance away. They had just slid into the ditch when they heard a few of the ATO bottles and 20 mm cannon rounds go off.

Three minutes later, fire engines arrived and began to foam down the developing inferno. They fought the fire for ten minutes, then left the area. Ten minutes was the limit of time allotted for fire fighting involving an aircraft carrying explosives. It was unknown to science if nuclear weapons or thermonuclear weapons would produce a nuclear or thermonuclear yield under these conditions.

The plane from Naples was coming around on a new heading on its flight to NAS Port Lyautey. The slight banking caused Turner to stir from an unusually long nap, stretch, and look out the window next to his shoulder. Puffs of fair-weather cumulus clouds were everywhere. He was well rested after an idyllic stay of two and a half days with Laura. The relationship, which had been building for the last year, had matured to the point for them to come up for air and examine the reality of their situation. Their physical and intellectual attraction for each other was strong and, they thought, immutable. During their last afternoon at the villa, they tried to cover all the contingencies they could think of that could threaten their relationship, starting with time away from each other and ending with either one becoming a casualty of covert operations in the cold war. Their conclusion: proceed as before, accept inevitable uncertainty, and get on with it.

He turned away from the window and saw the co-pilot coming up the aisle purposely.

I wonder why he's looking at me?

The copilot stopped and leaned over the passenger next to Turner, "Burt, we need you up front."

"What's going on, Pete?"

He repeated, "We need you up front."

Turner excused himself as he stood up and tried not to step on the other passenger's toes and followed the copilot to the cockpit door. The copilot opened the door, allowing Turner in first, and followed, closing the door behind. The copilot gestured to the navigator at his table, and the navigator handed Turner a set of earphones and a microphone. After putting on the earphones, he heard the pilot in conversation with Lieutenant Commander Bello.

"Yes, sir, he just arrived."

"Put him on."

"This is Turner, sir."

"This is Commander Bello, Turner. We have an emergency situation at Sidi Slimane. There's a B-47 on fire on the runway. Firemen have knocked down the fire substantially, but the ten-minute limit for fighting an aircraft fire with the possibility of explosives on board is about up, and the fire fighters are preparing to retire from the scene."

It's loaded with one of their thermonuclear weapons.

"The commanding officer out there has asked us for assistance. Your team is waiting for you on the tarmac. Chief Williams has the HUP ready to go. Your airplane is scheduled to land in four minutes. Do you have any questions?"

Yeah, I have a lot of questions, but they are all classified. I'm sure he doesn't want to reveal anything to someone monitoring this frequency. I could ask if the guys brought my field clothes. I'd hate to go to work and ruin my blues.

"No, sir."

"Very well. Out."

The pilot came back on the intercom. "Hey, Burt, what's a frogman going to do out in the desert?"

Without thinking, he answered, "Make miracles happen."

Sitting in his seat, he didn't remember anything between handing the radio equipment back to the navigator and walking back to his seat. His hands were folded in his lap. He wasn't excited or apprehensive. It sounded like the people whom he understood to be in charge and in control of things weren't.

The R-5D landed and taxied to the terminal. When the cabin attendant unlatched the door, he was the first out, and on the way down boarding stairs, almost fell when his flight bag caught between his leg and the railing. He collected himself and ran down the flight line to the HUP. The HUP's rotors were turning slowly, and he could see Flint Williams through the Plexiglas at the controls. The exec, Yeoman Fry, Gallegos, and Cole were waiting for him near the HUP's entry hatch.

The exec yelled over noise, "They're expecting you, Turner. The air base CO and Lieutenant Colonel Knox will meet you at the control tower. You should know the air base is being evacuated of everyone except essential personnel. If you need anything, call us." He looked hard at Turner and added, "This is a maximum effort operation, Mr. Turner." He turned to Yeoman Fry. "Take Mr. Turner's flight bag. He won't be needing it."

Turner handed his flight bag over to Fry, then the exec and Fry walked away from the HUP, holding their hats as the rotor downwash increased. Gallegos and Cole climbed on board, followed by Turner. Williams, seeing all were on board, called out, "Secure your belts. Turner, get up here next to me where you belong."

Turner looked around and saw that Gallegos and Cole had accurately anticipated what gear they were going to need and had loaded it on board.

Cole, said, "Sir, we thought you might need these." He held up Turner's rough-side-out boondockers and socks, with one hand, and in his other hand, soiled field-clothes from Turner's locker in the EOD shop. By the time the HUP was at altitude, Turner had taken off his blue uniform, stowed it in a compartment in the back of the HUP, and had changed into his field clothes. Before going to the cockpit, he looked at Gallegos and Cole and said, "Look at the fine mess we are getting ourselves into!"

Gallegos replied, "It is only because we are the most capable, Olie."

They all laughed.

He went forward and unsteadily worked himself into the copilot's seat. He fastened the seat belt, put on the helmet, adjusted the microphone, and said, "Gosh, Chief, thanks for the ride."

"Well, Mr. Turner, when I found out it was you, I figured you would be up to something interesting again, so I bumped the pilot on duty, and here we are."

They were heading east and Williams said, "Look ahead, there must be hundreds of red tags coming down the road from Sidi Slimane." (Red tags were red license plates designating American military dependents attached to American military bases in Morocco.)

"My exec said they're evacuating everyone except essential personnel."

Approaching the air base, they could see the smoldering B-47 about a quarter of the way down the runway; five more B-47s were lined up behind. The last two in line were being jockeyed around by tow tugs to be towed back and parked on the flight line. A staff car, two jeeps, and a number of fire engines were parked near the control tower. Farther away, an ambulance with lights flashing was leaving the area.

Williams flew directly to the control tower, and as the HUP settled to the ground, three air force officers and an enlisted man were holding their hats against the downwash of the rotor blades. Williams shut down the engine, the team left the HUP and walked over to a group of extremely apprehensive men. Salutes were exchanged, and Turner introduced himself and his team. In turn, the senior officer, a colonel, replied, "I'm Colonel Sharp, the base executive officer. I'm in command. Our commanding officer is attending meetings at the Pentagon. This is Lieutenant Colonel Stephenson, our Operations officer and Lieutenant Colonel Knox, who runs our weapons division. Master Sergeant Powers is our fire chief."

Lieutenant Colonel Knox added, "We met before. Lieutenant Logan gave Lieutenant Turner a tour of our shop a while back."

Colonel Sharp ignored the connection. "We have a very serious situation here, Lieutenant. We have already lost an officer and an enlisted man and are now facing what may turn out to be catastrophic. The SAC EOD team at Nouasseur is out on a training exercise and is being called back. We don't have a runway, so they will have to be heloed in, which will further delay them. We need something to happen now, so let us know what you need."

Turner noticed the three air force officers were wearing wings. Colonel Sharp wore command pilot wings. The two others wore senior pilot wings. The pilots and master sergeant were obviously very experienced. They wore campaign ribbons signifying risks taken perilously and survival. This was new to them. They were unprepared and clearly in a situation beyond their control. The strain was obvious. Because of his training, Turner had a technical sense of the situation, but being young and inexperienced, had no sense of how terrible the situation was.

Colonel Sharp asked, "Lieutenant Colonel Knox, will you explain the situation?" He turned and stood, looking at the smoldering airplane about a half mile away.

"About a half hour ago, we were having a Coco Alert." Then Knox began to describe what the Strategic Air Command Coco alert was about. Turner interrupted to save time, and told him Lieutenant Logan had earlier explained the exercise.

"Well, good enough," Knox said and continued. "The aircraft was the seventh in line and experienced a casualty of the rear main wheel assembly causing, the tail to settle. The rear fuselage forward of the tail buckled just behind the horse collar containing thirty ATO bottles, fuel cells ruptured, and a fire started. The three-man crew had some trouble abandoning the aircraft, but they got out just before the fire crew closed with the aircraft and began to fight the fire. They fought the fire with some success until the obligatory ten-minute "safe" period for explosives on board was up, then pulled back to where you see them now. You can see from here there is a minor fire in the left wing tip and smoldering elsewhere."

Turner asked, "What do you have on board, sir?"

"An MK-36 Mod I thermonuclear weapon in the strike condition, a full load of 20 mm HEI in the rear turret, the ATO bottles, and a large amount of unburned fuel."

"When you say in the strike condition, you mean the plutonium capsule is ready for arming the weapon for thermonuclear explosion?" Turner asked.

"Yes."

Out of the corner of his eye, he could see Gallegos and Cole talking quietly about what they just heard.

Then Turner asked, "Is Lieutenant Logan nearby, sir?"

"Unfortunately, he was with the fire crew when they tried to move the front section of the fuselage off the runway. There was a flare-up. Joe and one of the fire crew were severely burned and taken to the base hospital."

He stepped back in shock, got a hold of himself, and asked, "Master Sergeant Powers, is there anything we should know about from your end?"

Master Sergeant Powers, deferring to Lieutenant Colonel Knox said, "Sir . . ."

Lieutenant Colonel Knox answered, "I was with Lieutenant Logan when they put him in the ambulance. Before losing consciousness, he said there could be a partial nuclear yield."

Cole pulled on Gallegos's shirtsleeve and quietly said, "You hear that, Chief?"

"Loud and clear, Petty Officer, loud and clear."

Turner asked, "Is there anything else, Master Sergeant?"

"Well, sir, it's just about what you can see from here. The fire started at the rear of the airplane and spread forward to the wings real quick. We were able to knock it down substantially, and as the lieutenant colonel said, the only fire is a small one in what remains of the left outer wing. The problem is, along with aluminum, there is a substantial amount of magnesium in the structure of the airplane. Because of the foam we put down and already-burned materials, the metal is pretty much insulated from the air right now. But the magnesium is still hot and, if exposed to air, oxygen will cause reignition and we will have an inferno. The 20 mm HEI and what's left of the ATO bottles will cook off again, and there is going to be hell to pay with that bomb."

"Thank you, Master Sergeant."

Colonel Sharp returned, looked at Turner intently, and added, "I want what's on board that aircraft rendered safe as quickly as possible. I want to emphasize we are not mission capable until that aircraft is bulldozed off the runway and the runway is made operational. We can't carry out our mission as part of the strategic response plan for this part of the world without that runway. Right now, we are out of business until that aircraft is bulldozed out of the way."

He paused, and in a slightly different tone, he added, "The base is yours, and we will do anything we can to help you." This all-encompassing statement, out of desperation, was not wasted on Turner.

He saluted and said, "We'll get our gear on and get started, sir."

Gallegos and Cole had already unloaded the "first out box" of equipment from the HUP and laid out three sets of protective clothing, including modified gas masks. The mask filter canisters offered some protection from smoke, but were of dubious protection against radioactive particles below a certain size. The team donned their protective clothing, took turns taping the seams, and slipped protective booties over their footwear. Turner picked up the AN/PDR-27 gamma radiation detector; turned it on, and made sure it was working properly.

"Well, let's have a look, gentlemen."

They pulled their masks over their heads, adjusted the straps, then pulled the hood of the protective clothing over the straps. After a final check of each other's protective clothing, they went out to the wreckage. Turner's adrenaline rush wasn't helping him as he tried to remember the bomb's electronic fusing system.

They stopped at the edge of the field of yellowish foam and looked at what was once an unusually beautiful aircraft. The vertical stabilizer, with its identification number 20242, and the midsection of the fuselage remained relatively intact.

They went into the field of foam and walked slowly around the aircraft. Under the wings, the six engines, with their nacelles burned away, were still attached to their pylon engine mounts. Near the tail were the twisted remains of the horse collar and ATO bottles.

In a voice muffled by his mask, Turner asked, "What do you think, guys?"

Cole answered, "I think we are not going to be able to keep this protective clothing on for very long. It's too hot, and we can't hear each other."

Gallegos answered, "You're right, but keep it on Cole. Have you any indication of radiation, sir?"

"Nothing so far. Let's go look at the left side again. I want to look at the fuselage under the trailing edge of the wing."

On the way, Gallegos stopped and looked at one of the engines. "Look at this." He slipped a turbine blade from its holding groove in the engine. "This is how heat resistant the turbine blades are—they still look like new."

They went around the twisted skeleton of the left wing and stopped about twenty feet from the foam-covered fuselage. There was an opening in the foam that could lead to the bomb bay.

Cole said, "Be careful over here. We have a few ATO bottles peeking out at us from under the foam."

Looking around, Turner asked Gallegos, "What do you think about pushing the tail section out of the way and dealing with the ATO bottles and ammunition before we do the bomb?"

"Well, sir, move anything, and we're probably going to have a fire. If we had the fire crew standing by ready to foam, we might be able to cut away what's left of the fuselage section overlaying the horse collar and the ATO bottles. Once the tail section is out of the way, we could deal with the ATO bottles. We really are taking a chance if we don't have fire crew standing by."

Cole had gone to look at the tail turret; returning, he pulled his hood back, pulled off his mask, and said, "The ammunition belts from the magazines are burned some. We just have to be careful."

Turner pulled his hood back and took off his mask. "We can't work out here with this stuff on. If you want to take your hoods and gas masks off, do it, but let's keep the protective clothing on as long as we can." Gallegos and Cole pulled their hoods back and took their masks off.

"What do you think we need for equipment, Chief?" He asked."

"We need a bulldozer, a cherry picker, and heavy-duty metal cutting equipment to begin with."

They took a last walk around the hulk and went back to the control tower. When they arrived Chief Williams was talking to Colonel Sharp; Colonel Sharp looked at Turner and said, "The chief informs us he just received word to return to the Naval Air Station."

Turner looked at Williams and said, "Have a nice ride back, Chief."

Williams gave Turner an uncharacteristic regulation "Aye, aye, sir," saluted, then climbed into the HUP. Turner didn't understand the gesture was given sincerely. Williams knew there was a good chance he wouldn't be seeing Turner and his team alive again.

As the HUP rose from the tarmac and swung to the west, Turner explained what the team's initial plan was and the equipment and fire personnel he would need. A nearby airman with a clipboard wrote down everything he said. Colonel Sharp turned to his Operations officer and said, "Give the lieutenant what he needs." Then, addressing the fire chief, he said, "Master Sergeant Powers, ask for volunteers for two fire trucks. I'll be in Operations."

The Operations officer and the airman with the clipboard walked over to a jeep where a junior officer was waiting. He spent a few minutes talking to the officer, who then picked up the handset of the jeep's radio and began to order up equipment.

Master Sergeant Powers had no trouble finding volunteers; they all wanted to go back in. He selected two trucks and crews, and after garbing up in protective clothing and masks, they were ready to go.

Lieutenant Colonel Knox and Turner talked for a few minutes, then Knox said, "Take my jeep, Lieutenant. The radio is tuned into the control tower. We'll be monitoring it."

The team loaded up the jeep and, with Gallegos at the wheel and the fire trucks in trail, they went to the site. As the incident progressed, there wouldn't be time to use the jeep's radio.

As agreed earlier, the fire trucks parked on the left side of the aircraft, about twenty yards out from the edge of the foam; Gallegos parked just inside the foam. When the team got out of the jeep, Turner said, "Chief, you and Cole to take a look at the wreckage covering the horse collar and ATO rockets. See if you will be able to disengage it from the tail section so the tail section can be pushed aside. While you do that, I'll check out the opening in the fuselage and see if there's access to the bomb."

Cole looked up and said, "The heavy equipment is rolling in."

A pickup truck, bulldozer, and cherry picker drove up and parked to the rear of the fire trucks. Gallegos and Cole went to the pickup and spoke to the driver; the driver called the other drivers over. The conversation was short; they quickly unloaded the pickup truck and, with the two other drivers wedged into the cab, drove away at high speed without looking back.

Gallegos and Cole went to the tail section, and Turner met with Master Sergeant Powers to explain what the team was going to do. Powers said he would back up Gallegos and Cole by repositioning the fire trucks in anticipation of a worst-case flare-up.

Turner returned to the jeep, picked up a small tool bag and the AN/PDR-27 radiation detector from the back seat, and made his way to the opening in the fuselage. After sweeping away the foam partially covering the opening, he was able to pull back a section of aluminum skin revealing the interior of the bomb bay. Then he put the AN/PDR-27 inside and checked for radiation; there was no indication of radiation. He looked inside and saw what was left of the tail of the bomb. The parachute retarding system was burned away and one of the four tail fins still remained.

He took the flashlight from his tool bag, turned it on, and worked his head and shoulders inside the opening as far as he could. He played the beam of light around and saw where the loom of detonator wires ran to the PETN detonators embedded in the explosive primary of the bomb.

The adrenaline rush had taken him this far, but now, having done its job, was subsiding and leaving in its wake a growing apprehension. He took several deep breaths, pulled himself together, and continued on. To the right of the primary, he found the arm-safe switch. He trained the beam of light on the window of the arm-safe switch; half of the window was green, half was red. *All we need right now is ambiguity.*

Raising the beam to the in-flight insertion device for the plutonium capsule, he felt a wave of panic. The plutonium capsule was partially inserted into the implosion sphere of the primary.

If fire reaches the weapon and the forty-eight PETN detonators set off the implosion sphere of the primary, maybe there could be a partial nuclear yield. Maybe when the forward fuselage twisted and split open, it may have caused some sort of electronic fault in the insertion mechanism. Sounds impossible.

He examined what he could of the weapon's fusing system, the X unit, and its connections, and knew there was no way he could tell if the fusing system's interior was heat damaged. He worked his way out of the confined space and walked over to where his men waited.

Cole asked, "Are we all going to disappear in a great mushroom cloud today, sir?"

He tried to keep from showing how worried he was, and explained what he saw—it was their turn to be worried.

Gallegos said, "A partially inserted plutonium capsule seems impossible."

Turner replied, "I can only think Joe saw what I just saw and that's why he said, 'partial nuclear yield.'"

Their training was the best in the world. Almost twelve months of highly technical instruction in the science of conventional, nuclear, and thermonuclear explosives, rendering safe procedures for all known types of weapons and weapon systems—placed, launched, or dropped, underwater or on land. Their training emphasized self-discipline in adhering to proven procedures, but not at the expense of resourcefulness when proven procedures were impossible.

Now this team was faced with a thermonuclear weapon problem compounded by other explosive ordnance that was also susceptible to ignition and explosion if exposed to fire. Weapon design scientists at Los Alamos Scientific Laboratory and Livermore Radiation Laboratory did not know how a thermonuclear or nuclear weapon would behave under the present circumstances. The team was presented with an opened-ended situation, which could result in their deaths and possibly the deaths of a great many others. Under the best of circumstances, they would not escape unharmed.

Turner summed it up. "Here are the possibilities: a thermonuclear yield in the megaton range, based on everything we know, is impossible. A nuclear yield, not likely. A partial nuclear yield with the primary exploding and the plutonium capsule partially inserted, who knows? Finally, an explosion of four hundred pounds of conventional explosive making up the primary if I make a mistake disconnecting something or a fire starts again—at least they will find our body parts, maybe."

They were in agreement with Turner on all counts.

Turner said, "If you two start taking apart the fuselage, I'll try to do something about the plutonium capsule, then disconnect some of the amphenol connections and disable any power sources that could give trouble."

After collecting the tools they might need, Gallegos and Cole went to the fuselage section where it was still partially connected and carefully cut through sheet metal and supporting structure. Ten minutes later, the tail section was free.

Cole got on the bulldozer, started it up, and under Gallegos's guidance, moved in position to push the tail section away. The fire trucks moved in closer to cover Cole. Gallegos climbed onto the cherry picker, started it, and moved it in position a short distance from the bulldozer. Cole edged closer to the tail section, contacted it with the bulldozer's blade, and began slowly pushing it away from the remaining wreckage of the fuselage.

When the tail section was about ten feet from its original position, there was a flash. As Master Sergeant Powers warned, previously unexposed hot magnesium met the air setting off an inferno. The bulldozer was caught in the center, and with the fire using up the available oxygen, its engine stalled. Cole stood up on the bulldozer's seat, screaming at Gallegos to get him out.

At the same time, Turner's attempt at extracting the plutonium capsule was proving unsuccessful. He tried several tools, and in final frustration, a small crowbar, also without success. A partial nuclear yield, although remote, was possible. He began unscrewing amphenol electronic connections he could reach when he heard Cole's scream and felt searing heat at his back. Forcing his way out of the opening in the fuselage, he snagged his protective clothing and was held fast. Trying to concentrate on freeing himself, he fumbled with the snag, then reached in a side pocket, pulled out his utility knife, and cut way the snag.

When he was in the open, he was horrified to see the bulldozer surrounded by fire and Cole standing on the bulldozer's seat. The firefighters were doing their best to knock down the fire as Gallegos began to move the cherry picker within range to lift Cole from the bulldozer. The chief came near enough to raise the small crane and drop a hook and cable to reach Cole. After two tries, Cole grabbed the hook, and Gallegos lifted and swung him out of immediate danger.

Turner yelled to the firefighters, "Get everyone the hell out of here. NOW!"

Several ATO bottles shot off, and 20 mm HEI canon rounds from the tail turret began to shoot off randomly.

Gallegos stopped the cherry picker at a relatively safe distance and jumped down as Cole dropped to the runway. Turner came by in the jeep, slowed, picked up his two men, then skidded around in the foam, straightened out, and followed the fire trucks away from the intensifying inferno.

The people at the control tower were watching the vehicles as they tried to escape the inferno when several ATO bottles fired; one landed in front of the lead fire truck and spun around.

When the team and fire fighters returned to the control tower, what was left of the aircraft was burning more intensely. The air force officers, Turner's team, and the fire fighters, had taken shelter behind the control tower as 20mm HEI canon rounds intermittently shot off. Gallegos looked at Turner and said, "If the bomb goes off with a partial nuclear yield, being here isn't going to do us much good, sir."

"If we were five miles away, it may not be much better," he replied.

Cole, brushing ash off his clothing, said, "Well, if the four hundred pounds of conventional explosive in the primary lights off, we are sure going to be close enough to know it."

As they waited for the worst to happen, Turner explained to the Operations officer, in detail, what he, Gallegos, and Cole had attempted to do, up to reignition of the fire, emphasizing the importance of the fire crew. Again, the airman with the clipboard was busy adding this information to Turner's initial assessment of the incident.

Thirty-five minutes later, all was quiet—there was nothing left to burn.

The group came around from the shelter of the control tower, and the Operations officer said, "It looks like it's all over."

Turner replied, "I'll take my men out and see if there is evidence of radiation or any unexploded ordnance. If everything looks OK, I think you can clear everything off the runway. Sorry about your bulldozer, sir."

The Operations officer replied, "Well, this will go down in the history books. No one expected something like this could happen, and no one expected we would get off so easy. Whatever you did when you were working on that weapon saved a lot of lives. We were very lucky. You and your team deserve a lot of thanks."

"I'm not sure I did much at all with the weapon. I do agree we were all very lucky."

Gallegos and Cole came by with the jeep, Turner got in, and they drove back out to the site. When they arrived, they slowly drove around the charred wreckage. Only the tail, with the aircraft's identification number 20242 scorched but still legible, was relatively intact.

When they got out of the jeep, Cole said, "Well, Chief, that really did it. I'm not sure there is enough left to take to a junkyard."

"I'm not sure a junkyard would want it, Cole."

Turner said, "If you and Cole check out what's left of the ATO bottles and twenty-millimeter rounds, I'll look over what's left of the bomb."

When he got to what was left of the bomb, he saw the primary was completely burned away, and the only thing recognizable was the extremely huge sausage-shaped secondary resting on what was left of the bomb's steel case. After experiencing intense heat, the secondary's uranium 238 was exfoliating like a boulder of granite. He put the AN/PDR-27 on the secondary and thought there might have been a slight flicker of the needle. He removed the instrument, looked around, and decided there was nothing more to see or do.

The AN/PDR-27 radiation detector was designed to detect radioactive gamma rays produced after a nuclear or thermonuclear explosion. The instrument was inappropriate for nuclear accidents with resultant burning of plutonium 239 and uranium 235 of the nuclear fission primary implosion sphere. Because of the lack of appropriate radiation detection equipment, an unfortunate series of events was to soon follow.

Gallegos and Cole found and stacked fourteen of what was left of the previous thirty ATO bottles and piled together a small number of 20 mm HEI canon rounds. The air force Nouasseur EOD team would deal with it. Cole picked up one of the 20 mm HEI rounds and pocketed it for a souvenir.

They met back at the jeep, and Turner radioed the control tower that the site was secure, and asked for a call to be put in to the naval station requesting helicopter transport for return of the team.

They took a last look around and began to get in the jeep when Gallegos said, "We have visitors."

Another jeep approached the site at great speed. Entering the field of foam, the driver, a major, slammed on the brakes, causing the jeep to slide out of control sideways and come to stop in a cloud of foam. The major jumped out, followed by a sergeant. The major yelled out, "Where's the cap? Were's the cap? Goddamn it, I signed off for it! Where is it?" He did this while trying to shake foam from his shoes and trouser legs.

Cole, in an aside, said, "That officer has some great dance steps, or maybe he has ants in his pants?"

Turner quietly answered, "Probably both."

Ignoring Turner and his men, the major, with the sergeant following in his wake, went to where the bomb bay had been. They looked at what was left of the bomb, then the major said something to the sergeant; they turned and looking carefully from side to side, slowly walked the short distance to the end of the runway, turned, and came back, repeating the exercise. They stopped for a moment, looked back up the runway, then walked over to the jeep where Turner and his men were standing. The navy men saluted the major, and without introducing himself, he attempted to return the salute but, overcome with an excessive sense of responsibility, demanded, "Where is the cap? I signed for it!"

Gallegos and Cole, trying not to be part of what they saw coming, stepped away from Turner.

"Ah, sir, I'm sure the capsule and uranium pit burned away with the explosive lenses of the primary."

"That, Lieutenant, is impossible. It has to be here some place. It has to be found. I'm not going to be court-martialed for losing it."

I bet he's going to say, "It must be here."

"It must be here!"

"Ah, sir, there were two fires. After the first, the capsule was probably still intact and in the retracted position in the AIFI. After the second, what was left is what you see now, the secondary of the bomb and nothing else."

Turner looked at Gallegos and Cole and said, "It's time to leave."

"I want your name and the names of your men!"

Turner gave his name and rank, and that of his men, saluted the major, and without further adieu, he and his men got in the jeep, with Turner at the wheel, and drove off. The last Turner saw of the major and the sergeant was when he looked back in the rearview mirror and saw the major facing the sergeant, waving his arms around, and the sergeant with hands on his hips, looking down at the major.

When they arrived at the control tower, Turner parked the jeep in the lengthening shade, and they unloaded their equipment. After packing the equipment back in the first out box, they were helping each other out of their protective clothing when Chief Gallegos said, "Mr. Turner, it looks like you and Petty Officer Cole had an accident."

They both looked down at the crotch of their pants. Cole said with a big grin, "I couldn't hold it til I got home. How about you, Mr. Turner?"

"I didn't know I did it," he said, sheepishly.

They had just finished stuffing their protective clothing in individual seabags, when the Operations officer and the airman with a clipboard came over.

"Lieutenant Turner, your ride will be here in about thirty minutes. I have your report up to your team's last reentry to the site. Let's finish it up."

The airman with the clipboard carefully copied down Turner's exceptionally detailed postincident report, including comments by Gallegos and Cole.

At the end of his report Turner added, "Oh, just before we left the site, a jeep drove up with a major and a sergeant. The major didn't give his name, but he was in a high state of concern about the plutonium capsule. He made it very clear he was responsible for the cap and, insisting it was intact, wanted to know where it was. I tried to explain I was sure the cap was in the AIFI initially, but the intense heat either melted it down with the aluminum and magnesium or burned up with the rest of the primary implosion sphere."

"Well, Major Cotter did sign off for the capsule in that weapon. He is the kind of officer that can be a bit obsessive, but, hell, that's what SAC's about.

I'm sure he will come around when the official investigation proves you right." He turned to the airman and said, "Peters, give the lieutenant his copies."

The airman had already separated out the copies, and after putting them in an envelope, gave the envelope to Turner.

The Operations officer said, "Here comes the food van. I'm sure you and your guys are hungry and thirsty. Lieutenant Colonel Knox ordered up sandwiches and drinks for you and the firemen."

The van pulled up close to the control tower. Two airmen got out and set up a table and laid out a variety of sandwiches, a coffee urn and mugs, and an urn of ice water and plastic cups.

Master Sergeant Powers held his men in check and motioned the navy team to go first in line. A few minutes later, a nonalcoholic picnic was in full swing.

A short time later, there was a distant *chump chump-chump*, signaling the arrival of their helicopter. The navy men shook hands all around, and as the HUP let down, the team could see Chief Williams at the controls. When he landed the HUP, he put his head out the side window and yelled out to Turner, "Your friends and neighbors are waiting for you at home. Get your gear on board!"

After loading and securing their gear, Turner was just climbing on board when Lieutenant Colonel Knox came down from the control tower and called out to Turner, "Wait one, Lieutenant!"

Turner dropped down from the HUP and met the air force Officer.

"Yes, sir, what's going on?"

"Lieutenant, we just got word Joe Logan died twenty minutes ago. I'm sorry."

Turner put his hands in his pockets and looked out at the remains of the world's first thermonuclear incident. Gallegos called from the cargo hatch of the HUP, "Come on, sir. We're leaving."

Knox touched Turner's shoulder and quietly said, "They are waiting for you, son."

Gallegos, knowing something was wrong, jumped down from the HUP and ran over to Turner. He took one look at Turner, then asked Lieutenant Colonel Knox, "Is anything wrong, sir?"

"Lieutenant Logan died a short time ago. He and Lieutenant Turner were friends."

Gallegos took Turner's arm and said, "We have to go now, sir."

Just before they got on board, Turner looked back and yelled above the sound of the engine, "What about Carolyn?"

"Carolyn was with him to the end."

Gallegos grabbed his hand, pulled him on board, and Chief Williams waved him to the cockpit. He stumbled his way to the copilot's seat, fastened his safety belt, and, with some trouble, put the helmet on. Through the earphones, he heard Williams say, "Had a rough day, huh, Mr. Turner? It isn't over yet. The CO of the air base, your boss, and others are very interested in hearing about your collaboration with the air force."

Hearing nothing in return, he looked over at Turner and saw a tear tracks going down his grimy cheek. At lift off, the team had been at Sidi Slimane for seven hours.

Chapter 15

When they landed, a sailor from NOF ran up to the HUP's open cargo hatch. "They want all of you up at the admin building. You're to meet with Captain Travis immediately. One of the yeomen is coming by with the commander's car."

Gallegos and Cole had just finished unloading their gear, and the bag holding Turner's blue uniform when Commander Hawkins's car pulled up with a screech. Yeoman Jenkins got out and yelled, "Where's Mr. Turner?"

Turner was still in the copilot's seat. Williams reached over and put his hand on Turner's shoulder. "Better get going, Mr. Turner." He didn't respond. "Burt, they are waiting for you."

Without saying a word, Turner took his helmet off, raised his right arm, and wiped his face with the sleeve. Then he pulled himself up and unsteadily made his way out through the cargo hatch. He walked over to the car, Gallegos opened the front passenger door, and Turner got in and slumped down in the seat. Gallegos closed the door, and he and Cole got in the back seat. Yeoman Jenkins put the car in gear and commented, "It smells like you guys just came from a very large barbeque." And then he drove off.

There was no reply.

Five minutes later, Yeoman Jenkins dropped the team off at the NAS administration building. Inside, the officer of the day was the same surly lieutenant junior grade who was officer of the day when Turner came back to give his report on the Sidi Yahia communications site bombing five months ago.

"Ah, Mr. Turner, I see you haven't developed a sense of pride in your appearance since we last met."

In an unthreatening tone, Turner replied, "I'm here at the request of the commanding officer of this base. Would you have one of your yeomen call and say we are on our way up, please?"

Ignoring his request, he answered, "I question your appearance, Mr. Turner, and if these are your men, I question theirs. As officer of the day, I represent Captain Travis. You and your men are out of uniform and quite filthy. Come back after you get squared away."

The two yeoman at desks a short distance from the back of the counter were looking on, one with his mouth wide open, the other with his elbows on his desk, hands holding his lowered head.

Gallegos and Cole looked at each other. Cole quietly said, "Oh boy, this is going to be very bad."

Not only were Turner and his men not in the uniform of the day, but they were grimy, sweaty, presenting a combination of odors, and very, very tired.

Displaying a lack of good sense, the OD continued, "I'm sure the captain will be glad to see you after you and your men deal with your appearance, and—"

"Look, you dumb fuck, call the captain's yeoman, and tell him we are on our way up!"

"But—"

"Don't say another word, you miserable piece of shit masquerading as a naval officer."

Seeing one of the yeomen picking up the phone, Turner said "Thank you" and, with his men in trail (with big smiles), went across the lobby and up the stairs.

Two pilots waiting for a plane were sitting on a bench on the other side of the lobby. Hearing the altercation, one said, "That was an interesting exchange."

The other added, "It would appear the OD may have exceeded his authority—"

"Or his common sense?"

"Yeah, and probably is regular navy."

On the second floor, they walked down the hallway to the open door of the captain's outer office. They went in and were greeted, with a smile, from the female yeoman first class.

"I just received word you and your men were on the way up. The captain said to show you right in when you arrived."

Cole and the yeoman exchanged a look that appeared to Gallegos to signal an unexpected familiarity. Turner knocked on the captain's door, heard a "Come in," and they went inside.

Standing near a table with the always-present coffee urn, cups, and saucers was Captain Travis; his exec, Commander Felix; Commander Hawkins;

Commander Peetz; and Major Larsen. A chief yeoman, with a tape recorder and steno pad, sat at the end of the conference table.

The captain saw the men come in, and ignoring their previously questioned appearance, he said, "Mr. Turner, why don't you and your men grab some coffee and sit down and tell us what happened."

The officers went to the conference table and sat down. Gallegos and Cole made themselves available to coffee and then sat next to Turner, who had denied himself of the same.

His pants were dry, but he wondered if he smelled of urine.

Captain Travis began, "This meeting is classified Secret—Restricted Data and the participants attending are here on a need-to-know basis. Are there any questions?"

There were none.

He continued, "I, along with Commanders Hawkins and Peetz, have been ordered to attend a meeting at 1400 tomorrow at the American embassy in Rabat. The meeting has been called to brief our ambassador on what is now being called the Sidi Slimane Incident. At 1600, he will meet with King Mohammed V and his advisors to explain what occurred at Sidi Slimane. Air force will take the lead on the ambassador's briefing. We will address the part this command played.

"What we understand so far is that shortly before noon, the acting CO at Sidi Slimane, Colonel Sharp, called us and said an aircraft carrying explosives was burning on the runway. He explained the nearest air force explosive ordnance disposal team was on a mission and had been called back, but would not be available on site for at least six or seven hours. He requested our SW/EOD team's assistance. For security reasons, in this case, explosives are a euphemism for also carrying a nuclear weapon. After meeting with Commander Hawkins, we agreed that the NOF SW/EOD team be immediately sent to Sidi Slimane." He looked at Turner, "Would you take it from there, Mr. Turner?"

Gallegos felt Turner was in no condition to give a detailed account of the incident. Cole felt whatever happened next was going to be embarrassing.

When the question was asked, Turner's preoccupation with the loss of Joe Logan fell away, and he proceeded to give an uninterrupted, detailed briefing that lasted forty-eight minutes. Gallegos and Cole were amazed at Turner's memory and riveting presentation.

Captain Travis commented, "Well, that was quite impressive." Looking around the table he asked, "Are there any questions?"

"Yes, sir."

"Go ahead Commander Hawkins."

"I want to congratulate you and your team for a difficult job. Well done."

The other officers demonstrated agreement.

He continued, "Do you have any further thoughts about the plutonium capsule that . . . let me see . . ." He looked at his notes and continued, "Major Cotter, deservingly, made such an issue about?"

Only Hawkins could have asked this question, he was the only one of the staff officers at the table having background in nuclear weapons.

"I feel strongly the capsule burned or melted or both and will not be found intact."

"Understanding you did not have radiation detection equipment other than the AN/PDR-27, which is unable to detect plutonium alpha emission, what is your best guess in regard to the extent of alpha contamination at the site?"

"If the cap melted, I think alpha radiation would be confined to the same area of the melted and resolidified metal of the bomb bay. If the cap burned, the downwind footprint of plutonium oxide might be a problem. I guess melting and burning could have occurred simultaneously. If alpha detection equipment becomes available, these possibilities could be narrowed down."

Captain Travis replied, "Gene, didn't you get word Los Alamos or Sandia was sending out a nuclear scientist with radiation detection equipment?"

Commander Hawkins replied, "Yes, sir, he will arrive day after tomorrow and will stay at our transient officers' quarters. He's bringing the latest radiation detection equipment for alpha, beta, and gamma and may be going to Sidi Slimane after he meets with us."

Commander Peetz asked, "You told us the cause of the accident was a problem with a rear-wheel assembly giving way."

"Yes, sir, that's how they explained it to us."

"Major Larsen and I have been very much involved in analyzing evidence of insurgent terrorism spilling over from Algeria, and we have been warned that Istiqual rebels may be a threat to our base. Did you get any indication from the air force people you worked with of a concern for possible terrorist activity?"

"No, sir."

Commander Hawkins asked, "Chief Gallegos, do you have any comments in regard to your team's action at Sidi Slimane?"

"Well, sir, other than being completely unprepared for dealing with a nuclear or thermonuclear weapon under the conditions we encountered, and not having the appropriate radiation detection equipment, I think we were very lucky. Indian Head will certainly use this incident as part of their nuclear weapons disposal curriculum in the future, and I am sure the teams in the field will be requesting alpha radiation survey equipment ASAP."

"And you, Petty Officer Cole?"

"Mr. Turner said it all very well, and I agree with the chief. I would say, though, that our protective clothing was totally inadequate. It was cumbersome, and we got overheated right away. The modified gas masks prevented us from communicating well, and we had to take them off to talk with each other and because of overheating. As the chief said, we were very lucky, but not only about the weapon not going off, but not getting beat up by the ATO rockets and 20 mm HEI canon rounds that Mr. Turner talked about."

Captain Travis commented, "Well, there were no casualties. I would say that in itself was pure luck."

Gallegos and Cole looked at Turner. Turner, with some effort, said, "I'm sorry, sir. I neglected to say there were two casualties. A first lieutenant by the name of Logan, Joe Logan, and an airman fire fighter. I don't know his name. Lieutenant Logan died of extensive burns, and I'm not sure if the airman died of his."

Commander Hawkins asked, "Is that the loading officer from the weapons division? Wasn't he a friend of yours?"

"Yes, sir, in both cases."

There was a murmur of voices and shuffling of feet.

"I'm very sorry, Burt."

"Commander Felix and Major Larsen, no questions?" Captain Travis asked.

There were no questions.

Captain Travis looked at Commander Hawkins and said, "I think it would be appropriate to take Mr. Turner with us tomorrow, don't you? Just in case?"

"Yes, sir, I think it would be wise."

"We are adjourned, gentlemen."

Turner got up and, not remembering where he was, said, "But my blues, my blues are wrinkled and dirty."

Hopefully, he was out of earshot; if he wasn't, his plaint was ignored.

As Turner and his men were going out, Commander Hawkins said, "Mr. Turner, ask the captain's yeoman to call Yeoman Fry. Tell him to pick you and your men up and come back for me in an hour."

"Aye, aye, sir."

After making the arrangements with the captain's yeoman, they left the captain's office complex, went downstairs, and were passing the reception counter. Out of the corner of his eye, Turner saw one of the yeomen standing at the counter, the other still at his desk. The self-important, troublesome OD was missing. The one standing gave a cheery "Good evening, sir," followed by the other's "Yes, sir. Have a good evening."

Turner gave a weak smile and replied, "Thank you, and goodnight to you both."

Cole nudged Gallegos.

When they were waiting on the lawn for their ride, Turner said, to no one in particular, "How the hell am I going to get my blues ready by tomorrow?"

Gallegos said, "We can take care of that, sir."

The staff car arrived and Yeoman Jenkins drove them up to the EOD shop, where they found their gear stacked next to the door—Turner's bag with his uniform was on top. They got out of the car, went up the four stairs, and Gallegos unlocked the door to the shop. Later, with the all gear stowed except the bag with Turner's uniform, which he carried, they returned to the staff car. Getting in, Gallegos said, "Jenkins, take Mr. Turner to the BOQ, you can let us off after."

On arrival at the BOQ, Turner got out and asked for the bag with his uniform.

Gallegos said, "Get some sleep, sir. We will take care of this." He added, "Driver, to the chiefs' club, *toute suite.*"

Turner went inside to the counter, rang for the steward, who came from behind him.

"Good evening, Mr. Turner."

He went around the counter and took Turner's room key from the pigeonhole. Seeing Turner drawn and grimy, as he handed the key over, he said, "It looks like you have been working pretty hard today, sir."

"It was a hard day, a very hard day."

"Good night, sir."

"Good night."

Walking down the hallway of the second floor, he passed Miller and Teipner's rooms. The rooms were closed and quiet. *Probably on a flight somewhere*, he thought. The door to Pierce's room was open, and Brahms's Symphony No. 1 was being played, at low volume, as he passed.

Pierce saw him and called out, "Is that you, Burt Turner?"

He kept walking.

"I say, is that you, Burt Turner?"

With some effort. he replied, "It is. Good night, Phil."

Pierce came to his door and said, "Turner, you must come in. I need to chat with you."

"I'm on my ass, Pierce." He walked on.

"It's about a coming visit of a representative from Los Alamos."

He stopped in his tracks and thought, *How could there be a connection between Phil Pierce, of all people, and Los Alamos?*

He turned around, walked back, and asked, "What's going on, Phil?"

"Come on in and shut the door, Burt."

Turner followed Pierce inside, shutting the door behind.

"Sit down, my friend."

Seeing Pierce wearing his professional face, Turner sat down on a small couch next to the Phillips hi-fi.

Pierce took an open bottle of red wine from his desk, refilled his glass, and filled another glass from a nearby shelf. Holding his glass, he reached over and put the other on a small wooden Moroccan table within reach of his bewildered guest. He sat down in an overstuffed red leather chair far too expensive for the usual resident of the BOQ, took a sip of wine, and said, "Without trying to instill guilt, I want you to know I have been waiting up for you."

"Why?"

"To inform you I am now your personal physician."

"What the fuck are you talking about?"

"About an hour ago, we received a message from Bethesda Naval Hospital saying they received a priority message from Los Alamos advising that you and your team may have been exposed to radiation."

How could anyone know this? How could Los Alamos know about the incident so fast? The air force at Sidi Slimane must have immediately reported an incident was occurring to SAC Headquarters in Omaha, and SAC notified Los Alamos. There was no nuclear yield. Why would they be concerned about radiation? Los Alamos must have gamed it out and come up with probabilities based on information sent to SAC Headquarters from Sidi Slimane. Oh shit . . . They must be thinking about alpha from the plutonium. The scientists won't be here with alpha survey equipment til day after tomorrow, and tomorrow is the meeting in Rabat.

Pierce had been talking to him; he hadn't been listening.

"I'm sorry. What did you say?"

"I said: Bethesda has directed me to collect urine from you and your team for seven days. Not one specimen a day, but all urine you produce in a twenty-four hour period. Each time you need to urinate, you will collect it in a gallon bottle. You are not expected to fill it, although the more urine the better. You and your men will turn the bottles in to me every morning, and I will give you another. Every other day, we will send what we have to Bethesda by air."

He paused for comment from Turner, who was too tired to comment.

Pierce continued, "Your bottle is over there." He pointed to the gallon glass bottle.

"Chief Gallegos and Petty Officer Cole were taken to the dispensary after you were dropped off here. Binki has the duty and will give them their bottles. She will tell them to get started tonight and meet in my office tomorrow morning at 0930."

"What do you think this is about, Phil?"

"I don't know what you and your men have gotten yourselves into, but this sounds like the preliminaries of an assay protocol for heavy-metal poisoning. Physiologically, a chelation process may occur if a heavy metal comes on board. The result can be detected in the urine. To make it simple, if a heavy metal enters the body, evidence of it being there may show up bonded to some other agent that may be on board naturally or artificially. The result of this phenomenon can be found in the urine. Have you been playing with a heavy metal that's radioactive, my good friend?"

"I can't tell you, Phil."

"Well, I'll just play along with Bethesda, unless I think my patients are being misinformed or mistreated."

They had a few sips of wine, then Pierce said, rather indifferently, "Commander Hawkins called just before you came in. He told me you may have trouble sleeping tonight but need to be at your best tomorrow."

He put his glass down, got up, and went to his desk, where he picked up an inch square paper envelope, opened it, and removed a small yellow pill. He then went to the room's small washbasin, took a glass from the shelf, filled it with water and, holding out the pill with one hand and the glass of water in the other, said,

"Take this now, and no questions, please."

Turner hesitated a bit, then did as he was told.

"Hopefully, you won't have to get up to pee before morning. If you do, make sure you go in the bottle. Any questions?"

Turner got up, picked up his bottle, and said, "No, I just want to hit the sack."

Pierce opened the door. On the way out Turner said, dully, "Thanks, Phil."

"Goodnight, Burt."

When he arrived in his room, he took off his sweat- and smoke-infused clothes, wrapped a towel around his waist, grabbed a bar of soap from the soap dish of the washbasin, and padded down the hallway to the shower room.

The shower room door was open, and clouds of steam were coming into the hallway. He went in, closed the door behind him, and made his way to the showers. Just before going in, he put his towel on one of the wall hooks, went around the corner, stepped over the tiled sill, and got under the first showerhead. Turning on the faucet, he looked around, and sitting on the tiled floor, farther down, were three junior officers he recognized as pilots from VQ2, the very secret electronic surveillance squadron. They were quite drunk. The one nearest was looking down between his knees at a large pool of vomit edging toward one of drains. The other two had their backs to the wall, one crying, the other consoling rather incoherently.

The pilot with his head between his knees looked up blearily and said, "Hey, Burt Turner, old man, how's your ass?" Before he could reply, the pilot said, "We lost another A3D. The fucking Russians came over the Turkish border and shot down Billy Murphy's plane. Jack Schakowski and a full crew were on board."

VQ2's mission was to fly from NAS Port Lyautey to the Turkish-Russian border and record Russian search radar and radio emissions.

"I'm sorry. That's really rotten, Larry."

"It's supposed to be a fucking cold war. Our guys and you and your guys, are being sent out to do shit we shouldn't be doing. You know that? If there was a fucking war, OK. But this is bullshit. You know that? Ninety-nine percent of everybody else is sitting on their asses. It ain't right. Flight pay and hazardous duty pay is so much shit! This isn't supposed to happen, man! Fucking rules of engagement don't mean shit!"

Turner could barely hear the pilot and didn't want to improve the situation. He finished, quickly left the pilots in mourning, and toweled off on the way back to his room. Inside, he lowered the shade and, after peeing in his bottle, put his shorts on, turned off the light, and fell into bed. Before he could think about the day, Dr. Pierce's yellow pill worked its magic, and he was asleep.

Two hours before landfall, the airplane to Paris was going down. The airplane hit the cold North Atlantic water and quickly went under with a full load of passengers trapped inside. Turner saw one of the emergency doors open over the wing. Joe was incapacitated and couldn't move. Turner struggled to get his friend to the opening. Not making progress, Joe said, "Burt, don't try to help me. Save yourself!" The water was closing about them.

A knock at Turner's door interrupted his dream. "Mr. Turner, sir. Mr. Turner, sir!"

He sat up with a jolt. "All right, all right!"

He almost fell as he got out of bed. He steadied himself, made his way to the door, and opened it. Standing in front of him was a steward, holding in one hand his freshly cleaned and pressed uniform and hat cover and in the other, his black shoes, polished to a high sheen.

"Good morning, Mr. Turner. A sailor from the chief's club just dropped this off at the front desk."

Bewildered, Turner took the uniform, hat, and shoes from the steward and asked, "How much was it?"

"He didn't say, sir, but there is a note pinned on the coat's lapel." The steward turned and walked away.

"Thank you, and thank you for bringing it up!"

Without looking back, the steward said, "No problem, sir."

He stood for a moment watching the usual commotion in the hallway as residents were on their way to the breakfast. He looked at his Rolex, it was 0705. He went back in, put his uniform, hat, and shoes in the closet and grabbed his damp towel and shaving gear. He was just going out when he remembered he was to pee in the bottle. He came back in, went to his bottle, did his part for the Bethesda Naval Hospital/Los Alamos National Laboratory research project, and went on to the showers.

Returning to his room clean and shaven, he put on his wash khaki uniform and went down to breakfast.

When he walked into the main room of the officers' mess, he saw Binki and her friends at their usual table on the far side. She noticed him and waved. He waved back and continued to walk down the aisle to his table. He took a seat across from Pierce, who was reading a four-day-old *New York Times* newspaper.

Seeing Turner over the top of the newspaper, he put it down and said, "Well, you certainly look well rested, Mr. Turner."

"Well, Dr. Pierce, what ever you gave me really put me away. I can't remember sleeping like that before."

"Better living through chemistry, Burt, better living through chemistry. Did you visit your bottle this morning?"

"I did. Do I have to take it to work?"

"If you are used to holding your urine over extended time, probably not. I would advise keeping it within range otherwise."

"Where are Miller and Teipner?"

"They flew some VIPs from Washington to Oran and Bizerte yesterday. They said they would probably be back this afternoon."

The steward came to the table and asked, "Dr. Pierce, what will you be having this morning?"

"I'll have the scrambled eggs and bacon, two slices of wheat toast, coffee, and orange juice. And how is your knee, Jason?"

"Much better, sir. I'll not be riding motorcycles for a while."

"I would hope not. You are lucky to have only a very bad bruise."

"And Mr. Turner?"

"I'll have two eggs on wheat toast, orange juice, a glass of your most excellent powdered Penguin Milk Concentrate and finish off with a cup of coffee. Thank you."

"Yes, sir."

During breakfast, Turner did his best to avoid asking further about what would happen if his urine and that of his men tested positive for something.

He and Pierce were just getting up to leave when Binki Bioconi came over. "Well, Burt, last night, I gave rather large urine collection bottles to Chief Gallegos and Petty Officer Cole."

"I bet that was interesting."

"Not really. The chief was stoic and quite cooperative, as expected, and Cole, embarrassed, to say the least, got into a monologue about how his privates may not work properly under procedures as advised. I didn't tell them anything except to collect their urine for seven days, and Dr. Pierce would talk to them this morning. You may get a call from them, Burt."

"I bet I will! Did they tell you anything about what they had been doing?"

"I didn't ask. They didn't volunteer anything."

Pierce said, "This whole thing is going to be very difficult if I am not allowed to know what's going on."

They walked out together and talked about the weather (it was getting cooler) and went their separate ways.

When Turner arrived in his room, he went directly to the closet and unpinned the note from his coat lapel and read,

> Mr. Turner, you owe a SCUBA lesson and ride on the AVR to Chief Steward Peabody.
>
> Respectfully, GMC Gallegos and AO1 Cole.

Chief Peabody was the man to know; he ran general services for the BOQ and officers' mess. Turner smiled and thought how remarkable his men were.

He was carrying his specimen bottle when he arrived at the NOF office complex. Smiling a little too broadly, Yeomen Fry greeted him. "Good morning, Mr. Turner."

Then Yeoman Jenkins, also with the same sort of smile, added his, "Yes, good morning, sir." The yeomen, being privy to all communication coming in and going out, knew exactly what was going on and, between themselves, called the SW/EOD team's undertaking Operation Aqua Yellow.

He went to his desk, took off his hat, and put it on his filing cabinet, put the urine bottle out of sight under the desk, and sat down. He looked at his IN box and sighed. Gearing himself up, he took a handful of papers from the stack, put them in chronological order, and was about to begin when Yeoman Fry came to his desk. "The commander wanted to see you when you came in, Mr. Turner."

Pointing to his stack of papers, he replied, "I have a week's work to catch up. If I go in there now, he's going to ask me to demonstrate the can-do spirit and give me things to add to this pile."

"Yours is not to reason why, yours is just to do or die, Mr. Turner." Fry walked back to his desk. At the other end of the office, Lieutenant Van Buren echoed, "Yours is just to do or die, Mr. Turner."

Ignoring the supply officer, he got up and, on the way to the commander's office, walked by the exec's open door. The exec was on the phone, a pencil in his hand, the other hand at his forehead, and with a stack of papers in front of him. At the commander's door, he knocked twice on the doorframe.

The commander glanced up from his work. "Yes, yes, come in, Burt."

He called me Burt again. He walked in and stood in front of the commander's desk. "Yeoman Fry said I was to see you, sir."

"Just a minute." He finished writing a paragraph on a yellow pad, put down his pencil, looked up, and said, "In regard to the meeting at the embassy this afternoon, I'll be riding with Commander Peetz in his car. You will go with us. We will leave NOF at 1245."

"Yes, sir." He turned to leave.

"Before you go. The recorded proceedings of yesterday evening's debriefing was immediately transcribed, sent, and received by the embassy in Rabat at 2200 hours last night, so the powers that be will be familiar with our part in the incident. Copies will have been made available to the naval attaché, Captain Andersen, and the air force attaché. Air force also sent proceedings of their debriefing last night, and copies will have been made available to both attachés.

"The proceedings are far too detailed for Commander Peetz and I to refer to at the meeting. I would like you to develop an outline of the incident by half-hour increments if you can. Rough it out, and give it to Yeoman Fry."

"Aye, aye, sir." The tone of his voice changed. "Captain Andersen will be there?"

"Yes, Mr. Turner, Captain Andersen will be there." He added, more quietly, "Let those of us who know about people like the captain deal with him. Be on your best behavior, young man."

He was about to leave the office when the commander said, "You were observed to have brought in your specimen bottle. Perhaps it would be best if you left it in the head."

"Yes, sir."

"That will be all, Mr. Turner."

Coming out of the commander's office, he saw Gallegos and Cole waiting at his desk. He went up to them and said, "Let's go to the conference room."

Leading them out of the office, they crossed the hall and went through the open door of the conference room. A seaman was sorting newly arrived mail on the floor. Turner said, "We need to use the conference room. Give us fifteen minutes. Shut the door on the way out, please."

"Yes, sir."

The seaman left, and they sat down at the conference table.

Turner looked sternly at Cole and said, "You don't have to put your dick in the bottle, OK?"

That broke the ice, and they laughed. For the next fifteen minutes, Turner told them of his conversation with Pierce. He answered their questions as well as he could and explained that nothing could be resolved until the scientist from Los Alamos came with his equipment. He also let them know that he would be accompanying Commander Hawkins and Commander Peetz of Fleet Intelligence Center to the meeting at the embassy in Rabat that afternoon. Finally, he thanked them profusely for dealing with his uniform problem, and he would comply with the debt to be paid. He sent them on to their appointment with Dr. Pierce.

It took over two hours to work up three variations and a final copy of the incident outline before he passed it to Yeoman Fry to smooth up and type for the commander's approval. The final product was classified Top Secret—Restricted Data. Two copies were made, one for Commander Hawkins, the other for Commander Peetz. When Commander Hawkins reviewed the finished product, he was moved to send a short memorandum.

> Mr. Turner, your outline is well done and will allow us to answer questions in ways helpful to the uninitiated.

> Commander Hawkins

He was pleased to receive the "attaboy" but he thought "helpful to the uninitiated" was a bit much. Then he realized the commander was referring to the "uninitiated" as those without a background in the technology of nuclear weapons. He reminded himself not to underestimate his CO.

He was able to leave NOF in enough time to change into blues and go to lunch in the officers' mess. When he came in, he saw Miller and Teipner were back and sitting with Pierce.

Taking his place at the table, he asked, "Where have you airedales been?"

"We had the pleasure of taking two State Department officials to Algiers and Tunis, Tunisia, and back," Teipner replied.

Miller added, "Another trip over the sands of the Sahara, the greatest beach in the whole world. We had the pleasure to skirt three sand storms. I must say, my copilot flew admirably."

"You jerk! You were my copilot on the way back!" Teipner replied.

Pierce looked at Turner and said, "Before you arrived, our aviator friends were telling of the current political situation in Algiers and Tunis."

The steward came to the table and took orders for the four. When the steward left, Turner asked, "Is there anything new going on?"

Teipner answered, "Three weeks ago, we knew things were coming apart for the French at home and in our part of the world. We know they have given up Morocco to try to hold on to Algeria and Tunisia. Well, now the French are really getting hammered by the Arabs big time. And the OAS, the Secret Army

Organization, has more French Army and Foreign Legion deserters joining with French civilians than ever. They want to stay in Algeria under their terms and are fighting both the Arabs and what's left of the French Army."

Turner asked, "What about Tunisia?"

Miller answered, "What's left of the French Army and Foreign Legion chased the Arab insurgents into Tunisia, and then, because they don't have enough men to seal the border, the insurgents came back over the border later and at different place. President De Gaulle accuses President Habib Bourguiba of harboring Algerian insurgents and not acting in good faith after France gave Tunisia independence two years ago. Habib Bourguiba says it is impossible for him and his tribal militias to seal the border and keep the Algerians out."

Turner asked, "And the French, they don't cross over and go after the insurgents because Tunisia is a sovereign state?"

"That, and they don't have the troops."

"I think that's what's happening on the Moroccan border too," Turner replied.

"The borders were artificially drawn up by Europeans based on mutual interests and in utter disregard for native tribal populations, which were nomadic for the most part. Colonies or protectorates were formed, and over time, the Europeans have been forced out or are being forced out, and in their place, new independent nations are formed. Just as in the Middle East: Lebanon, Syria, Arabia, Persia, Iraq, and Jordan," Pierce added.

Miller said, "If we occupied or colonized any of these countries, I wonder how we would do."

"Undoubtedly, the Arabs wouldn't tolerate us either for very long. I think the history of colonization/occupation, with security provided by military forces, isn't new. The Romans did the same thing," Pierce added.

Turner said, "But when the Romans came into North Africa, they let the natives become citizens of Rome, gave them the vote, and made the territories city states. I think this is the sort of thing the French attempted to do in Algeria, making it part of France."

Pierce replied, "Well, imperialism will become less and less cost-effective as native populations with leaders like Habib Bourguiba and Gamal Abdal Nasser forcefully retake, nationalize, and benefit from resources that were developed and held by French, British, and other Western powers."

"That's pretty heavy thinking, Dr. Lieutenant Pierce," Miller replied.

"Well, you can add to all this Christians being colonizers or occupiers of Muslim lands," Teipner replied.

Turner thought he had heard this all before from Laura and al Karim.

Miller changed the subject with, "What have you been doing, Burt. How was Naples?"

"Naples . . . the meeting at COMNAVACTSMED was formidable. Some of it resembled what we were just talking about. I can't say any more than that. Socially, it was wonderful though."

"You met Laura there, you rascal, didn't you? Teipner asked.

Turner's face turned bright red. "I did, and I learned about and enjoyed Mediterranean cooking."

After lunch, he was sitting at his desk, initialing, one by one, notices and memoranda, signifying he had read them, and putting them in his OUT box. Those he felt needed to be read again, he put in his HOLD box. Warrant Officer Fulkerson, as usual, made suggestions, recommendations, and did all the paperwork for running the mine shop. Turner would be giving him an Outstanding in every category of his annual report of fitness, as usual.

He heard a familiar voice talking to Yeoman Fry. He looked up and saw Lieutenant Bruce Franklin.

"Hey, Bruce, what are you doing here?"

"I am here to fetch you and Commander Hawkins for the ride to Rabat. Commander Peetz is waiting in the car."

"I was wondering who was going to drive. I thought it might be me."

Yeoman Fry said, "I'll call the commander and tell him you're here."

A few minutes later, the commander was on his way out of his office, giving Fry instructions for the exec, who was at lunch.

Seeing Franklin, the commander asked, "Well, are we ready to shove off, young man?"

"Yes, sir, we are ready to shove off."

Arriving at the car, Commander Hawkins motioned Turner to get in the front seat next to Franklin; he got in back with Commander Peetz.

On the way to Rabat, the two commanders were intensely studying Turner's incident outline, and the two junior officers involved themselves with inconsequential small talk. Then, in a more serious tone, Franklin said, "I read the transcript of your debriefing last night, Burt. That was quite an amazing adventure."

"It was a pretty damned awful mess."

"I understand two air force people were killed."

"One of them was a very good friend of mine," he replied quietly.

"I'm sorry, Burt. The transcript didn't suggest you knew anyone personally."

Franklin was distracted momentarily as a large intercity bus came up from the rear, overloaded with passengers inside, and with other passengers sitting perilously on the roof, holding baskets and bags. The driver honked twice and passed.

He continued, "You really did a good job at the debriefing. Your end of the matter is probably closed."

Lowering his voice, Turner replied, "I'm not sure about that. I think the worst is yet to come."

Franklin glanced in the rearview mirror at the two officers in the back seat, who continued to study their copies of the incident outline, lowered his voice, and asked, "In what way?"

"A scientist from Los Alamos is arriving sometime tomorrow with state-of-the-art radiation detection equipment. He could find something we don't know about. There might even be a political problem developing."

"What we know so far could turn out to be the tip of an iceberg?"

"Bruce, you know about the missions the team has been sent on. Each one was considered a success, but the consequences of every one—every damned one—were messy as hell. The consequences of this one could be far worse."

"Well, you guys are special. There is no record of an SW/EOD team ever stationed here or in the Med that has been tasked to do what you guys have been tasked to do. One wonders if the people sending you out not only understand the consequences of an unsuccessful mission but also understand there could be negative consequences accompanying a successful mission."

"My guys wonder, 'Why send us?'"

"You guys happen to be in the right place at the right time. It's all under the heading, Emergency Integrated Incremental Flexibility, or EIIF, found in the back pages of the Operation Scorpion Fish plan. Of course, Sidi Slimane wasn't part of Operation Scorpion Fish."

"Well, I hope not."

"But your upcoming trip to the Moroccan/Algerian border is."

"You know about that?"

"Hey, I'm Commander Peetz's right-hand man."

Approaching the usual traffic and people jam at the bridge between Sale and Rabat, he looked out his window and thought, *People here are simply trying to survive like everyone else. Most probably can't read or write, probably have never heard of a cold war or understand why we are here. They will never know what happened at Sidi Slimane.*

Franklin worked his way through traffic, crossed the bridge, then followed the river Bou Regreg east to Embassy Row and made a right turn into the driveway to the American embassy.

Before entering the embassy grounds, he stopped the car at a gate, where credentials were presented to Moroccan Army security guards, examined, and the car waved on to a second gate at the entrance to embassy grounds. Credentials were presented to U.S. marine guards, who, after examining them, used a nearby telephone to announce the arrival of the naval officers from Port Lyautey. Returning the credentials, the marine gave directions to visitors' parking adjacent to the main embassy building farther on.

Franklin drove to visitor parking and parked next to one of two U.S. Air Force staff cars. The naval officers disembarked, and Turner and Franklin followed Commanders Hawkins and Peetz into the main embassy building.

Stopping at a third security checkpoint, they again presented credentials, were given security badges, then assigned a marine security guard, who led them to the main conference room on the second floor. At the entrance to the conference room, a marine examined their security badges and each officer, according to seniority, entered. Turner was last.

Inside, he saw four air force officers sitting at a large most impressive polished oak conference table. Across from them, he was surprised to see Captain Dillon from COMNAVACTSMED. Commander Hawkins walked over and took the chair next to Dillon; Commander Peetz followed and sat down next to Hawkins. With the naval officers joining the air force officers, there remained eight chairs vacant at the end of the table.

Turner recognized Lieutenant Colonel Stephenson, Lieutenant Colonel Knox, and Major Cotter. Next to Stephenson and sitting directly across from Dillon was a colonel he hadn't seen before; he thought he might be the commanding officer of Sidi Slimane.

Franklin walked over to one of ten empty back chairs, parallel and a short distance from the conference table, and sat down.

Turner looked across the room and saw Lieutenant Colonel Bennett, standing alone, looking out a floor-to-ceiling window. He went over and saw a large circular lawn bordered by a broad band of beautiful flowers. In the center of the lawn was an impressive three-tiered water fountain with a bronze eagle perched on top.

"Do you have a view like this from your office, sir?"

Bennett turned, smiled, and said, "If there were headstones out there, it would be a marvelous cemetery, but no, my view is of an old red brick wall I can almost touch. How are you, Mr. Turner? You look rather worn."

"I'm fine, sir. I guess you are here about Sidi Slimane?"

"Well, as a matter of fact, I am. I was given a rather brief rundown of what happened before I left Paris. I thought you might be in the thick of it, and here you are."

He reached in his inside jacket pocket, pulled out a small white envelope, and gave it to Turner. Turner recognized the handwriting of his name, smiled, and put it in his jacket pocket.

"She says hello and would like to see you, but had to go to Egypt for something or other. I think we should take our seats."

Bennett walked over and sat down on the navy side of the table, two empty chairs below Commander Peetz. On the way to the back chairs, Turner passed near where the air force officers were sitting. Lieutenant Colonel Knox saw him and said, "Hello, Lieutenant Turner. I have something for you." He reached into a folder in front of him, searched around inside, withdrew a small pink envelope, and passed it over his shoulder to Turner.

"Ah . . . thank you, sir. It's good to see you again."

"You better find a seat. Maybe we might talk later."

"Yes, sir."

Major Cotter, sitting next to Knox, gave Turner a most unpleasant look. Turner with a smile, said, "It's good to see you again too, sir."

Cotter, with a grunt, ignored the courtesy.

Turner went on to the back chairs and sat down next to Franklin.

A few minutes later, a side door opened and Ambassador Ferrous J. Gates and two aides, all in carefully tailored, expensive dark suits, entered, followed by the air force attaché, a colonel, and the naval attaché, Captain Andersen—Turner's nemesis. The officers stood at attention as the ambassador, his aides, and the attachés went to the end of the conference table and sat down.

The ambassador was heavyset, about sixty, with flowing white hair. He was a Princeton classmate of the current speaker of the U.S. House of Representatives, who recommended him highly to Secretary of State Dulles, who, in turn, after vetting, suggested the appointment to the president. The ambassador was former CEO of an international construction firm that held the majority of construction contracts for overseas American military bases, which included three of the five in Morocco.

"Please be seated, gentlemen."

He took a pair of glasses from his handkerchief pocket, put them on, and held his hand out to his aide, who gave him a manila file.

He opened the file and read, "Thus, the duty of the Moroccan government is to put into action the resolution approved by the National Consultative

Assembly during its study for the foreign policy, and to realize the evacuation of the French troops and the cancellation of the American bases immediately and without delay. The danger of these bases was quite proved and clear, especially with the incident that happened when an American B-47 took fire at Sidi Slimane and was carrying an H bomb, as rumors said, something which spread fear among the people of the area that was threatened with full destruction."

He looked at the officers at the conference table, then folding back the page, he continued.

"To illustrate the permanent dangers that constituted these bases, here is what happened yesterday at the base of Sidi Slimane, near Kenitra, Port Lyautey. A bomber having caught fire, the fire was rapidly expanding. A siren alerted the families and civilians of the base to evacuate as rapidly as possible from the homes and offices. Two thousand cars, according to information journals, rapidly left the base, taking these American families far away. All this because we feared an explosion from an H bomb. Well, who alerted the civilian Moroccan people living in the area? Who would have taken care of them had the explosion really taken place? Why must the Moroccans serve as guinea pigs to these apprentice sorcerers?"

"Gentlemen, these are translations from this morning's *AL-RA-Al-AM* newspaper and the *PDI Weekly Democratic* newspaper. The Moroccan Communist Party's, *Espour* and the Istiqual Party *Al Alam* say much the same. The local radio stations are now exercising editorial vigor about the subject." He gave the newspapers back to the aide.

The officers at the table were stunned, the air force officers necessarily more than the navy officers. Franklin uttered a quiet "Oh shit" simultaneously with Turner's "Oh fuck." What Turner just heard made him think how naive he was when he considered the people in the streets of Sale as simple, uninformed, and never knowing what happened at Sidi Slimane.

Franklin leaned over and quietly said, "Lieutenant Colonel Bennett looks like the only one not surprised."

Turner replied quietly, "I think he always had the big picture and thought, eventually, something was going to happen—not necessarily a nuclear incident, but something big, outside the players' 'everything for the mission' orientation."

The ambassador continued, "As you have been informed, I will be meeting this afternoon with the king and his advisors in regard to the incident at Sidi Slimane. In preparation, we have carefully read the air force and navy debriefing reports. Other than a nuclear yield of some sort, I cannot imagine anything worse possibly happening as a guest of a country just emerging from colonization by a Western power. With that said, I have the following questions: First, how in hell can a rear-wheel casting fail on a B-47? Please tell me."

The colonel sitting next to Lieutenant Colonel Stephenson raised his hand slightly.

"Yes, Colonel Hogue?"

"Sir, as you know, I had the unfortunate experience of being at the Pentagon when the incident occurred. Fortunately, thanks to my staff officers and emergency personnel, and with help of navy personnel from the Naval Air Station at Port Lyautey, what could have been a far worse outcome was prevented.

"Now, the rear wheel casting. The Strategic Air Command has required the Boeing Airplane Company's designers and engineers to test extensively every part and combination of parts under all conditions that could be anticipated in the life of a B-47 airplane. Boeing continues to test, at the same high level, additional modifications for improvement of operational readiness and mission success of the airplane. Every B-47 accepted by SAC undergoes maintenance procedures far more exacting than maintenance procedures on other aircraft in the air force inventory. SAC maintenance personnel are the highest qualified in the air force and, like other SAC personnel, are frequently tested to assure they remain so.

"With that said, it is not impossible for a rear wheel casting to fail, but highly improbable. Boeing is sending out people to investigate the cause of the casting failure, but I hasten to add their work will be hindered by the effects of intensive heat on the rear-wheel assembly and what might be left of the wheel casting in point."

The ambassdor asked, "Colonel, has there ever been a situation where an aircraft carrying a nuclear or thermonuclear weapon in the strike condition crashed and/or burned? What I'm getting at is how nuclear safe, in relation to fire or aircraft crash, are our current nuclear weapons?"

"The scientific community has told us the weapons are inherently safe, and we tell our aircrews they are inherently safe. I would say this incident has proven the assertion to be true."

Turner sat up straight and looked as though he was going to stand up. Commander Hawkins was watching Turner, caught his eye, raised his hand up and down, and pointed a finger at Turner. Turner received the message and sat back in his chair.

"Colonel, I'm asking you, has an aircraft carrying a nuclear or thermonuclear weapon in the strike condition ever crashed and/or burned before?

"Beginning in 1950, there were a few incidents having to do with inadvertent drops, fires, and crashes. At no time was there a nuclear or thermonuclear yield, only detonation of conventional explosive, which was unremarkable." He paused, then added, "None of the incidents involved a weapon in the strike condition."

"So this is the first time a nuclear or thermonuclear weapon in the strike condition was in a fire or crash?"

"Yes, sir."

"In regard to the weapon's uranium and plutonium, should there be any concern of radiation aftereffects?"

"My best source in regard to your question is my nuclear security and safety officer, Major Cotter, sir."

The colonel looked toward Major Cotter. Cotter, obviously nervous, looked back at the colonel.

The colonel said, "Go ahead, Major."

"Well . . . there would be no concern for radiation levels of the uranium 238." He paused, looked at the colonel, and continued, "As to the plutonium 239, there would be no problem, if we could find the capsule."

Colonel Hogue and Lieutenant Colonels Stephenson and Knox gasped. Franklin whispered "Ohhh boy."

The ambassador glanced at his aide for a moment and pushed on, "It seems we have a conundrum." He reached his hand out to his aide; the aide gave him two thick files, each classified Top Secret. Holding one up in each hand, he continued, "Here we have two scenarios in regard to radiation. The air force scenario explains the plutonium capsule was intact and any radiation, alpha radiation, I believe . . ." He turned to his aide, who nodded his head in the affirmative, and continued, "Alpha radiation would be restricted to the immediate area of the plutonium capsule. The uranium of the secondary was essentially of no concern."

He handed the air force transcript back to his aide. "The navy scenario has a different point of view. The plutonium capsule melted and burned, with the possibility of alpha radiation particles being in the immediate vicinity or elsewhere undetermined. Because alpha radiation equipment was unavailable, there isn't a way to know the extent of alpha contamination. There is agreement about radiation from uranium within the air force report."

He looked at Captain Dillon, who glanced at Commander Hawkins.

Hawkins began, "We feel without alpha survey equipment we would be going down the road to misleading assumptions that could later be regrettable. I would like to add that in the most recent conferences I have attended at Los

Alamos and Sandia National laboratories, the scientific community has been careful to say they don't know if a nuclear or thermonuclear weapon in the strike condition would be nuclear yield safe in a fire or crash."

The air force colonel was wise not to pursue the commander's answer.

The naval attaché raised his hand, "Mr. Ambassador, I would like to ask a question of Major Cotter, sir."

"Go ahead, Captain Andersen."

"Major Cotter, I have heard plutonium alpha radiation can be stopped by a sheet of paper, but if inhaled or ingested, it is the most poisonous substance known to man. Is that true?"

"From what I understand, yes, I believe it is true, sir."

"If the plutonium capsule was removed from the automatic in-flight insertion mechanism, the AIFI, during initial rendering safe procedure, could a potential catastrophic area of contamination have been avoided?"

"Sir, a catastrophic area of contamination is not possible. The plutonium capsule is yet to be found. We will find it!" He paused, then continued breathlessly, "If the capsule falls into communist hands, it would be catastrophic. The ungodly communists are out to destroy our way of life and seek to dominate the civilized world. They are out to steal the hearts and minds of our young people. I can't think of anything worse than one of our plutonium capsules in their hands."

Franklin looked at Turner. Turner said, "I have heard someone else hallucinate along those lines."

The naval attaché continued, "Mr. Ambassador, the point I want to make is, an investigation must be made with respect to possible negligence demonstrated by the officer in charge of the navy special weapons/explosive ordnance disposal team that deployed to Sidi Slimane. I believe there is ample evidence about a gross error in his rendering safe procedure, which would account for loss of the plutonium capsule. The young officer involved has a history of incompetence and endangerment of others at great financial and political cost to the United States."

Everyone in the room was aghast except Major Cotter, who was thinking about other things.

The ambassador stood up and said, "OK, we're done here!" He left the room, followed by his aides and the air force attaché. The Sidi Slimane air force officers were quick to follow. Captain Andersen remained, making notes in a small notebook.

Dillon got up and walked over to Bennett, who stood looking at Andersen, sitting near the head of the conference table. He spoke to Bennett, and they both left the conference room. Then Andersen finished with his notebook, got up, and proceeded to the doorway.

Commanders Hawkins and Peetz were away from the conference table, talking quietly about what just occurred. Commander Hawkins glanced over and was disturbed to see Lieutenant Franklin grab Turner's arm as he made a move toward Andersen. Commander Hawkins walked over to Turner and quietly ordered, "Stop right there, young man. This is not your battle. Don't make me ashamed of you!"

Turner took a deep breath, relaxed a bit, and Franklin let go of Turner's arm.

Meanwhile, Lieutenant Colonel Bennett, in company with Captain Dillon, was waiting in the hallway.

Lieutenant Colonel Bennett asked, "Excuse me, sir, a moment please?"

"Yes, yes, what is it?"

"Captain Andersen, what in God's name was that all about?" The attaché stared at Bennett and didn't reply.

Then Captain Dillon said, "Captain, I want you to know as part of my report to Vice Admiral Horner, COMNAVACTSMED, I will include your unprofessional and out of place comment in regard to Mr. Turner. I am sure what I write will not be ignored by the admiral."

Lieutenant Colonel Bennett gave a hard look to Andersen and said, with utter disgust, "Let's get out of here, Captain Dillon."

They were well down the hallway when they heard, "You haven't seen the last of me! I have friends in high places!"

After diffusing what was leading to a catastrophic confrontation between Turner and the naval attaché, Commander Hawkins looked at Commander Peetz and said, "Well, Tom, the ambassador was easy on us. I'm sure air force upper echelons in Washington will be unfairly taking a lot of heat about the incident for a while."

"There is no easy way out of this. Unfortunately, I'm sure some heads will roll. Let's get outta here."

On the way to the car Turner thought: *Joe Logan and an airman were killed. No one said anything about this. Self-inflicted amnesia until international politics are dealt with?*

They were just north of Sale when Turner removed the envelopes from his jacket. He opened Laura's first.

My darling, I am on my way to an archeological conference in Alexandria as an observer. The conference has to do with Phoenician ports in Syria, Lebanon, and Egypt. I just found out I will be returning to the U.S. earlier than we thought. The way it looks, I will be leaving the museum in three weeks. Is there any way we can meet in Paris to finalize our plans before then?

Love, Laura

He opened the second envelope.

Burt, SAC is flying Joe back to Delaware tomorrow morning. I will accompany him. I am having his funeral and burial near my parent's home in Annapolis. Joe thought the world of you. He told me several times he had never met anyone like you. I guess I never had either. Two weeks before the incident, we found out I was pregnant, so I will always have a part of Joe. I will be living with my parents in Annapolis. If you are ever in the area, you are required to stop by. My dad's name is in the Annapolis phone book under Admiral Fletcher Smith, Ret.

Carolyn

He folded the notes and put them back in their envelopes and looked out the side window. *Why am I here and Joe's gone? It's so unfair. It's all wrong. Someone said that God's dead. Is there a God?*

It was almost midnight when the lieutenant junior grade from Operations drove up in a staff car and parked a short distance from the visitor's entry to the NAS air terminal. The VR24 R5-D from Paris taxied in, came to a stop, and the cockpit crew finished shutting down the aircraft's four engines. As the last propeller stopped windmilling, two ground crewmen pushed air stairs to the passengers' hatch, and at the same time, an air crewman from inside swung open and locked the hatch door in place.

The first passenger disembarking was a disheveled civilian. Hanging from a shoulder strap on his right side was an aluminum container about the size of a breadbox; he carried a leather suitcase on his left. The passenger was the expected scientist, Dr. Timothy Rowen (PhD, nuclear physics, University of California, Berkeley, 1950) from the Theoretical Design Division, Los Alamos National Laboratory.

Stepping down the last stair onto the tarmac, he tripped and almost fell. The ground crewman stationed at the bottom of the airstairs for just such an event steadied him and asked, "A little too much food and drink in Paris, sir?"

The scientist was showing the effect of flights from Albuquerque to Port Lyautey lasting almost twenty-six hours. Adjusting the shoulder strap, he answered, "I didn't have the pleasure, thanks."

The lieutenant junior grade came up and introduced himself. "I'm Lieutenant JG Thompson from Naval Air Station operations, sir. Are you Dr. Rowen?"

He glanced at the wings of gold on Thompson's jacket and replied, "Yes, I am."

"Captain Travis, the Naval Air Station CO, asked me to meet your plane and transport you to the transient officers' quarters. I'll take your suitcase, sir."

"Thank you."

When they got to the car, Thompson put the suitcase in the backseat. Dr. Rowen preferred to hold on to the aluminum container. As they were driving away, Dr. Rowen saw the other passengers from the plane, officers, enlisted men, and a few in civilian clothes, walking toward three battleship gray school buses parked between the terminal and the control tower.

"How far is it to transient officers' quarters?"

"About five minutes, sir. We have you all checked in."

"Can you give me some idea of when and where I will be meeting folks?"

"Tomorrow morning, one of the stewards will wake you at 0645. Breakfast begins serving at 0600. I'll pick you up at 0815. You are scheduled to meet with Captain Travis and his staff at 0830."

He replied wearily, "Well, that's expeditious."

When they arrived at the transient officers' quarters, Thompson assisted Dr. Rowen in picking up his room key and escorting him to one of three VIP suites on the second floor. Then he unlocked the door to the suite and handed Dr. Rowen the key.

"Here you are, sir. In the event you need anything at all, there's a phone in your room, and you can call one of the stewards at the reception desk. If it's associated with your mission here, have them call me. They have my number. If need be, I can be here in fifteen minutes. I have been assigned to you for the next twenty-four hours." He smiled and added, "I will continue to be expeditious, sir."

When the duty officer handed over the scientist's leather suitcase, he also gave him a manila envelope bordered in red and stamped, on front and back, in red, SECRET—RESTRICTED DATA.

"Sir, I was told to give you this."

Dr. Rowen looked at the envelope and said, "How nice, thank you." And then he went into his room and shut the door.

He smelled coffee, looked around, and on a low coffee table in front of a lounge was a silver service coffee pot, sugar bowl, and creamer on a silver tray and a ceramic coffee cup (blue anchor on its side) and saucer next to the tray. He dropped the suitcase and put the aluminum container on the desk near the closet. After taking off his shoes and his trousers, he went over to the lounge with the classified envelope and sat down. He closed his eyes and rested a few minutes, then reached over and poured himself a cup of coffee. It was surprisingly hot. He added cream, sat back, unclasped the envelope, and withdrew Turner's incident outline clipped to an abbreviated transcript of the navy debriefing. With the cup of coffee in one hand and Turner's incident outline in the other, he began a long read.

At 0815 the next morning, Turner and Franklin were sitting across from each other at one end of the conference table in Captain Travis's office. Captain Travis was at the head of the conference table. On his right was the captain's exec, Commander Felix. Next to Felix was Captain Dillon, then Lieutenant Colonel Bennett and Dr. Lieutenant Pierce. On the captain's left was an empty chair, saved for the scientist from Los Alamos, then Commanders Hawkins and Peetz. They were all drinking coffee and chatting, with the exception of Turner and Franklin, who knew they were out of place in the group. Dr. Pierce didn't necessarily ignore Turner, but was preoccupied with the aches and pains of Captain Travis (prostatitis) and Commander Peetz (recurrent gastric reflux).

At 0825, the door opened, and Dr. Rowen entered the room. The shoulder strap attached to the aluminum container was wrapped around his right hand, with the container dangling next to his leg; in his left hand was a thin black briefcase.

He was wearing a royal blue sweatshirt with CAL in gold letters on the front, Levis, and Mexican sandals over white athletic socks. Turner and Franklin smiled at his attire; the other officers acted as though they didn't notice. He was about six feet tall, looked quite athletic, and made a statement with his long brown hair reaching almost to the collar of his sweatshirt. The officers stood up in greeting; Captain Travis made introductions and invited the scientist to sit next to him.

Captain Travis began, "Dr. Rowen, we know your journey was tedious, long, and exhausting. Please understand we will do everything in our power to help in your inquiry while you are with us."

"Thank you, Captain Travis. Before I left Los Alamos, people from State Department and the Central Intelligence Agency talked to a few of us about what they knew of the incident. It wasn't much. However, thanks to Dr. Pierce's quick response to our request for urine samples, I was able to acquire the results of the team's initial urine analysis before leaving for Port Lyautey. With the urine analysis, coupled with the very informative incident outline and abbreviated proceedings of the navy debriefing, I have been able to come up with a number of assumptions."

Franklin leaned across the table and quietly said, "Maybe Commander Hawkins and Commander Peetz didn't need the outline in Rabat, but the outline is getting exercised, old man."

"To begin with, the incident was a very noble experiment. No one knew how a nuclear weapon in the so-called strike condition, might behave if involved in a catastrophic situation such as this. Some thought a partial nuclear yield would occur. Some thought the PETN detonators would set off the Composition B and Baratol explosive lenses of the primary, but because of the asymmetric explosion wave, no nuclear yield could occur. Some of my more peculiar colleagues used the word *Armageddon*."

He reached down and brought up his briefcase, opened it, and withdrew two pages stapled together. "Gentlemen, the probability of plutonium contamination as a result of the incident, as reflected in the outline and abbreviated debriefing, is no longer a probability, but proven certain by the initial urine analysis."

He looked at the first page and said, "I'll summarize: Lieutenant JG Burt Turner has a third of a lifetime body burden of plutonium 239. Chief Gunner's Mate Manuel Gallegos has two-thirds of a lifetime body burden, and First Class Aviation Ordnanceman Jack Cole has a maximum allowed lifetime body burden."

Turner experienced a wave of panic.

"Most of us know how extremely hazardous plutonium can be if it enters the body. It's a bone seeker, and once in bone, continues to produce alpha radiation, having serious consequences on blood-forming tissue. In the team's case, having a lifetime body burden or less is somewhat worrisome, but would be far more so if they receive additional radiation in some sort of future event. At the present time, we feel there is an exponential increase in blood-forming tissue disease, such as leukemia, with additional exposure to plutonium.

"There is no doubt the SW/EOD team picked up the plutonium through inhalation and/or ingestion. In reading the outline and the abbreviated debriefing, it was painfully obvious the lack of alpha survey equipment indicating plutonium 239 at the incident site put the team at disadvantage and endangerment that could have been prevented."

He looked at Turner, "Were you and your team wearing protective clothing?"

"Protective clothing at all times, and modified gas masks only at first. The heat was intense, and we could not communicate with the masks on."

"Did you perchance ingest anything at the scene?"

He thought for a minute, then replied, "Air force brought sandwiches, coffee, and ice water to the command center. The center was about two hundred yards from the scene. We did eat what was offered."

"To sum up, I believe the highly radioactive plutonium capsule housed in the AIFI burned and released alpha contamination. I agree, the radiation detection equipment available to the team, the AN/PDR-27, was useless during the course of attempting rendering safe procedures.

"Obviously, the teams were not issued alpha survey equipment because those that ultimately make decisions about such things did not understand an incident such as this would happen. Their concern was for aftereffects of a nuclear exchange with the Soviet Union and release of gamma radiation. The instrument of choice was the ANPDR-27.

"Be that as it may, I believe the incident site and surrounding area is contaminated with plutonium residue. When Turner's team took off their masks and left them off, they became heavily exposed to that residue, airborne and on every surface, including their protective clothing." He paused, then asked, "Did you leave the protective clothing on the scene or bring it back, Mr. Turner?"

"We brought the protective clothing back in seabags. The seabags are in the EOD shop at the Naval Ordnance Facility."

"When you and your team were flown back, where did you go when you arrived?"

"My team went to the EOD shop, and I came here for debriefing."

"Here, in Captain Travis's office?"

"Yes, sir."

"Let's do an experiment."

He reached down, brought up the metal case, opened it, and lifted out a gray radiation detection instrument and said, "Gentlemen, this is a PAC-3G alpha radiation detection device, the instrument the SW/EOD team and air force teams needed, but didn't have. It could have been made available, if the possibility of an incident of this kind was considered by higher authority."

He turned on the PAC-3G, calibrated it, and asked, "Mr. Turner, after coming back from the incident, you said you came to this office. Where did you stand?"

"In front of the captain's desk."

Dr. Rowen turned the PAC-3G on, got up, and walked over to where Turner said he stood. He got down on one knee and rested the radiation detector on the rug. It immediately began to click at a high rate of speed.

He looked up and said, "Well, what do you know."

Captain Travis was livid. "For God's sake what do we do now!"

"Captain, we will continue to use the PAC-3G to find out what else has been contaminated by clothing and footwear worn by the team members. Objects contaminated will be gathered up, sealed in fifty-five-gallon drums, and sent back to Sandia. There is no doubt the interior of the helicopter they flew in from Sidi Slimane is contaminated, and must be thoroughly washed down with water. Any other vehicle they rode in will be examined, and if carpeting or other removable floor covering is contaminated, it will be sent to Sandia. Otherwise, washing down until contamination is no longer detected in the dried surface is the rule."

The CO's exec, very much on edge, said, "That's going to be a serious undertaking."

"Yes, it is. I would suggest we start now, gentlemen."

Three days later, with the help of the Naval Air Station's fire department, the task was complete. Seven fifty-five gallon drums were placed on board a special flight to the Naval Air Station at Patuxin, Maryland, for further transport to Sandia National Laboratories, Albuquerque, New Mexico. Dr. Rowen was the escort.

A special team with PAC-3Gs were flown from Hill Air Force Base, Florida, to the U.S Air Force Strategic Air Command at Sidi Slimane to conduct further decontamination operations.

Ten days after the incident, the editorials in the Moroccan newspapers had turned their attention back to the Algerian border incursion problem and communist conspiracy. The incident was unknown elsewhere.

The second SW/EOD team had arrived at the Naval Ordnance Facility. Ensign Billy Gibson, the officer in charge, was of unknown quality; both Gallegos and Cole held the two enlisted men, a chief boatswain's mate and a gunner's mate second class, in high regard, based on previous experience while serving with them.

It was 1600, Friday afternoon. Lieutenant Turner was standing with Commander Hawkins, looking out the commander's office window.

"I know you. Chief Gallegos and Petty Officer Cole have not been able to spend much time orienting the new team, but since they will be used in a more conventional way, what help you have given will have been sufficient. This is your last 'pee in the bottle' day, isn't it?"

"Yes, sir, it is."

"Well, the last report from Dr. Pierce told us there is no sign of plutonium in you or your men's urine. It's gone, except for what became locked up in bone."

"That's what I understand, sir. We may have dodged a bullet. I guess we have to learn not to think about it in the long term."

"Yes, I would suggest that. Are you ready to have a week in the great sandbox with Moroccan Air Force Lieutenant Bajda?"

"Yes, sir. We met with him and Sergeant Benabhou yesterday. We were very comfortable with them."

"What time do you fly out?"

"Oh-six-hundred, Monday, sir."

"And return the following Friday. We are not sure when you and the team will be deploying to Fort Tindouf, probably five or six days later. The Foreign Legion at Tindouf hasn't given us a firm date yet. You have the duty this weekend, don't you?"

"Yes, sir. It will give us time to make sure we are ready to go Monday."

Almost casually, Hawkins said, "Before you go, this morning we received word from the secretary of the navy's office that the secretary was aware of the fine work you and your team did at Sidi Slimane. You will hear more, later."

"Thank you, sir."

"On the way out, have Lieutenant Commander Owens come in."

"Aye, aye, sir."

When he arrived at his desk, he sat down and felt pleased with himself. He looked across the room to where young Ensign Billy Gibson was drowning in a sea of paperwork, and felt old and tired.

Chapter 16

2003

D r. Turner's thoughts about his tour of duty as a young naval officer in Morocco, over forty years ago, was interrupted by, "Ladies and gentlemen, this is your captain speaking. We are beginning our final approach to the Santa Fe airport. Because of a friendly jet stream, we will be landing ten minutes early. We hope you have enjoyed your flight, and we want you to remember that you are the reason that Southwest Airlines continues to be successful. Thank you for flying with us."

The cabin attendants were checking to make sure all passengers had their seat belts fastened as Turner snugged up his seat belt a little more. He continued to gaze out the window and thought, *It's been over forty years since Sidi Slimane. The situation in North Africa and the Middle East has gotten worse, especially with the rise of radical Islamic fundamentalism. Laura warned this could happen. She didn't realize the movement could have global implications though. This meeting is going to be like stepping out of a time machine and going back to another world.*

After landing, Turner's plane had to wait for an Airbus 320 to vacate the gate. It was a short wait, and his plane pulled in and parked.

Before the cabin door opened, the passengers had already left their seats and were muscling their carry-on belongings from the overhead compartments. Turner got up and nudged his way into the tightly packed aisle and removed his old flight bag from the overhead bin. The cabin door opened, and the march of the sardines began.

When he entered the terminal, he looked around and saw Brannen at a newsstand reading a paper. He approached Brannen from behind, put his hand on his shoulder, and said, "Are you going to buy it and read it, or read it and not buy it, Stephen?"

Brannen turned and laughed. "Well, there you are, Burt Turner. Actually, I just bought it." He folded the newspaper and put it under his arm. "It seems the feds are having success in surveilling Al-Qaeda's and other jihadist organizations' monies and communications. It's nice we have the capability to do these things."

"I hope the feds are never tempted to use that capability on us folks," Turner replied.

This thought went over Brannen's head. They shook hands, and Brannen said, "The car is just outside. Did you have an OK flight?"

"I am sure my flight was a lot more comfortable than your C-130 flight. There was some turbulence in the Denver area, but in general, it was a nice ride."

They left the terminal and made their way to the parking lot, where Stephen Brannen couldn't remember where he had put the car.

"Are you having a 'senior moment,' Stephen?"

"Burt, you can't believe how often senior moments visit me these days. It's like they say—'never pass a urinal, never trust a fart, and don't ever ignore an erection.'"

Turner laughed and replied, "I never heard that one before."

They both saw the car with U.S. government plates at the same time.

"There it is! Just where I parked it."

They drove out of the parking lot and, twenty minutes later, were leaving the beautiful New Mexican desert on their way up the winding mountain road to Los Alamos.

Turner commented, "I think it's colder here than in Reno."

"It's somewhat higher. Does our desert look different than your Nevada desert?"

"Quite different. The colors here are incredible."

"My wife and I have lived here for eighteen years. When I am away for a time and then come back, it always seems that I am seeing it for the first time. I never get used to the colors in combination with the terrain."

As they left the desert and drove up into the pine-fir community, they agreed that the mountain forest of the Los Alamos area and Turner's Sierra were very much the same.

Nearing the town of Los Alamos, Brannen said, "We are at about 7,200 feet. In 1942, General Leslie Groves, the director of the Manhattan Project, was looking for an isolated location to build a laboratory facility to develop the bomb. Robert Oppenheimer, the first director of the laboratory, told Groves he knew a very remote area that had a marvelous view. A perfect spot was in the mountains just outside of Santa Fe, New Mexico. He also told him there was a boys' school there that might be bought and used for housing the scientific and support staffs. Additionally, Oppenheimer said there would be plenty of room for building the research facility. The location was right here on Los Alamos Mesa. Groves was interested. Everything began to fall into place. The U.S. government negotiated with the school, bought the property for $440,000, and built the laboratory, or should I say laboratories. Oh, the property also included two trucks, fifty saddles, and sixty-odd horses. What a deal, huh?"

"Well, I knew about Oppenheimer and the history of the Manhattan Project's development of the bombs from studying nuclear weapons at Indian Head. But we certainly didn't learn about the boys' school, trucks, saddles, or horses."

"I can't imagine why not. This means you probably didn't know about the two tractors or eight hundred cords of firewood that were thrown in with the deal?"

"Christ, Stephen, where do you get all this?"

"Up here, there isn't an awful lot to do on cold winter nights. We have a wonderful library."

They entered the town and drove to the motel. Brannen turned into the parking lot and parked in the Reserved for Registration slot. As they were getting out of the car, Brannen asked, "Do you want to take a shower or anything before we go to lunch?"

"I have to go to the bathroom, that's all."

Registration went quickly. When they got to the room, Turner thought, *On a scale of ten, this is about a seven.*

Brannen had indeed made everything very easy so far.

They had lunch at a small restaurant near the motel. Hearts of romaine salad and Coke for Turner. Bacon, lettuce, and tomato on white bread (toasted) and water for Brannen.

During lunch, Brannen went over the plan of the day. They would meet the others in a secured conference room in the administration building at 2:00 p.m. Since there would be some time before the meeting, Brannen would take Turner to the weapons and technology museum. First though, Turner would need to go through security and sign for his security badge. It would not be required for the museum, but it was required for everything else.

He asked, "What level am I cleared for?"

"Top Secret/Restricted Data. The discussions could be rather wide ranging, and it was thought wise for you to be cleared for that level."

"How did I get cleared at that level so quickly?"

"The great powers started your background check after our first meeting at Gar Woods. It appears you continue to be a good risk. There was no evidence that you became a subversive type or joined any group that had subversive types in it. Well, excepting your college's faculty senate," he joked. "A few weird folks there. Actually, it appears you have become quite a loner these last four or five years."

Turner let that observation pass. He did say, "So I guess you thought I would show up here, even though I hadn't made up my mind about your invitation."

"We thought you might, and we wanted to make sure you were cleared for the interviews. You know, since the Wen Ho Lee/FBI fiasco, security is tighter than a drum here."

"Do you think that Lee gave classified information to the Chinese?"

Brannen shrugged, "Wen Ho Lee was working in the Weapons Design or X Division. It was alleged, and I emphasize *alleged*, that in 1999, he gave classified information on the W-88 warhead used in the submarine-launched ballistic missile Trident to the People's Republic of China. He was incarcerated for nine months during the court proceedings and under investigation for three years. The Department of Energy Office of Counter Intelligence, the FBI, and the CIA made a number of serious mistakes during their investigation of Lee. When the case went to court, the witnesses for the U.S. Department of Justice were unable to prove allegations of Lee's passing classified information to the Chinese. The news media really burned the FBI and CIA. Today, if anyone wants to take issue with these two agencies and how they go about their business, they start with the Wen Ho Lee case. Because the allegations could not be proven, Lee was released and allowed to continue his work at Los Alamos. Do I think Lee gave information to the Chinese? We know that he lied a number of times during the investigation, but the best information I have is that he didn't."

Changing the subject slightly, Turner said, "You know, the first time I was going through a security check, they asked me if I had ever been a communist or been involved in the Japanese Black Dragon Society, or some other groups I'd never heard of."

"You really date yourself. I remember that too."

They finished their lunches, and Brannen paid the tab.

They went to the administration building and spent twenty minutes in the security office. Turner received a Top Secret/Restricted Data clearance pass, laminated and with a clip to attach it to his lapel or shirt. The pass was to be worn when admitted to secure areas.

Turner was incredulous. "I can't believe this. The paperwork was all ready for my signature, and all I had to do was wait for my picture to be taken?"

"Burt, the government can work at the speed of light when it wants something. Few taxpayers will ever have a chance to realize this."

Brannen, pointing to a board on the wall next to the counter, said, "That's a check-in, check-out board. Your name is just below a fastener where you will clip your pass before leaving the building. Wear the pass at all times when in the building."

Turner put his security pass on the board. He noticed Brannen's below his and over to the right.

They had forty minutes to spend at the museum. The museum was unclassified, and there were a number of tourists, mostly AARP types, examining the story or history of development of the first nuclear device that later was exploded in 1945 at the Trinity Site near Alamogordo, New Mexico. Turner and Brannen skipped over this display to look at a facsimile of Little Boy, the gun-type nuclear bomb that destroyed Hiroshima in 1945. Next, they saw Fat Man, the implosion-type nuclear bomb that destroyed Nagasaki, also in 1945.

He thought, *Little Boy, 12.5-kiloton yield, 100,000 died. Fat Man, 22-kiloton yield, 140,000 died.*

There were a number of other examples of earlier nuclear bombs: the MK-6, first nuclear bomb to be mass-produced in 1951 with a yield of 40 kilotons, and the MK-8, with a substantially smaller yield. There were four or five other bombs and warheads of various sizes that Turner recognized.

Brannen disappeared around a corner ahead of Turner, but returned immediately and said, "Follow me, I want to show you something."

He followed Brannen around the corner and stopped abruptly. A chill went up his neck, and his heart started racing. Just in front of him, about ten feet away, was a facsimile of a thermonuclear bomb, a hydrogen bomb he was well acquainted with. Stephen Brannen read out loud from the bomb specification plaque.

"This two-stage thermonuclear bomb was operational between 1957 and 1962. Parachute retarded. Weight: 17,500 pounds. Yield: 10 megatons." Brannen turned around and said, "Recognize this?"

Turner swallowed. "I never thought I would see this thing again. It's been a very long time."

Looking closely at the information plaque, he said, "They got the yield wrong. It was 19 megatons. And they don't say anything about the damage radius. I think the damage radius was about twenty-one miles."

"Well, it's your bomb. At least, you rendered one safe like it. We have about ten minutes. Do you want a Coke or something?"

"Yeah, let's have a Coke."

Ten minutes later, after collecting their security passes and finding out where their meeting was to be held, they left the security offices. On the way to room 231, their security passes were examined three times—the first before entering an elevator down the hall from the security offices, the second after exiting the elevator on the second floor, and finally, a third before entering room 231.

Turner's powers of quick and accurate observation had subsided somewhat as he grew older, but his gift continued to give him a level of situational awareness well beyond that of the average person. Entering room 231, he looked around. There were no windows. There was a long oak conference table with six comfortable-looking leather chairs. On the conference table, there was a large pitcher of water with fresh ice and six glasses. Audiovisual equipment, including a laptop, were on a small table at one end of the conference table, a pull-down screen was on the wall opposite. The floor was made of polished but very worn green asphalt tiles. At each end of the room, in opposite corners near the ceiling, was an unobtrusive security camera. Two men were chatting at the other end of the room. One appeared to be in his fifties, the other somewhat older.

The older man turned and, recognizing Brannen, walked over.

"Ah, Mr. Brannen—and I believe this gentleman is Dr. Turner."

They shook hands as the other two men joined them.

"I'm Bud Gottlieb from Special Affairs, Department of State. The gentleman on my right is Nuri Shaalan, the assistant to the director for operations in North Africa and the Middle East of the Central Intelligence Agency."

They shook hands.

Gottlieb said, "Let's all sit down and chat a bit."

Turner and Brannen sat next to each other; Shaalan and Gottlieb faced them. Gottlieb had several file folders before him; Shaalan had one before him.

Gottlieb began, "First, what we will be talking about over the next few days is classified Top Secret/Restricted Data—TS/RD. Top Secret because the information, if compromised, could cause extreme damage to United States interests, both military and political. Restricted Data is in respect to nuclear weapon discussions. Additionally, only those who have a need to know, and are cleared for TS/RD, will have access to what we do here. All our meetings are being videotaped.

Now, with that out of the way, I would like to thank Dr. Turner for coming here to help us better understand what happened forty-plus years ago in regard to what has been called the Noble Experiment.

The operational reports submitted by what was then known as the Strategic Air Command of the air force, or SAC, and the navy Special Operations folks are quite conflicting, especially in regard to estimates of released radioactivity and its long-term effects based on the science and technology available at the time.

We have been forced to revisit the incident because it is in our national interest to reestablish a small military presence, in a number of North African countries, as part of our war on terrorism. There are those in high places that want to be prepared to deal with any questions that might tend to slow or prevent this reestablishment because of a misunderstanding of what happened a long time ago. We want negotiations to run its course and result in a program advantageous to the host countries, as well as to us, in preventing terrorist activities."

Gottlieb looks like one of those career State Department types, probably a heavy hitter. Gray hair carefully and expensively coiffed. Below the French cuff on his left wrist, a gold Rolex President and a simple wedding ring on his finger. He's very polished, and he makes me very uncomfortable.

"Nuri, perhaps you could give us your perspective."

Shaalan began, "We know if the incident you were involved in is bought up, Dr. Turner, it will be used by radical Islamic fundamentalists as an example of America's historical attempt at trying to gain hegemony in North Africa and the Middle East, at the expense of Islamic peoples. If this proves to be the case, we want to be able to provide historical information that terrorist activities, by extremist groups, had a great deal to do with the incident at Sidi Slimane."

He has the name. He has the look. He's an Arab. But he has a New England accent.

Gottlieb added, "It would appear that most people are overly impressed with what they assume to be the uniqueness of our times. The terrorism that the United States and other Western countries are concerned with today had its origins in the 1954-1962 Algerian war against the French. History tells us that as many as one million Muslim Algerians were killed in Algeria's successful bid for independence. Eighty thousand French soldiers and civilians were also killed. Terrorism on both sides was widespread."

From a file folder in front of him, Gottlieb withdrew an eight-by-ten-inch photograph of a young boy.

"This is a sixteen-year-old Arab boy. We think he and another Arab boy were responsible for the rocket-propelled grenade, or RPG, attack on the B-47 carrying the thermonuclear weapon at Sidi Slimane. Russian RPG-3s, along with other weapons, were supplied to various groups in the National Liberation Front, or FLN, by the Russians . . . not necessarily to be used against the U.S., but that's another cold war story. The boy's name is Owdi ibn Zahwahiri."

Turner didn't know where Gottlieb was going with this. He glanced at Shaalan; Shaalan was smiling. He knew.

Gottlieb withdrew another picture from the file folder and passed it around. The picture was of an older man with a white beard, heavy black eyebrows, and deep-set eyes. He was wearing a black turban and, with an arm raised, appeared to be speaking vociferously into a microphone.

"Today, Owdi ibn Zahwahiri is about sixty-six years old. He is a highly educated cleric and was an associate of Osama bin Laden when they were both fighting the Russians in Afghanistan. We think he is currently involved in masterminding Taliban activities in southeast Afghanistan."

Turner was flabbergasted and said, "Gentlemen, I don't understand how I can help you. I wrote the initial navy operational report about my special weapons/explosive ordnance disposal team's involvement. I am sure you have read it and have read any additional information that the navy provided. I didn't know that an RPG fired by terrorists caused the incident. In fact, it was explained to me that, as the airplane taxied for takeoff, a rear-wheel casting failed, and the airplane caught on fire."

Gottlieb replied, "I understand what you were told. But now you know what actually happened."

The rest of Friday afternoon was taken up with procedural matters covering the Saturday and Sunday meetings. Turner read classified documents and examined classified photographs supplied by Gottlieb and Shaalan. In one photograph, he could see himself garbed up in protective clothing and using a radiation monitor near the still-smoldering B-47. Initially, he treated the documents and photographs in a perfunctory manner, then became absorbed in long-forgotten details of that incredible experience and what was now supposed to be the cause of the incident. Finally, Turner finished reading the last document, put it on top of the others, and pushed them and the photographs across the table.

Gottlieb said, "Dr. Turner, we would like to meet here at 8:30 a.m. tomorrow, if that is convenient for you."

"I have nothing planned. All this is becoming very interesting—very disturbing, but very interesting. Eight thirty sounds fine."

Gottlieb turned to Brannen and said, "Stephen, if you will drop Dr. Turner off at security tomorrow morning, we will have a security guard bring him up to room 231." He added, "There is no reason for you to attend the meeting."

The introductory phase was over. It was 6:30 p.m.

After Turner and Brannen turned in their security passes and were walking out of the administration building to the parking lot, Turner asked, "Shouldn't you be at the meeting tomorrow?"

"I don't have a 'need to know,'" Brannen replied.

The parking lot was almost empty; the car was easy to find. Ten minutes later, Brannen dropped Turner off at the Los Alamos Inn. "I'll pick you up at eight. Get some sleep."

He waved and drove off.

Turner went into the motel and made his way to his room. Once inside, he closed the window blinds and lay down on the bed (usual motel-room quality). He was exhausted, mentally and physically. He closed his eyes. *This isn't so bad. It's fascinating to have access to all that information. I wonder if they will ask about the cooperative arrangement we had with the French Foreign Legion that led to our covert operation in support of the Moroccan government. Maybe they could make a connection with Russian-supplied intelligence and RPGs at Sidi Slimane. Real intrigue there. I have to get something to eat.*

Turner forced himself from the bed, washed up, and left for the nearby restaurant.

He ordered a cheeseburger (with everything), french fries (large), and a beer (Coors). For dessert, apple pie (institutional, but OK) and coffee (decaffeinated) with cream (real) and sugar (teaspoon and a half).

Helen would really be pissed. I should have had something lighter. When he came back to his room, he took two Pepcids for his expected gastric reflux, crawled into bed, and immediately fell asleep. It was 8:15 p.m.

He awoke at 7:00 a.m. with dinner still heavy in his stomach. After showering and shaving, he got dressed and made his way to the restaurant of the night before. For breakfast he had cantaloupe (quarter slice), two slices of toast (wheat, with strawberry jam), and a glass of milk (1 percent milk fat).

At 7:55 a.m., he was in front of the motel. Five minutes later, Brannen pulled up, and Turner got in the car. Fifteen minutes later, Brannen had dropped Turner off and Turner had gone though security and was sitting by himself in room 231.

A middle-aged woman came into the room with an oversized tray and carefully placed it in the center of the table. On it were three cups and saucers, two large insulated pots (coffee and hot water), tea bags, cream and sugar containers, four donuts (glazed), three bismarcks (nonglazed), and a stack of paper napkins. Finished with her chore, she smiled, pointed at the pastries with a frown, and said with a Hispanic accent, "You do know these things are not good for you."

Before Turner could say anything, she left the room.

A few minutes later, Gottlieb and Shaalan entered the room, each carrying a briefcase. They greeted Turner and poured themselves coffee (both black) and sat down.

Gottlieb, helping himself to a bismarck, asked, "Are your accommodations satisfactory, Dr. Turner? Did you sleep well?"

Turner, watching the oozing jelly from the bismarck dribble down Gottlieb's fingers, replied, "The accommodations are quite satisfactory, and yes, I slept very well."

Gottlieb picked up one of the paper napkins from the tray, fastidiously wiped the jelly from his fingers, and said, "Do keep track of your costs so we can reimburse you, Dr. Turner."

At this point, Gottlieb and Shaalan both opened their briefcases, took out legal-size pads of paper and several file folders. Some of the file folders were bordered in red, designating secret or higher classification. Shaalan reached back into his briefcase, took out a new pad of paper (also legal size) and a freshly sharpened pencil and gave both to Turner. He noticed their legal pads appeared to have the first page covered with one-line sentences—maybe questions or key subjects they wanted to cover?

Gottlieb said, "We are changing the format a bit. Earlier, we thought we would meet with you individually—Nuri first, then me. Last night, when we were comparing notes, we found that the information we would be covering was relevant to both our agencies, and we came up with what may be an interagency first in cooperation—it makes more sense for both of us to meet with you at the same time. Besides, from time to time, two heads may be better than one as we try to help you remember things you may have overlooked or forgotten."

Turner leaned back in his chair and said, "Let the games begin."

Gottlieb replied, "Yes, let the games begin." Looking at Shaalan, he asked, "Would you like to start, Nuri?"

"Yes, of course."

"Dr. Turner, some of our questions may seem far afield, but please bear with us." Then, glancing at his legal pad, he asked, "Could you tell us what you can remember about your initial contact with members of the French Foreign Legion? Perhaps start with why a contact was established."

"That does seem rather far afield. I'm not sure what that has to do with the incident at Sidi Slimane."

"We are grasping at straws here, Dr. Turner. We need anything you can give us," Gottlieb replied.

"Captain Arthur Dillon, I think it was, of COMNAVACTSMED, the Fleet Intelligence Center at Port Lyautey, and my commanding officer, Commander Gene Hawkins at the Naval Ordnance Facility, at NAS Port Lyautey were involved in planning a mission in support of a covert operation code-named Scorpion Fish. It seems the CIA station in Paris had passed information on to naval intelligence about a cell of Arab extremists in the FLN, the Front de Libération Nationale, who were strongly against the presence of U.S. military bases in Algeria, Tunisia, and Morocco.

"There was mounting evidence that these individuals were planning to target U.S. naval weapons storage and communication facilities in those countries for destruction or incapacitation. The covert operation was one of surveillance and reconnaissance and was designed to determine if there was a genuine threat that would deserve some sort of preemptive action, and to find if the Russians were supporting the Arab FLN insurgents with intelligence and weapons.

Because special weapons/explosive ordnance disposal teams were not trained in surveillance and reconnaissance, a plan was developed by liaison officers at the American and French embassies in Rabat for my team to accompany a small detachment of legionnaires who were expert in surveillance and reconnaissance. This was to be a training operation for us. Arrangements were made for my team, along with a squad of recon marines stationed at NAS Port Lyautey, to accompany the detachment of legionnaires on a night mission in the Rif Mountains. That mission was my team's initial contact with the French Foreign Legion."

Shaalan asked, "What were the recon marines doing with the French Foreign Legion?"

"As far as I know, there was some sort of cooperative agreement with the French Foreign Legion to develop realistic field problems for our marine detachment."

Shaalan sorted through what appeared to be reference material and said, "It appears this particular mission doesn't match our historic information—please go on Dr. Turner."

"Well, that is all I can remember about working with the Foreign Legion."

Shaalan made a note on one of the papers, turned it over, and read for a moment. Then he asked, "Was the Foreign Legion, in any way involved with the Larache mission?"

"There were no legionnaires with us. I would have had no way of knowing if they were involved in a mission in support of Operation Scorpion Fish."

"Were the Israelis?"

"No." *I think they were.*

The discussion turned to the security breakdown that led to the incident at the U.S. Navy Communications Site at Sidi Yahia. When Lieutenant Hamid al Karim's name came up Turner was informed that al Karim was now the Director of Moroccan Security Affairs.

Gottlieb glanced at his watch and said, "It's almost time for lunch. If it would be OK with both of you, I could order up lunch, and we could eat here."

Turner and Shaalan agreed to the proposition. They all decided on tossed salads, sourdough buns, and iced tea. Gottlieb checked the numbers on a card attached to a nearby phone and called in the order.

Then he said, "Dr. Turner, I know this is quite tedious for you, but your recollections about your covert operations with the Foreign Legion may have been one of the factors that led to the incident at Sidi Slimane."

Turner replied, "I don't know how that could be possible."

"Well, during your tour of duty in Morocco, it happened to be the time that the FLN was most active, probably because of a highly successful recruiting program targeting easily influenced sixteen- to twenty-two-year-old Arab and Berber males. It is now known that a small number of these recruits were trained to attack American military installations in response to the American presence in Morocco, Algeria, and Tunisia. Perhaps you were not privileged to know about these attacks?"

Gottlieb's monologue was thankfully interrupted by the delivery of lunch. In this more comfortable atmosphere, Turner learned that Shaalan was from Massachusetts, born to Jordanian parents who lived in Cambridge, went through public school there, then was admitted to West Point. He spent six years in army intelligence, the last two years at the American embassy in Lebanon. He left the army as a captain and was recruited by the CIA. He had been in the CIA for twelve years, was married and the father of two teenage boys who were driving him nuts.

Gottlieb was a graduate of the Air Force Academy. During the Vietnam War, he was a young aircraft commander of a B-52. Post-Vietnam, he quickly rose through the ranks, and after a number of assignments, which included a tour of duty at the Pentagon, he retired as a colonel and immediately joined the Department of State. He had been there for the last fifteen years. Gottlieb had a wife and no children.

Turner didn't have to share his story; Gottlieb and Shaalan were already quite well informed about him through a series of background checks that began a long time ago.

After lunch, Gottlieb continued, "We talked about the past. Now, fast-forward to the present. As part of their holy war, their jihad, radical Islamic fundamentalists are using extremely cost-effective terrorist attacks against the United States, Britain, Indonesia, Spain, Russia, the Philippines, and a number of other countries. You and a few others have historical information that can help form a chronology of events that will become part of a matrix for computerized game theory at the Pentagon, and the different service war colleges. We already have extensive information from the Israelis. The outcome of this gaming could give us military and political options for developing strategies to counter what is now called global terrorism. As we chat about the incident, if there is anything that might cause you to remember any experience you may have had with the Arabs, and/or with the legionnaires, let's talk about it."

It was 6:30 p.m. when the discussion ended. The three men were mentally exhausted. Their meeting had not been adversarial; the players were objective and to the point, for the most part. Dinner was on Gottlieb at the local steak house. They drank too much wine, Paraduxx, 1999 (Duckhorn Vineyard), forty-five dollars each, three bottles. It was close to midnight when they dropped Turner off at his hotel. They agreed to have Brannen pick Turner up at nine the next morning.

––––––––––––

It was overcast and very cold when Brannen arrived at the Los Alamos Inn. He was five minutes early. Turner, waiting just inside the entrance, came out and quickly got into the car.

As they drove off, Brannen asked, "How did you get along with your new friends?"

He knew enough not to ask Turner about the information covered at the meetings yesterday.

"Actually, quite well. It was rather grueling, but not adversarial. They treated me with courtesy and respect."

They pulled into the parking lot and parked where they had the previous day. They entered the administration building, and on the way to security, Brannen said, "I'm not sure if Gottlieb and Shaalan will be sitting in on this session, but Bob Davenport of archives will be there. I think a gentleman from weapons design is going to sit in too."

After collecting their badges at security, they made their way to room 231. The security officer stationed at the door checked the photographs on their badges and then allowed them to enter the room. Gottlieb and Shaalan were sitting at the table with a man in his forties sitting at the head of the table and a man much older than anyone else sitting at his right. Stephen Brannen took a seat at the end of the table.

The man at the head of the table stood up and said, "Dr. Turner, I presume. I'm Bob Davenport of archives, and next to me is Dr. Somers from Weapons Design X Division. It would be useful if you might sit across from Dr. Somers. Mr. Brannen knows Dr. Somers quite well. They are both interested in designing nuclear and thermonuclear weapons to be one-point safe when transported."

(A nuclear or thermonuclear weapon is considered to be one-point safe if, during an accident and the conventional explosive sphere of the weapon is detonated, there will not be a nuclear yield or partial nuclear yield.)

"Mr. Gottlieb and Mr. Shaalan expressed an interest to sit in with us. Now, this morning, the plan is to chat about the unfortunate occurrence at the SAC air base at Sidi Slimane in the late spring of 1960.

"Dr. Turner, we have all studied the air force and navy operational reports submitted after the incident and the analysis later written by our scientists here at Los Alamos. I know forty-some years have lapsed, but we would like you to try to think back and answer a few questions for us."

"I'll do my best," Turner answered.

"About what time did you arrive at the scene of the incident?"

"I don't quite remember." He thought for a minute, then said, "The team had already loaded the HUP—the helicopter, before I arrived. As soon as my plane from Naples landed, I boarded the HUP, and we took off. We were probably on the scene midmorning."

"After you landed, what was the situation? And if you could, would you mention names?"

"The air force base acting commanding officer, Colonel Sharp, and his staff were waiting for us at the control tower when we landed. The officer in charge of the weapons division, if I remember correctly, his name was Knox, Lieutenant Colonel Knox. He told us the airplane was moving down the runway and had a rear-wheel assembly casualty, causing the airplane to lean and settle to the runway, flexing and then fracturing the fuselage and breaking the left wing. Then the fuel cells in the fuselage and wing ruptured, starting the fire.

"He said there was an MK-36 thermonuclear weapon on board in the strike condition. He also said the fire crew had fought the fire for the regulation ten minutes allotted for the high explosive content of that particular weapon, and withdrew to a position near the control tower. After talking the situation over, my team and I put on protective clothing and went in to the site."

"Was the weapon on fire when you approached?"

"During our walk around, we saw a few small fires in the forward fuselage and forward of the tail in the area where the fuselage fractured. This area also was where the horse collar containing a number of assisted takeoff (ATO) rocket bottles were located. The bomb bay area was still smoldering . . . no, the weapon was not on fire."

"What was the condition of the weapon when you saw it?"

"About a third of the upper part of the radiation case was burned away, along with the polyethylene liner. Inside, the uranium secondary was intact, but spalling."

Seeing the quizzical looks on some of the others' faces, Somers explained, "Spalling, in this case, is like exfoliation or scaling."

Turner continued, "For some reason, the conventional explosive of the primary—the implosion sphere—didn't seem to be damaged. The electrical leads to the PETN detonators were undamaged, and the AIFI was intact, but the plutonium capsule was partially inserted in the primary."

"Are you quite sure about that, Dr. Turner?" Dr. Somers asked.

"I was sure enough that I tried to remove the capsule, Dr. Somers."

Hearing this, the men finally understood how dangerous the situation had been. An explosion of four hundred pounds of conventional explosive could have been expected, but a partial nuclear yield, though remote, wasn't out of the question for a weapon of this type back then.

Dr. Somers took over from Davenport. "What was the state of the arm-safe switch, and was anything left of the fusing system?"

"The arm-safe switch was intact but ambiguous, the card in the window was half green, half red. From what I could see, the fusing system, at least in the area where the X unit would be housed, seemed to be intact."

"Did you attempt to do anything about the fusing system?"

"I was unsure if the X unit or other electronics might hold residual current, so I disconnected as many cables as I could get to." He paused then said, "I must say that if this wasn't interesting enough, there were more than a few of the thirty ATO bottles, still exposed to the heat, that ignited and flew around, and 20 mm high explosive incendiary canon rounds from the rear turret cooking off. My men were very close to all of this."

As soon as he said this, he thought, *I'm sure they didn't need to hear all of this. They're only interested in the bomb, too bad.*

Davenport asked, "For the archives, what type of radiation equipment did you have, and what were its capabilities?"

"We had AN/PDR-27s for monitoring gamma radiation, possibly beta radiation."

"Were you able to detect any radiation?"

"Very slight gamma radiation near the secondary, but that could have been an anomaly in the radiation detection equipment we carried whenever we deployed, but I am sure there was significant plutonium contamination."

"You didn't have alpha radiation detection capability?"

"No."

Davenport looked at Somers and said, "This is the discrepancy that continues to surface and sours the final reports."

"I'm not sure what you mean by the discrepancy," Turner said.

"Other reports stated that, at the time of the incident, alpha radiation detection equipment was available, and negligible alpha radiation was detected near the weapon and not elsewhere."

Turner was getting tired now and erupted, "That's bullshit. Alpha radiation detection capability PAC-3Gs were not available until they were flown in from the U.S., and that was at least three days after the incident!"

Trying to calm Turner down, Davenport quietly said, "Dr. Turner, you're the key to this conundrum. We don't know why others disagreed with you, at the time or later. Please understand we are not trying to be adversarial. We need your help."

Turner relaxed a bit and said, "Look, when I wrote the incident report, I emphasized there was circumstantial evidence for widespread plutonium contamination. The scientist from Los Alamos came to the base at Port Lyautey. He carried equipment capable of detecting alpha radiation. He found plutonium contamination all over the place. Add to that—evidence of plutonium was found in my urine and my team's urine."

Somers seemed to ignore this and continued to bore in on Turner's explanation and asked, "Do you feel all the plutonium and uranium was vaporized and lost?"

"No. The firefighting effort dropped the temperature, which could have allowed for a change of physical state from vapor to molten metal. With additional cooling, anything remaining would have become amalgamated with the aluminum and magnesium from the airplane. But I feel strongly a large amount of plutonium oxide and uranium oxide was widely spread by personnel."

Until this point, Gottlieb had purposely stayed out of the discussion, but he now interjected with some irritation, "There is no doubt that Burt is right about this. It was four days later when the PAC-3Gs arrived and detected alpha contamination all over the place."

"And that was not in the reports," Davenport added.

Turner raised his voice. "Then operational reports were either gun-decked when they were written, or the information was expunged later, damn it!"

Somers, looking at Turner through tired, old man's eyes, calmly said, "I don't believe I've heard the phrase *gun-decked* before."

"It's an old navy saying for hiding information or lowering the importance of information in question."

"Oh my, that's very good, Dr. Turner . . . gun-decked." He looked down at his notepad and asked, "Dr. Turner, when the fire began again, do you have any idea why the fire didn't detonate the conventional explosive of the primary?"

Without hesitation, Turner answered, "No."

"Well, I think we could all agree that if it did detonate, we might have had a partial nuclear yield."

Somers sat back, looked around the table, and said, "At the time, we called it a noble experiment. We didn't have any way of knowing what could happen in an event such as this."

A long discussion began between Davenport, Somers, and Brannen about the inconsistencies in the operational reports: how and why the incident occurred, what immediately happened with the start of the fire, and what the actual degree of radiation contamination was. They argued that information of real scientific and safety value was lost, because of obfuscation driven by political necessity.

Turner, absorbed in the discussion, eventually noticed that Gottlieb and Shaalan had left the table and were in a corner of the room, in deep conversation. Gottlieb saw Turner looking their way and motioned him over. He rose from the table, and as he approached, Gottlieb said, "We thought we might have a little more time with you, Burt, but it's already 11:30 a.m., and it's obvious their session with you will go right up until noon. You have to leave then, right?"

"Yes, I have to be at the Santa Fe airport at about 1:30 p.m."

Gottlieb smiled and said, "Burt, as a history buff, I would be interested to get your point of view concerning the assassination of Ben Bella's attorney in Rabat."

"Maybe you might invite me to dinner again sometime, Bud?"

"Maybe I will, Burt, maybe I will."

Six weeks after the meetings at Los Alamos, Turner was at his desk putting the results of the protein synthesis examination in his grade book. He was quite pleased with his students this semester; they were bright and unusually responsive. The high grades gave evidence to this.

Earlier, less interested students dropped their classes to spend more time on the ski slopes. Turner wondered how the parents would feel if they knew they were subsidizing their children's winter sports at the cost of academic education.

It had been a good semester so far. The administration was supportive of the way he was running things. The biology faculty was getting along with each other, and the laboratory supervisor, Mrs. Connor-Wright, had been less confrontational with the biology faculty.

He closed his grade book, opened the middle drawer of his desk, and put the grade book inside and the graded test papers next to the grade book. He closed the drawer; leaned back in his chair; spun around to the window; and saw, on a branch of the Jeffrey pine, right there, a stellar jay annoying a red squirrel defending its right to a pine cone.

He thought about the kayak trip he was taking next spring in the Sea of Cortez. It was his fifth paddle trip to Baja, California. He signed up, along with eight other paddlers, for the one-hundred-mile, ten-day paddle from Loreto to La Paz. As usual, the group would be self-contained and camping on the beaches along the way. He hoped the afternoon wind from the northeast would be gentle—not much chance, though, at that time of year.

His desk phone rang. Still looking out the window, he reached around and lifted the handset.

"Burt Turner speaking."

"Dr. Turner, this is Cindy," his secretary said.

"Yes, ma'am."

"There's a naval officer here to see you. May she come in?"

He sat up in his chair and answered, "A naval officer, a woman?"

"Yes, sir, exactly."

Without asking who it was by name, he said, "Well, yes, yes, send her in."

He spun back to his desk and waited. There were two knocks on the door.

"Come in, come in!"

The door opened, and a very attractive middle-aged woman, a navy commander, entered. He rose from his chair and came around from his desk to meet her. As he shook her hand, he saw above the three gold stripes on her sleeve a gold leaf with a silver acorn center, designating the Navy Medical Corps. On her left breast, above three rows of service ribbons, were the gold navy wings of a flight surgeon.

He showed her to the chair in front of his desk, and as she sat down, he said, "A female navy doctor and flight surgeon, very unusual."

"Not so much anymore, Dr. Turner," she answered.

"What can I do for you, young lady?"

With a very sweet smile, she said, "I was attending a conference at the south end of the lake, at Harrah's Club. My mother told me you were a professor here, and I thought I might drop by. I'm Dr. Katherine Roberts's daughter. I have been told you are my father."

CPSIA information can be obtained
at www.ICGtesting.com
Printed in the USA
FSHW021308150120
66123FS

9 781436 325899